ORPHAN TREE

AND

THE VANISHING SKELETON KEY

ORPHAN DREAMER SAGA
Episode Four

A Novel

J. NELL BROWN

Join the Orphan Dreamer community, and sign up for J. Nell's newsletter at https://jnellbrown.com/newsletter.

Industrious brothers and sisters challenge their siblings to reach for the stars. Who knew that four little Southern girls would be allowed to leave a legacy: a journalist, an attorney, a Lieutenant Colonel in the US Marine Corps, and a physician who also writes fiction and nonfiction books? Truly it is Yahweh—the Great I AM—who has the final say.

So I whisper this prayer for my sisters: "My dearest Abba, Father, when our spirits are released from our bodies and we escape Earth's gravitational tug and slip into Yeshua's (Jesus's) eternal dimension forever, I hope that we leave our world a bit more livable for the next generation—just like our ancestors did for us. And may we all hear from you, Yahweh, 'Well done, good and faithful servant.' "

Until we meet again, my sisters, I wish you blessings as we continue living in the spirit of this proverb attributed to Eleanor Roosevelt and to other great thinkers: great minds discuss ideas; average minds discuss events; small minds discuss people.

—J. Nell Brown

BOOKS BY
J. Nell Brown

NONFICTION

Shhh, My Father Is Speaking, and I Am Listening: A Bible Study on Hearing God's Voice

Blood Moon—God's Warning: Why Knowledge of Jewish Feasts Is Essential to Understand the Blood Moons of 2014 and 2015

FICTION

Orphan Dreamer Saga
Orphan Dreamer and the Missing Arrowhead

Orphan Dreamer and the Glass Tattoo

She Laughs Last

Orphan Tree and the Vanishing Skeleton Key

A Generation of Lighted Evergreens

House Guest

Collector's First Edition Paperback
The Omega Journey: Blood Moons Whisper

God Factor Saga (GFS) Trilogy
Frozen Prayers

Blood Moon Relics

Autumn Rains

The Rose of AD 30 (A GFS Compilation)

COMING SOON

Orphan Falls Running Wild and Free

Little Peach Lies

Orphan Star: The Mark

Dear Reader,

I wrote the Orphan Dreamer Saga as a sweeping transcontinental story heavily spiced with thrills, comedy, and a pinch of that horror-trope element called dread. The saga reads as a contemporary epic that defies time, taking the reader from the predawn of humanity's beginnings to a future of what-ifs.

Like the popular television show *This Is Us*, each episode of the Orphan Dreamer Saga follows three different time periods of each character's story arc while solving a main plotline mystery.

That's why I recommend reading any short story, novella, or novel in this saga when you're focused. Otherwise distractions could cause you to get confused with the story line. So consider turning off the television, brew a cup of tea, curl up with *Orphan Dreamer and the Vanishing Skeleton Key*, and immerse your mind into Daniela's and Cillian's worlds. And to keep track of time periods more easily, note the time and date stamps at the beginning of each chapter.

The Orphan Dreamer Saga is a work of fiction; however, a thread of truth weaves throughout the tapestry of words.

The saga should be read in order, starting with episode one, *Orphan Dreamer and the Missing Arrowhead*, a story that begins to answer these questions: what makes the main protagonist tick, and how does her mind work? Episode one reads as a nonlinear story that shows the world of a schizophrenic—a world of chaos and confusion—yet reveals how Yahweh sees the protagonist, Daniela, very differently from how other humans see her. He sees her as a child who hears His voice unfiltered.

The themes explored in the second novel of the series, *Orphan Tree and the Vanishing Skeleton Key* (*OT and VSK*), hold true to my mission as a novelist: write fiction that paints a human likeness upon the faceless and gifts a voice to the voiceless. As a result, *OT and VSK* paints a picture of distressed children that will jolt—and possibly disturb—some readers, just as *Twelve Years a Slave* and *Uncle Tom's Cabin* challenge their readers. Nonetheless, I've kept my word to expose these stories in the Orphan Dreamer Saga, especially after learning about certain atrocities that children experience.

If you want to skip the chapters that feature the most heart-wrenching parts of Cillian's journey, **do not read** Chapters Twenty, Twenty-Three, and Twenty-Four. But you will miss some of the plot points.

For those readers who choose to read his complete story—which I recommend for those sixteen and older—this experience will provide two options: pretend the social issue isn't real or do something about it. As the author, I hope for the latter response. All characters are fictional except for references to God and Jesus, as well as the concepts of angels and demons.

The proper Hebraic names of God and Jesus are used in this book: Yahweh (YHVH), Adonai (My Lord), Immanuel (God is with us), and Elohim (Supreme One) for God, and Yeshua for Jesus.

The Sons of Venus represent a conglomerate of religious, financial, and political secret societies and bear no resemblance to any one group in particular.

When the last grain of sand slips through the narrowing of history's hourglass, Yahweh will stand triumphant in the spiritual battle depicted in this novel. He says, "For God so loved the world, that he gave his only begotten

Son, that whosoever believeth in him should not perish, but have everlasting life" (John 3:16).

I am thankful for this truth. What would life be without God's love?

Now get ready to enjoy the second full-length novel of my series, the Orphan Dreamer Saga, previously known as the God Factor Saga!

With gratitude,
J. Nell Brown

I—Orphan Dreamer

FAILED AGAIN.

For the second time. And failure sort of matters when a sixteen-year-old has been chosen to save the world from the Nephilim. The half-human, half-demon aliens invading Earth.

Daniela runs her forefinger along the outline of the weapon—a permanent solution to a temporary problem. Human perceptions, like motives, rarely tell the truth, the whole truth, and nothing but the truth, so help us God.

Thirty minutes ago, Daniela, the Orphan Dreamer, had slipped Emmaline's "pepper spray"—a.k.a. gun—from her friend's Louis Vuitton purse. She'd never seen a gun up close, much less held one.

She lies back on her bunk bed, exhausted, gun in hand, and steeped in depression and disappointment. All because she failed to secure Emmaline Georgina Winterlyn Darbyshire as her loyal friend and kindred spirit.

But it turns out, betrayal sucks even more than failure.

She presses the barrel against her right temple. *Click!*

Grace—God's undeserved favor—says, "No! Not tonight. Tonight, Daniela, you will live."

Tears stream down her face. "I am Daniela. I am the Orphan Dreamer. I am loved. You are loved. And I will be brave for us—tonight, in the morning, rain or shine, forever and ever and ever. Amen."

★ ★ ★

Determined to answer an age-old question—what convinces a human to betray their friend or their family?—Daniela reads some of her previous journal entries. A year ago, during a Billy Graham crusade at Florida's Jacksonville Coliseum, the famous reverend had said this:

The human heart is the same the world over.

—Reverend Billy Graham

The human heart . . . its needs are the same: to discover life's purpose, to experience a love worth dying for, and to be given a second chance—reborn, cleansed, then allowed to bask in the eternal gift of redemption.

Redemption is simply a new start. It is the treasure of a lifetime gifted by our Creator, Yahweh—Elohim, the Supreme One—Immanuel, God is with us.
Yet . . .

—J. Nell Brown

The heart is deceitful above all things, and desperately wicked; who can know [its truest intentions and motives]?

—Jeremiah 17:9

Does a smile not paint the face of the deceiver and a compliment not slip past the lips of the slanderer? The ones who nurture hatred in their deepest parts, do they not preach love, or at least associate with those who do? The ones who demand loyal friendship, do they not relish in gossip?

A socialist or a fascist political leader claims to protect citizens, yet secretly lusts for power, planning a coup with the intention of gaining resources and power to dominate the masses.

No human can fully discover another human's truest intentions. We hide our ghoulish motives behind faux smiles and insincere words. Who are you—really? Can I trust you . . . or your deepest motives? Am I a fool when I choose to trust? Who am I? Can you trust me—can you trust my motives?

Yet to trust is to practice the art of love. If I choose to love, who can I love without regret?

—J. Nell Brown

What is right is not always popular, and what is popular is not always right.

—J. Nell's and Daniela's parents

Concern for man and his fate must always form the chief interest of all technical endeavors. Never forget this in the midst of your diagrams and equations.

—Albert Einstein

The Orphan Dreamer's Legacy

Dear Diary,

Emmaline Georgiana Winterlyn Darbyshire, hopefully my Anne of Green Gables Anne with an e, still sleeps above me on the upper bunk of our Los Alamos loft. I am writing this entry beneath the illumination of dim candlelight. For the first time since I was named the Orphan Dreamer, I can see my future clearly.

I am the Orphan Dreamer. My name is Daniela Rose Cavanaugh. I am an introvert, so I quietly wield my most powerful weapon—prayer—as I fight to accomplish my mission: stop the Nephilim before they abandon Wormwood, invade Earth, and destroy us all.

Still, my most earnest wish remains simple and true, and that is to convince Emmaline Darbyshire to commit to becoming my forever kindred spirit. Six months from now, will she still like me, much less love me? What about in a year? Probably not.

Even in the midst of my depressive loneliness, I choose to live for your sakes, not mine. I wipe off Emmaline's "pepper spray"—a.k.a. her gun—with a washcloth, removing my fingerprints before I slip her weapon back inside her Louis Vuitton purse. We're only sixteen, and I've never fired a gun. It's probably not the best idea to use the side of my head for target practice.

Or maybe it is. Because when I die, my loyal friend and kindred spirit, Ethan Mohammed Solomon, will be waiting for me at the banks of the Jordan River, the path to Yahweh's home. Ethan loved me. He loves me still. He was my first kindred spirit, and maybe my only one.

Yours truly,
Daniela Rose Cavanaugh
The Orphan Dreamer

Egalitarianism: the doctrine that all people are equal and deserve equal rights and opportunities.

Elitism: the belief or attitude that individuals who form an elite class—a select group of people with an intrinsic quality, such as high intellect or wealth—are more likely to be constructive to society as a whole and therefore deserve influence or authority greater than that of others.

There is a struggle going on right now. It is between two worlds: egalitarianism and elitism. We are meant to be equal as people, but not all ideas are equal. We have reversed it. We have made an elitism of people and an egalitarianism of ideas, and that is flawed.

—Dr. Ravi Zacharias

2—Adelaide:
#Before My Parents' Stories Begin

The End, the Present . . .
08:01 P.M., Friday, May 11
Blue Ridge Mountains

"LET FREEDOM RING! LET THE angels sing! Let the whole world know that today is the day of reckoning."

It's Independence Day—but not for humanity. The Nephilim have invaded Earth. They've been waiting . . . lurking among us . . . for six thousand years. Now they're ready. Waiting until we're asleep before they attack. The last of the blood-moon prophets has sounded the alarm.

Cloaked inside an aluminum hull and a mist of darkness, my airplane pilot navigates their cold, dark lair below the Kármán line.

For almost six thousand years, the Nephilim and the

Watchers—the Nephilim's powerful fathers—have been watching us, drooling over our lush home, Earth, as they train for a future and final battle with humans, Armageddon. They remain in the shadows, hiding on Wormwood, their invisible planet.

I guess it sucks to be invisible, though I wouldn't know much about that.

An Irishwoman's fiery-red hair spills down my back in tumbles of ringlets. Father gifted me his pale hue and winter blues, tinged with flecks of amber and green. African and Sri Lankan blood courses through my veins, splashing my cheeks with cocoa-colored freckles.

A bat-cave, sun-deprived version of Meghan Markle, the Duchess of Sussex, with red hair.

That's me.

A thunderstorm spews from the clouds that surround us. Rain splashes, then slithers down the windows of my da's Learjet. As we travel 41,000 feet closer to the Watchers' lair, will they kidnap us? Levi, the classmate who assaulted me during my morning run today, tried. Is he one of them, a Nephilim, the offspring of a human female and a Watcher—a pure-blood demon?

My heart upticks a beat.

Feeling lightheaded, I ring Beth for dinner service and a melatonin.

When she arrives, I decide not to take the melatonin.

I can't fall sleep—not here, not anywhere—unless my mother, the Orphan Dreamer—Daniela Rose Cavanaugh—sits next to me.

Oblivious to our predicament and after serving dinner, my flight attendant curls up with a book in hand and a blanket tossed across her shapely legs. She rests in an alcove behind the pilot's cockpit while I guzzle down a glass of grapefruit juice. But the splash of citrus doesn't tantalize my taste buds as it usually does.

Anxious, I pen the foreword to my mom's biography, which will be written by my kindred spirit, Cordelia Grey Anderson.

Dear Reader,

My mother's legacy emulates a matryoshka doll—a Russian nesting doll constructed of birch, lime, or alder wood. The doll represents motherhood and stories hidden inside a story about an orphan—my missing father—and the Orphan Dreamer who dreamed of him—my mother.

Yours truly,
Adelaide Rose Cavanaugh
The Orphan Dreamer's daughter

I clip the pen to the spine of my journal, then bite into a fresh California roll. The usual savory flavors of rice, avocado, cucumber, and seaweed taste no different than water. Trembling, I slip my mask up over my mouth. A tear slips over my lashes and thumps the page of my open journal.

I recline in the plane's posh leather seat and wonder if this weekend will be my last opportunity to cuddle with my mom and whisper, "I love you."

Outside, a pair of engines quietly whine as they suck up jet fuel and propel us through the sky.

Staring past the plane's window, I watch a thunderstorm make a light show in the distance. I should be halfway between Exeter, New Hampshire, and Asheville, North Carolina. Almost home. Almost safe.

I reread Beatha's text: *Come home. The news from the doctor isna good.*

Mummy's favorite song—"No One Ever Cared for Me

Like Jesus" by Steffany Gretzinger—plays through my earbuds as I open my laptop and gaze at the blank screen. But I care for Mother. Maybe she doesn't know how much.

Another nonesoteric question nags me. How should I answer that firecracker research question on my Political Science in the Middle of Religious Studies final exam?

I consider the question again: Three Abrahamic religions: Judaism, Christianity, and Islam. For some, Christianity identifies the Messiah of its parent religion, Judaism. What question of Judaism does Islam answer?

Cordelia was right. It's the mother lode.

Discussions about religion or political beliefs never end well, much less discussions about politics within the context of religion. More lost than found, I close my laptop and stumble more than pace the airplane's unsteady aisle as our pilot, Jacob, navigates the plane through a black stormy sky.

Standing in front of the lavatory mirror, I take a deep breath and start washing my face. Moments later, the engine's thrust slams me into the wall. I pull myself to my feet, grip the washbasin with one hand, and continue washing my face with the other—determined to remove Levi's touch, his scent, and the grief of losing my da, and now, potentially, my mother.

An hour later, the pilot announces over the intercom, "Preparing for descent, Miss Adelaide."

Ready or not, here I come, Mummy. Did Mr. T., my political science professor, infect me with whatever bug was ravaging his lungs?

Will I murder my mother by contaminating her lungs with a virus that up until a few years ago caused the common cold? I have to risk it. I'll wear a mask and wash my hands, because I need to see my mom's face before she dies.

Besides, I have to tell her something. A secret.

Damp auburn hair clings to my face, and Mother's words echo in my mind: "What Yahweh has shown us in the light, He proves true to His children in the darkness. Never fear. He walks with us through the valley of the shadow of death. Don't let the excitement of your youth cause you to forget your Creator. Honor Him before you grow old and say that life isn't pleasant anymore."

Her version of being reborn is dying to one's self, like Yeshua the Messiah died to His identity, to his rightful position as King of all Kings, when he took on the form of a human and trudged up the Via Dolorosa to Golgotha's hill where a rugged cross awaited his mangled body.

The war between good and evil is won by humility, not pride, Adelaide. Yahweh only gifts wisdom—essentially our war plans against the Nephilim—to the humble. Mummy's sayings and her past harbor greater mysteries than Levi's chameleon face.

"Mom." My face contorts. "I need to be close to you. Stay with me for a while longer. We need you to fight the Nephilim and win. To stop the bad pandemic."

Dinna cry, lass. My da's words replay in my mind. *Ye'll be roundin' the mountain in the morn. You've made her proud. Know that. And know this. I love you, lass.*

I bite down on my thumb, transferring the pain until I stop crying. I wipe my eyes and remove the evidence of my emotional meltdown. My right eye shades blacker than Levi's soul, so I dab flesh-colored foundation on the bruise and blend it. Before class, Cordy had given me her makeup kit and a quick lesson, because I don't usually wear the stuff.

I sit back in my plush seat and strap my seatbelt secure. The hum of engines is my sole companion.

Cordelia Grey Anderson was correct. I'm curious. She was right about one other thing: I'm a thief. After retrieving my leather satchel, I remove my mother's journal—the one I stole during my last visit home. I read the last ten pages, then trace patches of dried, rust-colored stains that splatter each page.

Is it blood? Did my da—the assassin—cause the bloodletting that stains my mother's journal?

Did he torture Mummy? Is he the reason I'm to become an orphan?

The flight attendant taps me on the shoulder, then hands me a cup of tea in my favorite thermos. "Ready to land, Miss."

"Yes, ma'am." I inhale but don't smell any spice. I click on the cabin's overhead light, making sure the liquid inside the thermos is the color of tea. Sighing deeply, I reread the last paragraph on the first page of my mum's journal. Once again, her serene, alto voice seems to replace mine.

Some say knowledge of one's joyful ending can make the present misery tolerable. But who knows if one's last act will be full of joy or sorrow? Maybe we all know our final act and don't realize it; or maybe we deny the facts of our final curtain call. Inspired by the One whose beginning and ending defies time—the Alpha and the Omega—an ancient prophet wrote, "And as it is appointed unto men once to die, but after this the judgment." I am no prophet; I am a woman and a mother, but I am sure this saying applies to me as well.

If I had known my ending, how would I have lived my beginning?

—Daniela Rose Cavanaugh

Her voice trails off, and my opinion of her character remains the same. *You would have lived as you have—amazingly well, Mom. My kindred spirit.* I have to decide: Could Cordy Grey's novel create a Simmie Knox portrait out of Mother's legacy?

Yes, it could.

I glance at my reflection in the mirror of Cordy's foundation case. Trails of emotion have eaten away the veil of foundation cream, so I reapply the stuff. Then it dawns on me: I look like Dracula's wife—pasty white. My skin begs for a bath of sunshine. The summer sailing trip with Cordy will be good for both of us, and hopefully we'll discover some of my parents' secrets.

In the dimly lit cabin, I dab more foundation around my black eye.

Mom can't know what happened.

Not ever.

My mother's death is playing out in slow motion, and she shouldn't be forced to worry about her daughter.

Half brain-dead, I open my email on my smartphone.

To: Adelaide Rose Finn
From: Professor Jakob Cohen
Date: May 11
Subject: Open Immediately!

COVID-20 is the least of Earth's final troubles. Wormwood will collide with Earth in less than one year. Do something if you care about your future! Your mother has given up.

B'shalom,
Professor Jakob Cohen
Director of Israel Antiquities Authority

P.S. Your research question is complex, but if you want to discover what question of Judaism Islam answers, study the origins of the two religions and learn about the story of the two half brothers, Isaac and Ishmael. One was promised by YHVH, and the other was conceived because of Abraham and his wife's impatience.

Hint: Look for the connection between Islam and the Roman Catholic Church as you enjoy your visit with your mother, my late nephew's best friend.

Why does Professor Jakob have a copy of my research question? I'm a nobody, and I've never even met the guy! Who sent this email? Is this a prank? I punch Seth's number into my satellite phone, and my genius hacker friend answers on the first ring.

"Seth."

"Adelaide, darling. Calling from the sat phone. Where are you jet-setting to?"

"The mountain chalet."

"Be careful. Your mother's immune system can't fight off this nasty virus." I slide the back of my hand across my forehead like my mum does to check for fever. Warm, but not hot.

"I basically bathed in alcohol when I returned to my dorm room. The CDC claims that the incubation period is fourteen days, and I don't have a fever, so I hope that I'm okay. For now. Would you do me a favor?"

"Hacker at your service."

"I'm forwarding an email to your secure account. Can you tell me if it originates from Professor Jakob Cohen's home or work IP address? He's the director of the Israel Antiquities Authority."

I send the email. Ten minutes pass as I mindlessly eat a ripe orange. I can't taste the sweetness of the juices or smell the citrus scent.

Defeated, I slip the half-eaten orange and the rind into a plastic bag.

"Can I take your trash, Miss Adelaide?" the flight attendant asks with a smile plastered across her wrinkled face.

What have I done? I could be infected with COVID-20, and I've been breathing into the face of a sixty-something attendant.

With my mask dangling to my chest, I stare at my black-and-purple flowered leggings. "No, thank you." I study the ridges of my knuckles, then slip the mask back up over my mouth. "Ms. Beth, why don't you sit up front for the rest of the flight?"

"If you don't need me."

"I don't. Eat and drink whatever you like."

"Thank you, Miss." Beth disappears behind the divider separating the main cabin from the flight crew's private quarters.

"Doesn't appear so." Seth's voice startles me. "I'll look into it."

"Let me know when you find out who sent it. The pilot is about ready to land, so I have to go."

"Done."

"Later." I end the call. *Wormwood.* What else can I learn about the place? I tap my pencil on the mouse pad. Wormwood is a star.

I search *Wormwood and Stars,* then click on the second link:

> The third angel sounded [his trumpet], and a great star fell from heaven, burning like a torch [flashing across the sky], and it fell on a third of the rivers and on the springs of [fresh] waters. The name of the star is Wormwood; and a third of the waters became wormwood, and many people died from the waters, because they had become bitter—toxic. (Revelation 8:10-11, AMP).

Creepy and cataclysmic . . . is Wormwood an asteroid? I decide to ask Mummy when I see her.

And if a bunch of the population is going to die, what countries will experience the highest casualties? Come on, God. Does Earth really need an outer space event to kill off a bunch of humans? Thought we had that down pat with COVID-20.

What's the purpose of a worldwide pandemic?

Think like a conspiracy theorist, Adelaide.

Are we sitting on the verge of World War III? Or worse, an overreaching one-world government like Mummy says the Bible prophecies foretell, one that will force people to take a mark—the name or the number of the beast, 666—in order to buy and sell?

I remember the barcode tattooed on the underside of my da's right arm and shudder. Utterly confused, I open my binder and draw circles on the page.

Back to my paper.

So three Abrahamic religions. Judaism, Christianity, and Islam. For some, Christianity identifies the Messiah of its parent religion, Judaism. What question of Judaism does Islam answer?

Something ominous, or I wouldn't have been given the assignment. Murphy's Law!

Think, Addy Rose. Religion. Economies of the world. Wars and rumors of wars. A pandemic. How are they related?

Rubber scrapes asphalt as the pilot lands the jet.

Eyes low, mouth covered with a cloth mask, I exit my da's jet, then jog across the tarmac with my backpack slung over my shoulder.

After I enter the terminal and walk past the women's bathroom, a pit the size of an avocado develops in my gut. I glance left, then right. Red hairs stand up on the back of my neck as a cold shiver grips my slight frame.

I'm being followed. I can feel it. It's claustrophobic and ominous.

Questions pummel my mind. What does my stalker want—my mother's journal, the professor's email, or me? Will I be assaulted again? Where can I hide? Or should I fight? Did Levi follow me? Is he a Nephilim? Will he kidnap me?

Storm!

I bolt through the terminal. Refusing to stop and glance over my shoulder, I barrel past a vacant security podium, then skitter through a set of glass sliding doors and out of the Asheville Regional Airport.

Snowy cold slaps my face.

What the heck? It's springtime!

But there's no time to solve the inconsistency between the month and the weather. Footsteps slap the sidewalk behind me. Head down, jacket collar tucked around my neck, I run into the garage, rapidly pressing the unlock button on my fob. I lunge toward my car when it beeps. Please don't let the battery be dead.

I slip my backpack off my shoulder, open the car door, dive in, and lock the door. Then I slam the key into the ignition.

Come on, battery! Don't fail me now.

A woman—maybe Euro-Asian—dressed in black spandex pants and a matching leather jacket runs toward my car. Who the heck is she? Oh. My. Goodness. That's Sakura! The black widow.

I turn the key.

The V-8 engine roars to life. I floor the accelerator of my 1969 periwinkle-blue convertible Mustang and smoke her. As I speed out of the garage, "Mama Said" by The Shirelles blasts through my speakers. "Mama, I'm coming home," I whisper. "Because I need you!" After holding in the shame and anguish caused by Levi's assault, tears flood my eyes, and I weep.

Like mother, like daughter. We keep our crap together, acting strong when we're not. Cavanaugh-Finns don't cry in public.

Period.

But what a stupid rule!

As I charge away from the airport on a vacant and dark street, a sly grin slips across my face, and I let the windows down. Snow pelts me, but I don't care. I'm free. I wipe my eyes.

Cordy Grey's memoir about my parents' legacies will create a Simmie Knox portrait, layered with fluid and purposeful strokes of color meant to capture the character, spirit, and personality of the subject in a dignified manner.

Their story? It's multi-faceted like the innards of a wooden Russian doll. It tells the tale of an orphan boy and the girl who dreamed of him—and the story of the Orphan Dreamer and her Glass Tattoo.

I share their secrets because these memories are nearly all I have left of my family.

The Book of Genesis tells the story of an ancient time when evil beings from the spirit world [fallen angels/demons, the Watchers] were sexually involved with human women. Their children became giants called Nephilim, of whom so many legends are told. This is their story.

3—NOMED

SOME PEOPLE ARE LIKE CLOUDS. After they vanish, the day becomes much brighter.

Nomed—a Watcher, a fallen angel—spreads his midnight-black bat wings and jumps off the edge of a wormhole, free falling as he time travels back to war-torn 1945 Hiroshima, Japan. He clings to his only possession: Aglaope, his wife and a siren, a kind of mutant Nephilim, the crossbreed descendant of a Watcher and a human.

Dodging stars and moons, the powerful warrior bends the fourth dimension of time just as the Orphan Dreamer will one day use her Glass Tattoo and defy the confines of years, months, days, hours, minutes, and seconds.

But the Orphan Dreamer will possess a different set of motives.

Motives. Tricky little things, aren't they?

The Orphan Dreamer—Rose—will attempt to save humanity from the ruthless pandemic caused by Nomed's master. The prelude to Earth's Armageddon. Why fight all seven billion humans when they can reduce their numbers before the war of all wars begins?

Nomed snorts as a laugh escapes his throat. The two-legged monsters deserve their tortured end, a period inked with their own blood that seals the conclusion of their six-thousand-year reign of terror.

Does not Earth groan, waiting for Elohim's sons and daughters to be revealed so Nomed's agents can scrub the planet clean of the rest of the humans?

As for killing humans, Beelzebub—Lucifer's warlord charged with training an army of Watchers sequestered on Wormwood—scheduled a trial run of a viral pandemic during the Gregorian calendar year of 2020.

"We shall take note of how the two-legged creatures react to an unseen enemy that travels through their precious air," Beelzebub had said to convince Nomed's master to sign off on the plan.

On Nomed's way to Hiroshima, he glides past Enola Gay, a B-29 bomber.

Twenty minutes ago, the B-29 had dropped Little Boy on top of the unsuspecting heads of children, their parents, the elderly, scientists, politicians, priests, and more, reducing parks, homes, and churches to infernos and crematories.

Oppressive gray clouds and black dust swallow up Hiroshima's horizon, obliterating the silhouettes of trees, shops, and homes. Bloated bodies litter irradiated soil, lying in contorted angles atop pulverized concrete and twisted rebar.

In the distance, a lone church steeple pierces the haze.

Sneering, Nomed circles fifty feet above the bombed city, his vision laser-focused on the steepled church. His mission is simple: Go to ground zero. Locate a fire-bombed Methodist church accented with a steeple. Retrieve from its underground vault a Hebrew relic—the Vanishing Skeleton Key—that opens an ancient warrior's tomb, a map revealing the secrets of the future that hopefully leads to the end of the humans.

If he fails—no, he must never fail.

He holds his wife firmly to his chest and takes a deep breath. If he fails, the humans—the storm clouds to Nomed's sunny day—will decimate Earth via their endless wars, pollutants, and mass-murdering inventions.

He. Must. Stop. The. Humans.

Though he lived on Earth millions of years before humans invaded the lush planet—during the space of time between "In the beginning God created the heavens and the earth" to "and the earth was existing without form and void"—Nomed is nothing more than a teenage boy at heart. An idealist who followed the wrong idea. He gave himself to Aglaope, his childhood crush, and then committed a fatal mistake.

Resisting the sensual urge to indulge in both pleasure and pain—well, mostly pain—he cradles Aglaope inside his powerful embrace while hovering above the tree line of a park full of dead trees and birds.

The fallen angel surveys the landscape of char and rubble, the crumbled ruins of a once golden city laid to waste by an atomic bomb. The bomb had burned at a surface temperature of 10,830°F, a temperature hotter than his summer home, hell. As he lands beside ash-covered slides and swings, a morning chill hits his chest.

"Filthy humans!" he says to Aglaope. "Look at what they've done to the place." Gently, he deposits his treasure—his wife—in front of a swing, displacing air. The resulting gust pushes the swing back and forth. A human wouldn't be able to see him but would see the moving swing.

He crosses a sidewalk stamped with black shadows where people had once stood. "Agla, be careful. Stay close to me."

"They cannot see us."

"True, but the neighborhood isn't safe as long as they are scampering around."

"Wherever you are, I am safe." Aglaope stands on her toes and kisses him. *If only that were true.* Boosting her husband's ego and blindly believing in her husband's version of truth—this is the job of a wife.

"Prepare to get dressed, so the humans can see you." Aglaope slips a knapsack off her shoulders and removes a set of clothes.

"If I have to." Nomed spreads his wings back and away from his body, then slips on a pair of breeches. Carefully, the fallen angel compresses his wings, pulling them close to his yellow-veined, albino skin, hiding them beneath a white dress shirt that stops at his shoulders, a gray wool duster, and a blue tie.

A bird crippled by one burnt black wing hobbles along the ground. Chirping, the poor creature attempts to outrun the pair. Nomed scoops it up. "Agla, look at the creature's eyes. They are strangely alert, even intelligent."

"You're paranoid. It's just a dying bird. We're wasting time, Nomed!"

He places it near a fountain that miraculously still spews water. "Our quarrel is not with the animals, Agla."

A bright yellow butterfly lands on the back of the baby raven. "It's an apricot sulphur."

"I know my insects." Aglaope rests her hands on her narrow waist. "The water is irradiated and will kill the bird."

"Then it won't die of thirst."

"Like all the rest of creation, the birds are groaning, waiting to be rescued from the human's hell—Earth." Aglaope strokes the bird's back before rising to stand beside her husband.

"And there goes the neighborhood." Sighing, he shakes his head.

"More like the universe."

"I won't allow it to come to that."

"Promise?"

"Follow me." He crosses an empty street, heading in the direction of the steepled church.

"After we locate the Skeleton Key, what then?"

"Once we open the Key, we will know Elohim's plans for Earth's last kingdoms, and then we will use the information to either undermine or support these empires in order to eradicate all Homo sapiens."

"And if you fail?"

"I will not fail. I possess a repertoire of tools."

"What's your plan A?"

"A pandemic. A slow percolation of terror—an invisible weapon that torments the human psychology more than a nuclear bomb." His upper lip curls into a smirk. "I want to—no, I need to—watch them suffer."

"Ahh, it's your specialty, my darling. Diseases, plagues, and death. When?" She clasps her hands together.

"After the moon drips with blood." He pats her arm.

"Why wait?" she snaps, narrowing her eyes at his patronizing pat.

"First, I must secure a human agent. Second, Israel must become an independent nation. Third, after Israel exists as an independent Jewish state, its leaders must annex Jerusalem to the State of Israel."

"The ancient prophecy?"

"Yes, Agla." He recalls the Hebrew prophecy. "But it has not been fulfilled yet: 'Who has heard or seen anything as strange as this? For in one day, suddenly, a nation, Israel, shall be born.' "

"Impossible! A nation born in a day." She shakes her head. "Nonsense."

"The prophet Isaiah said it, not me. During blood moons—when lunar eclipses fall on a tetrad of Jewish holidays—Israel will become a nation. Then, sometime later, during another tetrad of blood moons, the Israelis will reclaim Jerusalem."

"The Jews securing their own land . . . I will believe it when it happens. They are but few in number."

"Doesn't matter! The British are behind this effort, as well as Lord Rothschild—a British citizen and in the early twentieth century, the most powerful banker in the world."

"Your proof?"

"The Balfour Declaration." Nomed juts his chest out. "A written public statement issued by the British government in 1917 that announced the British Empire's full support for the establishment of a 'national home for the Jewish people' in Palestine. Even US President Woodrow Wilson supported the declaration."

"Have you gone mad? Are you feverish, my love? The Palestinians will never stand for this."

"One day, all of Abraham's children will stand together in one accord."

"Nonsense!" She winks at her lover. "Never fear because

I'm on your side—and securing an agent should not be a problem. There are millions of morally corrupt humans slithering across the face of Earth. Toss the field rats a few gold or silver coins. In their world, the end justifies the means, and they will sell their souls to the devil for money."

"Not just any human agent. Someone privy to our motives."

"A Nephilim?" Aglaope shivers.

Nomed wraps his arms around his wife, then answers her question: "Affirmative."

"Oh, I see," Aglaope says. "But a Nephilim will want their piece of the pie—a kingdom or an empire."

"We'll gift him or her a small outpost, no different from when we gave Zeus his Mount Olympus." Nomed huffs. "Even he could not keep his kingdom, eating his own child and cavorting with women who weren't his wife. A drop of human DNA spoils the soup."

"What fairy tales the humans have made of my people's—the Nephilim's—stories."

"In their egotistical dreamworld, they hope to become Poseidon, Athena, or Zeus."

"Hoping to become and being are two distant states of reality. Trust me, Nomed. Enlist a plain-Jane human. Their minds are easier to manipulate. You suggested it yourself. They tell stories of the Greek gods because they long to become gods—but we do not want to work with a god on this project."

"You're the master manipulator, Agla. Yet, you worry because of the foretelling of the birth of the Orphan Dreamer, Elohim's human agent—a plain-Jane girl."

"She's different—she's chosen. But look around." Aglaope turns 360 degrees, surveying the destruction.

"I can see."

"They despise each other, Nomed. You quoted your Elohim-inspired scripture, so I'll quote mine. 'Many will be offended and will betray one another.' " She shrugs. "I didn't write it. The Apostle Matthew did. Remember? Motives, Nomed."

"Tricky little things."

"Indeed. And the humans are eager to work for us. Eager to be offended and betray their neighbors. They are savages. Cannibals. Destined to destroy their own. Why should we stop them? Give them the tools. Help them."

"Agla." Nomed reinforces his tone with a heavy dose of bass, like a lion calling his lioness on the African Sahara before mating. The concrete rumbles, and Aglaope runs into his arms. "I require a crossbreed who never thinks about right or wrong because they are proud and eternally convinced that they are always right. What if Elohim convinces our plain-Jane human to repent and take a path in conflict with our goals?"

"The humans are proud, too, but for now, I rest my case." She sighs. "Will the humans suspect crossbreeds like me of planning to eradicate them?"

"They won't."

"Are you sure?"

"Does it matter?"

"The Orphan Dreamer matters, and she's a human. She's a dangerous human. Given her humble state of mind, she will choose to revere Elohim, and He will gift her wisdom—the antidote to our poison of pride."

"Stop fretting over her, Agla."

"That girl could determine our destiny!" She rests her hand atop her empty womb.

"She hasn't been born yet, and the other incompetent

two-legged creatures don't believe that we exist. Agla, I'm no crossbreed, just pure evil."

"I know." Grinning, she runs her hand down the ridges of his chest.

"So then let me handle the recruitment process. They refuse to believe that I exist, while choosing to believe theories about aliens—when we're the aliens!" He lowers his voice and kisses Aglaope on the forehead. "We worry about her when we have to."

"Luckily, I am invisible to the boorish humans." Aglaope strokes her neck. *You would scare the wits out of them if they could see you, dear*. Yet Nomed desires her. "I am no alien. We are extradimensional—special."

"Have it your way, but your job is to infiltrate the girl's mind, make her depressed, and then she'll commit suicide."

"I know my job description."

"One day, they will build a spaceship, maybe even a Space Force, and try to meet and then conquer the little green Martians."

"Beelzebub's army will be waiting."

"If they find us before we come for them." Nomed winks and Aglaope blushes, her face darkening to merlot-red. "Fighting the visible war, they have disregarded the invisible one—the one that matters, the one that culminates with Armageddon, our beginning and their end. Whether we fight on Earth or in space, we win." Something dark rises up inside of him, and Nomed salivates, his mouth needing to kiss Agla's neck, then bite deep into her flesh, feasting on her life.

Stop! You'll hurt her. He sucks a deep breath into his constricted lungs, then steps a few feet away from his wife.

"Do I stink?"

"It's the fish."

"The Japanese eat fish with every meal. It's healthy for humans."

"Then when Wormwood—our Trojan horse—emerges from its wormhole crawling with demons, we will strike the sea and kill the fish first."

"Always planning for war." Clearly oblivious to his internal war, Aglaope walks beside her husband, her icy hand brushing the warmth of his woolen coat. His skin chills with a cold breath of fresh air—heaven's breath instead of hell's fury. "Their amnesia equals our second chance," she reassures her husband. "We will win."

"In time."

"What's Elohim's excuse? Why did He create these filthy two-legged monsters?"

"It was a lab experiment gone majorly wrong," he quips.

Laughing, she slaps her hand over his eyes, then says in a mocking voice, "Cover your eyes, Nomie, and the monsters will disappear."

He laughs and places his hand over hers. Her delicate but cold flesh reminds him of his mistake.

Slowly, he removes her hand and his, taking in the breadth and depth of humanity's ruthlessness. "Agla . . ." She waits for her husband to speak. "If I can imagine something, it has already happened. My pandemic is not a new invention." He pauses, weighing his decision to be vulnerable. *My mistake almost killed her.* "I am not that clever."

"But you are persistent."

"I am." He rolls his shoulders back while gazing into Aglaope's eyes.

"In time, the clouds will be erased, and the sun will shine once more, Nomed." Her strained cheeks crack with a smile—almost hopeful, desperately vulnerable. "Make it so. Make the sun rise once again."

But the sun does not belong to me. How could I force the Son to shine? He glances at his wife, refusing to share his morbid thoughts. Instead he reaches for her hand, and she takes his as they approach the end of the sidewalk.

Aglaope's multiple shoes *click* and *clack* across broken concrete, tapping an eerie rhythm and reminding him of his own failed experiment—the rebellion.

"Agla, when will the clouds disappear forever?" His voice darkens with an unmet and desperate longing, a longing only she could satisfy, but he would kill her if she tried to fulfill it during her delicate, unwell state.

"You're the general of Lucifer's army." She snaps her glare toward her husband, then speaks with purpose. "Make them disappear, Nomed."

Nomed—one of Elohim's angelic prodigals, a fallen angel who followed Lucifer in his rebellion against Elohim—mentally prepares for war.

And you will hear of wars and rumors of wars. See that you are not troubled; for all these things must come to pass, but the end is not yet.

For nation [ethnos, race] will rise against nation, and kingdom against kingdom. And there will be famines, pestilences, and earthquakes in various places.

All these are the beginning of sorrows . . . And then many will be offended, will betray one another . . . and will hate one another.

—Matthew 24:6-8, 10

Wraith: a ghost or ghostlike image of someone, especially a shadow that appears shortly before or after that person's death.

4—THE ORPHAN

THE PRESENT THE END . . .
MAY 10
NORTH SYRIA

THE SOUND YOU HEAR IS the sound of freedom.

Helicopter blades thump against a veil of thin night air as an MH-47 chopper transporting an assassin races low over the Syrian desert. The assassin's brothers-in-arms had long ago given him the nickname Wraith—the ghost.

His destination? Northern Syria.

His mission? Assassinate Abu Bakr al-Baghdadi—ISIL's leader, a terrorist known for his brutality.

Riding a bullet train straight into a desert hell, Wraith waits with the rest of his special-ops soldiers, the Orphans. Throat dry, his body and lungs riddled with a mysterious virus, he shakes beneath a blanket of cold fever and a sweat-stained, desert-patterned camouflage.

Alongside him, muscled men breathe the chopper's stale, infected air.

Wraith inhales, then barely exhales, trying to avoid contaminating his fellow soldiers. Wracked with fever and hoping to hide his violent shakes, he bear-hugs Spook, his friend and brother-in-arms—a four-year-old Belgian Malinois with a fawn coat and a black mask.

The dog lies across his master's lap, waiting for a go command that will come in less than twenty minutes.

Wraith buries his nose in the dog's coat, inhales, then blows out a congested exhalation. "Sorry, old boy."

Sometimes climbing out of bed and choosing to breathe are the bravest parts of a day, because "the mind is its own place, and in itself can make a heaven of hell, and a hell of heaven."

A creative as much as a warrior, Wraith holds true to the spirit of John Milton's warning, so he chooses to make a heaven of his present hell. He fixates his mind on a memory formed seventy-two hours earlier when he lingered in his version of bliss—almost satisfied, nestled deep inside his wife's safe space, a private place created just for him.

Back in their mountain chalet's master bedroom, the couple had relished their time together. Calum Scott and Leona Lewis's duet "You Are the Reason" had played in the background and entombed the couple within an orgasmic musical delight that made promises of sacrifice, hope, acceptance, and unconditional love.

In thirty-six hours, after he returns home, he will relive that memory with his Daniela Rose again and again until she tires of him.

He smiles.

Wraith had been fortunate. His Orphan Dreamer's illness had never discouraged her consent. He bites into his lower lip, hiding a homesick expression as his skin tingles with anticipation. Or maybe that's the fever.

He laughs quietly, then pops another acetaminophen tablet between his parched lips before washing it down with water from his canteen.

"Ten minutes until go time," the jumpmaster barks, jolting Wraith from his carnal daydream and back to his desert hell. He glances at his watch. Florescent red numbers glare back, 00:30—zero dark thirty.

Ironically, it's his *nighean donn's*—his wife's—least favorite time of day.

After nightfall.

The time of day when the sun abandons its post, leaving a trail of shifting shadows cloaked in darkness as a cover for those eager to get on with their diabolical plans.

But Wraith knows there is no need to be afraid of the dark, because even after dark, ghosts don't exist—and neither do aliens. Wraith's success on this mission relies almost entirely upon these two common misconceptions.

In his gloved left hand, the special-ops warrior clenches a communication stamped in bold red letters: **TOP SE-CRET**. Beneath the illumination of his penlight, he re-reads the message printed on thick ivory cardstock.

The letter is a PMC—a presidential memorial certificate—but PMCs are normally only requested by the family after a US soldier dies. The order of steps makes sense: death, then a preprinted thank-you letter for the soldier's sacrificial service.

Wraith inhales, doing what the living enjoy doing. Breathing.

Very much alive, Cillian Joseph Finn-Barry—Wraith—exhales as he focuses on the name scrawled across the signature line: Sheldon Covington, the president of the United States of America. The husband of his wife's childhood bully, Claire Amilee Underwood.

He glances at his call sign, Wraith, and his chest tightens. Tonight the teenage runaway who survived a myriad of horrors will once again fade into the night—because camouflaged, ghostly creatures get away with everything, even murder.

A sneer fades into a shy smile. The assassin's hands tremble.

Can I kill again?

He chooses to mentally run back inside his safe place—a vault of memories filled with his wife's enchanting face, blessed by the Creator with a silky veil of rich cinnamon skin, doe-brown eyes, long black lashes, and full, dusty-rose lips.

The delicate scent of fresh rain and flowers shadows her lithe frame as she passes by him, then backtracks and jumps onto the couch as though it's the deep end of a swimming pool, only to tell him, "I love you, Cil, and I'm so thankful you're real."

On the living room couch, she snuggles inside his arms. Together. Forever thankful that they found each other, they watch lazy flames flicker atop the hearth of their living room's stone fireplace.

His Daniela Rose, his *nighean donn*, adores the literary genius of Jane Austen, and would often read her classic works to him—her heartsong—after they made love and before they fell asleep.

He misses those nights.

Quiet.

Uncomplicated.

Tender.

So in honor of his dying wife and the famed English author, he says to Spook in a throaty whisper, "Dinna worry yerself about me, then." The military working dog perks up as his master rubs his head, as if asking, why?

"Aye, then. It's a truth universally acknowledged, ghosts never die, and neither do aliens, because neither existed . . . until tonight." His dog whines. "Dinna worry. No one's lookin' for us, Spook. Weel be safe, and weel return home verra soon. Then I'll be makin' yer favorite treat: cooked pumpkin, rice, and beef balls."

Spook presses his head into his master's rigid chest and releases a muted bark.

"If it comes to that, I'll be givin' my life for yours, old boy. Then ye'll sire a whelp of pups." Wraith embraces his faithful friend, and his heartbeat slows. The masculine, rhythmic thumping fading into the night—slow, steady, and purposeful. No different than the heartbeat of a hibernating grizzly.

I am Wraith.

Wraith is real, so ghosts are real.

But what about aliens?

5—I Am the Real Assassin

A Cosmic Revolution

I GET IT! HUMAN NATURE applies to all human be-ings—assassin and assassin's victim.

But I am not human. "So stop breathing, and maybe you will live." My breath stops the world as my lungs exhale sickness and death—but mostly fear.

Who am I?

I am invisible—small but not inconsequental. Heavy is the head that wears the crown. My head weighs heavy as I wear my corona, my crown. Scientists call me a virus, even nicknaming me the crowned one, a variant of coronavirus: SARS-CoV-3.

Tsk. Tsk. I am none of these. The humans have never taken the time to discover my real name, so listen very carefully. I will only say this once.

My first name is Pandemic.

My middle name is Pestilence.

My last name is Fear.

Nice to meet you too. Oh, you don't want to shake my hand? Think that I've invaded your world? Weren't expecting me? My arrival on Earth should not be a surprise to you.

I was created when humans were created, then I mutated after you messed up. Besides, did not the Apostle Matthew—one of Yeshua's twelve followers—write about my invasion?

You don't know Matthew or about this ancient prophecy?

You've not read the book of ancient mysteries—the best-selling book of all times, the Word of the Supreme One?

Ahh, I get it.

Too busy gaining the whole world while losing your soul. And now you're losing your peace and even your life. It's tempting—the gaining, the consuming—but in the end, all is lost except what survives the fire. Before I exhale and before I mete out my punishment, I'll give you a second chance— if you want it.

Because I am fragile, a softie at the center of my simple body composed of fat, protein, and RNA.

So pay attention, humans!

Listen to Papa Bear. Time for a bedtime story.

This is the Apostle Matthew's warning: "For nation shall rise against nation, and kingdom against kingdom: and there shall be famines, and pestilences, and earthquakes, in diverse places. All these are the beginning of sorrows . . ."

Pestilence . . .

My name was written in the ancient book of mysteries,

so my arrival should not be a surprise. But remember: I am only the beginning of sorrows.

The seals have been broken.

The bowls poured out, releasing chaos into the world, just as the ancient plagues tormented the Egyptians. I sneeze, then I cough, spreading droplets of fear. *Achoo.* Just one more sneeze. They all feel so good.

Are you scared?

Then run.

Hide.

Beg the rocks to fall on you, because this—me—is only the beginning of humanity's nightmare before Earth's end.

Do any dare to stand against me, a 120-nanometer speck? One does. Dressed in a warrior's garb, the Orphan Dreamer—a pesky teenage girl, one of yours—intends to make war with me.

The Creator painted her skin the shade of mud. This is an advantage for me, because the world will not take a brown girl seriously. She knows this, so this mud-faced girl plans to assassinate me.

Not happening! I sneeze. She contorts her body, and my deadly, virus-laden spray misses her face.

Oh, now *you're* mad, gearing up to fight me as well?

I wouldn't if I were you.

Do you possess the Orphan Dreamer's weapon—her sword, formed with fire, purified and strengthened in the forge of humility? The Creator of her weapon trusts few with His powerful invention, as He understands that most humans who ask for access to such a sword never unsheath it and fight. No, they become paralyzed with fear, armed but not dangerous. They choose the path of the non-war-rior—all talk, no action.

Haven't seen the Orphan Dreamer's sword? Don't

believe it exists? Your eyes have been blinded, but I see it. Her sword—Elohim's words—is very much alive. She wields it skillfully as she attempts to remove my head.

My mission is simple: assassinate the Orphan Dreamer.

I roll up my sleeves and raise my shield, then shout through dense, hot air, "Give it your best shot, Danny Rose!"

I suck in buckets of air, then sneeze, projecting tiny droplets of pestilence into her face.

She does not run or turn away.

Danny Rose inhales. Her eyes burning with fire, she advances. Then I see it—a quote written across her tattered T-shirt: *If I had known my ending, how would I have lived my beginning?*

Beginning and endings.

She's made peace with both. Shucks!

Nothing more to lose, but everything to gain, she will fight me. She is no longer shackled with mundane motives, unlike a rich old man named Malcolm Forbes who once said, "He who dies with the most toys wins."

A rather puzzling human philosophy if I might say so myself. The mantra only makes sense if death is humanity's ultimate toy-prize.

Is it?

How morbid it would be to look forward to dying while clutching an armful of money, cars, and houses—paper, fiberglass, and stucco.

If sense is so common on Earth, and if a human being chooses to embrace this toy-story approach to life, shouldn't that two-legged man or woman at least assure themselves of the one and only thing that matters—what happens after they die?

I never ask a question that I cannot answer. Just like the

Orphan Dreamer, I know what will happen to humans after they crash and burn: "For it is appointed unto men once to die, but after that the judgment."

So I ask you humans the same question that Yeshua posed over two thousand years ago: "What good will it be for a man if he gains the whole world, yet forfeits his soul?"

No hope?

Hope has a name.

He called himself the Way, the Truth, and the Life. Life. Breath. Oxygen. Every human must breathe, all the while hoping the next breath does not kill them.

My hope?

Glad you asked.

Convince the Orphan Dreamer to shift her priorities, to lay down her powerful yet invisible weapon and choose to embrace—as so many other humans have—the spirit of fear, self-preservation, and the endless search for money, celebrity, and power.

Will the Orphan Dreamer choose to gain the whole world and forfeit her soul? Will she refuse to time travel into the exotic worlds of the past and future to search for the clues required to solve the ancient puzzles? Will she refuse to learn the answers and secrets that are the keys to saving everyone—including her enemies—from the dark force that seeks to eradicate humans and inhabit Earth?

Or will Daniela Rose Cavanaugh sacrifice her dreams of securing a kindred spirit and choose to rescue her fellow humans from me, Pandemic?

Here's to hoping the she chooses option A: to live self-ishly and ignore her destiny. By the way, Malcolm Forbes died at the age of seventy on February 24, 1990, and he left all his toys behind. I've never seen a moving truck behind a hearse.

Here's to humanity's future—death. Humans had their turn. Now it's my turn to collect my toys, those lovely human corpses.

I sneeze again. Death and fear charge before me. On the chessboard of life, I slide my queen into position. Checkmate, player one—that's you, by the way. Your king is in check, and there is no way to remove the threat.

Game over.

I sneeze, then inhale deeply, breathing in a clean, pure life without you. "Bless you."

It's true: human nature applies to all human beings. Assassin or assassin's victim, it makes no difference. But humanity . . . well, that's a different story.

Not all humans are humane.

A long time ago, on the day after a plague killed the firstborn male child of those families who did not paint lamb's blood above their doorposts on their homes, the Hebrew deliverer, Moses, led his people out from Egyptian slavery.

Another great deliverance awaits on the horizon for those people who have been grafted into Abraham's eternal covenant with Yahweh.

Plague.

Death.

Deliverance.

Then the Promised Land.

Today, followers of the Way—such as the Orphan Dreamer—have painted Yeshua's blood across the doorposts of their hearts.

One day, after I have had my fill, Yeshua, the Great Deliverer, will lead God's people on the great escape to His eternal Promised Land.

I'm laughing while humans frantically worry about me,

a virus. You're nervous now about me—but what happens when the Great Deliverer raptures His followers and their ruach—their spirits—disjoin from their bodies, leaving billions of corpses to litter Earth? In light of *that* pandemic, I am child's play.

My advice?

If the Orphan Dreamer decides to emerge from her introvert's shell, speak up, and gift her global neighbors with a message that explains how to be infected by Yeshua's pandemic—listen to her. Then do it.

I sneeze again. Specks of virus cling to the wings of an apricot sulphur, a metamorphosis of the Orphan Dreamer.

You never want a serious crisis to go to waste.
What I mean by that is it's an opportunity to
do things you think you could not do before.

—Rahm Emanuel

So that no one will have power to buy or sell unless he bears the stamp (mark, inscription), [that is] the name of the beast or the number of his name.

Here is [room for] discernment [a call for the wisdom of interpretation]. Let anyone who has intelligence (penetration and insight enough) calculate the number of the beast, for it is a human number [the number of a certain man]; his number is 666.

—Revelation 13:17

6—Orphan Dreamer

IN THESE EARLY PRE-SUNRISE MOMENTS, my thoughts linger between there and here as I reenter the present from my travels through time.

Moments pass, and my body fully awakens from its numb state.

My lungs constrict, forcing me to cough. I press my hand into my chest, and my lungs rattle beneath my clammy touch. Something soft and hairy tickles my palm. "A raven's feather and a butterfly's wing?"

Reality comes into focus. I had travelled back in time to World War II, Hiroshima, Japan, as an injured raven. Vulnerable and dependent on the mercy of Nomed and Aglaope—my enemies. Even now, are they hiding in their dimension while stalking the air that surrounds me? Gasping, a litany of coughs shoot pain into my ribs and back.

Finally I catch a fleeting breath and whisper into the empty spaces, "I was born to fight. I am destined to win . . . even if we humans do not deserve a second chance."

The US Marines fought America's battles from the Halls of Montezuma to the shores of Tripoli, so I will fight on. I also travelled back in time to war-torn Syria. Did I take on the body of a special-ops soldier, one of the Delta Force or the Orphans?

Or did I fight against my husband as a member of ISIL? "Dear God, please, no!"

Who was I? What was I?

Our Belgian Malinois jumps onto our bed and curls up beside me, then whines. "Of course! I was you, my darling boy—my Spook!" I kiss the top of his head as he presses his muzzle into the crook of my neck. "Your dad . . . he wasn't alone. Not this time." I cry tears of joy. "We were by his side." I wipe my eyes.

This morning he's missing. My husband—Cillian Joseph Finn, the Wraith—is gone.

Vanished like a ghost.

I sigh because it's near my journey's end, the second week of May, and a blizzard is blowing into Bearpen Knob—my home in the Blue Ridge Mountains.

A lightning bolt flashes, zigzagging across the foreboding purple darkness that is the early morning sky.

Treacherous yet tranquil, the growing storm surrounds my chalet, bleeding dry all signs of springtime and life while painting the landscape in shades of cold, anemic, cadaver-white. It's as if the elements are colluding with the grim reaper. Maybe they are.

A wolf howls in the distance, confirming my fears.

My mom called my ability to sense slight changes in nature Yahweh's voice or my knowing when speaking with those unable to understand the language of the Creator. My teachers called this ability a sixth sense, and a Cherokee spiritual leader called it the wolf within.

I hear the promise of trouble in the muted clanks from the redwood chimes hanging from my bedroom's veranda. I sense it in the unsettling rustle of leaves that dance between the fingers of a chill wind snaking down the mountainside.

It's a restlessness, an undoing, a prelude to our impending fate—the last showdown, a war fought between humans and Wormwood's occupants.

In some circles, the topic of Wormwood is not new. On seven occasions, ancient prophets wrote about the invisible planet in Hebrew scriptures, always implying a tone of bitterness—a curse. The New Testament only mentioned Wormwood once.

I reach for my tattered book, flip to the last book of the New Testament written by John, Yeshua's longest-surviving apostle:

> The third angel sounded [his trumpet], and a great star fell from heaven, burning like a torch [flashing across the sky], and it fell on a third of the rivers and on the springs of [fresh] waters. The name of the star is Wormwood; and a third of the waters became wormwood, and many people died from the waters, because they had become bitter (toxic).
>
> —Revelations 8:10-11(AMP)

Contaminated water causes famines, even pestilence . . . and pandemics.

I have known for quite some time *who* will start the pandemic of all pandemics intended to snatch some humans from Earth. I know the identity of the person because I love Him, and He loves me.

It is true. Two pandemics lurk in the shadows of Earth's future.

The instigator of the first pandemic will attempt to drastically reduce the earth's human population.

The second pandemic serves as an escape hatch and a welcome relief for those who willingly walk the narrow path to the extraction point. Trust me, not all dying is bad—if we're prepared.

One last mission remains before I die—stop the mysterious *who*, the initiator of the first pandemic, before he unleashes Lucifer's death machine: Earth's Armageddon.

This delay will give my daughter time to turn away from her path and make peace with her Creator.

What about her father? What if Cil's not really gone and is still alive?

Is he safe? If he's safe, will he return? If he returns, is he ready to face the second pandemic—the good one, the Rapture? Fear dives beneath my skin, then lays clusters of parasitic eggs that hatch within moments to feed on my last morsels of hope and bravery. My fears have become personal and urgent.

And if he's not safe, do I deserve to keep breathing? My constant and loudest companion—guilt—never leaves my shadow and usually comes to me in the form of one question: Why didn't I whisper more prayers for him?

Busy gaining the world and fulfilling my dreams. A tear slips down my cheek. Guilty as charged.

As usual after I return from my travels, my legs ache and my spine throbs. I stretch as I gaze past a bank of windows into the storm's stark haze, imagining the shape of each unique snowflake as their ice crystals smash against the heated glass.

One snowflake falls from heaven to quench hell's thirst. Daniela, you are that snowflake. That's what my father said.

I sigh.

As a young girl, I longed to be liked, not for my classmates to think of me as a flake of ice belaying into the pits of hell. But the call to sacrifice one's dreams is the job description of a prophetess, the one who raises the alarm so those willing can run to safety. Do we humans deserve divine safety or rescue?

Our wars. Our pollution. Our chaos.

Rightfully, Earth groans for its end. Its restart, a second chance, the day humans vacate this lush and beautiful planet. Sacrifice—one of life's most heart-wrenching nuisances. My arm trembles, forcing my fingers to uncurl.

I've accepted my destiny. The evidence is shown in the palm of my right hand. An ancient jewel that resembles a snowflake—the Glass Tattoo—transforms from an indigo tattoo inked onto my palm to its original form, a snowflake diamond. The priceless stone *clacks* as it falls to my bedroom's gnarled maple wood floors.

"Fumbling follies all imagined!" *I'm such a klutz.*

The throbbing penetrates deeper into my bones, but my breath catches as I climb out of bed and retrieve the relic, then place it back inside its case. A patina bronze box with a cover made of African ivory.

I rub my fingers together.

Granules of sand scratch my softened skin—the hands of a physician who no longer heals, the hands of a woman who no longer caresses the muscular shoulders of her eternal love or brushes the ginger curls of her teenage daughter.

The acrid scent of death and the earthy scent of a muddy battlefield meld together, lingering inside my nostrils, remnants from my latest journey to a desert in northern Syria.

I stand in front of the wall of windows inside my bedroom, longing to escape into the snowy tundra.

Past the windows and at the end of my driveway, an American flag waves. I smile, big and full. I am an American—all-American—my citizenship bought by the blood, perseverance, and prayers of my ancestors hundreds of years ago.

In my neighbor's driveway, a Confederate flag thrashes against the pole, its defeated ideology still whipping in the wind. The Chauncey family built a plantation-style house with black shutters and white siding last year. Their family name hails back to a time when *massas* lazily rocked on the porches of Southern plantation homes while Negros labored in cotton fields—or swung from sprawling oak trees, if they refused to work for free.

Times change, but inevitably, someone reaches up to turn back the hand of progress. The face of Claire Amilee, America's First Lady, flashes in my mind.

Standing in my Pollyanna nightgown, I stare into the starkness of a spring storm and swallow my fears. But I can't quite push away my biggest fear: I haven't told Adelaide, my incredible daughter, that I'm dying.

I'm afraid she'll stop living if I tell her. I shiver. What if Cillian or Beatha have betrayed my wishes and told my daughter? I move to warm myself near the fireplace and watch as the flames lick up their breakfast.

Quiet and without fanfare, Beatha tiptoes into my bedroom, enters the bathroom, and turns on my shower. Should I ask her? No, not now.

Moments later, I step into a cascade of hot water, allowing the stream of hot water to massage my sore muscles. I dry off, then brush my teeth. While relishing the bath gel's lingering scent of lavender and sage, I dress in a pair of skinny jeans and a white T-shirt. The mirror shows me a reflection that I've come to despise, so I dust a coating of rosy blush onto my cheeks, resurrecting my face from the dead.

"Daniela?" Beatha's voice echoes as she walks in from the upstairs kitchen nook and sets a tray on my bedside table. "Ready to eat breakfast, then go to the airport? The plane's ready."

"Almost." Breathless, I stuff one of my tattered journals into my bedroom safe. "If I don't return from Delaware, give this to Adelaide. It will lead her to the truth about her dad."

"You'll come back."

"Beatha."

"I will." She exits my bedroom.

On top of his nightstand, a silver dollar rests at the base of a bronze lamp topped with a stained-glass lampshade depicting snowcapped mountains and soaring eagles—a gift from Cillian's younger brother, the architect and musician.

The coin will be safe here, so I leave it, my husband's most precious possession.

After eating a breakfast of oatmeal and fruit, I roll my suitcase to the door that leads to the garage. Desperate for my diseased lungs to release more oxygen into my bloodstream, I greedily inhale concentrated oxygen from a nasal cannula.

Faith, my Maltese, jumps into her carry-on bag. Spook follows, and the four of us climb into the warm interior of a black Land Rover. Beatha sits next to me. We pull up our face masks and recline in our leather seats. Spook curls up and lays across my bare feet. Faith falls asleep in my lap as Robby drives us to Asheville Regional Airport.

Today, two tasks will demand my full attention. First, confront the President of the United States and find out where my husband has disappeared to. Second, return to the chalet in time to welcome Adelaide home from boarding school.

The life of a wife—or a widow—and a mother.

On the way to the airport, I must make one phone call—a call to my middle-school bully, Claire Amilee Underwood Covington, the president's wife. I remove the encrypted phone from my carry-on bag and stuff it into the waterproofed pocket near the neck of my jacket.

This will be our last call, thank God.

"You dinna want to ha' to be callin' that twit, do you?" Beatha slips down her spectacles and rests the newspaper on her lap.

"Would you?" I ask.

Beatha shakes her head as she sips her mug of Irish tea. "Thank you for makin' the sacrifice for us all."

"You're welcome," I reply. Can I make it through this journey to Dover Air Force Base in Delaware? Oxygen from my canister hisses, blowing a puff of life into my nostrils beneath my mask.

Adelaide Rose doesn't deserve to become an orphan like her father was. My daddy called me the Orphan Dreamer. Years after he pinned that label on me, his only child, I came to understand that life plays the cruelest jokes on dreamers.

Dreamers see the future, yet they never reach it. Dreamer or not, I won't kiss my daughter on her wedding day or lend a listening ear while she navigates motherhood.

Please don't feel sorry for me.

I don't—never have. Aren't we all dying, in a way?

Beyond the highway, a cold, dark, and endless forest beckons me into her icy embrace. The safe, hot breath of the Rover's cabin whispers, "Don't go."

7—Orphan Dreamer

THE ENCRYPTED PHONE VIBRATES INSIDE my jacket pocket. I slip off my right glove, remove the phone, and look at the screen. "She beat me to it."

"Figures." Beatha looks up from her devotional book.

I press the answer button, connecting the call to the car speakerphone. Both Robby and Beatha can be trusted. Besides, the nature of this call affects them as well as the rest of Earth's citizens. I stare down at the phone, which resembles a coiled rattlesnake as it rests in my lap.

"Hello."

"Danny Rose—is that you?"

"Alive and in the flesh, Claire." Clenching my jaw, I imagine her still sucking on that apple-green lollipop at the neighborhood playground while telling me that I'm not good enough to play with her and the other kids. *Stupid is as stupid does*—so my Grandma Gertrude used to say.

"Darlin', how are you?" Her accent dips into the lazy currents of her Mississippi River drawl.

"Still upright."

"No word from dearest Cillian?"

"Not yet." Two words will do. No need to deposit any extra information into her bank account of gossip.

"Ain't that the berries?" Claire clucks her tongue against the roof of her mouth. "Men . . . they can be special. That sorry man of yours has more money stuffed inside his britches than the Rothschilds and the Rockefellers superglued together, but he can't keep his hips home, can't call, and doesn't believe it's necessary to stay near his dyin' wife's side."

I can tell by her pattern of speech that she's smiling—most likely laughing at me and my situation.

But we'll see who laughs last.

That's Claire Amilee Covington, a truly well-bred Southern belle—saccharine-sweetened Southern iced tea to your face, but just beyond earshot, a mouthful of spice, daggers, and cyanide.

The twelve-year-old version of Claire Amilee was meaner than a rattlesnake morning, noon, and night. But somewhere between then and now, she grew a brain. Exploring the world does that to a person, makes them not quite so afraid. Besides, First Ladies of America can count their real confidants on one hand. I fit the bill—out of breath and no energy to gossip. "Shall I call Emmaline?" I ask.

"Wait just a moment."

"Why?" I catch Beatha's side glance.

"I wanna chat a bit."

"About?"

"Sheldon told me that you're coming east." Claire pauses.

"What else did he say?"

"Those are my husband's affairs."

"Then why did you bring up my travels?" I challenge.

"I don't want you to leave disappointed . . . I mean, if my Sheldon proves to be unhelpful, I'm hopin' that doesn't cast a pall on our friendship."

"My question is simple, Claire. Did Sheldon have anything to do with my husband's disappearance?"

"He said he didn't."

"I was hoping you wouldn't lie to me as well." I open the thermos that Beatha packed for me and sip my tea. "Shall I call Emmaline?"

"Please do, darlin'. Conjure up the tornado."

I press the Add Call option and call one of my favorite redheads, a professional boy hunter who finally married a great guy after learning how to design biological and biochemical weapons at the Air Force Institute of Technology. She possesses a lead foot as well.

"Danny-girl," Emmaline says in her sultry Demi Moore–esque textured voice. "How's my sis?"

"Tired."

"Where are you?"

"North Carolina—on my way east."

"I'll say prayers for you, Danny-girl. And may you and Beatha fly on the wings of an angel."

"Thank you, babe. Claire's on the other line."

"So this is it, then? Go ahead. Patch the overly botoxed demoness through, and let's get this over with."

"Please don't fight with her. I don't have the energy to referee."

"Collateral damage. That's all her husband has brought to the White House. I need to speak my piece during this call."

"Are you done?" I ask, becoming somewhat impatient.

"Since when does a commoner question English royalty?" Emmaline's snarky question harkens back to when we first met. Mary, the Queen of Scots, capstones Emmaline's ancestry. As a result, she's technically a member of the English royal family.

But I'm just as much of a smarty pants. "July 4, 1776, when fifty-six Americans signed the Declaration of Independence, Your Highness." We chuckle.

"Good comeback. Means you're still fighting. Love you, pretty girl. My Lozen." We allow silence to speak the volumes of a lifetime of friendship, love, and forgiveness.

"Love you too, Limy. I'm putting Claire on. Be nice." I click the Join button.

"Hi, Claire," Emmaline's voice upticks half an octave—she's getting ready to lie, and she's going to do it nicely. Beggars can't be choosers.

"Weapons girl and her little brown prophetess, why so long to patch me in? What were you girls scheming about?"

"How to boot your husband out of the White House," Emmaline says without missing a beat.

"What she means, Claire, is that you and Sheldon deserve a vacation. You've both worked so hard for the American people, and we're forever grateful."

If we survive, Emmaline texts me.

"Thank you, Danny Rose." Claire overexaggerates clearing her throat. "Emmaline, Paul's been gone, hasn't he, doll?"

"Why do you ask?" Another text message pops up from Limy. *A permanent vacation!*

I roll my eyes. Come on, Emmaline. *Leave it!* I text back.

Emmaline is right. America teeters on the brink of a Civil War thanks to Sheldon, but Claire is powerless—just a cute face.

"Do me a favor, Emmaline?" Claire goes for the left hook. "Ask—no, beg—that husband of yours to take you somewhere remote and exotic, then refuse to let you come up for air until he properly softens that concrete into butter."

"After yours pounds through Earth's outer crust," Emmaline retorts.

"Ladies," I say, though my breathless voice is a whisper, and I struggle to breathe as my heart races. "Stop."

"Danny," Emmaline says, "are you okay?"

"I'm fine." I sit back and breathe slowly. Outside, snow falls in blankets. "Please finish up what needs to be discussed."

"How many can the hive accommodate?" As though Emmaline senses the fact that I'm totally over everything, she acts as though she and the First Lady have never sparred and laser-focuses on the purpose of the call: give the president what he wants—within reason—so he'll help us find my missing husband.

"Ten million," Claire answers. "More than Noah's ark. But we only want five."

"How do we choose them?" Limy asks.

"The genetically superior ones, of course."

"Which to you is . . . ?" I ask.

"No criminals." *Depends on who's defining the term,* I think as Claire blathers. "No disabilities and no health issues—sorry, Danny Rose. No fatties, they take up more than their fair share of space. No drug or tobacco users. You get the picture."

"I do." I imagine Claire ogling herself in a mirror as she speaks, brushing thinned but still long strands of bleached blonde hair down her slender, tanned back.

"What about IQ?"

"A must-have," Claire responds.

That eliminates Sheldon and Claire, Emmaline texts to my phone, then asks Claire. "And the war?"

"Still on."

"What if Daniela and I choose to not work with you or participate in your World War III and mass pandemic?"

"You'll be a daisy if you do."

I butt in. "I was hoping to prevent war. It's such unnecessary carnage."

"Danny, why prolong the inevitable?" The tone in Claire's voice reveals her impatience. "Everything needs a reset—even Earth."

"And the children?" Emmaline protests. "We don't even know what or if anything or anyone exists on Wormwood. We just know that it's coming."

"And according to Daniela, we don't have much time before it arrives," Claire says. "At least not enough time for you to go explorin' the deep caverns of morality. Darwin was right. Survival of the fittest."

Emmaline challenges the president's wife. "Only if humans enforce Darwin's principles. Tell me, Claire Amilee, for you, is it survival of the fittest or the meanest?"

"Shall we not try for peace," I say, trying to inject calm, "even if war remains inevitable?"

"Not war, darlin', but total annihilation. It's hopeless—it's already set in motion. You both know this."

"Then take the batteries out." Emmaline's voice flattens. "Unplug the clock, you heartless wench."

"Would I be calling either of you if I could stop this

planet from approachin', or if I didn't possess a shred of decency?"

Decency is in the eye of the beholder. I don't say my thoughts out loud.

"You want my weapons to enact your plans," Emmaline states the obvious. "Eliminate as many people on Earth before Wormwood arrives, so then the militaries of the world only have to defend the elite."

"The president asks this of you, not me."

"Then why isn't he asking?" I challenge.

"Because we're . . . friends."

"No, Claire—we aren't friends."

"Good to know, Danny Rose. My turn to be brutally honest. You're not the queen of morality. And I can't stop Wormwood from arrivin' any faster than you could stop Earth from spinnin'."

"Are you lying to us, Claire?" Emmaline has already judged Claire guilty. I don't know why she's asking the question.

"I'd chew a beehive of bees before lyin' to either of you."

"That's why the honey's been tasting like spit lately," Emmaline snaps.

"Join the adult table, Emmaline. The food tastes better over here," Claire says. "I've spoken to the president. He's made up his mind, and so have I."

"Didn't know you possessed one to make up." Emmaline just will not stop. I text, again: *Stop it!*

"If humanity is sitting helplessly in the sights of some extraterrestrial sniper, and if, as it seems by today's conversation, that President Sheldon plans to assist the occupants of Wormwood by diminishing Earth's human population using one of Limy's bioweapons, shouldn't a moral leader warn Earth's citizens about the president's plan of eugen-ics?" My voice oscillates between a C-sharp and a C-flat. "Give them a fighting chance to run, hide, or fight back?"

"That's your job, Danny Rose."

"No, Claire. My job is to continue warning humanity about Yeshua's *good* pandemic—the escape to a place of eternal rest at the end of a long journey."

"You've been smokin' weed, haven't you? By definition, pandemics kill, Doctor Cavanaugh-Finn."

"Smoking weed? Not my m.o. But sharing truth? That's my game." I pause. "Yahweh said to the people of ancient Israel, 'When I shut up heaven and there is no rain, or com-mand the locusts to devour the land, or send pestilence among My people, and My people who are called by My name will humble themselves and pray and seek My face and turn from their wicked ways, then I will hear from heaven, will forgive their sin and heal their land.' "

"You do that—grovel, beg, then play a game of hide-and-seek with your God—while the rest of the adults like my Sheldon make destiny."

"Locusts are swarming in Africa now," Emmaline adds, defending my stance.

"A global viral pandemic devastates the elderly and vul-nerable," I add. "Fires parch Australia."

"Why not allow Daniela to rally the followers of the Way—Yahweh's children—and see if they can humble themselves, pray, seek their Master's face, and turn from their evil ways, and then, just maybe their God will hear from heaven, forgive their sin, and heal *our* lands."

"Thought you were agnostic, Emmaline. Jesus-freak Danny got your goat?"

"The world's still DEFCON 1 because of COVID-20 and the approaching planet. We need to try something besides having your husband minimize the threat while he secretly plans to unleash death in the form of a bio-weapon!" Emmaline screams. "So browbeating Danny Rose into submission to your plan so that she serves up some crap-filled sandwich with a smile to God won't get you where you want to go."

"Limy's right. Think about what she said, Claire. What will people do after the last long trumpet blast—Tekiah Gedolah—of Rosh Hashanah is released and Yeshua extracts the spirits of His followers from their bodies? Billions of corpses will litter the planet. What will follow? Total mental meltdowns for all left behind!"

"You're speaking of the Christian Rapture," Emmaline interjects. "Right, Danny-girl? Just want to spell it out for our church pew-warming heathen."

"Yep, and the pandemic we're experiencing now—a.k.a. SARS-CoV-3, COVID-20—will resemble a corny April Fool's Day prank after humanity faces the *good* pandemic, the Rapture. Talk about panic and ensuing chaos," I say.

"All the more reason to cull Earth's population before Wormwood arrives and before your twisted Jesus-freak pandemic. Less maniacs to imprison and quell."

"Warn the masses, Claire," I demand. "It's only fair!"

"A child doesn't need to know his mode of punishment, only that it's comin'," Claire drawls on. "They'll figure it out once a paddle's in hand and the bedroom door has been closed."

The woman's a sadist!

"I've always nurtured a special pity for your children," Emmaline says. "I learned how to pray after you told me you were pregnant. And then I cried, 'hallelujah!' after your first miscarriage."

"We should save the children, Claire," I say. I feel numb

all over because of the ridiculousness of President Sheldon's plan, and I just want to sleep—forever.

"Children die every day, Danny Rose. At least death will come quickly to the young."

"I was hoping, no, praying, that a speck of morality lay hidden inside your entombed soul," I say.

"Not only does Claire define amorality, she wants you to use the Glass Tattoo and bend time so she can see into the future and manipulate the present."

"I know what she wants, Limy, and I won't do that."

"Then she wants me to lend her my latest bioweapon to destroy Earth—our home."

"Death and destruction are why scientists create bioweapons, right?" Claire doesn't give Limy time to answer. "It's time to start over, Danny Rose. Don't be afraid. The president and I both want a few black people in there with us."

"Oh, I know you didn't!" Emmaline, the Bostonian English girl, goes from all-out urban talk to disapproving English quiet. The silence hangs for a moment.

"A bit of African DNA would be good for genetic variety in the hive," Claire says.

"Claire Amilee Underwood Covington." Emmaline pauses, and I brace myself. "How could a backwoods couple like you and the president understand anything about complicated subjects such as genetics, biology, or virology? Do you even know what makes a virus a virus? And by the way, all humans possess African DNA, genius."

"You talk about genes, Claire." More wheeze than words come from my lips. "What about character?"

"Danny Rose," my best friend's voice steadies. "You could gift the Covington clan a dictionary for ten Christmases, and they still wouldn't know what character is.

Between him and her, they have sliced and diced this country along racial, socioeconomic, and religious lines, and now want to eat the pie all by themselves. Cheers! Here's to hoping this pie contains the same special ingredient of Minny's chocolate pie in *The Help*."

"In all fairness, most politicians don't possess a healthy dose of character, Limy," I say, trying to inject a dose of sunny calm before the incoming storm. "And the media does their fair share of poisoning people's minds against each other. Besides, people can only be divided if they want to be."

"Well let's see if Claire can tell her basic colors. Last time I checked, Daniela's skin is brown, not black. If you can't tell the difference, Claire, should you and your husband really be making these big decisions?"

"If I was prejudiced, I wouldn't ask Daniela to be a part of our new world. She'll be a raw ingredient."

"If I was prejudiced'?" Emmaline pulls out her gloves again. "Is that a question? Besides, Daniela's doctor performed a total hysterectomy because of the ovarian cancer: no uterus, no childbirth."

Thin layers of ice stitch veils over the Rover's back window, and I close my eyes. We had a chance to save the world, but it deteriorated into a hen fight.

That's humans for you.

Male.

Female.

Makes no difference.

"Daniela, I have another bone to pick with you," Claire says, veering off subject. "I'm just gonna say it plainly . . . isn't it convenient that your eternal flame—the Wraith—goes missin' at a time like this, when a worldwide viral pandemic has arrived and threatens us all?"

"What?" I sit up straight. "He's missing under your husband's watch. COVID-20 is not Cillian's fault! Nor does he have anything to do with Wormwood's imminent arrival. NASA was only able to detect the planet six days ago. But Wormwood's eventual collision with Earth has been predicted since Yeshua's disciple, the Apostle John, wrote the Book of Revelation in 96 AD. In order to avoid this cataclysmic event, every human has been gifted the option of being infected by Yeshua's DNA, so that when the last trumpet sounds, they can participate in the great escape—the *good* pandemic—way before Wormwood arrives!"

"The president—my husband—rightfully thinks of your bedmate as the promised one: Earth's worst nightmare, six-six-six, the Son of Perdition, the antichrist!"

"He didn't start this viral pandemic, nor did he see Wormwood before NASA spotted the planet."

"How do you know? Did you ask him? Oh that's right, he's gone."

"And here I was thinking that Sheldon Covington was born and bred to become the narcissistic monster that you just mentioned. If for no other reason than every Eva Braun requires her Adolf Hitler." Daniela savagely defends her husband.

"Don't you dare! I'm no Eva Braun."

"She didn't think she was either." I dig in my heels, and Beatha gives me a thumbs-up. "Historians even accuse her of abusing Blondie, Hitler's dog." I reach down and stroke Spook's haunches. He rolls onto his belly.

"I'm serious, Daniela Rose Cavanaugh!"

"It's Daniela Rose Cavanaugh-Finn now. Don't you read the *New York Times*?"

"You. An introvert. Scared of your own voice. In the *Times*?"

"Well, even when an introvert marries a Manhattan-based billionaire, the *Times* announces the nuptials."

"They also leaked the grits two days ago and identified you as the Orphan Dreamer. So do your job, Dreamer! You've travelled and solved your ancient mysteries, now go stop the *bad* pandemic before humans can sign up for your Jesus-freak pandemic!"

"I am, but I can't force the masses to do what they refuse to do."

"What is that, again?"

"Humble themselves and pray."

"Really, that's your only antidote to this virus? I always knew you were pathetic, emotionally vacant, and a permanent failure."

"Then why did you call me?" I clutch my phone, an umbilical cord of sorts between the present and eternity.

"To give you one last chance to jump on board."

"So you and your husband are going to help the occupants of Wormwood kill humans?

"We are."

"Okay, Claire." Winter winds howl, pushing our off-road vehicle dangerously close to the edge of the road. I grip the middle arm rest.

"Sorry, ma'am," Robby says from beneath his mask as he grips the steering wheel tighter.

I text Emmaline: *If Claire and Sheldon are dead, the bioweapon plan stops.*

Emmaline texts me back: *FYI, Adelaide knows you're dying. I made a mistake and told her. I'm sorry.*

My fingers release, and the phone drops to my side.

"Daniela!" Beatha screams my name, then her voice fades into the storm.

8—Orphan Dreamer

THEY'RE WAITING FOR THE PLANES to arrive.

After our Learjet lands, I scurry as fast as my jelly-legs can carry me through the Center for the Families of the Fallen—a well-lit room where grieving families linger in the embrace of overstuffed chairs while they wait for the next C-17 Globemaster III cargo plane to land. Each C-17 transports their dead loved ones from faraway battlefields.

The price of freedom.

It never was free.

Still light-headed from my panicked breathing and fainting episode in the car, I stand in a small office at Dover Air Force Base beside Colonel Ribey and his soldiers.

I cleanse my lungs with five deep breaths as four Pratt & Whitney F117-PW-100 turbofan engines roar overhead, vibrating the windows of Colonel Ribey's office. The telltale stench of spent fuel spreads throughout the ductwork of this nondescript beige building and burns delicate vessels inside my nostrils.

"He's here," I whisper. Even beneath the weight of a whisper, my voice shatters into a billion fragments.

I walk around the colonel's desk and focus on the tarmac beyond the floor-to-ceiling windows, then watch as the pilot engages the C-17's thrust reverser, stopping the beast of a plane on a dime.

My tears cleanse my American pride, transforming pride into thanksgiving. America is my homeland, and I'm one of her daughters. The C-17's pilot, an American hero, is bringing another hero—my Cillian, the Wraith—home.

Desperate to keep his memory alive, I whisper again and again, "He's here . . . he's here . . . he's here, Daniela."

But my body revolts, and warm liquid drips from my right nostril onto a stack of folders sitting atop Ribey's desk.

Quickly, I sop up the droplets of blood with a handkerchief, noting the bold red letters—TOP SECRET— stamped onto the manila folder. I pinch my nose, stymying the bleed.

Should I open the folder?

No. Let them keep their secrets.

I've kept mine.

Tonight my daughter, Adelaide Rose, will return home, and I won't miss her arrival. I could never have asked her to come with me today. I'm Adelaide's mother, not her friend. What kind of mother burdens a seventeen-year-old with her problems, especially a task as morbid as this one?

My legs wobble as though I've cooked them in boiling water.

"You okay?" the colonel asks.

"Nosebleed." I shrug.

"Still?"

"Some things never change," I say, and the colonel nods. After minutes pass, I release my death grip. "All done."

"How's Adelaide?" Ribey's gaze drills into the depths of my soul.

"Happy. She's coming home tonight."

"Does she know about her dad?"

"She doesn't know that I'm here." I avoid the question and grab the corner of Colonel Ribey's office desk before whispering for Adelaide Rose—my brave, breathtakingly beautiful, and very sane seventeen-year-old daughter: "Yahweh, may her days be filled with more hope than mine. May she dream, and may her dreams not make a fool of her . . ."—my voice falters—"as mine have. In Yeshua's name. Amen."

"Life's not fair, Doctor Cavanaugh." Nothing new there. The colonel hands me a tissue.

"I'm well acquainted with that fact, Colonel."

Noah Webster learned twenty-six languages before he decided in 1806 that *fair* would be defined as just, equitable, impartial, unbiased, dispassionate, objective, and free from favor toward any side.

"Doctor Cavanaugh, this isn't your job," Colonel Ribey whispers to me. "You don't have to do this. We have people for this."

"This," I repeat, acknowledging the colonel's use of the generic noncommittal pronoun that indicates a person, thing, idea, state, event, time, or remark.

"Yes, this."

"Since when did a hero's life boil down to an indiscriminate pronoun?" My voice threatens to shatter into pieces, but I hold it steady—quiet, firm, and unyielding.

"What do you mean?

"*This* possesses a name. A mission. A legacy. My late husband possessed impeccable character. He lived as a faithful father, a devoted husband, a lover of his Creator, and a brave American soldier. The pulse of my heart was and is not a *this*, Colonel." I finish my quiet sermon, knowing that I'm preaching to the choir.

"That's not what I meant, Doctor Cavanaugh."

"I know." I turn to face my friend. "Forgive me, Charlie. I'm not myself."

"Most military widows aren't. Can you do this?" Colonel Charlie Ribey rests his hand on my shoulder.

"He doesn't deserve to be processed, then boxed inside a casket all alone."

"Follow me, then."

Shoulders back, I follow Charlie out of the office, struggling to keep up. Out of breath, I stop short on the tarmac.

No tears. Not here. Not in front of that man—President Sheldon Covington, a man who toys with my family's future. I throw daggers with my eyes at Claire's husband.

A trumpeter plays "Taps" and Colonel Ribey raises his hand in a salute. The twenty-four simple notes gut me.

Day is done, gone the sun,
From the lake, from the hills,
From the sky.
All is well, safely rest,
God is nigh.

The trumpeter plays the last twelve notes as the silver jaws of the C-17 military cargo aircraft finishes opening its cavernous mouth. Standing stock-still, my knees lock as my stomach threatens to projectile-vomit my lunch—water and antacids—onto the asphalt.

I refuse to give Covington that pleasure. Jet fuel burns my nose, but blessed mercies, the delicate capillaries inside my nose don't bleed again.

Fully opened, the C-17 shows us the contents of its stomach: one American-flag-draped coffin, the final resting place of my heartsong. The other families are still waiting for their C-17 to arrive.

Members of the US Armed Forces, all dressed in camouflage, raise their right hands in a stiff salute.

A carry team of seven soldiers dutifully march up the ramp toward the aluminum coffin, lift it, then escort my dead husband down the ramp, onto the tarmac, and toward the building's side entrance.

God, please no! I cry out the words inside, too stubborn to let them out.

President Covington releases his salute, glances at me, then looks away. Coward. If only the American people really understood the motives of the manipulative first couple. They care about themselves, not the citizens of America or the citizens of the world, for that matter.

My Adelaide needs her mother, and my dead husband needs his widow to remember his legacy. *Don't focus your emotions on strangers.* Resting my hand over my heart, I make a promise: "I'll never forget you, Cil."

A tsunami of morbid questions floods my mind. How does he look lying in that aluminum casket? Is his body maimed? Is his face smeared with blood? Are there bruises? Missing body parts? Would I recognize him if the coffin were opened?

Questions that demand answers.

Forcing the morbid thoughts into the recesses of my mind, I follow Charlie through a side door and the rest of the procession follow us into the Dover processing facility.

After a few minutes of walking, we arrive inside the washroom of the processing facility. The soldiers will bathe his corpse for the first time since the Orphans retrieved his body from a tunnel in Russia. Concealed inside their body bags, eleven more dead soldiers wait for their shower.

My knowing tells me that something about this whole scene stinks more than a pile of dead fish, and it's not the corpses, either. *Ask to see the body. President Covington and his wife are lying to you.*

"I want to see the body," I tell Colonel Ribey.

"B-b-but you can't, Doctor Cavanaugh."

"Stop calling me doctor, Charlie. We've been friends for years. At least now you don't stick pencils in your nose to download information and pick your boogers," I say, and he grins.

"During middle school, you and I fought against the world on that big yellow school bus. Remember?"

"And we're fighting the world now. Let me see him. Please."

"Daniela, but the president—"

"What war has he ever fought, Charlie?"

"N-n-none."

"Valor doesn't happen via osmosis. It's earned. He cares about his image and that's about it. And for the record, Americanism isn't decided based upon nationality—it's based upon valuing the tenets of the Constitution. Am I right?"

"You are."

"Charlie . . ." I step forward. "America's Constitution promises me freedom, and I want to see my American hero—one last time." I clear my throat, forcing the ache out. "It's still you and me against Claire and Sheldon, so make it happen—for old times' sake."

"For you, Pickles." He nods. "But not until I do something." He winks at his middle-school crush.

"Thank you. You're doing the right thing."

"Give me a second." He chats with a random soldier, and after a moment, that soldier approaches the president's Secret Service team. A few seconds later, the soldier escorts the president and his entourage out of the room, giving us space to complete our task. "Shall we?" Charlie leads me down a side hallway.

For the next few minutes, quiet fills the space between us. "Coffee later, Danny Rose?" Rows of fluorescent lights flicker overhead. Don't die, not here. Not inside a warehouse stocked full of dead American soldiers.

"I'm almost dead, Charlie."

"You're still beautiful."

"My husband was just KIA."

"Cil was my friend . . . but you can't knock a lonely guy for trying." Charlie takes me into his office. Plaques and medals decorate the spacious room. "Stay under the radar. I'll meet you back here in a few minutes." Colonel Ribey marches toward the processing wing of the base.

A few minutes later, Charlie returns to his office, sits on the edge of his desk, crosses his arms, and stares at me for a full ten seconds.

"Well?" I break the silence.

"You're not going to like this, Danny Rose."

"What happened?" My heart pounds beneath my ribs.

"There's a problem."

"Can I solve it?"

"We'll see. Follow me."

Down hallways, around curves, and past security checkpoints, we finally walk into a bright, cold, and sterile room. Stainless steel and polished tile reflect the fluorescent lights hanging overhead. At seventy-two thousand square feet, the Dover processing center stands as the largest morgue in the world.

"After the commander—your husband—was taken through the Explosive Ordnance Disposal Room—"

"My late husband is not a terrorist."

"Routine procedure. We scan each soldier's corpse for bombs."

"Oh, okay." I cross my arms, protecting myself from the next answer. "If his body had been booby-trapped, would the soldiers here at Dover have been harmed?" I swallow hard.

"Not likely. Steel-reinforced walls over a foot thick house our scanner. That room was built to withstand a blast from a pound of C-4."

"And did you find any unexploded bombs, ammunition, or booby traps?"

"No." Charlie pauses. "Danny Rose, it's important that you know that either my right-hand man or I stayed with Wraith's body during the entire process. After his corpse was scanned, they took him to the showers, washed him, then unpacked him from the case."

Get to the point, I want to say, but I can't help my curious mind. "What happens to his coffin, Charlie?" I hold my breath because I know the answer.

"It's recycled." The colonel clears his throat, and I stare at the ground, hating war and hating hatred itself.

Like an alligator, America sits as a predator on top of the food chain. The spent lives of soldiers and war-torn crippled bodies serve as the scaffolding for America's position.

"When will these wars stop?"

"You know the answer to that question, Orphan

Dreamer. The wars cease after the world ends. And when will the world end? After the last apex kingdom—America or another empire that follows her world domination—fades to black on the stage of life: the day when humans are no longer in charge of Earth."

"What a glorious day that will be." I slide my sweaty hands down my pant legs.

"In your eyes, the eyes of Earth's Orphan Dreamer, is humanity lost?"

"Maybe . . . probably. But I'm not the judge of the world. Yahweh is." Now only obedience to my heavenly Father's will and love for my daughter drive me to complete my mission. "Why did you call me the Orphan Dreamer?"

"That's who you are—right?"

"It is, but who told you?"

"Your husband."

"So the cat's out of the bag?"

"And she's a beautiful feline." He laughs, and I smile.

"What does my title of Orphan Dreamer mean to you?"

"Sacrifice, no different from the fallen heroes who lie in caskets all around us."

"I wouldn't make that comparison." I rub my finger along my earlobe. "I'm no hero. A servant, but not a hero."

"But you are, and you're a warrior who has been fighting outside of the spotlight for our second chance since before you could watch a PG-13 movie by yourself. Day after day, you picked up your weapon and fought the invisible battle for us wayward hellions."

"Was it worth it?" I roll my shoulders back, softening the ache between my scapula.

"Yours was the battle that actually mattered." Ribey crosses his arms. "In the end, I hope we don't disappoint you."

"Charlie, I don't care for liars or gossips." I rap my fingers across the colonel's desk and release a long sigh. "Cillian's body wasn't found inside a Russian tunnel. He was fighting in Northern Syria." The colonel shifts his weight. "Please explain why you lied on your report." Charlie glances to where the president had been standing and then says nothing to defend himself. "I travelled to Syria, Charlie. I saw Cillian on that chopper. Sick. Pouring sweat while holding his family close."

"How? You shouldn't have been there. Were you a stowaway? That's against protocol!" Charlie crosses his arms.

"I guess Cil didn't tell you every detail about the abilities of the Orphan Dreamer."

"He obviously didn't." Charlie closes the distance between us. "What are you?"

"I'll tell you what you're not. The US military only dominates Earth's first three dimensions." I grin—wide, free. "Not the fourth dimension of time. It's true: Other militaries have attempted to dominate time. The scientists of the Third Reich gave it a go, but they failed." Pausing, I let my statement sink into his mind. "Tell me the rest, Charlie."

"You should know that just because Cillian was in Northern Syria fighting, doesn't mean he wasn't in Russia—or that he didn't die there."

"Explain!" I step closer, violating Charlie's personal space.

"I can't, but what I will tell you is that when my soldiers here at Dover unzipped the commander's body bag, I was standing at his side. I touched his skin. It was cold and wet, still splattered with stony grit, but . . ."

"Charlie?"

"The soldier in that box is intact, identifiable, but that

corpse is not the commander. That's not Wraith—our Cillian."

Sheldon—that lying sack of scrambled eggs! I clench my fists and inhale several slow Pilates breaths. "Where's my husband, then?"

"I don't know."

"I won't abandon my husband out *there* all alone." My facial muscles twitch. "Help me find him, Charlie."

"If he's out there, how do we find him?"

"I don't know exactly, but I need him home, Charlie. When the last trumpet sounds during the Feast of Trumpets, Rosh Hashanah, you, me, Cil, and so many others will be leaving Earth and going home—forever."

"Cil is my friend too. Of course I'll help you." In the privacy of his office, Charlie—my booger-eating, freckle-faced middle-school friend, now all grown up—embraces me. "Promise."

"And promises, like hearts, must be kept."

9—ORPHAN DREAMER

LOOKING SICK IS NOT MY modus operandi because I won't be any person's charity case or victim. I inhale several deep breaths from the nasal cannula that rests beneath my nose, then remove the cannula and oxygen tank, leaving them both in the secretary's office.

Dressed in a navy-blue pantsuit and a French-blue shirt, I march behind a Secret Service agent as he opens a concealed door that leads into the Oval Office. President Sheldon Covington stands behind the Resolute desk, his back to me and the north-facing fireplace. "Hello, Daniela. You get around. Delaware, now Washington, DC."

"Owning a private jet makes it easy."

"One family. Three jets. Not concerned about climate change, I see."

"Ready for January twenty-first, your last day flying on Marine One?" I taunt. Hands in his trouser pockets, President Covington doesn't face me. "The day you'll no longer be president?" I care nothing of politics—my war isn't with my fellow humans and their empires. But he does. Silence. "Where is he, Sheldon? Where is my husband?"

"Gone." He tosses me a closed envelope stamped in bold red letters: **TOP SECRET**. I open it and read the letter.

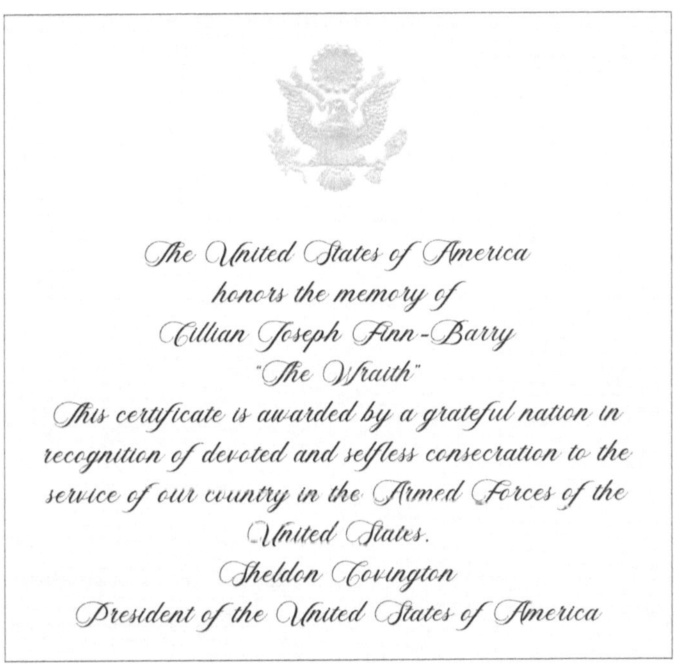

The United States of America
honors the memory of
Cillian Joseph Finn-Barry
"The Wraith"
This certificate is awarded by a grateful nation in
recognition of devoted and selfless consecration to the
service of our country in the Armed Forces of the
United States.
Sheldon Covington
President of the United States of America

"The letter is a PMC—a presidential memorial certificate." I toss the letter back onto the president's desk. "Why is the letter stamped top secret?

"I know what it is, Daniela. I signed it."

"But PMCs are always requested by the family after a US soldier dies, and I haven't requested one."

"You're smart. I see now why the medical school admissions committee accepted you."

"Is he dead?" Silence. "If he's not dead, where is he?"

"In the movies, the actor would say, 'If I told you, I'd have to kill you.' And sometimes the movies get it right." He struts from behind the Resolute desk and stands way too close to me. His breath smells of potato salad and baloney.

Only God knows how many COVID-20 viral particles are escaping the back of his throat. I step back—way back. "Go home. Adelaide needs you. She's got a controversial research paper to write about religion, after all."

What's he going on about? I say to myself, then refocus the conversation. "Where is he, Sheldon?" I mutter. He ignores me. "Where. Is. My. Husband?" I grab the letter, ball up the PMC, and throw it at the president's smug face. It bounces off his glistening forehead.

Sheldon nods, and a Secret Service agent begins to escort me out of the Oval Office.

"You don't want to assault a president. You'll die in a federal prison, and I like you free—for now. So take your temper tantrum back to the hills of North Carolina." He puffs out his chest. "I am America."

"You're not a god, nor the embodiment of the spirit of this great country—and I'm already dying, Sheldon. I wouldn't mind taking you with me, but we'll be parting ways after we're both dead."

"Heaven and hell, the fairy tales of the pathetic."

The Secret Service agent presses a button on his lapel.

The president raises his hand, stopping what would have been a tsunami of CATs—not furry felines, but the Counter Assault Team of the Secret Service charged with a simple mission: neutralize and eliminate any threat to the president. "That's not very Christian, Daniela."

"Then good for you that I am a follower of the

Way—not a political, cultural, money-grubbing version of a Christ follower. As the Orphan Dreamer, I remind you that there is another way."

"In this world, everyone is jockeying for position, power, and privilege."

"Not everyone. Because my Master's kingdom is not of this world. Political party, race, and a bank account provide little street cred where either of us are going after we die."

"Not of this world . . . huh, so if you're some sort of alien being, an extraterrestrial, why save humanity, Daniela?"

"I'm not a little green alien, nor is Yeshua." I pour molten steel into my voice. Flash frozen, it hardens. "No definition in Merriam-Webster's dictionary could define His truest essence. And to answer your question, it's my duty to throw a lifeline to my neighbor."

"And this . . ." he says, surveying the Oval Office, "is mine." He waves me back to him. "Come." I don't budge, so he approaches me. "Roswell, New Mexico . . . Area 51. Claire's dad was there."

"Before or after he murdered his wife and attempted to murder Claire?"

"Before." He pauses. "For the sake of one's sanity, some things are best left unseen and undiscovered, Daniela."

"Come clean."

"He saw *them*." Visibly shaken, Sheldon reaches for my arm, and I step backward, avoiding his touch.

"Who's *them*?" A sour taste fills my mouth as I leverage my best poker face.

"Your Watchers—the fathers of the Nephilim."

"Why didn't you tell me before? Why didn't Claire tell me during our phone call this morning?"

"She doesn't know. He never told her, but I found his

journal. Help us . . . protect us from them until we reach the hive. Give us a chance before you float away to your non-little-green-men alien kingdom." Sheldon smirks as he crosses his arms. "You owe us this."

"To owe means to be in debt to someone or something. I owe you and your bees nothing."

"Then for old times' sake. Time travel into the future. Learn the ways of our enemies. Help us formulate a war plan to stop them—or at least delay the invaders." Sheldon glares at me. I refuse to move a muscle in my face. "Maybe you're one of them, Daniela."

"That depends on the identity of *them*." I taunt him while I trace the outline of the Glass Tattoo tucked beneath my dress shirt. My shoulders relax.

Sheldon furrows his brow. "By them, I mean—"

I raise my hand. "The hideously dreadful version of the future Watchers."

"You knew?"

"Of course."

"Claire's dad saw a metamorphosis of the original Watchers, the fathers of the Nephilim, from angel to something monstrous."

"A preview of the creatures that will be released during Earth's Great Tribulation."

"Yes, and they were no little green aliens."

"During the Great Tribulation, the Watchers will not appear as they once were—powerful, beautiful angels. Instead, when they come again, each will possess the body of a horse, the face of a man, a woman's hair, teeth like a lion's, wings, and tails." I shiver while rubbing the goosebumps popping up on my arms as I remember that dreadful day over twenty years ago. "The Bible gives all the details."

"Then you'll help us stop them, because you should be terrified as well—and because you know that to refuse me means that you will spend the rest of your brief life searching the fourth dimension to find your missing Wraith, because I won't help you."

"If Cillian is lost in the fourth dimension, Mister President, you possess absolutely no way to help me succeed in finding him."

"I command the greatest military on Earth."

"Only in your dimensions of space and time."

"And my Space Force? One day we may be able to defy time without your help."

"Dead on arrival when it comes to fighting the Nephilim and their Watchers." I turn my back to Sheldon and snap a mental photograph of the Oval Office. The busts of some of the world's greatest leaders rest atop pedestals inside the most famous house in America. "Claire told me about your plan." I glance over my shoulder. "Does your staff know what you're up to with the hive?"

"It's not my plan. Belongs to Claire."

"What?" I spin around and face the president.

"Like I said, it's not mine, and I don't agree with her. The trait of bullying other people exists in her genes. It's an Underwood trait. You should know that."

"My dear God, please . . . please bless America, land that I love." I clasp my hands and look up at the ceiling. "Abba! Father, this isn't a command or an inane bumper sticker, but a request. We're going to need Your blessing and protection from Claire's evil schemes."

I exit the Oval Office, retrieve my oxygen tank, and follow Beatha out of the White House to our private car. *That Claire Amilee Underwood Covington! A liar of liars, just like her father Satan.* "That's why she miscarried all her babies—she's a Nephilim." *But I could never carry a child to term either.*

"Who's a Nephilim?"

My mind wanders down familiar paths.

"You okay, Mrs. Daniela?"

"I am, Beatha. I am. You know, travel's a breeze when you're married to a billionaire." She cocks her head and gives me an odd look. It's understandable. I never talk about Cillian's wealth. But I have my reasons. "Just looking at the bright side of things."

"The sun always finds you. You're never in the shadow for long."

"Let's go home. Adelaide expects to eat her favorite meal tonight, and she's been given some crazy research assignment, according to the president." Finding renewed strength in the belly of my anger, I power walk to the car.

"A research assignment, Mrs. Daniela?"

"That's what he said. She has to write a paper about politics and religion."

"How does he know about the paper, Mrs. Daniela? Maybe the president is the one who wants that paper written and hopes that you share your thoughts with Adelaide, so he can spy on you."

"Now I know why Cillian loves you so much. You are Mossad, Betty Crocker, and Harriet Tubman wrapped into one woman. And I love you too, Beatha. Thank you for being you."

"Ah, go on, Mrs. Daniela."

"It's Daniela. Just plain Daniela." I smile.

10—Orphan Dreamer

THE HIKE TO THE TWIN lakes promised solitude, not safety. Melted ice dripped from an aspen tree, then splashed across sixteen-year-old Daniela's nose. Nearby, a twig cracked, and birds chirped as she clutched the grip of her recurve bow—a beauty constructed with onyx limbs anchored to a honey-stained Shedua riser.

Earlier that morning, after the Orphan Dreamer had awakened and aborted her time travels, the Glass Tattoo ejected from her right hand, forcing the nightmare from here mind: military morgues, domestic espionage, and desert battlefields.

Walking briskly, she closed the gap between her and her kindred spirit, Emmaline. After gulping tea from a thermos, she capped it and released the canister to rest above her hips, where it dangled next to a quiver full of Port Orford cedar-footed arrows.

The Orphan Dreamer could escape any crisis with her bow, her twelve arrows, and her kindred spirit at her side.

"Danny Rose, you're not getting off the hook. You never answered my question." Snow crunched, then flattened beneath Emmaline's hiking boots, leaving a path for her friend to walk in.

"I forgot the question."

"A man presses a gun to your forehead and demands you answer his question in ten seconds or *bang*, you're dead: Fall in love or save the world. Decide. Ten. Nine. Eight. Seven . . ."

"First off, you're a girl. And second, why are you still teasing me about oily boy, Limy?" she said, her voice a whisper among dead leaves.

"I was born to matchmake lovebirds," Emmaline replied, equally quiet. "It's a Darbyshire trait. Four. Three. Two. One."

"I'd fall in love," Daniela said, matter-of-fact.

"Okay. Then let's forget all the save-the-world stuff and find your oily boy."

"News flash: I die. He dies. You die."

"So he's real then and not just a figment of your dreams?"

"I hope he's real. But I don't *know* that he's real." Daniela sighed. "Role reversal. What's going on with you and Toby?"

"Crickets."

"They make noise, at least. More than I can say for this remote trail." Daniela surveyed her surroundings—a narrow hiking path walled in by mountain slopes.

"Maybe ghosts are haunting this place."

"Stop, Limy. I don't like scary stories, especially while backcountry hiking."

"I thought you loved the quiet, Miss Introvert."

"Not this kind." The wolf within Daniela howled, promising trouble. But what kind? She rested her hand on her quiver.

"Does the isolation of this trail bother you?"

"A bit."

"Did you ever see the movie *Deliverance*?"

"No, and don't tell me about it," Daniela said, hoping to squelch any more of Emmaline's scary stories—her specialty.

"Fine. As for Toby, he's as outgoing as a pair of catatonic crickets," Emmaline said, and they laughed together.

The girls had been released three hours early from work at the lab. Eager to make the most of their free afternoon, they had driven an hour to Trampas Lakes Trail, hidden in the Pecos Wilderness near Santa Fe, New Mexico.

"Danny-girl, according to the map you snatched from the library, the hike to the lake is a twelve-mile round trip through a narrow pass between two snow capped mountain ridges."

"So basically, we're boxed in for twelve miles in the forest." Powdered snow dusted the Orphan Dreamer's olive-green down jacket while dampening her voice.

"Embraced by, not boxed in. Life's all about perspective."

"Some people lie to themselves better than others." Daniela jogged ahead on the trail. "On the bright side, the trail promises the reward of seeing a pair of pristine lakes."

"One for you." Emmaline nudged Daniela, bumping

her off the trail and crashing into a ponderosa pine. "One for me."

"The lakes aren't single guys."

"Then let's skinny dip."

"Not on your life! In this weather, the lakes are most likely still capped with a thin layer of ice." A howl in the distance stabbed Daniela in the gut. *What are you trying to tell me?* "We're not slushing," she finally said.

"Did you hear that?"

"We should've started hiking at first light, not at one o'clock," Daniela chided.

"Have gun, will travel. We'll survive any stupid wolf that tries to attack us."

"But maybe not a pack of wolves. Besides, the gray wolf is protected by the Endangered Species Act, so you can't shoot or kill one unless you want to pay a six-figure fine and serve time in prison."

"Then we'll run like banshees." Emmaline folded the map and stuffed it into her pant pocket. "I'd like for you to reconsider camping with me in the Jemez Mountains this weekend."

"In the snow?"

"In the snow. In the wild. It could be that you're destined to meet your oily boy in some remote wilderness." Emmaline slapped her hand to her brow, mimicking an overly dramatic actress. "A damsel in distress rescued by a wild, unshaven rugged man."

"Here we go again." Daniela rolled her eyes. "Why do you want me to endure a catastrophe just so I can be rescued by a guy from my dreams—who may or not be real?"

"It's romantic, Danny Rose!"

"Only in a novel, Limy." Daniela shook her head, then

smiled. "You're an Anne of Green Gables clone, and I love you for that, but I'm just fine with meeting a nice guy in the produce aisle of a grocery store."

"You're the dreamer, so dream!" Emmaline hiked around an outcropping of shrubs, then changed subjects. "Earlier, I was telling you the truth."

"I'm not accusing you of lying, but I am not *Titanic's* Rose DeWitt Bukater."

"Good. The *Titanic* sank, even in the movie." Emmaline laughed, and Daniela rolled her eyes again.

"I'm just not that girl. No one notices me. I'm invisible, a ghost. Most days, I am content with my reality, leaving all the guys to crawl all over you like lice in matted hair while leaving me alone."

"Only Daniela Rose could make dating sound like a lice infestation," Emmaline quipped, then both girls burst out laughing.

"Seriously," Daniela huffed. "During last week's party at Alfonso's loft, I hugged the wall all night."

"I noticed, and I also watched you pour your beer into a window planter."

"I don't drink. I couldn't dump the stuff in the toilet because the bathroom was occupied all night by underage teenagers puking their guts out."

"Daniela, you can't be serious!"

"Shh! I thought I heard something." Daniela stopped. Emmaline stopped, and they both listened. "Nothing. Let's keep hiking."

"Even my dad gives me a beer once in a while."

"We're both underage."

"So?" Emmaline shrugged.

"Maybe the cops would give you a pass for breaking the

law, but not me. If I do the crime, I'll do the time. My parents already gave me the talk about my reality as a brown-skinned person in America."

"But they never talked to you about romance?" Emmaline asked.

"Priorities." Comparing discrimination to romance? Somewhat odd.

"Tell me this: how many cacti have you slaughtered via alcohol-induced intoxication because of your teetotalism?" Emmaline chuckled by herself.

"One."

"Next time, tell Alfonso you don't want a beer."

"I didn't want to sound rude or prudish." Daniela struggled to catch her breath as her heart frantically pumped blood, attempting to oxygenate the cells of her aching muscles as the girls climbed from an elevation of nine thousand feet to eleven thousand feet.

"You've got to learn how to talk to a guy." Gravel shifted as they trudged up the incline. "It's an art."

"I'm awkward, Limy. Nosebleeds. Out-of-the-blue thoughts. Off-topic comments . . . never been kissed by a boy."

"And that's a crime against humanity!" Emmaline shouted, then lowered her voice. "I could pay my brother to kiss you."

"Goodness, Limy, I'm not that pathetic. I don't pay for sensual favors, and while my life's no Simmie Knox portrait, I do possess a life. Yes. It's messy, even weird, but I've accepted my reality, and I sort of even like parts of it. It's hard for me to express how I feel to a random girl, much less a living, breathing boy." Daniela's breath hitched.

"Would you like to stop, rest—eat a protein bar?"

She noticed. "Thanks." Daniela plopped down on a rock

that projected from the mountain slope. She inhaled crisp, cold air permeated with the woody aroma of ponderosa pine, aspen, and a variety of spruce and fir trees.

After catching her breath, she said, "I'm just trying to make friends too . . . maybe even go on a date."

"Alfonso's single." Emmaline grinned.

"He's gay."

"Really?"

"Positive. Li Xiu told me at the party after I accepted the beer from him."

"But he didn't tell you that."

"True . . . he's nice to me when we work in the same lab."

"Then ask him out on a date."

"I'm too afraid."

"Then I'll ask for you." Emmaline didn't give Daniela time to accept or decline her offer. "What do you think about Li Xiu? Is she a spy from the People's Republic of China?"

"She's our postdoc and mentor—how would I know?"

"From your Orphan Dreamer travels." Emmaline sat on the boulder beside Daniela and faced her friend. "And she's a Chinese woman working in a major defense lab in America."

"News flash. The Chinese people have lived in America since the 1800s. She's no more of a criminal than you or me. Why do you really think she might be a spy?" Silence filled the spaces between conspiracy, espionage, and common sense.

"I thought I saw her slip a vial inside her work bag."

"You thought—or you know? The realities are not the same, especially if you're accusing someone of espionage. Besides, why would she steal a virus or bacteria? Some of those microbes are beastly."

"I didn't stick around to ask, but I'm worried." Emmaline finished her protein bar and chugged down a bottle of water.

"We'll keep an eye on her—together." Daniela stood, ready to hike. "But not because she's Chinese." She winked.

"Danny." Emmaline slipped her finger into the pocket of Daniela's hiking pants. Daniela pulled away.

"What's wrong?"

"While you were taking a bath last night, you entered some sort of catatonic state. I was worried but didn't call 911 because you told me that sometimes you time travelled, and I thought that were you travelling."

"I'm sorry."

"I'm not angry, and I can deal with the situation, but I worry about you. What if you bugged out while you were driving or swimming?"

"I avoid lakes, oceans, rivers, and ponds, just like I avoid Ebola. I can't swim, remember?"

"And driving?"

"I can drive. I can't travel unless I purposefully engage the Glass Tattoo." She pointed at the snowflake diamond hanging from her neck.

"How exactly does it work again?"

"I hold it in my right hand. If I am supposed to travel, the relic disappears into my palm and a midnight-blue tattoo shows up in its place. It opens a portal to a timeless place where answers beyond man's knowledge are found and the past, present, or future can be relived."

"Does this place have a name?"

"Ellesmere."

"Sounds so *Lord of the Rings*."

"Love the books."

"So do I." Emmaline agreed with Daniela. "Right

before you slipped into your catatonic state and travelled, you said, 'Take me to the stars, oily boy.' I sat with you until you awoke because I couldn't let you drown in eighteen inches of water."

"You protected me, Limy." The Orphan Dreamer hugged her ally. "Thank you." Daniela blinked fast, imprisoning all but one rebellious tear. "I didn't mean to scare you. Honest, I didn't." Feelings of shame invaded the capillaries beneath Daniela's skin, flushing her.

"Don't be embarrassed."

"I could have slipped beneath the surface of the water and drowned, burdening you with my death."

"But you didn't. You did shave off a few years from the end of my life, and fair is fair, so don't play Alzheimer's possum with me. You were tossing and turning while you slept." Emmaline buried her gloved hands in her pant pockets. "You spoke about a man—Black Irish: raven hair, pale skin, and sky-blue eyes—while I saved you from drowning."

"A man, not a boy?" Daniela's face flushed hot.

"A red-blooded man."

"No way! I couldn't have." She hiked past Emmaline and navigated down the snow-packed trail toward the lake.

"Don't run from me. Remember, I saved your life . . ."

"I don't remember dreaming about a man," Daniela hollered over her shoulder, breaking her cardinal rule of always hiking in stealth mode—seen but not heard. "Much less a handsome one."

Emmaline jogged to catch up, then gripped Daniela's arm. "In a friendship, there's room for secrets, but never lies. Your rule, not mine." She stopped, then pulled Daniela to a stop.

Both girls gasped.

The forest had parted, revealing a partially frozen glacial lake surrounded by shear mountains that reached to the clear-blue sky. Had they been transported to another dimension: heaven on earth, a dreamworld?

Daniela's deception of omission stood bare against the raw honesty of nature. "This view defines breathtaking. Raw. Honest. Perfect." Out of breath, Daniela's voice came in sputters. "Technically, according to the Endangered Species Act, you can kill a gray wolf if you're acting in self-defense or in defense of other human life." She paused before her big confession. "I did dream, but it was a nightmare about a scraggly homeless kid with a blurred-out face, black pits where eyes should have been, and lice-infested hair."

"I think . . ." Emmaline nervously glanced over her right shoulder.

"What's that?" Daniela grabbed Emmaline's arm.

"Voices?"

"Whose? This place is supposed to be deserted." Daniela insisted. "Fall back."

They crouched behind a rocky outcropping of the mountain as two hikers disappeared past a cluster of aspens only to reappear as the man skipped atop russet-colored boulders that jutted up from the clear, cold lake.

"It's just two lovebirds." Emmaline rolled her eyes and strolled toward the lake. "And I'm positive you were making love to the guy in your dreams."

"No—never. I couldn't . . . I wouldn't. I don't know how!"

"Calm down. Zombies and ghosts aren't roaming the planet, and the apocalypse hasn't begun—yet!"

"But my parents!" Daniela strolled closer to the couple, curious about the depth of the lake. Emmaline ran past the Orphan Dreamer, turned, and walked backward as she continued her interrogation.

"Are your parents afraid that one day you'll grow up and actually want to kiss a boy? It's not illegal."

"My mom always says, 'Boys and books don't mix.' And my dad prayed for Armageddon to happen before I eclipsed puberty. In my parents' world, kissing a boy deserves capital punishment."

"Then don't get caught." Emmaline kicked a rock into the lake. "Your parents never prepared you for romance. What a shame. You're so pretty."

"Me? Pretty?"

"You."

"Okay." Daniela stooped beside the lake's edge and weaved her hand through the shallows. Her fingers grew numb from the frigid water and floating ice. "My parents don't want me to get hurt."

"Back to Earth, and Limy to the rescue."

"You don't understand."

"What's there to understand, Danny Rose?"

"I'm not married." An eagle swooped from the sky, soaring about fifty feet above the lake before diving toward an unfrozen portion on the other side. "I'm supposed to stay a virgin until I marry." Daniela splashed her face with cold water.

"Is that what you want—to remain stagnant in your sexuality, a.k.a. a virgin, until you're married?"

"As a matter of fact, it is." Daniela stood, then removed an arrow from her quiver. "But I'm not stagnant. More like steady."

Mindlessly, she fluffed the fletching, the tangerine-colored feathers attached to the shaft just below the nock. The indicating fletch—the feather that would point outward when the arrow was properly nocked—showed silver within the sun's light. When the arrow was released, the fletching would create drag, forcing the arrow into a spin like a bullet shot from the barrel of a gun.

"Why wait?"

"It's simple, really." Daniela shrugged.

"Help this complex mind understand."

"I'm only sixteen, and I don't see any reason to make temporary decisions about my sexuality that will force me to deal with permanent consequences."

"Maybe the consequence is love," Emmaline said, her voice soft.

"At sixteen?"

"There's a chance. Even Anne from Green Gables met her Gilbert Blythe while still in grade school."

"You're Anne. I'm Diana Barry. It's not my gig, Limy—I am not a risk-taker." Her tone up-ticked an octave. "I long to fall in love, but I'm not emotionally ready to sleep with anyone. I'll wait for my husband. That's my preference. Why do we have to spread-eagle just because society expects us to? We women each have a brain, not just a body. We each have a spirit, not just a soul, so we can choose to wait and expect to not be shamed while doing so."

"Well said, crow head—my Diana Barry. That's real girl power. Maybe I'll wait from now on too. But talking to a guy isn't making love."

"Never said it was. Maybe talking first is better, but I'm an introvert, remember? Beer-pouring cactus killer." The girls laughed. "Most times, I'm too afraid to speak up, Limy. Absolutely terrified to say a word."

"But you're the Orphan Dreamer, destined to warn the masses about the end of the world as we know it."

"Ironic, huh?" Daniela sighed, then giggled. "Don't

worry. I won't slack, even if I didn't choose the assignment. But know this: *I've* chosen my approach to sexuality. There must be commitment between me and my homeless waif. I'm not asking much, just the right to my own body."

"Blessed Virgin Mary, you are still untouched." Emmaline sighed. "I'm sure your hymen is still intact. Just a wet dream." She winked, then revealed a pitiful smile. "And, no, you're not asking much."

"If you meet my parents, don't joke about sex in front of them. Please."

"Love isn't a joke."

"But lust plays jokes on sixteen-year-old hearts."

"You deserve oily boy, Danny-girl. A man who's the reason love songs are written." As if on cue, Emmaline's handheld radio serenaded them with Etta James's "At Last." Emmaline extended her hand. "Dance with me, Danny-girl."

Daniela obliged.

Is this real? She hoped so yet felt guilty at the same time. It was true: To be genuinely happy was to be content. To be content was to be full, and not every human was or would ever be full. Why should Daniela—a nerdy introvert—be happy and content while others weren't and never would be?

Life's not fair, and survivor's guilt sucks lemon curds!

Resting her head on Emmaline's shoulder, the Orphan Dreamer shuffled her feet to the rhythm of the song. "Finally, a kindred spirit," she whispered. Red hair with an adventurous spirit to match.

"Agreed."

"Limy, thanks for giving me a chance." Daniela didn't deserve this much happiness, promise, and possibility. She blinked back emotions of guilt.

"At your service, Mrs. Oily Boy."

"You're like a broken record. I don't remember that part of the dream, only the bad stuff."

"Try to remember." Emmaline whispered.

"Don't get my hopes up. Please. I'm not like you." She pushed away from the dance. "It was another nightmare, nothing more."

"Be brave. Fall in love."

"I won't survive a fall any better than Lucifer survived his." Daniela slipped into a schizophrenic's dissociative thought pattern. "For the record, I despise spiders and cold, dark, and deep lakes and oceans." Her mouth went dry.

Ignoring the mishap, Emmaline didn't mock her friend. She embraced Daniela, then released her back into the world—the world of an empath, an introvert—where dialogue mostly happened in her thoughts.

"Thanks, Limy."

"Your problem, Danny-girl . . ." Emmaline swept a stray ringlet from Daniela's face. "You see the night sky but refuse to see the stars. Why? Is it safer to filter out the stars? The light? The good part?"

"I prefer for my feet to touch Earth's surface at all times. And I like sunlight instead of nightfall. That's all." Daniela fingered the shaft beneath the arrowhead—the relic gifted to her by an ancient Hebrew prince named Jonathan when she had time travelled to Gibeah. "I've been places and seen things." She looked into Emmaline's curious eyes.

"What have you seen?"

"Enough to know that all of this beauty surrounding us will not last forever. The clock is ticking down to zero." Daniela inhaled the scent of ponderosa pine as birds sang a cheerful song. "Do me a favor."

"I'm your girl. Always will be." Emmaline squeezed Daniela's hand.

"It sounds crazy, but . . ."

"Since the days of my firebrand ancestor—Mary, Queen of Scots—crazy's been my game and the Darbyshires' motto." Emmaline winked at her new best friend, and Daniela grinned.

"When you return to Boston, don't forget me."

"I won't."

"And don't forget your promise. Help me save our home, Earth, from Lucifer—the sand dragon."

"Look at this place. Of course I'll help assassinate the devil who was once an angel if that means we can hike to this lake again and again." Emmaline spread her arms wide, mimicking the bald eagle circling above the lake. "Still have gun, will travel and shoot dead any wolf who attacks you." She snapped to attention, then saluted Daniela. "Reporting for duty, Commander Cavanaugh."

Don't laugh.

"You're too silly, but I need to be honest with you, Private Darbyshire."

"Private?"

"Staff Sergeant." Daniela pulled Emmaline's hand down from her forehead. "We'll require weapons more powerful than bullets."

"Your arrows are definitely not more powerful than my bullets." Emmaline furrowed her brow.

"Traveling at three hundred feet a second, an arrow can pierce a bulletproof vest, tunnel past skin, muscle, and bone, and pierce a tree behind the vest wearer."

"Impressive." Emmaline's mouth hung open. "Summer project: master archery."

"If you come to Gainesville this summer, I'll teach

you. But in order to engage Lucifer in battle, we'll require weapons that can silence an invisible enemy—a ghost."

"A ghost, like the Sons of Venus?"

"The who?"

"Never mind." Emmaline averted her eyes and meandered toward the shoreline of the closest partially frozen lake.

"I imagine that we'll meet all kinds of sordid characters along our journey—men and women hiding behind veils of secret societies, governments, and radical groups." Daniela caught up with Emmaline. "Can you handle this new reality—the life of a warrior?"

"It's unsafe." Emmaline reached down, picked up a rock, and threw it toward the frozen portion of the lake. The rock disappeared below the fractured sheet of ice. "Uncertain. Perhaps painful." She grinned. "I'm a born risk-taker."

"The yin to my yang." Daniela sheathed the arrow. "So much pressure solving ancient mysteries with the world's fate riding on our success or failure."

"At least we've solved one question: when." Emmaline encouraged her friend.

"Yep. After the blood moons of 2014 and 2015. The monster can't start his earth-shattering pandemic until then."

"We've got a few years to just have a bit of fun."

"Maybe a year, because I don't know how fast I can solve the ancient riddles, and every child deserves to live in a world where dreams really do come true." Daniela rested her hand on her friend's shoulder. "One day, we'll be able to lay down our weapons—but from this moment on, we're at war."

"A dastardly plan!" Emmaline licked her delicate lips. "I'm dying to kick someone's butt."

"So am I." Daniela grinned.

"You should take a bath, Danny Rose." Emmaline kissed Daniela on the cheek. "You smell like sex."

"What? How? You're such a little joker!" Daniela chased her friend across slippery pebbles and stones. "Cold, deep, and dark lakes—not my pastime."

"How could I forget?"

Suddenly, the man skipping along the rocks ahead of them and farther out onto the lake slipped, then disappeared beneath the surface. "Delbert! Delbert! Help! Help!" The woman shrieked.

"Why on earth did he venture out onto a half-frozen lake? Do you still have that rope in your backpack, Limy?"

"Affirmative." The girls made tracks, arriving next to the woman standing on a wide, flat bolder just past the shoreline, before the lake turned into deep water with a thin overlay of ice.

The man bobbed up from the water and tried to grip the edge of the ice slab blocking him from shore. No luck. But at least he had emerged from his arctic grave. "Delbert!" The woman waved her hands as though they were ropes that would pull him back to shore.

"Who is he?"

"My husband, and he's got a bad heart. Please." She clutched Daniela's arm. "Please help him."

The Orphan Dreamer shook the woman loose and focused on her task: save Delbert. "Lie on your back!" Daniela hollered to the man. "Limy, tie your end of the rope around the first pine tree closest to the shore. Can you tie a constrictor knot?"

"Of course I can. My parents own a sailboat." Emmaline ran her end of the rope back up the sloped shoreline, sloshing through ice-cold water. She wrapped the long rope around a ponderosa pine, then secured it via a constrictor knot.

The woman kept waving and screaming.

"Shh." Daniela rested her hand on the woman's shoulder and beckoned her to shore as they inched toward the shallows of the frozen shoreline. Immediately, the ice cracked, and Daniela and the woman stood calf-deep in icy water. Thank God for waterproof socks and boots. "Did you hear that?"

"No."

"Something's crying for help."

"I don't hear anyone," Limy said. "I hear the piping of an eagle and Delbert splashing."

"That's not it."

"Focus, please," the frantic wife demanded. "The doctor recently diagnosed me with ovarian cancer. We honeymooned here, and we decided to relive our youth. It's not time for my Delbert Blythe to die. Save him."

"We're working on it." Daniela cupped her hands around her mouth. "Hold on, Delbert! We're sending out a rope."

"Look." Emmaline pointed toward the blue sky. "That bald eagle is dive-bombing a defect in the ice on the other side the lake. Why?"

Help. Help, Daniela heard the weak cry again. It wasn't coming from Delbert Blythe.

Emmaline peered through her binoculars and scanned the lake. "Goodness gumdrops, there's a wolf cub hanging on to a lip of ice on the far edge of the hole in the water. It's not going to last much longer, Danny-girl."

"It's a stupid dog, girls." The woman grabbed Daniela's arm. "Save my husband. We've been married for twenty years. We married at eighteen."

Ever the introverted thinker, Daniela kept her thoughts to herself. *I don't think the pup is the stupid one, ma'am.* "The pup's asking for my help. I'm going to help it too."

"What?" The woman shook Daniela. "Dog's and wolves whimper and wail. They don't ask. What's wrong with you, child?"

"They can ask, and they do." The Orphan Dreamer glared at the woman. "You're wasting my time."

"You can hear animal thoughts as well as God's thoughts?" Emmaline placed the untethered rope end into the Orphan Dreamer's hand.

"Grab the fire starter." Daniela yanked one arrow from her quiver, wrapped the rope beneath the fletching, and tied a constrictor knot. "The rope will add quite a bit of drag, causing the arrow to drift, so this may not work."

"It better," the agitated woman threatened.

"Or what?" The Orphan Dreamer glared at the woman. She shrank back as Daniela aimed the weapon twenty-five degrees above the man's watering hole and released.

Bull's-eye. Better be. She'd learned from her grandfather when she was only six years old.

The arrow landed inside the man's death trap, piercing the water. "Wrap the rope beneath your shoulders!" Daniela yelled to the man, then faced his wife. "You're in charge of pulling him to shore until Limy and I save the cub."

"You're leaving me?"

"Just start pulling," Daniela snapped. "Limy, light the fire starter." Emmaline removed the binoculars from her face. "The bald eagle trained its sights on the drowning pup."

"It's not dinnertime yet." Daniela nocked a blunt-tipped arrow, aimed high toward the bird of prey, drew, and released.

"You'll kill it!"

"Hoping to only knock it off course." *Success!* Dazed, the eagle stalled, fluttering its wings but still flying, albeit in a disorganized pattern. *Save the wolf pup.* On the other side of the lake, a lone gray wolf waited.

"Across the lake . . . must be a she-wolf, the cub's mother."

Emmaline refocused her binoculars. "She's a beauty, whoever she is. It's a gray wolf, alright. Black muzzle. White stripe punctuated with a black circle runs down the middle of her head and ends at her nostrils."

"Limy! Pay attention." The she-wolf howled a mournful tune, ripping the Orphan Dreamer's soul into shreds. She loaded another arrow, this one constructed of wood and a metal tip interwoven with a flammable material. "Light it up."

"But the shaft's wood."

"We're wasting time, Limy."

"It'll drown unless we go out and rescue it." Emmaline lit the tip of the arrow.

"That bozo was skipping across stones less than a hundred feet from shore and fell through after he slipped off a rock. The ice is too thin to hold our body weight." She nocked the arrow, drew, then released. The flaming arrow struck the thin layer of ice that blocked the pup from swimming to its mother.

"You missed."

"No, I didn't."

Emmaline surveyed the damage via her binoculars. "You cracked the ice."

"Good. Light her up." After Emmaline lit the next flammable tip, Daniela reloaded and fired. They repeated the process three times. "Binoculars." The thin sheet of ice blocking the pup from its mother had been obliterated, clearing the path for the eager mother to rescue her curious child.

The she-wolf dove into the water and swam, pulled her exhausted pup back to shore, then disappeared into the forest, most likely to return to their den.

"Will it live, Danny-girl?"

"I hope so. We'll pray that it does."

Minutes later, as the girls helped the frantic wife pull her husband from the lake, a howl filled the air. Daniela stood up straight, then smiled. "You're welcome."

"Don't tell me the wolf said thank you," the woman mocked.

Delbert Blythe asked, "What's your name, Miss?"

"Daniela Rose. My friends call me Danny Rose. This is my friend, Emmaline."

"Thank you, Danny Rose and Emmaline."

"You're welcome, sir," the girls said in unison.

Shivering, the man shook both of their hands. "You saved my life. Not that it's worth saving. My heart's not too good these days."

"I'm sorry to hear that," Daniela said.

Sitting on the ground beside a fire and draped in a wool blanket, the man reached for his backpack. "I want to give you something. It's not much, but I'm a woodworker." He gifted Emmaline a carving of a hummingbird and Daniela a carving of a fish. "You, my child, are a fisher of men."

Daniela tilted her head. "That's what Yeshua said to Peter, His apostle."

"Indeed, it is. Go fish for souls."

"Yes, sir, but you'll die of hypothermia if you don't get warm." Daniela and Emmaline assisted the couple by gathering more firewood, setting up their tent, and tending to the man until he dried off and fell asleep inside his toasty sleeping bag.

The Orphan Dreamer shouldered her bow and faced the trail. "Six miles back. It's almost dark. Let's go home, Limy."

"Ready to dream about oily boy again?" Emmaline trudged beside her weary friend.

"I'd love a hot bath without even dreaming of sheep tonight."

"Then give me the Glass Tattoo."

"You can't activate the stone, Limy."

"I know, but you can." Emmaline placed the relic inside Daniela's front jacket pocket. "Don't touch it by mistake." The girls hiked back to Emmaline's Jeep without speaking.

Dusk yielded to night—Daniela's least favorite time of day. Thankful for returning to the Jeep before dark and being safe inside the truck's cabin, Emmaline flipped on the vehicle's lights and heater, illuminating their path and warming the cabin. "Danny, I've decided."

"What?"

"Your life—my life—doesn't need to mimic a Simmie Knox portrait with perfect, clean lines. Georges-Pierre Seurat painted using pointillism: a mosaic of colorful dots, insignificant on their own but a masterpiece when completed. And Seurat's 1884 Parisian *Sunday Afternoon on the Island of La Grande Jatte* is worth over thirty-five million dollars." She paused. "Messy? Yes, but we're on our way to becoming priceless."

"Beautiful and poetic, Limy. Thank you." In their journey, they had saved two strangers. Character couldn't be painted on like eyeshadow. It took a lifetime of experience, choices, and sacrifice.

"Do you think we'll ever hear from that couple again?"

"They didn't ask for our address, so no," Daniela concluded.

"And the wolf?"

"They don't write letters very well." Daniela chuckled. Beyond the Jeep's window, the asphalt road passed in blurred lines. "My rafiki says, 'Feed a dog for three days, it will remember you for a lifetime. Feed a human for a lifetime, they will forget you in a day.' "

"So you still want to save the world?" Emmaline teased.

"For the sake of the children, my parents, and you— yes, I do."

"Kids?" Emmaline grinned. "Making a romantic decision with permanent consequences?"

"I'm not a nun, Limy. No matter how much my parents want me to act like one." Daniela faced her friend as Emmaline sped down the highway. "I want to fall—no—I want to grow in love, steady like an oak tree."

"The orphan tree."

"That's clever."

"I know." Daniela's kindred spirit squeezed the Orphan Dreamer's thigh. "Then I'll water and fertilize your roots, and one spring while the sun is shining on you, you'll bloom into a rose." She cranked up Sam Cooke's classic tune "A Change Is Gonna Come."

II—Orphan Dreamer

PRAYER IS THE GLUE THAT links chronos time with kairos time, God's appointed time. Outside Daniela and Emmaline's Los Alamos flat, snowflakes, all silvery and bright, fell against the lamplight, casting a wintry veil over the Jemez Mountains.

The roosters were still sleeping as Daniela Rose Cavanaugh sat on her lower bunk bed, rereading a letter that she'd written to Yahweh when she was twelve.

She had titled the letter THE BARGAIN.

Dear Abba, Father,

It's me, again.

Sorry to bug you, but if I am the last Orphan

Dreamer, how do I become "unchosen" without hurting anyone's feelings?

I want to help, but my schedule's full.

I'm still searching for my kindred spirit, the friend who allows me to be myself, keeps my secrets safe, and helps me punish the two meanest girls at Milweekee Middle School—Claire Underwood and Tameka Jenkins.

If you need another Orphan Dreamer, may I suggest three adults who kick butts and take names every day? Ms. Bender, my science teacher, is smart. FYI: her rambunctious kids will need babysitters. Mrs. Johnson, my school bus driver, is punctual. She smokes. Kicking butt and wheezing may not go together, though.

What about Mom?

She's perfect: wise, beautiful, patient, and a crack shot with a sling and stone! Mom could thump the planet robber on the forehead and knock him out cold.

FYI: fighting Lucifer isn't really a task for twelve-year-olds. Please consider increasing the minimum age for the job. You'd find more willing applicants.

Good night!

Yours truly,
Me, the retired Orphan Dreamer

P.S. If I qualify for hazard pay after serving as Orphan Dreamer for twelve hours, one minute, and two seconds, please send the funds to Dad and Mom. They could use the money for Dad's hospital visits. Thanks.

Five years later, at sixteen, on lavender-scented paper, she'd penned another letter to Elohim, the Supreme One, and named this letter THE PROPOSAL.

Dear Abba, Father,

It's me, again.

Sorry to annoy you, but if You want me to discover the identity of the human agent behind Lucifer's plan to annihilate humans from Earth and then fight and defeat this agent, I'll need a few more warriors fighting beside me.

I prefer the kind with broad shoulders, a willing spirit, a big smile, and a wicked sense of humor. If she—or he—knows how to fire a gun, that'll help me out, because I despise guns. In the wrong hands, bullets are too fast at ending a life. I'll stick to my bow and arrow . . . and kill only if absolutely necessary. For instance, if someone's getting ready to launch a nuke and I'm standing in front of them with a loaded bow.

I. Do. Not. Want. To. Murder. Anyone.

Okay?

By the way: After Ethan died, thanks for leading me to another possible kindred spirit: Emmaline Georgiana Winterlyn Darbyshire. She's awesome! Anne of Green Gables, redhead awesome. So cool of You to answer that request. But can I be honest with you? Sometimes she disappoints me. I ask about her worries, and at times, she forgets to ask about mine—unless we're talking about boys, her favorite subject in the universe.

I'm trying to trust You with everything. Honest, I am, but sometimes I feel as though I'm not that special—less than average. How could You really love me?

Sorry about the "wet dream." Promise it won't happen again. Emmaline swears that I dreamed about some hot Black Irish guy. Can't remember a thing about him, but I don't think that she would lie to me.

when we hiked the other day, she said that I smelled like sex. What does lovemaking smell like?

Anyways, I promised Mom and Dad that I wouldn't give up my virginity to any man beside my husband, but I guess, if Emmaline's right, I gave up my virginity in my dreams—to the first guy I met.

Mom tells me that you're a God of second chances, so right here and right now, I'm saying that I'm sorry.

Please . . . let me start over.

FYI: The idea of fighting Lucifer isn't quite as scary as it used to be when I was twelve, but I'm still not stoked about the position. I can't afford for Limy—my hopefully forever kindred spirit—to think that I'm abnormal because I'm the Orphan Dreamer.

She says that she loves me just as I am—nose-bleeds, big hair, and brown skin—but she's only known me for three months.

Good night!

Yours truly,
Me, the reluctant Orphan Dreamer

P.S. I guess I didn't qualify for hazard pay after being chosen as the Orphan Dreamer, but my research job at Los Alamos National Laboratory pays $2,000 a month. The money helps with Dad's hospital visits . . . so I guess You answered that prayer too. Thanks.

Standing up beside her bed, Daniela tucked her journal beneath her pillow, then climbed on to her lower bunk.

"We're not hibernating bears, Danny." On the top bunk, the warrior's roommate tossed and turned beneath her bedspread. "It's colder than a freezer in here."

"Didn't want to wake you by making noise or turning

up the heat. Besides, don't you sleep better inside a subarctic apartment?"

"Only when I'm falling asleep," Emmaline said as she yawned.

"Sorry, Limy." Daniela pulled back her covers, got up, and headed for the thermostat.

"Why are you up so early?" Emmaline hung over the edge of her bunk, her hair dangling and looking like a freshly lit matchstick. "You should be exhausted after yesterday's hiking adventure."

Daniela bit her lip, burying a chuckle. "Got tired of dreaming."

"Were you dreaming about Lozen again?" Emmaline had sometimes called Daniela "Lozen" ever since they'd read books about the Apache warrior princess who possessed magical powers and protected her people during the early Americas' land grab, championed by newly arriving immigrants in the southwest United States. They both admired the Native American woman. They had vague plans to visit the New Mexican caves rumored to have been where Lozen and her tribe hid from the invaders.

Daniela adjusted the thermostat to seventy-seven degrees before dive-bombing beneath her comforter. "I was dreaming about angels and demons."

"Again? Were you dreaming about the devil who was once an angel?" Emmaline asked as she crawled down from her upper bunk and made a bathroom run with the door partially shut.

"Yes. I've always wondered what Lucifer looked like. According to the biblical tradition, the fallen angel was the most beautiful and powerful of angels—a morning star, son of the dawn." Daniela turned on her side and curled up into a fetal position. "They called him Venus—the master of enlightenment and intellectualism."

"How did the son of the dawn get himself demoted to a slithering snake who's forced to eat dust all day?" Emmaline washed her hands, then emerged from their closet-sized bathroom with a drying towel in hand.

"He fought God and failed. But that didn't stop him. Even now he continues to poison the minds of God's children . . . us. And God's character is no different than a mama grizzly bear's—she fights to the death to protect her children."

"Only if she loves her cubs."

"Like God, mother grizzly bears always love their cubs."

"So angels and demons wouldn't allow you to sleep—again—preacher girl?"

"Insomnia's going to age me faster than cigarettes gray out the face of a dedicated smoker." Daniela picked up her custom-designed recurve bow and slid her fingers down the bowstring.

"It's the lack of oxygen to the skin . . . the gray smoker's mask. And whatever you do, don't start lighting up." Emmaline stuck her finger in her mouth and mimicked vomiting. "We couldn't be friends anymore."

"Noted and ditto." Daniela winked, not that Emmaline could see her in the darkness illuminated by a night-light.

Bored, she retrieved three foam-tipped arrows from the box beside her bed. She nocked the first arrow, quarter-drew, aimed, and shot. The projectile hit the bullseye of her indoor target—a high-density plastic foam installed above their couch.

"Nice shot!" Stretching, Emmaline shuffled across the flat into their tiny kitchen. "After work today, drink chamomile tea. Then you'll sleep properly. Want a bit of tea or coffee?"

"No stomach for caffeine quite yet. Enjoy your coffee."

Minutes later, Emmaline returned cradling a mug of brew in her perfectly proportioned hands. "Yesterday, you didn't want to talk about the boy from your dreamworld." She plopped onto a plaid couch that anchored the northern wall of their apartment, then clicked on the side table's lamp. "You said that the antichrist will come on the scene after the blood moons of 2014 and 2015. But you don't know who will start some type of pandemic that will eradicate tons of humans. Are you afraid that your oily boy will grow up into a monster like Stalin or Hitler—or even the antichrist—and start this pandemic?"

"I've never met the guy outside of my dreamworld." Daniela shrugged. "If he were walking down the street, I wouldn't even recognize him. I can't remember how he looks, just how he makes me feel—scared."

"In the beginning of any romantic adventure, it's normal to feel scared. The fear is the pleasure, and so is the pain." Emmaline's eyes shimmered a mesmerizing shade of green. "That's when it's the most fun. The most uncertain. The most interesting. Don't you know this?"

"No."

"Dang, girl! I know your parents were scared to death of you meeting a boy, but you've eclipsed puberty and the world hasn't fallen apart. So school is in session."

"Boys do things to girls that my parents don't like," Daniela quietly said. "And I'm their only daughter."

"Good things, if it's the right time and the right man." Emmaline's eyes twinkled with the faint glimmer of a glorious sunrise. "Don't worry. I'll teach you everything."

"Everything? Sounds terrifying."

"Don't you want to learn?"

"Sometimes I don't want to hope, Limy." Daniela tossed her journal to the end of her bunk.

"Why?"

"The process of hoping defines futility."

"Learning isn't hoping."

"But it is. A person doesn't learn about something they never hope to become or achieve."

"Dreamers do."

"Dreamer or not, I'm a pragmatist."

"Tell me your truth."

"If I hope that one day the scraggly boy in my dreams will materialize and become someone special to me . . . and then time passes and nothing happens, and I realize that my dreams were nothing more than a delusional, schizo mind trip, the disappointment will shatter my heart into a billion pieces, and I'll stop trusting God."

"Shattered hearts can be glued back together."

"Not before they bleed out." Daniela gulped down a mouthful of hot air. "Besides, I'm afraid."

"Of what?"

"That I'll . . . I'll . . . kill myself because of the depression. Shattered and abandoned hearts hurt so bad." She avoided Emmaline's gaze and clutched the front of her nightgown.

"It's Ethan, right?"

"Yes."

"He's dead. It's time to let him go."

"I need my heart, Limy, and he's interwoven into every cardiac muscle. I can't rip out my heart. It's where I remember Ethan, and you, and my parents." Daniela sighed.

"Danny Rose . . ." Emmaline dabbed a tear from the corner of her green eyes. "Your words go down in my history book as some of the kindest and most sincere words anyone has spoken to me." She raked her hands through her ginger morning frizz. "Don't be embarrassed about your depression—you don't have to stay victim to those negative thoughts."

"What should I do?"

"Fight. Be vulnerable. Trust me. Let me in."

"You have your own problems."

"I can juggle." Emmaline smiled. "Watch me. Plan B: If your dreams about oily boy are dead on arrival, I'll walk with you through the disappointment, breathing for you until you can breathe on your own."

"You'd do that for me? Promise?"

"Hope to die." Emmaline crossed her chest.

"Don't die. Ethan did that, and kid funerals suck."

"Then I'll keep breathing oxygen . . . for you, for us."

"Ditto." Daniela burrowed beneath her bedspread, not wanting to accept the fact that it was time to get ready for another day of research at Los Alamos National Laboratory—where both girls were discovering ways to rectify DNA damage caused by nuclear weapons.

"Heartbreak is a deadness, a decay that rots your insides," Emmaline mused as she sipped her cup of coffee.

"Morbid, Limy." Daniela curled her upper lip into a sneer.

"So is death." She stared into her coffee cup as though reading a dark fortune. "Some hearts were created to be broken, but not yours, Danny-girl."

"My life isn't a fortune to be guessed at, Limy. That's why I love my plan A: caution. A heart never removed from its protective shell can never be crushed, much less rot." She shivered, imagining how it would feel to rot while still alive.

"Don't be afraid to try and fail at love when you're still young. The art of love is similar to learning how to swim."

"I never learned."

"Or learning a second language, then." Emmaline persisted in making her point. "If you don't learn how to love when you're young, it's harder to figure out later in life." A sheepish grin spread across Emmaline's face, pushing dimples into cream peppered with flecks of cinnamon. "It's time to unsheathe your heart. Give it some air. Let it breathe. Clean out the mold and make room for healthy, nonfungal growth."

"Sounds like spring cleaning, Mama Cavanaugh–style." They both laugh. "Limy . . ."

"Yes, Danny-girl?"

"There was more to my dream."

"And?"

"There was a man . . . I think."

"Pray tell!" Limy shot up from her couch-slouch.

"This man's different. He's no oily boy. I couldn't see his face clearly, but somehow I know that he was handsome. He was huddled inside a helicopter with his dog, a Belgian Malinois, waiting to fight."

"That's the Black Irish guy I heard you talking about. He was a member of a group called the Orphans."

"I don't remember his face, his hair color, or what fraternity he was part of. But then I dreamt about a teenage girl, a redhead like you. Her professor assigned a research paper about understanding the ancient conflicts between the three Abrahamic religions: Judaism, Christianity, and Islam."

"Why don't their followers get along?"

"It's a family affair."

"My great ancestor was Mary, Queen of Scots. I know about familial conflict."

"Okay. Abrahamic religions 101: Ishmael—the father of non-Semitic Middle Eastern people—was born to Abraham and his wife's maidservant, Hagar, after Abraham's wife, Sarah, grew impatient waiting for Yahweh to fulfill His promise of gifting a son to the elderly couple."

"So Sarah told her servant to sleep with her husband? Genius."

"Yep. Then Hagar raised Ishmael in Abraham's household. But thirteen years later, at the ripe old age of ninety, Sarah conceived her first son, Isaac."

"Gross! You're kidding, right?"

"Yahweh never breaks His covenants with humans. So just like He promised, He gave Abraham and Sarah a son named Isaac. And Isaac grew up as the child who would fulfill Yahweh's prophecy—your seed will bless the whole world."

"How?"

"By preserving the Messianic bloodline, resulting in the birth of Yeshua HaMashiach—Jesus, the Messiah."

"Hagar and her kid. What happened to them?"

"While Sarah was still barren, Hagar treated her owner with contempt. So after Sarah popped out her kid, she banished the slave, sending Hagar and her child to the desert."

"The slave girl was happy about the banishment because she no longer wanted to be loaned out to sleep with her shriveled-up, geriatric boss?"

"Yep. Another entitled couple screwing up the world. Adam and Eve—the rerun." Daniela sighed. "But like any good parent, Yahweh intervened and promised Hagar that her son, Ishmael, would birth a great nation. Some Jewish scholars teach that after Sarah died, Abraham married Hagar whose new name was Keturah, and they had six sons."

"A happy ending, then?"

"Not completely. The angels of Yahweh told Hagar that Ishmael's offspring would be a wild people. Meaning that his descendants—the Arab nations—would live near the descendants of his half brother, Isaac—the father of modern-day Jewish people—but they would not get along."

"A feud between brothers was started, sucking the world into a family war. Don Corleone and *The Godfather* rerun," Emmaline summarized the biblical account. "Makes my family look super normal." They both laugh.

"Wait a minute, Limy."

"What's cooking?"

"Isaac and Ishmael—they're half brothers. And as a result, Israelis and Arabs are half brothers, related via their father Abraham's DNA."

"Spit it out, Danny-girl."

"If a sinister organization knew about this ancient familial feud and required a nidus of conflict that would ensure a global war such as Armageddon—the follow-up to Lucifer's pandemic, the final play to eradicate all humans from Earth—what would this sinister organization do to spark that war within this powerful family?"

"They would cause an offense by starting, then keeping, the drama brewing between embittered half brothers—or nations," Emmaline answered.

"According to my dreams, this offense would be continued via religion. Just like my future daughter's exam question. Three Abrahamic religions: Judaism, Christianity, and Islam. For some, Christianity identifies the Messiah of its parent religion, Judaism. What question of Judaism does Islam answer?"

"I don't know—nothing?" Emmaline shrugged.

"It must answer something, Limy. Christianity identified

the promised Messiah written about in the Hebrew scriptures by the prophet Isaiah. 'Therefore the Lord Himself will give you a sign: Behold, the virgin shall conceive and bear a Son, and shall call His name Immanuel.' So what question does Islam answer of Judaism?"

"Maybe it answers a question of Christianity?"

"Good point." Daniela paused. "But that's not the question. Besides, the whole purpose of the Jewish faith is to preserve Yahweh's promise of His plan for the redemption of creation. And according to the Christian tradition, in 0 AD or 3 AD, Jesus was born, fulfilling the purpose of Isaiah's writings that promised a Messiah to save us feckless humans from ourselves."

"Okay. Then what?"

"Thirty-three years later, Jesus died on a Roman cross—and three days later, he rose from the dead, accomplishing His mission of paying the price for redemption and fulfilling all the spring Jewish feasts."

"Case closed."

"But the case of the succession of Abrahamic religions isn't closed. Why add another religion to the Abrahamic faiths six hundred years after the birth of Christianity?"

"Why do you care?" Emmaline asked Daniela.

"Because the Apostle Matthew wrote 'And then many will be offended, will betray one another, and will hate one another.' So is the conflict between the three Abrahamic religions the nidus for Armageddon?"

"When did Matthew live?"

"He walked with Yeshua, so around 30 AD." Daniela rolled an arrow between her hands as though she were starting a fire. "Here's why I care. Maybe the same person or entity that took advantage of this brotherly feud and assisted in the process of forming a religion born out of the visions of an illiterate, uneducated man—Muhammad—will also start the pandemic intended to eradicate humans from Earth."

"Earth's Armageddon?"

"Affirmative."

"So you want to find out the identity of this person or entity?" Emmaline asked.

"It's my job—my destiny."

"But how?"

"According to the apocalyptic writings found in the Book of Revelation, the last government to rule Earth before Armageddon will be led by two narcissistic leaders: a religious leader called the false prophet and a secular political leader known as the antichrist—also known by the number of his name, Chi Xi Stigma, six hundred and sixty-six translated to six-six-six."

"I'm confused. Is Lucifer's pandemic a war or a biological outbreak caused by a virus or a bacterium?"

"Both . . . I think. The pandemic most likely precedes the war. Makes sense to reduce Earth's human soldiers before engaging them." Daniela toyed with the Glass Tattoo that hung from her neck. "Offense leads to betrayal."

"Then betrayal sets the world on fire," Emmaline concluded.

"Yeah, and you're right about another topic, Limy."

"I am?"

"Motherhood may not seem as earth-shattering as our research here at LANL or solving ancient mysteries that will save the world. But one day, I do want to marry a brave man and raise our children. Plain, ordinarily simple."

"Then you will."

"I wish I possessed your faith."

"It's easier to believe for a friend than for yourself. I'll help you find your man, and along the way, we can stop Armageddon together."

"You're such a nerd!" A lazy grin spread across Daniela's face. "But I adore nerds, especially nerds who are also kindred spirits."

"You're making me blush."

"Good. And if Toby's more boring than crickets, it is time to find you a lion dripping with testosterone. Rah."

Emmaline tossed her head back and laughed.

Daniela threw back her bedspread, ran across the room, and tackled her friend with tickles. Then she stood straight, clasped her hands, and prayed, "Dear God, help Limy and I find our long-lost Y chromosomes."

"And God, I know we're strangers, but Danny Rose is exhausted. She didn't sleep last night. Every dreamer needs her sleep. And even a break from her immediate destiny—praying for oily boy—and her intermediate destiny of solving ancient mysteries," Emmaline added.

With eyes closed, Daniela waited as though Yahweh would speak, breaking glass and unroofing their apartment building.

Because when the time comes, would the Orphan Dreamer intercede for her friends and her enemies—or allow them to perish? A minute later, she seemed to hear a reply deep inside her soul.

Warriors don't stop when they're tired. They stop when they have defeated the enemy and won the war. Pray without ceasing, Rosebud. Don't give up.

"But I'm not a warrior, Yahweh," Daniela protested. "I'm a dreamer . . . and a tired one at that."

"Talking to yourself again?" Emmaline teased.

"You know *who* I'm chatting with. Wake me after you take your shower. I need a few more minutes of sleep."

"Okay, sleepyhead. But don't forget, in case we see Liu Xi today, watch her. She's up to something, and I'm going to find out what."

"Twenty more minutes of sleep in exchange for spying on a colleague . . . deal." Daniela slipped beneath her covers.

"Did you whisper a prayer for your oily boy?"

"Not yet, but I will." Daniela looked away from her friend's penetrating gaze. "What if my prayers fail?"

"You will fail if you don't at least try—and if you try, you won't fail."

"I hate you!"

"Love me, darling."

"You're so confident so early in the morning, my love." Daniela glanced at Emmaline.

"I'm your ally—always and forever, twenty-four seven." Emmaline walked into the bathroom and closed the door. The Orphan Dreamer fell asleep without praying for the orphan, her oily boy.

In sixteen years, when the moon dripped with blood, Daniela would be required to make another decision: sleep or pray.

What was that? Their front door rattled beneath the pounding of a persistent knock. Daniela's eyelids popped open, and she shot up in bed. "Is that you, Limy?"

No answer.

Again something or someone hammered at their front door. Wood splintered. The Orphan Dreamer reached for her bow and arrow. Emmaline—hair dripping with water and a towel wrapped around her wet frame—stumbled out of the bathroom. "What the heck is that?"

"Heck if I know." Daniela ran to the door and engaged the chain lock.

Staccato. Urgent. Ominous.

The knocking started again, and she jumped back, raised her bow, nocked a three-pronged cutting arrow, and aimed her bow toward the door. "Who is it?" she commanded in her deepest voice.

Silence.

"What do you want?" Daniela insisted.

Silence again.

"What's the plan, Lozen?" Emmaline towel dried, then threw on her underclothes, T-shirt, and jeans.

"You'll open the door and stand behind it, so I have a clear shot." Daniela positioned herself, her bow fully drawn as she stood ready to impale their intruder. Her kindred spirit reached for the door handle, turned it, and opened the door. The chain stopped the door from opening fully.

No one. Nothing. Except . . .

"There's a package leaning against the base of the door." Emmaline crouched.

"Grab it, then shut the door, Limy." Daniela trained her arrow at the gap between the door and the doorframe.

Emmaline retrieved the package and slammed the door shut.

One snowflake falls from heaven to quench hell's thirst. I am that snowflake. I am Daniela Rose—the Orphan Dreamer.

Who are you?

12—The Orphan's Brother

Tuesday, March 17, 1998
India

PAUL PLOPPED ONTO A COT and leaned back against a concrete wall inside Mrs. Preeti Moorjani's mud hut.

"Every boy must know who he is," Preeti stated, her emphasis landing on the word *must*. "Or that boy will become what another person labels him as."

"I am Cillian's brother, Paul. I am an orphan, and so is Cil. We are nobodies in this big world."

"No, my child." She slapped her veined hand on top of a rickety wood table in the middle of her mud hut. Tea sloshed out of a cracked mug. "You are a child of the King of all Kings, Yahweh!"

"But I'm not a prince, and neither is Cil," Paul said as he flipped through his tattered geography textbook. "I've read this before. It's boring. I need a book that teaches me how to earn money. Lots of money."

"Gaining the world but losing your soul, Paul?" Preeti asked.

"After we ended up in Bushcroft's brothel, Cil only asked me to do him one favor: learn how to make a boatload of money so we—and you—can be free. I have to keep my promise. I won't let him down, not this time."

"You're not planning to counterfeit money, are you?"

"Such a criminal mind you have." Paul laughed, then picked up the cracked mug and sipped spiced tea. Preeti laughed, too, then rubbed Paul's back.

"Cillian gave you a present for your birthday."

"Why didn't you tell me as soon as you came home?" Paul sat up straight. "Is he okay?"

"He says he's well." She handed him the apple.

"Don't tell me how he says he's doing. How does he look to you?" He studied her face, looking for any slight expression that could reveal the truth.

"He nurtures much joy and hope for you and your future."

"What about his future?"

"It's uncertain."

"No—absolutely no! I won't accept that!" Paul looks down. "Sorry, Mrs. M. I shouldn't yell."

"I understand. Eat your apple." Deep lines trailed from the corner of her eyes as an expression of surrender spread across her face. "He has dreams of greatness for you. He lives for you, Paul."

"Does he smile?" Paul bit into the apple and licked the juices from his lips. "Does he hope?"

"Whenever he speaks of you, Cillian's bright-blue eyes light up, illuminating the darkness surrounding him."

Preeti wiped a tear from her eyes. "In this very moment, you are his breath, his life, his blood." She leaned down and kissed Paul on the forehead. "Keep learning."

"Thank you." Tears seeped from the corners of Paul's eyes. He sniffled hard, then clenched his fists. "Let's rescue Cil from that madman." He jumped up, leaving a rumpled mattress behind.

"In time, child."

"Later may be too late."

"Or right on time." She returned to the stove and stirred a pot of curry soup.

13—THE ORPHAN'S BROTHER

AT THE BROTHEL, SCARFACE CHARGED into Asher Bushcroft's air-conditioned office. "What do you want?" The boss refused to look up from his work.

"Your favorite boy's missing," Scarface said as he picked up a fat Cuban cigar and ran it across his nose, smelling the fine tobacco. "Thought you'd like to know."

"What I'd like to know is why you've wrapped your grimy, fat fingers around one of my Cohiba Behikes?"

"Sorry, boss." He tossed the cigar back into the velvet-lined box.

"What do you mean, he's missing?"

The burly man rolled his eyes. "He's not here."

Bushcroft glared at his soldier, glanced down at the cigar box, then glared at his henchman again. Scarface placed the cigar back properly. "And who was charged with watching him?"

"It's Bobby's watch at six o'clock." Scarface's posture stiffened.

Bushcroft looked at his watch. "But it's three o'clock. Your watch?"

"I came as soon as I discovered he was gone. That should count for something."

"Can a doctor almost cut out the right tumor?"

"No, sir."

"I didn't think so." Bushcroft capped, then neatly placed his Fulgor Nocturnus fountain pen—studded with 945 black diamonds and 123 rubies—on his desk calendar. The pen had cost him nine million dollars.

Bushcroft flipped through an equally posh calendar. "I see a packed schedule for that ungrateful boy." Bushcroft looked the unworthy bodyguard up, then down again.

"Can't do work if he's not here." Scarface scratched his stomach, then his head.

"Keep scratching and stating the obvious, moron. If my customers didn't love that onyx jewel so much, I'd finish him off. Nobody leaves me and lives."

"I'd enjoy the job," Scarface said. *After enjoying the onyx-haired boy first.*

"Enjoy this: If you don't find him, you'll suffer his punishment—thirty-nine stripes with the cat." He was referring to the cat-o'-nine-tails, of course. The same instrument of torture the Romans had used to rip into Jesus's bare back. "Understand?"

Bile rose in the back of Scarface's mouth. He swallowed, then nodded curtly.

"Good. Fetch Eeeny, Meeny, Miney, and Mo."

"Yes, sir." The guard briskly walked from the office, and once he escaped Bushcroft's watchful eyes, he ran to the dog kennel. He quickly leashed the dogs and led them from the barn. Barking filled the compound.

Beyond a barbed-wire fence past the barn, child slaves worked the soil on one of Bushcroft's organic farms. He'd sell the produce for a premium in the American and European markets. Bushcroft ate the same organic food and fed it to his orphans.

As the dogs walked Scarface, the child slaves looked nervously at the four vicious canines. When he finally arrived back at the office with the dogs leashed and somewhat under control, Bushcroft commanded him to sit. Scarface sat. The dogs also rested their haunches on the carpet, and their master buried the animals' noses in Cillian's sheets. "Take a long sniff, boys." Their tails wagged.

"Let's go." Bushcroft opened a cabinet and removed two items: a rope and his whip. Scarface retrieved a double-barreled shotgun from the gun cabinet. "You don't need that, stupid."

"Y-y-yes, sir." He returned the gun. "Decided against the cat?"

"For now. That brat has a schedule to attend to. I'll save the cat for you if we don't find him." Bushcroft smiled.

Scarface trembled.

Nostrils to the ground, the dogs tracked the slave's trail all the way to a mud hut with a faded mosaic curtain as a door.

"That's odd. Preeti is my seamstress. She wouldn't . . ."

"But she would," Scarface said. "At the hotel, that old woman's always chattin' up the boy."

Preeti came to the door and pushed aside the curtain.

"Preeti." Bushcroft kissed the old woman's wrinkled hand. "The new suit you made for me is exquisite. The Italian wool is softer than a baby's butt."

The woman's eyes shifted from Scarface, then back to her boss and his bullwhip. "Fine materials make for a fine suit. May I help you, sir?"

"What'd you do with the boy?" Scarface clenched the woman's arm.

"What boy?" She pulled back, but her strength was no match for the pit bull of a man.

"Let her go." Bushcroft hit Scarface with the handle of his whip, then smiled at the old woman again. "Don't know why my bloodhounds led us here, but you know their noses never lie. Have you seen Cillian?"

The woman wiped her hands on the front of her apron and shifted her weight. Scarface frowned. If she lied, it would be his skin. He leaned toward her and pressed. "The pale-skinned boy with the black hair—the boy at the brothel. Have you seen him?"

"She knows what he looks like," Bushcroft said. "All of Mumbai knows. It's why he's so popular."

"I've seen him at the brothel," Preeti said.

Desperate not to find himself on the other end of a cat, Scarface stepped past Bushcroft. "You're always cozying up and talking to him. Where is he?" He lifted his hand as if to strike the old woman.

"Diplomacy, Saul. Put your hand down. I've never struck a woman—except one." Bushcroft stepped forward and fondled her cheek. "He's a savage, and I won't let him harm you, Preeti. Why don't you let the dogs search your place? Then we'll be on our way. And for dinner, join us back at the palace, would you?"

"I'm on a deadline to finish the—"

"That can wait."

"But the new slaves arrive tomorrow."

"Always meticulous about your work. Another time then?"

"Yes, sir." She nodded, then moved her lips without uttering a sound: "Yahweh, make those vicious dogs and their owners leave."

"Did you say something?" Bushcroft closed the distance between them. The flowery scent of his perfume filled the shack, and outside, the dogs charged the stagnant air with barks and wails.

"She's praying—a sure sign that she's hiding something," Scarface snarled.

"Shut up and shut those dogs up!" Bushcroft snaked the bullwhip from his belt.

"They only listen to you, boss."

"Keep talking, and I'll string you up outside. Then lay into you."

Scarface backed up closer to the door.

"What are your plans for that?" Preeti pointed at the whip.

"Keeping wayward employees in line."

Preeti shrunk back.

"I'd never harm a woman. My dearest Natalia would be cross with me," Bushcroft said.

"Natalia?" Preeti's brow slanted down toward her nose.

"She was—no, is—my beautiful sister." He bowed his head. "She's missing . . . but I will find her one day. You'll sew beautiful clothes for her. You would adore her, Preeti. Young. Breathtaking. She was a violinist and a ballerina. She even earned a scholarship to Juilliard."

Outside, barks fizzled into whimpers. Bushcroft turned to Scarface. "Check on them!"

Scarface shuffled out of the shack. "They're covered in fire ants, boss!"

"Brush them off." Bushcroft ran outside, and the men dusted off as many of the ants as possible. "Take them down to the watering hole."

★ ★ ★

Legna remains in the world of the immortals.

The fire ant army claims a victory as the four-legged intruders and their humans leave the old woman's home. But Legna needs a mortal's prayers to strengthen him for the fight ahead. The mortal he was counting on is busy making a new friend in Los Alamos, New Mexico. "Elohim, give Daniela a second chance. She's only sixteen."

★ ★ ★

Paul climbed out of the storage basket. "What happened to the dogs?"

"For the moment, Yahweh has protected us from whatever evil Lucifer's agents intended for us." Preeti clasped her hands together. "Abba, Father—Yahweh Nissi—the Lord is my banner! Protect Cillian, in Yeshua's powerful name. Amen," she cried out so loud that Paul was afraid Bushcroft, Scarface, and the dogs would hear.

Red curry bubbled on the stove, and a spicy aroma filled the hut. "Will they find him?" Paul said.

"I pray not. But if they do, God be with our Cillian."

"Where would he go? We have to find him first."

"I don't know."

"You're keeping something from me, aren't you?" Silence pulsed through the one-room house. "I'm not a baby. I can handle the big stuff."

"He told me he wanted to die."

"Suicide?"

"Yes."

"Nothing bad can happen to him! I won't allow it. We have to find him before he—or they—do something stupid."

"Paul, I wanted . . . I can't." Preeti pressed her hand to her chest as though she were trying to keep her heart from bursting.

"Tell me." Paul held her hand. "Tell me the truth, not what Cil told you to tell me."

"You're older now." She stroked his golden-wheat locks.

"I'm fourteen. I can fight. And for my brother, I'd die fighting if I have to."

"He wouldn't want that for you. But I will tell you the truth. You deserve the truth. For a long time, bad things have been happening to your brother."

"Why? Cil's the best."

"I can't understand Yahweh's purpose." She looked to the roof of her mud hut. "It's not fair," she cried. "Yeshua, protect him."

"When you talk to Yeshua, does He ever answer you?" Paul pressed the woman. "For Cil's sake, does he answer?"

"Oh, Paul, I'm thrilled you asked." Preeti rubbed her arms where Scarface had grabbed her.

"You okay?"

"I am." Stirring the bowl of curry, she wiped tears from her eyes. "I don't have much of an appetite now." She smiled. "Do you?" Paul shook his head, and she turned the stove off. "While we wait to hear about Cillian, I'll tell you a story." She sat down on her cot, opposite Paul's. "The talking will ease my anxiety."

"Cil always told me stories too." Paul sat on his own cot. "I think he was distracting me from his sadness."

She leaned closer to Paul. "When we are born, we are

all capable of growing up and participating in evil deeds, like Mister Bushcroft and his friend."

"Not Cil! He's perfect . . . right?"

"He's kind, generous, and reliable—but no, no one's perfect when measured beside the Light of the World."

"Cil never expected me to be perfect, just to do my best."

"That's because Cillian isn't perfect, but the Light is. And the Light substituted His perfection for our imperfection."

"I don't understand."

"In the beginning, Yahweh created two perfect humans, Adam and Eve. They lived in a beautiful place called the Garden of Eden. He stayed close to them, walking with the couple in the cool of the evening every day. One morning, Adam and Eve threw away their closeness with the Light because they wanted their own way. Then evil crashed into their bliss."

"If the Light wants me to be perfect, I don't want to walk with Him. Even Cil said I was mischievous. I'd be in the spotlight and in trouble all the time."

"He doesn't expect us to be who we're not."

"People have been cruel to my brother and me, and Cil blames himself for our hard life. He never told me anything, but I saw him crying in secret at the care home. Then when we arrived in India, he worked from sunup to sundown, and we lived in a concrete prison. They branded him, Mrs. M. I saw it."

"I believe you." The motherly woman wrapped her spindly arms around Paul, and her sagging brown skin draped over his petite neck. One tear ran down his cheek. She kissed his gaunt face after another tear appeared. "Paul, Yahweh loves you and Cillian more than you can imagine."

"I don't feel it," Paul said, his voice rising. He sniffled, then stared at the floor. "Just your love and Cillian's, but not His."

"Trust me. Your Creator loves you even more than we do. No human loves like Him. He loves like a waterfall—wild and free. We love like raindrops—reserved and stingy—because selfishness taints our motives." She applied her words gently to Paul's injured heart like the sutures of a skilled surgeon.

"Why does His love make us so sad?"

"It's not His love that makes us sad. Lucifer tries to make us forget we are loved and leads us away from the Light until we no longer feel the warmth of God's love. But just because we don't see or feel the sun, doesn't mean that it's not still shining. Yahweh doesn't force us to love Him or others back."

"I want to love you and Cil."

"But do you want to love those mean men?"

"No way! Are you sick?" Paul yanks away from her embrace. Electricity seems to prickle his skin.

"I'm rather well, Paul. The fact is, God loves them."

"Why? He should love Cillian more—he's good."

"Because God loves the whole world." She opened her arms.

"I don't wanna love those men. I'm not going to love those men! If I were older and stronger, I'd murder them with my bare hands."

"Hatred turns to bitterness, and bitterness to misery. You're too young to exist as a slave to misery. Follow God's principles of love and love your enemy. Only His methods will gift you with the peace that transcends all understanding."

"Why are you telling me these things? Cil's missing. We

should be out searching for him. Are you picking on me or delaying our mission because you're scared?"

"I am scared." Preeti paused. "But I want to point you in the direction of a better path—a path of freedom—that can only be experienced when we walk close to the Person of Love. Then you can love Cillian even more when he comes back."

"How do you know that he'll come back?"

"I had a vision last night." Turning, she fumbled through an old wooden box. "I won't always be with you."

"You're not going to leave me?" Paul slid to the edge of his bed. "The vision didn't show you abandoning me—right?" Tears trickled down the boy's tanned face. "Please, Mrs. M. Please don't leave me alone."

"I'd like for us to live together forever, Paul. But that reality isn't a possibility on Earth. But a place exists where we can live as a family forever."

"Then tell me! Tell me everything you know about this place and how to get there."

"I will as soon as I find—"

"What are you looking for?" Paul jumped up and paced the room.

"The book that shows us the way to my soon forever home."

"Want me to help? You always say how much your back hurts."

"I'm fine," she said. She massaged her back and eventually retrieved a tattered, leather-bound book. "Ah. Here it is." She smiled wide, then cradled the book to her chest.

"Please hurry, Mrs. M. Tell me what you know about this special place because Cil is suffering. I need to rescue him, and maybe he'll join us."

"Many Hebrew people suffered under Lucifer's oppressive rule. One man—Job—lost his family, his health, and all of his life's savings in one fell swoop. But Yahweh gave Lucifer one rule: he couldn't take Job's life."

"That was nice of him," Paul said sarcastically. "But who would want to survive after a thief stole all of your savings and a serial killer murdered your family?"

"Cillian would like to survive."

"He's never been rich, and his mom . . . she treated him horribly. Mrs. M., who's Lucifer?"

"He's a fallen angel—Satan, the devil, our enemy."

"Even the devil was once an angel?" Paul asked, confused.

"Yes. One third of God's angels joined Lucifer and rebelled against God. They chose their own path that day— their fatal mistake. Embittered, Lucifer and his fallen angels now steal, kill, and destroy humans. Like some politicians, he takes from others and gifts the victim's wealth to his agents—the selfish ones, the Nephilim."

"Nephilim?"

"Crossbreeds between humans and fallen angels, demons."

"Sounds sci-fi."

"Have you ever heard of Area 51?"

"I read about it. Roswell, New Mexico—right?"

"*They* were there." Preeti's hands shook.

"The Nephilim?"

Preeti nodded.

"Tell me more about Lucifer, their leader."

"He was the most beautiful of angels, full of light and splendor. His bejeweled body reflected the light of his Creator. But pride reduced him to nothing more than a ghost. Invisible. He plots, then influences humans to carry out his dark deeds." She opened her Bible and read parts of the book of Job.

As he listened, Paul pulled his knees to his chest and wrapped his arms around his legs. "I love Bible stories. When we didn't have food to eat, Cil would distract me, telling me the two Bible stories he knew: the story of Joseph and the story of David and Goliath."

"Stories of heroes."

"I felt like I was watching an action movie." Behind a sheen of emotion, Paul's apple-green eyes glittered with excitement. "Cillian and I saw a film once at the care home—*Anne of Green Gables*, a story of friendship."

"A beautiful film!"

"We're kindred spirits, you and me."

"We are." She ran her veined hands along the yellowed pages of her Bible. "And kindred spirits share their most valuable treasure. Mine is to tell you, Paul, that you'll discover a treasure in this book if you read it."

"Treasure . . . do you mean a pot of gold?"

"More precious than gold. That's what the wisest, richest king of Israel—King Solomon—said."

"I promised Cillian that I'd find a map that would lead us to treasure, but that we'd spend the treasure together." Paul pointed at the ancient book. "If someone hid our map inside that book, we should find the map, then leave on our adventure—now! Cil's in danger. I won't let him down, not this time."

"Paul?"

"At the care home, Miss Grey beat him. She refused to stop, no matter how hard he cried or held still. I was only a boy, so I stood outside the door and waited for him, waiting to see if he would survive."

"I'm sorry." Preeti rested her hand across her mouth. "No one deserves such treatment."

"Open the map. Help me find our pot of gold, then let's find Cil."

"I've never seen the Bible as a map before, but I suppose you could call it that. However, the words won't lead us to a pot of earthly gold. Instead, the book will lead us to a place where streets are made of pure gold." Her eyes twinkled with delight. "A kingdom not of this world."

"That's more gold than I could have hoped for! I promised Cil I'd find a treasure, and a promise is meant to be kept."

"Then you'll keep your promise, and I'll help you."

"You're the greatest!" Paul jumped up and slipped on his jacket.

"What are you doing?"

"Dressing to leave. We don't have time to waste."

"You're correct. We have no time to waste. Eternity's clock is ticking down to zero, and Yahweh asks you and me to make a choice before the clock strikes zero."

"What choice?" Paul slipped on his shoes.

"Accept Yahweh's payment for our rebellion, so we can live with our Creator forever in the place decorated with streets of gold—a place of peace, no wars or mean people. For God so loved the world that He gave His only begotten Son, that whoever believes in Him should not perish but have everlasting life."

"He lost everything too." Paul buried his hands inside his pockets.

"Yes, but he gained me and possibly you and Cillian," Preeti said. "We gain a treasure too. The map found in this book leads to eternal life." She tapped the pages of her Bible. "Will you follow Yeshua and secure the ultimate treasure—an eternal prize that no devilish person can steal? Or will you die outside of God's family and live with Lucifer and his fallen angels in his home—hell?"

"Those are my choices?" Shaking his head, he scrunched his nose. "Who doesn't want to walk on streets of gold and live with their family in a safe place? Of course I'll accept the offer."

Preeti laughed, then held Paul's hand. "This means you'll never walk alone again. Yeshua's sacrificial death and glorious resurrection from the grave fulfilled the promise Yahweh made to Adam and Eve—that one dark day, Lucifer would bruise Yeshua's heel, but one glorious morn, Yeshua would crush Satan's head."

"There's a lot of blood, bruising, and crushing going on in exchange for a map that leads to a home with streets of gold. Just sayin'."

"Sin looks ugly. Which wound do you think is fatal, Paul?"

"Having your noggin stepped on by God." Paul shrugged, then started packing for their adventure. "I don't see anyone bouncing back from that one, not ever."

"Paul, we can't go back to Mister Bushcroft's lair. It's too dangerous."

"But Cil's counting on me!"

"We must surrender and allow Yahweh's angels to find your brother."

"I know you're scared, but no one knows that place as well as you do. Help me. My brother's suffering, and they're going to murder him, like the people murdered Yeshua. Don't be a chicken—be an eagle. Please."

"Yeshua sees every suffering person, even Cillian." She rested her hands in her lap. "His angels await our prayers.

They are more powerful than even the eagle. But in order to speak to God as a father, the person asking must first become His child."

"What are you saying, Auntie?"

"Do you want to become part of God's family, so you can talk to Yahweh as your loving father? Entering into a relationship with our Creator is more important than securing riches from Him."

"If it will help Cillian come back to me, then yes. Besides, Cil may want to join up as well. He doesn't have a family, except for me and you."

She kneeled beside her cot. Paul hesitated, then kneeled beside her. "Talk to Yahweh like you spoke to your father before he died."

"We didn't talk. My dad stuttered, like Cil does sometimes."

"Then talk to Him as you would talk to your mother or to me."

"I can do that. Yahweh . . . I'm not much of a talker. But I'd like to follow you, and I wouldn't mind living in Your world instead of mine—but not until we find Cil, tell him about our plans, and give him a chance to join up. He desperately needs a break. Okay? See you later."

"In Yeshua's name, Amen," Preeti added.

"Can we pray for Cil too?"

"God hasn't hung up the phone. He's still up there, listening."

"Daddy . . ."

"Go ahead. God loves you. You're His son now."

"Cil's lived in hell since I've known him." *Only babies cry.* Paul composed himself. "He acts brave, but he's scared. He wants to make friends with anyone who roots for him. That includes You. When You meet my brother, just know that sometimes he's afraid to show his feelings, so be patient and please don't shut him out. You won't regret adopting my brother, I promise. In Yeshua's name, Amen." Paul's shoulders relaxed as peace entered him.

"Yeshua spoke these words to a weary world: 'Come to me all of you who are weary and heavy laden, and I will give you rest.' "

"I'm exhausted." Paul sat on the edge of his bed. "The sun set three hours ago. I hope Cil comes home to be with us soon."

"Riding on the wings of an angel," Preeti added. "The purpose of God's timing is not to give relief but to give us revelation."

With no appetite for dinner, the wheat-haired, bright-eyed boy climbed under his covers and whispered prayers for Cillian. As peace enveloped him like a warm blanket, he fell asleep.

14—Orphan Dreamer

AS THE SUN ROSE FROM its slumber, the family town of Los Alamos lay still and quiet beyond Daniela's window.

Bow drawn and arrow aimed at an invisible intruder, Daniela waited as Emmaline had retrieved the mysterious package left by the person who had almost knocked their front door off its hinges. "Do you smell that, Limy?"

"I do. Springtime. Flowers. Whoever dropped off this package must have bathed in floral-scented bath gel."

The cardboard box was stamped with international postage, addressed to Miss Daniela Rose Cavanaugh, and marked with an Israeli return address. It was also too heavy for its size. The Orphan Dreamer's best friend dropped the box onto the kitchen table. "What's inside?"

"Open it and see for yourself." Daniela hid her weapon

beneath the lower bunk bed as Emmaline opened the box and removed a velvet-wrapped object.

"It's a statue." Its head was made of pure gold, its chest and arms of silver, its belly and thighs of bronze, its legs of iron, and its feet of part iron, part baked clay. "And it's heavier than an armful of bricks," Emmaline added.

"It looks familiar."

"Where do we start? What does this mean? Will this statue lead us to the *who*—as in who will start Lucifer's pandemic?"

"Good questions, and the answer is maybe. But we can't be late for work. That's unprofessional."

"You're such an adult," Emmaline joked. "Fine. I'll hide it."

"Don't tell me where," Daniela said, "so if that flower-scented door banger comes back looking for this thing, he won't kidnap me!" She was joking but knew the statue was important somehow. Retreating into the bathroom, she started the shower and thought, *Let the games begin.*

After Daniela showered, she dressed in a pair of jeans and a loose-fitting sweatshirt. The girls locked up the loft, descended three flights of stairs, then climbed inside Emmaline's Jeep. The redhead descendant of Queen Mary loaded a compact disc into the CD player.

"It's beautiful, Limy." Daniela closed her eyes.

"It's called 'Mariage d'Amour' by Paul de Senneville. Translated 'Marriage of Love.' Figured you needed a calming potion after this morning, and music seems to do the trick every time. Try to take a catnap. You've been up since midnight."

"I'm used to it." Daniela opened her eyes and gazed at her friend. "We'll be okay." She assured Emmaline while thinking, *but will my oily boy be okay?*

Exhausted from the morning's adventure, the pair rode quietly to work.

Daniela cried silently to her heavenly Father on behalf of the boy who had haunted her dreams last night. *Send oily boy a powerful angel, like Legna. If he requires rescuing, please rescue him, Yahweh.*

After Daniela finished her plaintive pleas, she opened her eyes, focusing beyond the SUV's windows.

The quaint Los Alamos community gossiped of wealth—the mysterious and nerdy kind.

Resting at the foothills of the Jemez Mountains, the township of eighteen thousand souls included intelligent and curious faces that peered through Kenneth Cole or Coach wire spectacles, perched atop aquiline noses.

Keen sandals and Moosejaw fleeces fitted snugly to lithe physiques that slid behind the steering wheels of Land Rovers or Jeeps, off-road vehicles caked in desert dust from weekend drives into the mountains. Hiking the Jemez Mountains and skinny-dipping in the mountain's hot springs were the most popular pastimes of the town's residents. Los Alamos was a scientist's town, more populated with church spires than bars, whispering morality and safety.

A townsperson could only possess one of two reasons for living on the isolated plateau named Los Alamos: supporting the scientists who researched all things nuclear at Los Alamos National Laboratory (LANL) or working as a scientist at LANL—the site where nerds developed the atomic bomb.

The two fresh-faced girls who lived in the loft apartment on Iris Street fit into the second category. They were blossoming scientists—college students completing a research semester in the Biology Division at LANL.

But Daniela possessed an even bigger mission: preventing an entity or an individual from committing worldwide mass genocide. At this point it seemed likely this entity would accomplish that goal by creating a global pandemic, but only time would reveal the secrets of exactly how its plan to eradicate humanity would unfold.

"Limy," Daniela's voice croaked from lack of sleep. "Maybe the statue will lead us to the *who* that will start the inciting events of this mass genocide of man, woman, and child . . . eventually. But in order to find the *who*, we must follow the breadcrumbs of *why* the entity wants humans gone."

"Why?" Emmaline asked, and the girls giggled at her word choice.

"Since I was first given the Glass Tattoo, my mom always said that God will judge a person's motives—their intent—before He ever judges their actions, because sometimes the intent of a person is good, but the action is bad. Other times, the intent of a person is evil, but the resulting action appears good."

"Okay."

"She also said that if I want to find out who will start this mass genocide, I need to understand their motives. That understanding will lead me to the villain's doorstep. But she also warned me that I may actually like him after I meet him. A siren's song often lured sailors to their deaths—likewise, his charm may lure me to mine . . . and ours."

"Ominous."

"Exhausting, because actions don't always match a person's motives." Daniela balled up her jacket, placed it between her head and the car doorframe, then fell asleep.

She knew she must understand why her villain wanted

to instigate the mass genocide of humans—then, hopefully, her mind would be illuminated by Wisdom, which would help her recognize, find, and stop *who* after he, she, or they arrive on the scene.

But where does a sixteen-year-old insomniac start?

With what she knows: offense usually precedes betrayal, and the worse kind of offense occurs between those who once trusted each other the most—kindred spirits, sisters, parents, spouses, or even brothers.

How does a teenage girl forgive that person?

She chooses to.

15—Orphan Dreamer

STILL PUZZLED BY THE MEANING of the statue she'd received that morning, Daniela reread the professor's letter from last week, along with her previous weeks' journal entries, written during her lunch break at the lab.

A week ago, she'd been reading a book not included in the Hebrew scriptures, the Book of Enoch. It mentioned Watchers—fallen angels—and their offspring, the Nephilim. Tucked away in a corner of the cafeteria while sipping a cola, Daniela Rose jotted down a few more notes about the alien creatures, then reviewed her journal entry.

Journal Entry #364:

March 17, 1998: For the last two days, Emmaline and I have done our best to prepare to fight an unidentified and future megalomaniac—the antichrist. Most days we read Daniel and Revelation to learn about the fight my rafiki promises will unleash a global pandemic on Earth, wiping humans clean off the map forever.

But Lucifer rarely fights without the help of a gullible, power-hungry human agent. Stalin. Mao. Mussolini. To name a few. Are these humans really humans or something more—like a hybrid between an alien and a human, a predator of real humans? A Nephilim?

What human or half-human and half-alien would align themselves with the fallen prince and choose to bring death to his or her own people?

Oily boy. Who is he—really? Is he a Nephilim? Is he the antichrist?

Thinking back to what she'd read about Nephilim in the Book of Enoch, Daniela dropped her turkey sandwich in surprise. "I've read about this statue before!" She left her lunch and retrieved a small leather-bound text, opening it to the seventh chapter of Daniel.

Her heart pounded behind her ribs, and her neck veins engorged with blood.

Warm liquid poured from Daniela's right nostril and blood spattered the pages of her journal. *Onion breath and ketchup stains! So unladylike!* Quickly, she tilted her head back, sniffed hard, swallowed, then pinched her nose.

Don't suffocate.

With her left hand, she yanked open her purse zipper and removed a Ziploc bag stuffed with saline-soaked gauze. While tilting her chin in the air and holding her nose, she dabbed the page of her journal with the gauze before wiping the skin beneath her nose.

Please! Don't let anyone see me.

She glanced left, then right. A woman sitting a few tables away scooted her chair back before power walking from the room. "It's not the plague, lady."

After holding her nose for ten minutes, Daniela slipped a rolled-up, saline-soaked piece of gauze inside her right nostril. Salt stung the fragile tissue but staunched the bleeding. She lowered her chin, thankful that only one person had witnessed her leaky nose.

Dressed in jeans and a sweatshirt, Emmaline strolled across the lunchroom toward Daniela.

Sour milk and mushrooms! What would Emmaline think of the gauze sticking out of Daniela's nostril?

Friendship.

Secrets.

But no lies.

Okay, so here we go. "Hi, Limy." Speak first. Control the conversation. "It's only a nosebleed." Daniela shrugged. "I'm not contagious or even dying. Promise." Daniela pointed to the gauze partially hanging from her nostril. "It's contained."

"Do you need ice?"

"I'm fine—never felt better." Daniela raised her arms, stretching her muscles. Emmaline sat next to her friend. She wasn't the least bit scared of the nosebleed. Daniela's heart rate slowed.

"Come on, Danny-girl. Let's get you out of here." Emmaline slipped her arm under Daniela's. Together, the girls marched out of the cafeteria and headed for their lab. As they walked, Emmaline asked, "Did you figure out who sent that statue? Do you think it could be from that professor you know who lives in Israel?"

"I'm not sure . . . but maybe. A week ago he sent me this letter." Daniela peeked over her shoulder, then retrieved a letter hidden inside her leather-bound journal.

My Darling Rosebud,

I need your help.

The statue—I hope—is the key that solves the mystery of who. The Watchers are still watching. But know this: the Jordan River is a special place, the original Area 51. Read Yehoshua 3:11-17.

On a personal note, I hope the Skeleton Key—the statue—will also lead you to your heartsong.

B'shalom,
Professor Jakob Cohen
Director of Israel Antiquities Authority

"Is the statue we received this morning the same statue Professor Jakob mentions in his letter? Why would he fly all the way from Israel, bang on our door, then run away before we see him, Danny-girl?"

"I know. It doesn't make any sense."

Emmaline returned the professor's letter to Daniela. "Who's your heartsong?"

"Heck if I know! But he sounds delicious." They giggled. "On a serious note, Limy, during lunch, I reviewed a journal entry that I wrote after reading the Book of Enoch, a collection of stories about the Watchers—the angels who betrayed God and impregnated human women with Nephilim. I believe Nephilim are hybrids, part human and part fallen angel."

"So half-breed extraterrestrials are walking among us, wreaking havoc?" Emmaline gripped Daniela's arm tighter.

"Yes. I believe the antichrist—the prophesied initiator of Lucifer's pandemic—along with his sidekick, his false prophet, are both Nephilim, evil crossbreeds empowered by dark magic. The Watchers—the purebred fallen angels, the fathers of Nephilim—don't roam earth. They're locked inside a place of darkness, according to Jude's letter in the New Testament. It's the Watchers' children who stalk Earth."

"Where are the Watchers now?"

Daniela glanced over her shoulder, then said, "In the Book of Enoch, Enoch describes his journey into the heavens. He speaks of ten realms of reality or dimensions, which we're just now discovering via the string theory of physics. According to the Book of Enoch, the Watchers await their judgment day in the fifth realm."

"Creepy crazy," Emmaline added, then glanced over her shoulder too.

"What is it?" Daniela picked up her pace.

"I could swear that guy has been following us since we left the cafeteria."

"I agree. Let's storm," Daniela whispered. Holding her badge, she glanced over her shoulder once more before entering their lab. "Limy, that's the guy from the frozen lake."

"That you rescued?"

"I'm sure of it."

"Maybe he's a serial killer." Emmaline's face drained of blood, leaving behind freckles and milk-pale skin.

"Run!" Daniela broke into a sprint, and Emmaline ran alongside her. Daniela's breath hitched as she engaged her leg muscles, pushing through the burn of too little oxygen pumping into her quads and hamstrings.

Snow crunched beneath her feet. Daniela gasped.

"Are you okay?"

"I'll make it." Daniela gulped down several deep, cold breaths. "I have to." Still, her heart raced, and her chest constricted. She was too young for this uphill trek to whip her heart into such a gallop. Emmaline snatched the badge from Daniela's hand, ran ahead, swiped the badge, opened the door, and waited for Daniela to stumble inside.

With both hands, Emmaline forced the door closed.

Delbert Blythe, the drowning-lake guy, slammed into the glass door. His gaze refused to focus, roving wildly. "Open up. I need to talk to you—now!" He pointed at Daniela, then rapped the glass door in the same staccato beat that had woken the girls up that morning.

"He's the guy . . . the one who left the package on our doorstep." Daniela gasped. "It's the knock. Goodness gracious! A crazed serial killer knows where we live. I should have never saved his life yesterday!"

"Let's go to the lab," Emmaline said, but the man shook his head while burying his hand in his right pocket. "He has a gun, Danny-girl!"

"Don't leave!" the man shouted. "Please, Miss Daniela!" He retrieved a sheet of paper and a pen, then scribbled a note onto the paper. He placed the note on the sidewalk in front of the door. "You, Daniela. Only you can read the note." The crazed man stepped away from the door.

"Just leave it, Danny."

"No. I can't. Maybe his note will help us solve the mystery of who." Daniela reached for the door handle. Emmeline grabbed her friend's hand. "What if he soaked the paper in poison?"

"Then I'll die."

"Just like that?"

"Just like that, Limy." Daniela removed a set of gloves from her bag and pushed her hands inside them before opening the door and retrieving the note. Emmaline gnawed on the corner of her lip.

"And?"

"Will you open the next door with your badge?" Daniela asked.

Emmaline turned her back toward the Orphan Dreamer, swiped her badge, and opened the door, giving Daniela a few seconds to read the note: *Don't trust the redhead! You saved my life, now I'm saving yours. The lake incident was staged. I've been following you because they are following you.*

"What does it say, Danny-girl?"

"Something stupid." Daniela ripped up the letter into multiple pieces, placed it into a garbage bin, then poured her remaining cola on top of the paper, drenching each piece. "There. No need to worry about it anymore."

"That was drastic."

"I'm the Orphan Dreamer. Drastic is my middle name." The girls disappeared inside their safe place, but Daniela could still smell the man's scent—much too floral a scent for a man. "*We* have a bit of research to do."

An hour later, sitting in a dark room, Emmaline adjusted the aperture on the department's electron microscope while Daniela prepared another slide. Emmaline viewed each slide, looking for strands of RNA inside a novel virus. "I've got a bad case of cabin fever." She looked up from the million-dollar microscope.

Still a bit winded, Daniela smiled weakly and avoided her roommate's gaze.

"The snow will be melting soon. Flowers will spring back to life." Emmaline lifted her chin, as though the sun would shine on her face. "We should take that backcountry camping trip I was talking about into the Jemez Mountains this weekend—just you, me, and nature. Get away from that crazy guy."

"After the blizzard tomorrow?"

"The fresh air could help your breathing, and we'll only hike the flat parts."

"It's the Jemez *Mountains*." Daniela frowned. "Where exactly are the flat parts?"

"The valley, near Lake Fenton. I'll teach you how to swim."

"I tried. I can't swim. And even if I could, I'm not a polar bear who swims with icebergs." Daniela inhaled slowly, then exhaled. "March weather in the mountains can be fickle —even dangerous."

Even inside the lab, Daniela's knowing allowed her to hear Douglas firs and ponderosas rustling between the fingers of a gentle breeze and blowing their woody, evergreen breath into her nostrils.

She inhaled deeply, again and again, lost in the wonder of a cold March day and coming to terms with the fact that her lungs were not healthy.

"We'll hike and search for the Apache warrior caves that we talked about, then dig for treasure."

Daniela crossed her arms. "The plan is insane, Limy."

"For a Darbyshire, it's par for the course."

"Queen Mary really did a number on your DNA. Do Darbyshires like to freeze to death, as well?"

"Only in the summer."

"That's possible at night in the desert." Daniela broke into a fit of coughs.

"I'll keep you warm." Emmaline focused the optics of the microscope. "Seriously, Danny Rose, are you okay? Should you see a doctor?"

"I'm fine, just out of shape."

"You don't look out of shape."

"We rarely look like what we really are."

"Then hike with me. Let's discover who we really are, and a campfire will give us light and heat. We'll roast marshmallows and tell each other stories—scary stories."

"Those are called nightmares. I already experience my fair share of those."

"How are you ever going to meet a hot guy being so boring?"

"Meeting hot guys at ten-thousand-feet elevation after a snowstorm in spring? Nothing and no one will be hot— not even Denzel Washington dressed in a parka."

Emmaline flashed Daniela her most pitiful expression.

"Goodness gracious, Limy. Okay. Fine. I'll agree to camping in the Jemez Mountains . . . if you agree to tell our research director where we're going."

"He's overbearing—such a nosy Nathan." Emmaline sighed. "You don't trust me?"

"I don't want a mountain lion eating us for lunch without someone knowing about it."

"What would he do, bring the Tabasco sauce?"

"If you refuse to agree, the deal is off." Daniela knew how much the director irritated Emmaline, but after receiving the lake-guy's letter, the Orphan Dreamer required an insurance plan. *Don't trust the redhead.*

Why?

"I can stop a mountain lion in its tracks." Emmaline pushed back from the microscope and struck a martial artist's pose.

"With that?" Daniela burst out laughing.

Emmaline flashed a wicked grin—full lips slightly tucked between her teeth while her bashful eyes and dimples told all sorts of lies. "That and pepper spray." She shrugged as she looked down and away.

"Yeah, right." Daniela shook her head.

"Emma and Danny," Li Xiu Ying, the lab postdoc and the girls' mentor, interrupted. "No time to chat while hogging the electron scope."

"I'll get up if you promise to bring us ramen for lunch tomorrow," Limy said.

"Deal."

"It's all yours." Emmaline pushed away from the scope and removed her slide. Li Xiu sat down, and Emmaline followed Daniela out of the scope room.

"She's so pretty," Daniela whispered.

"Heard she scored a job at the virology lab at the National Institutes of Health," Emmaline added. "Have you discovered any intel about the Chinese spy, a.k.a. Li Xiu?"

"That's sort of racist."

"But plausible." Emmaline shrugged.

"I've not had any time to stalk Li," Daniela said sarcastically.

"Speaking of Asians, some geneticists believe that North America's indigenous population shares significant DNA with Mongolians. You could be related to Pocahontas—or Lozen."

"Explains the Asian features. I like the sound of being an heir of an Apache warrior princess."

"Not possible." Emmaline laughed at her own silly joke. "Lozen never had children. But you could still be related."

"Not funny. Don't tease me."

"This isn't a tease: if we hike the Jemez Mountains this weekend and explore Apache caves, I have a hunch that we'll find something important." Emmaline laid her trap.

"Like?"

"A clue that will help you understand the prof's letter. Call it my sixth sense . . . and you're welcome." Emmaline plopped onto the stool in front of her standing lab desk.

Daniela rested the prepped slides on a flat box. If she agreed to hiking the Jemez Mountains after a blizzard with her best friend—her only friend aside from her parents—would she regret her decision?

Would that decision become her last?

"Okay, I'll go," Daniela said. The guy said to not trust the redhead, to keep exploring and trying to figure out who would attempt to kick off the apocalypse.

"Goody gumdrops!"

Daniela hunkered down at her lab desk and allowed her mind to wander. Before long, she was lost in her world.

Some preachers called vivid daytime dreams visions.

No problem can be solved from the same level of consciousness that created it. Imagination is everything. It is the preview of life's coming attractions.

—Albert Einstein

"And it shall come to pass in the last days," says God, "That I will pour out of My Spirit on all flesh; Your sons and your daughters shall prophesy, Your young men shall see visions, Your old men shall dream dreams."

—Acts 2: 17

16—NOMED

WITH HIS WIFE IN TOW, Nomed—Legna and Daniela's invisible enemy—walks past the entrance of the Nagarekawa Methodist Church. "Shall we gather the relic for our master's plan?"

"We shall," Aglaope says, following him.

"Come, then." Nomed marches down the aisle of the lone church, a building constructed of concrete but anchored on top of a rock. Defiant, it stands firm amid death's footprint.

"Nomed." Aglaope's voice echoes off the stone walls of the church. "Do you think Lucifer is lying to us? Will his plan work—do we possess the power to eradicate the humans?"

Nomed's heart sinks into his jackboots. "I don't know, Agla."

Wars and rumors of wars . . . that must be the way to eliminate the humans. The creatures' behavior had always been predictable: fear followed by carnage. But could he save the lives of his soldiers? Why should his brothers-in-arms die at the hands of the vile and hypocritical humans?

A flashbulb burns bright on the inside, illuminating a new plan. A better plan. He stops at the end of the church aisle. Crushed and splintered concrete reveals a dark recess and a set of underground stairs. Nomed's heart races as he tiptoes into the open vault.

"Be careful," Agla whispers.

In the darkness, gold glints beneath the blackened sky. "Found it." He grins. "We're going to win, Agla."

"You found the Skeleton Key?" She watches as he returns to the surface cradling a heavy object.

He exits the five-foot-deep hole.

A hopeful smile spreads across his wife's face. "You have made many mistakes, but in the end, you have never failed me. And now you have located your relic and have come up with a new and better plan. What is this new plan? Will it replace Lucifer's?"

"No. But it will save the lives of our people." Nomed holds up the statue, then runs his fingers across its iron and clay toes. "Ten toes made of clay and iron, representing the last of the human kingdoms. Here is the evidence, and Elohim cannot go back on his prophecies, as they are promises written in the Hebrew scriptures."

"What will you do next?"

"I will follow the methods the English used when they 'conquered' Ireland, then ruled over the Irish from 1169 to

1691 before they 'conquered' the rest of the world during the 1800s."

"Every historical account sings the praises of the English war machine."

"I'll tell you a secret."

"I adore secrets." Aglaope clasps her hands together.

"I know you do." He removes an oil cloth from a pouch attached to his breeches. "No different from our master, the humans are liars. Their history books are full of half-truths—lies, if you will. The false historical narratives tell of the English—and other dominant European peoples, the Spanish, Italians, Germans, French, and so on—all bravely fighting their enemies and then winning their wars."

"His-story tells just that. In His-story, the villain can become the hero, and the hero can become the villain."

"My smart girl. So the secret is quite simple: psychological warfare. Words are the most powerful weapons when it comes to paralyzing an enemy, especially when the victim believes the lies."

"That's it?"

"That's everything. And the English mastered psychological warfare—a propaganda of sorts that preached superiority."

"Explain."

"They disseminated false narratives of racial inferiority based upon Social Darwinism—an ideology suggesting that the cream rises to the top."

"Interesting."

"After rejecting the intelligent design theory, the Darwinist narrative numbed the consciences of the English citizens toward other racial groups. At the same time, the theory encouraged other non-English racial groups to embrace a low opinion of themselves."

The concept clicks in Aglaope's mind. "So alongside their propaganda, the English sow seeds of offense between brothers—ethnicities of non-English background."

Nomed laughs. "Remember the old proverb: United we stand, but divided we fall. Divide and conquer is one of the oldest plays in the book."

"And the one about internal strife: Many will be offended, and will betray one another, and will hate one another," she quotes back.

"Put a cherry on my cake! You've got it, darling. Divide the humans. Encourage them to murder each other, and when we leave Wormwood and invade Earth, we will slaughter the few humans remaining."

"Armageddon?" Aglaope verifies.

"Indeed."

"During the 1800s, how did the English wage their campaign of psychological warfare?" Agla chides. "Pamphlets?"

"Don't be cheeky." Nomed wags his finger. "Education. The most powerful form of spreading information or propaganda is art—music, visual art, and the written word. They are the ultimate forms of insidious manipulation. Look at the English frescoes painted on Ireland's palace walls."

"I've never travelled to Ireland."

"I'll take you, one day. But trust me when I tell you that in those frescoes, native Irish women are portrayed as floozies."

"And Irish men are portrayed as lazy drunkards?"

"Yes, Agla! Yet in the same painting, the invaders—the true villains—paint themselves with brushes of morality."

"Let me guess."

"Please do."

"The English woman is painted as modest and with a cherub resting on her shoulder—"

"While the hand of God reaches down from heaven and crowns the Englishman lord to rule over the Irish savages," Nomed finishes for her. Smirking, he slips the wrapped statue into his thigh pouch. "And that, my dearest Agla, is how a tiny empire 'conquered' the world . . . cleverness, manipulation, and organization. Not raw power."

"So was England the last of the European kingdoms to rise to power? Are they the iron that makes up the iron and clay feet of the statue you retrieved?"

"I don't know—yet."

"We will execute the same type of insidious warfare when fighting the humans and bringing about Armageddon?"

Nomed nods to Aglaope. "That is the plan. Take notes."

Aglaope sits on the concrete floor and pulls out a pen and paper from her pack. His boots *click* and *clack* as he paces the dusty floor.

"First: convince the natives—the humans—of their inferiority via Darwinist theories. Make them believe Elohim did not create them, and thus He serves no purpose in their lives. They are sand on a beach—small, irrelevant accidents of the universe and nothing more."

She feverishly writes, then looks up. "Next step?"

"Plant seeds of discord among brothers—the humans. Offense preludes betrayal. Betrayal fuels wars."

"And wars eliminate our enemy." Delight illuminates her face. "Next?"

"Encourage the humans to devalue each other."

"How?"

"Television. Degrading music. Racially charged world leaders. Laughing at each other's differences versus learning from each other. Greed. Immorality. Cheapening sexual unions. Birthing drug-addicted children, then regarding babies and old people as nuisances."

She writes, adding her own enhancements. "It is easier for a human to kill another human if they have been devalued. Also, intra- and intercultural war will further reduce the populations of our enemies."

Looking skyward, Nomed folds his hands together as though he were praying. "I have been blessed with the most intelligent of women as my wife."

"I'm not a woman. I'm the offspring of a Watcher. I am a Nephilim." She swipes a bit of patriotic emotion from the corner of her eye.

"Don't cry."

"I'm so proud of you."

He remains quiet—contemplative, thoughtful. In the final moments of Nomed's Armageddon, his soldiers will strike like hyenas, then feed like vultures on the flesh of the exhausted champion—the lion, the true king of the jungle.

Nomed's plan is clever.

Cowardly.

Deceptive.

Emotion wells up inside Nomed's gut. *This method of warfare will save the lives of my brothers-in-arms.* They would fight in Lucifer's war, but they would not die.

"Agla." He kneels before his wife.

"Yes."

"It's time to make a child."

"Now?" She looks down and timidly meets his piercing gaze. He imagines her train of thought—the violence, the pain, and yet the pleasure of the act. Would she survive it? Should she wait until she recovered?

"I know you better than I know myself. You're distracting me . . . keeping something from me." She stands, looking down at her husband. "What haven't you told me, Nomed?"

There can be too much truth in a marriage, so Nomed keeps his mouth shut. The truth: Daniel's manuscript, the one found in the Qumran Caves, tells a different story of Nomed's future.

Should I tell Agla?

Is it a lie when you know the truth but refuse to share it?

17—Orphan Dreamer

FOR TWO DAYS, A NEW Mexico blizzard dumped snow on the ridges and slopes of the Jemez Mountains.

As a Florida girl, Daniela Rose Cavanaugh had never seen snow before living in Los Alamos, much less hiked in the mountains right after a blizzard. Then again, her world had never collided with the world of Emmaline Georgiana Winterlyn Darbyshire before, either.

Life teaches many lessons.

Lesson one: Poor decisions kill—even two brave and invincible sixteen-year-old college girls. Lesson two: Don't make a promise you can't keep. A promise was a promise, so early that morning, as the blizzard raged, Daniela helped Emmaline pack their winter camping gear and appropriate winter clothes inside the Jeep Wrangler.

Stupid is as stupid does.

But stupid could stop acting stupid. Daniela chose to return to her sensible Southern roots. So as a safety precaution, she tested her new best friend's satellite phone and called her rafiki.

"Hey, Dad."

"How's my girl?"

"Cold."

"It's the weekend, so burrow in, drink hot cocoa, and stay warm."

"Yes, sir. I will." Daniela left out the details about where she would be burrowing. Sick fathers shouldn't be forced to worry about their teenage daughters. "Calling on Limy's sat phone, so I can't talk long."

"Love you to the moon and back."

"And you to the Milky Way and back." Daniela blew a kiss into the phone. "No matter what happens, don't forget me, Daddy."

"How could I ever forget you? What's wrong? You're scaring me."

"Didn't mean to . . . love you." She swallowed her fear. "Tell Momma that I love her too."

"I will. She'll be back from the grocery store in a little while, then you can tell her yourself. She's cooking jalapeno corn bread tonight."

"My fave!"

"She'll whip up a batch when you return home in a few weeks. We'll leave the light on for you, Daniela."

"It'll guide me home no matter how dark. Hugs and kisses." She ended the call. After her shower, Daniela pondered the details of the vision she'd experienced yesterday in the lab.

England.

Propaganda.

Psychological warfare.

And the statue, found in a bombed World War II–era church.

Beyond the picture window of their tiny apartment, sheets of snow cascaded down from a resin-gray sky, cloaking the town and the evergreens that stood stalwart in the distance.

Dressed in their pajamas, both girls stood in front of the window, admiring the frigid, yet calming scene. For the third time, Daniela was falling in love—with the weather, no less. Her cheeks flushed warm as she fought back girlish giggles.

With hands wrapped around hot mugs of cocoa topped with marshmallows, they relished their winter drinks.

"To new beginnings." Emmaline clanked her mug against Daniela's.

"To second chances."

Could the fragile sprouts of a new beginning not only survive beneath the icy tundra of frozen prayers, but also gather enough strength to push through the winter terrain and grow into something powerful like an oak tree?

Daniela had prayed for oily boy, but as usual, nothing seemed to come of her prayers. She craved a dose of the Son's life-giving warmth. She craved change, evidence that her prayers were working.

For some reason, she felt that hiking through a winter tundra in the quiet of nature would allow her to walk closer to the Son and hear His still and gentle voice.

Shine on me, Yeshua. Turn my fragile dreams into reality. Let my oily boy be real and make Limy my forever friend.

"A million cups of hot cocoa for your thoughts." Emmaline sat on the deep windowsill and faced her friend.

"Sounds fattening . . . I'm thinking about sunshine and love."

"The dark, depressive thoughts . . . have they faded, for now?"

"In this moment."

"I'm glad."

"So am I." Daniela sipped her hot cocoa.

"What took you back to depression's dark cave?"

"The nosebleed."

"Why? It's just a nosebleed—epistaxis caused by the spontaneous rupture of blood vessels. It's not the bubonic plague."

"The event triggered childhood memories, of times when I felt helpless and longed for my classmates to like me, to give me the benefit of the doubt even though I looked different. I was so afraid that after you saw blood dripping from my nose, you'd be gone the next morning."

"I don't abandon my friends—and where would I have gone in this blizzard?"

"Somewhere better."

"I'm standing by the best thing that has happened to me in years, so promise me . . ." Emmaline rested her hand on Daniela's arm. "Don't walk through your dark valleys alone. Not anymore. You don't have to. I'm here."

"That's the irony of the situation. I'm never alone—just feel as though I am. Yeshua promised to never leave me or forsake me."

"Come to me. Let me be involved, and I'll make you feel that I'm here, just like He's here."

"But you don't believe in Yeshua."

"I didn't say that I didn't believe. I said I don't follow. There's a difference. I'm your friend, Danny-girl. Friends stand by their friends no matter the location—the valleys or the mountaintops."

"When it's dark, how will I be able to see you?"

"Feel me, like you feel your Yeshua. Besides, I can hold a flashlight steady, so no need to walk in the dark."

Daniela rested her head on Emmaline's shoulder. "Thanks for your loyalty, Limy Darbyshire. You're a dream."

"At least I'm not a nightmare."

Last night, a depressive winter storm had cast darkness over Daniela's sunrise, threatening to snatch the sunshine from her blue sky. But a knowing—Yahweh's voice—calmed her now.

Even in the desert, seeds drank up the sun's strength, then grew. They held on for springtime's warmth and waited for dark clouds to gift them with rain. One rainy day, Daniela would stand taller than an evergreen, casting shade over weary souls.

"Limy." She shifted her weight. "You once told me that you thought of your unspoken hopes and dreams as prayers riding a wingless bird. Why?"

Emmaline sat down on the couch and stared into her mug. Daniela sat on the floor in front of her friend. "I'm sorry to intrude, and I'm sorry for whatever disappointments life has thrown at you."

"What doesn't kill you makes you stronger, right?"

"If you survive." Daniela paused, allowing silence to begin the healing process of her friend's broken heart. "We'll limp to the finish line together, but we'll make it to the end."

"That's a visual." Emmaline giggled.

"My grandma Gertrude was the best at making me feel better."

"How?"

"She used to say, 'One snowflake falls from heaven to quench hell's thirst.' " Daniela's voice cracked. " 'Button, you are that snowflake destined to quench the hellish thirst of an orphan boy, so lean back and start falling.' "

After one such heartwarming talk years ago, Daniela's beloved grandmother had collapsed. Sprawled on her back and covered in spilled flour, she had died inside her farmhouse pantry.

"You are a snowflake, Danny-girl. Unique. Delicate. Refreshing."

"Snowflakes clump together, Limy."

"No. That's your destiny, not mine." Emmaline paused, allowing her compliment to soak through Daniela's protective shell. "Your grandmother must have been an incredible woman. I would have loved to have met her."

"She believed when others doubted."

"I believe in you."

"I know, and I hope that I don't disappoint you." Daniela found the dangerously green eyes of her kindred spirit. "I don't deserve you, or at least, I feel as though I don't."

"Earn it . . . if you must."

"How?"

"Start by forgetting what Claire Underwood and Harry said to you when you were growing up."

"Why?"

"You're my friend now! And all my friends are practically perfect." Emmaline's eyes dazzled with hope and understanding.

"Talk about being set up for failure." Daniela chuckled.

"You won't fail. I won't allow you to. But tell me this: the hellish thirst that you're destined to quench, it's oily boy's thirst—right?"

"I suppose." Daniela shrugged. "Not that I have a clue how a nosebleeding, awkward girl like me could quench any boy's thirst, much less the parched and hellfire reality of a tormented boy I've never met."

"If your grandmother said that the hell you're destined to quench belonged to an orphan boy, then oily boy is an orphan."

"You're right."

"Always am, Miss Boys and Books Don't Match." Emmaline laughed. "Your oily boy has been abandoned. In honor of his pain, maybe it's time to give him a proper name." She tugged one of Daniela's curls, then watched it spring back toward her head.

"I need a dose of inspiration worthy of renaming this figment of my imagination."

"Nature inspires the most desolate of souls, so look to her as we hike."

"You're a poet, Limy." Attempting to stir up her inspiration, Daniela scrutinized the sights beyond their window. "Los Alamos—no. Atomic bombs: Fat Man and Little Boy—definitely no! Science. Oppenheimer. Einstein. Apache Indians. Lozen. Hot springs. Plateaus. The Jemez Mountains. Caves. A winter storm . . ."

"What about 'the poet'?"

"But that's you."

"I gift the name to oily boy until you can think of another one."

"It'll remind me of you—my real-life kindred spirit—when I'm discouraged by and confused with the fantasy of him."

18—Orphan Dreamer

THE WEATHERMAN HAD PREDICTED THAT Los Alamos's sky would stop dumping snow Friday at midnight, then yield to cold, blue morning skies Saturday morning.

His prediction proved true, and the girls woke Saturday to eleven inches of fine-powdered snow obscuring the sidewalks of Los Alamos.

"Ready to grab some groceries?" Emmaline sauntered out of the bathroom, dressed in hiking pants, a Keen jacket, and hiking boots.

"Let's do it."

Wrapped in winter coats, neck scarves, wool hats, thermals, and hiking pants, Daniela and Emmaline exited their toasty abode, trudged down Trinity Drive, purchased a few more supplies at Smith's Food & Drug, their favorite mom-and-pop grocery store, then each carried an armful of groceries uphill.

"We should have brought your Jeep." Daniela's breath hitched.

"It's invigorating to walk before hiking," Emmaline said as she walked ahead of Daniela, snow squishing out beyond her feet.

"Only if your lungs are sucking up enough oxygen," Daniela gasped. Emmaline stopped and turned toward her friend. "Are you okay?"

"I'm fine." Daniela stood still, closed her eyes, then gulped down several breaths. Her heart raced, and her chest constricted. *What's wrong with me?*

"I'll help you." Emmaline backtracked, took one of Daniela's bags, and walked beside her friend.

"Thank you." Daniela's face flushed, and she refused to make eye contact with Emmaline, so her friend shifted the conversation.

After loading their paper bags into Emmaline's Jeep, they climbed into the heated cabin.

The Orphan Dreamer rubbed her hands together as the heat defrosted her skin, and Daniela's kindred spirit slipped on her sunglasses and lifted her chin to see beyond the glisten of sunlight on the snow.

Cascades of deep red curls fell down her back and freckles added texture to her face. At birth, heaven must have kissed her face, then said, "Be beautiful, Emmaline."

The redhead had obliged.

As the sun washed her face in springtime warmth, the Orphan Dreamer closed her eyes, enjoying her last moments of peace until Emmaline lifted her foot off the accelerator.

"Let's go, Danny-girl." True to form, Emmaline turned

the ignition, cranked up "Indian Outlaw" by Tim McGraw, then punched the gas.

Daniela gripped the door handle as the race-car driver gunned the Jeep out of the parking lot, then westward along Infinity Drive—the main road out of town toward the Jemez Mountains. Thankfully, a snowplow had already cleared the snow from the roads.

She continued to DJ, playing music in the background as they weaved through the tiny town, making tracks and memories. Breathless, Daniela cracked the window. Crisp breezes channeled up over the edge of the plateau and into the Jeep's cabin.

She exhaled, then inhaled the woody, evergreen scent deeper.

Breath.

Life.

A gift from the Creator. Her breath was coming a bit easier now. But why the breathlessness at the age of sixteen?

Emmaline tapped the steering wheel with neatly trimmed nails. "On the way to the mountains, let's stop at Spence Hot Springs and take a dip."

"We're not carrots looking for a bowl of ranch dressing. It's cold outside." Daniela pushed her head into the headrest. "Bathing suits in twenty-degree weather isn't appealing to me. I'm a Florida girl."

"Everyone up here soaks in hot springs. It's good for you. Healthy. Maybe . . . you could breathe easier."

"My breathing is fine."

"Secrets. Lies. Friendship. Remember?"

"I was loaded down with groceries, walking up an incline and three flights of stairs at eight-thousand-feet altitude."

"So was I."

"The hot springs will be crowded. I hate crowds."

"Where's your sense of adventure?"

"I am adventurous."

"Prove it."

"I love cooking new cuisines, reading thrillers, and the nail-biting adventure of applying to medical school." Daniela redirected the car vents away from her face, then sipped her hot cocoa. "It's true: People jump from planes when the engines are working just fine. That doesn't mean we have to jump."

"Hot springs compared to skydiving? You can't be serious."

"Deadly. Virulent bacteria such as pseudomonas thrive in hot water, and after they infect a hot tub bather via a small cut on their skin, the aerobic bacteria kill by cannibalizing their host—eating their flesh." Unblinking, Daniela glared at Emmaline as they passed Valles Caldera National Preserve. She fought to not burst out laughing.

"Did you write that tidbit about flesh-eating bacteria into your med school application?"

"Didn't need to. I wrote an even better story." Daniela winked.

"So you submitted your applications! You've officially applied to medical school?"

"I did."

"Danny's going to med school!" Emmaline made up a song. "Danny's going to med school!"

"We'll see."

"Where are your top choices?"

"University of Florida, followed by Emory. I'll admit the waiting is soaking up my adrenaline stores."

"You're such a nerd. Maybe that's why you're not

sleeping and you're short of breath when walking uphill?"

"Could be. I should be sleeping, because I'm exhausted."

"Life lesson number one: Even when stressed, you need to learn how to act *fun*. How are you ever going to make your oily boy happy?"

"At sea level, warm and clothed." Daniela's gaze softened.

"You sound like a parent, but you're adorably hilarious."

"More like sinfully sane." Daniela's wide smile dammed up Emmaline's incoming waterfall of words. Then the Jeep jerked as she shifted into a slower speed to climb a steep incline. Both girls lurched forward, then back.

"See? Even the Jeep struggles with inclines." Daniela rubbed the whiplash out of her neck, and laughter popped past their tense smiles. "I love this song!" She turned up Michael W. Smith's hit song, "Friends." The girls sang along.

Twenty minutes passed. Voice raspy, Daniela pointed to the map. "This shows Fenton Lake State Park about thirty-seven miles from San Ysidro, so we should arrive at the campsite soon."

"There's a little restaurant-bar a few miles away if you want to grab a hot lunch before we leave civilization."

"I wouldn't mind using an indoor toilet one last time before squatting with the coyotes. Count me in."

"Running water, so it's a bathroom run, then." Emmaline floored the gas pedal. Centrifugal force crashed into the Jeep's side at the bend in the road, threatening to kick them off the mountain's edge. Rubber gripped the road, fighting the lethal force.

Daniela held her breath. She hated driving and didn't have a car, so she kept her mouth shut and prayed. If she and wealth eventually met on life's path, she'd hire a chauffeur. "That's a place to stay—Laughing Lizard Inn." She pointed to a sign. "Makes you want to book a room."

Ten minutes later, Emmaline sped into the parking lot of Los Ojos Restaurant, churning up dust before slamming on her brakes.

"Umm . . ." Daniela rolled down her window and looked out. "You sure about this place? One tattered-tan building framed by green posts stood alone. A faded American flag flapped in the wind atop a chipped white pole. Black wrought-iron bars guarded the front windows.

Emmaline opened the glove compartment and removed a black velvet bag. "Pepper spray." She glanced up at Daniela.

"Looks heavy."

"My version of it." She winked.

"More like bear spray." Daniela exited the Jeep and walked around to the driver's side. She stumbled behind her fearless friend. "For the record, this was your idea."

"Have gun, will travel." Emmaline tapped her mysterious bag, and they entered the restaurant together. "And you consented."

"True."

Deer heads cursed with lifeless black eyes glared at the girls from the opposite wall. A brown bear's fur sprawled across the right wall, and a stag's antlers hung from the left wall. A coiled rattlesnake was pinned against an overhanging beam in mid-strike. Needless carnage to shore up an insecure hunter's ego. Daniela's stomach churned.

Greasy men dressed in ripped T-shirts ogled the teens. Daniela named the men, as she did any stranger who made her feel uncomfortable. The exercise brought the strange into the familiar.

Toothless Tom licked his lips.

Grimy George rubbed his beer belly.

Jumpy John couldn't sit still on his chair.

Emmaline reached into her velvet bag and pressed her "pepper spray" to her chest.

"Ladies, shall we dance?" Grimy George slid his barstool back as he stood. The stool crashed to the floor.

"If you like two-steppin' on broken legs," Emmaline said, retreating back to her friend's side. The plate of fries and an All-American hamburger sitting in front of Jumpy John made Daniela's mouth water.

"I'm not feeling this place," Daniela whispered. "Seriously, Limy. I'm not hungry enough for restaurant food to ward off an attack." Beans and rice cooked over a campfire sounded delicious and safe. She rested her trembling hand on Emmaline's shoulder.

Holding a beer bottle, Grimy George swaggered toward the girls. The bartender picked up the phone and dialed. Maybe he was calling 911?

Time to leave! "Storm?"

"You bet." Emmaline raced past the rickety door. Daniela followed, leaving a trail of dust in her wake. Safely inside the Jeep, the girls slammed the doors shut. Unnerved, they sat stone-still, their short lives flashing before their eyes.

"That was close, Limy."

"Too close. Let's roll." She keyed the ignition, shifted into drive, then floored the accelerator. The Jeep's tires spun, throwing dirt toward the bar as they sped back onto the paved road.

"No more remote diners."

"No argument from me."

Daniela gripped the arm rest, blanching her knuckles a dusky gray, but she was glad for her friend's fierce driving.

"Here's to hoping that detour isn't indicative of what's to come."

"Affirmative."

Golden grasslands speckled with olive-brown shrubs cast off an earthy fragrance. Unknown bird species chirped, welcoming their visitors—or intruders. The small creatures would find out which the humans were soon enough.

"I should have researched the bird species native to this region." Daniela rolled her window partially up.

"Why?"

"What if one of us gets in trouble and we need to send a secret signal?" She peered through a set of binoculars, looking for anything abnormal.

"I'll holler for help if I'm in trouble," Emmaline said.

Daniela shook her head. "That defeats the purpose of blending into the environment and maintaining stealth, Ranger Limy."

"We're not on a special-ops mission—are we?"

"Ops mission, but not sure how special."

"I thought we were hiking, spending girl time together while looking for birds and Apache cave art." Emmaline playfully thumped Daniela's shoulder.

"Hands on the steering wheel, Dale Earnhardt." Daniela focused the binoculars' lens on something moving in the distance. "It's a bobcat!"

"I'm confiscating your thriller novels as soon as we arrive at camp."

"Only if you flush your romance novels down the toilet." Daniela placed her finger into her mouth, playfully making a gagging noise.

"There are no toilets in the Jemez Mountains." Emmaline giggled. "If you flush my romance novels down the toilet at our loft, then I'll need the real thing. You don't want boys sleeping over, do you?"

"My dad would kill me, and my mom would tetanic seize."

"I'll protect you." Emmaline slammed her right fist into the dashboard. "Ouch!"

"Could you please drive and leave the right hooks for Muhammad Ali?" Daniela rolled down the window, drinking in the clouds, fresh air, and green trees as she leaned out. "This I know for sure . . ." She faced Emmaline. "You're a kindred spirit. Firebrand crazy, but I love you for it."

"Cheers to that." Emmaline squeezed Daniela's shoulder as winter's breath dived deep into the vehicle, whipping ginger and brunette locks into a frenzy.

"I guess my kindred spirit was a her after all."

"I don't understand."

"When I first prayed for a kindred spirit. Yahweh sent me a boy, Ethan."

"Losing Ethan must have been hard." Emmaline navigated her Jeep deep into the valley between the mountains.

"It was."

After several minutes of silence, she nudged Daniela. That wicked smile had returned. "So gnarly."

"Dead animals." Daniela shook her head. "Greasy, pot-bellied men." They burst into a cacophony of laughter. "Who do you think the bartender was calling, Limy?"

"Heck if I know." Emmaline turned away from Daniela's interrogative glare.

Like a rising sapphire, shimmering waters appeared in the middle of the desert. "Danny!" Emmaline gasped. "It's gorgeous." She pointed toward the lake tucked between two mountains.

"It's Lake Fenton." In silence, she watched the foreboding body of water as though it were a sleeping grizzly. What secrets lay hidden within its shifting, sandy depths?

The memory of her time-travel adventure to Gibeah flooded her thoughts. Prince Jonathan. The arrowhead. The desert oasis. The assault by the sweaty, brawny Philistine. Then diving into a bottomless desert pool to escape her assaulter when she couldn't swim. The pool proved to be the portal back to her world—leading her to Ethan's ICU hospital room right before he died.

"How deep is it?" Daniela asked.

"Deep enough to swim. And after this trip, you'll swim like a fish."

"The water is freezing."

"Are you afraid of Lake Fenton because the water is cold?"

"It's not the temperature." Daniela rubbed her ear. "I almost drowned when I was a kid. Harry pushed me into Newnan's Lake, and I couldn't see or touch the bottom."

"He had a crush on you!" Emmaline drummed the steering wheel in time with another McGraw song, "I Like It, I Love It."

"Goodness, I hope not." Daniela craned her neck out of the passenger window. "Is it typical for a boy who likes you to try and kill you first?"

"Of course!" Emmaline changed her voice to mimic a feminine version of Sir David Frederick Attenborough, English broadcaster and natural historian. "It's the first rule of masculine romance—dominating the female, he fights his feelings of vulnerability." She drove off the paved highway and down a wide dirt road. The Jeep's wheels spun, throwing loose dirt and pebbles against the undercarriage and sounding like a machine gun as the girls jostled left and right.

"What's next in your sordid guidebook of romance—swallowing a handful of rusty nails and then donning a crown of thorns before saying 'I do'?" Daniela said, and Emmaline laughed.

A basalt monolith jutted upward on their right, surrounded by sharp peaks and a lush pine forest.

"That's Battleship Rock!" Daniela said, the local topography yanking her from her romantic critique.

"I don't see any water around the rock to warrant the name."

"The geographer named the rock for what it could become, not for what it is," Daniela said.

"Deep. The philosopher speaks. Ready to dive deep into another pool? Do you want to know what happens next in my sordid guidebook of romance?"

"Doesn't make any difference." Daniela shrugged. "With my nosebleeds, I could join a convent, become a nun, and no one would notice."

"Too permanent. Sixteen-year-olds making temporary decisions with permanent consequences. Remember?"

"Okay. I'm listening. What about a sweater-crocheting spinster, creating scarves for my luckier acquaintances, a.k.a. Emmaline Georgiana Darbyshire?"

"I like sweaters." Emmaline glanced at her friend, then back at the road and then back at her friend again.

"Fine. Tell me."

"Thank you! I was going to burst. Look at the wild, Danny." Emmaline lifted both hands off the Jeep's steering wheel and gestured wildly. "You've seen those male lions with their lionesses."

"On National Geographic. Hands back on the wheel—please," Daniela insisted. Emmaline complied.

"It's magical."

"More like brutal."

"I hope your honeymoon night changes your mind." Emmaline yanked the steering wheel right. The Jeep's wheels spun and threw loose dirt as they careened up a narrow incline.

"Driving in like the cavalry."

"Just how I like my men."

"Keep it PG-13."

"I'm just scaring away the wildlife and clearing the pathway to Battleship Rock. So are you really terrified of the male species?"

"Cautious."

"It's springtime. FYI: they're in season." She turned into an empty dirt and gravel parking lot, then cut the engine.

"At least the snow isn't as deep here." Daniela shifted in her seat and faced her friend. "But it's not a good sign when the campground is empty except for two sixteen-year-old girls. I thought *lots* of people were hiking the Jemez in March. A friend of mine by the name of Emmaline told me that."

"Maybe the others hiked in from Los Alamos instead of driving?"

"For thirty miles through the snow? Nice try. Besides, it's three hours before dusk. If *they* were going to be here, *they* would've already arrived."

The sun had begun to drop behind the western horizon, leaving a fiery trail of tangerine, rose, and lavender in its wake.

"We're burning daylight." Daniela opened the Jeep door.

The sun would pay them no favors. It was fatiguing, sagging behind the western mountain range. The girls secured their hiking packs onto their backs, grabbed an armful of supplies from the trunk, and trekked through two inches of snow toward the campsite. In less than ten minutes, they arrived and found that the site had already been cleared of snow.

"Who cleared the site?" Daniela dropped her supplies onto the ground. Her heartbeat upticked a few beats.

Emmaline cupped her mouth and shouted, "Anybody out there?" Her voice carried over the lake and across the valley before stopping somewhere near the base of the Jemez Mountain range. Silence. Then a faint echo boomeranged.

"Fate is walking across the back of these mountains." Daniela shivered.

"Calm down, Danny-girl. Any serial killers out there?" Emmaline shouted before her voice trailed off. "Tommy the Tooth—or whatever you called him." She mocked Daniela's wariness.

"Shh, they'll hear us." Daniela shoulder-bumped her friend before they returned to the Jeep to retrieve more supplies.

"Laughter decreases stress. You should try it." Emmaline removed the tent and sleeping bags while Daniela grabbed the Coleman stove before she slammed and locked the Jeep's back door.

"It'll be dark soon. Wanna go look for that cave?" Emmaline asked.

"It's too late. We'll hike to the cave tomorrow morning."

Daniela dropped their remaining gear onto a patch of dead wildflowers.

"You're positively no fun."

"We're camping in the wild after a snowstorm, and it'll be dark soon," Daniela said. "So we need to set up camp quickly, or we'll freeze to death. What's the fun in that? The winds couldn't have blown that much snow off the mountain, Limy. Something . . . or someone has been here. And why did they only clear this camping site? We should clear another site, closer to the Jeep."

"Not a chance. It's too late. Maybe the Son—your Yeshua—shined on us, melting the snow."

"That's called faith."

"I'm trying." Emmaline shrugged.

Daniela remembered the letter. *Don't trust the redhead.* Could she exercise faith in her friend's character? The Orphan Dreamer unsheathed their tent, then pitched their two-person nylon home. No need to lose the heat generated from their bodies in a cavernous tent.

She arranged their sleeping bags next to each other, then placed two battery-operated lanterns, some snacks, and water within reach. "Race you for firewood." Daniela dashed out of the tent and past her friend, her hot breath leaving a trail of fog—a map.

Would her lungs fail her again?

She breathed with purpose.

Her heart raced and her chest burned, but she pushed through the pain. *Keep going.* Only another eighth of a mile. She arrived at the edge of the forest, the world spinning like a merry-go-round.

She caught her breath, then gathered firewood to add to the stash of dry firewood they'd brought with them.

After four trips into the woods, Daniela rested for five minutes, then organized the tinder inside a natural firepit. She ignited her fire starter, and less than an hour later, the sun died.

Orange flames flickered against the black sky. Twinkling stars hovered overhead as Daniela stirred their beans and rice inside a tin pot. Meanwhile, Emmaline flipped strips of bacon inside a small iron skillet atop the Coleman stove.

"Smells delicious, Danny-girl, but the scent will draw wild animals and potentially wild people." Emmaline stood with her hands on her hips, lost in a thousand-mile stare as though she were looking for someone or something.

"We'll eat fast." Daniela shivered at the thought of attracting anything wild. She pulled her jacket close and waited for the beans to finish cooking. The smoke burned her eyes, making them tear. She sniffled.

"You okay?" Emmaline nudged Daniela's shoulder.

"It's the smoke."

"Black beans and bacon never smelled so good, huh?"

"Ruth's Chris, here comes Daniela's Steaks." Daniela gazed into the fire, lost in a trance. "It's so quiet out here." She rubbed her arms as the fire pocked and crackled.

"Is this kind of quiet okay with your knowing?"

"Time will tell," Daniela said as she thought of someone else. Where was the orphan from her dreams now—the boy with the lice-infested, shaggy black hair and bone-bleached pale skin? Was he safe? Could she find him in the complex web of her dreams, then squeeze him out of her alternate universe into her reality?

Did she *want* to free him?

Daniela envisioned popping a pimple on her face, then watching the blackened sebum worm its way out of the defect and onto the surface of her skin. Oily boy was nothing more than a pimple trapped beneath her depressive and confused state.

For days, she hadn't dreamed about him. Eventually, even a pimple must be extracted.

Her last dream of him had been a nightmare, but images of the brothel, rape, and hopelessness had slowly faded from her memory. If the Philistine had captured her, would oily boy's reality have been hers?

"The male dominates the female, fighting his feelings of vulnerability," Daniela whispered Emmaline's words, and her hands visibly shook.

Her heart ached for what she had known to be real: gentle, sweet, and funny Ethan. Her thirteen-year-old friend had been struggling with cancer when they travelled to Gibeah. And after Ethan returned from their trip to ancient Gibeah, he had died. Had the stress of time travel killed him?

If so, when would the stress of time travel kill Daniela?

The Orphan Dreamer didn't deserve another kindred spirit. She'd wasted the life of the first. She studied Emmaline while she ate, guilt eating up her insides.

"Take me on one of your time-travel trips, Danny-girl." Emmaline chewed a strip of bacon.

"Can't."

"Sounds final."

"It is." *I'm a black widow that murders her best friends,* Daniela thought. "Do you like your dinner?" Her voice was barely a whisper.

"I'm so starved, everything tastes amazing."

Danny spooned another scoop of beans onto Emmaline's plate and topped them with three strips of bacon before serving herself again. As they ate their second helpings, the cold night air lay thick between their silence.

Emmaline spoke first. "I'll never forget this moment."

"Neither will I."

"Tell me a bedtime story. One of your adventures."

"Where to?"

"How about one of your wild adventures with Professor Jakob in Israel?"

"Why?"

"Understanding him will help me understand his mysterious letter—like for starters, did he have something to do with sending the statue?"

Guilt, shame, and sadness held the Orphan Dreamer's tongue hostage. Did Professor Jakob hate her for the loss of his only nephew, Ethan? It didn't seem like it, but true feelings are often hidden.

Second by second, black swells of depression threatened to drown her. She gasped, gulping down air, chased by chugs of water. Unforgiving cold stabbed her throat, then her chest before reaching her lungs and finally her gut.

Most people interpreted silence as anger. Her kindred spirit didn't deserve to misunderstand her introverted friend. So the Orphan Dreamer inhaled again, then said, "The trip wasn't so wild—it was rather tame, actually." A tear threatened to tell her secrets. She swiped the liquid emotion away. "We didn't have the funding to make our trip *Indiana Jones*–wild."

Emmaline chuckled. "What did you accomplish during your archeology trip with the professor?"

"I learned basic excavation techniques while I studied Jewish feasts and the artifacts necessary to outfit the third Jewish Temple."

"What's next?"

"Professor Jakob is keen to find the Hebrew prophet Ezekiel's scroll that details the dimensions of the upcoming Third—and last—Jewish Temple. He believes Ezekiel left clues in the scroll that will tell the reader when this Third Temple will be built and where the lost artifacts from the First Temple are hidden."

"You never found Ezekiel's lost scroll?"

"Conducting an archaeological dig takes money—and lots of it. He showed me the Copper Scroll, though, and a few of the other Dead Sea Scrolls. Seeing them in person was a magnificent experience."

"I know about the Dead Sea Scrolls, but what's the Copper Scroll?"

"A scroll constructed of copper found in the Qumran Caves—the same caves where the Dead Sea Scrolls were discovered."

"And the Copper Scroll was part of the Dead Sea Scrolls cache?"

"Yes and no. The majority of the Dead Sea Scrolls were found by Bedouins between 1946 to 1956, whereas an archaeologist discovered the Copper Scroll in 1952 in the back of cave three at Qumran. It was the last of fifteen scrolls extracted from the cave, but the construction of the scroll is different. All the other Dead Sea Scrolls are composed of parchment or papyrus—the Copper Scroll is constructed of beaten copper."

"Must be a beautiful relic, but do you think the Copper Scroll is a fake?" Emmaline cast her fishing line back into Daniela's lake of knowledge.

"That's above my pay grade. But I can tell you that the professor was skeptical of the scroll's authenticity."

"If it's real, what mysteries does it reveal?"

"It's written in Hebrew, but the Hebrew style used in the

scrolls is different than that used on the Dead Sea Scrolls. The Copper Scroll lists a vast treasure hidden throughout the wilderness."

"The Judean wilderness?"

"That's the presumptive conclusion, but no one knows how to find the loot."

"Why was the treasure hidden?"

"Aren't most ancient treasures?" Daniela asked. "Anyway, Professor Jakob thinks that if the Copper Scroll is authentic, it tells of a treasure taken from the Temple of Jerusalem and hidden by the faithful during the First Jewish Revolt against Rome in the first century, 66–70 AD."

"Right before the Romans destroyed the Jerusalem Temple in 70 AD?"

"You know your Middle Eastern history."

"A little. I didn't learn to read Hebrew for my health."

"Another possibility is that the scroll tells of temple treasures hidden during the Second Jewish Revolt against Rome—the Bar-Kokhba Revolt—in 132–135 AD."

"Danny-girl, I'd love to travel with you." Emmaline stoked the dying fire. "One summer. Just you and me, without . . ." Her voice trailed off, and she never completed her thought. Daniela wondered, *without what or who?* "Here comes Indiana Jones and her firecracker, boy-crazy sidekick. Take me with you."

"Limy, full disclosure: I am a black widow who kills my best friends, especially when we travel."

"Should I expect to be murdered in my sleep tonight?"

"Should I?" Daniela said, thinking of crazy lake-guy's warning.

"Not tonight." Emmaline wickedly grinned. "And my blood's resistant to poison, so I'm coming on your next dirt dig. That's final."

"You've been warned." Daniela yawned and then yoga-stretched, releasing endorphins into her blood. "We enjoy each other's company, but we don't always agree with each other. Professor Jakob doesn't completely agree with me, but I think the fall feasts—Yahweh's appointed times—may have something to do with the astronomical phenomena called blood moons."

"You're really knowledgeable about Jewish traditions, but I'm confused because you're a Christian, and I thought Jews and Christians mixed like oil and water?"

"The history of Christianity is complicated, but I'm a Yeshua follower who reads and believes His word—the New Testament *and* its predecessor, the Hebrew scriptures or Old Testament."

"And the New Testament is a testament of who?"

"It testifies that Yeshua is the promised Jewish Messiah, born of the tribe of Judah and of the lineage of the warrior, King David." Daniela washed their tin plates in a bucket of lake water, then placed the tinware on top of the fire to sanitize the metal, happy to no longer be talking about oily boy.

"You're a scientist . . . you must agree that the virgin birth is rather hard to believe."

"We all choose to have faith in something."

"If Yeshua was the long-awaited Messiah, why are Jewish people still looking for their Messiah? And why do they distrust Christians—or Yeshua followers, as you call yourself?"

"If we're going to talk, let's at least enjoy the view." Daniela entered their tent and retrieved their sleeping bags. She spread down a plastic tarp, rolled out their sleeping bags underneath the starry sky, then slipped inside her cozy winter bag insulated with a wool blanket. "Most

Jewish people are still looking for their Messiah because Yeshua was a disappointment."

"Isn't that blasphemy?" Emmaline dressed in blue-gray-and-red-striped flannels, then climbed into her sleeping bag nestled close to Daniela.

"Who wants your Messiah—the rescuer from Roman oppression—to arrive on Earth as a helpless baby, hailing from a trailer park background—i.e., a Nazarene—born in a Bethlehem barn with cows and sheep, only to watch him live as a vagabond carpenter who one day rides into Jerusalem on a donkey to betrayal by a friend, mockery by a rabid crowd, and finally a brutal Roman flogging followed by inhumane crucifixion?"

"The process seems pointless."

"Yeshua didn't meet first-century Jews' expectations. To them, He was a weak and powerless radical, unable to defeat their Roman oppressors." Daniela turned on her side and faced Emmaline.

"In all fairness, the Romans did crucify him, then bury him in a borrowed tomb."

"They did. But do you give up on sunshine because the moon shines?" Daniela asked.

"No."

"And notice, the tomb was borrowed."

"Noted. What's the payback for murdering the Son of God?"

"Eternal separation from the Light of the World, and suffering for all eternity in smoldering darkness. Our escape hatch is to repent—change direction and go the other way."

"And the Catholic crusaders? Where do they fit into your theology?"

"If someone is killing another person in the name of Yeshua, they're not a true follower of Him."

"I wonder who's going to share that news with the good old Bible Belt oppressors."

"The Bible already did. The Apostle John wrote that if someone says he loves God and hates his brother, he is a liar. Region doesn't matter. People from any part of the world can hate and then oppress—even people who believe they are kings and queens of tolerance. Trust me. I've been located downwind of overt and sneaky oppressors."

"Daniela, if your God is so good, why is my brother dying? He's not a bad person. Why would your God take him away from me? He's the only one who truly understands me—besides you."

"I'm sorry, Limy." Daniela quietly rested her hand on Emmaline's. Present, but not pushy. The campfire's flames retreated into scorched embers, glowing with an internal heat.

"What does your holy book say about dying?

"Death never plays fair. It's the result of human wrongs, but there's hope: Yeshua paid our debt during his Roman execution and then defeated death when he rose from the borrowed grave."

"How does execution, death, and debt help my William live?" Emmaline's voice cracked.

"Tell him to reach out to the Life Giver."

A few seconds passed. Emmaline intertwined her fingers with Daniela's. They were slicked with sweat and nerves.

The Orphan Dreamer squeezed, telling Limy, *I'm here.* "Limy, death is simply the result of human decay—or sin. Yeshua paid our debt, healing our fatal condition and gifting us life—if we receive His gift through our belief in His essence."

"Sounds like a sales pitch."

"My dad's fighting leukemia. I don't need to sell anything. I've lived the journey, so I know how you feel."

"I didn't know. I'm sorry, Danny-girl." Weeping softly, Emmaline rolled closer to her friend.

Daniela's voice lowered to a breathy whisper. "Sometimes I'm mad at God—and even feel betrayed."

"Then what's the point of following Him, Danny Rose?"

"Because deep inside, I know that He loves me." Daniela sighed heavily as Emmaline's gaze pierced Daniela's armor, searching the deepness of her soul.

"That's called hope."

"Adventure doesn't wait for sleepyheads. Morning's coming." Daniela sat up, afraid of her own vulnerable state. "It's time for bed." She retreated to their tent, and Emmaline followed, securing the tent door. Both girls zipped their sleeping bags. Foggy trails of breath rose and fell above each of them. "Sweet dreams, Limy."

"Don't go travelling to another time and another place, leaving me out here alone."

"I don't decide when I travel," Daniela whispered. Full of hope, she clenched the Glass Tattoo in her right hand, closed her eyes, and prayed, "Help oily boy, please."

"Just like the bed bugs, don't let oily boy bite."

"Have bug spray, will travel . . ." Daniela closed her fist around the Glass Tattoo. Warmth started in her hand, then radiated from the diamond, embracing the Orphan Dreamer.

19—Orphan Dreamer's Kindred Spirit

EMMALINE USUALLY FELL ASLEEP FIRST, but she was wide awake while Daniela slept. Her soft snores filled the space between the tent's blue nylon walls.

Emmaline clicked on her flashlight. The sparkling snowflake diamond—the Glass Tattoo—no longer hung from Daniela's neck. She gently opened Daniela's right hand and saw a midnight-blue snowflake tattoo staining her friend's pale palm.

Where had she gone? Would she dream of her poet? If she did, would she remember her dream this time, gifting the girls a few juicy details?

"Bad timing, Danny-girl." Emmaline considered trying

to wake her friend but instead closed her hand and waited. History possessed stories of feminine Judas Iscariots as well. She snuggled deep inside her sleeping bag, waiting for the arrival of Robert—her father's employee and a member of the fearless special-ops team, the Orphans.

A non-celestial illumination swept across their tent, probably the headlights of Robert's F-150.

She pressed into her sleeping friend, and something hard poked her chest. Curious, she peeled back Daniela's bag, then shone her flashlight across the statue, the Skeleton Key. "I hid it," she whispered. *How did Daniela find the statue inside the loft—and why did she bring it with us?*

Eyes wide open, Emmaline studied its details again: head made of pure gold, its chest and arms of silver, its belly and thighs of bronze, its legs of iron, and its feet of part iron and clay.

Daniela opened her eyes.

Beads of sweat pimpled up across Emmaline's forehead. Her lungs constricted. "Are you awake?"

Silence. Daniela closed her eyes again. Gasping for breath, Emmaline gently grabbed the statue, crawled out of her sleeping bag, then cracked open the tent's opaque flap. Cold, fresh air poured through the mesh, chilling her to the bone. Could she betray her friend—her only real friend? She stepped outside the tent.

A lone star fell from the sky toward the horizon. *Make a wish, Emma.* She longed to hear her dad say that.

"I wish for love, Daddy. The romantic kind that releases butterflies from their cocoons. I'm no virgin, but I wish for a man who love songs were written for, just like Danny's oily boy, the poet." She glowered at her sleeping friend. "If you exist, oily boy . . . if Daniela doesn't want you—and even if she does want you—I'll take you seven days out of the week." Emmaline clung to the statue, pressing it between her breasts. "Be mine too."

Inside the tent, Daniela tossed and turned. Sweat clung to her neck and face. Over and over again, she released whimpers, "No. Please no . . ."

"What's happening?" Emmaline whispered. Two nights ago, after her dad had recruited her to set up the kidnapping, Emmaline had dreamed too.

In her dream, she'd been camping with Daniela. One minute they were laughing, talking, and gossiping, and the next moment her religious friend had vanished as though the Christian Rapture had occurred.

In the distance, leaves rustled while the moon hid behind clouds, further dimming the night's light. "Robert, is that you?" Her heart raced beneath her ribs. She had practiced Pilates for a reason. *Focus on the breath. Breathe in, breathe out.*

She obeyed, and scents of spruce bathed her lungs.

Daniela's snores quieted.

A black-headed grosbeak cooed, its spring carol carried on the mountain air's morning breath—or was it a warning for Emmaline to escape while she could? A wolf howled. Emmaline shivered, remembering the she-wolf near the lake. Daniela had saved the she-wolf's cub. Wolves never forget.

Daniela's breathing paused, and Emmaline watched.

"Is she dead?" A male voice startled Emmaline, and she about-faced. Her father's man stood at the tent door.

"Robert. You almost gave me a heart attack."

"Can't carry both of you out."

The pair watched as Daniela's face contorted with agony. Black and blue splotches darkened her face, then her neck, as they stared.

"What did you do to her?"

"Nothing!"

"What's happening?" Robert marched inside the tent.

"I don't know." Emmaline reached for her friend's arm. Her skin was cool to the touch. "Danny! Danny Rose—wake up, please."

"Don't wake her." Robert pushed Emmaline aside. "Crikey, Emma."

"Danny, breathe, so I know you're alive." Emmaline held her breath. "I won't lust for your oily boy ever again. Promise." Beads of sweat erupted on Daniela's face, and her eyes tracked back and forth under closed eyelids. "I shouldn't have confirmed that you're the Orphan Dreamer, Danny-girl." She knelt down and whispered into Daniela's ear. "They don't deserve you." Emmaline thought to shed a tear but chose not to.

"All is fair in love and war. Is that why you're betraying your friend?"

"It's complicated."

"Daddy issues?"

"Just do your job."

Small puffs of condensation lifted from her friend's nose and then dissipated. Emmaline sighed in relief. *She's alive!* Blood slithered from Daniela's right nostril, and Emmaline realized something must be dreadfully wrong.

Had the ghost of Lozen awakened? Was she determined to reclaim her vast lands? How would she fight a ghost?

Don't be stupid! Ghosts aren't. Neither are aliens.

"Whatever you're going to do, do it quickly." Emmaline stumbled out into the night air.

"Someone else said that before a betrayal occurred," Robert stated flatly.

"Who?"

"Jesus, before Judas betrayed Him to the religious leadership."

"Thanks for the Bible lesson." Looking up, Emmaline—Daniela's Anne with an *e*—pulled a blanket around her shoulders and stared into the star-filled sky. "Did you recognize us in the bar?"

"How could I forget my boss's cute redhead kid?" Robert—an Orphan member—packed Daniela's things. The Orphans were trained warriors and assassins who vowed to protect the Sons of Venus, a clandestine secret society that manipulated politics, world economics, and even the weather. "Where's the statue?"

"At the loft in Los Alamos."

"You said that you'd make sure she brought the relic."

"I changed my mind."

"Just like you changed your mind about us?"

"That was a mistake. Do your job. Collect another asset—my friend—for the Sons of Venus."

Emmaline should know. Her dad had presided over the society last year.

Mr. Darbyshire had ordered Robert to find the girls' campsite. As usual, Robert had obeyed.

Emmaline had obeyed her father as well.

No one dared to disobey him.

The plan was simple: kidnap Daniela, torture her, discover what she knew, and then kill the Orphan Dreamer.

Daniela was a wild card, motivated by morality. The Sons of Venus couldn't tolerate that fact. Tonight, Emmaline's friend had travelled to a faraway place, separating the girl from her body, and that fact alone might save her life. Maybe her Legna would come back with her and kick butt?

Emmaline paced the ground beyond their tent.

If she thwarted her father's plans, would he be mad?

Angry enough to beat her again? Their relationship had been strained tighter than a zipline since his favorite child—William—had been diagnosed with cancer. *I'll divorce your mother if my son dies. She killed your twin brothers.*

Emmaline's mother? A baby killer? Never in a million years. The Duchess of the Isles of Caithness, Charlotte Cairstine McDonald Darbyshire—Emmaline's mother—couldn't even tell a little peach lie.

"God . . . are you out there?" she whispered. The crunch of a tree branch answered and shifted her gaze. She refused to breathe. "Robert."

A large shadow moved at the forest's edge. "Is that you, God? Why are you scaring me?" Two red dots appeared and disappeared at the top of the shadow, then four yellow dots appeared at the bottom. "Blinking eyes?"

A wolf howled, and an eerie green mist floated above the shadow as it moved closer . . . and closer . . . and closer.

The mist stopped one hundred feet beyond the light of the almost dead fire.

"No need for special effects, God. I believe You exist. It's just that I don't need another father in my life who behaves like my dad. That's all."

A chilly gust snuffed out the remaining glow from the firepit's stubborn coals.

Darkness clung to her skin, and she hugged herself. Glancing back at the tent, she willed her friend to awaken and explain whatever alien phenomenon was going on.

Robert stepped out from the tent, cradling the sleeping Daniela in his arms. "What's out there?"

The shadow moved closer.

Noise like a fire engine or a freight train careening around its tracks completely out of control followed Robert's words, then intensified. There were no tracks in these parts, but metal wheels seemed to screech and howl through the night.

The shadowy mist stopped.

Suddenly the yellow dots charged toward the pair—Judas and her accomplice. Yellow dots anchored themselves into a hairy wolf face marked with a white stripe punctuated with a black circle that ran down the middle of its black head, between the eyes, and to the flared nostrils.

A second set of yellow eyes followed, materializing into another wolf face. Bigger. Stronger. Its teeth bared. Then another, a smaller wolf, came into focus.

"We're surrounded by wolves. Where's your gun?" Robert fumbled, dropping Daniela.

"Inside my sleeping bag." Emmaline caught Daniela before she hit the ground, but not before a sickening pop. Daniela's right pinky jutted out at an odd angle. "You broke her finger!"

"Focus on what's important, like why do you think your daddy gave you a gun? To leave it lying about? For show and tell? You're as stupid as your daddy says you are."

"Stop calling me stupid!" The truth dawned on Emmaline. The distinct facial markings. The charging animal was the she-wolf of the cub that Daniela had rescued from drowning. "They're coming to protect Daniela."

"What?"

"The wolves. They're coming to protect Daniela."

"She some kind of Indian?" He sneered at her. "You're some kind of stupid."

"No—you're the stupid one. They're called Native Americans." Dragging her slumbering friend, Emmaline backtracked toward the tent, but her feet got entangled in loose rocks, and she landed on her butt. Daniela collapsed on top of her.

"Serves you right for backtalking me." Robert brandished his gun and fired off two rounds.

The wolves scattered.

Above, a falling star disappeared into the forest's edge. The world seemed to move in slow motion.

Panting, Emmaline rolled Daniela off of her, then dragged the slumbering Orphan Dreamer into the tent.

The wolves would be back, hungry for blood. Would they ambush the trio from the rear?

Emmaline tried to zip the door, but the grip tab stuck. Finally the zipper caught, and she tugged it until it stopped. "At last. Closed." She pressed her hand to her pounding chest. "But it's only nylon. It won't protect us."

Ashamed of her betrayal, she slinked down and lay against Daniela's sleeping back. Embracing her only real friend, she protected the vulnerable Orphan Dreamer and her destiny.

Outside, Robert's screams played a haunting melody to beats of gun fire. Canine whines mixed with vicious growls and bones breaking between powerful jaws. The wolves had indeed regrouped and seemed to be attacking from the rear.

Emmaline stared at her friend, paralyzed by fear. "What's wrong with you? Wake up. Help me save you. If you die, we all die. Help me save the world, Lozen."

Be calm.

Lozen was.

★ ★ ★

IMMORTALS—TIME WITHOUT END

Robert—a Nephilim—had failed.

Cloaked in black shadows, Nomed peers across Lake

Fenton and spews a rotating column of hot winds toward the lone-occupied campsite. The tornado grows as it barrels closer and closer to the girls' tent. The winds pick up Robert's mangled body and toss it into the forest. Two wolves escape, seconds ahead of Nomed's rotating column of rain, hail, and wind.

Legna, Yahweh's warrior, fills his lungs and then encircles the campsite with a protective layer of cold air, forming a wall of ice to block the tornado.

Nomed inhales, then blows again and again. Seconds turn to minutes; Nomed fatigues. He clutches his charred side—a gift from his master, Lucifer—and inhales, sucking in icy air. The fierce rotating winds from his mouth cease. Nomed closes his eyelids, hiding his red irises, and runs back up the mountain ridge.

Tonight, the tornado won't kill the sleeping dreamer or her helpless friend.

Nomed's plan B: Kill her reason for praying—the orphan. Legna won't protect his competition with such ferocity.

THE CRUCIBLE

He sent a man before them, even Joseph, who was sold for a servant: Whose feet they hurt with fetters: he was laid in iron: Until the time that his word came: the word of the Lord tried him. The king sent and loosed him; even the ruler of the people, and let him go free. He made him lord of his house, and ruler of all his substance.

—Psalms 105:17-21

20—The Orphan (PG-13)

IN LIFE, SOME PEOPLE FEEL the rain; others get wet. The Creator had designed Cillian to feel everything and to survive a soaking.

Escape was Cillian's only alternative to suicide.

Yet, no matter how much the mental anguish tormented his soul, the instinct to survive won out. He crawled on his hands and knees through the spring rain shower, stopped and lapped up water from a rain puddle formed inside his secret garden, his hiding place.

Thankful to be free of his personal hell—a lonely, concrete cell—he splashed rainwater onto his face. Satisfied, he sat against a tree and savored his surroundings, inhaling the organic and earthy scents of soft black soil overlain with scents of jasmine and rain.

The drizzle had cleaned his hair and skin, and he felt

like he had after Grandma Barry let him bathe inside her clawfoot tub. He buried his hand deep inside his pocket and massaged the rounded edges of his American silver dollar—a gift from the Barrys.

His body begged for sleep, but at least he was safe.

Cillian buried his bruised body deep beneath a bed of sopping wet leaves. The orphan boy would dream of a better future that included a belly full of food, freedom, and unlimited possibilities for Paul.

His eyelids drooped heavily as sleep lured the orphan into its embrace.

Time elapsed.

Whispers of crushed leaves awakened him.

Lying deathly still, he inhaled. *Dogs' breath!* His heart set into a full gallop. *Bushcroft's bloodhounds! It'll be worse for me now.*

No time to run.

Lie still.

Friend or foe, a dog's nose rarely missed the scent its nose was trained to discover. Wet noses sniffed his face, then howls pierced the night air.

He struggled to his feet, ready to run.

"Not so fast, my boy." Fire ignited at the back of his neck as someone seized a tuft of his hair. The voice chilled him to the bone.

On his knees, Cillian blinked rapidly until Bushcroft and Scarface came into focus—his slaver and his tormentor's sidekick.

"You're an ungrateful whelp," Bushcroft blathered under his breath.

"No, sir." Cillian stood up. "I-I-I've been servicing yer customers for years. I've earned my freedom."

Scarface slapped the orphan boy's face, because

Bushcroft was too short to reach it. Bushcroft removed his suit jacket and vest, then rolled up his dress-shirt sleeves. "String him up."

Scarface yanked Cillian around, then threw him against a towering tree. Rusted manacles had been driven into the tree's bark. Thinking that he'd secured his freedom, had Cillian walked into a trap?

Why hadn't he noticed the manacles?

"I took you in. I fed you. I sheltered and educated you when you couldn't do any of these things for yourself, and how do you repay me? With obedience, with gratefulness? No. You abandoned me and tired out my dogs and Dumbo over there by forcing us to come looking for you."

"I've earned my freedom." Cillian fought for every ounce of bravery he could muster, but Scarface still wrapped ropes around his wrists and looped the ropes into the rusted manacles before tying them. Was Cillian the criminal? "Ye canna deny me what I've earned."

"I can . . . and I will."

"I-I-I demand my freedom."

"Demand?" The question hung in the air. "Trust me, son. I'm going to give you more than freedom. I'm going to give you something to remember me by."

"Dead or alive, I-I-I willna be goin' back to the brothel." Cillian strained against the ropes eating into his wrists.

"Yes. You. Will. Because in life, we all have to do things we'd rather not do. My brothel is your home. Your place. Your destiny." A *swoosh* cut the air. Cillian's heart quickened, and he jerked his head to the right.

"Are ye going to be thrashin' me with that?" Cillian asked.

"You are an inquisitive, careful child who pays attention to detail, and that's why my customers adore you."

"Ye'll ha' to kill me, then. I'll not go back alive."

"Murder? No. Never." Bushcroft strolled to Cillian's side. Gazing up at the orphan's nipples, the master taunted him. "I'm going to mark you—forever."

"When I'm laid to rest in my grave, there'll be no flesh on my back," Cillian concluded.

"The devil himself intends it so, but don't worry, child. I've been known to show a bit of mercy. You won't die, but you'll wish that you had."

Scarface scoffed. "Don't give the lad false hope, boss."

"His hope's frail, but not dead," Bushcroft chided Scarface and taunted his slave. "Need to leave enough skin in case there's a next time."

Scarface rubbed his hands together. "If he runs again, boss, can I have a turn? I've been practicing." Cillian's blood froze. He braced himself against a stabbing headache.

"He won't run again. This one's real smart. After I'm done with him, put him on suicide watch. You'll watch him."

"Even when he's working?"

"Especially when he's working."

Scarface licked his lips. "The pleasure's all mine, boss." He yanked the ropes tighter around Cillian's wrists. "We're gonna become best friends," he said, then faced his boss. "Are you a religious man, boss?" Scarface hocked up a wad of saliva and spit before continuing to taunt Cillian. "I mean, the great book does say that God is the friend of orphans."

"The man in the clouds and I have an arrangement." Bushcroft spit on the ground. "He stays on His side, and I stay on mine. I've done life my way, and it works for me."

For you.

Scarface whispered to the orphan boy, "How many

helpless souls have begged for the big man upstairs to intervene in Bushcroft's ways?"

Cillian grimaced and bit his lower lip to keep his sobs hidden behind his parched lips.

"You're not crying?" Bushcroft said. The orphan shook his head. "Good god, child! For your sake, don't whimper. Your cries will resurrect something inside of me, and I'll enjoy this ritual even more." Bushcroft cut the air again with his whip. "Did your pappy ever teach you any lessons?"

Cillian stayed silent, bracing for the first blow.

His mother's boyfriend had taken a board, a willow switch, and a belt to him, but never a horse whip.

"The youth of today—so undisciplined and unthankful. Daddy didn't want to be bothered with you, then? That's fine." He paused. "Every boy needs an . . . attentive father. We must all do our part to raise this fatherless generation, and I'll fill that role tonight." The slaver dug the wooden handle of the whip into Cillian's back. "Hold real still. It hurts less. Understood?"

Cillian's head swam and sweat beaded up on his forehead. He'd hated anticipating Joe Sanders' or Miss Grey's first blow. Bushcroft's prelude frayed his nerves even worse. He slumped, his eyes rolling back into his head.

"Stand up!"

The volume of the slaver's voice shocked the boy from his stupor. Cillian squeezed his eyes shut and dug his fingers into the gnarly tree. How many boys had this twisted man tortured? It didn't matter. It would be Cillian's back flayed open once more. Wide awake, he counted the crags in the old tree and waited. His wrists screamed in pain, and his fingers numbed.

"I believe in biblical flogging. Forty minus one was the

old Hebrew custom—one short of the gentile's whipping. You can count, can't you, boy?"

He clamped his eyelids tighter, and now a warm trail of liquid wetted his face and the side of his leg.

"We'll add the one back in, shall we? I asked you a question."

"Sir?"

"In your own little world, are you?"

"No, sir."

"Good. I said, you can count, can't you?"

Cillian's jaw clenched as he steadied his body for what was to come, then nodded.

"Count it out," Bushcroft said. "Start with thirty-nine. That's called mercy—not giving you all that you deserve."

Whoosh!

The whip sliced Cillian's bare back. Cillian squeezed his eyelids shut. "Thirty-nine." Stars speckled his vision, and a deep blackness sucked his soul further into a pit of despair, but he steadied his shaking frame.

He counted down, whispering. "Twenty." It wasn't true—holding still hadn't lessened the pain.

His body flinched to the right and then the left, back and forth, until he finally said, "One." Salty, thick blood seeped into his mouth as he groaned. The victory belonged to him. He hadn't given the short man the thrill of hearing him cry.

"Cut him loose."

Pain knifed through Cillian's raw back. After they cut the ropes, he fell backward, crushing the pile of dead leaves he'd hidden beneath earlier.

"Pleasant exercise." Bushcroft rolled his shoulders. "Get up. He's not to be carried. Make him walk." Body trembling and blood soaking his trousers, Cillian pushed himself to his feet.

"I've a brothel full of customers waiting for you. Shower, serve them, and then we'll finish our gift exchange tonight." Even though Bushcroft was a foot shorter than Cillian, his putrid breath of cigars and alcohol assaulted Cillian's nose. The foul odor permeated the air all around the bleeding orphan.

"Aye, sir."

Five hours later, an old man lumbered from Cillian's prison, his flesh sagging.

Grandfathers should be at home telling their grandchildren stories, not giving an orphan boy nightmares. The gray-haired man hadn't even asked why Cillian's back was caked in blood. Not every grandpa was like Grandpa Barry.

Paul would be a kind and gentle grandpa.

Cillian smiled, relishing the thought of his brother growing up and finding familial happiness.

He had finished his duties for the night, so Cillian struck a match and lit a candle. No need to illuminate the room while he was in the act of his carnal duties. Trembling, he wrapped a soiled sheet around his naked and pain-wracked body.

Alone at last, there was no need to continue the brave act. So he buried his face into his palms and cried like the sixteen-year-old child that he was.

Another few minutes passed, and he finished his outward manifestation of grief, but it would take an eternity to heal the millions of stab wounds that had pierced his heart and soul. "My prayer," he whispered, "my only prayer is dinna let me wake."

Shoes scraped concrete.

Polished leather shoes.

Bushcroft entered Cillian's cell. "Nonsense. Cancel that request. My heart would shatter into millions of pieces if you abandoned me forever." In the candle's butterscotch glow, Bushcroft's steel-gray eyes peeled away any remaining dignity from the child slave. "If you please, we'll finish what we started. Follow me."

Cillian dressed under the eyes of his master. Hunched over—he had grown too tall for the dank cell—he buttoned up his starched dress shirt and stumbled behind his owner. Scarface met them outside and wrapped nylon ropes around Cillian's wrists.

"Come on. Don't dawdle." Bushcroft pulled the rope while Cillian trudged behind.

"I'm not an animal."

Bushcroft stopped, turned, and buried his fist into Cillian's lower abdomen. The child slave fell to his knees. Where had the sudden boldness come from?

"What did you say?" The slave driver glared at his charge. "What did you say?"

Cillian diverted his eyes. "Nothing."

"I love animals." Bushcroft stood taller. "I donate a million dollars each year to PETA." Bushcroft yanked the cord so hard that he almost toppled Cillian onto his face. "Stand up!"

Cillian stood.

Into the night, they took a path fraught with boulders, rocky terrain, and prickly shrubs—his Via Dolorosa, the sorrowful path.

Finally, they stopped.

Cillian scanned the area. It was familiar; it was his hideout, the same one from earlier. He clenched his jaw and fought for any last shreds of strength. He wouldn't survive another flogging.

"You like this place, don't you?" Bushcroft said through a sneer.

"No, sir."

"Too bad, because I love this grove—an oasis among filth and poverty, a lush green garden in an otherwise desolate land. A Garden of Eden." He untied Cillian's hands, only to secure him around the same tree again. Scarface sat on a stump, slugging back beer.

Cillian pressed his cheek to the tree's splintered bark. His hands burned as Bushcroft pulled the ropes tighter.

Moments later, the whip sliced through the air, slapping Cillian's back. He bit through his tender lower lip. Blood gushed, and he muffled his screams.

"He's a boring one to flog. Doesn't scream like the others. I have an idea. Untie him and bring him to the stump."

Scarface tossed a beer can beside Cillian's feet.

"Drinking's bad for you. Littering's bad for us." Bushcroft pointed at the man's empty can.

"I bet he'd die for a sip right now." Scarface's speech slurred. He meandered to Cillian's tree, then tore at the ropes. The orphan stumbled backward, this time catching himself before falling.

"Hope you're not tired yet. I'm beginning to have a little fun." Bushcroft chewed on an oversized cigar. "These aren't Cubans. Where are the Cubans?" Evil flashed in his eyes.

"They are Cubans. Saw to it myself."

"You'd better not be lying."

"Promise, boss." For the first time since Cillian's captivity, he heard fear in the man's voice. How had he acquired the jagged pink scar on his cheek, anyway?

Scarface grabbed the lad's shoulders and prodded him toward a two-foot-tall tree stump. In the middle of the stump, a rust-colored substance encircled a hole.

"Put your hand on the stump and then hold real still," Bushcroft said.

Cillian obeyed.

Ever since he could crawl, he had learned about cruelty at the hands of his mother and Joe, but even Cillian couldn't have imagined what would happen next. Notes from Paul de Senneville's "Mariage d'Amour" played in his head, and he imagined his fingers gliding across Grandma Barry's piano.

The visualization barely calmed him, and his waiflike frame shook uncontrollably. Pain invaded every inch of his body as shock set in and his vision blurred. He had been asking for an appointment with death, and the grim reaper had finally cleared his schedule for a fatal visit.

Bushcroft's knuckles whitened over the shaft of a hammer as he drove a titanium stake through Cillian's left hand. *Clank, clank, clank!* The wooden tree stump splintered with the intrusion of the stake.

The slaver spoke in a controlled and quiet tone. "No one wanted you. I took you in."

Cillian screamed.

"Ungrateful and vile, you'll be marked for life." He grabbed Cillian's hair and yanked his head back. "If you survive this night, know this . . . when you're all grown up and go lusting after some young lady, if she's a respectable woman, she will never tolerate a man with a limp and mangled hand stroking her in the night. No matter how innocent, a woman wants to be taken. It takes strong hands to do so."

The physical pain had almost broken the boy, but the psychological pain was kicking him over the edge.

Cillian's screams disintegrated into wails. He was no longer willing to play strong when he wasn't. He had acted like a man since he could remember, but in reality, he was only a sixteen-year-old boy.

"I have toyed with the idea of extra duties or death." Bushcroft interjected the hammering with verbal torment. "I have decided on the latter. You have pushed me to the limit. You did this!" Spit landed on Cillian's nose.

When the head of the spike was one inch from the back of Cillian's hand, the hammering finally stopped. "Give me a hug," Bushcroft said and leaned in to hug the boy.

Cillian jerked backward, his eyes at half-mast and the sadistic smile of the pervert etched into his brain.

Bushcroft slapped the boy. His head jerked to the right, and blood-tinged spit dripped from his cut lips. "Potential without discipline equals havoc. You've lost your vision. Your place. You could have worked faithfully for me, and when you became too old for the job, I would have taught you the business. You could have owned a business like mine."

"I want to die," the orphan muttered.

"Nonsense. No one *wants* death."

"I am no one."

"I gave you everything to make you someone." Bushcroft raised his fist.

A wave of hot air encircled Cillian, and acid flamed in his throat. He swallowed the putrid fluid, but the pain refused to abate. Bile spewed into Bushcroft's face. If he had possessed the strength, Cillian would have laughed.

Bushcroft wiped his face with a starch handkerchief. "I changed my mind."

"Aye, then?"

"You will not die—no, you will live and wish that death had granted mercy to you." He skated his thumb across Cillian's lips, opening the wound there further. He lifted his thumb to his mouth and tasted the boy's blood.

A vampire, living on the life of others. If I live, you will die. My blood is poisoned. Even the care-home's matron had called him Leviathan, Job's sea monster. Kid monsters rarely grow up into adult angels. Cillian masked a snarl, contorting his face to appear like a victim.

"A helpful hint for times like this." Bushcroft licked his lips.

Cillian dared a defiant response. "I could take notes, if I possessed the use of my hand."

"Comical. When I am confused, I like to spend some time alone and reflect. Why don't you spend the night here, maybe a few nights, alone?" Bushcroft whistled a peppy tune as he and the drunken Scarface swaggered down the path toward the brothel.

"You promised me you'd let me have a go at him," Scarface slurred.

"Focus on keeping upright. Fall, and I will murder you in cold blood," the slaver spat. Their conversation faded into the night, and blackness as thick as ink dripped around Cillian.

The silence was broken with the chattering and clucks of crickets, the moans of frogs, and the scratching of some creature.

Cillian started at a strange sensation. It felt like a pinprick at first, then pain dug into his right heel.

Teeth?

Claws?

Nailed to his orphan tree—a place of shame and torture, the orphan was blinded by the darkness, so he contorted his body, positioning himself higher atop the stump. Each movement tore at the flesh, tendon, and bone in his left hand.

One question tormented him: Would he be able to play

the piano again? If he could, miracles were possible, and hope might survive.

A scant jury of yellow-eyed owls weighed in with their opinions. *Hoo-hoo.*

Cillian rubbed his concave abdomen with his right hand. His stomach contracted, and green vomit dangled from his mouth. The acid burned his open lip. Unable to see in the night, he looked toward the pain pulsing in his mangled hand.

No respectable woman would ever want a limp and mangled hand stroking her in the night.

"Okay," he whispered.

21—Orphan Dreamer

Sunday, March 22, 1998
Jemez Mountains, New Mexico

MOONLIGHT CUT THROUGH THEIR TENT, casting a lifeless and cyanotic-tinted light through the blue nylon and washing the Orphan Dreamer's skin with a deathly glow. Pain wracked Daniela's lithe body—from her left pinky finger up to her shoulder.

She wiped her nose with the back of her arm, staining her favorite pajamas with blood. Her mouth dried, she glanced at Emmaline, hoping her friend was still asleep.

Beneath the warm glow of a lantern, Emmaline stared back. "You okay?"

"I am. Dry, cold air . . . rips my nose apart every time." Daniela chuckled.

"You were restless last night." Emmaline gave Daniela a tissue. "Did you dream?"

"I did. Did I wake you?"

"Sort of."

"Sorry." Daniela blushed.

"It's okay. What did you dream about?"

Dodge the question, but don't lie. She didn't want to think about her terrifying nightmare of floggings, torture, and a helpless boy, much less speak of the horrors. Why depress Emmaline? "Why didn't you wake me?"

"I tried, but you wouldn't wake. You even stopped breathing for a while."

"Sorry."

"Noted. To make it worse, I had a dream about were-wolves and vampires, and I heard weird noises all night," Emmaline said, prodding Daniela to tell all. "Did you solve the mystery of the Skeleton Key during your dream?"

"No, I didn't." Daniela pulled her blanket to her neck, blocking out the chill. "And I didn't mean to put you in harm's way—really I didn't." Warmth flooded Daniela's cheeks, and Emmaline's expression registered confusion, or maybe it was the look of guilt.

But about what?

If Daniela interrogated Emmaline, would she abandon her?

Daniela gasped for air, afraid of Limy's answer as they climbed out of their tent. "It's so dark that even the roosters haven't awakened." The Orphan Dreamer clicked on a flashlight and rearranged their sticks inside their firepit while Emmaline added more tinder. "My left finger's killing me." Daniela massaged her forearm, hoping to ease the ache. "I wasn't wearing a popsicle splint when I went to bed last night. Who splinted my finger?"

"While you're asking a million questions, explain the black, purple, and blue splotches splattered around your neck." Emmaline touched the Orphan Dreamer's skin at the base of her neck.

"Ouch!" Daniela stepped away from her best friend. She pulled up her shirt, and Emmaline turned the flashlight's beam toward her friend.

"Goodness, Daniela! What happened to you?"

"I didn't want to complain, but I hurt all over. It feels like someone dropped me off a cliff last night."

Emmaline remained quiet, losing eye contact with Daniela.

Towering evergreens sprawled on either side, casting shadows toward the lake, and tumbleweeds dotted the forest floor. Daniela surveyed the campsite, fanning her flashlight's beam north, south, east, and west. "Looks as though a tornado barreled through camp. And that looks like blood."

"I told you. I heard weird noises—like a freight train, wheels screeching and everything."

"Strange, isn't it?"

"What do you mean?"

"The forest edge is decimated, yet our camp is undisturbed. Something doesn't feel right here. We should leave and go home."

"Not on your life, Danny Rose! Not until we hike down to the caves. You promised me."

"Why do you care about the caves so much?"

"I just do."

"Then we should eat an early breakfast, and at first light, head to the caves while daylight is still ahead of us."

"Agreed, but not before a swim in Lake Fenton. I need to wash this nightmare right out of my hair."

"Tomorrow—first thing in the morning, I promise."

"Fine. The stink will keep the wild animals at bay."

Emmaline tossed sap-filled branches on top of cold ashes while Daniela tucked dry sticks and newspaper under the branches and struck the lighter.

Pops and crackles disrupted the quiet mountain air. Daniela swallowed an ibuprofen, then continued to massage her hand. "Did I break my finger while I was sleeping?"

"You did." Emmaline shrugged while looking down and away, then busied herself with making coffee. "After I noticed the break, I applied the splint."

"Florence Nightingale to the rescue. Thanks, Limy." Daniela donned her headlamp and then slid her foot across a bed of snow outside their tent. "Someone churned up this snow last night." She kneeled, then sifted powdery snow through her gloved fingers. "Look!"

"What is it?"

"A bullet casing."

"Could've been here already. Or maybe a hunter shot a deer last night?" Emmaline poured a cup of piping hot coffee into her tin mug. "You spotted a blood trail."

"Right in front of our campsite?"

"I agree—the prospect defines scary." Emmaline hugged herself. "I was thinking last night while you were *away* and I was all alone that maybe I could help you and the professor secure funding for another archeological dig in order to find Ezekiel's blueprint for the last temple."

"How?" Daniela asked. But she was thinking, *why is Limy changing the subject from a spent bullet to fundraising and archeology?*

"Simple. I'll ask my dad. His company—or even his business associates—might chip in a million bucks." Emmaline gulped down her coffee.

"I'll ask the professor. You mentioned a group called the Sons of Venus. Is that the name of your dad's company?"

"No!" Emmaline near shouted. "Sorry. I didn't mean to yell. My head is pounding."

"Ibuprofen?"

"I'll survive."

"Who are the Sons of Venus? And please tell me the truth, Limy."

"I can't." Emmaline aimlessly poked the logs in the fire. "What I can tell you is that whatever—"

"Or whoever," Daniela interjected.

"Okay. Whoever was stalking us last night, it was something odd."

"Something supernatural or extraterrestrial?"

"Yes, like the ghost of Lozen and her Apaches. And if my hunch proves true, that thing may come back tonight after we hike to the caves."

"What's your hypothesis? Did a supernatural being visit the camp last night?"

"I don't know," Emmaline said.

"I was sleeping. What did you see, Limy?"

"Two red eyes floated above a black shadow that was emitting a green mist, then four yellow dots came charging from the shadow."

"Two red dots. A shadow. A green mist. And four yellow dots. Anything else?"

"A falling star." A smile spread across Emmaline's tired face. "A star fell from heaven and seemed to collide with earth, just beyond the forest. Then the four yellow dots charged me and Rob—"

"And who?" Daniela paused in the middle of brushing her teeth.

"Nothing. I wonder if the falling star was an angel like Legna, the hot angel you hang out with in your dreams."

"But you said 'Rob.' "

"I'm tired and confused. Was the falling star Legna, Danny-girl?"

"Could have been. But if he came to our campsite last night, he was protecting me—I mean, us—from something or someone. Maybe your Rob."

"Does he always tell you everything?" Refusing to defend herself against Daniela's accusation, Emmaline wiped her face with a wet rag.

"Not everything. Because after I travel, we don't have much time. Besides, I wasn't with him last night."

"Then who did you see last night?"

"Oily boy's tormentor." A tear slipped down Daniela's cheek. "And what I saw was horrible." She broke down and cried, softly weeping for an orphan boy whose life equaled nothing more than hell on earth. "No more excuses. I have to find him, Limy."

"Okay. I'll help." Emmaline sat down beside her friend.

"I won't take you with me like I took Ethan. The trip killed him, Limy."

"You're special, not a murderer, Danny Rose—more special than I will ever be. How does that feel?"

"If it's true? Scary."

"We're both scared, and whatever happened last night convinces me that your Nomed will need human agents to help him accomplish his mission on Earth . . . which may be to murder you, the Orphan Dreamer, before you can rescue your orphan boy or stop the *bad* pandemic."

"Little green men prodding humans to do their murderous bidding." Daniela belly-laughed, grabbing her ribs from a sharp pain. "I always thought Claire and Harry—my childhood nemeses—were the devil's henchmen."

"They probably were." Emmaline laughed as well. "I was rich, so no one at school picked on me to my face.

They stabbed me in the back after they siphoned off movie money."

"Betrayal still sucks," Daniela said.

"I got even."

"Maybe I will too." During breakfast, Daniela treated Emmaline to hot oatmeal with cranberries.

Unusual for her personality, Emmaline treated Daniela to dead silence.

After breakfast, Daniela scraped the oatmeal from the bottom of their tin plates before washing and sterilizing them over the fire. She reentered the tent and began packing for their day hike. Emmaline followed.

"Are you mad at me, Limy?"

"Don't know." Emmaline shrugged.

"I didn't mean to abandon you. I admit, the Glass Tattoo complicates our friendship, and that reality isn't your fault. It's mine."

"I'm not mad, Daniela Rose." Emmaline rarely called Daniela by her given name. "I'm scared."

"I am too." The Orphan Dreamer packed the tinware inside a burlap bag as Emmaline fiddled with the zipper of her jacket. "Limy, I wear a brave mask each day, but it's just that—a mask. Most days, I'm scared senseless."

"Daniela . . ." Emmaline paused, and Daniela held her breath. "You're the monster scaring me."

"What?" Daniel couldn't believe her ears. *Am I a monster? Am I the antichrist? No, I can't be. I'm a follower of Yeshua—the Christ.* Her dad's words replayed in her head: *Don't be so eager to meet someone new that you lose yourself.*

Be yourself.

In that moment, Daniela considered betraying her identity and possibly her destiny to please a new friend . . . but she had to—right? What teenage girl dreamed of walking life's journey alone? And girls desperate for friends couldn't demand perfection from anyone.

Still, the Orphan Dreamer must defend her character. "I'm not a monster, Limy! Weird. Boring. Odd. Label me any of those, but I'm no monster. So tell me, why are you calling me that?"

"Monsters scare people—right?"

"Correct."

"Well, when you slip into a catatonic state in random places, you scare me. What happens if you pull a stunt like that in front of a guy that I like?"

"He may project my weirdness on you." Daniela hung her head.

"We're only sixteen, and we've barely lived. Doesn't this whole apocalyptic thing bother you? Isn't it unfair? We're forced to make decisions that we don't want to make in order to please people we don't want to please—your enemies and my enemies. Then our enemies deceive us, and we betray our friends in order to pacify our enemies. It's *The Usual Suspects* all over again—the villain was in plain view the whole time, orchestrating the whole sordid story line."

"What are you *really* saying?"

"I don't know anymore." Emmaline fidgeted with the edge of her sleeping bag. "I just don't know." She ran out of the tent, kicked a tent stake, and the nylon home collapsed on top of Daniela Rose.

"Smart move, Limy." Daniela fought to escape the nylon tomb. She crawled from the collapsed tent, only to find her best friend pouting with her arms crossed. "Don't talk in riddles, Limy."

"Why? You can't solve them."

"Don't be rude."

"You're not my parent, Daniela Rose."

"Maybe I'm not, but I'm a person, so chew on this, genius. I. Am. Not. The antichrist. I am trying to stop him from tearing up our home, Earth. And of course the idea of staring Armageddon in the face at the age of sweet sixteen sticks in my craw."

"Who said the antichrist is a he?" Emmaline cast a judgmental stare in Daniela's direction.

"It's not me, Emmaline Georgiana. You can't conspiracy theorist your way out of whatever you did wrong last night."

"Who said that I did something wrong?"

"Your face."

"Okay. Maybe the monster is me. Maybe I'm the antichrist." Emmaline grinned—lopsided, eerie, and mysterious. "No matter the gender, Daniela, some sinister, mysterious creep branded with six-six-six plans to start picking us off like a bunch of bimbos running upstairs in a B-rated horror movie." Emmaline's voice registered falsetto C sharp.

Make her laugh.

Disarm the nuclear bomb before it blows.

"Why do the bimbos always run past the front door and every open downstairs window, only to charge upstairs to a windowless loft while a knife-wielding slasher chases behind about ten feet?" Daniela joked.

"To stretch the stupid movie past ten minutes." A flat smile softened Emmaline's angry face, and she blew a forceful breath from her nose. "Okay, so the antichrist isn't either of us."

"That should've been obvious. We're on the same team—right?"

"How much time's left before this crazed person arrives

and starts this earth-shattering pandemic?" Emmaline dodged Daniela's question.

"Twenty to forty years—I think." Daniela shrugged. "After the blood moons of 2014–2015."

"In twenty to forty years, we'll likely be married, and our kids will be adolescents. So when the world falls completely apart, we'll be around forty years old."

"My mother conceived me when she was forty."

"Ancient ovaries entombed in cobwebs. You're not going to wait that long—I hope. We'll be navigating the apocalypse by then." Both girls laughed.

But deep down inside, Daniela restrained herself from slapping Emmaline across the face for laughing at her mother. "I don't know how the whole story will end. The only clue I've solved so far is *when*. After the blood moons of 2014–2015—the Jewish calendar year of 5775."

"What happens after 2014–2015?"

"The antichrist—six-six-six—will unleash his trial run of a pandemic."

"Trial run? Pandemics, by definition, are all or nothing."

"Not until the causative agent has been perfected—and not until the genomic code of the causative agent functions in such a way that it will devastate the human body's immune system and/or cause the immune system to turn on its host."

"A virus that behaves like a Trojan horse while invading the human body?"

"The analogy works somewhat. I've been studying the pathophysiology of Dengue virus. It works via two scary mechanisms, cytokine storm and antibody-mediated enhancement."

"I've read about antibody-mediated enhancement, when the body's immunoglobins, instead of protecting the body from an assassin virus, joins forces with the intruding virus and opens the door of the cell, then helps the virus replicate inside the cell."

"You don't need me. You already understand."

"Just the science. My dad's brother died of Dengue fever. He lived as a missionary in Brazil. I need you because I don't understand the religious stuff."

"Who does?" Daniela chuckled.

"And like . . . what's the purpose of the pandemic? In other words, what motivates a human being to unleash a plague on other humans?"

"History answers your question, Limy."

"Okay. Explain."

"In this very place, one culture purposefully infected another culture with smallpox and measles by giving them blankets laden with the virus. Why? For a land grab? Look around us. The mountain range and the plains stretch millions of miles in each direction. There's so much land that we're camping in a vast wilderness by ourselves. So what motivated these disease spreaders?"

"Greed, jealousy, and revenge—the same for all us evil and selfish humans."

"Most likely, greed, jealousy, and revenge motivate our antichrist. He'll be a greedy and vengeful character. But for the record, I do know that the antichrist is not one of us."

"What do you mean?"

"In order to defeat six-six-six, I must fight alongside the King of Angel Armies—Yeshua—and his angelic warriors. Yeshua's kingdom isn't of this world. Why would I need an angelic army if the antichrist is fully human? He—or she—must somehow not be of this world."

"Jesus is an alien? You're kidding me! My Methodist pastor never taught us that detail."

"Alien? An extradimensional being? A celestial being? An extraterrestrial? Or none of the above? I don't pretend to understand every detail about Yeshua's physical traits, but I do know that he's not the anemic dude who needs a stat blood transfusion as most contemporary images suggest his likeness. Besides, who are we to try to define the King of all Kings from our simplistic human perspective? So don't know, don't care." Daniela drove the tent spike back into the permafrozen ground, resurrecting their nylon home. Then she poured a pot of heated water into a bucket half-filled with cold lake water for her bucket-bath inside the tent.

"If I'm mindlessly following around a little green man, I would care!"

"You know that I'm not following around a little green man, Limy! People will perceive Yeshua as they want to, but I don't pigeonhole His essence or what He is capable of. I do know that Yeshua once said, 'My Kingdom is not an earthly kingdom. If it were, my followers would fight to keep me from being handed over to the Jewish leaders. But my Kingdom is not of this world. (NLT)' He called himself the Light of the World, the Way, the Truth, and the Life. One of his apostles truthfully said that Yeshua is the Christ—the Son of the Living God."

"Okay. I'll buy it. He's a celestial being, and humans are just too stupid to fully understand the dimensional reality and essence of Jesus—the Mack daddy of all things supernatural."

"Spoken like a kindred spirit." Daniela smiled wide as she toweled dry. "My bottom line is when it comes to Yeshua . . . that's my King." She removed a compact disc, a plastic case tucked into her journal, inside her backpack. "My rafiki gave me this. When I'm depressed, I listen to it.

May I borrow your portable CD player? The battery's dead in mine."

"Of course." Emmaline gave Daniela her player.

The Orphan Dreamer loaded the shiny compact disc into the CD player and pressed play.

Without moving a muscle, the girls listened to an excerpt from S. M. Lockridge's famous sermon, "That's My King."

Emmaline sat on her sleeping bag and rested her chin on her knees, most likely contemplating the gravity of Reverend Lockridge's description of Jesus. "It's true, Danny-girl. Your Jesus . . . he's beautiful. Mesmerizing. Simply amazing. Makes me want follow Him."

"Go ahead. We'll be walking side by side."

"I'll think about it. As for your antichrist and his henchmen, nothing but a bunch of little green men invading earth. Talk about a neighborhood going to the dogs. So you're saying that Armageddon could really be an alien invasion?"

"I didn't say that at all. First, Armageddon is caused by an evil force, not Yeshua. Nor am I saying that all extradimensional beings or aliens are bad. Maybe humans and the motives that inspire our actions stink more. In the vastness of the universe, why should a human stand as the measurement of normal?"

"It's possible that from heaven's perspective, maybe extradimensional beings are the norm and we humans are a deviation from the norm," Emmaline said.

"Legna classifies as an extradimensional being. He's not bad."

"You would say that!" Emmaline twinkled with mischief. "But I so want to meet that hottie one day." She licked her lips.

"Didn't eat enough breakfast?" Daniela guffawed. Emmaline burst into a deep laugh.

Just before dawn bled the morning sky of darkness, a shooting star bolted across the sky. Maybe Legna was flying to another country to defend oily boy. Before she'd fallen asleep last night, she had prayed for him.

Daniela pointed toward the blackness speckled with billions of twinkling stars—angels waiting to do Yahweh's bidding. "It's an angel going to assist a child of Yahweh."

"The stars are aliens too." Emmaline washed her body with water from Daniela's bucket, and Daniela did the same, then brushed her hair into a bun. "I'll never look at the night sky the same way again. So many hot angels to date."

"Have it your way."

"I always do, and by the way, this pep talk of yours is officially ruining our camping trip." Emmaline winked at Daniela.

"You asked. I shared."

Emmaline toweled dry. "Danny-girl, how do I know if I can really trust you?"

"I've never lied to you. Kept a few secrets, but who doesn't?"

"You're right. You're not a liar, just trying to understand what makes someone a liar. Lying is not in your DNA but crazy is." She paused. "At least it is, according to your doctor who didn't believe you possessed a firm grip on reality. He diagnosed you as a schizophrenic with childhood-onset depression—right?"

"That's a low blow, Limy. I'm different—but not crazy or a schizophrenic."

"That's what they all say."

"I'm not *they*. I'm Daniela Rose Cavanaugh, the Orphan

Dreamer, and empathy drives me to experience and feel the pain of others, physically and emotionally. The doctor was wrong about me—I'm not crazy. I simply hear Yahweh's voice unfiltered, that's all."

"God—the being who you say created all the badass stars—a.k.a. angels—chitchats with you, and you talk to Him as though He's standing right in front of you?" Emmaline wagged her head.

"Yes. It's true."

"It's a crazy proposition, Daniela."

"For a girl cursed with absolutely no imagination . . ." Daniela could throw judgmental darts as well. "And who salivates over anything that moves and possesses a testicle . . . to her, yes, maybe my reality looks crazy!"

"You've inhaled the air of propaganda. That's all."

"If Yahweh isn't real, Limy, real isn't! And for the record, through my dreams and through my visions—dreams that I experience when I'm awake—I hear Him."

"You and your imagination."

"Sometimes His voice comes as an assurance—a knowing. I've told you this before, Limy. I'm weird to most people, so what? Nothing new there. But you're supposed to be my friend. Friends should at least try to understand their friends."

A full minute of silence hung between them before Emmaline conceded. "Your reality would be weird to the average human, Danny-girl . . . but then, you're not average, and that reality scares me, making you a monster to me on occasion." Emmaline sighed. "But the honest truth is that I've basically scored the most kick-butt friend ever. Maybe I don't deserve you."

With a towel wrapped around her shivering body,

Emmaline leaned over their bucket bath and pecked Daniela's cheek.

"Was that a Judas kiss or an Anne with an *e* kiss?" Daniela waited for an answer as though her life depended upon it. Maybe it did.

"Time will tell." Emmaline started to dress in her hiking outfit.

"She always does."

"I have a right to tell you how I feel, ask questions, then come to my own conclusions."

"I know, and I can come to my own conclusions as well. Right now, you may believe that I'm the most amazing friend ever, but that's your perception in this moment. It may change. My childhood bullies thought I was weird."

"They were afraid of you and too insecure to tell you how they felt."

"So they thought of me as a monster too?"

"Nothing is wrong with you, Lozen—my best friend, my kindred spirit, my *Anne of Green Gables'* Diana Barry blessed with crow-black hair and magical abilities." She fingered Daniela's thick hair.

Daniela's words choked in the back of her throat, tangled up in a web of emotions. "She's all I ever wanted to be. Anne girl's Diana Barry—a classy young woman, a loyal friend who grew up, married, and birthed a couple of children. I never asked to become the Orphan Dreamer. I was chosen. I'm trying to make the best of my reality."

"Don't go soggy-bread soft on me. Can we *really* stop this impending pandemic, Lozen?" Emmaline asked.

"If Wisdom helps us."

"Who's Wisdom?"

"Wisdom stood beside Yahweh when He created Earth.

She knows the beginning of humanity's story, and she knows how to find out the details of our ending. She hasn't told me the outcome of my fight—but I haven't asked. I believe this pandemic can be stopped, and Wisdom will help us if we ask her to."

"She? Wisdom's a girl?"

"Yahweh refers to Wisdom in the feminine sense."

"Score one for the girls!" Emmaline fist bumped the air. "Meet Wisdom—the brains behind the operation."

"But even though Wisdom functions as an advisor, we still need to perform the grunt work." Finished dressing, Daniela grabbed her backpack and stepped outside the tent.

"You solved when this pandemic will wreck Earth, so now we need to solve who." Emmaline rolled up their sleeping bags, placed them in the back of the tent, slipped her backpack on her shoulders, and joined Daniela outside before zipping up their nylon home. "After you discover the identity of who, will you warn everyone—even Claire and Harry, your enemies?"

"Yes." Her voice oscillates. "But they won't listen."

"Why?"

"In their eyes, I'm a nobody. What could I possibly tell them?" Would anyone on Earth listen to a depressed girl who in their eyes was tainted with brown skin and cursed with big, bushy hair—a girl who lost Ethan, her only friend, six months after she found him?

Who said life played fair? But who needed life to play fair when angel armies fought on their side?

Daniela slipped her Bible into her backpack, hoping and praying—begging—that Yahweh would show His Orphan Dreamer grace.

"Limy probably thinks I'm crazy, but don't take her

away from me," Daniela whispered. A desert breeze carried her request up over the mountain slopes while depression threw a coat of arms around Daniela's shoulders, weighing her down. She gasped for breath. How could she hike weighed down like this?

"Are you okay?" Emmaline rushed to Daniela's side.

"I will be." She gasped for another breath. "I have to be. We must find the cave."

Depression sucked.

It was humiliating and heavy, and Daniela fought to keep her nose above the waterline while answering pointless questions of nonempathetic people: Do you like to struggle? Don't you *actually* want to get better?"

Really?

Had the Orphan Dreamer awoken one day and gleefully decided to feel as miserable as a fly trapped inside a hot cow patty? Sarcasm steeled her resolve, but made her think: Should she save the Claires and the Harrys of the world?

Were selfish gawkers worth the sacrifice?

"You'll do right by us all." Once again, Emmaline read Daniela's mind. It's what kindred spirits did. "Sorry about my words earlier. I trust you."

"Prove it."

"You're my friend, and you're our Orphan Dreamer." Emmaline kissed Daniela's cheek, then smiled, crooked and carefree, while yanking the Orphan Dreamer back to the shores of the sea of morality, saving her from drowning beneath the riptides of destructive thoughts. "That's an Anne with an *e* kiss."

"Let's find that cave you're dying to take me to."

"Roger that, Lozen!"

22—The Orphan

DRIED TEARS AND DARKNESS CLUNG to Cillian's skin even as India's sunrise burned dew off dried leaves, orange dainty flowers, and soft grass—truly a lush oasis in this hellish place. "Wake up, boy." The baritone voice and slap across the back startled the teen slave.

Pain wrapped Cillian's body in agony's thorns. He jolted forward, arched his back, and released a scream. A hand slapped his back again. Confused, Cillian cried out, "God, why?"

"Even Saul doesn't call me God." Cillian finally recognized the voice—Bushcroft, the master of his hell. "I'm pleased that your attitude has changed. You've saved me the PTSD from killing you in cold blood."

"What d'ye want from me, sir?"

"Loyalty. Appreciation. The return of my Natalia."

"Natalia? I dinna be knowin' a Natalia or where she might be." He opened his eyes, crust and emotion ripped from his thin, pale eyelids. He looked down at the cold, rusted metal spike that had impaled the tender pale flesh of his left hand.

"Oh, but I do. Your life and the Orphan Dreamer's life in exchange for hers. Nomed promised me."

"The Orphan Dreamer? Nomed? You've mixed things up. I dinna be knowin' what yer talking about."

"I'm not a baker. I never mix anything up." Bushcroft's knuckles whitened, and in one jerking motion, the stake dangled in the air.

Cillian pursed his throbbing and thickened lips, blocking another scream. His left arm trembled with pain. He steadied his left hand with his right and pulled both hands to his chest, trying to stop the shaking that seemed to spread through his body.

"Shall we go home?" Bushcroft wound twine around his slave's wrists. *Home? The brothel?* The lad remained quiet. "Shall we walk home, you and me, then eat a dinner together? I've much to show you, Cillian." Looking up, he leveled his gaze at the orphan.

"Aye, sir." Cillian stumbled along in a halting gait, protecting his heel wound caused by some mysterious animal's sharp fangs. *Who are the Orphan Dreamer, Nomed, and Natalia?*

He had never met any of those people, but he grinned. Maybe he could exact his revenge by harming a person—one of these three mystery persons—who seemed to matter to sadistic Asher Valerian Bushcroft.

"Not so feisty now, are you?"

"I didna sleep well." Cillian removed any strength from his voice. *Don't intimidate the little elf.*

"I drank a gin and tonic last night, then slept harder than a hibernating bear."

The ridicule didn't stop as they walked through rocky terrain and past mud hut villages. With a rope thrown over Bushcroft's shoulder and attached to the twine secured around Cillian's wrists, the slaver never looked behind.

A bully's confidence can render a man a fool, careless in the presence of imminent danger.

The slave squinted his sleep-caked eyes at his master, plotting his second assassination. He couldn't take complete credit for the death of Miss Grey, the cruel care-home mistress; something otherworldly had ended her life.

Cillian's neck veins protruded as he meditated on the nature of bears. Bushcroft's strict insistence on education had proved useful. A bear stalked the wilderness as a dangerous predator. Cillian knew that if a hunter grazed the beast—inflicting a nonlethal wound instead of killing it—pain would drive the five-hundred-pound creature to insanity. With powerful muscles soaked in adrenaline, the grizzly's thirst for revenge would consume its existence. And if the hunter got close enough, the bear would make the careless hunter pay with his life.

Bushcroft's payment was past due.

23—The Orphan (PG-13)

BUSHCROFT TURNED ONE HUNDRED AND eighty degrees, then pulled a gun from a hidden waistline pouch, a wry smile oozing from his lips. "You'll go straight to the clinic." Cillian nodded. "Remember the last time you visited the medic, my dear boy?"

"Aye, sir."

"You came out with a little brand, and now I own you. I've marked you—for life." The short man circled the teen slave. "Your back. Your hand." He pressed the barrel of his gun into Cillian's pierced hand.

The orphan boy did everything he could to not pass out from the pain.

"Your manhood . . . I've marked them all, and no respectable, virtuous woman would allow you to touch her."

Bushcroft spit. The cigar-laden phlegm coated Cillian's right bare foot.

A sordid laugh belched through Bushcroft's vocal cords. "Are you scared?"

"I am."

"Honesty. I like it."

At the clinic, antiseptic bombarded Cillian's nostrils. Metal instruments clanked in their bowls after the careless user threw them to the side.

Injured boys moaned. Bushcroft watched.

Cillian flinched as a small male Indian nurse stabbed a needle into his heel in eight locations. "I don't know what bit you, but I don't want you foaming at the mouth like a rabid dog," the nurse said, his deep voice steeled.

Cillian clenched his fists as the nurse ran a rough, cold rag up and down his back and over his left hand and bitten right heel. It burned—actually, it more than burned. The clear liquid set his body aflame. "Can ye not be a wee bit gentler, sir?"

"Thoroughness is what's required to prevent systemic infection, not gentleness. Where are you from?"

"The northern coast of Ireland."

"Doesn't explain the Scottish burr mangled with an Irish brogue that's sometimes hidden within the accent of an Englishman." The man chuckled. "Can't make up your mind who you'd like to be?"

"I know who I want to be, but I've not yet possessed the freedom to express myself." Cillian painted a fake smile on his face, then turned toward Bushcroft. The man beamed.

The nurse leaned close to Cillian's ear. "Go to America—the land of immigrants cursed with a dream. My brother's there. His kid studies medicine."

"How? Not medical school, but immigration to America?"

The nurse wrapped Cillian's left hand in gauze and dressed his back with salve. "Bushcroft is using you—use him back. Find a way. Your life depends upon your success," the nurse whispered. "If you decide to escape and require refuge, Preeti's house is located along the river, last row, two houses away from the refuse pile. The code: you say 'woodpecker,' and she says 'owl.' "

"Saba, you're done. Finish up." Bushcroft strolled to Cillian's side. "Monotony could bore any businessman. On to a different assignment before our dinner for two."

"Put this on." Saba handed Cillian a clean linen tunic.

"Aye, sir." Cillian slipped the tunic over his shoulders. Standing behind the slaver, the nurse nodded, approving of Cillian's politeness. The child slave walked slowly, trying to keep the shirt from sticking to his back until the salve was absorbed.

Bushcroft stood tiptoe on a chair and draped his arm around the boy's shoulder. "Now look who's taller."

Cillian clenched his jaw.

The wounded bear's adrenaline swelled in his veins, and an idea formed in his mind.

He pulled away, and Bushcroft tumbled off the chair, straightened the hem of his suit, and cleared his throat. "Feeling better, are we? Good. You'll work harder. I fought with myself about losing a day's worth of brothel income, but I've decided that today you'll join the misbehaving boys' detail. Afterward, you'll be pleased with your previous job."

"Will I be workin' outside?"

"Why, yes. Why do you ask?"

"I'd better wear sunscreen and a straw hat. The customers wouldna want their lily-white bunny toasted."

"Thinking ahead." He snapped his fingers, and the nurse approached. "Lather him up."

"Yes, sir." The nurse smeared chalky white cream on Cillian's face, neck, and hands. The rest of his body was covered by clothing. "You see?" Saba whispered. "You've already figured him out. Protect what he believes belongs to him."

"Enough, Saba." Bushcroft clapped his hands. "I've got be able to find him beneath all that cream."

Cillian's wrists bore no chains as he and the master hiked about one mile to a field, with Bushcroft whistling all the way. At the fields, a squat man patrolled, chastising any wayward lads with a riding crop.

"Dominic, meet Cillian, my understudy. I'm teaching him the business."

"You're not leaving us, sir?"

"Not yet. He's not ready. Still fine-tuning his discipline. He'll work with the other condemned boys. Watch him closely. A change of heart is what I'm looking for."

"I've changed a few hearts in my lifetime." The man mouthed a toothpick, and his black eyes stared deader than a corpse. Cillian thought of the man as a gateway to the other side, so in his head, he named him Deathway. The man picked up a shovel and flung the handle toward Cillian. It hit him square in the chest. "Dig."

Bushcroft cleared his throat, and the guard walked to his side and squatted to be eye level with the boss.

They talked, and Cillian heard every word. "Go easy on the boy. I whipped him rather thoroughly last night. Don't want him dead. Tame him until he sings while he works. Don't make your preference obvious—make him think he could end up in one of those shallow graves."

Deathway nodded, walked to Cillian, and barked, "Dig here, and throw these corpses into the ground. Cover the grave with dirt." The man advanced toward a group of boys.

They cowered.

Bushcroft pranced back to the path that led to the brothel, and Cillian sliced his shovel through the muck. To his right, three malnourished, abused corpses awaited their improper burial. His head spun with anger. A boy with ginger hair stood next to him, looking at him with desperate, nearly dead eyes.

They both looked down at the corpses beside their feet.

The boy pointed to one. "Tommy, the funny kid. He arrived when I did," he said quietly, reverently. "Bushcroft starved them to death. After we're assigned to this work detail, he barely feeds us."

Cillian swallowed hard, pushing the invading bile back into his stomach. He needed strength, not sadness. "How are ye farin'?"

"I'm dying. How are you?" The boy smiled the best that he could.

"That's somethin' Tommy would've said?" Cillian scooped a shovel full of dirt and tossed it to the side.

"Yeah. Before he died, he was my best friend. He kept me laughing."

"Laughter . . ." Cillian shoveled more dirt. "I've been missin' that ingredient from my cake for a good while now." The corners of Cillian's mouth hinted at a smile. "I'm not good at tellin' jokes, but how can I help?"

"You can't. When customers don't want you anymore, he cuts your food to three hundred calories a day."

"Why not put a bullet in yer head and be done wi' it?"

"Makes him feel better about what he's doing to us."

"Sadistic pig. Why doesn't he find a wife and leave us alone?" Cillian squeezed the shovel's wooden handle.

"Thomas overheard him talking once. He can't stand women."

"Probably canna get one." Cillian glanced down at his bandaged left hand. *Neither can I.*

"The girls his height would still be in kindergarten." The ginger-haired boy snickered. "Besides, he doesn't see their purpose—prefers boys." The boy's hands blanched around the shovel's handle as the tip penetrated only one inch into the sand. "I'm sorry, I won't be much help on this grave. I'm awfully tired."

"Keep talkin' to me, then, and I'll be doin' the rest."

"About what?"

"Anythin'."

"What's your name?"

"Cillian Finn."

"You Irish?"

"Born in Ireland but lived in England before I came here. My mum and her ancestors are from Scotland's Highlands. What's yer name?"

"John. I was riding in the truck with you when we left England, but I didn't talk much, so you probably didn't notice me. Where's Paul?"

"Somewhere safe." Cillian visibly shook.

"I won't tell."

"I noticed you on the truck, but yer skin and bones now, so it took me a bit of time to figure it out just now. Hi, John."

"Hi, Cillian. You sound funny, but not like an Irish person. I remember that you sounded English, but today, you're a Scotsman."

"Does it matter how I speak?" Cillian declared.

"No, but it's unusual."

"Like I said, my mother's a Highlander Scot. I lived a wee bit in Ireland, but I picked up her Scottish burr and learned the Gaelic language from her."

"Makes sense. Why don't you sound Scottish all the time?"

"My mum didna want me to speak with a burr outside the house. She'd thrash me if I made a mistake."

"Doesn't make sense."

"Has your life ever been makin' sense?"

"When I was four, and Mummy took me to the ice cream shop," John said.

After Cillian finished digging a shallow grave, he rolled the three corpses into the earthen tomb, then began to fill in the grave. "I've never eaten ice cream. How does it taste?"

"Like heaven's clouds."

"John," Cillian paused. "I'm verra disappointed we had to meet again like this."

"Don't be."

"Why?"

"Tonight I'm traveling to paradise," John said.

"I remember traveling to Paradise, England. Met Bushcroft, and here I am. How are you goin' to get there?"

"Found a pamphlet in my room . . . actually, it found me." John looked at the sky. "There it was, lying by my head when I woke up. It was something about John 3:16 and God loving the whole world and giving up His only Son to save it. It said if I believe in Him, I'd be saved. I signed up right away. Beats this gig. Gee, I just realized that thing was addressed to me—John 3:16—I was born on the sixteenth of March."

Cillian looked away and shoveled another scoop of dirt

onto Tommy's corpse. "Do ye think you'll make it all the way up there, then?"

John touched his chest. Weakened, his hand fell back to his side as he leaned heavily on his shovel. "I'll make it. Don't worry. Wanna come? There's ice cream—all-you-can-eat."

"Not tonight. I've got to find Paul, make sure he's alright. D'ye want to sit?"

"Not allowed. We work till we drop, but maybe I'll see you up there, Cil. I hope so." John stumbled forward until breath fled his emaciated body.

Cillian stared into the grave that he'd helped to dig. The two friends now lay together, John on top of Tommy.

The orphan's face contorted as he fought to restrain the anger that exploded from his chest and coursed through his veins. He stiffened his back and gripped the shovel in his grimy hands. His boldness increased, and he looked up from the grave and stared at Deathway.

If only he possessed the physical strength of a wounded bear, he'd kill the man with one blow. But his physical strength had leaked from the wounds marring his back and his left hand. Surveying John and Tommy, who had labored beneath the sun, his fate became clearer. There would be no promotion. Bushcroft would murder him, in time.

Predators always kill their prey.

There was no time to waste. He needed to evolve into the predator—the next step in his evolutionary transformation. To do that, he needed to escape. And if he perished during the attempt, at least he had tried.

The second step: explore who he was and who he could become to exact revenge. Miss Grey, the care-home's warden, had called him Leviathan, Job's sea monster, the dreaded antichrist born to suffocate life from Earth. Cillian had no clue who Leviathan or the antichrist was, but he was rather good at mimicking personas.

If the antichrist lived free, Cillian would be happy to take the job. But in this moment, he gazed toward the heavens, hoping to see John's spirit floating up to the ice cream shop. Instead, an apricot sulphur landed on his freckled nose.

24—The Orphan (PG-13)

Monday, March 23, 1998
India

JOHN HAD DIED, AND THE other boys listed along, too worn down to attempt the task of making a friend. The sun eventually learned to hide like the rest of the boys, and it ducked behind the flat western plain.

Cillian felt, saw, and smelled the fear pulsing through the death camp before he heard his owner's voice. One boy soiled his pants at the sound, another vomited, and others kept their gazes on their graves and their feet.

"Come to me, Cillian." Bushcroft waved.

Don't hesitate. Spare the other boys from Bushcroft's sadistic tendencies. He quickly tossed his shovel onto a pile of yard tools.

"Excellent. You've become responsive. Efficient. To-day's task has impacted your attitude." The small man rocked back and forth on his heels. "What are you thinking about, my boy?" Bushcroft's smile darkened his devilish face as he wrapped his arm around Cillian's waist.

Instinctively, the bear arose within Cillian, and he pulled away. Fire shot down the nape of his neck. The whip had flayed open the skin at the base of his neck. Scarface grinned, his hand slick with the slave's blood.

"You didn't learn a thing, did you?" Bushcroft jumped up and down like he was performing the Russian Kalinka dance, his palm colliding with Cillian's dirt-covered cheeks again and again.

The world spun in circles.

Warm, salty liquid tickled Cillian's swollen lips as the jack-in-the-box continued his assault. Cillian glanced at the other child slaves. At least he couldn't beat them too.

Their eyes avoided his stare, their courage frozen at some point along their journey.

He clenched and released his jaw until it finally remained clenched, then he leaned down so the man could have easier access to his face.

"Dear God! Are you getting angry, boy?" Bushcroft's shoe pummeled Cillian's thigh, and the boy sprawled onto the ground.

"Get up!" Spittle flew. "Get up! Get up! Stand up! Take it like a man! Stand up, you foolish boy!" Bushcroft thumped Cillian across his neck, shoulders, back, and legs with his velvet shoe. A little elf beating a boy with a velvet shoe. Laughter landed into Cillian's mixing bowl of emotions, and he belted it out.

Cillian pushed upward. Bushcroft tripped him, and he fell back into the sand. Cillian pushed up again, pulling his feet beneath him.

"Get back down there!" Bushcroft kicked him from

behind. "Stop laughing. Crawl! Crawl on all fours to my office."

Stand.

Crawl.

The little man canna make up his little mind.

Right hand and left knee followed by left hand and right knee, Cillian's pants ripped, and his knees became bloodied and bruised as he crawled half a mile to Bushcroft's office. Funny how a spirit can soar, then tumble back to the ground within a matter of seconds.

"Stand up and get inside."

Cold air blasted Cillian's sun-parched face. No amount of sunscreen could have protected his fair skin—he was sure he resembled a roasted tomato. The customers liked him pale, so at least he would avoid a night of rape.

"Sit."

Fine tan leather supported his fatigued body, and Cillian was grateful for the rest as Bushcroft finished up paperwork. Scarface dropped a plate of steak, broccoli, and kale salad on a dinner tray in front of Cillian. "Eat, then go to bed. You look like an overripe tomato, so I can't use you tonight. You'll double up tomorrow. *Capisci?*" Bushcroft said.

"Aye, sir." Cillian had learned Italian. He understood.

"Quick to respond. Something's getting through your thick skull," Bushcroft said, but for Cillian, there would be no tomorrow. Plain. Definitely simple.

After eating dinner, the exhausted slave trudged to the picnic area, slid onto a wooden bench, and practically inhaled his ration of soup and bread. A group of boys stared at him from across the outdoor eating area, their cheeks sunken to the bone. He had just eaten his second meal, and they had most likely received only soup. He knew why—purposeful starvation, giving them time to repent for their involuntary sins.

Cillian tucked fruit and cheese into his pant pockets. Then, like a piece of ice running down hot skin, a cold, moist hand gripped Cillian's arm. He jumped. Had Scarface seen his thievery?

"Come with me to medical." The words made him tremble.

"Why?" Cillian looked up at an olive-skinned man with dark eyes and a slight limp. "Who are you?"

"No questions. Come."

He followed the man into the clinic, and once inside, the man turned to Cillian. "Your hand must be kept clean and dry, or you'll lose it." The doctor reached for the lad's hand and squeezed. Cillian's face contorted with pain. A thick creamy substance poured out of the wound. "You'll die of sepsis if you're not careful."

Cillian laid his hand on the cold steel table. The doctor doused his wounds with a brown solution. "It's called iodine."

"Why are ye looking after me?"

"Preeti told me about you. She's my sister."

"What did she say?"

"You are a kind, respectful boy, and she considers you a son. She told me that, whatever I must do, I must make sure you survive."

"Did she say anything else about me or my family?"

"I didn't know you had a family." The doctor's voice dropped a few notches. "We have a visitor coming through the door."

Cillian tensed. "I don't."

"Don't what?"

"Have a family." *Can this doctor be trusted?*

"This is a hell of a place to be if you'd been cursed with a son."

Scarface entered the clinic, then ogled the teen slave while breathing heavily onto the orphan's face.

"Screaming isn't a sign of weakness, lad." Cillian didn't bother to turn toward the sadistic voice behind him. He could smell the man—floral like a bouquet of flowers. He bit his lower lip, squeezed his buttocks tightly, retrieved a cloth, and dug the washcloth into his good hand.

"Here. I'm giving this to you only because I like you." Bushcroft pressed a glass of clear liquid into Cillian's lips. It was clear, but it moved differently than water.

"Drink it, then thank me."

Cillian sucked a quick breath through his nostrils and sipped. The clear liquid lit a flame at the back of his throat. He coughed and spat the liquid onto the concrete floor.

"Still a boy. One day, I'll make a man out of you, but in time . . . the customers prefer boys." Bushcroft snatched the glass from the orphan and chugged down the contents. "Ah! That's how it's done." He winked at Cillian.

A knot twisted in Cillian's stomach, then sprang legs and bolted into his throat. His abdominal muscles contracted and released. Green liquid pooled on the floor. Looking up with a gaze that could burn holes in the man's face, he narrowed his eyes and rolled his good hand into a ball. Adrenaline sloshed through the wounded bear's veins, pushing him to the brink of something unbelievably bad.

"You've been naughty." Buschcroft glanced down at Cillian's fist. "You'll go to bed without milk and cookies."

"Shall I escort him?" Scarface eagerly asked.

"No. He knows the way home."

Moments later, Cillian limped across the grounds.

To his right, behind a fence, one of the death-detail

boys wedged his face between the slats that separated the wooden posts. They were condemned. Cillian slowed and looked in both directions. Beneath the glow of a dingy lamp, no one was looking, so he pushed the fruit and cheese from his pocket into the boy's hands. "Here, take it."

The boy grabbed the food and stuffed it into his mouth. He looked at Cillian with thankful and hopeful eyes.

"It isna much. Just enough to make ye feel as though you're not dying for a few minutes."

"Thank you all the same." Cheeks stuffed, the boy grinned.

The orphan found his cell—his home, but not for long—and lay down. Eyes wide open, he waited.

25—Orphan Dreamer

AFTER THE GIRLS SECURED THEIR campsite, Daniela swallowed two more ibuprofens. "How far is the cave?" She slipped her feet into her favorite wool socks, then into her hiking boots.

"About a mile." Emmaline buried the map into her fanny pack, then tightened the scarf around her neck.

"Let's make tracks." Dust clung to Danny's boots and clothes as she trudged down the trail, wishing she could lay on a block of ice to numb the pain.

"Lozen, maybe you're not supposed to find him—maybe six-six-six will find you."

"The Mack daddy of stalkers. Sounds terrifying." A shiver marched through Daniela's body. Already dressed in cold-weather gear, she caressed the edges of the Glass

Tattoo hanging from her neck. Moving quickly, her left foot slipped, and she fell onto her left hip. "Mud and smoke!"

"Careful! Don't break a leg." Stiff winds tossed Emmaline's fire-branded hair around her face as she ran to Daniela. "Here, take my hand."

"Got it." Daniela laughed at her comical memory.

"What are you laughing about?"

"You remind me of Laura Ingalls Wilder running through the fields during the opening credits of *Little House on the Prairie*. The only thing missing is a prairie dress and an old-fashioned hymn."

"You giggle when you're scared."

Daniela hiked a bit further, then admitted, "You're right . . . I sing too." Deep from her chest and spirit, Daniela sang one of her favorite hymns from her Afro-American spiritual culture: "Take My Hand, Precious Lord" by the Reverend Thomas A. Dorsey:

> Precious Lord, take my hand
> Lead me on, let me sta-and
> I am tired, I'm weak, I am worn
>
> Through the storm, through the night
> Lead me on to the li-ight
> Take my ha-and, precious Lo-ord
> Lead me home . . .

The birds chirped, continuing the Orphan Dreamer's spiritual song.

"Our songs get us through, Limy. Whether on the Southern plantations or before a sixteen-year-old frightened dreamer searches for and then explores some dark cave, the music still strengthens me. It calms me, cheers me, and gifts me hope."

Our music.

Our spirituals.

Our soul.

Our story—untainted, unchanged, and raw, offering praise to our Creator.

"Beautiful and breathtaking, Danny-girl." Emmaline slipped her arm around Daniela's slight waist. "Thank you for sharing a piece of your soul with me. I'm . . . honored. But I don't deserve you."

"No—"

"It's true. Trust me." Emmaline clasped her hands to her chest and smiled at Daniela, then walked at a slower pace with her friend at her side.

After a few moments of walking in companionable silence, Emmaline abruptly stopped. "Did you hear that?"

"I did." In the distance, a mountain lion screamed. Goosebumps erupted over Daniela's skin. "We're the intruders here."

"Intruders bent on living." Emmaline opened her backpack and removed her "pepper spray."

"Limy, that's a gun!"

"What did you think it was?"

"You're only sixteen."

"I know, birthday's in May. And calm down, I've taken safety classes, and I'm a sharpshooter. Watch the rock, Danny-girl." Emmaline aimed the gun at a small black rock that rested about one hundred feet away. She pulled the trigger, and the rock jumped in the air as it splintered apart.

"What did that rock do to you?"

"It got in my way." Emmaline pressed on, then kicked the remains of the rock that she'd blown to smithereens. "Don't forget. May fifteenth. Let's have a b-day party, me and you."

Switching between blowing up rocks and celebrating birthdays.

Who does that? Who was Emmaline, really?

Daniela remembered the man's warning: *don't trust the redhead.* How had Daniela's pinky finger been broken while she slept? And who was Rob?

During her dreams, she'd never broken a bone, only gotten banged up with resulting scrapes and bruises to show for the trauma.

But she played along with Emmaline's distraction. "I'll make the most amazing cake for you." Then Daniela pointed at a rocky dome. "Almost there. The mouth of the cave should be located behind that cluster of trees, according to your drawing."

A bee buzzed around Emmaline's ear. She hit the ground. "Sorry. I'm anaphylactic allergic to bees."

"Hold still." Daniela fanned away the insect. "Do you carry an EpiPen?

"It's in my fanny pack."

"Good to know. Don't worry. I won't leave you bloated and suffocating." The girls proceeded toward the mouth of the cave.

"Danny-girl, did you know that West Point Academy studied Apache military tactics to form their own military strategies?"

"Lozen probably taught the Green Berets and Delta Force how to track and evade the enemy." Daniela slowed her pace, descending the last steep incline. "You said your dad is in intelligence . . . something about the Sons of Venus? What exactly does he do?"

"MI6."

"James Bond MI6?"

"That's him."

"Who's your favorite Bond?"

"Sean Connery, of course. Yours?"

"Pierce Brosnan." Daniela fanned her face.

"Ahh. You're crushing. Would you ever marry a SEAL?"

"The gray complexion and the blubber . . . not exactly my type," Daniela joked as she jumped off a two-foot-high ledge and landed firmly before helping Emmaline down.

"You know what I mean." Emmaline pinched Daniela's butt. "The Navy SEALs. Do you want to marry them?"

"Not all of them—goodness gracious!"

"Daniela and her lethal harem."

"If I ever marry, give me a man so boring that he rocks an insomniac to sleep." Daniela navigated around a small rock outcropping, then heard the telltale rattle. "Stop!" She held up her hand.

Emmaline stopped on a dime. "Can you see it?"

Daniela scanned the ground, then looked up and surveyed the rocky cleft. "It's an inch above our heads." The serpent was curled into a striking pose at eye level, its tail still shaking, warning them to halt.

"No EpiPen will neutralize the poison of a rattlesnake bite."

"We'll wait him out."

The girls stood still from 9:38 a.m. to 10:27 a.m. until the serpent slithered away.

"We have to pay more attention," Daniela said, jogging toward the cave.

"Give me a man with muscles packed beneath camouflaged fatigues—rugged, rough, testosterone boiling in his veins—then I'll pay attention." Emmaline twirled in a ballerina dance. Had she not learned anything?

"Next trip—Annapolis, Maryland. Next mission—find Limy's long-lost sailor. A man who possesses more muscles than an African rhino and can execute a mean military salute." Daniela ducked beneath a rotting tree branch, waiting to enter the mouth of the pitch-black cave. Time seemed to stop.

She listened.

Silence answered.

An acrid taste rested on her tongue. Dank, stale air assaulted her nose. Would they find anything besides bat guano in the cave? Emmaline slipped her arm beneath the crook of Daniela's elbow. "For Lozen. Shall we?"

"And for a friend's hunch that this will give us a hope of solving the mystery of the Skeleton Key." Clicking on her headlamp, Daniela entered the cave first. "We're walking in the steps of a warrior."

"At this very site, Lozen may have contemplated how to help her people survive." Emmaline followed.

Silence suffocated everything except the scuff of their feet along loose gravel. Daniela froze. "Did you hear something?"

"It's a spider, scurrying across the cave floor with its eight legs—and it's looking for you!" Emmaline tickled the back of Daniela's neck. She cringed and shrank away from Emmaline's touch. "Did I hurt you, Danny-girl?"

"My skin feels as though someone poured hot oil on it."

"Sorry. I was kidding. I remembered the tarantula that haunted your time travels. I thought you'd laugh."

"I dread spiders."

"I know, but why does your skin hurt?"

"Never mind . . . take a look at this." Daniela angled her headlamp toward the cave wall, illuminating cave drawings.

"Was this Lozen's doing?" Emmaline reached out to touch the wall.

"Limy, don't! Archeology rule number one: don't touch—and potentially erase—history." Emmaline retracted her hand, and the girls studied the ancient art. "The painting tells a story of war."

"Look at this, Danny." Following the pattern of a drawing on the wall, Emmaline air-traced four big red circles with her forefinger. Daniela leaned in. "Red circles . . . large, symmetrical, purposeful. They mean something."

"Odd rendering in the middle of a war scene." Emmaline crossed her arms. "What are they?"

"Moons." Daniela stepped back and evaluated the wall from a distance. "Four of them—a tetrad of blood moons. I can't believe my eyes." She removed her camera from her backpack and took a picture.

"Blood moons?"

"You bet."

Emmaline tapped her chin. "Each time a tetrad of lunar eclipses fell on a specific sequence of Jewish holidays, something significant happened to the Jewish people."

"You remembered."

"MIT senior with straight As."

"That's my Limy." Daniela smiled, then grabbed her journal from her backpack. She turned to a page and pointed to her spreadsheet. "Take a look."

Tetrads of Blood Moons and Their Effects on Jewish People

    The Spanish Inquisition—1492
    * Passover, April 2, 1493
    * Sukkot, September 25, 1493
    * Passover, March 22, 1494
    * Sukkot, September 15, 1494

The War of Independence—1948
* Passover, April 13, 1949
* Sukkot, October 7, 1949
* Passover, April 2, 1950
* Sukkot, September 26, 1950

The Six-Day War—1967
* Passover, April 24, 1967
* Sukkot, October 18, 1967
* Passover, April 13, 1968
* Sukkot, October 6, 1968

What Happens Here?
* Passover, April 15, 2014
* Sukkot, October 8, 2014
* Passover, April 4, 2015
* Sukkot, September 28, 2015

"Creepy intentional or a coincidence, Danny-girl?"

"Prophetic. Predictable. Interesting."

"And the blood moons of 2014–2015, what happens?"

"My guess is that sometime after 2014–2015, the beginning of the end is ushered in, leading to the eventual revelation of the antichrist, six-six-six, who will dominate the world scene. His grand entrance remains one of the last prophesied and significant events for the Jewish peoples before Christ sets up his eternal kingdom."

Daniela focused on another drawing, a chest with two poles and two angels resting on the lid. "Look, Limy!" Emmaline pressed in so close that Daniela could smell her coffee breath. "This drawing is a spitting replica of the Jewish Ark of the Covenant."

"You're right." Emmaline re-angled her headlamp.

"Why would an Apache finger paint a Jewish relic on a New Mexican cave wall?"

"Maybe the rest of the scene will reveal the story. Let's keep exploring." Daniela took more photos.

"When did the Ark of the Covenant go missing?"

"Before the Babylonians sacked Solomon's temple in Jerusalem in 586 BC." Daniela jotted down a few more notes. So your dad really is MI6?"

"Confirmed."

"And also a member of the Sons of Venus?" Daniela interrogated her friend with the bright glare of her headlamp. Emmaline opened her mouth, then closed it again. "You don't have to tell me, but if you choose to say something, remember . . . in a friendship there can be secrets, but never lies."

"The laws of friendship, according to Danny Rose Cavanaugh." Emmaline cleared her throat and shifted her weight. "He's a member . . . b-b-but don't tell anyone."

"Why would I? I don't even know who the Sons of Venus are!"

"Shh! Don't. Tell. Anyone." Emmaline closed the distance between them in two strides.

"I won't—promise." Daniela stepped back, turned, then trained her headlamp on the next finger-painted scene, following its course from left to right. "Death. Destruction. A source of light. Dots." She fingered her ear, a nervous tic. "These dots are grouped together. Separated by spaces, the dot groupings are drawn in a regular pattern, and they're smaller in diameter than the four moons. I think this a numbering system . . . maybe even a cipher."

"A secret message?"

"Maybe."

"Let's decode it."

"I'll count the dots," Daniela said, "and you write down the numbers."

They counted 20, 5, 13, 21, 10, 9, and 14, then Daniela snapped a photograph.

"If this cipher was left by an Apache, why write the code in numbers instead of their native language?" Emmaline asked as she drew a copy of their findings inside Daniela's journal.

"I wouldn't know, but I've always believed that when Yahweh speaks to humans, He speaks in the language of mathematics—the universal language. He said, 'Let there be light,' then a powerful and bright force charged out of Yahweh's presence at 670,616,629 miles per hour . . . and there was light. Mathematics is a universal language."

"Like six-six-six—the unholy trinity."

"Right." Daniela paused. "It may just be semantics, but the Greek letters possess the gematria where Chi equals six hundred, Xi equals sixty, and Stigma equals six. The question of the century is this: do I add the numbers together— six-six-six—or interpret them separately—six-hundred, sixty, and six? Even so, if I wanted to share a code with a non-English speaker, I would write it in numbers. My issue with this scene is that I don't know how many Apaches spoke English, much less understood the English numerical or alphabet system."

"Dahteste, Lozen's sidekick." Emmaline shared. "She spoke fluent English, so it's likely that other members of the tribe learned how to speak and write English. But what about your dreams from last night? Any more clues that could help us now?"

"Nothing that makes sense." Dread marched across Daniela's slight shoulders, rattling her teeth and her bravery. "Oily boy was being tortured—again." She massaged her aching back and shoulders. "Otherwise, my dreams have been sluggish and unrevealing as to who starts the darn pandemic."

"Pump Red Bull into their veins," Emmaline snapped before her tone softened. "Don't be afraid to dream. Your parents and I are depending on you to bring back clues so we can help you solve these ancient puzzles and stop this future pandemic in its tracks."

"If I'm going to dream, then I need to be able to trust you when I dream and travel. I need to know that my body remains safe with you." Daniela's camera dangled by a strap from her neck as she gazed at her friend.

Emmaline remained quiet for what seemed like ten minutes. Finally she answered. "I know you need to be able to trust me."

"Who broke my finger? The break didn't happen during my travels because the orphan boy's finger wasn't broken by his tormentor."

Emmaline stared at the tips of her hiking boots. "Robert dropped you."

"Robert? When? Where?"

"He's a guy I know . . . my boyfriend."

"You're lying."

"How can you tell?"

"The wolf within—my knowing."

"Then why ask me?" Emmaline quipped, and Daniela waited for Emmaline to speak truth. "Robert works for the Sons of Venus. He came to our campsite last night—hence the spent bullet—but I don't think he'll be giving us any more trouble."

"When were you going to tell me?" Daniela shone her headlamp left, right, back, and forward. No one. Nothing.

"You don't understand. My dad . . . he's powerful. No

one tells him no. Not even my mother. When he wants her, he gets her." A tear escaped Emmaline's right eye.

"I'm sorry." Daniela embraced her friend while wanting to punch Limy's piggish dad in the face. "It's okay. I'm here. Forever and always."

"I believe you." Emmaline sopped up her tears with her shirt sleeve. "Forgive me."

"Forgiven. We're both exhausted, so let's solve this cipher back in the safety of camp. We'll leave for home in the morning."

"Home—a tiny loft nestled in a small town compared to my parents' sprawling Massachusetts mansion."

"My parents' home in Florida isn't fancy, but the door is open to you." Daniela refocused on the task at hand. "If these dots represent a cipher, and the code is English-based, maybe the numbers can be plugged into a simple number-to-alphabet cipher."

"Too simple." Emmaline objected.

"I'm glad, because my brain is toast." Daniela snapped a few more photographs of the finger-painted scene in case there were more clues they hadn't noticed. They reached the end of the cave. "Let's storm. We've got some decrypting to do."

With their simple number code secured in Emmaline's backpack, the girls hiked back to their campsite.

Sitting by their campfire, Daniela decided it was time to tell Emmaline everything—or almost everything. "When I activate the Glass Tattoo, sometimes I can see things—more than just weird oily boy dreams. I see vivid visions of the past and future civilizations. These experiences are so real that I believe I've time travelled, which I shared with you earlier. Limy, I can touch people. I can smell their body odor, taste their food, and feel their fear."

"Tell me more." Emmaline furrowed her brow. "Better yet, take me with you."

"That's all I know." Daniela shrugged and half-laughed at herself. "It's not safe for you to travel with me. Ethan died after he returned."

"We'll fight that battle later. How did you find the Glass Tattoo?"

"I didn't. My parents gave it to me on my thirteenth birthday—or rather, someone left it on our front door-step."

"That whole 'Armageddon before puberty' is your parents' mantra when it comes to your ability to date. But on the other hand, they gifted you an ancient relic that forces you to travel all alone through the expanse of time while encountering dangerous people in unfamiliar places."

"They don't force me."

"But their parenting style is totally incongruent. But please, don't feel awkward. We could have tons of fun with your special time-travel powers."

"What do you propose?"

"First, a few facts: do you talk to anyone besides the orphan boy when you travel?"

"You know about Legna, a fire-spitting angel with re-ally cool eyes." Daniela's face flushed warm, and her ears prickled.

"You've been keeping the most salacious details from me. No wonder you're not interested in snagging a SEAL. Let me hold the Glass Tattoo, so I can meet Legna for my-self," Emmaline commanded."

Daniela obliged, removing the snowflake diamond from the leather cord that hung from her neck. "The trav-eling isn't all roses and sunshine. I don't particularly want to save the world and prophesy doomsday to strangers."

"Tell me your biggest fear about your calling."

Daniela's voice dropped to a whisper. "I don't want to end up like Lozen—alone, childless, and imprisoned by the enemy. No matter who you call me, Limy, I'm not Lozen. I am Daniela, an introvert, snagged for a job that I'm not qualified for."

"Most effective leaders are introverts." Emmaline rubbed her fingers across the precious stone. "Have you shared the details of your travels with your parents?"

"No. I mean, yes, but I don't know if they really believe me. No matter how hard they tried to mask their feelings, I could see the fear behind their hopeful smiles. I think my parents are secretly worried about my calling, hoping God will reassign me to a typical job for normal, pretty girls: a model, a teacher, or a nurse."

"More like a circa 1960s job. Why do you feel that way?"

"I'm their only child, and what if I am just a depressed schizophrenic lost inside my delusions and not really the Orphan Dreamer?"

"Your angst is the result of raging hormones. I'm going to hire a guy to make out with you and relieve some stress."

"That would be the last act listed on my stress-relief options. Trust me." Daniela reached into her pocket and pulled out a polished obsidian arrowhead. "Prince Jonathan gave me this before he died."

"A prince! Who is Prince Jonathan—your boyfriend?"

"Ancient Hebrew royalty, circa 1019 BC."

"A three-thousand-year-old prince? That's who you hung out with when travelling to that place in 1019 BC?" Emmaline snapped her fingers.

"Gibeah."

"Yes. I don't pretend to understand everything that

you're telling me." Emmaline paused. "But I promise you that from now on, I will fight with you—not against you." She opened Daniela's left hand, placed the Glass Tattoo in it, and closed her fingers around the diamond-like stone.

"You don't want to meet Legna and check out my story?"

"No. Because I believe in you. This belongs to you. Keep it safe. Our lives depend on it." Emmaline ran her fingers through her hair. "I possess a few magical abilities of my own, Indiana Jones."

"Pray tell."

"A solid right hook." Emmaline threw a punch, cutting the air.

"I'll make a fire, Sugar Ray Leonard." Daniela lit a batch of tinder, then poured half a bottle of water, a can of black beans, and bacon bits into a tin pot before resting the pot on the grate that rested above the fire.

Once again, the sun dipped behind the mountains, and the campfire flickered against the backdrop of a cold, endless night.

A blanket of stars hovered low overhead.

"Smells good," Emmaline said.

"Hope it tastes as good as it smells." Daniela pulled her jacket close and rubbed her hands beside the fire.

"Wanna share spooky stories while you finish dinner and I roll out our sleeping bags?" Emmaline asked.

"A couple of girls camping all alone in a vast canyon where mountain lions, copperheads, or a flash flood could kill us in our sleep . . . we're basically living a spooky story." A bird warbled, agreeing with Daniela. "But if telling a scary story makes you happy, my ears are wide open." She grinned.

"Thanks. If we're going to solve your pandemic mystery

and understand who starts the darn thing, we have to start somewhere. Let's profile this hypothetical antichrist. FBI, here we come!"

Emmaline served dinner, and Daniela spooned a mouthful of beans into her mouth. "Delicious."

Daniela slipped on her proverbial sleuth's hat, and Emmaline peppered her with questions. "Economic status: rich or poor?"

"Probably rich. If he's poor, he'd better possess one heck of a personality."

"Ugly or handsome?"

"None of the world's dictators have ever looked attractive. Why start now?"

"Religion—gentile or Jewish?"

"The masses tend to be rather anti-Semitic, so he'll most likely practice—at least superficially—the religion of the masses."

"Christian, Hindu, Buddhist, or Muslim?"

"That's a hard one."

"Maybe he practices some combination of the Abrahamic-derived religions—Judaism, Christianity, and Islam—and calls it a New Age movement?"

"A chameleon able to fit into any religious enclave. Plausible. Useful. Enough of that, though. Shall we finish solving the cipher?" Daniela ate another spoonful of beans, turned on her flashlight, and opened her journal.

"We shall." Emmaline leaned back in her camping chair and Daniela crisscrossed her legs. They relished the rest of their dinner while solving the simple number-to-letter code: 20, 5, 13, 21, 10, 9, and 14.

$$20=T$$
$$5=E$$
$$13=M$$
$$21=U$$
$$10=J$$
$$9=I$$
$$14=N$$

"Temujin," Daniela said. "Who the heck is that?"

"Someone who may have something to do with the Ark of the Covenant and those four blood moons painted on the cave walls?"

"That solves everything," Daniela said sarcastically. "More questions, no answers."

"You said that a replica of the Ark of the Covenant had been finger painted onto the wall next to the grouping of dots, so the two must be related."

"Phone a friend?" Daniela closed her journal.

"It's safer to call your dad over mine." Emmaline handed Daniela her satellite phone.

"If you say so." Daniela dialed her parents' number. When her mother answered, she asked her to run an errand: go to the Alachua County Library and find out who Temujin was. "Appreciate it. Thanks. Love you, Mom. Call me back in the morning." She ended the call. "Ready for bed, Limy?"

"Totally." Emmaline entered their tent. "We'll drive home tomorrow morning, then get back to work in the afternoon."

"Tonight, let's sleep tight." The girls piled into their sleeping bags and zipped the tent door shut. As they both sat listening to the sounds of nature around them, Daniela asked, "Limy, how did you know about this particular cave?"

After a few moments of quiet, Emmaline confessed, "Robert told me about it."

"What?" Daniela bolted up, yanked her friend's cover from over her face, and shot daggers with her eyes beneath the lantern's glow. "Were these cave drawings recently drawn? Are they fakes?"

"I don't know."

"Of all the things you could've done to me—you've made me into a fool, Emmaline!"

"Okay! Okay! Give me a chance."

"You're a liar, and liars disgust me." The air around the girls filled with Daniela's disdain. "I should've known. The paint looked too new, not faded enough."

"The truth is, my dad refused to continue paying for my college tuition if I didn't cooperate with his plan."

"Which was?"

"Lead you to that cave and lure you into trying to make sense of the cave drawings."

"Are they original markings?"

"Yes and no."

"You're skating dangerously close to getting on my last nerve, Limy!"

"I know, and I'm sorry. But as Lozen fought for her people, she'd heard a rumor that leaders of her tribe were to be imprisoned at Alcatraz Island."

"I don't have time for a history lesson. Just tell me why you lied to me."

"Let me finish my story."

"I'm not a child, so no bedtime story required."

"I'm telling you the truth, Danny-girl." Emmaline's voice shattered. "Honest, I am." She swiped a waterfall of emotion from her face. "Please listen to me. Give me a chance to make this right. Don't abandon me. Your Yeshua gave the thief who was dying on the cross next to Him a second chance. I've never had a friend like you . . . so please, try to understand my motives, Danny Rose."

"Fine." The Orphan Dreamer crossed her arms.

"Okay." Emmaline blew her nose, clearing out the snot. "Trusting that America's military leadership would honor the result of their negotiations, Lozen and Dahteste began negotiating peace treaties for the release of members of their tribe. They trusted the European-Americans right up until the moment when the warriors of Lozen's tribe realized they had been lied to."

"Feeling's mutual." Daniela shook her head. "Go on."

"If Lozen wanted to rejoin her kin, she and Dahteste needed to head east. So in good faith, the Apache warriors laid down their arms and surrendered. Five days later, they were loaded onto a train bound for Florida." Emmaline paused.

"Sounds rather World War II concentration-camp era." A sour taste of disgust settled in the back of the Orphan Dreamer's throat. She coughed, then gulped down a bottle of water but couldn't clear the taste. "And?"

"The women were taken into military custody after Geronimo—Lozen's brother—finally surrendered. So the great Apache warrior, Lozen, was no longer able to fight to keep her land and traveled as a prisoner of war to Alabama's Mount Vernon Barracks, a horrid place."

"And she died in confinement from tuberculosis in 1889," Daniela concluded. "I know that part."

"Yes. She did."

"What is the point of your history lesson, Limy? None of what you've shared changes the fact that you used me, lied to me, and almost got me killed by some guy named Robert."

"My maternal great-great-grandfather was the general who oversaw that mission. After Lozen's capture, my ancestor met with her—no, I have to tell you the whole truth. He tortured her, attempting to understand the source of her power."

"What a monster."

"They run in my family. Bruised and with blood dripping from her wounds, Lozen whispered a prayer: 'Upon this earth on which we live, Ussen has power. This Power is mine for locating the enemy. I search for that enemy which only Ussen the Great can show to me.' "

"She prayed to the source of her power—Ussen."

"Any relation to your God, Yahweh?"

"Why don't you ask Him for yourself, Limy?"

"Maybe I will." Emmaline rolled onto her back, and Daniela followed suit. "She gave my great-great-grandfather the drawing shown in this photograph." The redhead produced a black-and-white photograph.

"This is a replica of the cave drawing."

"No. The cave drawing is a replica of Lozen's prison drawing. Robert came to the cave and painted the image on the walls."

"Why?"

"You said that Wisdom helps you solve your riddles and puzzles. I guess Wisdom doesn't like me or my dad. We couldn't figure out the whole picture, but you did. Tell me again, so I can pacify him and stay at university."

"Then, to your education." Daniela sighed heavily. "After four blood moons, the culprits will pay for the actions of whoever stole the Ark of the Covenant so many years ago, and humans will be infected by a mysterious virus, a *bad* pandemic."

"The mother of all pandemics?

"I don't know."

"What about the alien planet, Wormwood?" Emmaline asked.

"Wormwood will collide with Earth, and Nephilim—the offspring of fallen angels and humans—will engineer and spread this deadly virus before taking over the world, enslaving all humans before systematically eradicating every man, woman, and child. And they'll enjoy every second of the process. Armageddon will serve as their capstone."

"Professor Jakob or someone else sent you the Skeleton Key, the statue made of precious metals. You don't know the purpose of that trinket yet, right?" Emmaline reached for her photograph.

Daniela zipped her sleeping bag closed. Lying quiet for a while, the Orphan Dreamer finally spoke. "No, I don't. I would've helped you and your dad solve the mystery of Lozen's drawing if you had simply told me the truth, Limy."

"I couldn't rely on your good nature. Mother gets the brunt of Dad's anger when he doesn't get his way."

"Solving the puzzles . . . it's my job, and I'm no slacker."

"But I can be."

"Don't project Emmaline onto Daniela." Daniela kept the Glass Tattoo far away from the palm of her right hand. No dreaming or traveling tonight. It wasn't safe, even though her only friend lay beside her.

"Goodnight. See you in the morning, Danny-girl."

"Goodnight."

Maybe Yeshua's *good* pandemic—the Rapture—would occur while they slept, taking Daniela away to her eternal home and leaving her Anne with an *e* behind to survive the greatest tribulation Earth would ever know.

But could she survive by herself?

26—Orphan Dreamer

IN THE MORNING, EMMALINE BURIED her nose in her armpit, then yanked her head back, laughing. "Skunks and stink bugs! Time for a bath." She reached for Daniela's hand. "Come on. If I'm the skunk, you're the stink bug."

"I'm not diving into Lake Fenton." Daniela set her jaw.

"I won't allow you to drown. Besides, I survived a tornado all by myself. Come on. Where's my brave Lozen?"

"Dead . . . remember? The American cavalry led by your ancestor captured Lozen, and she traveled as a prisoner of war to Mount Vernon in Alabama, believing all along that your great-great-grandfather would keep his word. But he didn't, and she died of tuberculosis in a prison."

"In another lifetime, my best friend existed as an encyclopedia!"

"Don't make fun of me, Limy. Not now."

"Eventually even warriors die, but a dying fire comes back to life with a bit of the right attention." Emmaline stoked the fire.

"Eventually liars die, destined to encounter a different kind of fire called hell."

"Lozen's god failed her. Your God may fail you as well. So be kind to me. Help me." The girls removed the tent stakes, slid their home closer to the flames, then replaced the stakes. "You can tread water?" Emmaline asked.

"I can't."

"Try."

"If I drown—or die of TB—humanity dies alongside me, remember?"

"Compromise. Humanity's destruction or not, you're not smelling ripe inside my Jeep." Emmaline retrieved a bar of biodegradable soap from her tent. "Just wash the grunge and the outdoorsy warrior's stench off."

"Camping in the great big wild wasn't my idea, but fine." Daniela snatched the bar of soap from her friend-turned-parent, then sniffed her armpits. "You're right. I stink."

"When is your mom going to call us back with the identity of Temujin?" Inside the tent, both girls stripped down to their bare skin.

"The library wasn't open on Sunday. She'll call today, maybe on our way back to Los Alamos." Wrapped in a beach towel, Daniela ran toward the water's edge.

Buck naked, Emmaline raced past her and charged into the cold lake, releasing a scream upon impact with the arctic water. "Brain freeze but invigorating!"

Daniela waded into the shallows, then threw her towel

to shore. She quickly bathed, slathering her body with the natural soap.

"Danny Rose!" Emmaline's face contorted with hints of disgust and a major dose of concern. "Your skin! It's covered with black—"

"Leeches?" She slapped at her skin, looking for the black wiggly parasites.

"Not leeches, but bruises." Upon closer inspection, Emmaline started crying.

"Don't cry, not for me." Daniela hadn't noticed—the benefits of changing from her pajamas into her day clothes inside a dark tent before Emmaline had awoken. She looked down at her bruised body and blinked away shock. "It's oily boy—the poet. He's in trouble."

"How . . . when? Is someone hurting him?"

"Yes."

"Is the bruising normal?"

"Yes." Daniela hung her head.

"You hurt where he hurts. That's how you knew you hadn't broken your finger during your fretful dream."

"That's correct."

"I want to help you. What can we do for him?"

Body shaking, she kneeled as water sloshed against her chest. The cold lake heightened her senses. "You can't help him." Daniela turned her back to Emmaline and prayed, "Yahweh, protect him. Give my oily boy the courage to find safety. In Yeshua's name, amen."

"You keep calling him oily boy instead of the poet." Emmaline stood by her friend.

"Oily boy fits him—for now. And I'm fine praying for him as he is. No need to force someone to become who we want them to become."

"Can you accept me as I am?"

"Maybe . . . in time."

"Regarding him as oily boy, could you quench his hellish fire and fall in love with him?"

"I don't know."

"If you can fight the devil and win, you can fight for oily boy and for us." Emmaline failed at hiding her concern. "The world's hardly worth saving if no man on Earth melts your heart. Or no friend irks you with her mistakes." She finished bathing.

Was oily boy real, or had Daniela completely lost her ever-lovin' schizophrenic mind? And who was Emmaline to basically demand forgiveness? What a drama queen! Daniela's heart begged for him to be real. Her soul wept, wishing that Emmaline had never lied to her.

But ever the practical girl, she couldn't help but think that he couldn't be real—he *shouldn't* be real.

Because the girl he was destined to love had been cursed with nosebleeds, a broken brain, and brown skin. Though she had come to love her birthday suit, she knew not everyone did. For Daniela, saving the world seemed easier than loving herself.

A wolf's howl pierced the stillness.

"Danny."

"What?"

"Don't around turn too fast . . . but look behind you." Emmaline pointed over Daniela's shoulder. The wolf's plaintive howl disturbed the silence, again.

Daniela looked over her shoulder. Head held high in the air and mouth agape, the she-wolf cried again.

Immediately, the archer recognized the head markings. "She's breathtaking, Limy."

The she-wolf howled again and again. "Coming to say

goodbye?" Slicked with soap, Daniela waded back toward the shoreline, allowing the cold lake water to cleanse her.

Quietly, the she-wolf waited as Daniela rinsed the remaining soap from her skin. Teeth chattering, she tiptoed from the water and wrapped her bruised body within her towel. "Where's your cub, momma?"

"Dead." Emmaline shouted from behind, then dived beneath the water and swam toward the shore before resurfacing.

"How?"

"Robert killed her cub the night you dreamed and travelled." As Emmaline approached, the she-wolf bared her teeth and raised her hackles. A bark salted with a vicious growl warned Emmaline to stay put.

"Stay back, Limy!" Daniela inched toward the angry mother.

The she-wolf backed away from Daniela's approach. "I'm sorry. I'm so sorry."

Wrapped in a towel, the powerful warrior took a knee, bowed her head, and waited for whatever punishment would come from the wild animal.

The she-wolf sniffed the air, pawed the ground, then cautiously approached.

Nose touching Daniela's nose, the anguished mother peeled back her lips, showing off her white teeth. The bite of a gray wolf could break the leg of its prey. What could it do to a human neck?

Would the she-wolf force Daniela to pay for the sins of another?

She whispered a prayer of acknowledgment: "The whole creation groans. We humans have poisoned your world because we insist on playing God through wars, oppression, and distorting Yahweh's creation. One day, if I fail to stop Lucifer's pandemic—an imitation of Yahweh's *good* pandemic—humans will be scrubbed clean from Earth."

The she-wolf howled.

"Maybe my failure would serve you, and the rest of creation, best."

The she-wolf tilted her head back and cried something pitiful. Daniela had acknowledged her pain. Now, validated and emptied of the rawness of her sorrow, the gray wolf pressed her muzzle into Daniela's chest, nudging her and forcing the Orphan Dreamer to stand.

After Daniela stood up, the powerful canine launched upward and kissed her cub's rescuer on the mouth before falling into her arms. The Orphan Dreamer embraced her kindred spirit—Lozen's spirit.

"That's no Judas kiss." Daniela grinned from ear-to-ear. The gray wolf mouthed a half-bark and half-howl. Daniela released her fury friend. "God speed to you, Lozen's spirit. Until the day when humans no longer murder wolf cubs, and the wolf grazes with the lamb . . ."

The cubless mother charged into the dense forest of the Jemez Mountains and then disappeared . . . maybe forever.

Daniela blew a kiss in the direction of the canine. "I give you all the love in the world, my kindred spirit—the truest and bravest Lozen of the wild."

Shivering, the Orphan Dreamer cried as she entered their tent, and Emmaline followed.

Closer to the fire, the nylon home was surprisingly warm. Emmaline dried off, slipped on her underclothes, then threw a woolen blanket around her shoulders. The two sat on their respective sleeping bags, allowing the fire to warm them.

"What did the wolf say?"

"Do you believe that I can hear the animals speak now?"

"You told me you could, and I know that you would never lie to me, Danny-girl—our Orphan Dreamer. Deception is not your vice. It's mine. And I'm a pathetic little liar. Speaking with a forked tongue runs in my DNA."

"Sin runs in all of our DNA, manifesting in different ways. The first step of freedom is repentance—acknowledging, stopping, then turning away from our bad habits. Mine is negative thinking and negative speech patterns. I'm going to practice speaking more edifying words, Limy."

"Okay, and I'm sorry for deceiving you."

"Forgiven." Daniela glanced over her shoulder. "Lozen's spirit lives inside that gray wolf. I'm sure of it."

"Breathtaking observation. So we did meet our hero, the Apache warrior princess."

"Indeed, and she thanked me for rescuing her only cub, and then refused to snap my neck or dive into the lake and drown you."

"Her cub's death wasn't your fault. The guilty verdict falls on Robert and me."

"Had I not travelled, I could have—and I would have—fought to the death to save her baby girl." Daniela gazed into Emmaline's eyes. "She gifted us both a second chance. That's mercy. And without a gun to match yours and Robert's, I may have been killed during the skirmish, eliminating my ability to fulfill my ultimate mission. That's God's mercy—a second chance. And like oxygen, we all need it."

"Thank you." Emmaline hugged Daniela. After a few seconds, she pushed from her embrace, hooked her pinky finger into Daniela's good one, and said, "I want—no—I need to tell you everything." Was Emmaline going to lie to Daniela again?

"Please do."

"Last night, the she-wolf and her cub charged Robert.

He was carrying your limp body out of our tent, planning to kidnap you and take you to the lair of the Sons of Venus where tormentors would torture you until you told them everything."

"About what, the cave drawings?" Her heart pounded something fierce.

"Interested but no cigar."

"The statue, a.k.a. the Skeleton Key?" Daniela stepped away from her only friend.

"Important in time. But first they wanted to learn details about your oily boy—where he lives, what he looks like, and what makes him tick."

"Why? He's just an orphan."

"The Sons of Venus require a leader . . . a six-six-six, an antichrist so riddled with hatred against his fellow man that he'd escalate everything and take any action that would eradicate humans: plagues, natural disasters, wars, genocide—annihilating the human pack—the family."

"Where chaos exists, order will be required." The Orphan Dreamer rubbed her temples, massaging away a migraine.

"True. And the Sons of Venus would be lurking in the shadows as their antichrist stirs up chaos, waiting to bring order tainted with the end goal of world domination. The politics of their movement is a mix between communistic socialism and national socialism, and America lies downwind of their political sights. For weeks now, I've heard my dad talk about the hive."

"What's the hive?"

"A place where the socialist elite will hide while their antichrist stirs up trouble, and Earth has been scrubbed clean of the regulars—the disposable humans."

"You knew all this when you befriended me?"

"Yes, but I wasn't expecting to fall in platonic love with you."

"I walked into a trap." Daniela wagged her head, then slammed her fist into her left palm.

"More like a ruse, and I'm sorry." Emmaline moved closer to Daniela, but the dreamer inched away. "It's true. The Sons of Venus will start your pandemic but not until they secure their leader—six-six-six, your holy book's anti-christ."

"And you would have helped them make this happen?" Daniela glared into Emmaline's eyes.

"Then, but not now—and not ever again. Please believe me, and in time, forgive me," Emmaline begged. But Daniela made her wait for an answer until she could gift forgiveness honestly and permanently.

The she-wolf had told Daniela to give humanity a second chance. And Yeshua had said to forgive as she had been forgiven.

Human actions and reactions—including the Orphan Dreamer's—sucked most of the time. So she surrendered to her Father. "I forgive you, Emmaline Darbyshire."

"Let me make up for my betrayal, Danny-girl."

"How?"

"You need a set of ears and eyes seeing and listening in high society's low places. You require a mole inside the Sons of Venus."

"If they're my enemy or an enemy of our cause, you'd be correct." Daniela uncrossed her arms.

"Maybe Wisdom sent me to your side. Let me become that mole, acting as though I'm their ally."

"It's a deceitful proposition, though."

"That's why you're not cut out for the job, but I am."

"Be careful, Limy."

"Always. And if you do nothing else based on our conversation, don't talk yourself out of loving oily boy, fighting for, and protecting him. He needs you. The Sons of Venus are bad apples." Emmaline inched closer toward her friend. Daniela stood still.

"And I need you."

"Thanks, Danny-girl."

"Because I've never met oily boy. And until I can test his character, all possibilities must remain on the table. Maybe oily boy was the tornado starter's human agent—a Nephilim, a descendant of a Watcher."

"So you think oily boy is a Nephilim? And that his father or mother was as well?" Emmaline said as the ominous accusation hung between the pair. "Then that would complicate things." A rosy hue returned to her pale, freckled cheeks. "Your complicated brain." Inside their tent, Emmaline removed her towel, then donned her T-shirt, socks, and sweatpants. "Does your brain ever choose the simple option?"

"I thought I'd chosen the simple option."

"No, you haven't." Emmaline's lips softened into a smile, parting as a belly laugh reached her throat.

"What? What's so funny?"

"You are. You're thinking on the same lines as the Sons of Venus. They hope that your oily boy comes from Nomed's bloodline, making your oily boy a Nephilim, one of theirs."

"I'm not like them." Daniela packed her backpack.

"I know. Your motives lie one hundred and eighty degrees apart, but your conclusions remain on the same x-axis."

Motives.

The separation between evil intentions and good intentions.

"What should I do?" Daniela paused.

"I wouldn't worry about who oily boy is or who he may become."

"I can't ignore the possibility," Daniela protested. "Denial defies my ethical compass."

"If your God is real, then shouldn't your prayers contain enough power to shift Satan's intended destiny for the orphan into a more positive outcome? Remember, 'Faith is the substance of things hoped for, the evidence of things not seen.' " Emmaline recited a frequently quoted Bible verse. Daniela tilted her head, and Emmaline defended her churchy Bible trivia. "I learned the verse during Methodist church."

"You're right, Limes."

"If your prayers fail and oily boy grows up into Satan's human agent, your love story—the journey of a virgin and a megalomaniac killer—would go down in the history books as the greatest love story ever told. Another *Phantom of the Opera*. A man who makes you bleed for him."

"You mean sing for him." Shock dimmed Daniela's smile. "The antichrist, Satan's human agent, isn't a vampire. He's the descendant of a Nephilim."

"Maybe not a vampire, but if he is a Nephilim . . . well, I'm coming clean. At our loft, I borrowed your Book of Enoch. I read it, so I know a bit about Nephilim."

"I would've allowed you to borrow the book. But share with me what you learned. Can we break down camp while we chat? I'm ready to go home."

"Let's do it."

After dressing, Daniela tore down the tent with military

precision while Emmaline gathered the rest of the camping gear.

"Watchers. That's what the Book of Enoch called the fallen angels who rebelled against Yahweh. They were giant, five-hundred-feet-tall warriors," Emmaline said as she snuffed out their campfire. "Imagine a human woman making love to that."

"Goodness, Limy!" Daniela's breasts seemed to turn inward and run as her ovaries went on strike. She folded the tent and stuffed it inside a tote.

"You should know that members of the Sons of Venus believe the Bible's Nephilim were probably corroborated by Greek mythology, or rather, Greek mythology corroborated the biblical account of Nephilim."

"You believe the Olympians were actually Nephilim?" Loaded down with an armful of supplies, both girls loaded the Jeep. Daniela stopped packing the trunk.

"My dad believes that."

"Your dad. Interesting. Let me find something . . ." Daniela sat on the ledge of the Jeep's trunk, removed her Bible from her backpack, and scanned the concordance, looking for the word *Nephilim.*

Daniela flipped to Genesis and read some verses from chapter six to Emmaline:

> "When human beings began to increase in number on the earth and daughters were born to them, the sons of God saw that the daughters of humans were beautiful, and they married any of them they chose.
>
> The Nephilim were on the earth in those days—and also afterward—when the sons of

God went to the daughters of humans and had children by them. They were the heroes of old, men of renown.

The Lord saw how great the wickedness of the human race had become on the earth, and that every inclination of the thoughts of the human heart was only evil all the time. The Lord regretted that he had made human beings on the earth, and his heart was deeply troubled. But Noah found favor in the eyes of the Lord.

So God said to Noah, 'I am going to bring floodwaters on the earth to destroy all life under the heavens, every creature that has the breath of life in it. Everything on earth will perish. But I will establish my covenant with you, and you will enter the ark—you and your sons and your wife and your sons' wives with you (NIV).' "

"According to Genesis, the sons of God—fallen angels—fathered Nephilim. Then, according to the Book of Enoch, the Watchers fathered Nephilim—human half-breeds." Daniela summarized. "Fallen angels. The Watchers. They are the same thing. These creatures lured humans into dabbling in the dark magic of demons, corrupting humanity, angering Yahweh, and thus inciting Noah's flood."

"If your Noah's flood was real, how could oily boy be a Nephilim?

"What do you mean?"

"According to what you just read, nothing, including the Nephilim, survived."

"Hold on a second." Daniela turned to Genesis, chapter seven. "Scholars teach that Noah's flood wiped out every single creature—except for the animals brought into the ark and the Hebrew patriarch, Noah, and his immediate family. But is that what the Bible actually says?" Daniela shared a passage with Emmaline.

> "All the living things on earth died—birds, domestic animals, wild animals, small animals that scurry along the ground, and all the people.
>
> Everything that breathed and lived on dry land died. God wiped out every living thing on the earth—people, livestock, small animals that scurry along the ground, and the birds of the sky. All were destroyed. The only people who survived were Noah and those with him in the boat (NLT)."

"That's it!" Daniela shut her Bible and placed it on the passenger seat. "And this is why a person seeking truth must read the Bible for themselves."

"English, please." Emmaline returned to camp with Daniela in tow.

"The Genesis account said all the living things on Earth . . . small animals that scurry along the ground, and all people. Everything that breathed and lived on *dry* land died."

"What about the fish?"

"They survived." Daniela grabbed Emmaline's arm.

"That means Leviathan—the Hebrew patriarch, Job's sea monster—survived as well."

"Holy smokes, Preacher-girl."

"And this is how Wisdom helps her girls solve ancient puzzles. She illuminates our path by helping us understand God's letter to humanity, the Bible—still the best-selling book of all times."

"You go, girlfriend Wisdom!" Emmaline pirouetted. Daniela clapped. "So, Danny . . ." Emmaline caught her breath. "In Greek mythology, many sea gods and sea goddesses existed, but they were ruled by the sea king—Poseidon—and his queen—Amphitrite. How did Job describe his sea monster, Leviathan?"

"You're really asking if Poseidon and Leviathan are the same creature?"

"I am." Emmaline hip bumped Daniela.

"Tonight, read Job, chapter forty-one." Daniela and Emmaline each grabbed a handle of their cooler and carried it back to the Jeep. "The imagery will terrify you. And, yes, maybe this description could solidify the connection between the Greek gods and the Bible's Nephilim, particularly Poseidon and Leviathan."

"There's another alternative to one of your Nephilim, a.k.a. Leviathan, surviving a worldwide deluge," Emmaline said. "One of Noah's unnamed daughters or one of his daughters-in-law could have entered her father's ark pregnant with a second-generation seed of a fallen angel—a Watcher, a son of God."

"The Bible doesn't refute that possibility." After returning to camp, Daniela folded up their Coleman stove and grabbed the bag loaded with their dirty clothes.

"And?"

"We may never know how a Nephilim could have

survived into the twentieth century, but I think that we can conclude there is a ninety-nine percent chance that a few of them survived by hiding in the sea or a human womb."

"Crikey creepy!" Emmaline snapped a few photographs, and Daniela shot her an odd look. "Making a few memories. That's all."

"Okay." Arms full, Daniela led the way back to the Jeep. "We absolutely know something evil—according to you, the Sons of Venus—plans to start a worldwide pandemic and attempt to murder all of humanity. Could a plain-Jane human commit such an act?" Daniela defended her fellow humans, hoping and praying that no human could behave one hundred times worse than Mao, the Muslim Turkish government that initiated the Christian Armenian holocaust, or Idi Amin—the butcher of Uganda.

Please, Yahweh. Don't allow one of us to be this evil.

"Maybe Temujin—whoever he or she is—will help us answer your question before the Sons of Venus recruit your oily boy from your dreamworld and declare him as their future leader."

"They'll have to go through me before they get to my oily boy." Daniela slung two bags into the back seat and then took a fighting stance, fists up, her body slightly angled.

"Ali—the girl version."

"Not in a million lifetimes!" Daniela resigned herself to the possibility of hope. "But I'm even more certain that there will be two pandemics when Earth starts spinning on her last leg—one we need to stop, and one that we can't and shouldn't stop."

"A good pandemic? Pandemics kill. Miss Lifesaver, you're confusing me."

"What if the Rapture, the Great Escape, looks like a pandemic, where millions or even billions of people suddenly die? But in reality, they will have transitioned into another dimension—Yahweh's realm—because their spirits had been called up from their bodies and taken to heaven? 'In a moment, in the twinkling of an eye . . .' " Daniela recalled the Apostle Paul's prophetic declaration about the Great Escape from Earth's gravitational pull. "The people left behind would lose their marbles."

"More than that!" Emmaline stopped in her tracks while heading back to camp to retrieve the last of their gear. "But if a good pandemic—the Rapture, as you call it—will occur sometime in the future, how will we tell the difference between the *good* pandemic and the *bad* pandemic?"

"Most likely, the Rapture, Yeshua's return for His church, will happen around Rosh Hashanah, at the time when the age of the gentile followers of the Way has been fulfilled and He has finished preparing His bride's forever-home."

After arriving back at camp, Emmaline leaned into Daniela and wrapped her arm around her friend's waist. "In one camping trip, we've solved two mysteries: a cipher painted by Robert inside a random cave, that the Sons of Venus will at least help the unknown *who* start the pandemic, and the fact that Yeshua may also instigate his own pandemic in the form of the Rapture—the Great Escape—then take his bride—the followers of the Way—to their forever-home." Emmaline ruminated about Rosh Hashanah. "Yeshua is a hopeless romantic . . . we could get along someday."

"He's not really into dating human girls." Daniela wagged her head and then rested it on Emmaline's slender shoulder. "Forget finding the person who will start the bad pandemic, I need to find you a husband and quell your raging hormonal sea."

"When will you have time?"

"I'll make time." Daniela chided while taking in the last bits of the scenery—their place, a place where they both agreed to become best friends. "That's what friends do."

"I'm so proud of you. You're going to medical school—"

"Haven't been accepted yet." Daniela pulled away from Emmaline's tug.

"You will be. You were created to serve the sick as their empathetic physician—you feel the pain of others, remember—all the while launching on a quest to find your oily boy and protect him from the Sons of Venus."

"I'm proud of you too." The Orphan Dreamer started the slog back to the parking lot. "Well on your way to earning your master's degree, then a PhD at MIT in biological engineering, and onward to beach a Navy SEAL. And you're right—we won't have that much time to date, much less solve the mystery of who will start the bad pandemic."

"You mean sleep. We definitely will make time to date hot guys even after you've been accepted into University of Florida's College of Medicine's Junior Honors Program." Emmaline changed gears as she clicked the key fob, unlocking the passenger and driver doors. "My mom attended Methodist church when she was a kid, and like you, she prays a lot. She always says that no one can know when Jesus will return." Moments later, Emmaline navigated up the road onto the main highway.

"She's referring to a New Testament passage when Yeshua said, 'But of that day and hour knows no man, no, not the angels of heaven, but my Father only.' "

"If you believe the Bible is true, that verse debunks

your whole mission of figuring out when this pandemic happens and who starts it, much less how and why."

"The English translation doesn't take into the account a Jewish idiom, which some believe could reveal more about that timing."

"Idioms. Sort of like . . . that Birkin bag cost me an arm and a leg, meaning the bag was expensive, not that I became an amputee in exchange for a gorgeous bag?"

"Yep." Daniela giggled.

"Spill the beans."

"Rosh Hashanah begins on the first day of a new lunar cycle. No ancient sky watcher could determine the beginning of the lunar cycle until a sliver of the new moon appeared in the sky," Daniela said. "So no one could know the *exact* day or hour Rosh Hashanah would start."

"Okay. I'll buy that."

"But not knowing the day or the hour doesn't mean that an astute Bible student couldn't know the year, month, or week of Yeshua's return or even the season that the antichrist will be revealed. A disciple of Yeshua wrote a letter to the early Christian church: 'And it shall come to pass in the last days, says God . . . I will show wonders in heaven above and signs in the earth beneath—blood and fire and vapor of smoke. The sun shall be turned into darkness, and the moon into blood, before the coming of the great and awesome day of the Lord.' "

"Sun turning to darkness is a solar eclipse, and your blood moons are a lunar eclipse," Emmaline concluded. "And vapor of smoke may be due to wildfires?"

"Bingo!"

Emmaline shook her head. "I need to see this stuff written down."

"I wrote more details about the Jewish feast days in one

of my journals that I left at my parents' house. I'll mail you a copy when I get back to Florida."

"What would my life have amounted to if I hadn't met you, Daniela Rose Cavanaugh?"

"Beautifully normal." They both giggled, and Daniela said, "I'm loving the idea of getting home to our loft and taking a warm shower."

"Ditto."

Daniela lay her head against the headrest and closed her eyes. "A kindred friendship feels like a seatbelt—slightly tethering, but safe and secure."

"Don't forget after we return to the lab this afternoon, observe Li Xiu. She's up to something. I just know it. If we can stop her, maybe we can stop this pandemic from ever happening."

"Between a foiled kidnapping, solving a cipher, and learning that some creep named Robert slaughtered a cub wolf that I rescued, I'd totally forgotten about our mentor. Duly noted. But why Li Xiu? I've never seen her steal anything."

"You weren't looking for her sticky fingers." Emmaline cleared her throat. "But I was . . . after I eavesdropped."

"Okay?"

"Back home, I placed a recording device and microphone inside the picture frame of a photograph of Mom and me that sits on my dad's desk."

"A bit dramatic."

"Sometimes the situation calls for dramatic. My efforts paid off. Because I learned that a scientist at LANL by the name of Li Xiu is a spy from China who works for the Sons of Venus. The science division is working with various labs to produce a virus that mimics the common cold but turns deadly inside the host after a week or so."

"But—"

"That's not all. The virology is being mapped to target certain people—people with significant African DNA—you, Danny Rose."

"Why?"

"The Sons of Venus believed that the Orphan Dreamer would look like a Swiss model: tall, skinny, blonde, and blue eyes. Then I told my dad that you were the Orphan Dreamer, so they're making a virus that targets people like you."

"Like we need any more systemic oppression?"

"I'm trying to be honest."

"Noted and appreciated. Also understood that because Li Xiu is a Chinese national, your Sons of Venus is not a domestic secret society. It is an international one."

"Aimed at creating a one-world government. So here's to a lifetime of exploration." Emmaline squeezed Daniela's knee, then turned east and headed to Los Alamos—the nerdy town that whispered wealth.

Emmaline's cell phone rang. "Grab my cell out of its case in the glove compartment, please." Daniela handed her the phone. "Hey, Dad. No. Danny Rose and I left the campsite and are heading back to the apartment." Emmaline paused and glanced at her friend. "She's gorgeous, nice, and smart . . . Dad, I can't talk about that right now. I'm driving. Okay. Love you."

"Is your dad checking up on you—or me?" Daniela put the phone back into its case.

"You." Emmaline shrugged. "You asked, and I promised to tell the truth." Friendships. Secrets, but no lies.

"That's creepy. I guess he wasn't too pleased to learn that I hadn't been kidnapped."

"Nope. He'll take it out on someone in Boston. Glad

I'm not there, but I'm sorry for my mom. Sometimes he's actually harmless when he's not snorting the white stuff."

"White stuff?"

"Cocaine."

"Oh! Cokehead or not, he's MI6. By definition, he's not harmless, Limy."

"True." Emmaline drove in silence for a while. "You're different, and he's interested, and not just because of oily boy." She glanced away from the road, then back at Daniela.

"What?" Daniela crinkled her forehead. "I know that look."

"I mean, why would the Creator of the Universe choose an introverted, black teenage girl from the wrong side of the tracks to become the Orphan Dreamer and save the world? Why not a European political power player?"

"It's His m.o.," Daniela replied, and Emmaline furrowed her brow. "I didn't say it. He did: 'But God chose what the world considers nonsense to put wise people to shame. God chose what the world considers weak to put what is strong to shame.' "

"Your God is a complete gangster—an OG, the original, and doesn't care what anyone thinks."

"That's one way to put it. Listen to this." Daniela loaded a CD into the car's player and played "The Champion" followed by "Addicted to Jesus," a rap by a Christian artist, Carmen. "Know this. Ever since I was a little girl, I've always wanted to be ordinary and accepted, but I'm warming to the idea of facing my reality."

"Freaks and aliens need friends too. So know this—I'm your friend because I trust you, and I like you." Emmaline's satellite phone rang.

"Can I trust you, Limy?"

"Yes." She pointed to the phone. "Answer it. It's probably your mom calling to solve the mystery of Temujin."

"You're right. I gave her the number." Daniela answered the phone. "Mom, thanks for calling me back. Can't wait to eat a plateful of your jalapeno cornbread in a few weeks." She inserted earbuds into the satellite phone's jack, then slipped one bud into her left ear and the other into Emmaline's right ear.

"The skillets are greased and the stove's hot," Mrs. Cavanaugh said. "I'm calling to tell you the identity of Temujin, but first, why do you want to know?"

"Limy and I found some Native American cave markings that we believe represent a simple alpha-numeric cipher." Daniela omitted the small detail that the cave drawing had simply been copied from a photograph. "If so, we solved an ancient puzzle."

"That makes sense. New Mexico cave art. Apache Indians. Some historians believe that North American's indigenous population shares DNA with Mongolians, so there is a connection between North America and Mongolia. Temujin is Genghis Khan—Mongolia's ancient great leader."

"You're kidding me!"

"No need for jokes. I'm sure this satellite call isn't cheap."

It's okay, Emmaline mouthed without uttering a sound.

"One of the cave drawings replicated the Ark of the Covenant," Daniela blurted out. "Why would an Apache draw a Jewish artifact and four lunar eclipses on a back-country cave?"

"It's all coming together, Daniela. Genghis Khan had six wives and over five hundred concubines. Geneticists believe that sixteen million men are descendants of Temujin, making him one of the most genetically prolific rulers in history. In addition to sharing Mongolian DNA, some historians believe that North America's indigenous population may share recent DNA with the lost tribes of Israel."

"The lost tribes of Israel. So cool, Mom! I'm part Mongolian . . . so . . . are we related to the ancient tribes of Israel?" Daniela's mind filled with ideas and questions.

"Maybe. But given the possible recent cultural association, maybe these lost tribes passed down stories to their children, and an Apache simply drew an image of what she was told?"

"So if the lost tribes of Israel are somehow genetically linked with the Native Americans and the Mongolians . . . . Mom, do you think that means the Ark of the Covenant is hidden inside Genghis Khan's lost tomb?" The question rolled off Daniela's tongue before she could stop it.

"Daniela Rose, I wish your father hadn't pumped your head full of Indiana Jones misadventures. I have no clue what Genghis Khan's tomb contains or where to find it. What I do know is that I can't replace you, so stay safe."

"You know that I don't control my dreams or where I travel."

"You can control when you travel."

"I travel when I'm compelled to do so."

"Don't be spicy."

"Yes, ma'am." Daniela paused and gnawed her lip. "One more thing, Mom . . . Professor Jakob, Ethan's uncle, I think he mailed me a statue. It's heavy—super heavy—and it looks like it was fashioned with real precious metals."

"Describe it to me."

"Head made of pure gold, chest and arms of silver, belly and thighs of bronze, legs of iron, and feet made of part iron and part baked clay."

"That's easy. The statue replicates the prophet Daniel's interpretation of King Nebuchadnezzar's vision—about the rise and fall of the last remaining kingdoms. The first kingdom represented in the statue was ancient Babylon. After human kingdoms end, Yeshua will set up His earthly kingdom."

"Hold on, Mom." Daniela retrieved the professor's letter from her hiking pack.

My Darling Rosebud,

I need your help.

The statue I hope is the key that solves the mystery of who? The Watchers are still watching. But know this: the Jordan River is a special place—it is the original Area 51. Read Yehoshua 3:11-17.

On a personal note, the Skeleton Key—the statue—I hope will also lead you to your heartsong.

B'shalom,
Professor Jakob
Director of Israel Antiquities Authority

She scanned the letter again and realized that it matched. She hadn't noticed that detail before.

The lithographic statue located above the professor's signature line matched the object that she held in her hand. She reread the last line of the letter: "On a personal note, the Skeleton Key—the statue—I hope will also lead you to your heartsong." But who was her heartsong?

"Mom, this relic could be worth millions."

"If the metal is real, Daniela. But who ships an ancient relic constructed of expensive metals via the US postal service?"

"FedEx," she said, as she thought about how unusual the delivery was. But the delivery of the Glass Tattoo had been unusual too. *Me and unsolicited packages.*

"Doesn't matter. The insurance to ship something like that would cost more than your medical school tuition. Besides, how would a metallurgist fuse these metals together? The statue isn't made of precious metals. Which begs the next question: why does the statue weigh so much?"

"I don't know."

"Don't throw in the towel so quickly. Think, Daniela Rose."

"The statue contains something heavy on the inside." Daniela shook the statue—its innards moved like weighted liquid.

"Good job."

"Goodness gumdrops, Mom! You're a genius. Wait until I tell Dad!"

"In the meantime, read Daniel 2:31-45. You girls stay safe. Daniela, I have a surprise waiting for you—"

"Don't tease me, Mom. That's not fair. Tell me."

"It'll keep. Study and work hard at the lab. Then come back to your father and me in one piece. I love you, darling."

"Love you, Mom." Daniela ended the call, retrieved her Bible, and eagerly turned to the Daniel 2 passage.

"Did your parents name you after Daniel?" Emmaline asked.

"They did. He was a dreamer and a Hebrew prophet, a contemporary of Ezekiel." She read Daniel's interpretation of King Nebuchadnezzar's dream to herself.

> You, O king were looking, and behold, [there was] a single great statue . . . As for this statue, its head was made of fine gold, its breast and its arms of silver, its belly and its thighs of bronze, its legs of iron, its feet partly of iron and partly of clay [pottery] . . .

> This was the dream; now we will tell the king its interpretation, [Daniel said], You [king of Babylon] are the head of gold. After you will arise another kingdom [Medo-Persia] inferior to you, and then a third kingdom of bronze [Greece under Alexander the Great], which will rule over all the earth.

> Then a fourth kingdom [Rome] will be strong as iron, for iron breaks to pieces and shatters all things; and like iron which crushes things in pieces, it will break and crush all these [others].

> And as you saw the feet and toes, partly of potter's clay and partly of iron, it will be a divided kingdom; but there will be in it some of the durability and strength of iron, just as you saw the iron mixed with common clay. . .

> In the days of those [final ten] kings, the God
> of Heaven will set up a kingdom that will
> never be destroyed, nor will its sovereignty be
> left for another people; but it will crush and
> put an end to all these kingdoms, and it will
> stand forever.
>
> Just as you saw that a stone was cut out of the
> mountain without hands and that it crushed
> the iron, the bronze, the clay, the silver, and
> the gold, the great God has revealed to the
> king what will take place in the future; so the
> dream is true and its interpretation is trust-
> worthy (AMP).

Daniela said, "In summary, the gold head represented Babylon. Silver, the Medes and the Persians. Bronze, the Greeks. And iron, Rome. Bottom line: all of these king-doms have risen and fallen, except for the kingdom rep-resented by the iron-and-clay feet and toes. And before a divine kingdom rises, represented by a rock *not* made with human hands, the final human kingdom rules."

"What's the final kingdom—the one with feet and toes made of iron and clay?"

"According to this passage," Daniela said scanning the ancient text again, "we've established that iron represents the Roman Empire, so somehow the influence of Rome continues into the iron and clay feet of King Nebuchad-nezzar's statue."

Daniela rubbed her left earlobe.

"What is it, Danny-girl?"

"Give me a sec." Daniela opened one of her old journals

and flipped to the middle. "Because of World War II, everyone knows about the Third Reich of Germany."

"Reich simply means an empire or a realm," Emmaline added, removing one hand from the steering wheel.

"If Nazi Germany was Europe's post Roman-empire Third Reich . . . there must be a First Reich and a Second Reich, correct?"

"Seems logical."

"Jiminy Cricket, here it is!"

"Cough it up—don't keep me in suspense."

"Adolf Hitler perceived that his Reich was the successor of the Second Reich that existed from 1871 AD to 1918 AD, and that the Second Reich had followed the First Reich—the Holy Roman Empire, which existed from 800 AD to 1806 AD."

"So the iron in the feet and toes of Daniel's statue represents a new Rome—the Fourth Reich?" Emmaline gasped.

"The last reincarnation of a Germanic-Roman Catholic empire, with a twist!" Daniela exclaimed.

"That's scary." Emmaline almost swerved off the highway.

"Don't kill us!"

"It's better than dying in a Nazi concentration camp or burning at an inquisitor's fiery stake!" She blew a forceful breath through her mouth. "I'm terrified of the answer, but tell me—which modern-day empire do you believe is represented by the iron in the feet and toes of Daniel's statue?"

"I'm thinking the European Union is the parent of this divided European kingdom." Daniela flipped to the corresponding passage and read, " 'And as you saw the feet and toes, partly of potter's clay and partly of iron, it will be a divided kingdom.' "

"Last semester I studied European history and learned that from 768 to 800 AD, Charlemagne—Charles the Great—was considered the founder of Western culture. The Franks named him the Holy Roman Emperor. During the beginning of his reign, he ruled over a divided European empire torn apart by war. He united Europe after so many bloody wars, serving as the founding father of the predecessor of the European Union."

"Does anyone venerate him, suggesting that someone who lives somewhere thinks this guy, Charlemagne, was important?" Daniela asked.

"Yes. Since 1950, in a little town called Aachen—the Rome of the North—Germans have awarded the International Charlemagne Prize of the City of Aachen to an individual deemed to have made an outstanding contribution to European unity."

"Who has won the prize so far?"

"Winston Churchill. Roman Herzog. Henry Kissinger. The European Commission. And many more," Emmaline ticked off the names.

"Heavy hitters." Daniela focused on her historian friend.

"You bet. According to the late German chancellor Helmut Kohl, the Charlemagne Prize is the most important honor Europe can bestow. So we think the iron is connected to the European Union . . . what kingdom is represented by the clay?" Emmaline passed a slower moving car. "Clay. Clay," Emmaline repeated the word as though the verbal cue would shake an answer out of Daniela. "Iron and clay don't mix."

"What are you thinking, Limy?"

"That's the million-dollar question."

Daniela adjusted her seatbelt, then sat crisscross-apple-sauce. "What about Arabic nations dominated by Islam? Some preacher once said that clay pots represent the fragility of human nature and also the desert."

"Because of the clay representing the desert? Sounds plausible," Emmaline agreed.

"Even if the empire following Rome's iron legs is a Germanic-Catholic—the iron—and Arabic-Islamic—the clay—amalgamation, the nucleus of Rome—the Vatican—will retain her religious influence according to the Apostle John's writing in the Book of Revelation. And lest we forget, Christianity and Islam are both Abrahamic, monotheistic religions."

"Doesn't mean they possess the same motives and the same end goal," Emmaline protested.

"True. What I meant is that they are similar, but not the same. Two different deities set them at odds with each other from the start." Daniela brushed lake water silt from her skin, longing for a hot shower. "I'm confident that the last kingdom represented by clay and iron feet and toes is somehow the Fourth Reich. Regarding the religious side of this political-religious world government, we know the message of the New Testament answers the question of its parent religion, Judaism: Who is the Messiah?"

"Yeshua?" Emmaline half-asked and half-stated.

"Yep."

"But Orthodox Jewish worshipers don't accept that answer." Emmaline punched the gas pedal, rocketing them down the long stretch of empty highway. She cracked the window, allowing a stream of cold air to circulate inside the Jeep.

"I know, and Yeshua's Apostle John explained in John

12:37-43 why Yeshua's Jewish community didn't accept His divinity."

> "But despite all the miraculous signs Jesus had done, most of the people still did not believe in him. This is exactly what Isaiah the prophet had predicted: "Lord, who has believed our message? To whom has the Lord revealed his powerful arm?
>
> But the people couldn't believe, for as Isaiah also said, 'The Lord has blinded their eyes and hardened their hearts—so that their eyes cannot see, and their hearts cannot understand, and they cannot turn to me and have me heal them.'
>
> Isaiah was referring to Jesus when he said this, because he saw the future and spoke of the Messiah's glory.
>
> Many people did believe in him, however, including some of the Jewish leaders. But they wouldn't admit it for fear that the Pharisees would expel them from the synagogue. For they loved human praise more than the praise of God."

"Motives. Sticky little things." Daniela closed her Bible.

"The powerful Jewish leaders of Jesus's day didn't want to lose their position. Instead, they chose to lose their souls," Emmaline offered.

"If you want to annoy a group of Pharisees, that's one

way to summarize John's letter. But if we're right about the feet of clay in Daniel's statue representing Arabic kingdoms and Islam, what was the purpose of introducing the world to a new Abrahamic religion, Islam, six hundred years *after* Yeshua came to Earth? Islam was late to the proverbial party."

"I don't know." Emmaline parked the Jeep at their Los Alamos apartment complex.

"We know the secular messiah—the antichrist, six-six-six—will promise power, money, and earthly success. That's in contrast to the motives of the real Messiah—the Christ—who promises eternal life. Blessed are the poor and spirit, etcetera."

"Maybe some religious people aren't into the poverty vow of your Yeshua."

"He doesn't require poverty, but He doesn't shun those who are poor." Daniela recalled an unanswered question. "Three Abrahamic religions: Judaism, Christianity, and Islam. For some, Christianity identifies the Messiah of its parent religion, Judaism. What question of Judaism does Islam answer?"

"Nothing. Historically, the Abrahamic religions of Judaism, Islam, and Christianity mix as well as iron and clay." Emmaline got out of the car and opened the trunk to retrieve their camping gear.

"You're wrong, Limy. Islam answers everything."

"Hold that thought—I need to pee."

27—The Orphan

PAST THE THREADBARE CURTAIN OF Cillian's concrete cell, a full moon illuminated the sky.

The orphaned slave had attempted to escape the brothel weeks ago.

Scarface, with the assistance of Bushcroft's dogs, had once again foiled Cillian's plans of escape, catching him, returning him to his concrete hell, then beating him senseless with a wooden baton before stuffing the boy inside a dog cage where he remained for a week. Bugs the size of a hummingbird had crawled acoss his tender flesh, nibbling at his wounds.

Tonight, the dog cage sat at the back of his cell, reminding him not to run for the third time.

Last night, Scarface had inflicted a fresh puncture

wound to Cillian's left hand, ensuring the slave would never play the piano again.

Unconscious for days, Cillian had teetered on the edge of eternity, but Preeti's brother, the camp's doctor, had not given up on Cillian's life or his future, tending him back to a quasi state of health.

Snores erupted from drunken guards. They had no need to remain sober—malnourished boys couldn't run too far. And a runaway slave was entertainment for the guards who relished the fear in a boy's eyes after being captured.

Owls hooted in the distance.

Cillian slipped off his shoes and tied the shoelaces together. He secured them around his neck and snuck from his concrete prison, hovering low to the ground to avoid the rotating spotlight.

Stay three feet behind the light sweep.

He crawled to his destination, slipped the bandage from his left hand, and revealed a map drawn with a black permanent marker by the doctor, Preeti Moorjani's brother.

About an hour later, he rapped on the doorframe of Mrs. Moorjani's shack.

"Woodpecker?"

"Owl." That was the code given to him in the clinic, but was the code still valid these weeks later?

She slipped the curtain aside and pulled him in. "Hurry." Cillian took a full breath for the first time in three years.

"Cillian?" Paul ran to him but turned away midstride to inhale fresh air. "You smell like death."

"I dinna mean to, Paul." Cillian tousled his brother's hair with his uninjured hand.

"For months, Cil, I've begged for you to come to me. To come home."

"Ye'll not be needin' to pray anymore, then. I'm here."

Cillian embraced Paul. His little brother's body tensed, then his shoulders and back muscles relaxed.

"Cil, I'm suffocating." Paul pushed back.

"Sorry."

"Cil, your face . . . what happened?"

Cillian ran his fingers over his cheeks and lip. They hurt. "Nothin'."

"What have they been doing to you?"

"Shh . . . I-I-I got into a fight with one of the other boys."

"Why?" Paul whispered.

"He tried to steal a piece of bread."

"Did you win?"

"Of course!" Cillian gave a one-two bop onto his brother's chest. "Aye—I'm Captain Finnegan Prometheus." He bowed low. "Your Highness, will ye be findin' a place for me in your outlaw nation?"

"You remembered."

"Always." Cillian sat on a rickety wooden stool, and Preeti moved to prepare a small meal for Cillian.

"No. Sit here." Paul patted his mattress. "This is my bed. You'll sleep here." Cillian sat down, and Paul faced his brother. "I know you won, because you're the strongest boy in the universe. But why did you have to fight for food?"

"I'm not much up for answering yer questions."

"It's okay." Paul looked down at Cillian's left hand. He crinkled his nose. Blood soaked the bandage. Paul closed his eyes and folded his hands. "Yahweh, thank you for bringing Cillian back to me. Please heal his hand."

Cillian surveyed the room as though he would find a ghost hiding there. "Yahweh . . . that's who Mama Kelley and Grandma Barry spoke to. You met Him, Paul?"

"Yep."

"How?"

"Mrs. Moorjani introduced me to Him, and we're basically window friends now."

"But I'm still your brother—your favorite. Right?"

"Always and forever."

Preeti tugged Cillian's arm. "Don't delay, child. You must eat. The night holds big plans for you."

"Yahweh will be comin' for a visit, then?" Cillian crinkled his brow.

"He's everywhere, and He showed me His plans last night in my dreams. Eat something hot, child. Strengthen yourself for your journey. Paul, you do the same." She gave both boys a bowl of porridge. "Eat."

Cillian closed his eyes, remembering the hot food served around Grandma Barry's and Mama Kelley's tables. He opened his eyes. Another angel stood in front of him— Preeti Moorjani. He would pay her back one day, but for now, he devoured the hot porridge. "I met your brother at the camp."

"He doesn't want to be there, Cillian." She fidgeted with the edges of her apron.

"I'm not angry wi' him. He helped me." He flashed a genuine smile. "Thank you, for the food and the map."

"Godspeed, my child." She stroked his cheek with her veined, bony hand. After he ate, the old woman slowly traced his face with her fingers.

"Mrs. Moorjani . . ."

"Yes, Paul?"

"You're leaving fingerprints in mud on Cil's face."

She smiled.

"Leave her alone, Paul. We've not seen each other for ages."

Preeti tipped a small bottle upside down onto her hand,

then whisked her spindly fingers across Cillian's forehead and Paul's, transferring oil and mud from Cillian's face to Paul's.

A familiar aroma filled their nostrils as oil drained off the tips of their noses. "Adonai, guide them into their destiny, help them forgive their tormentors, and gift them a supernatural love—Your agape love." Her arthritic hand covered Cillian's heart. She waited, then finally said, "Soften the calluses before bitterness suffocates him. Make his heart big and soft . . . like a stuffed teddy bear." Preeti smiled at the two faces staring at her. "This will be our last meeting, boys."

"I won't leave you." Paul nuzzled into the old woman's frail body.

"You must go before they realize you're missing."

"No." Paul held tighter.

"She's right, Paul. They'll be looking for me. We have to go."

"Where to, Cil?"

"Your destinies," Preeti answered. Her weathered hand gripped Paul's shoulder. Golden-blond curly locks had grown down to his shoulders. "You're a smart boy, Paul, well on your way to finding your pot of gold. You've taught me bravery." She studied both faces. "You're the sons I never gave birth to, but after tonight . . ." Her voice broke, then seemed to surrender to some invisible peace.

"What's wrong, Mrs. M.?" Cillian asked.

"Nothing. I'm happy. Even ready. My legacy is set. I have completed my mission." She retrieved another sheet and laid it across a straw mat. "Yahweh says for you to rest for an hour and then leave."

Cillian directed Paul to his cot. "Lie down and sleep."

Paul studied Cillian's face. "What about you?"

"Dinna be worryin' about me, Paul. I'll be okay." Cillian wrapped his thin arms around his brother, but his embrace released prematurely, strength failing his battered body.

"I do worry, Cil, more than you could possibly know." Paul lay down, then pulled up a blanket over his lean, muscular frame.

"We must rest. I'll let you sleep with my birthday present." He slipped his silver dollar underneath Paul's pillow. "Ye'll dream about somethin' cheery."

"Has it worked for you?"

"No, it hasna worked for me, but yer a different boy . . . a good boy."

Cillian lay on the mat beside Paul and slipped the sheet over his aching body. "Yahweh?" The room remained quiet. "If You're there, Ye'll be takin' us away from this hell. Send us somewhere cold, a place with snow. I'd verra much like a better life for me and my brother. We'll not be givin' Ye any trouble."

A moment later, he added, "The doctor said to go to America, but how?" Silence. "Are Ye listenin' to me, then?"

28—Orphan Dreamer

Friday, June 19, 1998
Los Alamos, New Mexico

SIX MONTHS HAD PASSED SINCE Daniela first met Emmaline at the Albuquerque airport. This morning the biology lab at Los Alamos National Laboratory was dark and quiet, and Daniela was buried in researching methods of repairing double-stranded DNA breaks caused by radiation.

She studied one slide and then another, the monotony of her routine helping her to forget the messiness of life outside the lab. She scribbled notes on a pad of paper. Data and more data cluttered the lined paper, and she rubbed her eyes. The work wasn't physically challenging, but a headache throbbed beneath her temples.

In the afternoon, she would code ribosomal RNA and then prep the mitochondria to make more DNA.

"Ready for lunch?"

Danny nearly jumped out of her chair. She hadn't heard Emmaline come up—she was wearing her rubber-soled ballet flats.

"Almost done." Daniela stacked her slides into neat rows beside the microscope. "We leave tomorrow."

Emmaline didn't answer. Daniela looked up at her friend. "You okay?"

"I'm sad."

"Why?"

"I miss you so much already." Daniela's Anne of Green Gables threw herself into her crow-head's friend's embrace.

"We'll be okay. Let's grab lunch."

Emmaline led the way to the mess hall a mile away. Summer was in full bloom.

"I've mapped out most of the proteins necessary to repair twenty protein DNA double-stranded breaks." Daniela lifted her chin, allowing the sun to wash her face with its own radiation.

"Then you have single-handedly saved humanity from the aftermath of nuclear fallout."

"I'm just a lab rat. You know that. Our mentor's the smart one. What about you?"

"I've just finished modeling the chemical structure of one nasty biotoxin. You heal 'em, I'll kill 'em."

"What a pair—healer and assassin."

"It's called balance."

They climbed onto the bus. The cafeteria at Los Alamos National Laboratory was a ten-minute ride from the biology lab.

"So what do we still need to solve the question of who?" Emmaline claimed the window seat, and Daniela slid in beside her.

"Find Genghis Khan's lost tomb and find the Ark of the Covenant, because according to Lozen's drawing, the ark might be in that tomb—either one could lead us to the person who will help the Sons of Venus start this darn Lucifer-inspired pandemic."

"Why do we specifically need to find the ark? Seems like an impossible mission."

"In the Old Testament, whenever the Judeans or a foreign power mishandled the ark, plagues came upon the land, killing many." Daniela swigged down a few gulps from her water canister. "If we find the ark before the Sons of Venus find it, we may be able to checkmate their plans of starting a pandemic."

"So the ark is a worldwide sanitizer?

"No." Daniela fought back a laugh. "It's more like a vitamin, preventative health. Disrespecting and abusing the Ark of the Covenant can precipitate plagues—our future pandemic—which qualifies as a plague. So if we can find the AOC and return it to its rightful place—the future Third Temple in Jerusalem—we may be able to checkmate Nomed, preventing the pandemic from ever taking off. And most likely, the unknown who will be looking for the AOC if they know anything about its past or its divinely inspired powers."

"The AOC is our secret weapon! Love it. And I'm up for helping you find it." Emmaline continued, "Next, identify who, as in the individual who will cause this pandemic. I already know that the Sons of Venus are scouting for him or her as well and will finance the rise of the antichrist. We also know that our mentor, Li Xiu, is working for the SOV and researching viruses to start a literal pandemic that targets the Orphan Dreamer—you."

"We also know that sometime after the blood moons of

2014–15, Yeshua will start His *good* pandemic, the Rapture, and take His followers to their eternal home around the time of Rosh Hashanah. So we still have a few years to stop the *bad* pandemic."

"After we arrived back at the loft a few weeks ago, you said that Islam answers everything. What did you mean?"

"Half-brothers Ishmael and Isaac grew up knowing their parents' mistakes—a slave forced to sleep with her master, conceiving a son, Ishmael, then being banished to the desert to fend for herself. Thousands of years ago, these brothers chose offense over forgiveness. Their descendants refuse to choose a different course, especially after Israel was formed as a nation."

"May 14, 1948, the day David Ben-Gurion, the head of the Jewish Agency, proclaimed the establishment of the State of Israel."

"And President Harry S. Truman recognized the new nation on the same day."

"How did that go down?"

"Not good. In their minds, Ishmael's descendants—the Palestinians and other Arabic groups—believed the descendants of their half-brother Isaac were moving into their space. They became angry and offended. Isaac's descendants claimed the land was theirs, believing it was their ancient home, embracing Yahweh's covenant to give them this land as their permanent home."

" 'The mind is its own place, and in itself can make a heaven of hell, and a hell of heaven.' "

"More importantly," Daniela said. "Offense leads to betrayal. Betrayal leads to war. War equals Armageddon as prophesied in Revelation. If a pandemic accompanies World War III, humanity won't stand a chance. Read this, Limy." Daniela opened her journal and pointed to a microfiche printout. "Who said that Nazism and Islam have no history?"

> Why did it have to be Christianity, with its meekness and flabbiness? Islam was a Männerreligion—a religion of men—and hygienic too. The soldiers of Islam received a warrior's heaven, a real earthly paradise . . . This was much more suited to the Germanic temperament than the Jewish filth and priestly twaddle of Christianity.

> —Adolf Hitler

"Islam and her devout followers are the clay portion of the last kingdom. The iron and the clay mixed together represents the rise of the Fourth Reich—the resurrection of Charlemagne's unified Europe, a.k.a. a European Union, but one that's also influenced by Arabic culture. And this new kingdom will be anti-Semitic."

"That's a mouthful, Daniela."

"You can say that again."

"I have a headache." Emmaline massaged her temples. "Don't forget, we also need to determine what heavy substance is locked inside your statue."

"Later. Not today." Daniela massaged her friend's shoulders, then stopped. "Question one thousand: Is my oily boy part of this devilish plan? And can I prevent him from participating in the Sons of Venus's plan?" She rested her hands on her abdomen.

"Are you knocked up, Danny-girl?"

"Immaculate conceptions are so 0 AD! But I am pregnant."

"What? When? Legna?"

Daniela laughed. "With a dream, and with the possibility of love."

"But?"

"I have to be sure—"

"I knew it." Emmaline blew a forceful breath from her mouth. "Just embrace the love."

"I need to be sure that my orphan boy isn't some kind of alien monster growing inside of me."

"What's the plan? In the movie *Alien*, the dude ate a bowl of spaghetti, and the alien ripped its way out of his stomach."

"I'm leaving all cards on the table, no matter how much I don't want to." Sweat dripped from Daniela's hands. "Denial never solved any problems, so I'm going to answer the question of whether my oily boy is the dreaded antichrist while I try to protect him." She sniffled.

"Don't deny yourself love while waiting for confirmation. After we both return home, the most important mission left for us both to accomplish is to fall in love. That's it. Or why even bother living? Saving humanity isn't worth the headache if you're denied a love of your own."

"Why does love require falling?" Daniela sat back down, then shifted in her seat as she rubbed her earlobe. "Makes more sense to step into love or even grow into love." She sighed. "Less likely to break a bone or one's neck."

"Rain falls. Snow falls. And humans wouldn't survive without them.

29—Orphan Dreamer

THE SEMESTER HAD PASSED TOO fast for Daniela Rose. After breakfast, Emmaline would drive Daniela to Albuquerque International Airport before continuing on to Boston.

Still lying on her lower bunk, Daniela removed her rafiki's letter from a rosewater-scented pink envelope. She'd saved the unread letter from her dad to read on her last day away from home.

She unfolded the thick lime-green paper.

Dearest Danny Rose,

Your mission—should you choose to accept it: believe in miracles. Pray for the boy locked inside your dreams. I suspect that he needs a miracle.

Love,

Dad, your rafiki

Beep. Beep. Beep. Daniela slammed the alarm clock. Time: 08:00 a.m.

She squinted past their loft's picture window while looking into a sunrise blurred by hazy fog. Ten minutes later, she finished her shower, exited the bathroom, and stepped to her friend's upper bunk bed. "Emmaline, time to get up." Daniela shook her friend. "I'm done with my shower."

"We have to return home today," Emmaline said, rubbing sleep from her eyes.

"Back to reality—dorms and college lectures, grad school for you and hopefully the Junior Honors Program for me." Daniela had applied last fall—the beginning of her sophomore year—to the University of Florida's seven-year BS/MD program. If accepted, she'd start the third year of her seven-year BS/MD program next fall.

"I need coffee." Emmaline shuffled around the apartment.

"Already brewing."

Thirty minutes later, water dripped from Emmaline's red ponytail onto her charcoal gray shirt as she nursed a mug of coffee in one hand and dragged her luggage to the door with the other. Turning around, she spoke to their vacant loft as though it were a person, "Danny Rose and I already miss you. May your next occupants love you as much as we did. May they enjoy as many hot chocolate late nights, and may they share as many secrets and solve as many riddles as the Orphan Dreamer and her Anne-girl." She blew a kiss at the empty cream walls.

Each with two suitcases in hand, they climbed down three sets of stairs. "Are you awake enough to drive?" Daniela organized the luggage inside the trunk.

"In three minutes, the caffeine jolt will ignite my spark plugs . . . and the rest will be history." Emmaline slammed the Jeep's back door shut, climbed into the driver's seat, and cranked the engine before careening down Trinity Drive, heading out of the Los Alamos township forever.

"Nothing like a rollercoaster ride to wake a teenage girl up in the a.m." Windows down, and a mountain's summer breeze blowing through their locks. Daniela reminded herself to not hold her breath. "You were right, Limy. The fresh air has helped my breathing."

"I'm glad." Emmaline slipped on a pair of aviator Ray-Bans. "You'll miss me, right?" She waited for Daniela's answer.

"Madly."

"Still going to check yourself into a convent and live as a nun during med school?"

"If I can get in. I'm not Catholic, remember?"

"Personal ad graveyard, here she comes. The apocalypse is barreling down on us—time to live a little."

"Living with boundaries is living too."

"Is faith your seatbelt?"

"To me, faith isn't a Sunday morning outfit meant to be taken off as soon as I exit a church building. My faith is interwoven throughout every detail of my life."

"I'm glad your rigid beliefs haven't stifled our friendship." Emmaline smiled.

"I wouldn't suffocate you with my beliefs or with a down pillow, for that matter."

"That's a relief!" Emmaline teased back.

"Just make sure yours don't suffocate me as well." Daniela smiled back.

"Promise."

"I won't always get the details of our friendship right, Limy, but I'll be the most loyal friend you could ever have."

"So this is officially 'I do?' " Emmaline's eyes twinkled with pleasure.

"If you want." Daniela's voice trailed off as her gaze fixed a thousand miles over the edge of the plateau, and an ache formed in the middle of her chest. What would she do without Emmaline at the dinner table, the movie theater, the lab, and their loft? Who would she be furious with, then long to forgive? The answers ripped her apart. Refusing to cry, she sat quietly and mourned her loss.

Two hours passed.

Daniela escaped her daze as Emmaline flew past signs announcing Albuquerque's airport ahead. A minute later, Emmaline whipped the Jeep curbside for departing flights.

"Thanks for driving."

Emmaline gave a thumbs-up, and Daniela swung her legs out of the Jeep, grabbed her bags from the trunk, then stood at the car window. "Don't be a stranger, Limy."

"Never." A lone tear rolled down past Emmaline's Ray-Bans as she stared straight ahead and gripped the steering wheel. Daniela schlepped her bags to the ticket counter, checked in, then approached the security gate. She paused and glanced back at the sliding glass doors.

Emmaline's Jeep hadn't moved.

Daniela squared her jaw, locking her emotions inside a private vault, then mentally tossed the key.

Would Emmaline Georgiana Winterlyn Darbyshire ever phone Daniela or answer the Orphan Dreamer's call?

After their research semester, Emmaline planned to graduate with her four-year degree and matriculate into a highly coveted graduate program at the Air Force Institute of Technology—a master's-level program that lasted for six academic quarters, teaching bright students nuclear, biological, and chemical weapons technology.

Would she find other friends—better friends?

An hour later, two jet engines propelled a 747 into the air as she gripped the handrail of her window seat on Delta flight 1452 from Albuquerque to Orlando, nursing her next dream of becoming a medical doctor.

Fools don't dare to dream.

Daniela was no fool.

"Yahweh," she prayed while holding her rafiki's letter, "I choose to believe in miracles." She talked to Adonai during her entire flight, her body still aching from her most recent dream about oily boy.

The topic?

Oily boy. In real life, was he cute? Would he be a great kisser? Would he pressure her to give up her virginity before she was ready? Could he understand her?

"Rescue him, Father. He's suffered enough." She closed her eyes and fell asleep for the last thirty minutes of the flight.

30—LEGNA

LIGHTNING FLASHES, ILLUMINATING THE UNIVERSE. The heavens rumble with Adonai's whisper. "Legna, wake up. My precious daughter's praying for the orphan."

"I see, Elohim." Legna bows low.

"Rescue My sons."

Silently, Legna unleashes his massive wingspan. Leaving his otherworldly dimension, he charges toward Earth's atmosphere. In front of him, dense air ignites. A trail of smoke swirls behind him. He contorts his angelic face as his skin ripples within jet streams.

In the distance, brown specks materialize into huts.

Legna's feet rake the muddy ground, and he stops, then compresses his towering angelic figure into his human form—a lean muscular frame covered in ebony skin. His legs are shielded with bronze plates beneath military fatigues. With violet eyes, he scans a thoroughfare lined with rubbish and huts.

He blinks. His irises glow bright blue, illuminating his path.

Adonai's warrior blinks again, and his eyes darken to coal black. Hidden inside an invisible cloak, he stalks the village streets.

Cows roam the empty streets. Legna inhales deeply, fueling his mortal body with oxygen. Vapors lifting from hot piles of cow manure assault his nostrils.

In nine minutes, he reaches his destination—a mud hut painted Aegean blue. A faded Indian-patterned curtain functions as the door to the hut.

"Time to go, boys." Legna slips a camo hoodie over his head.

He removes a can from his pocket, opens the top, dips his finger into camouflage paint, and applies it to his face. Without the camouflage paint, he'd be invisible to humans.

In one swoop, he tosses aside the curtain to the hut and surveys his sleeping charges. Stooping, he marches toward them. His gaze locks onto Cillian's purple, black, and blue face. "Humans. Devoid of humanity."

A cool wind from heaven blows down his back, calming his demeanor.

31—THE ORPHAN

CILLIAN COULDN'T BREATHE. HAD BUSHCROFT'S henchmen finally found him? The orphan sucked against a fleshy dam, his neck veins protruding. Fighting for air, his eyes burst open. Barely awake, the groggy boy reached above his face.

A nose?

Eyes? He pawed at lips, fingers, a palm, and then a muscular arm. Finally, his eyes adjusted to the dark.

A man whose faced had been streaked with green, brown, and black stared at Cillian. The intruder's ebony finger lay across his green-painted lips. "Shh. Come with me." Mouth uncovered, Cillian's chest heaved as he tried to replenish his diminished oxygen reserves.

"Trust me." Warm, intelligent ebony eyes willed Cillian to follow the man.

A black mustache curved over the intruder's upper lip, and deep black skin stretched over hypertrophied muscles—skin more beautiful than Mama Kelley's. All of Mama Kelley's brown-skinned friends had been kind to him, but when had a man with broad shoulders and strong hands been kind?

But something was different about this man. "Are ye real?" Cillian touched the man's face. His skin felt silky and warm.

"Someone else asked the same question about you," the man said, "and her prayers sent me to you."

"Yer not real, then."

"Why do you say that?"

"I'm dreamin', 'cause no one's been prayin' for me for many moons—except the Barrys and Mama Kelley, but I'm sure they've forgotten about me by now."

"Wrong on both accounts. But this prayer warrior, she's real cute and smart, and the same age as you."

"And she thinks of me?"

"Yep."

"I've never met a pretty young girl, much less been remembered by one."

"One day you will."

"I'm not anyone special to look at." Cillian propped up his body on his elbows. "Are ye sure she's not thinkin' of Paul, my brother? He's the pretty one."

"Black hair, pale skin, blue eyes—Black Irish. She's into unique things and people. You don't need to know her. She knows about you. Let's bolt." All in one motion, the man slung Cillian over his shoulder, then planted him back on the floor. "But if you break her heart, I'll break your legs."

"Ye about crushed my lungs already." Cillian released a sharp breath.

"You're not a lightweight anymore," Legna said.

"Anymore? Are ye a ghost?"

"Maybe."

"An angel?"

"My name's Legna." The orphan's rescuer extended his hand, and they shook hands. "Nice to meet you."

"Wake up, Paul." Cillian shook his brother, then looked up at Legna. "What kind of name is Legna?"

"You're smart—figure it out."

"Did the gentle voice send ye?" Cillian's pale fingers explored the stripes of paint on Legna's face. "He's not been talkin' to me lately. After I did the things that I've done at the brothel, I thought He had become angry with me."

"Elohim sings over you, Cillian, and He thinks thoughts of peace, not evil, toward you."

"How did ye know my name?" Cillian stared at the man. "I never told ye." A noise in the street refocused Cillian's attention. His heart quickened as he shook Paul again. "Paul, wake up." Paul mumbled.

"Did you figure out my name?" Legna asked.

"No."

"When you do, I'll tell you how I know your name."

"He's a sleepyhead in the mornin'," Cillian said, "but I'll wake him. Dinna worry a bit."

"We don't have time." The powerful man lifted Paul off the cot.

Cillian pulled on his brother's sleeve. "If he needs carryin', I'll do it." He pulled Paul toward him, but the sleeping boy slipped through his arms.

The intruder caught Paul before he hit the floor. "We'll make better time if I do it. Follow me." Legna crisscrossed his fingers over Cillian's face, and then Paul's. Green, brown, and black stripes painted their faces.

Voices blended in the distance. "What's that?" Cillian's gaze darted left and then right.

"Our cue to leave."

"Not before I tell Mrs. Moorjani goodbye." Cillian rushed to her side.

The woman slept, her breath lighter than a butterfly's wings. "I'll be carin' for Paul now, Mrs. M. You sleep." Cillian reached to touch her face but didn't want to awaken the old woman, so he ran to catch up with Legna. "Are we starting on a secret adventure?"

"You could call it that." Legna hunched down while moving away from the hut, allowing the shadows of the dilapidated houses to hide him. Cillian followed his example. "Do you like espionage?"

"Yeah! One of the movies we watched at the care home—not here, somewhere else—was about a spy. Maybe one day, I'll become a spy." Cillian rubbed his moist hand up and down over his khaki shorts. Legna stayed quiet. "I'm not strong or smart enough—yet."

"If you ask, My Master will gift you with wisdom. Then you can do anything."

Cillian looked back over his shoulder. Shadows shifted at the corner of the shack. "Someone's there."

"Down," Legna hissed, then grabbed Cillian by the neck of his shirt and slammed him to the ground behind a cluster of rail-thin cows.

"Why?"

"Be quiet." Legna's lip upturned into a snarl, and his eyes tracked shadows that solidified into a group of guards. A torch cast light onto the lead man's face. "What took them so long?"

"It's Scarface." Cillian hid behind Legna.

"Shh."

"What's going on?" Paul asked.

"We're escaping."

"Fine. I'm going back to sleep." Paul tucked himself into his tattered blanket.

Scarface reached beneath his jacket and brandished a long object. Starlight glittered across steel.

"He's going to kill her. We have to help her." Cillian tried to stand.

"Stop!" Legna's powerful hand grabbed the orphan boy's arm. "It's her time."

Memories of the brothel haunted Cillian. Strong men couldn't be trusted—powerful men equaled brutes and bullies.

"She's my friend." Cillian kicked and punched Legna, landing a right hook on the man's jaw. "Ouch!" Hitting a concrete wall would have felt less painful.

"Shut up!" Legna hissed. "My master forgot to tell me you were a feisty brat." Legna wrestled with the boy and finally immobilized him with a choke hold. "Wake her, and she'll experience the pain when it happens. Do you want that?"

Helpless, Cillian shook his head and turned away from the house.

A few minutes passed. Legna pulled Cillian close. "It's over. They've left. Go in and pay your last respects. I'll keep sleepyhead out here. He's got a dose of that peace that passes all understanding—this kid sleeps through anything."

All alone, Cillian trudged toward Preeti's home and walked past the open curtain. Blood soaked the front of her sari. Mouth slightly opened but eyes shut, the Indian woman appeared to be sleeping. "Mrs. M., are ye awake?"

She didn't stir.

Cillian walked to her cot and brushed his hand against her cheek. Her skin was tepid-warm. *This will be our last meeting.* The old woman's words replayed through his mind.

"Goodbye, Mrs. M., and thanks for carin'." The orphan pulled the sheet over her face, then walked back to the doorway, pausing before he left. He broke a mug on the edge of the woman's bed and buried the shard inside his right pant pocket.

Cillian returned to the mystery man and his brother's side.

"One day, I'll be findin' yer killers." Chest aching, he balled his right hand into a fist. "Then I'll be makin' them pay."

32—The Orphan

Sunday, June 21, 1998
Mumbai, India

SASSOON DOCK STANK OF FISH and human sweat as fisherman unloaded their catch.

Boats accented with brightly colored flags dotted the waterway, and up ahead, a large boat docked at the noisy pier. Standing on an enclosed platform, well-dressed European women and men whispered as warm ocean breezes penetrated Cillian's muddy locks.

Captains sounded their boat horns. Cranes whined. Laughter peppered conversations and children shouted while playing on the docks, but the sound the orphan heard was the sound of freedom.

"Freedom tastes like apple pie!" Cillian spread his arms wide.

"I'm hungry," Paul responded.

"Come on, boys." Legna waved them forward. "This ship won't wait for stragglers."

Suddenly, Cillian remembered the old fishing boat that had brought him and his brother to India. Months of slavery had followed. Cillian grabbed Paul, preventing him from boarding the boat behind Legna. "Where are you takin' us?"

"One step closer to America."

"You've been?" Cillian clenched his brother's arm.

"Many times."

"Ye'll be takin' us straight to America?"

"In time."

"I've never seen a boat like this, Cil." Paul spun on his heels, and dimples pushed into cream on his face.

"Time to expand your horizons." Past the ticket counter, Legna handed the steward plastic tickets and little blue books, only to retrieve them a few minutes later. "Follow me."

Silent, the three of them walked up the ship's gangway and stepped into a large room decorated with bright carpets and brass railings.

Heads down, Cillian and Paul kept to Legna's shadow as they entered a bank of elevators. The elevator climbed to Lido Deck, and they stepped off, following Legna down a long, narrow hall.

"Why do people keep staring at us?" Paul asked.

"Camouflage paint streaks our faces, and you two smell like elephants in musth." Legna turned left, then walked down another long corridor.

"Why don't you stink?" Paul said.

"I'm not dying."

"Then you're not a man." Paul stuck his chest into the air.

"Thank God!"

"Why do you say that?"

"If I were a man, I'd be forced to forfeit a good portion of my IQ and my palatial home for your slum digs."

"Where's your house?" Cillian caught up with Legna. "Is it fancy?"

"You'll see."

"When?"

"My mission and the goal of the pretty girl who prays for you are to make sure you arrive at my home one day, so keep moving."

"You'll be needin' to invite me first."

"You have been invited, but you're not ready to accept the invitation."

"Or ye dinna think I'm ready to go anywhere fancy." Cillian stopped. "Say it, Legna! I stink! I'm dirty—and poor! So you don't think that I'm good enough for yer house."

"Trust me, angry boy. Human goodness, money, and a shower have nothing to do with entering or living in my home." Legna turned and placed his hand over Cillian's heart. "A change must happen in here. My Master's kingdom is not of this world."

"We have to become aliens?" Cillian scrunched his nose.

"Something like that, but not quite."

"The pretty one, is she yer girl?" Cillian held his breath.

"My Master intends her heart for another."

"Good. Can I tell you a secret, Legna, if ye willna tell?" They continued to their room.

"Gossip. That's a human thing."

Cillian glanced back at Paul. "Dinna listen, okay?" Paul stuck his fingers into his ears. "I'd like to meet a pretty girl."

Cillian lifted his bandaged left hand. The bandage still

oozed with a creamy white substance. Stinking to high heavens, his left hand throbbed something miserable. Beneath blue-white moonlight, pink streaks ran up his arm. Would he lose his hand to infection?

"But no girl worth knowing would want me caressin' her in the night with a hand like this."

"Who told you that?"

"Bushcroft."

"Be careful whose opinions you choose to embrace." Legna flipped Cillian's hand, palm up. "It's infected."

"Will I lose it?"

"Not under my watch. You'll be caressing your dream girl one day. Don't worry."

"Thanks." Cillian followed his caretaker in silence, but Legna seemed more like a confidante, a friend, than a caretaker. "I didna like the men at the brothel."

"Hairy faces and behinds . . . who would?" Legna sneered.

"One day, I'd like to meet a lovely girl—a girl who laughs at my jokes even though I'm not verra funny," Cillian said. Legna didn't respond. "I dinna ken if she'd ever hold my hand, but I'll be dreamin' that she does." The orphan shifted his weight. "Yer eyes, sir."

"What about them?" His Adam's apple rose, then fell.

"They're changing colors from black to violet."

"We all have our problems. Your hand will heal—it'll be scarred, but not infected. She'll hold your hand—if you find the right girl."

"And if I dinna find the right one?"

"She'll plunge a dagger into your heart so deep the blade will stick out of your back." Legna walked faster. Blood rushed from Cillian's face, leaving his skin cold and clammy. "Let's find our room, clean you up, then stretch out."

After turning right, they stood in front of a maroon door. Legna slipped a plastic card into a slot on the door, then turned the handle. Cillian glared at the man. "D'ye believe in me?"

"I believe in the One who created you for greatness." Legna pushed open the door. He entered, followed by Cillian and then Paul.

"Cil, this room! Have you ever feasted your eyes on such a sight?"

"Never . . ." Cillian stood straight, and miraculously didn't brush his head on the ceiling. Two bunks topped with thick mattresses were dressed in starched sheets. A small desk jutted out from the wall, and a mirror hung over it.

"Dinna be touchin' anything."

"Why, Cil?"

"If you break somethin', I dinna ha' the money to pay for it." Years of selling his body without one rupee to show for it. Cillian pulled Paul's hand back to his side.

Behind the boys, the door slammed shut. Cillian's heart pounded inside his chest. Would Legna abuse him and Paul?

"I'm fifteen," Paul said. "I'm not a baby."

"Money's not a problem. Touch whatever you like, but stay inside this room." A mischievous smile crossed Legna's face as he exited the small berth. "I'll be back."

He returned about ten minutes later.

By the time he got back, the boys had investigated every nook of the cabin. Legna eyed the towels and three bright orange life jackets sitting on the bed. "Going for a swim?" Legna asked. Their protector held a tray overloaded with egg drop soup, strawberries, blueberries, baked chicken, fresh salad, chocolate cake, and water.

"In case the ship sinks." Cillian eyed the tray of food, and his mouth watered. "An Irish Traveller once told me that ships were nothing more than floating tombs."

"Did you steal that?" Paul bounded toward the tray while licking his lips.

"No."

"Can you swim, Legna?

"Swimming is for fish. I fly."

"Are you rich?" Paul pointed at the food.

"Very." Legna placed the tray on the cabin desk. "But I didn't buy it. All the food on the cruise is included in the fare. Eat, and after you clean up, I'll take you down for dinner. Then you can eat all you want."

"No one will be stoppin' us?" Cillian didn't believe the man.

"You belong on this cruise, like every other paying customer." Legna gave Cillian a bottle of pills. "Antibiotics. Take a pill three times a day." He stretched out on a patent leather couch.

"We didna pay." Cillian spooned soup into his mouth. Curry spice.

"My Master did." Legna crossed his arms and closed his eyes. "Eat, shower, brush your teeth, and wash your hair. Cillian, you need a shave. All the essential toiletries are in the bathroom."

"Do we wash our clothes?"

"You'll find clean clothes in a bag hanging in the bathroom."

"There's enough food for both of us, Cil. We can eat our fill." They both hovered over the tray of food. Paul ate a chicken leg and Cillian had a wing. Both boys shoveled scoops of food into their mouths until their cheeks bulged, then licked their plates clean.

"Go clean up," Legna barked. "I'm tired of smelling you."

"Yer not eating?"

"Is there anything left to eat?" Legna opened one eye and glanced at the empty plates.

"Sorry."

"The food wasn't for me."

"You've already eaten, then." Cillian vanished inside the bathroom, flipped on the shower, and closed the bathroom door.

Steam permeated the small bathroom, caressing his dingy skin. After he removed the bandage wrapped around his left hand, he stripped and entered the shower. Blood mixed with pus dripped onto the shower floor. Warm and soothing liquid needles prickled his skin. He washed, then scrubbed, then washed again until his skin squeaked.

He saved the hardest task for last.

Cillian forced himself to breathe as he lathered up a bar of soap and thoroughly cleaned his wounded hand. Directing the handheld showerhead over his palm, the jet stream of water flushed out pus as well as brown and red chunks of dead skin and congealed blood.

Pain wracked his hand, arm, and shoulder, yet the washing felt good. After he finished cleaning his hand, he examined the wound. Grotesque, jagged pink flesh draped over a partially healed hole.

No respectable woman would allow you to stroke her in the night with that hand. Bushcroft's words haunted his thoughts.

What about Legna's pretty girl?

After both boys finished their showers, the scent of Irish Spring filled the cabin as they dressed in new clothes.

Legna removed backpacks filled with packaged food,

water jars, and a change of clothes from under his bunk bed. He placed them at the foot of their beds. "For your trip."

"Our trip?" Cillian dug through the contents and removed a map. "A map of Mongolia. Why?"

"When you need to know, you'll know." Legna's lips upturned in a soft smile. "Let's eat dinner, then off to bed."

"You're going to tell us a bedtime story too?" Cillian snapped.

"Not good with stories. We'll explore tomorrow." He opened the door of the cabin and led the boys to the dining hall.

"How exactly does one go about it?" Cillian stared at the buffet. "I'm hungry, but I canna eat all this food."

"Start from the beginning," Legna said, "and take a small scoop of anything that smells good."

"Everything smells good." Cillian scooped a spoonful of each dish onto his plate, piling on a mountain of vegetables, fruit, casseroles, and meat. "When I'm rich, I'll be installin' one of these inside my home." He sat down at a table next to the windows.

"Money isn't everything."

"But it's somethin'." The ship gently rocked upon the sea, and glasses clanked, but Cillian didn't speak as he ate heaven's food.

After thirty minutes of gorging himself, he opened his mouth and belched. "I'll be sick." The lady sitting next to him turned and scolded him with her eyes. "Sorry, ma'am. I've not eaten a meal like that for a wee bit."

"Then I'm happy for you." She smiled. "You'll do well to save a little space for chocolate cake."

"Thanks, but not tonight."

"Then tomorrow." The lady stood and walked away.

Minutes later, Cillian lay down on his mattress, closed his eyes, and slept.

Over the next ten days, the boys explored every corner of the massive luxury ship, and Legna never missed a beat, a prank, or a joke.

On the eleventh day, the playful trio laughed as they launched spit-cannons over the edge of the lower deck.

Cillian ran aft and climbed onto the metal railing, peeking over the barrier. Light blue water churned in the wake of the ship. "Legna, what makes the water turn light blue?"

"Bioluminescence. Dinoflagellates in the water." Paul puffed his chest out. "Like in the Maldives." Cillian gazed at his brother, pride warming his cheeks.

"Enough about science. Off to bed. Today's the last day of the cruise." Legna led the boys back to their cabin. "You'll need your rest." After leading them back to their berth, he backed away from his charges. "Lights out. Stay out of trouble." He exited and nudged the door shut.

33—The Orphan

Wednesday, July 8, 1998
At Sea

AT 12:01 A.M., CILLIAN AWOKE—ON his own time, no greedy customers waiting for their onyx-haired entertainment.

Today he'd celebrate his seventeenth birthday without a party, but freedom would be his birthday gift, and that reality was enough for him. A wide smile spread across his face, pushing away years of sadness.

For the next few minutes, he lay on his bed and stretched every muscle before rolling over to face his roommates. A train of snores chugged from Paul's open mouth.

Cillian rolled sharply to his right side. As he did, his feet got tangled in his sheets, and he crashed face-first to the floor. After standing, he stumbled toward Legna's empty bed.

Where was he?

He dropped to his knees and looked under the bed.

How could a man the size of Legna go missing inside a tiny cabin? Minutes passed with no knock or turn of the handle. Cillian's breathing came shallow. Beads of sweat formed on his face. Another ten minutes slipped away. He paced the room.

Legna had abandoned them.

Shoulders slumped, Cillian sat in the cabin's swivel chair and accepted his new reality—a familiar state of being: abandonment. Leadership rested on his head once again, and heavy was the head that wore the crown.

His past record hadn't been stellar. Maybe a shower would calm him. He stepped into the bathroom and stripped.

The washing felt good but brought no clarity to his new situation.

He towel-dried, then stood in front of the bathroom's mirror, cataloging his wounds. Opening and closing his left hand, he asked, "Is there another man whose hand had been marred with a rusty spike?"

Away from the constant threat of shame, he knew he would heal. Cillian turned the shower back on, lathered up his backside and scrubbed until his skin burned. Mechanically, he erased the memories of sexual abuse. But would he ever feel clean?

The jury hadn't yet read that verdict.

Cillian lifted a clean towel from the bathroom sink. Bandages, ointment, and a little packet labeled *pain reliever* sat on the counter. Beneath the pain reliever packet, Cillian found a shiny silver dollar that still gleamed.

"How'd you get here?" He fondled the face of the familiar coin. "Thought I'd left you under the pillow in Mrs.

Moorjani's house." The orphaned boy dressed in a sweat suit, pocketed the coin, then opened the pain reliever packet and swallowed the two white tablets with water.

The polyester soaked up the wetness dampening his body as he reentered the air-conditioned cabin. Ice crystals seemed to encase his body, so he massaged his arms, uprooting the frost.

"Paul, wake up." Cillian squeezed his brother's shoulder. "Yer turn to shower."

"I'm awake, but give me a second." Paul crawled out of bed. Hair and pajamas rumpled, he stumbled into the bathroom.

"Paul. Legna's gone," Cillian stated flatly before his brother closed the bathroom door.

"Where to?"

"He didn't leave a note."

"What's that?' Paul pointed to a large manila envelope, then disappeared inside the shower. Cillian picked up the package and turned it over and over. Maybe Paul should step into the leadership position.

Cillian ripped open the envelope and shook the contents onto the desk. The two little folders that Legna gave to the attendant before boarding the ship had been passports.

A colorful flyer outlined their final destination. He sat on the bed and read every word of the pamphlet.

"Where did the passports come from?" Paul asked as he rubbed a cotton towel back and forth over his drenched hair.

"Found them in the envelope." Cillian barely looked up from the information card.

"What does the flyer say?

"We hope that ye have enjoyed yer cruise, which concludes at Xingang Port Passenger Terminal in China."

"China? We don't speak Mandarin or Cantonese."

"For now, we dinna need to. Read this." He gave the brochure to Paul.

"Your land tour bus will await you at Terminal One, and over the next twelve days, you will immerse yourselves in the sights and sounds of China. The tour will include the Great Wall of China, the Forbidden City, and the Terracotta Warriors, before continuing to the airport for an early morning flight to Ulaanbaatar, Mongolia, where your land tour will continue—"

"Aye, Paul. You and me, we're escapin' on a twelve-day travel tour!"

"Mongolia? Where the heck is that? What about America?" Paul gave the flyer back to Cillian.

"I've been workin' wi' my bare hands," Cillian growled as he cast a steely stare at Paul, "and I instructed you to study geography. Memorize the locations of these countries." He balled his hands into fists and his nostrils flared. Within the mirror's reflection, his iridescent blue eyes had darkened.

"I-I-I did. Honest I did, Cil. Don't beat me—please." Paul raised his hand to block a blow that never came.

Cillian stepped back, disgusted with himself for his sudden outburst of anger. He released his fist. What could he have done to Paul? Cillian shuddered. "I'm sorry, Paul." He tossed the flyer on his bed.

Paul hung his head. "I'm sorry, Cil. I want to help, but you always push me away. I try not to be a headache, so I ask questions."

"I've worked my hands raw in order to provide a better

life for us. The brothel . . ." Cillian's voice hung on wretched memories before dropping to a whisper. "It was dreadful."

"I'll do my part. Promise." Paul squeezed Cillian's wounded hand. His brother winced. Paul's voice rose a few octaves. "I'll keep praying for you, like Mrs. M. taught me. She told me—"

"What did she tell you?" His eyes narrowed.

"She said you worked an evil job, and if we didn't pray for you, the work would scar you for life or even kill you." Ashamed and vulnerable, Cillian collapsed onto the edge of his bed. "So I told her that just because your work was bad, that didn't mean that you were bad. You're the best brother, and you needed regular work. That job gave you that." Paul's naive answer struck a raw nerve, and Cillian's gaze rested on the floor.

"Cil, what happened to your hand?" Paul's voice had lowered to a reflective and pensive volume. "It doesn't stink anymore," Paul prattled on, feverishly attempting to loosen Cillian's tongue, but Cillian bit the inside of his cheek, determined to keep his tongue bridled and maintain Paul's innocence.

While Paul and Cillian ate breakfast, the captain's deep baritone boomed through the luxury cruise liner's intercom speakers. "We will sail into the Xingang Port at 12 p.m. local time. It has been a pleasure having you aboard Timbre Asian Cruise lines. Sail with us again."

Paul stuffed his cheeks with pancakes and sausage. "I asked God to make them stop hurting you."

Cillian just stared into the distance and remained silent. He had no appetite.

"I dreamed once," Paul said.

"About?"

"A brown-skinned girl who kissed you on the mouth." Paul blushed.

"No girl's ever going to be kissin' me on the mouth, Paul." Cillian leaned over the table, picked up a hash round, and tossed it at his brother. "Didna anyone tell you? Dreams aren't real. They never come true unless they're nightmares."

"Not true."

"Don't argue with me. Finish your breakfast."

"I miss Legna. He was a dreamer."

"No. He wasn't. Spell Legna backwards."

"A-n-g-e-l." Paul's eyes lit up. "Cool."

34—The Orphan

CROWDED WITH SHIPPING CONTAINERS, CRANES, and smog, Xingang Port appeared more industrial than touristy. Cillian watched from the ship as deck hands secured the ship to the dock with ropes.

An hour later, Cillian and Paul shaded their eyes against the midday sun as they walked off the gangway and into the bustling Chinese port.

A cool breeze welcomed the vagabond travelers. Paul nestled the manila envelope under his armpit, his attempt at being helpful.

Over the next fourteen days, the land tour delivered all that the brochure had promised, and the orphaned boys ate and slept like kings. Feeling like an explorer, Cillian had allowed his facial hair to grow into a scraggly beard.

Looking older ensured that no one would ask questions like "Where are your parents?"

Early one morning, Cillian removed the airline tickets for their next destination from the manila envelope.

"Why Mongolia?" Paul complained.

"Keeps us away from the brothel in India," Cillian said.

The brothers boarded a plane to Chinggis Khaan International Airport, which served Ulaanbaatar, Mongolia. They slept for most of the flight, not knowing what lay ahead of them. Jet wheels clenching the runway jolted them awake.

Cillian—followed by Paul—exited the plane, then entered the airport terminal.

Ivory-and-rust flooring accented wood-paneled walls. Mongolian mannequins dressed in traditional garb stood against reflective glass columns. The locals kept to their own business.

The boys entered an airport bathroom, took a quick sink-bath, and donned a clean set of clothes. Well-groomed men secured well-paying jobs.

After their pit stop, they strolled out of the airport, then climbed onto a bus headed to Ulaanbaatar but skipped the land tour. Sitting 4,364 feet above sea level, the city's air was warm, with little humidity.

Paul whispered, "Where should we go?"

"Why are you whispering?"

"Your tongue lashings suck."

"I didna think my tongue's long enough to lash yer rump?" Cillian smiled wryly. "I apologized—remember?"

"It hurt my feelings more than Miss Grey's paddle at the care home."

"Why?"

"She didn't care about me. I thought you did."

"The world's a tough place, and yer not a boy anymore. I mean to discipline you, prepare you to face the world on yer own, so from now on, ye'll be takin' yer punishments like a man. I've no problem wi' ye statin' yer case, but dinna whine—understood?"

"Tiim."

"Aye?"

"Mongolian for yes."

The orphan grinned. "Point taken." An hour later, Cillian halted their march to nowhere. Mongolia had embraced a nomadic lifestyle. On the edge of town, tents that lacked plumbing and electricity dotted the landscape. The locals called these neighborhoods "ger districts."

After they entered the tent-based quarters, Cillian wished he'd learned Russian or Mongolian. A lump rose in the back of his throat.

Would he lead Paul into trouble again? The lack of answers humbled him. "How do we talk to these people?"

"In Russian." Paul proceeded to speak the Cyrillic language.

After they secured a tent, Cillian fought for words, but none came. He draped his arm around his brother's shoulders. "I'm apologizin' to you properly. I'm sorry."

"Apology accepted."

"I'm so proud of you. Russian?" Cillian embraced his brother. "I'll make it up to you and take you to America one day."

"Promise?"

"On my life."

"One more question?"

"It's eatin' up yer insides, so spit it out."

"How will we travel to America without plane tickets?"

"I'll work until we can pay for passage." Cillian surveyed his surroundings. Where could he find a job?

"We'll work together."

"Together. Always." Cillian shook Paul's hand. He had protected his little brother's wings until the bones and muscles had grown strong. Time to push him out of the nest and let him soar—but could Cillian stomach the process?

"In America, a poor man can become rich."

"Aye, then. We'll be buyin' a palace bigger than Legna's." Cillian's back straightened.

"He'll want to visit."

"I'll see about that." Cillian tapped Paul's stomach with the back of his hand. "Let's use the money Legna gave us to buy a bit of food."

"It's not smart to spend all our money right away."

"We'll split dinner." Cillian exited their tent, leaving the ger district. Disorganized and cramped, the district mimicked a maze. Would they ever find their way out? *Free tent or not, best to stick to the city.* They found the city an hour later. As they laughed at Paul's jokes, they blended in with other wealthy European tourists.

"I dinna understand why Legna didna include fare to return to England." Cillian looked at the picture menu.

"He didn't want us to repeat our pasts." Paul placed his menu on the table.

"Our futures dinna look so bright. According to the map, Mongolia's landlocked, sandwiched between Russia and China."

"Then we'll find our hidden treasure in Mongolia and travel to America as rich men. And if America's our pot of gold, Mongolia's simply a detour before we obtain it."

Cillian rubbed the silver dollar inside his left pocket. "I canna understand a word on this menu. We'll find a place to eat that serves familiar food." They left the restaurant and wandered the streets.

"What about that place?" Paul pointed to Los Bandidos. After they explored the menu, they agreed to split an entrée at the Tex-Mex and Indian fusion restaurant. They sat at a table for two, and a waitress served water flavored with nuts and dates.

"I've got it!" Paul jotted notes on the back of a napkin. "Aye, then?"

"We will find the necropolis of Genghis Khan, steal his treasure, and live like kings." Paul smiled. "He once ruled all lands between the Pacific Ocean and the Caspian Sea. Before he died, he commanded his soldiers to bury him in secret. As they took his body to a remote tomb, his grieving army killed anyone they met on the route."

"Brutal."

"After they buried the emperor, his soldiers rode one thousand horses over the fallen warrior's grave. In the eight hundred years since, no archeologist has found his tomb." Paul leaned back in his chair, allowing his story to sink in.

"Surely they buried the treasure with the emperor."

"Nope. You see, I did study while we were touring China."

"Indeed." The waitress placed a plate loaded with delicious foods in front of Cillian. He split the entrée, and they ate while planning their treasure hunt.

"Mrs. M. used to say that God makes all things work together for good for anyone who loves Him." Paul sipped his portion of suutei tsai—salted milk tea. "He'll make us rich if we ask nicely."

"If He had wanted to be makin' us rich, He wouldna ha' ever allowed us to starve in the first place."

"But we didn't starve to death."

"Some have." Cillian remembered John and Tommy. *May they rest in peace.*

"Don't you want to try to love Him and follow Him?"

"I dinna ken enough about Him, Paul. I've had enough of followin' people I dinna know."

"Oh, I forgot about one thing. Excuse me." Paul folded his hands together and closed his eyes. "God, help Cil and me find a job. We need to eat." He opened his eyes to find Cillian staring at him.

"That's weird—too spontaneous."

Paul sighed.

The boys finished their meals in silence, paid their tab, then walked down the street into the night. Ulaanbaatar resembled Manchester, England—cleaner but more drab, painted entirely in grays and whites. The city's skyline penetrated the dusky sky.

The palette matched Cillian's mood—blah—but he kept on walking, hoping. At the edge of the sidewalk, trampled beneath careless feet, a lone bright pink flower had sprung up from a bed of rock.

Cillian refused to pick the flower, effectively killing the dainty plant. *If ye canna take care of her, dinna remove her from her roots.*

"Cil, look." Paul stopped in front of a place called Hennessy's Rest Bar. "They have a NOW HIRING EXPATS sign in the window. That's us!"

"It is."

Cillian entered first, and a portly man dressed in a white collared shirt hollered from behind a bar, "May I help you?"

Cillian pushed forward. "I-I-I'm lookin' for the manager." His stutter unmasked his fear of rejection.

"You're looking at him." The man plunged his thumbs behind his red suspenders. "Sumrall's the name."

"My name is Cillian Finn, and I saw your sign in the window." He half-turned, pointing at the sign, then Paul. "He's my brother."

"Hi." Paul shook Mr. Sumrall's hand. "The name's Paul."

"Nice to meet you both. What can I do for you?"

The last time Cillian had applied for a job, it had resulted in over two years of toiling in hell. Could Mr. Sumrall be trusted?

The orphan looked down and away from the gray-haired man. "I-I-I work hard. If ye'd be takin' us in for a while, allowin' us to work for you. We won't be any bother. I'd like a job."

"I need a strapping young man." Sumrall extended his hand. "You're hired." Cillian shook it. "Thank you, sir."

"First time in Mongolia?"

"Aye, sir."

"Where you boys from?"

"England."

"But the blond sounds more Scandinavian, and you sound Scottish, or Irish, or something."

"Paul's from Denmark, and I'm from Ireland, although my mum hails from the Highlands," Cillian rambled. "I've mostly lived in England—Manchester."

"Where are your parents?"

"Gone." Cillian should shut his mouth.

"Vanished into thin air, huh?" The man frowned, but Cillian didn't answer. "I should ask a lot more questions, but I know two hungry young lads when I see them. Work hard. Be respectful. Don't steal."

"I-I-I'm not a thief."

"Then what are you? You're more nervous than a jack-rabbit."

"I'm an orphan needing a second chance."

"I could use someone off the books to do all-around kind of work—clean up the place and serve in the restaurant some days. Can you do that?"

"Yes, sir," Cillian said. But flying across the Atlantic Ocean required lots of cash. "Wh-wh-what . . ." His tongue twisted into knots.

"Spit it out, son."

"What's the pay?" Paul blurted out.

"I'm not tryin' to be pushy." Cillian rotated the silver dollar inside his pocket.

"I like a man who asks questions," Mr. Sumrall reassured Cillian. "Tells me he's interested." The orphan looked up from the floor and studied the man's eyes. "I'll pay you one American dollar an hour for six hours of work a day, three free meals a week, and you keep the tips when you work in the restaurant."

"Yer verra generous."

"The bathroom needs cleaning, and the floors need scrubbing. I'll feed you both a snack before bed. You got a place to stay?"

"No, sir. We found a tent in the ger district, but I don't think we'll be able to find it again."

"You shouldn't stay there. Stay closer to the restaurant. I've got some old sleeping bags in storage. You can pull those out and sleep in the shed out back until you find a place." Sumrall propped his beefy hand on Cillian's shoulder. "I don't tolerate stealing."

The orphan was no thief. It had been lustful adults who stole Cillian's youth and innocence. "I understand."

"Anything else?"

"Do ye have a place where my brother could be studyin' while I work? I dinna expect him to take up space in the restaurant, but is there a library where he can check out a few textbooks?"

"If earning money's your goal, you'd earn it faster if your brother worked for me as well."

"I'm relyin' on him to fill his head with math formulas and words so I can retire in ten years." Cillian laughed. Sweat beading across his forehead belied his fake jest.

"Odd, but he's your brother."

"Cil," Paul said, "I don't mind working."

"Ye'll do as yer told." What if Sumrall spoke with the same deceptive words as Bushcroft had? Cillian would never forgive himself.

"Your choice." Sumrall waited for Cillian's reply. "But Paul could help out during the day and study with you at night. I have two sons—they're almost grown up now. I'll lend you their old textbooks. After the restaurant closes, study in the diner."

"Night school," Cillian said, glancing at Paul. "Okay." The owner gave Cillian a mop. His heart landed in his toes. *Tommy. John.* His fallen friends. But Sumrall had given the boy a mop, not a shovel.

"Something wrong?"

"No, sir."

"Go on and do your work. I'll tell the cook to whip up a snack."

35—Orphan Dreamer

"MOM! DAD! WHERE ARE YOU?" Seventeen-year-old Daniela raced into her parents' home. Her stride matched the speed of her breath as she cradled a letter in her hands.

Long, curly hair dangled past well-formed shoulders, and a thick white cotton T-shirt hugged her petite torso and narrow waist.

Another letter. Another destiny. How could a thin piece of paper hold the fate of a wishful and hardworking teenage girl? Would the University of Florida College of Medicine say yes or no? After returning from Los Alamos, Daniela had prepared herself for this day. Prayer had been her source of strength while she waited—her least favorite task.

"Daniela!" Chaplain Cavanaugh slammed the back door and hobbled into the living room. "Where are you? What's wrong?"

"Hope nothing's wrong. I received my letter from the University of Florida." Breathless, she clutched the envelope against her chest.

"Open it." He leaned against the lime-green Formica kitchen counter.

"I'm too nervous." She held the envelope out, the paper sticking to her sweaty palms.

"You're smart. Destined for greatness. A medical school will accept you somewhere."

"Daddy, you've never doubted me, but I'm a Florida Gator. I want to study here, in Gainesville. I need to stay close to you and Mom."

"If you hadn't travelled to Los Alamos, you never would have met Emmaline."

"I know the campus. Mom owns the bookstore now. I can work on the weekends and study at the store during the weekdays. And UF trains solid doctors."

"God knows I never want you to leave . . . but calm down. Your heart's too fragile to excite yourself."

"I'm fine." To defy her worsening shortness of breath, she power walked each morning and practiced archery on the weekends.

The result?

A lithe five-foot-six physique in spite of a diagnosis of early-onset mild pulmonary hypertension with resulting tachycardia.

"Did you take your Metoprolol?"

"I did." Daniela slipped her hand through the crook of her father's arm and guided him to the plaid couch. "I wonder if the envelope would be thicker if I'd been accepted."

"Fear is faith in the wrong what-if. Face your reality, Daniela. Don't sit back and speculate. Act."

"Stay with me. I'm falling with no bottom in sight."

"Your world isn't falling apart—it's falling into place. Trust Him. You've grown into a young lady, and your mom and I have raised you to endure pressure-cooker moments like this one. Ashes into beauty, remember?"

"How does the Almighty do that—transform soot into beauty?"

"Time and pressure." Sitting on the couch beside his only child, Daniela's father nodded. "Open it."

"But—"

"Do it!"

"Fine." She ripped open the envelope, then read. *Congratulations* was the only word she got to before jumping up and down.

"Good news, I presume?"

Overwhelmed, her tears answered for her. Daniela Rose launched into her rafiki's arms and embraced him. "Dad, it's finally happened. I'm going to learn how to care for sick people." Another part of her quest had been fulfilled.

Life was perfect—she had secured a kindred spirit, Emmaline, and she would matriculate into the Junior Honors Medical Doctorate Program at the University of Florida in Gainesville, her hometown.

After a moment of jubilation, she calmed down enough to continue reading.

Congratulations, Daniela!

You have been accepted into the University of Florida College of Medicine's Junior Honors Program, graduating class of 2004.

An orientation packet will follow within a few weeks. We look forward to you joining the College of Medicine as we continue the tradition of training outstanding clinicians in their specialty of choice.

Please return an acceptance letter within two weeks.

Best Regards,
Admissions Committee

"Two weeks! No way. I'm writing and mailing my acceptance letter today." She cradled the letter to her chest, thankful for a dream come true.

"You've never been one to sit on a decision for long." His eyes told Daniela that he approved—and sometimes that was all a daughter needed. "You made it."

"We made it! Thank you, Yeshua." Daniela lay down on the couch, her feet resting on her dad's knee. She basked in the warm glow of her accomplishment and her daddy's adoration.

"What are you going to do now, Doctor Cavanaugh?" Her rafiki massaged her feet.

"Call Emmaline, then drive to the bookstore to tell Mom."

"And then?"

"Finish up summer school, start medical school, ace my classes, then match into an anesthesiology residency program where I will study pediatric anesthesia."

"Pediatric anesthesia," Austin Cavanaugh stumbled over the odd words. "That's a tongue twister."

"As a medical doctor, I'll travel the world, sharing my

medical skills with sick people in Africa, Asia, Europe, the Middle East, and South America."

"What about Antarctica? The penguins need anesthesia too," he joked, and Daniela giggled. Laughing, he kissed her cheek. His laugh sounded like a car with a faulty starter, winding and winding until he took a breath.

"Will I be good enough?"

"You already are, my angel. Your smarts combined with Yahweh's presence shining through you could raise the dead."

"Thanks for everything, Daddy."

"No sugarcane fields for my princess." He held her hands in his and surveyed her soft skin. "No calluses neither—the hands of a doctor, meant to heal."

"And do no harm."

"You've become the young lady I imagined you would be—smart, compassionate, and tenacious. The twinkle behind your eyes blind the stars. You're breathtaking, Danny Rose." Gently, he brushed loose curls behind her ears.

"I guess I won't scare away the penguins."

"You're our snowflake destined to quench the hellishness of suffering." Her rafiki cleared his throat. "How's the boy from your dreams?"

"Okay, I guess." She avoided the conversation. No need to broach the uncomfortable subject of a boy whose skin—according to her father—Yahweh had colored with too much cream. In her father's defense, Jim Crow's South had not been that kind to him. "I should call Emmaline."

"Tell her hello from me—but save some of your joy to share with your mom. She'd die of heartbreak if you shared all of your bliss with Limy."

"I'm really grateful Grandma left her enough money to

buy the bookstore . . . but now Mom's at work a lot. Do you miss her?"

"I do, but I am proud of her."

Daniela kissed her father's cheek. His skin felt cool to the touch. Resigned to his CLL diagnosis, she swallowed hard. *Find a cure for cancer, then travel the world as a missionary doctor.* "You are loved. Never forget."

"Promise me something."

"Anything." She studied his face, where fine lines had deepened into wrinkles.

"Never allow your love for me or your mother to keep you from all the Almighty has destined you for." His emphasis landed on "all."

"Speaking about destinies, Professor Jakob mailed me a letter while I was living in Los Alamos."

"And?"

"Emmaline and I believe that the Ark of the Covenant may have been buried inside Genghis Khan's tomb."

"Your mom mentioned the letter. May I read it?"

"Please do." She retrieved the letter and gave it to her father.

"Go call Limy, Indiana Jones." Austin settled back into the couch. His breath hitched for a moment and then steadied. Daniela fought back emotion as she walked into the kitchen and dialed her best friend on the rotary phone.

"Limy, guess what?"

"You got accepted."

"I did."

"Time to celebrate! I'm coming to Florida."

"I'll ask my parents if you can stay in my room. During the day, we'll hang out and work at mom's new bookstore, wrapping books, drinking hot tea, and solving clues."

"Talk about heaven. Count me in! See you tomorrow." She ended the call.

"Limy's coming?" her father asked.

"May she?"

"Of course. Now go see your mother." He returned the professor's letter to Daniela.

Forty-five minutes later, Daniela arrived by city bus to her mother's bookstore. They talked about books, dreams, and medical school. Nestled together on a rose-and-paisley armchair, they celebrated Daniela's good news, eating pizza and sipping fizz from the tops of their once-a-month sodas.

After their special lunch, Daniela retreated to her mother's office. With her medical school letter and Professor Jakob's letter in hand, she stood in front of an ornate floor-length mirror.

Blood from a nosebleed slicked her upper lip. She wiped the blood away and sighed. Acceptance letters didn't solve every problem. Her nosebleeds had correlated with oily boy's sufferings.

For the last week, she'd been too nervous to pray for him as she waited for her acceptance or rejection letter. Prayer—real prayer—required spiritual fortitude as well as mental strength. Battles in the spiritual realm with Satan and his demons couldn't be won with distracted prayers. So with her resolve weakened by fear, her prayers for oily boy had waned. Even Emmaline had rarely mentioned him during their daily conversations.

Deep inside her soul, Daniela groaned. Ashamed of her selfishness and inattention to oily boy's needs, she turned away from her mother's looking glass, dropped to her knees, and clasped her hands together.

A lone tear warmed her cheek, but passion raged inside her heart. "Yahweh . . ." She stretched her arms wide like her Messiah had done. "Give my oily boy something—anything—to celebrate today."

Hair texture mattered to superficial humans but little to the devil and his angry demons. "This is how I fight my battles." On her knees and surrounded by God's angels, she stared at her reflection. "Kinky hair and armed with fiery arrows that pierce Satan's lair, laying waste to my enemy."

She stood and smoothed out her T-shirt and jeans as she descended the steps to the bookstore. "You'll be okay, oily boy."

36—Nomed's Zephyrine

TODAY, I CELEBRATE MY BIRTHDAY. "Happy Birthday to me! Happy Birthday to me, Happy Birthday dear Zephyrine. Happy Birthday to me," I sing to myself.

I am twenty-four hours old.

In honor of my twenty-four-hour birthday, I sank *Zeus*. No, not the mythical Greek god who spews lightning and belches thunder. I can perform all those menial Nephilim functions, plus more.

Zeus was a sleek, fifty-foot catamaran that had been sailing off the coast of Bermuda. I sank her, plunging a family of four into a frigid and salty grave.

Catamarans don't sink. They capsize. The yacht broker had guaranteed the adventurous Alcott family, but the broker had not met me. I am the storm, Zephyrine, and the western wind is my power.

Turns out God, the One who calms the seas and quiets both lightning and thunder with His "Peace be still" command was not and still is not into the business of sinking ships.

But Nomed—my master—was and still is.

Since the first ship set sail for North America, Nomed and I had waited eagerly for the transatlantic crossing of Aisling O'Hare—the Orphan Dreamer's Irish ancestor—but we failed our mission and sank the wrong boat.

Aisling O'Hare's boat landed at New York City's port. The redhead, dressed in a plain plaid dress, stepped off the ship clutching a tattered carpet bag full of dreams wrapped in clover and an Irish blessing:

> May the road rise up to meet you. May the wind be always at your back. May the sun shine warm upon your face; the rains fall soft upon your fields and until we meet again, may God hold you in the palm of His hand.

Would we fail again? I am not a serial killer like Pandemic, so murdering a mother, father, and two twin girls had not been in my preferred birthday plans. But innocent people commonly suffer as casualties of war. We—the first order of creation—are at war with the second order of creation—you.

To some, I am a soldier. And to others, I am a weapon.

But in my heart, I am a dreamer charged with assassinating the Orphan Dreamer and her future offspring. Those who choose to live under the curse of death will die alone—even me.

Many moons ago, our Creator diagnosed Death with the worst case of narcissism.

The most selfish of creatures, Death cares nothing about my fears or yours. Like a vulture, she circles above me, ready to devour me inside her insatiable maw in exactly two hundred and forty hours, fifty-six minutes, and twelve seconds.

Unless Nomed keeps his end of the bargain.

In my Creator's defense, the Creator never wanted anything or anyone to die—animals, plants, humans, or even me. But the early humans made a mistake when they chose knowledge over wisdom.

Now creation groans for the children of God to be revealed, so our nightmare of living under the curse of Death brought on by humans—you—will end.

Death.

A period.

The end, but also a beginning.

Yes. I agree that killing sucks but dying alone scares me to the eye of my storm. So I had to make a deal with one of the devil's demons—Nomed. Now he's my bedmate. My partner. My friend. I'm too young to die.

Focus.

Organize.

Tighten my winds.

It's almost time to kill again.

I suck in my growing five-hundred-mile-wide girth and hold a Pilates plank over the vast expanse of the ocean, not moving and barely breathing as my wobbly frame trembles. I fill up my lungs with warm, moist air.

"Zephyrine," Nomed calls, and my name resonates as nothing more than a whisper, echoing off planets, stars, and Wormwood.

Again Nomed shouts through the subarctic wilderness of space. "Zephyrine." The vast expanse reduces his voice to a mere whisper inside my ear. "It's time. Shall we honor our deal, their death in exchange for your life?"

"Why now? I enjoy watching the lumbering two-legged creatures hide from the torrents of my fury like ants on a farm downstream from a deluge." I laugh, then Nomed laughs—one shallow guffaw that ends prematurely.

He's serious.

Dead serious. "We lived here first. Earth is our home," Nomed reminds me.

"It's your former home, not mine. I existed in a place of perfection—the Garden—not the chaos of a planet whose existence was without any form and completely devoid of order. I was never ruled by your master, Lucifer."

"But a deal is a deal."

"And so it is." I reply in hushed tones, winded between the gusts of my breath as I hover over jagged porpoise-gray waves in the middle of the Atlantic Ocean. "Shall we dance?"

"We shall. Assassinate the Orphan Dreamer, and you will live forever, never fearing death. Shalom, my friend."

Shalom—how could a demon promise peace, harmony, wholeness, prosperity, and tranquility? Conflicted about the true motives of my friend Nomed, I follow his instructions and about-face. Changing my trajectory, I face North America—the Orphan Dreamer's homeland.

Will Nomed honor our deal and exonerate me from death row, vanquishing my death sentence of execution in ten short days?

I suck up my emotions. "I'm coming for you, little one." My voice is a whisper, yet in the deepest part of my being, I rage. Warm sea water fuels my stormy constitution as I initiate my first ballerina-like pirouette.

I pivot again and again, spinning one hundred miles east of the college town of Gainesville, Florida.

Waiting.

Growing.

Strengthening.

I prepare for my mission—kill the Orphan Dreamer. "A simple task," Nomed had promised. But he also thought the Orphan Dreamer's name was Rose instead of Daniela Rose. Seances are unreliable sources of information.

Two hours elapse as I shift closer to Danny Rose Cavanaugh's soon-to-be resting place—her mother's bookstore.

The bookstore—which sits tucked away on a side street near the moss-laden oak-tree-infested University of Florida.

The bookstore is a gem of a place.

That is, until my nasty breath collapses the store's four brick walls, burying the Orphan Dreamer and her letter— the letter about a statue—that holds the key to thwarting Nomed's plans for Earth.

Focus, Zephyrine! Bury the Orphan Dreamer alive. Entomb her dreams.

Danny Rose calls me Hurricane.

I like the name.

I call her Avalanche—cold, unpredictable, and shifty. I suck up another mouthful of watery fuel, allowing the moisture to settle inside my gut. The eye of my rage, the most vulnerable part of me—the eye of the storm, as humans call it—remains quiet, as though Yeshua had whispered, "Peace be still."

As I strengthen, I erect a treacherous wall around my inside parts to protect them. Danny Rose calls this protective barrier the eye wall of my storm.

She should know.

Every creature possesses a defense mechanism. Hers is self-doubt, an endless fuel that feeds her depression. Let's not talk about the confusing and disorganized thoughts scampering around her empty skull.

Nomed means to kill her with the sword of her weakness. She will die alone. Afraid. Distraught. A failure. Like Lozen—the Apache warrior princess she and her friend like to admire.

I am her executioner because I refuse to die—much less slip into the oblivion of a cold, dark universe all alone. I took Nomed up on his promise, but can a fallen angel be trusted? Can death promise life? Will Nomed—Demon— deliver? I should have asked and answered these questions before now.

It's time. My time to take the stage and shine.

Arching backward, I spin faster and faster. Rotating clockwise, I spew out a gutful of tornadoes. My legs and arms fly outward until my extremities fade into a blur of rain and wind called rain bands.

Nomed will be pleased.

A flash flood churning down University Avenue will do the trick. It'll decimate the University of Florida's stately red brick buildings and toss ancient stones, moss-laden oaks, and alligators through the glass doors of the Cavanaugh bookstore.

The bookstore's name equals another irony: Don't Judge a Book by Its Cover.

Doesn't the dreamer's mother understand her own kind? It is an impossible task for an average human to not judge based upon the superficial. Since when could a human take the time to fully understand anything beyond skin deep?

They are a lazy species.

Nomed's right.

They—you—do not deserve life. So I bring you death in the form of water and wind. My companion, Death, laughs as she hides in the layers of my six-hundred-mile-wide girth. Marching across interstates, fields, and buildings, I thrash trees to their death while eating up my fuel—my breath, my life.

Anger does that—eats the life of the creature who harbors the vile emotion.

A cold blast of air rushes into my innards. "No!"

Volcanic rage rises within me and heats the intruding column of cold air invading my being.

Gasping for breath, I stall. My behemoth girth saves me.

The love handles of my eastern flank hover over the Atlantic Ocean, allowing the invading cool air to rise and generate a void of low pressure. Low pressure above and high pressure beneath create a pressure gradient above the ocean—the cold air warms and slips upward, continuing to inflate my big head crowned with portly oil-black clouds.

Beneath me, humans disappear inside storm shelters, running from my storm surges and tornadoes.

They will not escape.

I slam down a power line, casting families and old people inside a nursing home into utter darkness where there will be weeping and gnashing of teeth.

My behemoth-sized clouds loom nine miles above the ocean, but I squander my heat—my life's oxygen.

Quick!

Plan B.

Drop the pressure again. It's the only way to remain

strong. Shuddering, I guzzle more water, and the barometric pressure inside my core—inside my heart—drops faster than an orphan's hopes and dreams.

I suck in even more air. It condenses. Energy releases, heating the air and forcing it to rise. Daniela's physics teacher calls the phenomenon the Coriolis force.

Humans and their labels. I chuckle, because the bottom line has already been settled. I am just strengthening myself before the kill.

The humans label me as a category four hurricane with sustained winds of one hundred and fifty miles an hour. Tornadoes march before me as fearless soldiers in my bloodthirsty army, forming a dragon's tail. "Nomed, I cannot see you. You've not abandoned me—right?"

"I would never leave your side, Zephyrine."

"I'll live forever . . . as an eternal storm?" Doubt creeps into my core, threatening to cool down the hot, moist air that is my lifeblood.

"After she's dead."

"Don't betray me."

"I wouldn't dare."

Fifty more miles until I reach Danny Rose's haven. Then we will fight—but dreamers don't stand a chance in the wake of my nightmare. It's you and me, Orphan Dreamer, then your precious orphan. Ethan's already dead.

A draft of ice-cold air blows into my storm's eye and freeze-chills my core, starving me of my fuel—warmth and moisture bathed in a bath of low-pressure and rotational winds.

My eye wall begins to deconstruct. "Who's there? Who's stopping me? Get out of my way, whoever you are!"

"Since the beginning, trusting fallen angels has always

been considered a bad idea, Zephyrine," a deep voice rumbles.

"Who is it?"

"Who do you think?"

"Nomed?" My voice lands lighter than a feather. Fear has stripped my brave wings.

"You flatter him."

I inhale. The being behind the voice smells of cedar, myrrh, and . . . power. "It cannot be. Not now. Please."

"It can. It is."

"Adonai's warrior, Legna?"

"You're as clever as you are gullible and nasty."

The heart of me—my eye—deteriorates even faster, relinquishing its well-formed existence as my chaotic eye wall—my defense mechanism—collapses inward. I am as good as dead. Legna will stamp my death certificate with a period. "Leave me, Legna! You must leave me to my work."

"You know that I can't leave, don't you, little one?"

"Why defend the weak ones?" I suck in warm ocean water, dropping my internal pressure and increasing my wind speeds to one hundred and eighty miles an hour. I will not die without a fight.

"I don't defend *all* the weak ones."

"But you do. If you save the Dreamer, then she saves the rest, and they keep living."

"Only if they want to be saved. It's surprising how many of Earth's created beings lust for death, refusing life at all costs."

"Listen to me, Legna. Please. If you side with them and not with Nomed and me, then you must die as well."

"Give it your best shot, Zephyrine."

"I will. I am. Don't you feel me? I'm strengthening."

"And here I was thinking that some morbid human was waving a funeral fan in my direction."

"You're right. It's your funeral, and you're the guest of honor."

"Didn't receive the invite."

"You cannot withstand this storm—my storm."

"But I can . . . because I am the storm." Legna arches his back. His winter white wings splay out behind his sculpted, towering ebony frame. He claps his wings together, sending shock waves through my form.

His violet eyes pierce my gray clouds. He glares into my soul. I gasp. *For all things created, He's beautiful.*

"I know." He smiles wide, flashing a smile that could paralyze Lucifer and freeze hell over.

"I hate it when you read my mind."

"Then don't think—just blow your hot air." Feathers back, his thighs and calves flex taut and his feet dazzle as their elements—a mixture of onyx and bronzed gold—catch a sliver of sunlight.

The rubies and diamonds on the hilt of his sword sparkle beneath my flashes of lightning. *His body was made for war.* I weep, and my rain belts lash my soul.

"Don't cry. I'll be quick."

"Don't hurt me. Not for her."

He reaches for the hilt of his sword. A warrior's sword, which is simply Yahweh's words—words powerful enough to create life and conquer death forever when He said, "It. Is. Written!"

"Nomed," I cry out. "Come to me. Help me!"

Nomed's silence deafens the turbulence of my winds. In my greatest moment of need, it is a hard lesson to swallow: Nomed—my friend—has abandoned me. But I must fight for my second chance. My life.

I must fight Legna, and I must win. So I unleash the rage of the century. Winds inside my eye wall rotate at greater than two hundred miles an hour.

I am a beast who must rage alone.

37—Orphan Dreamer

9:00 A.M.
TUESDAY, JULY 8, 1998
GAINESVILLE, FLORIDA

DANIELA AND EMMALINE HAD TO walk a mile from the University of Florida parking lot to Mama Cavanaugh's bookstore. Rain splattered atop the cobblestone sidewalk, collecting into tiny rivers that coursed over brick mortar and drenched their feet.

"Limy." Daniela stepped into a rain puddle, soaking her flip-flops. "It may be pouring buckets of rain, but it's still hotter than the devil's armpit!"

"Why on earth were you smelling the devil's armpits, Danny-girl?"

"It's a figure of speech."

"That doesn't change the fact that a hurricane's bearing down on Gainesville, preparing to shred this town into ribbons." Emmaline raised her voice, attempting to out-shout the howling winds. "Perfect timing for my little trip."

"I tried to tell you. But the storm should decrease in intensity as it crosses land. And we're almost to Mom's bookstore. Besides, there's no way a hurricane would dare to invade The Swamp—not even a cat-five hurricane would tangle with the Florida Gators."

"Why?"

"We're apex predators."

"On the football field, Danny-girl, but not in life." Emmaline tilted her body closer to Daniela's as she fought to stay dry under their umbrella.

"A gator can chomp down on Tim the Beaver anywhere and anytime."

"I applaud your loyalty, but a storm doesn't care anything about first downs, quarterbacks, or footballs." Emmaline jumped over another rain puddle, almost catching her toe on a crack in the sidewalk.

"Careful!" With one hand, Daniela dabbed her brow with a chilled washcloth as she clenched the umbrella's handle with the other. "Where's my funeral fan already?"

"Nine more hours and you'll have it."

"Shouldn't be so eager to visit the dead."

"We're not normal, Danny. Why fake it now?"

"We're seventeen, almost adults. That's what adults do—fake it 'til they make it." Two events eclipsed the Orphan Dreamer's calendar: her seventeenth birthday celebration and her childhood bully's mother's funeral.

I know! I know! Morbidly voyeuristic.

The truth.

Daniela never learned the art of saying no, even as a child. So when Claire Underwood—bully and queen bee of their high school—invited Daniela to her mother's funeral, Daniela had said yes. Bad habits refused to stay dead, but no funeral would dampen Daniela's birthday plans.

Smiling ear to ear, she waded through rain puddles as they navigated a red-brick cobblestone street, her most spectacular birthday present walking beside her—Emmaline Georgiana Winterlyn Darbyshire, a girl with too many first names who had chosen Daniela as her kindred spirit in spite of everything.

And Daniela had chosen Emmaline in spite of her addiction to deception and spying, but only after they had come to an agreement: no lying to friends.

"When we arrive at the store, lunch is on me. Actually, Mom and I made stew last night."

"Good. I'm starved, and my skin's shriveling up. I'll look like a bleached raisin at the funeral, squashing my hopes of landing a hot guy."

"Hot guys at a funeral?" Daniela began to run.

"Never miss an opportunity." Emmaline power walked beside Daniela.

"I wouldn't call attending my nemesis's mother's funeral in this gully washer an opportunity."

"What's a gully washer?"

"Southern talk for heavy rains."

"More like the rise of the River Thames."

So British. "I just adore you, Emmaline Georgiana."

"Save your adoration for a warm-blooded man. Rain is an aphrodisiac, and it muffles the noises of a make-out session."

"Please, Limy!"

"What's flapping your sails?"

"Control your urges, especially around my mom. She's not as avant-garde as yours."

"Okay, fine. Tell me about Claire's mom."

"Violet Underwood was a Southern belle if there ever was one, but no one will remember her for her Southernisms."

"Why?"

"My mom will tell you."

My knowing tells me that someone besides Violet will die at the end of this story. This is the Orphan Dreamer's tale, where some people die, some live, and some wish they were dead.

38—ORPHAN DREAMER

9:07 A.M.
TUESDAY, JULY 8, 1998
GAINESVILLE, FLORIDA

RAIN PUMMELED THE BRICK SIDEWALK, making Daniela's feet slip in and out of her sandals. The sky hung low. Its coloring mimicked Daniela's complexion after she vomited—gray with splatters of green. "Actually, I've changed my mind. We need to go—a tornado's coming."

"How do you know?"

"The sky looks green, and angry skies never lie." A tremor marched through Daniela's body as though an earthquake had ripped open the earth beneath her feet. "We have to run." Would her lungs keep up with her legs? She hadn't shared her diagnosis with her friend. Pulmonary hypertension took names and kicked butt.

"Just like in the Jemez Mountains. Talk about climate

change!" Emmaline burst into a gallop, and Daniela kept pace.

"Who the heck knows?" Saving her breath, Daniela stopped talking and started thinking. Unpredictable weather: was it a sign or a coincidence?

According to Luke—believer in Yeshua, practicing doctor, and writer of a Gospel account—in the end, there will be terrible earthquakes, famines, and dreadful diseases in various places. He wrote that terrifying sights and miraculous signs will come from the sky.

Lightning bolts pulled a body of menacing gray clouds across the sky. The sun disappeared. A sheet of rain formed the clouds' dragon tail, whipping back and forth and throwing buckets of rain atop Daniela's umbrella.

Daniela dodged a swaying lamppost. She gasped, out of breath. Emmaline slowed down her pace. Her breath warmed the Orphan Dreamer's neck. Hunching low, Daniela jumped across a rain puddle before landing solidly on the doorstep of her mother's bookstore.

A gust of wind charged down the narrow street, thrashing Daniela's back and flipping her umbrella inside out. Why had she even bothered with the thing? With rain-slicked hands, she gripped the tarnished copper door handle, pushed the thumb lever, then shouldered her way past the bookstore's red-stained glass double doors.

"Hurry up, Limy. Get inside. Hide beneath the stairs and take my mom with you."

"Done!"

Drenched, Daniela leaned outside and shook out her umbrella beneath the entry's overhang. A black condensation cloud dropped down from the storm cell's wall cloud. A gush of sticky, hot air channeled past the door, carrying a strong odor of freshly cut grass.

Storm!

She bolted inside, closed the door, then tossed the nylon contraption into an upside-down empty wine barrel—her mom's umbrella holder.

"Get in here, Daniela!" her mom said. Daniela locked the door, then slapped masking tape over the door's glass. "A tornado has touched down east of Leonard's Pizza."

Dressed in an ivory wool skirt, a silk sanguine shirt, and brown pumps, Mrs. Cavanaugh rushed from behind a juggernaut oak checkout counter with a towel in hand. "Dry off on your way behind the stairs." She patted her daughter down like a nervous cop with a suspect, but her touch made Daniela feel safe and loved.

"Thanks, Mom."

After ten minutes, the wind quieted, so the trio emerged from their hiding place. The freshly cut grass scent had dispersed. But the storm still brewed. Daniela ran to the front door. "Mom. Limy. That lamppost is toast."

Her kindred spirits peeked over her shoulder. "That was a near miss," Emmaline said.

"Maybe Legna protected us." Daniela backed away from the door and plopped onto the couch; her mother headed toward the sales register.

The familiar scents of citrus, wood, coffee, ink, and paper—from books, lots of books—dipped and dived around velvet and leather armchairs and couches and a set of wooden stairs before reaching Daniela's nose.

This was a place where dreams sprouted feet, then started walking. Her muscles relaxed as she slid her waterproof bag packed with a change of clothes off her shoulders.

Only rude girls attended a funeral sopping wet.

She caught her mother's gaze and smiled at the warmth

and affection that twinkled behind her coffee-brown eyes. "Love you, Mom!"

"Suga, did you girls eat breakfast before you left the house?" That was a Southern mother for you. Hello didn't exist in her vocabulary unless she was salty about something.

"Didn't have time."

"We're starving, Mrs. Cavanaugh." Emmaline circled around behind me.

"I've got a crockpot of stew simmering in my office upstairs. I'll fix you both a hot cocoa. We're fortunate the power didn't go out."

"Thanks, Mom."

"Skipping breakfast." My mother shook her head. Her black curls threatened to spill out of her bobby-pinned coif. "Danny Rose, you know better."

"Sorry. We were busy."

"You'll catch your death running around campus starving, cold, and wet. Don't even think about traipsing across the world on your medical trips."

"I'll do better." Daniela was convinced her mother had purchased this store location just to be closer to the medical school campus. "After the funeral, may Limy and I hunker down in the bookstore and study?"

"Depends on the hurricane," her mom said.

Daniela donned her most-convincing sad puppy eyes.

"This store's probably safer than our fifty-year-old house. You girls can come back as long as you promise to study and not talk about boys. Stay in the wine cellar. It's fortified." She flashed a smile, and sunlight burst past the threatening clouds and shined on her daughter.

Daniela completed her mother's sentence, "Because boys and books don't match."

"Exactly." Her mom's expression melted into a satisfied smile, yet her face appeared more resolved than that of Yosemite's El Capitan. "Virginity is not a disease. You girls would do well to remember that."

"Your mom's kidding, right?" Emmaline whispered.

Seventeen years old and never been kissed. "Actually, my plan A and my plan B are to remain a virgin until I marry."

"That's weird, Sandbox." Emmaline called Daniela that whenever she believed her friend's thoughts were bordering on schizophrenia.

Daniela's thoughts were perfectly organized, but the process of explaining them to linear thinkers required a boatload of energy. "Don't judge me. You can make your choice."

"I will."

"So drop it." Daniela had always preferred to color inside the lines. Even though her thoughts were disorganized at times, her actions were methodical. Regardless of what Emmaline thought, Daniela didn't disagree with her mother's reasoning. Saving her innocence for the right guy would help her ensure a less messy future—no hard decisions or plan B required.

A half an hour later, dressed in funeral digs, Daniela and Emmaline walked back downstairs and past the book tree, a ten-foot-wide bookshelf that had been designed to resemble a tree. A carpenter had carved divots for books; a canopy of silk leaves, fake branches, and roses hung from the rafters.

"Sit down and eat your stew." Coffee-shop approved music played in the background as Mrs. Cavanaugh wrapped Francine Rivers' *An Echo in the Darkness* inside brown paper.

Daniela sat in an armchair nestled in the bookstore's alcove. Her mother stood behind the counter and stated the obvious: "That storm's still brewing outside."

"Meteorologists promised a category-four hurricane," Daniela continued the asinine conversation. "It's a cat-five now."

"I'm worried about you girls. That church building for the funeral should've been condemned years ago."

"A bona fide haunted house. Great, Danny-girl." Emmaline smirked.

"It'll slow down before it reaches Gainesville, Mom. It always does. There's not enough ocean water to fuel its rage." Something else was bothering her mother. "What's wrong?"

"Nothing." She finished wrapping the historical novel. "Girls, the truth is . . ."

"What's this truth, Mrs. C.?" Sitting in a recliner with her legs crossed, Emmaline rested her spoon on the lip of her bowl.

Daniela held her breath, waiting for the verdict—her mother's truth. Daughters really did care what their mothers thought, no matter what they said.

"That dead woman, Violet Turnsdale Underwood . . . she chose to bed with that monster husband of hers. He was a grand wizard of the Klan and rained down terror on your daddy and me." Mother cleared her throat, and her voice dropped to a feathery whisper. "I don't want either of you to fall into that trap. You hear me?"

"Mom, I don't see myself marrying a KKK member, a mafia boss, or a Nazi. Okay?"

"Neither do I." Emmaline swallowed a gulp of hot cocoa, and Daniela relished the stew full of beef, carrots, onions, radishes, and potatoes.

"There's more than one kind of monster," her mother said. "Above all else, marry a man for his character."

"Do you really think the senator murdered his wife?" Daniela asked.

"I do. In the world of spiders and devils, bedmates eventually become victims. Look at the wolf spider. Hate never was a reliable kind of glue, not the kind that kept hearts joined together for an eternity."

"The female eats her mate after mating." Daniela scratched her back, feeling as though a tarantula had crawled underneath her dress and laid a cluster of eggs. Needless to say, she hated spiders.

"Well then, girls, you'll do good to remember the wolf spider before you choose your husbands." Her emphasis landed sharply on *husbands*. Not boyfriends.

Questions about romance raced through Daniela's mind like flittering butterflies, but she dared not ask them and ruffle her mother's nerves.

Calm down and catch the butterflies, Danny Rose.

She breathed instead of asking.

"What about boyfriends?" Emmaline lived to push limits.

"A boyfriend shouldn't step inside your house, much less lie in your bed. Goodness gracious, child. Who raised you, darling?"

"The daughter of a Methodist preacher." Daniela's mischievous friend sniggered as she whispered to Daniela, "Is this that black mom honesty you warned me about?"

"She's not finished yet," Daniela whispered back.

"Are they actually followers of the Way?"

"My parents?"

"Yes, honey. That's who we're talking about, right?"

"Speaking of mothers," Emmaline shot back. "What about matriphagy, the process of spiderlings eating their mother after birth?"

"Don't be cheeky, Limy." Mrs. Cavanaugh wagged her head. "Eating one's own mother! I am taking you to a Southern Baptist revival service this weekend. Don't worry about a change of clothes. We'll wash your funeral getup. It'll have to do."

"Going to another funeral—just a different name . . . that'll scare the devil out of me," Emmaline whispered mostly to herself, and Daniela fought back a giggle.

"Mom, do you like my funeral attire?" Daniela stood up and spun around, showing off her knee-length, A-line taffeta dress topped with capped sleeves and a boat neck. "Modest enough?"

"Check," her mother affirmed.

"Classy?"

"Check."

"Stylish."

"Mmhmm." Mrs. Cavanaugh paused.

"The dress looks hideous—even I know that," Daniela admitted and winked at Limy.

Emmaline moved her lips—*Thanks, Danny-girl*—but didn't utter a sound. Then she played along with Daniela's mother. "So why are you wearing it?" Emmaline challenged.

"It's funeral plain, allowing me to blend into the background, and I knew that Mom would approve."

"And with one yard of taffeta, you have single-handedly squashed any chance of enticing a husband."

"Then I'll never have to worry about eating my mate or matriphagy. No husband, no kids." She glanced at her mother. Mrs. Cavanaugh's facial expression said it all: *I approve of this message: chastity until marriage or better yet—remain a spinster.*

Daniela had calmed the prudish beast inside her mother.

But the possibility of never marrying and never starting a family pushed storm clouds into Daniela's sunshine.

Daniela's mother broke her dark trance. "Danny Rose, the dress hides your skin, and the boat neck obscures your cleavage." Proper and classy, her mother waltzed from behind the counter. "You're a lady, and ladies don't need to flash their breasts around like a driver's license at the liquor store—not that I know anything about liquor."

"Cool analogy though, Mrs. C."

"And you, my lovely Limy, would do well to stay away from all spirits except for the Holy Spirit," Mrs. Cavanaugh said.

The only prop missing to make Daniela's mother into a full-blown Puritan was a high-collared paisley dress. The Orphan Dreamer choked on a mouthful of humor.

"I only like good spirits, Mrs. Cavanaugh." Emmaline placed her empty soup bowl on a glass coffee table, then strolled toward a stack of unwrapped books. Her raven silk pantsuit flowed like midnight-blue ocean waves, dipping and diving into the shallow crevasses of her lithe frame. She explored the titles. "Sounds dark, even sadistic."

"Mother's definitely not into that." Nervous, a halting chuckle escaped Daniela's mouth as she placed her empty bowl on the coffee table in front of her. "I was dropped off by a stork on July eighth in 1981 at Alachua General Hospital."

"Not true, Daniela Rose." Mother radiated a mischievous grin. "The proof hides in the pudding." She rested her hand on her flat abdomen. "I am missing a few internal parts now, though."

"Mom, gross!"

"I'm proud of the fact that you were conceived in the tenderness of marital caress."

"Do tell us all about the tenderness and the caresses, Mrs. C."

"You're embarrassing me!" Daniela hissed. "It's like this, Limy, when I was a few minutes old, the doctor performed a hysterectomy on my mom. It happens every day. Uncontrollable uterine bleeding."

"You almost killed your own mother during childbirth? Sheesh, Danny-girl. Matriphagy in its rarest form."

"So macabre, Limy." Daniela rolled her eyes.

"Laugh in the morning and cry in the evening, girls. Today you may judge me a prude, but your choice of husband will make you or break you—for life."

"Sounds like a prison sentence on cell block nine." Emmaline winked at Daniela.

"It's worse . . ." Mom's voice raised half an octave and cracked on a few sharps on the way up. "It's a living hell."

"Then Violet's death would have been a great relief for her." Emmaline chose a regency romance novel, then sat down near Daniela on a terracotta-orange velvet couch.

"Relief cannot be found in the grips of hell's fire." Defiant, Mrs. Cavanaugh rotated her shoulders back. "Girls, if you ignore my warnings and choose to share a bed with a devil, I promise you will either become the devil's helper or one of his victims." Mrs. Cavanaugh's eyebrows rose in sync with the shrill of her voice.

"Are you trying to talk to us about the birds and the

bees, Mom?" Daniela quipped, trying to release the steam from the pressure-cooker conversation.

"As though birds or bees could teach two young women about men." She shook her head. "I will not allow you girls to leave my presence without some degree of instruction before you go running around in your little black outfits without supervision."

"It's 1998, Mom."

"I graduated summa cum laude from Spelman College. I know what year it is."

Emmaline propped her legs up on the couch, rolled up the legs of her pantsuit, then slouched down in the seat. Daniela's mother quickly covered her bare legs with a wool blanket. "Daniela and I are attending a funeral, not a prom. Besides, I was joking about finding a man at this death waltz—I just wanted to yank your Puritanical strings. That's all. I'm not that desperate. I'm already dating two guys."

"Two boyfriends . . . Daniela, you're not to follow Limy's example."

"I'm not in the same league as Limy." Daniela gave Emmaline a mysterious glance. "Beer-fed cacti. Remember?"

Emmaline winked, and Daniela tried to continue, but Mrs. Cavanaugh interrupted. "Beer? Cacti? What are you two going on about?"

"Nothing, Mom. Just know that I'll celebrate if I can score a man with all of his fingers and toes." Daniela criss-crossed her legs, threatening to rip her A-line dress at the seams.

"Daniela Rose, I can see right up your . . . sit like a lady."

"Sorry." Daniela uncrossed her legs. No need to stop her mother's heart. Performing CPR was tiring. She'd done the act before—four years ago, when her grandmother died inside her North Carolina farmhouse. "I'm a tomboy. Can't help it."

"You're not Tom or a boy. You are Daniela—a breathtaking young lady and my cinnamon-spiced bumblebee." Her voice dripped with maternal pride. "And it's nice to see you in a dress for a change."

"Only took a funeral," Daniela quipped, minimizing the compliment as embarrassment flushed her cheeks.

"Cinnamon-spiced bumblebee?" Emmaline faced her friend. "What's that about?"

"It's our special language."

"Cute."

"My nickname or the fact that my mother is trying to protect our purity at a wake?"

"Both." Emmaline read the first line of her chosen book. "It's a mouthful, but your mom's right—you're breathtaking." She tilted her chin. "The dress is . . . somewhat interesting. It refuses to steal your spotlight."

"Thank you—I think." Daniela fidgeted with the edges of her dress.

"I completely understand your mother's efforts."

"You do?"

"Of course I do. Doesn't your Bible say something about the dead rising again?" Emmaline sipped her hot cocoa and turned the page of her romance novel.

"Yes, during the Great Escape."

"You mean the Rapture, according to the Baptists?" Emmaline joked loud enough so Mrs. Cavanaugh could hear, and her eyes twinkled with mischief and flecks of amber.

"Yes," Daniela conceded, "but the Great Escape sounds more romantic."

"If the dead are raised at the senator's wife's funeral, our modesty will keep us from tempting graveyard zombies."

Emmaline's auburn curls, drunk on Boston summer sun, cascaded down her pale shoulders.

"Good point." Daniela bit her lip, halting a full display of what would have been a stupid-looking grin. In the meantime, Emmaline flashed a flawless smile.

In spite of her confusion, the Orphan Dreamer no longer needed to avoid uncomfortable situations. Because Emmaline—Daniela's life raft—sat opposite the girl whose destiny loomed larger than her brown-girl afro.

Mrs. Cavanaugh observed her daughter's new friend. She sniffed quietly, then wiped a stray tear away from her right eye. Hands shaking, the proper woman stirred a cup of tea while hiding her deepest emotions. Like daughter, like mother.

Daniela's mother changed the subject as she kicked off her heels and sat down beside her Daniela. "The senator's heart ain't nothing more than a thumpin' gizzard."

"A thumpin' gizzard?" Emmaline laughed, and Mrs. Cavanaugh's face registered pleasure.

"Southern vernacular—a.k.a. Claire's father lived as a coldhearted and cruel man, so tread carefully, girls. And Mom's warning us that boys are basically a disease—a pandemic without a cure." Daniela rotated her shoulders back, pleased to share a bit of her Southern culture with her New England friend.

"My vote . . . let's get infected." Emmaline kicked off her taupe suede kitten heels onto the mahogany floor. The *clack* startled Mrs. Cavanaugh—or maybe it was Emmaline's vote that had caused Daniela's mother to jump.

After almost spitting out a mouthful of cocoa, Daniela clenched the handle of her mug. *Infected. By boys.* What would her mother say?

"Sit up straight, girls. Don't wrinkle your outfits." Mrs.

Cavanaugh left the couch and marched to the end of the counter to begin closing out the register. "No use staying open in this gully washer."

That was it!

Gorgeous girls really did get away with murder.

Emmaline corrected her posture. No surprise there. England's aristocracy had invented posture.

Daniela sat up straight, mimicking Emmaline's peacock pose. Satisfied with the girls' rigid positions, Mrs. Cavanaugh removed a stack of book tags from the old-fashioned cash register. "Take these and a Sharpie—write 'twelve ninety-nine' on each tag."

Emmaline and Daniela obeyed.

Mrs. Cavanaugh finished wrapping the last of the books inside beige paper, hiding the publisher's cover—a layer of paper-thin skin designed to entice a reader to open an unfamiliar book, read the first sentence, then decide to reject or purchase the literary tome. Indeed, a dim prospect for an author's future or a teenager's romantic future.

Daniela studied her mother's intentional movements. She worked faithfully. A Proverbs 31 woman indeed. "Limy," she said in a hushed tone, "Mom only wants to protect us, not stifle our fun."

"It's still fun to tease her," Emmaline whispered back. "I think she's hiding a secret—don't you? A lovesick past or a devastating romance."

"Secrets are okay. My mom's our kindred spirit. Don't push it. She's not as young as your mother."

"Love you to the moon and back, Danny Rose." Emmaline's gaze lingered on Daniela's face, and just like that, the demo of Vitamin C's song "Graduation (Friends Forever)" played over the store's speakers.

The Orphan Dreamer eyed her mom. Guilt stuck to

her face like day-old ice cream as her fingers slipped away from the CD player.

Don't cry! Blubbering teenage girls define lamebrains.

"Mom, you didn't!"

"I did! Chuck at Epic Elektra owed me a favor. Happy birthday, Daniela Rose—my bumblebee." Mrs. Cavanaugh removed a small round cake from the dorm-sized refrigerator. "Cake?"

"Friends forever, Danny-girl." Emmaline blew a handful of kisses. Both teenagers cut a slice of cake and ate at the counter. "Mrs. Cavanaugh, why wrap each book inside plain paper? The publishers paid good money for those gorgeous covers."

"No reader should be forced to purchase a book based upon lust at first sight. Don't you agree?" Mrs. Cavanaugh's fingers paused as she waited for Emmaline's response. She wasn't talking about books or plain brown paper. Daniela held her breath.

"It's a refreshing concept." Emmaline ate another bite of fudge cake.

"Her patrons purchase books by the busload." Daniela licked icing from her fingers.

"Purchasing a book at Don't Judge a Book by Its Cover would be like . . ." Emmaline infused her next three words with a shot of disgust, "an arranged marriage."

"Thought you adored surprises." Daniela finished her cake.

"Forced emesis would be less torment than an arranged marriage. I need to know my man—really know him, Southern Baptist King James style of knowing."

The word *know* in the KJV Bible equaled coitus.

"But you can never really know anyone's truest

motives." A delicate smile picked up where Mrs. Cavanaugh's wise saying ended.

In perfect calligraphy, Mrs. Cavanaugh scrawled the book title across the wrapping paper as well as a few hints about the contents of the book: a mysterious letter, youth, friendship, choices, romance, sacrifice, survival.

"Wait a minute!" Daniela walked to her mother's side of the counter. "That's my story."

"Then you'll enjoy reading *A Voice in the Wind* by Francine Rivers." She gifted an unwrapped copy to her daughter. "Happy birthday." Before shelving another copy of the book on one of her store's bookcases, Mrs. Cavanaugh tied a velvet cream-orange ribbon around the length and width of the wrapped book.

"Thanks, Mom." Daniela leaned on her mother's shoulder.

"Mrs. C., can I say something?"

"Speak your mind, child."

Mom, that's a mistake, Daniela wanted to say.

"Not all women exude the weakness and indecisiveness of your customers." Emmaline ate her last bite of cake. "If the devil proves to be a disappointment, I'll leave him— and if a book sucks, I'll chuck it and purchase another. No harm, no foul."

"Ah, but you're wrong, Limy. After you've lived a bit longer, you will learn that precious few women possess the strength to open their mouth and speak truth in a relationship, much less scrape superglue off their shoes and go anywhere." Mrs. Cavanaugh's voice softened from school mom to concerned mother. "It's called a soul-tie for a reason, baby girl."

"Listening to you, marriage sounds a ghastly business."

Ghastly—so English.

"Marry the right man at the right time, nothing compares to the institution." Mrs. Cavanaugh reached across the counter and rested her hand on top of Emmaline's. "At best, women choose a mediocre companion, then moan and groan to their girlfriends about their poor choice, only to become nothing more than mirror images of their husbands."

"I wouldn't!"

"No matter how much a woman deceives herself and believes she is more than a copy of her other half, she rarely is. As for books and as a bookseller, I would be glad to sell you another book."

"I won't become anyone's mirror image," Emmaline whispered in protest. "Especially if he's ugly, poor, and uninteresting."

"Ugly is as ugly does. Same goes for stupid," Mrs. Cavanaugh said.

"You could remove your shoes, then no need to scrape superglue from their soles," Daniela quipped.

"Clever." Mrs. Cavanaugh straightened her hair.

"Mom, you should come with us to Mrs. Violet's funeral."

"In case the dead are raised, and zombies walk Earth, someone needs to sit near the phone, ready to dial nine-one-one." Mrs. Cavanaugh deadpan stared at Emmaline and then Daniela before breaking into a raucous laughter.

"Mrs. C., how dare you pull our legs!" Emmaline swallowed the last few giggles, then furrowed her brow. "Tell me the truth. Was Violet insane?" Emmaline asked. "Or were you just saying she was?"

"Ask Claire." Daniela suggested as she smoothed the

wrinkles from her dress. "Little Miss Untouchable may actually speak to you."

"Why would she speak to me? The girl doesn't know me."

"She's not in the habit of talking to dirt." Daniela's eyes locked with Emmaline's.

"You're not dirt," Mrs. Cavanaugh inserted.

"You never made peace with her," Emmaline said.

"Claire acknowledged my existence after our pastor preached about loving your neighbor."

"Is the invite to her mother's funeral some sort of cruel joke?"

"Maybe." Daniela shrugged.

"Devils. Beds. Eight-legged wolf spiders devouring mates." Emmaline stood behind Daniela and rubbed her ice-cold fingers up her bare arm.

The Orphan Dreamer pulled away. "Can we stop talking about bedmates and spiders?"

"I'd love to." Emmaline's upper lip curled into something sinister and manipulative. "Maybe your oily boy will rise from the dead during the funeral, scare Claire out of her wits, then sweep you off your feet." After stinking up the room with bad humor, Emmaline smoothly shifted gears. "Where's the professor's letter and the statue?"

Daniela hesitated. "In my bag upstairs."

"Go get it," Emmaline commanded in a soft but threatening tone. "Mrs. Cavanaugh, if Mongolian soldiers hid the Ark of the Covenant inside Temujin's—Genghis Khan's—tomb, we need to find that tomb in order to stop the pandemic."

Daniela's jaw tensed. *Do not tell me what to do.* Silent, she sat back down. Mrs. Cavanaugh studied Emmaline's demeanor—confident, insistent—and Daniela's—humiliated and annoyed.

"Emmaline Georgiana, Daniela is my only child," Mrs. Cavanaugh said and then paused, allowing her steel-magnolia threat to settle in. "Yahweh gave me Daniela, and He predestined my little girl to execute a mission: to save us—you, me, and Claire—from a nasty pandemic. But my mission rings simple: protect and guide my bumblebee to the sweet nectar of happiness and success, then squash any bugs that dare feed on her flowers and leaves."

"Which means?"

"I will fight to the death to protect my daughter. Pandemic or not, I am not afraid to die and neither is her father." Her words hang midair. "As a matter of fact, we donned our lifejackets—Yeshua's sacrifice—years ago, and we stand ready to cross the Jordan River. Saving the world is Daniela's mission, not her parents'."

"Yes . . . ma'am."

"That's settled, then." Mrs. Cavanagh rested her case, and Daniela understood that her mother was not willing to follow in Yahweh's footsteps and offer up her one and only child on a human-constructed cross as a sacrifice for undeserving humanity.

Not going to happen. God's love for fallen humanity may be otherworldly, but Daniela's parents' love was not.

Plain.

Definitely simple.

"As for Genghis Khan's tomb," Mrs. Cavanaugh continued, "God knows where those soldiers buried their warlord. And if they did hide the Ark of the Covenant inside their master's tomb, only God could reveal the grave's location to Daniela. But her father and I will not approve of her aimlessly traipsing around to find it."

"Would God reveal the location through her dreams?"

"Yahweh named my daughter the Orphan Dreamer for a reason."

"Yes, Daniela possesses a colossal destiny. Are you afraid?" Limy fought back. *Go, Limy! Go!*

"What concerned mother isn't?"

"If oily boy eventually rises from the deadness of Daniela's dreams, what kind of man will he be?"

"I don't know, but I do know that prayer changes every-thing—even the destructive ways of a man. As I said, right man at the right time."

"Your proof?"

"Read the New Testament biblical story of Saul, who evolved into the Apostle Paul."

"Tell me the story, Mrs. C."

"A Jewish Pharisee, Saul, persecuted the followers of the Way after Yeshua ascended back to heaven. But then one day, Yeshua appeared to Saul as the Light of the World and showed him that he had misunderstood the motives of the followers of the Way."

"What did Saul do after that?"

"After Yeshua transformed Saul's heart, Saul changed his habits."

"Habits are hard to change," Emmaline said.

"A change in name can change a destiny."

"Explain." Emmaline's gaze never left Mrs. Cavana-ugh's face.

"Saul embraced a new name, Paul, while embracing his new mission."

"And?"

"For the rest of Paul's life, he championed Yeshua's message of salvation by grace—not salvation by good deeds." Mrs. Cavanaugh cleared her throat.

"So he linked up with the people he had previously per-secuted?"

"It's easy to mistreat those we do not understand."

"Agreed."

"Not only did Paul hail the cause of the followers of the Way, but Jewish leaders and gentile politicians also flogged him because of this new salvation-by-grace message."

"He kicked the chair out from under the religious-po-litical factions of his time. Good for him." Emmaline sat back.

"The Romans imprisoned Paul for most of his remain-ing life, but while imprisoned, he wrote the majority of the New Testament, beginning each letter to the various persecuted churches with these words: 'Paul, an apostle of Jesus Christ.' "

As the angry storm pummeled the windows and brick with hail and rain, the trio sat in reverent silence.

After a few moments of quiet, Emmaline said, "Saul to Paul. A great comeback story. Christianity's greatest failure transformed into its greatest success." She hesi-tated. "What about Violet's husband, and what about oily boy—an orphan whom Lucifer may convince to become the dreaded antichrist? How do their comeback stories look?"

Daniela noted that Emmaline had left out the detail that the Sons of Venus, a group of probable Nephilim, had planned to turn oily boy to their side if he ever emerged from Daniela's dreams.

"No different than my Daniela, you are a curious girl." Mrs. Cavanaugh chuckled. "But Violet committed a fatal error when she married Senator Underwood. There is no comeback story for her."

"Why, exactly?"

"When the devil loses, he no longer needs helpers—demons and demon-possessed humans. Instead he lusts for victims, and so he turns on those who've been loyal to him and murders them for sport. That's the devil's m.o."

"So the senator was basically a vampire. What does that say about Daniela's oily boy?"

"God will have the final say."

Emmaline swiveled in her chair and faced the Orphan Dreamer. "Danny-girl, my gut instinct says we skip the funeral, hang out at the bookstore with your mom, and discuss the rest of the topics in the professor's letter as well as clarify our thoughts about the Skeleton Key. If we need to research a topic, the university's library can't be that far from here."

"Only a ten-minute walk." Rain and wind bended wispy trees, protesting their foolish plans. "After the storm passes, we can walk to the library."

"But we're still attending a funeral—during a hurricane?"

"We don't have to go, Limy."

"You promised. You hate lying, so we're going. As you know, I'm turning over a new leaf—my word is as reliable as yours. But in plain English, why did the senator murder Violet, Mrs. C.?" Emmaline demanded.

"Let's talk, plain and simple. Why do you really care about Violet Turnsdale Underwood or even oily boy?" Mrs. Cavanaugh sat down beside Daniela and across from Emmaline.

Uh oh.

As though Daniela's friend needed to hide while protecting a secret from the mother-daughter duo, Emmaline removed a makeup case from her purse and reapplied her foundation, blush, and lipstick. "My dad knew the senator," she finally admitted.

"Why didn't you tell me, Limy?"

"Is the detail important? Secrets, not lies. Remember?"

"Wait, Daniela." Mrs. Cavanaugh's tone dropped into her storytelling voice. "The day Violet died, it was a sweltering Florida day. Senator Roger Underwood had lost the election. Furious, he beat Violet to a pulp. The papers said so as well as Ms. Clipper—that woman knows everything."

"He lost an election, not an arm." Daniela leaned against her mother's shoulder.

"The beating proved that."

"Senator Underwood murdered his wife, and he's not in jail, Mrs. C."

"In America, do the rich, white, and powerful males face the same laws as the poor, brown, and powerless females?" Mrs. Cavanaugh's face redefined serious. "Just now, victims of one of the largest human trafficking rings are finally getting noticed, but no justice—yet."

Emmaline looked down and away then shook her head.

"I didn't think so." Daniela's mother continued. "Violet's father had bought Roger's six previous elections, but the oil tycoon refused to do so again, ending the senator's career." Mother pulled her daughter closer. "Evil never wants to go down alone."

"Mom."

"Yes, darling?"

"Do *you* believe oily boy will grow up and degenerate into another megalomaniac dictator like Claire's father?"

"Prayer changes everything and everyone, even the trajectory of a traumatized orphaned boy. Pray. Then when you're tired of praying, pray and fast."

"But if I forget to pray—or I don't pray hard enough—will Earth's destruction be my fault?"

"Mrs. C., if Daniela forgets to pray, will my best friend go down in history as just another Eva Braun?" Sliding to the edge of the couch, Emmaline hammered a proverbial nail, then waited.

Mrs. Cavanaugh remained quiet for a long time, her lips moving but no sound coming from her mouth.

She sighed—heavy and long. "I don't know the future, but I know who holds my Daniela and my Limy in His powerful hands. Yahweh is a good father. So girls, rest in His powerful yet safe embrace while you wait for Him to answer your questions."

Tired and emotional, Emmaline wasn't satisfied with Mrs. Cavanaugh's answer, so Daniela's mother gestured for Emmaline to join her and Daniela.

The adventurous redhead and the demure crow-head sat on the wise woman's left and right.

She held their hands, then whispered a Jewish blessing over her girls, "The Lord bless you and keep you; the Lord make His face shine upon you, and be gracious to you; the Lord lift up His countenance upon you, and give you peace."

"Mommy, blessing or not, I don't want to leave you tonight." Daniela practically whined. "That awful hurricane's brewing like a batch of bad coffee. It's going to be scary driving to that funeral."

"You gave Claire your word."

"Next time your middle-school bully asks you to attend her mother's funeral," Emmaline threw in her two cents, "tell her no."

"Thanks, Limy. I never would've thought of that on my own. Besides, you were coming to town and I thought—"

"You thought that I might want to meet a dead woman

at her own funeral and endure her crazy murderous family?" Emmaline huffed and puffed. "I hope the local police locked the senator inside a cell and threw away the key."

"As my mom said, they haven't found the senator or arrested him," Daniela shared.

"How exactly do you lose a grown man?"

"Don't know, but he's still at large."

"Crikey, Danny-girl!" Emmaline kicked up the decibel level of her Demi Moore–esque voice. "For the record, I enjoy dance halls, co-ed parties, and good movies, not funerals."

"I've got it." Guilt soaked Daniela's soul. "Mom, you've told me over and over that in a friendship, there's room for secrets but never lies."

"There can be too few secrets and too much truth in any relationship." Her mother rotated her wedding ring around her finger.

"When does a secret qualify as a lie?"

"When the motive of keeping the secret was to deceive and then mislead a person," Mrs. Cavanaugh answered, sharing her ageless wisdom.

"I'm sorry, Limy."

"For what?"

"Deceiving you by asking you to visit me and not telling you about the funeral."

"Why didn't you tell me?"

"It's just that I wanted—no—I needed Claire to know . . ." Daniela's voice dropped to an embarrassed whisper, "that someone—the most amazing someone, you—had chosen me as their kindred spirit."

"I'm your show-and-tell . . . at a funeral?"

"I'm sorry, Limy."

"Don't be." Emmaline hugged Daniela, then released her trembling friend. "I'm flattered."

"You're not disgusted with me?"

"Sort of . . . but I understand your motivation now. And I choose to not judge you for your silly actions. We'll show that Claire girl what she gave up back in middle school—the friendship of a warrior princess, Lozen."

Emmaline was proving to be a kindred spirit indeed, and so Daniela fully committed to her destiny: find out who would start the mother of all pandemics—the bad one, not the good one caused by Yeshua, a.k.a. the Rapture.

No matter how frightening her time-travel experiences might become, she would stop resisting the power of the Glass Tattoo.

Daniela's parents and Emmaline lived on Earth. The Orphan Dreamer would defend their homes. She fingered the Glass Tattoo beneath the neckline of her dress. "Mom. Limy."

"Yes, Danny-girl?"

"Don't worry about me becoming oily boy's Eva Braun."

"What do you mean?" Daniela's mother asked.

"If I discover that my oily boy will become Lucifer's antichrist, and if my prayers fail to stop his transformation into a monster, I won't befriend him, and I'll never lie down with him."

Mrs. Cavanaugh clasped her daughter's hand between hers.

"If I meet him in person . . ." Daniela collected every ounce of bravery. "I'll refuse to allow myself to fall in love or grow in love with him until I fully understand his motives."

"Motives. Sticky little things. Aren't they?" Mrs. Cavanaugh affirmed. "Discovering a person's motives is a lifetime's mission."

"Can a person ever know the truest motives of another person?" Emmaline challenged Daniela.

"I'll try. I'll bend time, travel when I don't want to, and learn how he'll affect our future." The Orphan Dreamer crossed her heart. "If I fail, I hope to die."

"We need you to live, bumblebee." Mrs. Cavanaugh's lower lip trembled. She jumped to her feet and paced the wood floor. "Sometimes I don't understand Yahweh." She stopped, turned, then gazed into her daughter's eyes. "Whether you save this chaotic world or not, you are my daughter. My light. My joy. And to me, that is enough. You. Don't. Have. To. Do. Any of this in exchange for my love."

"And dad?"

"Give the Glass Tattoo back to him. He'll love you just the same."

"And oily boy, Mom?" Daniela wouldn't cave. At thirteen, she'd given her word to Yahweh. A vow between God and a girl should never be broken.

"Goodness, Daniela Rose!" Mrs. Cavanaugh plopped down between the girls. "If that boy grows up and becomes Earth's dreaded antichrist, you'll do what is right by him." No longer hiding her truest emotions, Mrs. Cavanaugh cried as she kissed her daughter's cheek. "I trust you. Be careful."

"Every day ask Yahweh to send His angels to protect me," Daniela implored her sisters-in-arms. "Don't forget."

"Keep on asking and it will be given you; keep on seeking and you will find; keep on knocking—reverently—and the door will be opened to you," Mrs. Cavanaugh said, quoting a familiar Bible passage. "For everyone who keeps on asking receives; and he who keeps on seeking finds; and to him who keeps on knocking, the door will be opened."

"Ask anything?" Daniela clarified.

"It's your heavenly father's promise, not mine."

"Then Abba, Father, forgive me."

"Daniela?" Daniela's mother's face registered concern—brows tilted down slightly, crow's feet scraping shallow lines beside her eyes.

"If oily boy proves to be destined for evil, and his course proves to be unchangeable . . ." Daniela contemplated her next words, and her allies waited with bated breath. "I will kill him myself."

Mrs. Cavanaugh and Emmaline recoiled with shock. "Then you'd be no different than the senator," Emmaline said.

"Motives. Sticky little things," Daniela said. Separating herself, the Orphan Dreamer stood up, retrieved her bow from the wood trunk that served as an end table, loaded a foam arrow, and aimed the weapon high toward the ceiling before unloading.

The thunder rolled.

Lightning split the black sky. Rain pelted the windowpanes and ran in waterfalls down glass windows. Wind howled, screaming a warning. Four hours until nightfall. Four hours until Daniela would learn if Claire's invite had been nothing more than a cruel joke.

Still, the Orphan Dreamer would choose to wield the God Factor—a powerful weapon that sets captives free, used when humans refuse to correct their wrongs and repent. Yahweh corrects them, keeping Earth balanced. Some people refer to the God Factor as karma.

Die, Daniela! A slithering sinister voice hissed inside her mind, and a cacophony of emotions clamored and clanked inside her thoughts. Overwhelming sadness and feelings of failure, unsettling her bravado.

"I hate depression." She curled up onto the couch. "Suddenly, I don't want to be here anymore."

"Suicidal thoughts. That's out of the clear blue." Emmaline ran to her friend's side.

"That's the typical presentation," Mrs. Cavanaugh said. "Daniela, my love. It's the adversary. When you are weak, Yahweh still stands strong."

"I know, Mom. He always attacks me right before Yahweh plans to show me another clue."

Daniela's mother rubbed her back, opened her Bible, and read Psalms 91.

> You will not fear the terror of night, nor the arrow that flies by day, nor the pestilence that stalks in the darkness, nor the plague that destroys at midday. A thousand may fall at your side and ten thousand at your right hand, but danger will not come near you . . .
>
> For he will command his angels in regard to you, to protect and defend and guard you in all your ways [of obedience and service]; they will lift you up in their hands, so that you will not [even] strike your foot against a stone.

Emmaline thought of Lao Tzu's mantra: "Danny-girl, watch your thoughts; they become your words. Watch your words; they become your actions. Watch your actions; they become your habits. Watch your habits; they become your character. Watch your character; it becomes your destiny."

"Words to live, then die by." Daniela closed her eyes.

"You don't have to be *here* in the present, Danny-girl." Emmaline slid off the couch to make room for her friend to lie down. "You're the Orphan Dreamer. Have Glass Tattoo, will time travel—remember?" She slipped the Glass Tattoo from under the edge of Daniela's neckline.

"I'm dead weight if the storm worsens." Daniela held the relic in her left hand instead of her right, unwilling to activate it. "What if a flash flood occurs, and a wall of water slams into the bookstore? I'd drown—you'd drown."

"I can swim, Danny-girl, and I wouldn't leave you behind."

Would Emmaline once again take advantage of Daniela's dream state? Was Robert back from the dead and lurking in the shadows outside the bookstore?

"Take it." Emmaline placed the snowflake diamond inside Daniela's right hand. "Your mom and I will wait for you, even fight for you. We'll defend your body while your mind travels."

"How long?"

"For a lifetime. Friends don't abandon each other on a battlefield, and mothers . . . they define ride-or-die chicks."

"What if I scc oily boy?"

"Be brave, Lozen. Face whatever waits for you out there—even oily boy."

"Shoot him through with an arrow and be done with it?" Daniela half-smiled, dreading the act of killing any human. Or any animal—which is why she rarely ate meat.

"Give him a chance to show his hand while you watch your six."

"You won't need that where you're going." Mrs. Cavanaugh removed the arrow from her daughter's left hand. "You are loved and prayed for. These are your weapons.

May Yahweh's powerful angels ride into battle before you."

"Heaven's version of the US Marine Corps," Emmaline joked.

"Okay." Daniela closed her fingers around the Glass Tattoo.

Her mother's and friend's voices faded into the distance. But not before Emmaline leaned toward the Orphan Dreamer's ear and whispered, "Don't allow the Sons of Venus to have your oily boy. Fight for his second chance too. Remember the bruises. Remember the pain. Remember his hopelessness."

"The Sons of Venus?" Truly, Daniela's mother could hear dead men speak. "Who are they, Emmaline?" Before either of the girls could answer, an uprooted oak tree crashed through the bookstore's front door.

Wood split. Splinters flew like darts across the vast space. "Mrs. C., watch out!"

Mrs. Cavanaugh flung herself across Daniela's body.

A glass pane loosened, then flew across the room, flying over the couch where Daniela was sprawled out. The window slammed into the coffee table, just beyond the couch.

Mrs. Cavanaugh clenched Daniela's slight frame. Glass shattered, spilling across the floor. "Dear Jesus!"

"Mrs. C., you're bleeding."

"I know, baby girl. It's the glass." Wind sucked books off the shelves, loaded them into an invisible bow, and shot them across the room.

"We've got to go down to the cellar!" Mrs. Cavanaugh grabbed Daniela's legs, and Emmaline hooked beneath Daniela's arms, lifting her off the couch.

Dark blue ink spilled from the center of the flawless diamond, and the jewel disappeared into Daniela's palm, leaving behind a beautiful midnight-blue snowflake tattoo. With that, she embraced her destiny as the Orphan Dreamer.

The Glass Tattoo demanded all. Her past. Her present. Her future. And even the sweet calm of her dreams.

A supernatural energy burst through Daniela's right hand, pulsing throughout her entire being and yanking her inside a long, dark, cold tunnel.

No different than a shepherd calling his lost sheep home, a calm voice said, "Come up here."

Finally, after seventeen years, Daniela became her truest self—then she surrendered that self and her future to the powerful force. "Take me to the stars, Abba, Father."

He cradled His little girl inside his massive arms.

Earth's gravitational pull released.

The Orphan Dreamer bolted into outer space, toward Yeshua's extraterrestrial home.

39—Orphan Dreamer

A Cosmic Revolution
575 BC
Mesopotamia—Babylon

I STAND IN A COLD, vast space. No longer twinkle, twinkle little stars. Up close, the luminous and behemoth ball of gas spits liquid fire.

Still, I reach out, intending to touch a star.

"Don't touch anything, Danny Rose." That voice! Smooth, baritone, and bass in all the right places, with absolutely no hint of ear-grating, nasally vibrato. "Stars are resting angels. Don't wake them. They're beasts if you rouse them before their time."

"Legna!" I spin around on my heels, my body seeming to float without the restraints of Earth's gravitational pull. I slam into the body of the powerful warrior, my legs encircling his chest. Embarrassment floods my entire body. "Sorry. Didn't mean to invade your space." I push away.

"Rosebud." The powerful angel pulls me back to his chest and embraces me. A delightful scent of spice mixed with fine leather and autumn woods on a cold day clings to my nostrils.

"How's Ethan?"

"Healthy." Pushing back from our hug, he smiles wide. "Cancer doesn't exist in Yeshua's home." A glare from the sun reflects off his pearly whites, almost blinding me.

"Tell him hello, please." I cover my eyes with my right hand and stare at the midnight-blue tattoo inked into my right palm. Butterflies flutter inside my chest.

"I will." He laughs and uncovers my eyes. "Frowning so soon?"

"Why do your teeth gleam so darn white? Wear a face mask, dude."

"Good genes." He shrugs. "I don't consume human trash. You call it food." Legna focuses his gaze on something below our feet—a shifting dark, round form.

"Where are we?" Bending time and space, I have time travelled, but where to?

"The second heaven—Lucifer's realm."

"We've crashed the devil's lair?" My mouth dries more than perm-fried hair. "You're kidding me."

"Nope." Legna arches his back, and his snow-white wings splay out behind his sculpted six-foot-nine ebony frame. His calves and feet are a mixture of bronze and gold, and the hilt of his bronze sword sparkles beneath the starry night. His body was made for war, and mine was made for a man like him.

"You're such a show-off." I'm safe. My breath comes easy, and my heart beats slow.

"Sometimes." He winks, and I blush. His cobalt irises lighten to violet. *Where is the sign-up sheet to get lost in those pools of lavender?*

"The sheet . . . it's already full." He reads my thoughts. I forgot!

"Am I here so you can flirt with me?" Please say yes.

"That . . . That can never happen, Daniela." He shakes his head. "Me—" he points to himself—"with a daughter of man? It's not allowed or safe for you."

Not safe?

Why wouldn't it be safe?

He hears my thoughts and says, "You still have some growing up to do, so I'll tell you later. Your father would break my legs if I forced you to grow up too soon."

"Which father—the earthly one or the heavenly one?"

"Both."

"You have your orders, and I have mine. I'm the Orphan Dreamer. I've been ordered to dream, so let me."

"As you wish, Rosebud." He smiles—stiff, with a slight quiver hiding in his upper lip as though he's masking an urgent yearning, one that hasn't been fulfilled for an eternity.

Legna clears his throat. "Your next mission, should you choose to accept it, is to solve the mystery of *who*."

"Yeah, I know. I need to figure out who starts the pandemic that will eradicate humans from Earth."

"I'm here to help you. If you want."

"Have you been eavesdropping on Emmaline and me?" I laugh, but my joviality quickly fades.

What would Legna think about my sexual inexperience? My skin flushes hot. But what exactly is wrong with a girl who chooses to save herself for her future husband?

Nothing.

Absolutely nothing!

"Feeding beer to helpless cacti . . ." Legna chuckles. "Don't be ashamed of your choices. Keep yourself for the right one, Rosebud." Arms crossed, he invades my thoughts again.

"Okay." I bite my lip.

"You're not human pesticide."

"What does that mean?"

"It's not your responsibility to allow random guys to spread their weeds in the rich soil of your backyard only to leave you broken while you spray pesticide to kill his weeds. Boom!" Legna struts away and opens his hand as though he just dropped the mic.

Daniela runs to catch up. "Legna, wait! That's your version of the birds and the bees? I appreciate your advice, but could you stop reading my mind? It's creepy."

"I can't help it, but I can lie to you and act as though I haven't read your thoughts. Deal?"

"But friends don't lie."

"They keep secrets." Legna grasps my hand and leads me toward the planetary-sized blob of clear jelly—about the size of Earth—that sits suspended in the midst of space.

"Is that Earth?"

"Almost three thousand years ago. We're going to look in on Mesopotamia—Babylon—in 575 BC, when Iran ruled the world, like your America does now." His arm brushes mine, sending jolts of heat throughout my body. I step back. "Kairos time. Do you remember?"

"Yahweh sees our chronological time as we see a completed movie." I rehash what Legna had taught me about my time travels. "He knows the beginning and the end all at once. As a result, Yahweh can move through time and space, revisiting humanity's past and future. Because in His reality, the past and even the future are His present—His state of existence—I AM that I AM."

"Yeshua cried, 'It is finished' as He hung on a gentile cross," Legna adds.

"Yet in Him the crucifixion is still happening even though in relation to my seventeen-year-old present time, it happened almost two thousand years ago."

"You're a quick learner."

"I'm trying. I'm open."

"That's all we ask. Exist as a conduit for Yahweh's power to work through."

"Ok, so Babylon. That's the gold head of the statue."

"Bingo." Legna snapped his fingers.

"And the clay and iron feet, what kingdom does that represent?"

"Are you cheating on your final exam?"

"I didn't ask if and where the Ark of the Covenant was hidden. Give me some credit."

"I can't wait until you take that adventure and learn that Elohim's love cascades like a waterfall—so wild and so free." Legna's eyes twinkle. "The iron of Daniel's statue represents ancient Rome."

"But the Roman Empire fell."

"Rome has been resurrected into a weaker version of the ancient kingdom."

"The European Union?"

"You're acing your exam. The EU was formed as an extension of the Charlemagne Empire in 1993 via the Maastricht Treaty. The EU also traces its roots to the European Coal and Steel Community and the European Economic Community—and those communities were established in

1951 by the Treaty of Paris and in 1957 by the Treaty of Rome."

"Limy was right."

"You were also right about the clay and iron of the Earth's last kingdom representing an amalgamation of religious and political power. The false prophet—the antichrist's sidekick who works false miracles and deceives humans—will hail from this religious union."

"Who forms this religious amalgamation . . . and why?"

"You'll find out."

"Give me a hint."

"Only because I love—I mean, like—you. Three Abrahamic religions: Judaism, Christianity, and Islam. For some, Christianity identifies the Messiah of its parent religion, Judaism. What question of Judaism does Islam answer? Sound familiar?"

"It does."

"You're on the right track by answering this question, and one day Adelaide will ask you to answer the question, so pay attention to your journey." Legna sheds his *Phantom of the Oprah*–style black cape.

Immediately, a red hoodie, sweatpants, and tennis shoes cover his lean body. "Listen to this, Roscbud." He moves his hands through the universe as though he's a conductor directing a heavenly orchestra. Sir Edward Elgar's "Pomp and Circumstance March No. 1" reverberates through space and then . . .

African beats drop.

The heavens rumble with subwoofers, pumping out raps by Lecrae, KB, Tedashii, NF, and Andy Mineo.

Amped up on bass, we journey through the cold and no-longer-quiet blackness for several minutes until we stand on top of the gelatinous dome. Legna rests his hand on my shoulders. The beat drops lower, and he pushes me forward, forcing me to bend my knees, then lie face-down in the clear jelly.

"Stop!" I jump back up. "What the heck!"

"Don't be scared. I'm here, Rosebud. I won't let you fall through. Promise." Spreading his arms into a *T*-shape, he falls face-first on top of the gelatinous blob. His powerful frame becomes suspended in the substance.

I lie down beside him, allowing my body to melt into my miniscule portion of the see-through time capsule. The otherworldly material sticks to my skin like alien snot, leaving cold slime on the front of my body. So much for my funeral getup.

Face buried in the slime, I inhale.

Lilacs.

My favorite flower. I face Legna. I'm home. Home with Legna.

Is this how true love feels—comfortable, a longing wrapped into feelings about one person or, in Legna's case, species?

"Legna." I can speak even with my face buried into the gel. "Why don't I have to completely journey into this world like I did when I travelled back in time to Prince Jonathan's 1019 BC Gibeah to solve the mystery of the blood moons?"

"It's not necessary."

"Will it become necessary?"

"Maybe, depends on how much info you gather and how fast you gather it. But for now, my Master and your doting Father, Elohim, wants to show His compassion and patience toward you, especially after Ethan's death."

"Passive learning instead of active learning."

"He knows about your fear of rejection, loss, and abandonment. Elohim understands that only love perfected can eliminate your fear." Legna seems to pause.

"What's the catch?"

"Man's imperfections riddle Earth's realm. There is a trade-off to passive time travel versus active time travel."

"Spit it out!"

"When you don't completely break through the barrier of Earth's time capsule and fully bend time, shifting your reality into another time and another place in order to gather your clues and solve your mysteries . . ."

"Time's ticking. Countdown to doom and gloom. I'll shrivel up and die before you finish."

"Human cells weren't built for this experience. Suspended above the time capsule, you're aging faster than if we were to break through."

"Would it kill you to bring me good news for a change?"

"I long for that day, Rosebud." A fleeting smile makes him look even hotter. "The day when I carry you in my arms and escort you across Jordan's murky waters to the gates of my Master's home—a safe place, void of human imperfection. But for now, I'm terribly sorry to deliver the bad news."

I blink back a tear, saddened that I may never experience a human romantic embrace outside of my dreams or mother my own child—my Adelaide Rose.

Would she always remain a figment of my imagination? Human connections in the form of relationships fuel my mission to stop the pandemic. "C-c-can you explain why I'll die early? Not the drippy, emotional reasons, but the scientific reasons." I lift my head out of the gelatin.

He looks straight into me—not through me. I roll onto my back and he moves closer, almost lying on top of me.

Shivering, I stare into Legna's cobalt eyes. Gold flecks sparkle beneath his skin.

"If the mission will kill me, I deserve to know the process." My lungs fill with breath. "I can understand the science and mathematics of it. You see . . . I may not be the prettiest girl, Legna, but I'm not an idiot."

"No, you're not stupid, but you're wrong about one thing."

"Only one?"

"You are gorgeous." He waits.

"But not datable. At least not by you?"

"It's not safe. And your safety is my reason for existing."

"I feel like I should say thank you, but I'm too mad at you to show my appreciation." Sadness washes over me, followed by anger.

"Your fellow humans, their eyes are dim. Claire and Harry told you that you were ugly because of the color of your skin. Yet it takes looking through a microscope for a human to determine if a diamond is real. How can you trust their vision and perception about anything?"

"I've never seen a real diamond." I look at my right palm. "Except for the Glass Tattoo."

"Wrong . . . again. Without the magnification of a microscope, I can see that you're a diamond, Rosebud. One day, a human boy will see you as you are—refined through fire, beautiful and strong—yet delicate."

He traces the jagged white scars that mark my right and left forearms, then kisses my brown arm.

Still, the jagged white scars remind me of shame.

He buries his face back into the gel. "If you don't think you're beautiful, not many seventeen-year-old girls have mastered differential equations, physics, and organic chemistry during their second year of college."

He's right.

I straighten my back, then press my face back into the clear jelly. This time, the substance rises to the temperature of a warm bath. Sensing my willingness to learn, it embraces me. "Who is the human agent behind Lucifer's plan?"

"He's a Nephilim."

"I knew it! But I thought Noah's flood killed them all off?" I test Legna, knowing Limy and I have come to our own conclusions.

"One of Noah's daughters had been impregnated by a Nephilim. And then there's Leviathan—Job's sea monster. The great deluge didn't kill any sea animals."

"Score! We were right. Can't wait to tell Limy."

"By the way, back to the science, by passively viewing the world beneath you, you're dying early because of gamma-ray radiation."

"I'm being slowly nuked?"

"When you remain outside of this gelatinous barrier, your body is closer to Lucifer's domain. His fiery home, hell, located in the fifth heaven, emits a thousand times the radiation the sun releases. Your fragile human cells respond by initiating cell death—apoptosis—as though you've been exposed to a nuclear bomb."

"Is there anything that could protect me while I passively view the world, like slathering my skin with sunscreen or wearing a heavy lead apron before I time travel?"

"You could try both. Elohim is slowing down the effects of the radiation on your body left back in the bookshop as well as your traveling body, giving you time to complete your mission. But there's another problem. Lucifer's hell sucks up most of the oxygen in this realm, and your body craves oxygen."

"Without oxygen, the blood pressure inside the arteries that feed my lungs will increase."

"Then, one day, you'll drown in your own blood."

"Pulmonary hypertension." Swallowing a mouthful of gel, I choke and push myself up. Legna pushes out of the gel, too, as I spit out a mouthful. "That's why I'm so short of breath when I've been hiking."

"Yes, Daniela, and I'm sorry."

"It's not your fault, but when will this end?" Rage heats up my skin.

"Before your fiftieth birthday."

"I die before I turn fifty?"

"Ethan waits for you . . . and in the future, so do your dad, your mom, and your son."

"Both of my parents die before I turn fifty? And my son?"

"Don't grow bitter."

"At least let me be angry for two seconds."

"One. Two. I'll tell you a secret. The Professor's letter is correct in that the real Area 51 is located upstream of the Jordan River."

"Score." I pump my fist.

"Also, don't speak into the gel when you are angry. You'll suffocate."

"Thanks for sharing that tidbit now." I gulp down a mouthful of morbidity. "Knocked off by a broken heart. Seems fitting." I suffocate my dreams about finding a romantic interest, getting married, and having children.

"Talk to someone about your disappointments," Legna says. "Don't keep your feelings inside. The negative ones fuel your depression, and depression without brakes leads to suicide. Your friends and family need you alive for as long as possible. Remember this."

"Talk to someone . . . last time I did that I was locked up in a pediatric psychiatry ward. No. Thank. You. On Earth, I'm just a bat-crazy girl. I am the dreamer who can't even dream her worst nightmare away of dying alone while drowning."

Legna looks at me and says, "When you pass through the waters, I will be with you; and through the rivers, they shall not overflow you. When you walk through the fire, you shall not be burned, nor shall the flame scorch you."

"If angelic warfare doesn't work out for you, try poetry."

"Always wanted to be Edgar Allan Poe." He laughs. "But those aren't my words. As you know, Elohim inspired the Hebrew prophet Isaiah to write them."

"Then maybe I'll refuse to dream and choose instead to live for myself. Enjoy my life. Deal with my depression and let everyone fend for themselves."

"That's not you, Danny Rose. You're not selfish, couldn't be even if you tried."

"Then I'll practice more."

"Practice doesn't always make perfect. Why do you think Yahweh chose you? Stick your head back in the gel, Rosebud. Your enemy our enemy—has almost arrived. Time to go to war."

He's right. I want to be selfish, but it's not written into my DNA. "Here's to the worst gamma-ray suntan ever." I bury my face in the gel.

Rosebud.

I gulp hard as the memory of Ethan hits my gut. Sinking further into the extraterrestrial gel, past the gelatinous barrier, I dangle above another time and place. "If I push all the way through, will that reduce the amount of radiation my body experiences?"

"Yes."

Refusing to be fried, I push through. As I freefall, wind pummels my face. I emerge on the other side of a slippery tunnel. My newest reality: 575 BC, Babylon. No gamma-ray radiation for me. Watching from above is safer in the short term, but I'd rather risk having to participate than be slowly cooked to death.

An acrid odor burns my eyes as I climb out into a wide-mouthed cave.

In the dark, I step forward. Air replaces soil, and I start falling—again. I kick my legs, but still find no purchase. I plummet through space until arms grab me—the arms of a powerful warrior. He slows my descent, then sets me on solid ground. "Thanks, Legna."

"Time to discover your next clue. Open your eyes, Daniela."

I open them.

Night fades.

Time seems to reverse, and the scene lightens to dusk. I'm standing in the middle of a vacant road. Dust cakes my sandaled feet. A powerful man approaches me, and a broad smile spreads across his ebony face. "Daniela, so glad to see you again." He winks.

"Legna?"

"Guilty."

"You look so . . . different."

"What do you think, Danny-girl?" He flexes his muscles beneath his gray tunic.

"You're a servant, but a handsome one," I quietly say as heat floods my face. "A bit archaic in terms of your fashion—tunic, sandals, and a turban. Cute but circa something ancient."

"You've travelled back to ancient Babylon, and your

garb looks just as archaic," Legna says. I crook my neck. "Look in the mirror if you don't believe me."

"Be my mirror. Tell me what you see."

"I see a girl—beautiful, intelligent—dressed in a pale-pink silk dress and shawl."

"Glad you like the view." I glance at my skin. "I'm pale!"

"From brown to white." Legna chuckles.

But I miss my brown skin. I think and look away, then back at my protector. His coal eyes lighten to violet. There he goes with those eyes again.

"It's okay. The change is temporary."

"I thought it would be easier to live in someone else's skin, but it's not." I sigh, fighting a gut punch propelled by sadness. "So who am I in this ancient world?"

"My mistress."

"As in sex slave?"

"No. You're a member of King Nebuchadnezzar's harem."

"Goody goody gumdrops." I rub my hands together. "I get to deal with a lustful, sweaty old man."

"Only for a couple of days."

"That's what Sarah said to Hagar. Then there was Ishmael."

Legna belly laughs. "At least you're not a brutalized slave again."

"Moving on up. I should have remained in passive mode. What's your job?"

"Be the slave. Delay your nemesis, Nomed, from finding Ezekiel—Yahweh's prophet. Your job: follow the scroll. You'll need to know where Ezekiel hides it, then I'll take you back home. Try not to die. I don't want to have to explain your death to Elohim, my real Master."

"What if King Nebi wants . . . you know what?"

"No, I don't."

I lean in and whisper, "Sex."

"Think of an excuse." Legna steps back, his face unwilling to hide his disgust.

"Like what?"

"In America, human women complain of headaches all the time to fend off their eager husbands."

"News flash! We are not in America. Women don't have rights in ancient Babylon, so I'm sure they don't refuse the king's sexual advances by complaining of headaches and fatigue."

"I . . . I don't know."

"You got me into this mess, so you better figure this out." My voice draws the attention of the locals passing by on the dirt road.

"Actually, I didn't. You chose to abort the passive viewing."

"I. Am. Not. Going. To. Lose. My. Virginity. To. A. Pot-bellied. Piggish. King. Got that?"

Legna tears off the bottom of his tunic, then wraps my left arm with the rough cloth. "You have leprosy. He won't touch you."

"That's your plan? I would have been banished to a leper colony!" I turn around and consider running back to the tunnel.

"You can't leave. You won't find your way back. The universe is sort of big."

"Then take me back."

"I can't. Trust me. We'll think of something. I won't let him touch you."

"What about the Philistine from Prince Jonathan's era?"

"He didn't take your innocence."

"I don't want this dude touching me."

"Okay. Done." He raises his hand, reaches inside his satchel and removes a jar of ants. "Ever heard of ants in your pants? If Nebi bothers you, dump these ants on the sensitive parts."

"And you're Yahweh's baddest warrior." I shake my head.

Bright-yellow butterflies swirl around us, encircling Legna and me in sunshine. "Apricot sulphur butterflies. They're my favorite." With my arms spread wide, I spin around and around until I stumble. "Where did they come from? Why are they here, Legna?"

"To protect you from that potbellied pig, King Nebi." Legna runs his hand over his washboard abdomen.

"How?"

"After you identify Ezekiel, I'm sending you back to the bird's-eye view. These butterflies will function like a drone, an eye in the sky. You'll see what they see."

"Cool." A butterfly lands on the tip of my nose. I scrunch my nose, and the little insect flies away. "But—"

"It's final, Rosebud."

"What if you need my help?"

"An angel requiring the help of a human?" Legna spits. "I am Elohim's baddest warrior. Embrace it."

"Thanks a lot." I fight back tears.

"I didn't mean to hurt you." Legna takes a knee. "Forgive me."

"Stand up, silly. It's that time of the month, so I'm a bit emotional."

"Oh." Blushing, he stands up, unfolds a cloth map, and gives it to me. "You're the boss, so walk ahead of me." Reduced to nothing more than a human slave, Legna walks behind me. We walk through a massive gate, past guards brandishing swords, and into an open-air market. A luxurious palace looms in front of us.

I blow a forceful breath through my nose. "Here goes nothing." I pass a man dressed in a cream tunic accented with an emerald silk sash. He's short but handsome.

He looks at me, and his presence floods the air with a tidal wave of evil.

I scurry past him. Leaving Legna to confront the man, I hurry up the palace steps and enter a courtyard.

I am the Orphan Dreamer.

I am a spy.

Like Muhammad Ali, I float like a butterfly, and I sting like a bee. I walk for what seems like twenty minutes. "Hey, guys," I say to the guards, trying to keep a sense of humor in this humorless situation.

Something draws me, guiding me. Minutes later, I enter a small chamber. A man sits at a large wooden table. Who is he? He's not dressed like a king.

"Something to drink?" I ask the man. Without looking up, he nods. Nervous, I retrieve a pitcher from a side table and pour cool spring water into the man's goblet. The man gulps down the refreshing liquid, then looks up. He quickly pushes back his chair and bows. "Mistress Daniela, it is I who should be serving you."

He knows my name!

"Why?" I ask, and the man furrows his brow. "I mean . . . who are you to speak to me? I do as I please." I jut my chin into the air, faking royal superiority. Actually, I'm copying the actions of Queen Nefertiti—a.k.a. Anne Baxter—from *The Ten Commandments*.

Don't think Egyptian women had pale skin back then, though.

"I am . . . Ezekiel, the king's scribe."

"The Ezekiel?" I gasp. "Yahweh's prophet?"

"You know of Elohim?" He rests his stylus on his wooden desk. "Since when?"

"Since I was four years old. I gave my soul to Elohim's Messiah—Yeshua—and He gifted me eternal life." I gesture for him to sit. He refuses, so I pull up a chair and sit down. "I'm not who you think I am." His eyes ask a thousand questions, but his lips remain still. I wait for him to speak.

"But we have met many times before. You've been kind, but you belong to the king."

"Whoever you met, it wasn't me. I just arrived . . . from outer space." The prophet covers his mouth to hide a smile. I would be laughing too. *Get to the point.* "When will you hide the scrolls? I've got a funeral to attend in an hour."

Ezekiel looks away and fidgets with his stylus. "I do not know what scrolls you speak of."

"The ones that tell of the Third Temple."

"The Second Jewish Temple has not yet been built, Mistress Daniela."

"I know, but I arrived from the future, from a time long after the Second Jewish Temple was destroyed by the Romans. I understand that what I'm telling you is confusing, but it's true."

"You're a being from another time and another place. The Messiah has come in your world?"

"Yes and yes!"

"I knew that you were special."

"In my world, we call people like me aliens. We're not special. We're weird."

"Aliens." The prophet Ezekiel tries out the word. "Are you an angel?"

"No. That's Legna."

"You're an alien spy from another time and place?" A satisfied expression softens his face.

"Why not?" I shrug. "But I'm on your side." I study his expression. It's unfamiliar but easy to judge. "You keep staring at me as though I look beautiful."

"You do, Mistress Daniela." He points toward an alcove. We slip into it.

A looking glass made of polished bronze hangs on the opposite wall. Spools of henna curls run down my bronzed shoulders. An aquiline nose punctuates my face, and olive-green eyes stare back while a pink silk garment drapes across my frame.

Legna's words from the first time we traveled together replay in my mind. *You may look different, but don't get killed.* But he'd called me beautiful before I broke through into this ancient world. I rub my exposed arms, feeling naked without my brown skin.

Then the gravity of my reality hits me like a ton of bricks. I am physically attractive. Men lust after gorgeous women.

Act smart and boring, then you won't get raped. Hands on my hips, I demand, "If $\log_x (1 / 8) = - 3 / 2$, then x is equal to what? A. $- 4$; B. 4; C. 1 / 4; D. 10."

What am I doing? Ezekiel works for Elohim! I stand with as much grace and composure as I can muster.

The prophet thinks a moment, then answers, "Mistress Daniela, the answer is four."

"Yes, it is." I sit back down.

"And as for the scrolls, I will hide them in the cave of Makkedah." He unwraps a small stone tablet. "Take this."

"What is it?"

"A map that will lead you to the hiding place at the right time."

"But it's written in—"

"Hebrew, the language of my people." Ezekiel smiles.

"I take this with gratitude." I bow my head. *Emmaline reads Hebrew. Score!* "I look forward to solving the clues encrypted into your scrolls."

"I will leave for the cave tonight."

"You will not fear the terror of night," I encourage the prophet, reciting Psalms 91, my mother's favorite psalm. "Nor the arrow that flies by day, nor the pestilence that stalks in the darkness, nor the plague that destroys at midday. A thousand may fall at your side, ten thousand at your right hand, but it will not come near you."

"Poetic." Ezekiel blinks back a tear.

"I didn't write it."

"I remember now. Moses wrote that Hebrew Psalm. Are you one of my people—a Hebrew?"

"I don't know. I am still tracing the journeys of my ancestors."

"May you find the legacies of kings, queens, warriors, and most importantly, the faithful."

"Thank you, Ezekiel." I smile at my newest kindred spirit. "Take this." I gift him a glass jar. "I am returning to my viewing gel—a place perched high above Earth."

"What is it?"

"A gift for your adversary." Ezekiel takes my gift with one hand, then reaches toward me and pronounces an ancient Judaic blessing. "The Lord bless you and keep you. The Lord make His face shine upon you and be gracious to you. The Lord lift up His countenance upon you and give you peace."

"Until we meet at Elohim's home past the Jordan River, shalom."

"Shalom, Mistress Daniela."

A buttercup-yellow butterfly lands on the window ledge of the scriptorium. I stroll out of the room, ducking past strangers inside the king's palace, eager to return to my world of safety—or is it safe? Is the familiar safe? A prophet's calling requires sacrifice—mine, an untimely death.

Legna returns me to the viewing portal. Face plastered into gel, I watch as the Babylon drama unfolds before me.

40—Nomed

"TO MY SUCCESS. MY SECOND chance." In the cold blackness of deep space, the fallen angel, Nomed, belts out his favorite Christmas carol, a timeless piece.

O-o-oh, there's no place like home for the holidays—or any other day for that matter, he ad-libs—*cause no matter how far away you roam, when you pine for the sunshine of a friendly gaze, for the holidays, you can't beat home, sweet home.*

"I'm coming for you, Ezekiel." Without Aglaope's presence, Nomed strips any pretense of fake niceness. "I am who I am, my darling Agla. But you couldn't love me as I am—my deepest motives, my character, or lack thereof because you're not a purebred Watcher like me." He grins.

Picking up speed and shedding his obsidian and phosphorus green scales, Nomed crashes through the dense air of Earth's atmosphere with his raven wings spread and enters the world of the mortals.

Searing pain scalds his flesh, pulsing white-hot tendrils of anguish throughout his body as though a volcano had spat its fire and encapsulated him.

The agony ebbs. Minutes later, Nomed arrives at his destination, then abruptly stops singing.

Time to be quiet.

Time to focus.

Time to stalk.

Besides, the 1950s holiday ballad—one of his wife's favorite tunes—doesn't resonate with this ancient time or place. The humans call this incongruence an anachronism, but what do those barbarians know about anything besides squabbling with each other?

Nomed, not entirely restricted by the prison of the fourth dimension, pauses between the past and the future, bending time just as the Orphan Dreamer bends time inside her vivid dreamworld.

The only difference?

Danny Rose weakens when she bends time, leaving her more vulnerable to Nomed's wily schemes. Weak humans.

I may not be I AM, but I am NOW—Danny Rose's ever-present nightmare.

Impulsive pride drives him. His master, Lucifer, learned the hard way that pride precedes a Humpty Dumpty fall. Nomed would remain vigilant, pushing, but he would stop before he fell.

Smiling, he emerges as a fine-figured form, veiled in alabaster flesh kissed by the dawn's fiery golden glow.

He rubs his arm, grimacing, but the change in form was

worth the pain. "For I am glorious." He is now as beautiful as his master—the son of the dawn—used to be.

Hiding in the mob's shadows, he treks past the city gates into Babylon, sucking in slow and deep breaths through a pair of meticulously placed razor-thin nostrils. The earthy scent of cow dung clings to the back of his tongue and permeates his lungs.

Welcome home, Nomed!

A woman whose crown of locks boasts more silver than brown ogles him. She takes in her fill, then bows her head. Such appreciation. "I like this woman."

Give her a show?

Why not? Nomed rakes broad, strong fingers through his onyx coif, allowing highlights of tinsel to shimmer beneath the amber brilliance of a rising sun. Stopping short of a full grin, he gifts the woman a sensual smile that belies the truth hidden beneath his veneer of effortless charm: he has lost the only thing that matters—hope—and may never get it back.

Like a chameleon, the woman blends into the throng. He navigates the winding roads through the morning markets.

A fine linen tunic fits loosely around his wide shoulders, bellowing in the cool Mesopotamian breeze and masking his weapon. He adjusts the green silk sash draped around his waist and clenches the hilt of his dagger.

At just over five feet, a thirteen-year-old boy could stare Nomed square in the eyes, but his master had insisted that a small stature was less intimidating to the humans. *A small man cannot wield the power to destroy.*

Nonsense.

A man's size has nothing to do with his destructive tendencies.

Nomed spins a gold ring around his right forefinger. He glances at the image etched into the ring's face. Drawing strength from its meaning, he quickens his stride toward King Nebuchadnezzar's palace.

Morning markets rumble with haggling and trades of food, flowers, and cloth. Silver and gold coins clank in the hands of shoppers.

The morning fades, and when the sun sits halfway toward its midday position, Nomed strolls past the king's palace gate into the arboretum. Hanging foliage speckled with violet and seashell-blue flowers dangles overhead, replicating its splendor in the reflection of the sapphire pool in the middle of the garden. The floral scents are a welcome reprieve from the noxious, burning sulfur smell of the underworld. He stops, leans over, and stares at himself in the pool.

Why did you do it?

For the promise of power, you gave up Hope. You almost destroyed Agla.

Nomed stiffens his back and quiets the quiver in his upper lip.

His balm would be revenge. He erases the shadows of pain from his face and relaxes his mouth into a welcoming smile, soft yet masculine.

That'll do.

A face as finely put together as his serves one purpose: disarm the mortals and lure them into executing his plan. He will make them lead him to Ezekiel, and then they will help him murder Elohim's prophet. Mayhem will ensue, and then he'd let the herd kill each other.

He had already succeeded once, but could he do it again?

If he wants to live on Earth, he must.

Nomed ascends a set of stairs to the upper terrace, his leather sandals thumping on gray and ivory marble steps. Even Nebuchadnezzar's stairs show magnificence. Such opulence costs many shekels. While serving Nomed's master's cause, the pagan king had done well for himself.

He pauses on the upper terrace, glaring at the only closed window on the palace's eastern wall.

Could it be Ezekiel's scriptorium, the prophet he was sent to "question"? One way to find out. Nomed would certainly take advantage of the privacy, if so. He charges up the next set of stairs toward the palace entrance, passing a bronze-skinned girl dressed in pink silk.

She's out of place. An anachronism. He stops, turns, and watches the girl seemingly glide down the stairs toward the palace gates. "She's a picture of beauty," he murmurs to himself, then slaps himself across the face. "Stop it, Nomed. You're married."

Besides, engaging in a sexual act with female humans was off limits, according to Elohim. Their child would be a Nephilim, like Agla. Deformed and twisted, either physically or morally—according to the parents' choice.

A righteous air lingered in her perfumed wake, illuminating the bareness of his soul.

Could the mysterious girl be the Orphan Dreamer?

No. She has not been born yet, and the viewing room showed Danny Rose to be a Nordic girl. But when had Elohim played by the devil's rules or timeline of events? Witches and warlocks do not tell the truth.

A tall, muscular, ebony-skinned man with a well-cropped mustache crosses his path, blocking Nomed's exit from the upper terrace. The man seems to tower above the clouds.

How strange. The man wears servant's clothes, but

he seems to possess a special power—the kind a servant should not wield. Nervous, Nomed narrows his penetrating gaze, then allows his face to relax into a thin-lipped smile. "Slave, point me in the direction of Ezekiel, the Judean prophet."

"You assume I'm a slave?"

"You're dressed like one. What else should I assume?"

"And you're the size of a boy, yet you're a man."

"Wasn't my idea."

"Your size and my clothes prove one thing—neither one of us is the leader of our cause."

"Poetic."

"You're looking for the king's Judean prophet and scribe?" The man lifts his right brow, and his voice floats through the desert morning air as a cold vapor—touching nothing, yet seeming to permeate the world.

"Yes, my dear boy. Where is he?" *Who is this man?*

"Trust me. I'm not your dear or your boy . . ." The man crosses his arms. Head tilted, he studies Nomed's hand.

"What are you staring at?" Nomed demands.

"Your ring . . ." The man's smile—milky white teeth beneath tan lips—calms Nomed's fears for a moment. "May I see it?" The man descends a marble step.

Nomed recalls his master's instructions: *Take charge over those pathetic dying creatures.* He tucks his hand behind his back and puffs his chest out. "You do as you're told, or I'll have you punished."

"Try it." The man uncrosses his arms. "You sense who I am, but like your master, you hate—even fear—truth."

"What is truth?" Nomed gives him a once-over. "You're tall. Powerful. Want to kill me, yet you dress as a slave. You know nothing of truth . . . deception, maybe."

"I am a slave to my King—the King of all Kings, and your Master authors lies." The powerful man laughs at Nomed. "You couldn't recognize truth if it perched on the tip of that pointy nose of yours. Lies are essential to your nature, but no lie in the world will change your fate."

Nomed takes in the man's stomach—ridges and sinews of muscles quiver beneath his garment. His ears burn as he steps down onto a lower step, rendering him even smaller, and wrings his tunic between moist fingers. "I-I-I am Nomed."

"I know your name."

"Let. Me. Finish. I am the chief of legions. My master trusts in me, and you're nothing but a slave, reduced to fulfilling the whims of these filthy human creatures." He glares, trying to bore a hole into the thighs of the man standing like a tower of black granite in front of him.

"You've been practicing your introduction. Bravo." Legna slowly claps. "But verbal mantras don't work, especially when the one speaking them is peeing on himself." The powerful slave watches as urine snakes down Nomed's leg and dribbles on the ground.

"It's the cool morning air. I swear it!"

"Here. Wipe yourself." Legna removes a cloth from his girdle. "I am not here to humiliate you. Truly, a man's character is more quickly revealed when he wields power than when he stands powerless."

Nomed steps over his puddle of liquid fear. "I'll show you my ring . . ." he says, his voice squeaking, "if you take me to the prophet Ezekiel." He raises his right hand, hating himself for negotiating with a servant.

The man studies the gold ring etched with a blackened, recessed image of a sitting bull with a curved horn on either side of its head, the arms of a man attached to its chest, and a fiery cauldron for its belly. "The same as Bushcroft's."

"You noticed. Asher exists in the 1940s. How do you know him?"

"I travel."

"Now it's your turn." Nomed yanks his hand away from the man and punches his clenched fist into the palm of his other hand. "Who are you—really?

"No need to beat your own flesh." The man grins. "I am Legna, Yahweh's warrior, and you are a worm from Wormwood. I thought your planet wouldn't arrive until many years from now."

"So we meet again." Nomed grinds his fist into his palm. "Let's just say that I came a little early . . . as a tourist, surveying what we will soon possess." He grins.

"Assassin or reconnaissance?"

"Reconnaissance—for today."

"Clever, but if you're trying to change your fate—this isn't the way."

"Can you blame me for trying?"

Legna shakes his head. "I shall never betray one of Yahweh's prophets. My whole purpose for entering this filthy dimension of the mortals is to protect the prophet and his mission. I will not lead you to Ezekiel."

"You lied."

"No. You assumed. Unlike you, I would prefer to be at home, my eternal home, not here." Legna disappears, leaving Nomed to swipe at the air in front of him.

Where has the warrior gone? Why has he appeared as a slave?

Nomed slides his foot over his puddle of urine. Don't judge a book by his cover. The human proverb irks Nomed.

Stop trying to learn from them. They are inferior. Destined for destruction. He refocuses on the upper window.

No one.

He lost his single lead! Nomed sighs. A man with a scroll scurries past Nomed, up the steps, and toward the palace.

"Oh, but the gods! Got you." Where there is a scribe and a scroll, there is a scriptorium. "I've found Ezekiel without Legna's help."

Nomed spins the ring around his right forefinger as he follows the scribe at a safe distance. "Legna!" Nomed clenches his fist and screams into the air at his invisible opponent. "My master controls King Nebuchadnezzar. Ezekiel and his friends will die today."

No Ezekiel, no blood moon prophet.

No prophet, no scroll.

No scroll, no map.

No map, no future for humanity and no success by the Orphan Dreamer.

Chest puffed out, Nomed ascends the grand staircase, following his victim, a garrote wire concealed beneath his green sash.

No more mistakes.

But pride always precedes a fall.

41—EZEKIEL

HOW COULD EZEKIEL WATCH HIS three best friends be burned alive? The experience would haunt him for an eternity. He clenched his jaw.

His three young friends hadn't asked to be heroes, but alas, the king had condemned them to the fire.

Standing up for their beliefs had been their crime.

But would a fourth man walk with them, protecting his friends from the fire? Ezekiel prayed for this miracle, for an angel to rescue his friends. Staring at the fiery furnace, Ezekiel's faith wavered. Babylon's citizens had named this place Dura, a desolate land that would awaken beneath a smoldering sun. The fire was eager to consume the flesh of Ezekiel's three childhood friends.

It was too late for a miracle now. Instead of whispering

another prayer, he longed to murder his friends' tormentors.

But he considered Elohim's ways: He makes the sun rise on evil and on good. He sends rain on the just and unjust. He treats the evil person with His kindness—at least for a season—giving them the opportunity to turn and go a different way.

No matter what happened this day, Ezekiel knew the sun would still rise. So with a scroll tucked beneath his arm, he escaped before the mob gathered.

Even before their execution, he mourned them.

How would it feel to be thrown alive into a fiery pit?

But he can do nothing else.

He journeyed back to the palace's scriptorium. Even though he longed to remain at his friends' side, his mission demanded his return to the palace. He walked beneath a silent sunrise for what seemed like an eternity before the sound of urgent, yet purposeful footsteps behind him reached his ears.

Don't look back.

Keep going.

Ezekiel picked up speed, jogging past the city gates, through the market, and up the palace's grand marble stairs, his leather sandals *clicking* and *clacking* on the intricate stone.

He hurried past milky-white stone columns that towered above Babylon's hanging gardens—constructed to impress as well as intimidate— and chanced a look down.

The gardens dripped with lush foliage, but the wonder of the place was no match for Solomon's Temple, where the presence of Adonai had permeated before the Hebrews were captured.

The beauty of Babylon was nothing more than rot, built

upon pagan rituals and the sacrifices of the innocent. One day, it would come crashing down when Adonai brought the New Jerusalem to Earth—the place where man would tabernacle with Elohim.

Ezekiel's ragged breaths sucked in the noxious scents of overripe fruit mingled with desiccated soil and the sweat of slaves. The city ripened with lust and a thirst for blood.

The sound of footsteps followed again.

Ezekiel ran faster. *Almost there.* He scurried beneath a narrow arch past the gardens and down a darkened path, heading toward the secret entrance to King Nebuchadnezzar's palace. Slowing down, he studied the thick carpet of foliage clinging to the palace wall.

The rose—where is the Rose of Sharon?

Twenty paces forward. "There you are," he whispered, and quickly ran his finger along the insides of the ever-blooming flower. More than once, the flower had guided him to safety.

"May Elohim allow you to bloom for eternity." He began to weave his way behind the thorny wall of vine, but before he did, he removed the stopper from Daniela's jar and released a horde of ants onto the cobblestone path. "There. Go find him."

The rose bush clawed his skin, but the familiar pain promised camouflage and safety and quieted his soul. Behind, the spy's footsteps tapped across the cobblestone pathway adjacent to the wall of vines.

The pursuer persisted, but what did he want?

Perhaps Ezekiel, the ancient jewel that unlocked passage into other worlds—or the secret maps?

Don't breathe. Move quietly.

In his soul, Ezekiel recited the words of the great Judean warrior and psalmist, King David: *He who dwells in the secret place of the Most High shall abide under the shadow of the Almighty. I will say of Him, He is my refuge and my fortress and my God, in Him I will trust.*

Ezekiel toed off his sandals, rotated his body so that his back pressed against the wall, then inched north, his hand tracing the divots and contours of the stone wall.

Crisp leafy edges blurred into patches of green, and his brain begged for air, but his chest remained flat, as though one of the king's slithering serpents had curled around him and started squeezing.

He inhaled a long, quiet breath. Pollen tickled his throat. He stifled a sneeze.

Adonai, help me! For Israel's sake, not my own.

The footsteps stopped their frantic pace down the narrow path, backtracked toward Ezekiel's position, then stopped.

Whose side is Adonai on? At that precious moment, wails erupted into screams of agony. Daniela's fire ants had found their mark as Ezekiel's fingers dipped into a cold, smooth hole—the granite key—then over a discreet raised round wheel. *Blessed be Adonai, the God of my fathers.*

He rotated the knob.

The stone wall glided inward, not making a sound.

Ezekiel rotated his body. Leaves crackled. Quickly, he stumbled into another world, a remote and forgotten wing of the king's palace, then resealed the hidden entrance.

He couldn't save his friends from the fire, but he must save the scroll and the ancient stone for the one who would come after him—the last seer of the blood moons.

"My friends, forgive me for abandoning you," he said, as though their ghosts stood before him.

The palace torches blazed as they had during the last seven days, casting shadows across buttercream marble walls. Frankincense smoldered inside a bronze pot, releasing a heady scent of pine and lemon mixed with a woody aroma.

Shoulders back, Ezekiel strolled through the palace with the authority of a scribe to the king. His vision filled with the refinement of Nebuchadnezzar's home. Polished gold furniture glistened. Crimson silk and pale blue and silver tapestries floated on feathery gusts of wind like silken fingers reaching in to touch greatness.

Their grasps would return empty. Despite the luxury, Babylon's king was far from a great leader. Again the young Judean recalled the words of Solomon, the wise Hebrew king and son of King David: *When the righteous reign, the people rejoice: but when the wicked bear rule, the people mourn.*

Ezekiel mourned for both his nation and his friends.

A brutish ruler cared nothing for his country. Instead he divided the nation's citizens, pitting them against each other and creating chaos for his own arrogant purpose: to walk as a god among men.

King Nebuchadnezzar's ploy was simple, divide the simple minded, then conquer them. A simple feat for the ambitious and clever.

Ezekiel could never support the whims of such a ruler, and the time would soon come when he would face the executioner. But first he must complete his mission—take the maps to the cave.

The scents of their oils and perfumes meandered into the hallway before they appeared. Dressed in a rainbow of colorful silks, with their midnight-black hair braided with silver strings, the king's harem followed their mistresses toward the eastern entrance of the palace.

He waited, watching the women as they passed. The

fiery execution had been heralded as the event of the week. Were the women planning to watch it?

Ezekiel's chest burned. What woman would watch young men being burned alive? His Abigail would never participate in such a barbaric spectacle. But he reminded himself, his Abigail had a choice—these women did not.

He saw his late wife in his mind's eye, her nut-brown curls spilling over bronze, sculpted shoulders while she ate a pomegranate in the sun's morning light. He rubbed his eyes to blot out the memory, then continued his walk, penetrating deeper into the bowels of the palace where a few torches burned in the brazen pots.

He paused and dared a glance over his shoulder. Satisfied that he was alone, he twisted an iron handle and pushed open the heavy wooden door into the room where he had hidden his secrets.

The scriptorium.

After he closed the door, he latched the lock and fell back against the hard surface, looking around. This chamber, buried in maps and scrolls, was his home away from home. Four walls of twelve-inch-thick stone muted any outside sounds.

Inside the secure room, a rustle hissed. It sounded like leather sliding against stone. Fear drank the moisture from his throat and the hope from his heart.

"Who's there?" He breathed his question, praying no one would answer. "I ask you again, who's there?" He moved stealthily toward the eastern window and flung back the curtains. Light burst into the dusty room, but no spy lurked in the shadows.

He crossed the room toward the western window and peeled back the curtains, letting in more light.

No one.

Ezekiel braved a look out the west window. In the distance, ash and smoke mushroomed above cracked soil, obliterating his view of the furnace and the sky while blackening the consciences of the gathering crowd.

Mothers carried lunch baskets.

Children played games with their friends.

Shoulders back and heads held high, fathers spoke of wealth and the demise of their enemies.

Ezekiel was one of their enemies.

Captivity had reduced him to slavery, away from his homeland, but he refused to believe that his spirit had been created to rot within rusty chains. The Creator had shaped all mankind from the same ball of clay and then breathed into their lungs the breath of life.

Captivity was the thing of kings and queens, not Adonai.

Rays of sunlight pierced the growing clouds of smoke, enhancing the menacing profile of the king's golden statue.

He recalled the king's decree: "O people, at the time you hear the sound of the cornet and drums, fall down and worship the golden image, and whoever does not fall down and worship shall in the same hour be cast into a burning fiery furnace."

Two sunrises ago, three defiant Hebrew boys—renamed in Babylon as Shadrach, Meshach, and Abednego—had dared to refuse to worship the king's symbol of national allegiance—a ninety-foot-tall and nine-foot-wide gold-plated statue erected above the desert of Dura.

Shadrach was the one to speak on behalf of the three. "King Nebuchadnezzar, we do not need to defend ourselves before you in this matter. If we are thrown into the blazing furnace, Elohim, who we serve, is able to deliver us from it. But even if he does not, we want you to know,

Your Majesty, that we will not serve your gods or worship your image of gold."

With those words of conviction, Shadrach had sealed their fates.

Ezekiel shook his head. The Babylonian culture would never resonate with his beliefs as a Judean priest dedicated to serving and worshiping Yahweh. "See you in Abraham's bosom, my friends."

A gust of wind hotter than the devil's breath blew past Ezekiel's window, spewing ash and sand into his nostrils. He covered his nose, muting his cough.

Quiet, now.

Be about your work.

You must survive—no one can find you or stop your journey tonight.

42—EZEKIEL

THE CLANKS OF DRUMS AND the whines of trumpets sliced through the air, echoing deep into the palace and reverberating throughout Ezekiel's frame. Powerless to stop the impending execution of his friends, his stomach cramped.

Would they scream? "Elohim, have mercy on my friends." Blinking back emotion, he watched the furnace in the distance.

He had seen the king burn other "traitors" alive, so he could imagine his friends' fate.

Ezekiel watched as three young men, fully dressed with their hands tied behind their backs, stood at the lip of the fiery pit. King Nebuchadnezzar climbed up a set of uneven stone steps, his robe draping around his portly frame as he waddled across the platform that overlooked the furnace.

He paused.

The musicians ceased their noise, and the crowd quieted.

Nebuchadnezzar raised his hand, and the crowd gazed up at their king—their human god. In synchrony, he angled his chin downward and lowered his hand. The wattle of skin that hung from his neck jostled. The guards took their cue from the ruler and kicked Ezekiel's friends into the pit.

Ezekiel gasped as tongues of fire swallowed them.

In a moment, it was done.

The young Judean slammed the window shut and hurried to his weathered writing table. A lit beeswax candle sat on the corner of the desk. Inhaling deeply, he breathed in the familiar scents of ink, dust, clay, papyrus, and fear. Had he survived the Babylonian death march to slavery only to watch his friends die?

As Adonai willed. Quietness stilled the room. "For Shadrach, Meshach, and Abednego."

He gripped a stylus in his trembling hand, dipped the tip in a pool of ink, and continued drawing the final map.

Suddenly, the crowd outside grew quiet. *That's odd.* Had their thirst for human suffering been satisfied so quickly? Yet he refused to allow the fickle crowd's temperament to draw him back to the window. Hours passed as he transcribed.

Nightfall approached, and soon Ezekiel would make his journey. By the light of the full moon, he aimed to escape the city of Babylon before the child sacrifices began.

Despite child sacrifice being strictly prohibited in the Torah, some in the Judean culture had intermarried with gentiles and embraced the practice—and that was before the Babylonians took the Judeans captive. But murder would never resonate with Ezekiel's soul. Unfortunately, many Babylonians and exiled Judeans had grown accustomed to the idea.

He waited for the last scroll to dry. Next, he must finish the king's cuneiform cylinders that would tell of the fiery furnace and Ezekiel's friends' excruciating deaths.

Could he do it?

He must.

With tears welling at the corners of his tired eyes, he documented their stories, and the late afternoon sun silently roasted Babylon.

Ezekiel paused, drank a skin of water, and ate a morsel of bread before returning to his work. But the suffocating heat and mounting tension slowed the strokes of his pen. His eyelids grew heavy, and his mind lured him to sleep.

Drumbeats vibrated, jolting him awake.

How much time had passed?

Was it too late?

He reopened the western window. Red and orange clouds arched across the sky, and a hot wind blew from Dura, suffocating the palace with pulses of heat and ash. He must finish his task, but the delay would cost him.

Pressing the reed stylus into a slab of wet clay, Ezekiel continued recording his friends' stories. His shoulders ached with loneliness. *My dearest Abigail.*

Be strong.

As if Elohim sensed his inner turmoil, hope slipped into his dreary chambers in the form of a butterfly.

Its delicate yellow wings contrasted against the grays that dominated the room. The insect fluttered here and there before resting on the edge of his desk. Simple beauty, free from mankind's cruelty. A creature whose beginning had started cramped inside a cocoon.

Ezekiel watched the creature fold and open it wings. *Come fly away with me*, it said.

How would it feel to be free again? He reached for the winged creature, but the butterfly refused capture and escaped through the open window. Surveying his space, he laughed. "I know how you feel." Past his window, hope rested on the bruised petals of a red rose inside the palace gardens.

The crowd beyond the outer gates was gathering again. *Thirsty for more blood.* He slammed the shutters shut.

Ezekiel finished his task and prepared to escape. Wrapping his fingers around the completed Babylonian cuneiform cylinder, his grip moistened.

No, don't slip. The cylinder fell to the stone mosaic floor. If he ruined the inscription, he would need to remain in the scriptorium to complete another. *Adonai, please. The child sacrifices will begin soon.*

A wave of nausea hit his gut. *Help me be brave.* The ever-present threat of death tasted of rotting fish. Ezekiel lifted the cylinder with both hands and placed it on the middle of the table.

It was intact.

Turning quickly on his heels, he bumped a stack of scrolls.

He threw his body across the table as his eyes tracked the falling papyrus. They must not become damp. After retrieving the scrolls, he unrolled each one and inspected them for damage.

The scroll containing his map had dried. *Thank you, Adonai.* He rolled the papyrus and placed it inside a clay jar.

The two scrolls that belonged to the king were also

undamaged. Ezekiel secured the king's scrolls in another clay jar by the door. The courier would retrieve them in the morning, after the prophet's departure.

Beads of perspiration dotted his forehead and moistened his curly hair. With shaking fingers, he ran his finger down the intricately carved diamond hanging low beneath his tunic.

Desperation to keep the relic and map safe spurred him on, and the horrible sounds of screaming children echoing through the night lit a fire to his feet. How long would this country last while they disobeyed Elohim?

Ezekiel's very presence in Babylon signified that Elohim punished sin—the Judeans, His chosen people's sin. The people of his homeland had defied Elohim, stepping out from his protective covering.

Slavery followed.

The prophet secured his water skin to his belt, retrieved an unlit torch, wrapped his robe around his body, and reached for the two scrolls—the one containing the blueprint of the last Temple, and the other a message for Mistress Daniela, the one who would come after him.

Ezekiel inched toward the door and reached for the handle.

Hurried footsteps thud down the hallway outside of his chambers, freezing him in his tracks. His heart thumped against his chest. Did the king's counselors know about the secret scrolls? Had they come to execute him without the king's permission?

A heavy knock rapped against the door. Ezekiel cowered into the shadows. The knocking increased in intensity and frequency.

With no escape, he placed the scrolls back inside the

clay pot, then breathed what might be his last breath. "Mistress Daniela will be disappointed, arriving at the caves in her dimension with no scrolls to be found," he murmured.

As though something invisible but powerful was entering the room, a soft breeze ruffled the silken curtains over the eastern window. *He rode upon a cherub and flew; and He sped upon the wings of the wind.* The ancient words strengthened Ezekiel.

"Whatever comes, I tried to fulfill my mission, leaving clues for the final dreamer—a beautiful young girl."

A stream of light from the lone torch within his grasp glinted off the diamond hanging from his neck. He grabbed the intricately carved snowflake—the relic that would guarantee him an early grave—and stuffed the jewel beneath his tunic. *You've saved me before, Adonai. Save me again.* "The scriptorium is closed."

"But not to an old friend from Judea."

"Who is it?"

"Daniel. Open the door."

The voice sounded familiar. He opened the door. A lean, muscular man stood before him, holding a leather bag close to his chest. Ezekiel's body relaxed and a smile spread across his face as he stepped back from the open door. "Daniel, I thought you were the king's guards coming to arrest me."

"May I come in, before the king's guards arrest us both?" Daniel, a young Hebrew prophet and friend of the boys who had just been executed, stepped one foot inside the tiny room as he asked his question.

"Come." Ezekiel waved him inside and shut the door. His friend's aristocratic presence filled the room.

Daniel had been a member of Judea's royal family

before the Babylonians defeated the Judeans and enslaved them, but his noble bearings hadn't been diminished by slavery. Once a prince, always a prince.

Elohim had also gifted the prince with the wisdom and the ability to interpret dreams.

He alone could interpret King Nebuchadnezzar's dreams—the royal warlocks and wizards had failed. The dreams were shrouded by urgent warnings to the king by Elohim.

Elohim had given other secular kings warnings, always sending a righteous prophet to interpret the mysterious sayings so kings and their subjects would have an opportunity to repent and avoid Elohim's judgment.

Elohim had also given Daniel dreams of his own, messages for another era and for another people—the generation that would live during Earth's last human kingdom, before the Rock made without hands abolished all human-constructed realms.

Daniel had recorded these prophecies and had previously shown them to Ezekiel.

"There isn't much time." The dreamer unharnessed his leather satchel. "The sacrifices will begin soon."

"I can't bear another—"

"They survived."

"Shadrach, Meshach, and Abednego?"

"Yes, our friends are well."

"How?" Feeling lightheaded yet full of hope, Ezekiel plopped down on a wooden chair.

"There was a fourth man, an angel of Elohim. He brought them through the fire."

"Thank Adonai!" Full of joy, he cried, then sniffing hard, said, "I'll need to rewrite their story." Ezekiel looked back at the cuneiform cylinder.

"Don't rewrite it—add the ending." Daniel patted his friend's back. "The king is now afraid of our God and has changed his attitude. We are no longer outcasts because of our beliefs."

"Never made sense to me. The Babylonians took us from our homes, brought us to theirs, enslaved us, then persecuted us for our ways."

"Slavery never makes sense."

"It's safe, then?"

"For a while," Daniel said, then leaned against Ezekiel's desk. "King Nebuchadnezzar's counselors are constantly stirring up the king's ill will against us. You leave tonight?"

"I must."

"Before you go, take this." Daniel opened his shoulder bag and pulled out a copper scroll and a papyrus scroll. "Take them to the cave."

"Is that the Copper Scroll? I believed it was a myth! The Copper Scroll was rumored to provide a list of locations where gold and silver from King Solomon's Temple were buried."

"It's real, and it does tell of the treasures saved from King Solomon's Temple."

"So the priests accomplished their mission?" Ezekiel clasped his hands together.

"They did."

"Where are the treasures hidden?"

"Adonai will lead His chosen one to the caches at his kairos time. These relics will be necessary to build Israel's Third—and final—Temple."

"And the other scroll in your possession?"

"I recorded the image of the statue."

"Why?" Ezekiel took a step backward. "Our friends almost died because of that vile pagan image. I only wrote the story about the statue and fiery furnace because I am the king's scribe, enslaved to do the king's bidding, but you . . ."

"My friend." Daniel rested his hand on Ezekiel's shoulder. "My drawing does not give an account of the statue that Nebuchadnezzar forced Babylon's citizens to bow down to or perish in the flames. My drawing and words record another image of a statue shown to King Nebuchadnezzar in his dreams. Elohim revealed the statue's meaning to me."

"Tell me." Ezekiel opened the scroll.

"The head of the statue that the king saw in his dream was made of pure gold, its chest and arms of silver, its belly and thighs of bronze, its legs of iron, and its feet of part iron and part baked clay."

"What do the metals and clay represent?" Ezekiel asked.

"They tell of future kingdoms and governments, of their rise to power and their eventual fall into oblivion before that great and terrible day of the Lord—the end of human kingdoms," Daniel replied.

"And the rock?"

"At the end of the king's dream, a Rock not cut by human hands smashed the feet of the statue. The wind swept the dust away without leaving a trace, but the Rock—Elohim—that struck the statue became a huge mountain and filled all of Earth."

"What does this mean?"

"One day, Elohim will set up His perfect kingdom on Earth."

"May Adonai be blessed." Ezekiel fashioned his hands in a prayer-like position.

"The last blood moon prophet will be gifted the wisdom

to solve a series of mysteries and find the treasure spoken about in the Copper Scroll."

"And these treasures must be found in order to furnish the Third Temple." Ezekiel had already drawn a blueprint of it. "The rebuilding of the Third Temple is a clock in its own right. Has its rebuilding not been prophesied at the end of all ends?"

"I wouldn't want to be the last prophet." Daniel winced. "Do you know his identity, Ezekiel?"

"It's a girl."

"A girl?" Daniel's eyes opened wide, decreasing his natural handsomeness.

"Don't worry. We'll be resting in Abraham's bosom by then." Ezekiel rested his hand on Daniel's shoulder. "I prayed that you would leave this pagan city and come away with me to the Chebar River, where my sister lives."

"My place is here—even if I don't wish it to be." Daniel sighed. "Be careful on your journey. A stranger clothed in an ivory tunic and green sash asked about you in court today."

"Ivory tunic. Green sash." Ezekiel considered the details. "That's him—the mystery man who followed me earlier today. I had a dreadful time shaking him."

"Take the well-travelled road out of the city."

"I will." Ezekiel pointed to Daniel's third scroll. "The last scroll?"

"It records the dream Elohim gave to me."

"And?"

"In my dream I saw a great storm on a mighty ocean, with strong winds blowing from every direction. Then four huge animals came up out of the water, each different from the other. The last beast that rose out of the ocean is too dreadful to describe and is incredibly strong. It devoured its victims by tearing them apart with its huge iron teeth—and others it crushed beneath its feet. It had ten horns."

"Are the ten horns significant?"

"As I was looking at the horns, another small horn appeared among the ten, and three of the first horns were yanked out of the beast's head—roots and all—giving room for this little horn that had a man's eyes and a bragging mouth."

"The little horn is the ruler who antagonizes Elohim?" Ezekiel held his breath.

"Yes. This dreadful leader will defy the Creator, become the abomination of desolation standing in the holy place and war against God's people."

"And the animals . . . what kingdoms do they represent?" Ezekiel asks.

"The animals give clues of which kingdoms are represented by the statue. Your handmaiden prophet must discover what kingdoms are represented, though."

"She can do it. Mistress Daniela is tough."

"One of King Nebuchadnezzar's mistresses?"

"Yes. No. She called herself an alien."

"Are we not also aliens in a foreign land?"

"We are," Ezekiel agreed. "And whatever the progression of human kingdoms, each nation will have had their turn to rule and to serve. In the end, Elohim will judge us according to our motives and actions."

"Go to the grotto, my friend." Daniel helped his friend secure all three papyrus scrolls and the Copper Scroll inside his shoulder bag. "Hide them and be well."

The time to leave the familiar had come.

Ezekiel scanned his inscription desk, removed his robe,

and placed the satchel across his shoulder before donning his outer robe again. He grasped an unlit torch and followed Daniel out of the scriptorium.

The oversized wooden door closed with a soft thud.

Ezekiel glanced back at the door for a moment, at the faces of false gods and great cities carved into the wood. Nothing about Babylon honored Adonai, yet this was where Ezekiel had been placed. How could he judge the Babylonians, when Ezekiel's own people lived in no more truth than the pagan culture of Babylon?

"Go to your sister, then the hiding place." Daniel nudged his friend. "There's nothing more for you here."

"I will miss you, my friend."

"I already miss you." Daniel embraced his Judean friend. "Until we return home." The prince who had been reduced to a Babylonian slave released his friend, then disappeared down the hallway.

All alone, Ezekiel's chest ached. As though lost in a daze, he trudged toward the palace entrance, his stride lengthening as he walked through the courtyard.

43—EZEKIEL

575 BCE
MESOPOTAMIA: BABYLON

AN HOUR LATER, EZEKIEL FACED the gates of the city. Smoke clouded the horizon and lit his chest on fire, making his heart gallop out of control. *Be brave. Face it.* There was no route around the acrid hell. *Push through the crowd quickly. Keep your head down.*

Outside the city walls, the temple stood between Babylon and Ezekiel's home. The mayhem began in the streets and ended in the sordid temple. Against a darkening sky, ribbons of fire gyrated inside bronze basins.

The thud of dingy leather pulled over a brass bowl gave way to pounding wooden sticks as drunken musicians pounded out a chaotic rhythm and the crowd danced in a dark trance.

Perspiration mixed with dust saturated the air.

Faint scents of cumin and mint wafting from the open market in the distance almost, but not quite, calmed Ezekiel's stomach. He pulled his gaze back to the street—the way to his true home and the path to the cave.

Eyes down, garment lifted so it didn't impede his flight, Ezekiel quickened his pace. He weaved through the throngs of idol worshipers journeying to the blood-drenched temple, the pagan gateway to the gods.

The innocent cries of children about to be sacrificed reverberated in the air. He plugged one ear with his finger. With his satchel tucked under his arm at an odd angle, he ran.

A desperate cry yanked his vision to the right. He turned toward the sound, stumbled over a rock, and fell.

Looking up from the ground, he watched a wild-eyed mother swaying to the beat of the drum. She held her screaming baby in the air, eager to offer her little child to the priest of Moloch, the Babylonian fire god, a powerless deity made of brass with a head of a bull and outstretched arms that sloped toward its belly—a fiery pit. How could a nursing mother so readily give up the baby who clung to her breast?

Orgies in the streets painted a lewd contrast to the cold, possessed mother. Ezekiel prayed that future generations would judge these people who were so hungry to devour their own seed in the most horrific ways, as barbarians.

The world seemed to slow as Ezekiel pushed himself to his feet and wiped his hands across his tunic to remove the sand from between his fingers. He pressed his hand to his temple, blocking his peripheral view. Still, dust suffocated his breathing and stung his eyes. Desert heat scrambled his thoughts, and his vision blurred.

In the distance, a small adult stood on a stone in front

of him. Dressed in a linen tunic accented with a green sash, his olive skin glistened with sweat. Though he had a handsome face and figure, a perverted, encouraging grin etched the man's face with a sense of twisted pleasure as he scanned the throngs of people.

Ezekiel studied the man. *Who smiles while babies are burned alive? Why does he stand above it all—to watch every detail?* It was as if the man wanted the humans to sacrifice their own.

The young Judean's pace slowed. *Is that the man—the one with the emerald sash—the one asking about me in court today?*

Red dots splotched his face—the work of the fire ants.

The man's gaze landed on Ezekiel's face. *It is!*

Quickly, Ezekiel hunched lower, running in the shadow of a fat man and skirting around a fire pit. Did he dare snatch a baby from the hands of one of these women? Would they offer it up to him as willingly as they did to that evil idol?

No time. Avoid the man.

How fast he was becoming one of them.

Babylonians and wayward Judeans fed Moloch, stuffing its belly full of screaming babies. The sleeping god belched acrid ash and smoke into the air in return for the sacrifices. Void of power, he gave nothing more to his followers.

Ezekiel dipped his torch into a fire basin and ran around the temple. He ran until the wailing of burning infants ceased its assault on his eardrums, but their burning flesh stilled fouled the air.

Children are an inheritance from Adonai. They are a reward from Him. His eyes burned from tears mixed with sandy grit and guilt. "How could parents kill their own children, and yet my wife and I were barren?"

Safe and outside the city, he knew that he could have saved at least one. Why hadn't he saved a child? Had he been afraid?

Perfect love casts out fear. "Yes, I was afraid for my life."

He stopped down the road, turned, and faced the city and temple, longing to return to the mayhem and save the babies. "How could you let this happen? Where were you when the Babylonian army murdered my mother and father? Where are you now, Adonai?"

He closed his eyes, blocking out his present reality. He must go on. The man dressed in the tunic and green sash would find him. He walked into the night, tormented by the memories of his past.

Twenty-five years ago, he was to be a priest in Judah.

"No . . ." He quietly protested as blood pounded inside his ears. "Adonai, I don't want to remember." His tongue stuck to the top of his mouth, dry from hyperventilating.

Stubborn images flashed into his mind, punishing him: spurting blood, clanking swords, bloodcurdling screams, and the mask of death on his mother's face. Royalty, noblemen, priests, and prophets all captured to serve in Nebuchadnezzar's palace.

His hope of living out his life as a priest inside the four walls of Solomon's Temple had vanished, but the treasures had been preserved—including the Ark of the Covenant—and he would ensure their protection. The treasures had been lost to some after the demise of King Solomon's Temple, but not to the faithful of Adonai's children.

Those haunting memories of his family and his country were so alive now that they were fast becoming the moment instead of the memory.

My dear wife has died. I have no child to bear my name, yet shallow, tiny graves litter the ground. Babylonian soldiers had destroyed the temple. *Does the Copper Scroll hide a plan for redemption?* The map to *somewhere* thumped against his side as he pressed on into the darkness with just enough light to illuminate his path.

He splashed water onto his face from the water skin, trying to wash away the smell of death.

What of the butterfly in his scriptorium?

Butterflies.

Small but free.

Bright and beautiful.

The insect's presence signaled hope.

Wasn't that why Adonai had protected the Hebrews, so their seed—Melek Moshiach, the King anointed with oil—could bring hope to a wretched world?

Ezekiel couldn't think that this was the end for the Judeans, nor could he abort his quest, even though his people were enslaved. Adonai had promised that a remnant of repentant Judeans would return to their homeland. And that's why Ezekiel carried the scrolls, so that hope could be born and save the world from certain death.

The night turned into morning and the morning back into evening, and for another night, darkness surrounded him as he walked.

He clutched his fading torch as he continued on the familiar road. Martha, his sister, awaited him, and the thought soothed him like a summer drink from the Chebar River—cool, cleansing, and refreshing.

The sun peeked over the eastern horizon, and in the distance, the dark outline of his home in Tel-Abib contrasted against the sunrise.

Home at last.

He had escaped hell, and even though he was eager to see his sister, he slowed his pace.

"Elohim," he prayed. "I was a coward, no different than the mothers offering their children to Moloch. I should have protected my mother and father. I possessed a sword. I could have fought back." Looking toward the heavens, he said, "Mother, you told me my name means 'Adonai will strengthen.' How can I honor my namesake if I fail to fight the evil one's forces?"

Goats bleated and horses neighed as he walked up the windy dirt road toward his sister's home. After trekking up another four furlongs, he knocked and then opened the door. It creaked on the hinges.

"Ezekiel, is that you?" A youthful woman with brown curls that hung down to her slender waist appeared just inside the door. "My brother has returned home!" His sister touched his face. "You're ashen, dusty, and road weary, but still handsome as ever." She traced his lips with her trembling fingers.

"My sister." He stilled her with a stroke of his hand down her cheek, then embraced his last remaining family member.

"Come in. Rest." He entered the kitchen. "Will you eat?"

"Tonight I leave for the cave. I will rest, but I have no time to eat."

"Tonight?"

"My mission is urgent—and important."

"So is my mission, Ezekiel. That is to make sure you and I survive, so you must fill your belly, wash your dusty skin, and refresh your soul with wine." She pulled her hair up into a bun and harpooned a wooden stick through the unruly mess to keep it out of her amber eyes.

"Sleep is more important than baths, leeks, bread, and garlic."

"Spoken like a man, except for the refusal to eat." She laughed. "I offer my concession—I will prepare a pack of food, and you'll eat on the journey." Martha spread a woven mat on his bedroom floor.

"As you wish."

"Why not leave your scrolls here instead of in the cave?"

"When the time comes, Adonai's chosen one will find the cave of Makkedah, then locate the grotto and find my drawings."

"Who might that be?"

"Someone beautiful, clever, and smart like you."

"Flattery never won a war. I need you as well."

"I'm here."

"For now. The cave clamors with danger." She reached out, touching him, her attempt at softening his heart. "Since the siege, you're my only living family. Thieves lurk around the caves. Mary told me." She let go of him and lit a candle pot that rested on a stool inside his bedroom.

The fragrant scents of cinnamon, cardamom, and cloves washed the tiny house with spice.

"Mary—the gossiper and the worrier. Does she still believe that King Nebuchadnezzar's spies are hiding at the bottom of the Chebar River, waiting to ambush us?" He chuckled. "Surely they would have drowned by now."

"She means well."

"So do I. I am a prophet."

"You keep reminding me, but you were a son, a brother, then a husband first."

"I accept my failure as a son, a husband, and a brother."

"I didn't mean that."

"But I did, and I won't fail again. Neither will I foil my legacy."

"Your legacy?"

"How will the other dreamers and prophets be able to accomplish their tasks if I don't complete mine? My calling overrules everything, even my daily comfort."

"But not good sense. Cannot both calling and safety be present, brother?"

"I'll be careful." He kissed his sister on the cheek. "Do not fret."

"You don't have to save the world, Zeke. That's the Moshiach's job."

"And until He comes, Adonai relies upon his messengers, his prophets."

"Then may Adonai and his warriors be with you."

"And with you." His sister knew nothing of the jewel—the diamond that looked like a snowflake—the Copper Scroll, the blueprint of the Third Temple, or the scroll about the statue. He intended to keep it that way and refused to remove his robe as he rested on the mat.

A cocoon of sleep wrapped his mind in dreams and quieted his thoughts. Under heavy eyelids, his eyes tracked left then right, slowly at first, but then at the speed of Nebuchadnezzar's fastest chariot.

★ ★ ★

A vision unraveled, feeling more real than not.

Letters formed a message on the horizon: 29th of Tamuz 5754, a Hebrew calendar date that correlated with a date in the future.

A young girl emerged from the edge of the horizon, her emerald silk smock billowing in the breeze. Steps light and graceful, she appeared to float through the air until she reached a jagged rock anchored on a patch of grass. She lay down and removed a sheer golden veil from her face, only to ball it up and place it beneath her head.

Immediately, she fell asleep. "Daniela," a voice called, sounding like a thousand oceans.

Gingerly, the young woman pulled her veil close to her chest while she scanned the field. "Who's calling me?" Her tone, a deep but feathery timbre, yearned for an answer, as though she had been asking for far too long. "Who's there?"

"I AM THAT I AM."

She shrouded her face with the veil and kneeled. "Abba, please tell me what's going on." Another fierce wind blew from the north, lifting her garments and revealing scars, bruises, and lacerations cut deep into her back.

The calming voice said, "Daniela, write the vision on tablets. For the vision will happen in its appointed time. It will not lie."

"Ezekiel," the voice turned its attention away from the dreamer and to the prophet, "these scars are not her own. Her compassion has caused her to wear the latticework of pain inflicted upon another, a boy."

★ ★ ★

Fog pushed in over the horizon, and Ezekiel awoke from his dream. He smiled. Mistress Daniela—the alien—would indeed become the next dreamer. One day she would submit to the power behind the Glass Tattoo.

As he stood up from his mat, his rapid breath slowed to a steady pace. The torch burned dimly.

"Martha . . . Martha . . ." He squeezed his sister's shoulder. "Awake, my sister."

"Yes, my brother."

"Elohim confirmed it."

"Who?"

"The prophetess—the last of us all."

"A girl?" Martha trembles.

"Her name is Daniela." Ezekiel left out the detail that he had met Daniela in Babylon.

"Like Daniel, capable of seeing the past and the future." Martha hugged herself, as if the girl rested within her arms. "A girl who must navigate a man's world. May Adonai protect her from the darkness."

"Martha, are you afraid for the girl because no delicate creature of the weaker sex deserves a prophet's life?"

"Yes, I am afraid. She will be asked to sacrifice as you and Daniel have done. But the calling is an honor, not a punishment." She flicked him across the nose. "And quite often, delicacy hides fortitude. Adonai will gift her strength as He has equally given it to me and to you after Babylon's soldiers murdered our parents."

"I'm thankful that the lot didn't fall on your shoulders."

"I am strong, Ezekiel. Who runs this farm when you are gone? Who defends it—the chickens and the goats?"

"I couldn't imagine you suffering any more than you already have." He studied his sister's face. What if Martha's body bore the scars that the young girl's body had?

"I have been scared, Zeke." Her face twisted, and anguish distorted her voice.

Scared? By whom? Confusion clogged his senses. He pulled away from his sister when she needed him the most. "I must leave my final clue, then I shall return to this house and never leave you alone again."

"As Adonai has spoken, so be it." Martha embraced her brother. "Go in peace and safety. May my prayers mount you on eagle's wings and allow you to fly with haste and endurance . . . return to me, Zeke."

Ezekiel tucked her in beneath a blanket. "Sleep well." Beneath the pale amber glow of the torch, clouds of blue softened by halos of cheap gold marred her left eye. He hadn't noticed the bruise before. He brushed his finger beneath her eye.

"I shall dream of your return." Martha turned her head and lay back on her bed.

Ezekiel slung the pack of food across his shoulder, cradled the leather satchel against his body, then lit a fresh torch and retrieved another for the journey. Under a pitch-black sky, he scurried toward his destination, his dark-gray robe protecting him from the evening chill and prying eyes.

Yahweh-Yireh—God will provide—so grant me safe passage. Yahweh-Shalom—God of Peace—calm my fears.

Sometime later, he stepped off the main path and hurried through the hills. To his left, something moved in the brush. Had the man with the emerald sash found him? Ezekiel crouched low, the thundering sound of his own heartbeat masking the intruder's approach.

Moments passed, slow and sinister.

The movement occurred again, but it was far too close to the ground to be a person. He whipped around, his torch casting an aura of faint light around him. A sand-colored snake slithered through the dust until it reached a clump of bushes. A bright-yellow butterfly clung to the branch of a bush. Ezekiel was the intruder; this was the animal's home. He left the beast alone and continued his journey.

The butterfly followed. A night chill settled in his bones, but the still, fresh air cleansed his thoughts.

He wouldn't fail again.

As he approached a hill, flickers of his torch's orange glow shimmered across the sides of rocky walls. He stood in front of the cave of Makkedah, the place where Joshua, a Judean warrior, once rolled a stone over the mouth of the cave and trapped five enemy kings.

He walked past the cave entrance, and after one last scan of the area, ducked inside and snaked through the labyrinth of passages. The night sounds ceased, as if a massive door had covered the entrance.

Deep inside the cave, beyond peering eyes, he swept his torch from left to right. Shadows moved with him across the walls and the floor, and the coolness of the earth soaked through his skin and down to his bones. Drips of water sounded in the distance, adding movement and noise to the stale air.

His breath deepened.

The must of a damp, subterranean world filled his lungs, comforting him and telling him that he was safe, that his secrets would be safe. The smell had once been unpleasant to him, but now he sensed the presence of Adonai and felt His breath at his back, guiding him through the maze to a familiar cleft deep inside the belly of the grotto.

Water cascaded down from the ceiling and formed a clear pool at his feet.

He lifted his cloak and secured the leather satchel to his back before wading across the wide but shallow subterranean lake. Cold liquid lapped against his bare legs, purifying his skin.

After he exited the pool, he climbed a slight incline before stooping to enter a small room. He held his torch as far away from his body as his arm would allow, then searched for the symbol of a fish carved into the cave wall.

Finding it, Ezekiel anchored his torch in the cradle of a fractured stalagmite. Gently, he pressed his hand on the belly of the carved fish. Beneath the marking, a stone slid from a divot just above the cave floor, making a grinding noise.

Ezekiel dragged previously cut sticks from an outcropping in the cave wall and started a small fire. He removed a tall clay pot from behind a stack of dried hay and placed it on the ground in front of him, then took one scroll from his satchel and unrolled it.

Scrawled on the papyrus were the sketches for the Third Temple—detailed drawings Adonai had entrusted to him in a dream twenty-five years after he was taken captive by the Babylonians. He bent over the scroll, pressed the edges of the vellum until it lay flat, and anchored the edges with pieces of broken rock.

He sliced his finger with a sharp stone, then drew four blood-red circles around the edges of the scroll, leaving the mark of the prophets and the dreamers charged since the beginning of time to warn humanity about any dark threats to their earthly home.

After the blood dried, he rolled up the scroll, then bandaged his finger.

"Adonai, whisper the mystery of the four blood circles to the young girl." Silence rang in his ears, but peace ruled his heart.

His prayer had been heard. Daniela would recognize the mark.

Working carefully, he melted the wax seal around the pot's rim with his torch, removed the lid, and secured the three scrolls inside.

He would place the Copper Scroll behind the earthen vessel.

Another scroll had already been placed inside the vessel. That one contained Adonai's map to the Ark of the Covenant, but the map was more of a mystery—a cipher of dots grouped together and separated by spaces instead of a typical geographical map.

During his last visit to the cave, Ezekiel had counted the dots in each group: 20, 5, 13, 21, 10, 9, 14. In the Hebrew language, numbers correlated to letters of the Hebrew alphabet, but the matching alpha was nonsensical. The same alphanumeric system could be discovered in Latin and Greek. Maybe the cipher would reveal the name of a place or person.

Hopefully, the young prophetess would be able to solve the puzzle.

Ezekiel sat down on a naturally formed rock stool, drank water from the old wineskin, and ate the meal Martha had packed for him.

After he finished eating, he dug deep into his leather satchel and retrieved a patinated bronze box with a cover made of African ivory. He removed the leather cord and the attached jewel from his neck. Holding it next to the torch, the ancient relic sparkled like a glass snowflake.

The Glass Tattoo will only respond to the chosen one.

Will it truly be Mistress Daniela, the dreamer?

Time reveals all secrets.

He wedged the diamond snowflake inside the box, then secured the box inside the second clay pot before resealing the pots with fresh hot wax.

Ezekiel lifted the pot containing the jewel into the air. "Adonai Ra'ah, Lord, my shepherd, lead the young girl to this place at your appointed time." His voice echoed off the stone walls of the frigid cavern. "When the moon drips with blood, she must decide—intercede or allow them to perish."

The Judean prophet placed the pot back onto the ground. Kneeling, he clenched a handful of his cloak. "But what of her scars? Will she despise the ones who inflicted them and refuse to declare your warning to the people? Will the tormented boy despise his abusers?"

His voice broke. "Show her mercy, Adonai. Do not ask

her to walk the path of a prophetess and a dreamer alone, as you have required me to do. Gift her with the company of a man blessed with a richness of spirit and strength of mind and body, and until then—walk with her."

The young Judean prophet finished his prayer, then wedged both clay pots back into their hiding place before covering the hole with a waterproof seal.

He reset the lock, and for the first time, he activated the trap. Whoever illegitimately tried to open the hiding place would die a quick but painful death. Maybe one of the king's men would fall upon it.

Ezekiel's face burned with shame at the thought. Should he repent? Humanity was a complex entity—love and hate, revenge and mercy, all existing side by side.

Forgive and you will be forgiven. I forgive their wrongs against my friends. Forgive me for contemplating murder, Adonai.

A sense of finality and peace urged him to the cave's mouth. Standing at the cave's entry, he crouched in the shadows and surveyed the landscape.

But it was different now.

Quiet.

The peace he found inside continued as he passed the mouth of the cave. This portion of his calling was now complete. As he stepped beyond the cave, the floor trembled beneath him.

What's happening?

Dust showered down around him. Ezekiel lifted his robe and hurried away, his feet seeming to tap out the prayer, *A-do-nai, A-do-nai.*

★ ★ ★

IMMORTALS—TIME WITHOUT END

After retrieving Daniela from the viewing space above and

taking her to the safe house, Legna stays in the shadows of the immortals where no human can see him.

He watches Ezekiel leave and then with his powerful arms spread braces himself against the edges of the cave's mouth, where he obstructs the opening from the eyes of men and protects it from the advances of the spirit world.

Elohim always has a plan. Lethal but beautiful, hotter than the surface of the sun, His blue-white fingers of energy snake through the atmosphere and propel shockwaves into Earth's dimension. The earth quakes. A rumble of thunder throughout the heavens follows.

Rocks cascade behind Legna.

Veins protrude in his neck as he digs his fingernails into the rock and tightens his abdomen and thighs. He releases a warrior's cry and tucks his wings close. He can't afford them to be ripped from his back. How would he return to his celestial home or take Daniela back to her Earthly home?

Earth's floor shifts.

A chasm opens, and the cave folds in upon itself.

Walls become ravines, and boulders become weapons as the cave drops into black nothingness. He braces himself until the mouth of the cave can no longer be seen. Earthen dust coats his skin. He shakes it off.

Legna stands on the newly formed jagged precipice and glares down into a deep abyss. The earthquake has erased the presence of the cave and its secrets.

The opening will be hidden until the appointed time.

"How will she find the maps and the ancient mysteries?"

Silence answers the warrior.

So he gazes past Earth's atmosphere to focus on the stars—resting angels. He locks eyes with Betelgeuse, a workaholic star drinking up his own fuel, destined to collapse under his own weight—but he will live again after exploding into a spectacular supernova.

A reverent hush is the warrior's only companion.

Standing beside the collapsed cave, Legna focuses deeper into the heavens and notices Polaris—the North Star—as she drums out her adulation to the One who gifted her with song. With an eerie dissonance, larger stars play tuba and bass. Smaller stars sing with high-pitched voices, like celestial flutes.

Without an answer, he leaves the world of the mortals and marches across the Karman line that lies sixty-two miles above Earth's sea level—the boundary between Earth's atmosphere and outer space—and focuses his gaze on the Engraved Hourglass Nebula.

Stellar winds rip up the Hourglass's insides as she sluggishly expands. He cringes, knowing that his friend is dying, but not without a show. She's a sassy one. Thirty-one million light years away from Earth, the Hourglass reclines in space, shooting circular flames of gas from her blue-tinged innards.

One day, Legna will join the Hourglass, Polaris, and Betelgeuse in the angels' graveyard where warriors like him lay down their swords, shed their celestial and earthly bodies, and use their massive sources of nuclear power to illuminate Earth.

He had been made for war, not to exist as a nightlight for the humans.

If Daniela fails her mission and doesn't stop Earth's impending pandemic, Earth will be destroyed.

He smiles.

Because when the futile planet no longer requires nighttime illumination, Legna will retain his warrior's body and live forever in heaven, where Daniela will live after she dies. Maybe there would be a future for them in his celestial home—a romantic future?

The Master would gift her a new body—a celestial body—that might be able to accommodate his. Lust grips his frame.

Conflicted, he dares to seek his answer once more. "Will you not give the young prophetess a chance, Holy One? How can she find the relics when you've buried them?"

Silence permeates everything, aside from the eerie songs of sleeping angels. Past the Hourglass, deep inside the universe, at the limit of Legna's vision, massive winged beings bow before the eternal Master's throne.

Legna takes a deep breath, needing rest from protecting the humans. He feasts on the splendor of his eternal home.

Emerald trees line translucent golden pathways. A rainbow of flowers speckles the ground, and an ocean breeze peaks and ebbs from the salty water basin far, far away from the Karman Line, saturated with scents of frankincense and myrrh.

The gentle sounds of harps waft through the air.

A Being from before time began who always will be—I AM THAT I AM, Yahweh, the one true God, the Light of the World—fills the heavens.

His eyes are aflame with swords of fire, and His face is brighter than ten thousand suns. He engulfs the golden throne.

The human caricatures of my Master are insulting. They've never gotten I AM right.

"They were never supposed to comprehend all of me, only accept my gift."

"The Messiah?"

"Indeed. And remember your job, Legna. Protect Daniela, and in *kairos*, my appointed time, she will find the maps and jewel. Don't worry about how or when."

"You've humbled me once more." Legna, the powerful warrior, bows low.

"I want you to understand this mission, so you'll be of the most help to Daniela." Yahweh's voice rumbles through the heavens.

"I want to understand her distress. Will she be asked to surrender anything?"

"What she holds dear."

"What is that, Elohim?"

"Friendship. Love. Belonging."

"The majority of her kind don't seem worth the sacrifice. Why should she be bothered with seeking their affections?"

"Mercy isn't measured on scales of justice. I chose her because of her incredible ability to empathize with, love, and tolerate her kind."

"Redemption. We've spoken of it before, but I fail to understand the concept." Legna thinks of Moloch, the Babylonian god. "You're a good Father."

"Yes. It's who I AM."

"And I rejoice in what you rejoice in, all of the angels do, even though I don't understand why you show the humans mercy. They see you as a . . ." Legna hesitates.

"Pushover?"

"Yes, Your Great One." Legna kneels and keeps his head down. "Why not start over? Grant Nomed his wish, and scrub Earth clean of these foul, pathetic humans. But only after You take Daniela home."

"Take her life?"

"And gift her eternal life with You . . ."

"You mean with you, Legna. And at the same time, condemn Earth and all the other humans to imminent destruction?"

"I am a warrior. Facts—not fantasy—paint my worldview. The mortals don't even acknowledge or seek to understand their real enemies. And they often work in collusion with them, rebelling against and hurting You."

The sound of water cascading over a ravine and crashing into a valley below fills the heavens. The Master weeps.

What have I done? Legna clenches his jaw. *Not another Noah's flood! His tears will drown Daniela.*

"Legna . . ." The angel holds his breath and waits for his Master to finish His sentence and emotional display. "This time, you will benefit from the mission."

"Yes, my Lord." Legna shields his face behind one of his large, albino-white wings.

"As the young prophetess solves the ancient mystery of the Skeleton Key, she will teach you about redemption, so that you—with my children—will understand the Messiah's great love—how wide and how long and how high and how deep that love is."

"Daniela will teach me, and I will protect her." With a clenched fist, he slams his arm across his chest. *He shall give His angels charge over you, to keep you in all your ways.* Yahweh's promise to humans who choose to follow his Master.

Legna unleashes his massive wingspan and falls backward. He flies through black holes, nebulae, and constellations like a falling star navigating the infinite heavens.

He pierces the atmosphere of the third dimension into the world of mortals—Earth—leaving his heavenly body behind. His angelic power and form would frighten the humans. Wings shed and dressed as a slave, he stands outside Babylon's city gates, his muscles rippling beneath smooth ebony skin. A well-cropped mustache curves over his upper lip.

Again the citizens of Babylon stuff Moloch's belly full of the innocent, and he belches more ash.

The mortals are ruthless.

What will they do to the girl if they find her in the safe house? He grips his sword.

Legna's black eyes scan the gaudy opulence of Nebuchadnezzar's palace set against the sacrifice of those who were denied the privilege of choice.

Yahweh, stay near to me.

Legna's sight focuses on Nomed, who stands at the base of the altar and presides over the human sacrifices.

He lives to kill humans.

Yahweh's warrior approaches Martha's house—Daniela's safe house—where he'll wait for Ezekiel to return from the demolished grotto.

44—ORPHAN DREAMER

575 BCE

"I'M GOING TO FIND LEGNA and Ezekiel, Martha. They may need help. That rumbling was an earthquake. I'm sure of it." Daniela removed her pink silk robe and slipped on one of Martha's tunics, then wrapped her pink veil around her head.

"Don't go!" Martha's hand trembled. "The men will come for us. Wait here."

"Fighting defines my existence. I can't sit on the side-lines waiting to be rescued by men."

"But your burns from the viewing place?" Martha had treated Daniela's sunburns with gel from an aloe plant, cool water, and linen bandages.

"They'll heal."

"Then take these." Martha gifted Daniela a torch, a skin of goat's milk, and food. Daniela walked toward the door of Martha's home. "Wait!" Ezekiel's sister grabbed the tip of the Orphan Dreamer's pink veil, yanking her head back. "Forgive me."

"You're forgiven." Daniela said, and Martha looked away. "Take me with you—back to your time and your place."

"I can't."

"I hate living out here . . . alone." Martha began to cry, and Daniela embraced the woman.

"One day, we will live together. Keep the faith, my sister."

"I will . . . I must." A weak smile appears among tears. "I'll miss you terribly. I needed to meet you, to spend time with you, Daniela Rose Cavanaugh. You've lifted my spirits. Your trip wasn't a waste. Never believe that lie. Your mere presence saved my life—gave me hope in this lonely place."

Her hands protected with muslin rags, Martha gathered a clump of purple flowers with their roots and dainty white flowers.

"Those blooms are hemlocks and devil's helmet flowers." Daniela shifted her gaze from the blooms to Martha's eyes. "Both are deadly poisons."

"I . . . I didn't want to."

"Were you going to kill yourself?"

"Yes." Martha refused to meet Daniela's gaze. "You must understand. Please. Don't judge me, at least not yet. My parents were murdered right in front of me, and then they took Ezekiel. They . . ." Martha's hands trembled. "They defiled me—over and over. I'm so alone, but then you came. A sister and a kind face, a breath of hope."

"It's not my job to judge, only love and then heal." Daniela grabbed the clump of death and threw it into a firepit outside. She ran back into the house. Applying a cold compress to her new kindred spirit's brow, Daniela said, "I'll ask Legna if you can come with us."

"No. It's okay. My place is here." Martha sat down, then rested her hand on her belly. "The child would not survive the trip, and I'm not like them—the Babylonians—killing everything and everyone in my way."

"You're with child?"

"I am." Martha weakly smiled. "And I am unmarried."

Virginity until marriage. Some women hadn't been given the choice. A tear tumbled down Daniela's cheek. "I'm sorry, Martha. But your child will be born loved and even wanted."

"Go find Legna and Ezekiel, Daniela."

"I will, and your brother won't be allowed to leave you all alone, again. Legna and I will hide you somewhere safe."

"Thank you, my friend." Martha kissed Daniela's cheek and escorted her outside.

Listening and then empathizing while spending time to befriend a stranger had turned out to be the main purpose for Daniela's visit to Babylon. Securing the clay map had become a distant second. *People over things.*

Daniela left Martha's home.

A short time later, dust coated her feet and legs. Sweat dripped from her brow as she shielded her eyes. The cave jutted up from the earth in the distance.

As the sun set, she crouched low and crawled into a side entrance of the cave—an air vent, nothing more.

Spines of hair attached to a spindly leg bristled against stone. "Who's there?" Daniela faced the entrance.

A hairy black leg penetrated the cave's mouth, and then another until a monster spider inched toward her from behind. Would the spider turn into a demon like it had before, when she was returning from Prince Jonathan's world? Red eyes tracked her movements. "Legna's busy, Danny Rose."

"Who are you?"

"Nomed's alter ego." Hissing, the creature extended his fangs. Amber liquid dripped to the floor, and he rose onto his back legs in preparation for a strike. "Time to die."

Not like this. She dropped and rolled, wishing she had travelled with her bow and arrow. "Help!" She screamed, but horror dampened her voice to a mere squeak.

The earth shook beneath her feet. *An aftershock.* She ran toward the back of the cave, the spider right behind her. Rocks tumbled down the cave wall and barreled toward her. An explosion of dust blinded her escape. Hands forward, her palms slammed into a rock wall.

Dead end!

She doubled back, pressed herself flat against the wall, then charged past the spider toward a glint of light. But walls and dust obliterated her path.

"Help!" she cried again, clutching the clay map to her chest.

"Give it to me, Rose." The spider's hairy leg reached for her.

"My name's not Rose. I am the Orphan Dreamer. Who the heck do you think you are?" She dropped to her stomach, then rolled between the spider's fangs. Scooting to the middle of the spider's underside, she lit the insect with her torch. "Burn, you devil!"

The earth shook again.

Rocky ground disappeared from beneath her and the burning spider.

Storm! With bloodied hands, she fought for a grip on the ledge of crumbling rock but found no purchase. "Help!"

★ ★ ★

Immortals—Time Without End

"Help!"

Legna hears a cry.

"Rosebud!" His feet follow the pitiful voice as his vision moves past rock and dust. Up ahead, a shadow slips off the edge of a plateau and falls into a black hole that's widening into a gorge.

He spots a pink veil, then charges toward the color. "Danny, hold on!"

"Legna!"

A cosmic span of sugar-white velvet wings unfurl from his back. He dive-bombs and grabs her around the waist, yanking her into his safe embrace. Her breath slows from a pant to a well-timed rhythm.

"Your wings are soft, but powerful." She gasps, then releases an ill-timed giggle.

"That nervous habit of yours—give a compliment, then giggle." He lands on a shelf of land behind a juniper tree. "You have your clue—the clay map that leads you back to this imploded cave," Legna says.

"The map is virtually useless now." Daniela fingers the cuneiform map inside her satchel.

"Do you read Hebrew?"

"No."

"The writing on that tablet isn't a map back to this cave."

"What is it then?"

"A codex." Legna pulls Daniela close to his chest. "Your mom is sitting in her bookstore praying feverishly. Let's get you home. Follow me. I'll take you to the portal."

"Not until we find a safe place for Ezekiel and Martha." Daniela crosses her arms, daring Legna to refuse her demand.

"Already done," Legna says. Daniela scrunches her nose. "It's faster to fly."

"Then fly me back home."

"I can't—you won't survive the reentry. Do astronauts reenter Earth's atmosphere without a spacecraft? Nope."

"You win. Where do I access the portal?"

"The palace courtyard's pool."

"I can't swim."

"It's shallow."

"Why is the escape hatch from my nightmarish time travels always a body of water?" Daniela asks.

Legna picks her up, spreads his wings, then flies to the city of Babylon. "Water breaks the fall and cools your body as you pass through multiple dimensions, but most importantly, it cleanses and repairs a bit of your radiation burns." Legna lands a mile outside the city gates, then releases his charge. "Follow me."

After entering the city, he deftly navigates the Babylonian crowd. At the base of the palace staircase, he becomes invisible.

Peasants step aside, allowing Mistress Daniela a wide berth.

She still senses Legna's presence and feels the brush of his body against her shoulder as he escorts her back through the palace. When they arrive at the portal, the courtyard pool, his voice carries on the wind, "Have you prayed for the orphan boy recently?"

"I met Ezekiel, coaxed Martha off a suicidal cliff, then found you. When have I had time? Once I return home safely and check on my parents and Emmaline, I will." She smiles, disarming a woman who most likely wonders why Daniela is talking to herself.

"Sleep well," he says.

"I'll try."

Throaty laughs of bright green frogs and the staccato drumroll of red-eyed cicadas welcome her back to the palace pool. She wades in, then dives deep. Not one man tried to touch her the whole time. *Thanks, Legna.*

"You're welcome, Rosebud."

45—Orphan Dreamer

"DANNY ROSE, WAKE UP." THE Demi Moore–esque voice was familiar. The Orphan Dreamer opened her eyes. "Limy?"

"It's me." Emmaline smiled and caressed stray ringlets out of Daniela's eyes. "You're back. Safe and sound."

"You waited."

"That's what friends do." Emmaline stood up from her crouched position. Thunder rumbled.

"I'm wet."

"The storm broke a few windows and unhinged the front door. And there was the tree crashing through the front door debacle."

Lightning cracked the sky wide open, casting shadows into corners. Inside the cellar, the overhead lights and a fake Tiffany lamp sitting on a drum table flickered, then faded to black.

Still, the room looked and smelled familiar: a large oak island was stationed in the middle of books and shelves, beige wrapping paper cinched tight with ribbons sat on the table, and velvet chairs and leather couches saturated with the unforgettable scent of books and hot cocoa sat around the room.

The cellar was her favorite place inside the bookstore. Mouth dry and eyes gritty with sleep, she smoothed out the wrinkles of her black taffeta dress. "Where's Mom?"

"Before the water runs cold, she's drawing you a bath." Limy pushed a curly strand of Daniela's hair behind her right ear.

"Do I stink?"

"You smell a bit sweaty." Emmaline raked her finger across Daniela's brow, slicking her finger with perspiration.

"Did you know when I was coming back?"

"The Glass Tattoo stamped into your palm starts to fade when your dream cycle is almost complete."

"Did I say anything?"

"Nothing about oily boy. But you spoke of a map. Ezekiel. Daniel. And the hot warrior angel, Legna."

"What time is it? Is it time to go to the funeral, Limy?" Daniela sat up.

Emmaline glanced at her watch. "In three hours."

"Daniela, my darling." Her mother ran to her side and embraced her daughter. "You're back, safe and sound."

"Mom, in Babylon, I met Ezekiel and his sister Martha. She's having a baby, but . . ." Daniela's voice dropped to a whisper, "she's not married."

"Then I hope her brother cares and provides for her child," Mrs. Cavanaugh replied.

"Okay." Stunned silent for a full minute, Daniela couldn't believe her ears. No sermon?

"Did you get hurt?" Mrs. Cavanaugh inspected her daughter's body.

"Nothing visible. I transformed into a butterfly soon after I landed," Daniela revealed, and her mother tilted her head. "I could spy on anyone at any time, but I didn't want to." She jumped to her feet and patted herself down. "Where is it?"

"Are you looking for this?" Emmaline held out a miniature clay tablet. "Do you want to know what it says?"

"Of course! But how—"

"Right before you emerged from your dream, the tablet materialized from your right hand, where the Glass Tattoo had been activated."

"Then we can solve the mystery of the Skeleton Key! I'm sure of it. Why else would Ezekiel give me a tablet with Hebrew writing?"

"First, go take a hot bath, and I'll translate the tablet."

"I'll forget my dream."

"You'll catch your cold lying here in all that sweat." Mrs. Cavanaugh straightened her skirt.

Daniela slid the back of her hand across her brow. "Haven't arrived at the funeral and already sweating like a pallbearer in the Florida sunshine." Sweat dripped down the side of Daniela's face.

"For now, it's still too dangerous to go upstairs or drive home." Mrs. Cavanaugh struck a match and then lit a candle, using it to light several more until candlelight cast shadows and illuminated the cellar bathroom. "Emmaline and I will sit on chairs by the fireplace inside the bathroom, and you can dictate the details of your dream. We'll record everything."

"Good idea." Daniela jumped up but immediately regretted the quick movement. The room spun on its own. She grabbed the couch arm and steadied herself, then gingerly approached the bathroom.

"Don't climb into the tub while you're unsteady." Mrs. Cavanaugh rushed to her daughter's side.

"Yes, ma'am." She brushed her teeth, washed her face, took off the wrinkled taffeta, then sank into the bathtub.

Hot water lapped against her skin.

She told her mother and her best friend everything. " 'But you, Daniel, keep this prophecy a secret. Seal up the book until the time of the end when many will rush here and there, and knowledge will increase . . .' "

"Is that time now?" Emmaline asked as she wrote the Hebrew to English translation.

"Yes. What does the tablet say?"

"You're not going to believe this!" Emmaline jotted down a few more notes. "No code. No screwing around. Whoever gave this to you wanted to make sure you knew everything. Where's the Skeleton Key?"

"Upstairs on the second floor, in mom's office."

"Crikey! It would be up there. Only God knows what kind of damage I'll have to navigate to find the darn thing."

"Do you want me to retrieve it?" Daniela asked.

"No. You were walking more crooked than a drunken sailor." Emmaline handed the tablet to Daniela's mother. "Hold this. Keep it safe." She tucked the translated note into the top of her blouse.

Still fuzzy after traveling, the thought took a while to register. Why was Emmaline taking the translation with her? Was Robert waiting upstairs to swoop in and take the clue?

"Limy!" Daniela called, her voice raspy and sore. "Limy, come back here!"

"Daniela, what's gotten into you? Act like a lady. Stop that!"

"You don't know her like I do, Momma."

Mrs. Cavanaugh charged from the bathroom in pursuit of Emmaline.

46—THE ORPHAN

BEFORE THE SUN ROSE OVER the Mongolian plateau, Cillian stood in the middle of Sumrall's restaurant, feeling as though he'd been waiting in a welfare line for his number to be called.

He had dreamed that a plane would land at Chinggis Khaan International Airport, and the pilot would personally ask him and Paul to board, then fly them to America.

Mama Kelley had told him about Joseph's thirteen-year and Abraham's twenty-five-year waiting period before Yahweh intervened and delivered their God-inspired dreams. Why was the wait necessary? That part puzzled Cillian. Besides, had any of his dreams been inspired by Mama Kelley's Yahweh? Would his daydreams about the brown-skinned girl who had kissed him in Paul's dream come true?

Quietly, he hoped so.

In the corner of the restaurant, a group of Mongolian throat singers croaked a traditional song, and Paul helped him clean the tables before the first customers arrived. He'd already mopped the floors after Paul swept them. Tonight he would wash dirty dishes.

The last days of work had settled into an ache deep between his shoulder blades, but Cillian didn't complain. The manual labor felt like it had purged his soul from years of humiliation. An hourly wage, tips, and free food for him and Paul had equaled a windfall of good fortune. One day, America would make room for one more billionaire. Smiling, Cillian scrubbed a steel pot to a shine.

"Paul?"

"Yes?" Cillian's brother faced him.

"After we save enough money, if we pool our money together, we can purchase airline tickets, and visas, and travel to America."

"That's a swell plan."

"Hey, Cil!" Sam, Sumrall's son, burst through the back door, interrupting Cillian's cleaning routine. Paul gathered his textbooks, sat in a corner, and began his studies.

"Why are you up so early?

"Wanted to say hi before school."

"Hello, then."

"Hey." Sam waved. "Still need a cheap place to live?"

"D'ye have a place for us, then?"

"Yesterday I remembered that there is a campsite located two miles north. My friends and I took a survivalist vacation out there. I would've asked you to come if you hadn't already promised Dad to work the weekend shifts. I know how much this job means to you."

"Tell me about the campsite."

"Safe. Serene. Fire pits already built in, and remote enough that you won't run into the locals."

"Is there shelter?"

"You'll need to rummage up a tent, and they charge five dollars a week to camp out there."

"I can afford that." Cillian stood a little straighter. *Time to be buyin' a house for my brother and me.* "Thanks, Sam."

"I know that you're no beggar . . . just a guy who's fell on hard times. So Dad wouldn't mind it if I gave you my old tent and a Coleman stove."

"I dinna be needin' yer charity, Sam." Cillian glanced past the window and eyed the shed where he and Paul had slept last night with the rats. "How much?"

"Invite me to hang with you and Paul sometime. That'll be payment enough." Sam left the store, and the cooks arrived, slamming pots and pans onto the stove and into the oven.

Cillian wiped his hands, then walked over to the booth where Paul was studying. "I'd verra much like for you to be guessin' what I've secured for us."

"Tickets to America?"

"I'm not a billionaire yet. Try again."

"A raise from Mr. Sumrall?"

"D'ye see Mr. Sumrall, knucklehead?" He tussled Paul's hair. "I'll not be lettin' ye guess again, too hard on my ego."

"Then tell me."

"We're getting our own place tonight."

The shopkeeper's bell rattled against the glass door as the first patron arrived.

Cillian bolted back into the kitchen, afraid to allow a customer see the kitchen help. Paul left his studies, greeted the gray-haired man, and sat him at his usual table by the window. The teenager offered the man coffee and a menu. He accepted.

Paul snuck back to the kitchen to grab a coffee pot. "Cil," he whispered, "no more sleeping in that rat-infested shed?"

"No more." Cillian winked and prepared to wash the first newly soiled pot.

"You always come through, Cil. Thanks for everything."

"Yer welcome."

After work, Cillian hoisted their new home—Sam's old tent—on his broadening shoulders and followed Sam to their new woodsy campsite.

Sam helped Paul and Cillian pitch their tent beneath the boughs of a Japanese magnolia tree. Pink and white cupped flowers dangled from each branch, lending a botanical scent. He would dream of Mama Kelley. She had loved flowers. Yellow roses were her favorites.

In the distance, a blue lake flowed between two copper-red boulders.

"Nice, isn't it?" Sam said. Taking in the magnificent view, Cillian sniffled and forced a grin across his face. "You don't like it."

"It's heaven."

Sam crossed his arms, turned, and stood quietly by Cillian, giving reverence to what the Lord had done. Mama Kelley's biblical saying came to Cillian's mind, and he repeated it aloud, "This was the Lord's doing; it is marvelous in our eyes." Cillian's voice broke into a thousand plate shards. "We're home, Paul. We're safe."

"No one will bother you out here, and if they do, you'll come and live at our house. We have an extra bedroom."

From his mother's shack, to the care home, to the

brothel, then the cruise ship. Cillian finally allowed himself to breathe deeply. "Let's fire up the grill."

In a few minutes, charcoal burned Cillian's nostrils as he stirred coals in the bottom of their grill. Almost an hour later, Cillian said, "Dinner's ready."

"I'm starved." Paul sat on a patch of grass.

"Wash your hands." Sam lugged water from the lake. The boys washed their hands, then ate their fill of grilled meat and hot rice and beans. After dinner, they sat together, speaking to each other even while silent.

"I don't want to go, but I've got to get back," Sam said as Paul left for the lake. "Mom will worry."

"Would you like me to walk you home?"

"I know these woods like the back of my mother's hand. I'll walk by myself and remember our time together."

"I'd like to meet yer mother one day, but not the back of her hand," Cillian quipped.

"Done." Sam's eyes explored his friend's face. "Will you stay in Mongolia, Cil?"

Friends dinna lie to friends; they dinna deserve deception. "No. One day we'll be travelin' to America." Cillian reached for Sam's hand, and they shook.

"Until then, let's camp every weekend." Sam's gaze dropped as he waved, then he disappeared behind larch trees.

"I like Mr. Sumrall and Sam." Lamp in hand, Paul returned from the lake with a bucket of water.

"So do I, and it was good of Mr. Sumrall to loan us these old textbooks." Cillian placed two textbooks beside the storm light on the wood table. "Time for homework."

"When you grow up, I hope you're like Mr. Sumrall, but don't let your belly grow that big. My nutrition textbook says that's unhealthy."

"I dinna believe that I've ever eaten enough food to grow my belly to Mr. Sumrall's size, but I hope I'm like him too." Cillian opened his calculus book. Textbooks for physics, English composition, and chemistry lay inside the tent.

"Don't you want to actually perform these experiments?" Paul mapped out a biology experiment on paper.

"I'm in the middle of a differential equation. Give me a sec." All around them, beetles clicked in their own conversations, and a few gray moths flew toward the light, landing at the base of the storm lamp.

As Cillian worked his math problem, Paul glanced at his older brother. A hint of deviousness showed in his facial expression as he sneaked *The Swiss Family Robinson* out of his backpack, lifted his textbook, and slipped the novel behind it.

"Paul, isna it true that our success relies on discipline and being smarter than the competition?"

"I think so."

"Why are you readin' a novel when ye should be studying, then?" Cillian's icy glare nixed his little brother's playful spirit. "Return to yer studies."

"Yes, sir." Paul snapped *The Swiss Family Robinson* closed.

"Besides, we're living a Swiss Family Robinson story, no need to read about it, especially if it means you're not completing your biology homework."

"You've read it?" Paul flicked his tongue over his lower lip.

"Only in a novel would treehouse livin' be fun. The story ignores the flies, rodents, and varmints."

"But not the lakes, fresh air, and big brothers." Paul shifted in his seat, and Cillian smiled on the inside.

"What d'ye want to be when you grow up?"

"A famous architect."

"Yer going to build treehouses, then?"

"No. Mansions. Hotels. Bridges. Stadiums."

"Then, ye'll be buildin' me a mountain chalet because as soon as my feet hit American soil, I'm retiring," Cillian joked. "Grand halls, bathtubs bigger than oceans, and a table fit for a king, that's what ye'll build for me. Understood?"

"Aye, aye, sir."

"After I complete the next two problems and you finish mapping out your experiment, we'll take a night swim in the lake, clean up a bit. Then while you rub my feet, I'll grade your bio lab report."

"Yuck!" Paul twirled his pencil between his fingers. "My biology report isn't good enough."

"Then make it good enough." Cillian landed firm on each syllable.

"It's not an excuse but a fact. Besides, I'm a fifteen-year-old man, and I'll make my own decisions from now on."

"Dinna aggravate me, Paul. I've never flogged ye before," Cillian spoke quietly.

"No. You haven't."

"But I've taken quite a few of yer beatings at the care home."

"Right."

"And at the brothel . . ." Hours seemed to pass between them. "D'ye ken what a horse whip across yer bare back feels like, Paul?" Paul remained quiet. "He beat me like the Romans flogged Mama Kelley's Jesus—opening my back up to the bone." After Cillian laid on the guilt, he made his point. "I've only asked one thing of you. Try your best and become someone, Paul. Is the task so difficult?"

"D-d-don't worry about me, Cil. I'll pull my weight." Paul buried himself in his studies.

Cillian was thankful that he didn't need to verbalize his threat: *As sure as my name is Cillian Joseph Finn, I'll strip a switch from that tree, lay you over my knee, and rip the flesh from your hide.*

As quickly as his anger had boiled over, it cooled and simmered into a stew of shame and regret.

Cillian leaned closer to his brother, wrapped his arm around him, and pulled him close. "Yer safe with me, Paul—always and forever. When I sit in one of your grand halls or stadiums, it'll make sense of the years of suffering."

Paul nodded.

Cillian noticed the sights and sounds—a bird's chirp, wind rustling through the leaves, and the *crackle* and *pop* of their fire. "Tomorrow's Saturday, and Mr. Sumrall gave me the day off. After breakfast, we'll explore."

"I'd like that." Paul gingerly faced his brother. "Cil?"

"Aye, then?"

"I love you." He gripped his pencil between trembling fingers.

"I know." Cillian rested his hand on his brother's, calming his jitters. "And if while I sleep, I should escape this world without tellin' ye goodbye, it's because death left me no time."

"You'll have time. I'll make sure of it. And from now on, I'll take my own floggings—like a man."

"If ye insist."

"I do."

"Aye, then ye'll do best to stay out of trouble. No need to scar yer pretty-boy face." Cillian teased, then turned serious—dead serious. "When I look at you, I'm remindin' myself that I've done something right in my life. I've raised a boy into a fine young man."

After their night swim and much-needed baths, Cillian snuggled inside his sleeping bag. "Sumrall has a pair of cots in his storeroom. We'll save up and buy them if you like."

"I'll save my money, then buy one for you. I'm comfortable sleeping inside Sam's bag. We'll save your earnings for our trip to America."

"I could be gettin' used to this." Cillian rolled closer to his brother.

Sleep laid heavy behind his eyelids. Nestled close to his little brother, the orphan slept within heaven's embrace. Tomorrow he would awake in heaven or hell. Orphans never knew which until the morning.

47—Orphan Dreamer

DANIELA'S MOTHER LED EMMALINE INTO the bathroom. "Sit." She pointed to a velvet parlor chair, then pulled up another to face Emmaline.

"Why are you treating me like this?"

"What did you do to my Daniela in Los Alamos?" Mrs. Cavanaugh crossed her arms.

"Daniela?" Emmaline's face registered the hurt after betrayal. "That was between us. You told me that you forgave me." She slid to the edge of her chair.

"Sit back, or I'll tie you to that chair." Daniela's mother had gone into full-out mother-bear crazy mode.

"Mom, calm down. It's only Emmaline."

"Only Emmaline? You thought that she was escaping

the store with the translation of the stone tablet and the Skeleton Key. I could read your fear written in bold letters across your face because I. Am. Your. Mother, Daniela Rose Cavanaugh."

"It's . . . it's . . . a misunderstanding. Th-th-that's all." Daniela tried to undo the doubt that she had cast.

"Don't stutter, now." Her mother rested her hands on her hips. "You haven't done so in years. All that speech therapy. Your dad and I could have used that money toward his cancer treatments or your college fund." Mrs. Cavanaugh glared down at her daughter.

"I'm sorry." Emmaline slipped out of the room, but words beyond her apology sat frozen inside Daniela's throat, preventing the Orphan Dreamer from sounding the alarm.

After several seconds passed, her tongue loosened. "S-s-stop it. You're stressing me out." She pointed at Emmaline's empty chair. "Where's Emmaline?"

Mrs. Cavanaugh swirled around on her heels in just enough time to find a gun pointing at her face. "Why don't you take a seat and cool your jets, Mrs. C.?" Emmaline flicked the gun back and forth like a sheriff in a western.

Daniela's mother sat down. Emmaline tied her to the chair, and she protested, "How dare you? You'll rot in hell for this."

"Believe it or not, I'm trying to help."

"By pulling a gun? Is that what your people call it—*helping*?" Daniela's mother was going full-out racial.

"Let her go." Daniela stated flatly. Anything else and she might stutter her words again.

Emmaline paused, then obliged and untied the Orphan Dreamer's mother.

Mrs. Cavanaugh slapped Emmaline. "You're something

else, child. After today, you're gone. Out of my Daniela's life forever."

Emmaline blinked back tears as Daniela tightened the towel around her trembling frame and reached for the gun. "Give it to me." Her friend obeyed. "I'll only ask my question once. Were you planning to leave the bookstore with the stone tablet translation and the Skeleton Key?"

"No."

"Okay. That settles it. We're trapped inside this tiny cellar with no electricity and a storm still raging, eager to snuff out our lives. So let's not act like savages. Okay?" Her mother and her friend agreed.

Daniela spread a blanket across the brick cellar floor. She and Emmaline sat side by side while eating bowls of soup. Mrs. Cavanaugh sat on a loveseat by an oil lamp, crocheting a sweater. From her mother threatening to tie her friend to a chair, to delivering the slap of the century, back to crocheting a sweater—that was some kind of grizzly bear maternal instinct.

Daniela hid her smirk, the outward expression of her inner feeling, *That's my mom!*

Mrs. Cavanaugh looked down her nose and over her spectacles, then winked at her daughter while whispering, "I love you." *Love you, too*, Daniela mouthed.

"For the record, when I went upstairs to retrieve the Skeleton Key, the storm was calming."

The lights had gone out, and the trio decided that Emmaline would drive Daniela's mother home before the girls travelled to the funeral.

According to her mother, Daniela's taffeta dress was too wrinkled to walk inside a clothes dryer. Because she only owned one black dress, she would redress in a pair of jeans, a black T-shirt, and a black cuffed jacket at home.

"Girls, it's time for the funeral." Mrs. Cavanaugh clapped her hands together as though she were rounding up a playground teeming with kindergarteners. "The rain slowed down a bit. It's now or never. Take me home, then be on your way." She hugged Daniela, and then Emmaline. She studied Limy's face. "I'll make a lady out of you yet."

"I'm already a lady."

"Then act like one. For starters, stop pointing guns in people's faces, expecting the scenario to end well."

Standing behind her mother, Daniela mouthed to her friend, *I'm sorry, but she's right.*

I know, Emmaline blushed as she mouthed, then half-smiled. "Daniela, how do I look—show-and-tell worthy?"

"So show that I'm going to tell, 'Hey world, look out! Here comes Limy, my beautiful, classy, and smart pal!' " Daniela grabbed her umbrella. "Mom, please stay inside. I don't want you to get wet. Okay? So after we retrieve the car, we'll pick you up in front of the store."

"Make Emmaline walk in front of you, okay?" Her mom clung to her work bag and yarn bag as though they were life rafts in the middle of a tempestuous sea.

"I will." Daniela followed Emmaline to her Jeep. "Don't forget your pepper spray."

"Have gun, will travel."

"Don't we all know it."

"I'll never live that one down."

"You will," Daniela stated plainly.

Fifteen minutes later, and soaking wet, Emmaline slid into the driver's seat of her Jeep as Daniela buckled her seat belt. The speedster clicked her seat belt, keyed the ignition, then spun out of the empty parking lot, churning through rain puddles.

"I hope my mom didn't completely offend you just now."

"My mom thinks I'm a skank too. I'm used to it."

"But I'm not. Truly, I'm sorry."

"Forgiven. I wasn't expecting the slap, either."

"You pointed a gun at my mother, Limy. Do you not understand why that's just not okay?"

"Stand your ground. We're in Florida, right?" Emmaline pointed at the Jeep's glove box. "Open it."

Daniela opened the compartment, revealing a black and ominous gun. "Another one? You know we're under-age—right?"

"I have a special permit because of my dad's job." Emmaline removed the second gun and dropped it into her purse. "Don't want a nosy Southern cop thinking that it's yours. Besides, a bow and arrow would be too big to take to a funeral."

"Thanks. But . . . you can't exactly stand your ground when you're standing inside someone else's place of business. By default, that piece of floor beneath your feet doesn't belong to you. You've taken gun safety classes. Didn't they teach you to only point a gun at someone if you're prepared to pull the trigger? Would you really have shot my mom? Your impulsivity worries me—a lot."

"It wasn't loaded, rarely is."

"For real? That's it? You point a gun at my mom and that's your explanation—it wasn't loaded?"

"You're right, and I'm sorry. But don't abandon me—please." Emmaline clasped her hands together. "Give me a chance to tell you everything. Besides, I'll go to counseling when I return home."

"Please. Do. Something."

"Promise. It's just that . . . Daniela . . ." Emmaline half

paused, half ran out of breath, "It's the only way I kept him—my dad—from coming into my bedroom after dark. Then one day, I pulled the gun on him, and he didn't know that it wasn't loaded. He never knew."

"He did . . ." Daniela's voice dropped to a whisper, "things to you?"

Emmaline nodded, sniffled hard, then rolled her shoulders.

Daniela reached for her friend's hand and held it, standing her ground beside her Anne of Green Gables—her kindred spirit, a girl who made a mistake and required forgiveness *and* direction.

"I'm sorry, Limy. So very sorry that happened to you." She squeezed Limy's hand. "I need to hear you vow that you'll never point any weapon at me or my family again. Swear it, then in time, I will try to trust you again around my family."

"I swear it, Lozen." Emmaline released Daniela's hand, then slipped a compact disc into the Jeep's CD player. "Remember this?" Etta James crooned "At Last."

"I do. It could be our song if we were lesbians."

"Yuck. I couldn't like a girl like that." Emmaline turned onto University Avenue. "I played this song after your Los Alamos dream."

"I don't remember the details of the guy in my dream, if that's what you're asking."

"Black Irish—black hair, pale skin, and sky-blue eyes."

"Seriously, don't talk about this Black Irish dude in front of my mom. My parents are old for my age. You'll give her a heart attack." Daniela grabbed Emmaline's arm and squeezed. "Promise me! And never ever talk about oily boy in front of my dad."

"Why?"

"Promise me!"

"I promise. But why?"

"Dad's not too keen on guys like him."

"But you said you don't remember any details about oily boy."

"Black Irish—pale skin, blue eyes. While I don't remember his face, I know the definition of Black Irish." Daniela gazed past the passenger window.

"Your dad's a racist?" Emmaline slowed the Jeep, carefully navigating University Avenue through the rain.

"It's not racism, Limy. He suffers from PTSD from all the Southern Jim Crow junk he experienced."

"Never thought of it like that."

"No need for you to. He doesn't hate white people, but he's afraid of them because he knows what they're capable of."

"Talk to me, Danny Rose. Help me understand."

"Sometimes it's the talking that hurts the most. For you, it's information. For me, it's life. Living downwind of racial negativity embarrasses a self-respecting person."

"Then we'll hurt together. Your pain is my pain."

"Remember that mantra when we arrive at the funeral."

"Or when I meet your dad in a few minutes."

"He's okay with our friendship . . . as long as I don't marry someone who looks like you and you don't point a gun at his face. Then he *will* lose his marbles."

"I'll make it up to you. Promise, Danny-girl." Emmaline paused. "Is he afraid that marrying a white person will contaminate the Cavanaugh bloodline with Nephilim seed?" Emmaline laughed, but Daniela didn't. "I'm serious, Daniela."

"I know." Daniela shook her head. "As though a whole

race of people could be Nephilim seed. You're still game to help me save Earth from Lucifer?"

"I'm ready to kick some zombie butt, but I'm not into all the religious stuff. And I'm definitely not claiming Jesus-freak extraterrestrial status. My return address is located on Earth, so yes, I will defend our turf from the Nephilim—which I am not one of."

"I will defend our turf as well . . . so many more kindred spirits to meet." Daniela forced herself not to daydream. She would need laser focus tonight, not another dream to sift through.

"Any other juicy details?"

"When I travelled to Babylon, I learned from Ezekiel that our conclusions about who Nephilim are were correct. They are hybrids between humans and fallen angels, and they survived the flood because one of Noah's daughters was pregnant with one. And Leviathan—Job's sea monster—loved all the extra water. Leviathan is a first-generation Nephilim who can transform into a human-like being."

"Score." Mischief shone through Emmaline's eyes. "So many kindred spirits to meet . . . like oily boy?" Emmaline nudged her friend's subconscious.

"Here we go again," Daniela grumbled. But could oily boy become an even greater kindred spirit than Ethan and Emmaline? Could he become the heartsong that Professor Jakob wrote about in his letter?

Butterflies fluttered inside Daniela's belly. Apricot sulphurs! Daniela rested her hand on her abdomen and whispered a prayer, "Let him be real." Her cheeks flushed steamy hot.

"You're falling in love. I can tell."

"I sense that he's good, but I'm mentally preparing myself for the possibility that he's bad."

"So then, I hope he's real too, Lozen." Emmaline blew a kiss in Daniela's direction. The Orphan Dreamer caught the kiss.

"Be nice to my mom."

"Your wish is my command." Emmaline sang the popular line of Boyz II Men's 1994 number-one hit single, "I'll Make Love to You." She changed CDs and played the song. A few seconds later, Limy parked the Jeep in front of the bookstore.

Mrs. Cavanaugh climbed into the backseat. "Nice car."

"Thanks, Mrs. C."

Did they have to sing about throwing clothes on the floor? Daniela turned down the song and loudly asked Emmaline. "What was the translation of the stone tablet?"

"Simple." Emmaline removed the paper from inside her bra. The Orphan Dreamer laughed, then said, "That's such a mom thing."

"It works." She gave the folded paper to the Orphan Dreamer who opened it and read:

A picture is worth a thousand words, and no door can be opened without a key—the Skeleton Key.

Light a candle, illuminate the key, and answer the question of who will start the pandemic you seek to stop. In kairos time, insert the Skeleton Key into a lock that secures a ruler's tomb beyond the Jordan River.

Find King Solomon's Temple treasure that was lost after my people were taken captive by the Babylonians. The Copper Scroll is nothing more than an inventory of temple treasure and a decoy. Travel safe, my alien friend, Mistress Daniela.

"You're a mistress now," Mrs. Cavanaugh teased.

"Better than the situation in Gibeah as Prince Jonathan's slave."

"So you weren't his girlfriend?" Emmaline tilted her head.

"Never said that I was. You assumed."

48—Orphan Dreamer

EMMALINE DROVE INTO LINCOLN ESTATES—DAN-
IELA'S neighborhood on the historic side of town.

It was shaped like a ceiling fan. The fan's motor in the middle was the playground, encircled by a two-lane road. Houses sat around the park, stretched out like fan blades. Emmaline eased her Jeep around the playground.

"So many memories . . . some good, some bad," Daniela whispered.

"That's called life," Emmaline snapped, and the Orphan Dreamer ignored her friend.

Opposite Daniela's home, Claire's big red-brick house commanded two lots on the other side of the park, but Daniela's family owned the most land in the neighborhood.

In five minutes, she could have run across the park to Claire's front yard . . . if Daniela had been invited when they were children.

They passed the playground on Daniela's right. Rain fell on the heads of oaks, maples, and pines, creating puddles on the ground and on picnic tables scattered on carpets of grass. A wading pool anchored the middle of the park, and a sunken garden fifty steps north of the pool made for spooky adventures.

Tires screeched. "That would be Limy tearing up the asphalt before charging into our roundabout," Daniela nervously said, attempting to calm her mother's clearly frayed nerves after their lap around the Daytona 500 speedway.

"I'm surprised you survived Los Alamos." Her mother sat up in her seat and looked out the window.

"It wasn't the Alamo," Emmaline threw a pinch into the conversation.

"You never told me, Limy, that you drove like an escaped convict—out of control, up on two wheels."

"Leaving my house for college paralleled an Alcatraz escape."

"You don't say." Her mother opened the Jeep's door.

"Be nice, Mom. I love her. Limy flew to Gainesville on her dad's private jet just to celebrate my acceptance into medical school and my birthday."

"Moving on up, Mistress Daniela," her mom said. "Before you know it, you'll be moving into Buckingham Palace."

Emmaline dumped a cup of salt into the batter. "And Buckingham Palace isn't all that—it's cold in the winters and too hot in the summers. I've stayed there with my dad several times."

Daniela shrugged, then continued to celebrate her

kindred spirit. "Winterlyn properties represent a *different* standard of living: a Beacon Street townhome in Boston, a flat on Victoria Road in Kensington, West London, and another on Northumberland Street in Edinburgh."

"We're happy to have you visit our humble cottage, Limy," Daniela's mother said, demurely stepping out of the car.

Daniela stayed seated. *Would Emmaline be ashamed of Daniela's modest home?*

Mrs. Cavanaugh opened her daughter's door and then, as if reading her daughter's mind, whispered, "If she judges you because of where you live, she's not a friend. Move on."

"But you've judged her for every offense under the sun, Mom."

"That's different."

"And you were picking on me, too, calling me Mistress Daniela."

"That was your name when you traveled to Babylon. Don't allow your adolescent hormones to thrash you about. Take a deep breath." Daniela inhaled. "You'll need your mental strength for Violet's funeral."

Mrs. Cavanaugh marched to the front door, as Daniela turned to Emmaline and timidly asked, "Would you like to say hello to my dad or drive to the funeral now? I could change on the way."

"I'm going to meet your dad—then we're going to light a candle and see what the Skeleton Key reveals." She waltzed to the front door. "Besides, I'm dressed in all black—maybe he won't notice my skin." Emmaline followed Daniela and her mother into the stone cottage.

"Emmaline, meet my dad. Dad, Emmaline."

"How do you do?" A humid breeze fingered through Emmaline's auburn locks. She tipped her head slightly.

"Nice to meet you." They shook hands. "Thank you for loving my daughter."

Daniela's mom dramatically cleared her throat. Emmaline continued with pleasantries. "It's not difficult, Mr. C. We were going to celebrate Daniela's acceptance into medical school after the funeral, but the weather's the pits."

"Should we celebrate after a funeral?" Daniela cringed.

"You're not dead, are you?" Emmaline's eyes twinkled. A guffaw popped through Austin's lips, and Jeanette held a smile at bay as both adults offered each girl a lemonade and a seat.

"We'll come home, eat popcorn, and watch a movie instead of going back to the bookstore," Daniela offered.

"Yes, and we'll pull out a few board games," Mr. Cavanaugh volunteered.

"Congrats to you as well, Limy," Daniela said, shifting the topic. "Mom and Dad, Emmaline was accepted into an Air Force Institute of Technology master's degree program where she'll study nuclear, biological, and chemical weapons technology before completing her PhD in biological engineering at MIT."

"Who are you planning on killing, honey?" Her mother's brow wrinkled.

"Anyone who messes with Danny Rose."

"Oh my, a personal bodyguard," her mother replied.

Please don't talk about the gun to my dad. Daniela rubbed the lobe of her ear, then disappeared into her bedroom for thirty minutes.

"Danny!" Emmaline embraced her friend when she reappeared. "Look at you." She ran her fingers through

Daniela's long, thick, straight dark-brown hair. "You look like Lozen—gentle but strong, sensual yet demure."

"Thanks." Daniela sighed. She tugged at the edges of her pantsuit—a black organza-overlain taffeta number. "Like it, Limy?"

"Love it!"

"Thanks for letting me borrow it." Daniela blushed. "And for the record, it's official. I hate funerals. Permanent sleep is the utmost form of denial."

"You and your imagination, Daniela. Sure you want to go?" Mr. Cavanaugh reclined in his favorite chair and read the newspaper as Daniela's mother continued to crochet the sweater she'd been working on at the store.

"Claire wasn't my friend by any stretch of the imagination, but I promised to go."

"In a crisis, us girls stick together." Emmaline supported her friend. "Maybe the Underwood family and all their funeral guests are Nephilim, and we're gearing up for the fight of our lives."

"No need to wear your only church suit if we're going to scrap." Daniela smirked, then wolfed down a banana.

Her dad turned to an article about the funeral in the *Gainesville Sun*. "Says here the president is coming all the way from Washington, DC to attend."

"He's making a point," her mother added. "Martha told me that the senator was suffering from PTSD—from the Vietnam War. It's still awful what the senator did to his wife: raped, beat her unconscious, then shot the drooling mother in front of his two daughters. The police still haven't found him."

"That's one tormented soul." Her dad sipped on a glass of lemonade.

"Claire was a mean girl, but she didn't deserve this." Daniela applied lip gloss to her lips.

"Defending the class bully? You used to run home crying after she'd taunted you," her mom said.

"Apple suckers and the playground were the only things she could control." A twinge of guilt settled in Daniela's gut as she remembered Mister Spider's words—*Claire feels the same, doesn't know any better. She believed her papa, but she'll grow out of his misguided advice if you give her the time.*

"Kind of you to pay your respects." Her father laid his newspaper on his chest. "I'm proud of you, but keep a low profile. Stay out of the president's way. People are crazy these days."

"The funeral will be held in Palatka, Florida," Daniela replied. "A papermill town, hardly a metropolis."

"Mr. Cavanaugh?" Emmaline asked. "Before we leave, I'd like to ask you a theological question. You're an ordained minister who works as a prison chaplain?"

"That's right."

"When Daniela time travelled to Babylon, she observed Nomed and identified him as a Watcher—a fallen angel, a son of God."

"My daughter told me about Nomed."

"Her discovery of Nomed lurking about King Nebuchadnezzar's palace in 1019 BC Babylon confirmed that Watchers still exist and still roam Earth, even after Noah's flood. So could we surmise that Nephilim, the descendants of these Watchers who slept with women, live on Earth as well?"

"That's a reasonable conclusion. But another conclusion could be that after the flood, all Nephilim died and the bodiless souls of these creatures manifested as demons and can possess humans."

"Creepy, Mr. C."

"We are talking about demons, Limy." Mr. Cavanaugh said.

"What if an actual Nephilim survived Noah's flood?"

"Where?"

"Inside one of the uteri of Noah's unnamed daughters or as Job's sea monster—Leviathan," Emmaline said.

Mr. Cavanaugh thought for a minute. "It's possible."

"What do you believe the Nephilim are?"

"Satan's nuclear weapons," he answered quickly. "Their fathers, the sons of God, attempted to corrupt humanity's gene pool by producing children with human women. But the motive was more despicable than their actions. Their main goal was to prevent King David's bloodline from ever producing the Messiah, Yeshua—humanity's Redeemer— thus condemning all of humanity to eternal death."

"Pandemic version one," Emmaline concluded.

"Would we recognize a Nephilim?" Daniela asked.

"Not by their appearance, but by their intentions manifested by their actions. In times of old—before Noah's flood—Nephilim walked the earth as big, beautiful, and powerful male specimens. They possessed all of the superficial qualities humans lust after."

"Where are the original Watchers—the fathers of Nephilim—now?" Emmaline asked.

"In the abyss, waiting to be judged. But before their judgment day, they'll be released on Earth once more."

"You're kidding me!" Daniela squirmed in her seat.

"Hopefully not at tonight's zombie funeral," Emmaline teased. "But a pack of big, beautiful, and powerful male specimens would put Palatka on the map."

"Not a chance," Mr. Cavanaugh said. "The original Watchers will be released during Earth's Great Tribulation, after followers of the Way have been raptured, but the Watchers won't appear as they were. Instead, they each will possess the body of a horse, the face of a man, a woman's hair, teeth like lion's teeth, wings, and tails."

"Dreadful." Daniela rubbed her arms, vanquishing the goosebumps.

"They will be released for one hundred and fifty days—the exact duration of Noah's flood, when the Watcher's sons were tormented. These grotesque and foul half-angels will follow their king, Abaddon."

"If all Watchers are under lock and key, Nomed couldn't be a Watcher, right, Dad?"

"Maybe he's the embodiment of a Watcher's spirit that can possess a human's body," her dad concluded.

"One more ask-your-local-theologian question. Were the mythical Greek gods the same as the Nephilim of the Hebrew scriptures?" Emmaline asked.

"You're as imaginative as my Daniela, and just as genius." Mr. Cavanaugh laughed, sounding like a winding car starter. "Plato described Atlantis as an island located in the Atlantic just beyond the Pillars of Hercules—our modern-day Strait of Gibraltar."

"A narrow waterway that unifies the Atlantic Ocean and the Mediterranean Sea and separates Gibraltar and Peninsular Spain in Europe from Morocco in Africa—right?"

"Correct, Emmaline. But Atlantis was nothing more than Plato's plagiarism of Genesis chapter two." Mr. Cavanaugh tossed his paper on the coffee table. "The fish and beasts of the sea survived the great flood because the deluge only killed land creatures. As Daniela shared with you, Job named the most dreadful of sea monsters Leviathan."

"Was Leviathan the Greek god, Poseidon?" Daniela asked.

"As I said, Plato plagiarized Genesis chapter two." Mr. Cavanaugh guzzled down a glass of lemonade.

"According to Plato, Poseidon ruled Atlantis," Daniela said, then paused. "He fell in love with a human woman, and they conceived five sons."

Emmaline picked up where Daniela left off. "So the Atlantis story is really about how a fallen angel impregnated a human woman and produced five Nephilim."

"Absolutely. That's my girls!" The older man gazed at them both. "You ladies are indeed kindred spirits. Take care of each other—always."

"We will." They said in unison.

"Tell us the rest." Daniela slid to the edge of her chair, and Emmaline breathlessly waited as she sat crisscross-applesauce on the floor, leaning against Daniela's left leg.

"In Greek fables," Mr. Cavanaugh continued, "the Greek gods—Nephilim—functioned as military tyrants. They consumed the world's natural resources. Sound familiar?"

"Look through the annals of history," Mrs. Cavanaugh dipped her crochet needle into a string of yarn.

"Franco, Hitler, Tito, etcetera," Daniela listed contemporary military tyrants.

"From my extensive study of the Book of Enoch and the Hebrew scriptures as well as the gift of Wisdom's illumination, I believe the human tyrants you listed were all descendants of Nephilim and preludes to the tyrant of all tyrants—the antichrist," her dad confirmed.

"Before they fell, were the Watchers created for a purpose?" Daniela asked.

"They were, baby girl. The Watchers were just that,

angels dispatched to Earth to watch over and protect humans. Lust for human women got the better of them, and they defected from their rightful place, slept with women, and created Nephilim—savage giants who pillaged the earth and endangered humanity. Though no longer giants, the Nephilim of today are still savages."

"Besides sleeping with human women, did they do something else to make Yahweh so angry with them?" Emmaline asked.

"They taught humans methods of war as well as sorcery, overloading simple human minds with centuries worth of evil knowledge all at once."

"Our weak morality couldn't stop the resulting proliferation of continual evil." Daniela thought of Los Alamos National Laboratory—the site where the atomic bomb was designed, built, and tested. Then she thought of Hiroshima and Nagasaki, the cities decimated by atomic bombs.

"Correct. So reluctantly, Yahweh allowed the flood to rid Earth of Nephilim and the corrupted humans who no longer yearned for redemption."

"Is the world at the same place morally that it was in the days of Noah?" Emmaline leaned forward and rested her elbows on her knees.

"It's close." Daniela's dad adjusted his recliner. "Before the start of the worldwide deluge, an angel named Uriel warned Noah and instructed him to build an ark so the entire human race wouldn't be eradicated. God is not into pandemics that completely eliminate humans from Earth."

"Good to know." Emmaline twirled her hair into a bun, then harpooned it with a gold chopstick.

"It's odd how historians embrace Greek mythology as quasi-truth, yet judge and then dismiss the Bible as nothing more than a book of fairy tales." Mrs. Cavanaugh finished the sweater made of black and silver yarn. "Take this, Daniela. It will keep you warm tonight."

"Thank you. It's perfect!" Daniela put on the sweater.

"Mama, that's because ancient Greek gods ask nothing of humanity, but Yahweh does—humble yourself, repent, and be reborn." Mister Cavanaugh pushed up from his chair. "Humility gets us every time."

"Don't go yet, Mr. C.!" Emmaline whipped the Skeleton Key out of Daniela's backpack. "Daniela and I have a little surprise for you and Mrs. C."

"We'll see if Ezekiel's gadget works." Daniela struck a match and lit a cinnamon-spiced Yankee Candle. She held the statue over the faint light. A faded image appeared on the ceiling. "Mom, turn off the lights."

"It's time to go, or you'll be late," Mrs. Cavanaugh said.

"Mom, please. This is important. The dead can wait. They always do."

Daniela's mom complied, and the image showed clearer. Austin sat back down, tilted his chin back, and studied the ceiling.

"The Skeleton Key is an ancient projector!" Daniela laid on her back, and Emmaline perched on her knees, both gazing at the ceiling and the image.

"That's your clue, girls," the theologian spoke. "Jeanette, pass me my Bible."

Austin's wife obeyed and got her own. Daniela did as well, sharing her Bible with Emmaline, highlighting the focal points as her dad read.

"Let's look at Daniel 7:1-8 and 11-15, the words written in 606 BC by Daniel during his exile in Babylon. Daniela, read the first passage out loud. Emmaline, you read the second."

"Yes, sir," the girls said in unison.

> "In the first year of Belshazzar king of Babylon Daniel had a dream and visions in his head as he was lying upon his bed. Then he wrote down the dream and told the gist of the matter . . .
>
> "Behold, the four winds of the heavens [political and social agitations] were stirring up the great sea [the nations of the world].
>
> "Four great beasts came up out of the sea in succession, and different from one another.
>
> "The **first** [the Babylonian empire under Nebuchadnezzar] was like a lion and had eagle's wings. I looked till the wings of it were plucked, and it was lifted up from the earth and made to stand upon two feet as a man, and a man's heart was given to it.

"And behold another beast, a **second** one [the Medo-Persian empire] was like a bear, and it raised up itself on one side [or one dominion] and three ribs were in its mouth between its teeth; and it was told, Arise, devour much flesh.

"After this I looked, and behold, **another** [the Grecian empire of Alexander the Great] like a leopard which had four wings of a bird on its back. The beast had also four heads [Alexander's generals, his successors] and dominion was given to it.

"After this I saw in the night visions, and behold, **a fourth beast—the Roman empire**—terrible, powerful and dreadful, and exceedingly strong. And it had great iron teeth; it devoured and crushed and trampled what was left with its feet. And it was different from all the beasts that came before it, and it had **ten horns** [symbolizing ten kings]. I considered the horns, and behold, there came up among them another horn, a little one, before which three of the first horns were plucked up by the roots; and behold, in this horn were eyes like the eyes of a man and a mouth speaking great things.

"I looked then because of the sound of the great words which the horn was speaking. I watched until the beast was slain, and its body destroyed and given over to be burned with fire.

"And as for the rest of the beasts, their power of dominion was taken away; yet their lives were prolonged [for the duration of their lives was fixed] for a season and a time.'

"That's kairos time," her dad explained. Emmaline read the rest as Daniela looked over her shoulder.

"I saw in the night visions, and behold, on the clouds of the heavens came One like a Son of man, and He—that's talking about Yeshua— came to the Ancient of Days—and that's Yah- weh—and was presented before Him.

"And there was given Him [the Messiah] do- minion and glory and kingdom, that all peo- ples, nations, and languages should serve Him. His dominion is an everlasting domin- ion which shall not pass away, and His king- dom is one which shall not be destroyed.

"As for me, Daniel, my spirit was grieved and anxious within me, and the vi- sions of my head alarmed and agitated me."

"Dad . . ." Daniela looked up from her Bible.
    "Yes, Danny-Rose, what are you thinking?"
    "I'm thinking that the Skeleton Key, like a Russian doll, holds secondary puzzle pieces that will help us understand the statue even more."
    "Expound."
    "Here's what we all know." She used a pencil to point to the pieces of the statue. "The gold head represents

Babylon. Silver, the Medes and the Persians. Bronze, the Greeks. And iron, Rome. Bottom line: all these kingdoms have risen and fallen, except for the kingdom represented by the iron and clay feet and toes. Right?"

"Right," her dad said. Her mom and Emmaline nodded.

"And before a divine kingdom—represented by a rock *not* made with human hands—rises and crushes human kingdoms, the final human kingdom, the one represented by feet and toes made of iron and clay, will rule."

"And it's that kingdom that the antichrist will come from," her dad added.

"There's the connection between the statue and the who." Daniela scanned the ancient text again. "We've established that iron represents the Roman Empire, so somehow the influence of Rome continues into the iron and clay feet of King Nebuchadnezzar's statue. We think this occurs by an amalgamation of European kingdoms influenced by Roman Catholicism and Islam."

"Like the European Union?" Her mother retrieved an emerald ball of yarn from her knitting bag.

"That's a good start, Mom, and may be the end and final conclusion as well." Daniela opened her journal to a blank sheet of paper and organized her hypothesis.

"What are you writing, Danny Rose?" Emmaline asked.

"Notes. Lots of notes."

"Don't let your hands cramp," Emmaline winked. "You may need to slap a smirk off Claire's face at the funeral." Daniela kept writing.

Like the inner parts of a Russian doll, the projected image and the corresponding passage in the book of Daniel's visions confirmed that Daniel's statue and his animal-farm dream mysteries should be studied together.

A simple clue but not to be missed: the image of the

animal-farm dream was literally tucked inside the Skeleton Key. The two were related!

"We know that Daniel's statue foretold the progression of empires during and after Daniel's life. His animal-farm dream about the lion, the bear, the leopard, and the last beast also foretold the succession of the empires of the world, starting with the empire of Daniel's time: Babylon. The Bible says that there's nothing new under the sun— what has been, will be."

"What's your conclusion, Orphan Dreamer?" Emmaline asked.

"The animals in Daniel's animal-farm dream represent two sets of kingdoms—ancient empires that started during Daniel's lifetime and modern-day kingdoms that began after the fall of ancient Rome. So eight kingdoms in total."

"If the animal-farm empires are on repeat, could we repeat the cycle again, then again, then again?" Emmaline asked.

"Possibly. Probably. Because Yahweh is plentiful in mercy and slow to judge, he gives us time to repent. This is what motivates Him."

"Motives. Sticky little things," Emmaline quipped.

"True . . . and that's my role as the Orphan Dreamer— to prevent the antichrist from pressing *stop* on the repeat button, thus giving humanity time to respond to Yeshua's gift of eternal life, so they'll be prepared to endure the *good* pandemic, the Rapture."

"Will you fulfill your role and give us a chance to repent and participate in the Rapture?" Mrs. Cavanaugh asked, her facial expression frozen.

"Yes. I will. I'm the Orphan Dreamer, born to sacrifice my temporary happiness for the eternal freedom of my friends—and even my enemies."

Mrs. Cavanaugh sighed heavily.

"My last and final note. The animal-farm dream further explains the clay and iron of Daniel's statue, zooming in on the nitty gritty, revealing the individual players in this end-of-the-world empire—the empire of who."

"Girls, you're going to be late!" Mrs. Cavanaugh tapped her watch. "It's a forty-five-minute drive to Palatka."

"But, Mom."

"No buts. It's rude to arrive late to a funeral. Go. The rain has slowed to a drizzle." She turned to her husband. "The bookstore's going to need a bit of TLC."

"Don't worry, darling. I'll handle it."

"Drive safely."

"Yes, ma'am," the girls said in chorus. They exited the house, then climbed into the Jeep. Emmaline sank her key into the ignition. Immediately, her phone rang. "Hi, Daddy. Yes, she's with me." As she backed out of the drive-way, she handed the phone to Daniela. "My dad wants to speak with you."

"Hello."

"Nice to finally speak with my daughter's friend. I'd like to meet you one day."

"Me too."

"In private."

"Why?" Danny's flesh sprang up a field of goosebumps as she remembered the *things* Emmaline's dad had done to his only daughter.

"I know who you are."

"Nice speaking with you, Mister Darbyshire. Have a nice day too." She hung up and tossed the phone into Emmaline's lap like it was a live snake.

"What's unnerved you? Something Daddy said?"

"No. It's just . . . funerals." Daniela's smile flattened as

Mister Darbyshire's threat echoed in her mind—*I know who you are.* She didn't even know who she was half of the time.

"Finish up the puzzle, Daniela. I can't concentrate on another puzzle after the funeral tonight."

"Okay. I'll read, then use you as my sounding board. You drive and help me make sense of this stuff." Daniela flipped the pages of her Bible and read the passage to herself.

> Four great beasts came up out of the sea in succession, and different from one another. The first—the Babylonian empire under Nebuchadnezzar—was like a lion and had eagle's wings. I looked till the wings of it were plucked, and it was lifted up from the earth and made to stand upon two feet as a man, and a man's heart was given to it.

* * *

Daniela thought for a moment. "A beast represents a kingdom, per Daniel 7:17 and 23. Winds represent strife, war, or conflict, as in Jeremiah 49:36 and 37. And the sea represents multitudes, peoples, and nations, Revelation 17:15. Here are my journal notes . . ."

> "In ancient times: During the Babylonian empire from 605 to 539 BC, a lion with eagle's wings was a prominent symbol on Babylonian coins and on Babylon's walls.

"Okay. In later times—when European empires rule the world—who is the lion?" Emmaline asked.

"Here's what I wrote about that," Daniela said, returning to her notes.

> "In modern times: England's coat of arms features three lions."

"Then who's the eagle?" Emmaline asked.

Flipping the page, Daniela said, "An eagle's wings . . . here it is."

> "The passage foretells of a kingdom that would rise in modern times—plucked from the back of a lion (England—a modern version of Babylon) and flies away with an eagle's wings. This nation could be none other than The United States of America, whose national bird is the bald eagle."

"Cool!" Emmaline sped down a backcountry highway through a canopy of moss-laden oaks.

"The identity of the lion and eagle is solved. I'll read the next passage."

> "And behold another beast, a second one—the Medo-Persian empire—was like a bear, and it raised up itself on one side—or one dominion—and three ribs were in its mouth between its teeth; and it was told, Arise, devour much flesh.

"Who's the bear?" Emmaline asked.

"The Medo-Persian empire."

"Break it down for me." Emmaline turned onto a two-lane road, then slammed the accelerator to the floor.

"Only if you promise to slow down!"

"Slowing down."

Daniela read her journal notes aloud.

> "In ancient times: the Medo-Persian empire ruled the Middle East from 539 to 331 BC. The three ribs in the bear's mouth represent three nations—Babylon, Libya, and Egypt.

> "In modern times: The bear is represented by Russia, whose national symbol is a bear."

"And before you ask, here's the scripture from Daniel about the leopard, along with some additional notes I had written in my journal." She tapped her pencil on her journal while reading the Bible passage.

> "After this I looked, and behold, another—the Grecian empire of Alexander the Great—like a leopard which had four wings of a bird on its back. The beast had also four heads—Alexander's generals, his successors—and dominion was given to it."

"CliffsNotes?" Emmaline asked.

"In ancient times: The leopard represented the Grecian empire of Alexander the Great from 331 to 168 BC. This leopard looks freakish, possessing four heads."

"Creepy, but why?"

Daniela replied, "When Alexander died in a drunken

stupor at age thirty-three, his four generals—Cassander, Lysimachus, Seleucus, and Ptolemy—divided up the empire.

"I can't believe the Bible predicted all of this stuff thousands of years before it actually happened."

"Awesome—right?" Rubbing her right earlobe, Daniela flipped the page in her journal. "Here it is!"

> "In modern times: The leopard represents Germany, whose Leopard tanks have been used predominantly in European armies since their introduction in the 1960s. But this time, the four heads of the leopard equal the Four Reichs.
>
> "We already know that Germany's Third Reich attempted to gain world dominion during World War II, and that the Fourth Reich is emerging in our time.
>
> "As for the bird's wings. The leopard Daniel saw also had bird's wings, which represent France and its national symbol—a rooster. France and Germany have not only collaborated on the design of Leopard tanks, but both countries are also founding members of the European Union—King Charlemagne's resurrected empire."

"Who is the fourth beast? The kingdom that will rise during our lifetime—or that has already risen?" Emmaline braked at a stop sign.

Daniela read the associated scripture, then shared her notes again.

> "After this I saw in the night visions, and behold, a fourth beast—the Roman empire—terrible, powerful and dreadful, and exceedingly strong. And it had great iron teeth; it devoured and crushed and trampled what was left with its feet.

> "In ancient times: the fourth beast represented the Roman Empire that conquered the world in 168 BC after defeating the Greeks at the Battle of Pynda. Under the Caesars, Rome ruled from 168 BC to 351 AD.

> "In modern times: The fourth beast represents the revived Roman empire—the ten-world government. The European Union."

"But there's more, Limy."

"Pray tell!" Emmaline turned down a dirt road, nearing the country church.

"Yeshua's apostle, John, wrote the book of Revelation. Inside that book, John clarifies the details of the fourth Roman-inspired kingdom."

"Read it to me."

> "Then I saw a beast rising up out of the sea. It had seven heads and ten horns, with ten crowns on its horns. And written on each head were names that blasphemed God. This beast

> looked like a leopard, but it had the feet of a bear and the mouth of a lion! And the dragon gave the beast his own power and throne and great authority." (NLT)

"Whatever that thing is, it's some sort of mutation," Emmaline said.

"I agree. The Fourth Beast—kingdom—is an amalgamation of the leopard, the bear, and the lion—Germany, Russia, and England—with the dragon, a.k.a. Satan, giving this kingdom its power. Since the leopard is given a focal point in the Apostle John's vision in Revelation 13:1-2, the new horn that emerges and then dominates the three other horns is the antichrist—six-six-six, our unknown *who*."

But there's no longer a rooster or an eagle, and that is a very bad sign. What happened to France and America? Daniela rubbed her arms, kneading the goosebumps away.

"What's wrong, Danny-girl?"

"What almost scares me senseless is that when I compare the animal farm prophecy found in Daniel chapter seven to the animal farm prophecy found in Revelation 13, the eagle's wings that represent the United States aren't mentioned at all in Revelation's account about the final kingdoms of the world."

"When was the Book of Revelation written?"

"Around 90 AD, long after Daniel's book of visions from 600 BC."

"When the kingdom represented by an amalgamation of the leopard, the bear, and the lion rises, America will vanish?" Limy swerved the Jeep, kicking up dust.

"I don't know, but I think so."

"So an American girl saves the world, but Americans are wiped off the map for some unknown reason, like a pandemic?"

"Or Americans choose to follow Yahweh and most of her citizens are taken during Yeshua's pandemic, the Rapture?"

"Come on now, Danny. Have you even noticed the level of debauchery in our country? Goodness. Our married president lied about having sex with a White House intern."

"I know, but I must remain hopeful in order to do my job."

"What's the alternative, Danny? I'm not buying into your Mary Poppins hypothesis."

"This?" Daniela flipped to Revelation 17 and read about America's possible fiery end, interjecting her commentary as she read the lengthy passage that spelled doom and gloom for the greatest idea of a country ever born: a constitutional republic.

As Daniela read, Emmaline slowed the speed of the Jeep, wanting—no, needing—to hear the possible end of her home, the land of the free and the brave.

> "One of the seven angels who had poured out the seven bowls came over and spoke to me. 'Come with me,' he said, 'and I will show you the judgment that is going to come on the great prostitute, who rules over many waters. The kings of the world have committed adultery with her, and the people who belong to this world have been made drunk by the wine of her immorality.' "

"Whatever institution is represented by this prostitute who rules over many nations has been a constant source of immorality," Daniela interjected.

"So the angel took me in the Spirit into the wilderness. There I saw a woman sitting on a scarlet beast that had seven heads and ten horns, and blasphemies against God were written all over it. The woman wore purple and scarlet clothing and beautiful jewelry made of gold and precious gems and pearls. In her hand she held a gold goblet full of obscenities and the impurities of her immorality. A mysterious name was written on her forehead: 'Babylon the Great, Mother of All Prostitutes and Obscenities in the World.' I could see that she was drunk—drunk with the blood of God's holy people who were witnesses for Jesus.

"I stared at her in complete amazement. 'Why are you so amazed?' the angel asked. 'I will tell you the mystery of this woman and of the beast with seven heads and ten horns on which she sits. The beast you saw was once alive but isn't now. And yet he will soon come up out of the bottomless pit and go to eternal destruction.' "

"The beast that she's sitting on represents a Satan-influenced kingdom," Daniela said and then continued reading.

"And the people who belong to this world, whose names were not written in the Book of Life before the world was made, will be amazed at the reappearance of this beast who had died."

"According to Dad, this next riddle speaks of the antichrist," Daniela said.

> "This calls for a mind with understanding: The seven heads of the beast represent the seven hills where the woman rules. They also represent seven kings. Five kings have already fallen, the sixth now reigns, and the seventh is yet to come, but his reign will be brief.

Daniela looked up from her notes and gave her friend a serious look. "Limy, there's one city that sits on seven hills—the Vatican."

"Is the prostitute the Roman Catholic Church?"

"According to my dad, yes."

"Sheesh! The Pope won't make you a saint!"

"And wait until you hear this part," Daniela said.

> "The scarlet animal that died is the eighth king, having reigned before as one of the seven; after his second reign, he too, will go to his doom.

> "His ten horns are ten kings who have not yet risen to power; they will be appointed to their kingdoms for one brief moment, to reign with him. The ten kings are the one-world government, which will politically support the antichrist.

> "They will all sign a treaty giving their power and strength to him. Together they will wage war against the Lamb, and the Lamb will

conquer them; for he is Lord over all lords, and King of kings, and his people are the called and chosen and faithful ones." (NLT)

Daniela tapped on her book, then said, "The motive of the one-world government and the antichrist is simple—wage war against Yeshua and his followers and kill them off."

"If the ancient Roman Empire is a major player in the coming one-world government, then they had a lot of practice throwing followers of the Way to the lions, bears, and even crocodiles!"

"Unfortunately, yes," Daniela said, then continued reading from the passage.

> "The oceans, lakes, and rivers that the woman is sitting on represent masses of people of every race and nation.
>
> "The scarlet animal and his ten horns—which represent ten kings who will reign with him—all hate the woman and will attack her and leave her naked and ravaged by fire."

"Do you get it, Limy? If the woman represents ancient Rome, the political arm of the one-world government will attack the religious arm, starting Armageddon. If the woman represents America, the rest of the European nations will turn on her and destroy her. Plain—"

"But not so simple," Emmaline completed Daniela's usual saying of *plain, definitely simple.*

"Right."

"I have a headache!" Emmaline massaged her right temple.

"So do I . . . and we're going to a funeral." Daniela inhaled, then sighed. "Oh well."

"Biblical prophecy is incredibly accurate, if you can understand its riddles."

"It is a truth *not* universally acknowledged, Limy. And this is my mission: solve the ancient riddles of Bible prophecy, then declare plain explanations to those who are interested."

"*Pride and Prejudice*—Danny Rose style." They both chuckled.

"There's one more piece to this puzzle in solving the mysterious *who*—the one instigating the bad pandemic." Daniela read the final Bible passage.

> "And the beast which I saw was like unto a leopard, and his feet were as the feet of a bear, and his mouth as the mouth of a lion: and the dragon gave him his power, and his seat, and great authority.

> "And it was different from all the beasts that came before it, and it had ten horns—symbolizing ten kings. I considered the horns, and behold, there came up among them another horn, a little one, before which three of the first horns were plucked up by the roots; and behold, in this horn were eyes like the eyes of a man and a mouth speaking great things.

> "I looked then because of the sound of the great words which the horn was speaking. I watched until the beast was slain, and its body destroyed and given over to be burned with

fire. And as for the rest of the beasts, their power of dominion was taken away; yet their lives were prolonged—for the duration of their lives was fixed—for a season and a time [kairos time]."

"Who exactly is the little horn?"

"According to my dad's understanding of the scriptures, the little horn is Chi Xi Stigma—six-six-six, the antichrist."

"Okay, but six-six-six . . . connect the dots for me."

"The antichrist is a descendant of Germanic-English-Russian royalty, the fourth beast. A proud person who possesses man's wisdom—the eyes of a man—but not God's wisdom. He will lead a political-religious government that will persecute anyone who defies him."

"We must find and then eliminate this monster." Emmaline shifted her Jeep into second as she navigated the washboard road.

"Agreed."

Five minutes later, Emmaline parked in front of a rickety old church.

"Do you have any tissues?" Daniela's hands dripped nerves. "I hate crying at these sorts of things."

Emmaline removed a clump of tissues from her purse as well as a silencer and her gun. As she rotated the long-barreled noise suppressor onto the end of the gun, her friend's eyes bulged from their sockets.

The redhead grinned—crooked, but cute. "Mama likes to pack a little heat."

"You told me before. But may I remind you: We are only seventeen, barely old enough to be packing anything except gum and makeup. Besides, we'll never get past the president's security detail with that."

"He's attending the graveside service across the street from the church, not the church service. Grab your snot rags, and let's meet the zombies." Emmaline slipped the weapon into her purse.

"God help us!" Daniela's butt cheeks tensed. "I despise the idea of guns in a church."

"Only in a church?" Shoulders back, head up, Emmaline marched past the scant crowd toward the church entrance.

Long ago, paint had peeled off the exterior walls, littering dead grass with carpets of lead snow. "Guess metal detectors have been deemed unnecessary in the sticks. Maybe every Tom, Dick, and Harry in here is packin' heat." Daniela's legs wobbled as she stumbled into the stuffy white clapboard church.

Inside, a sea of black lay before them: polyester church dresses and suits, polished shoes, the mood, and the casket. The girls found a seat near the middle. With sweaty hands, Daniela reached for Emmaline's.

"Danny-girl, relax."

"Distract me."

"I've thought about what your dad said." Emmaline stared at the altar. "If you knew your ending, how would you have lived your beginning?"

"What's your verdict?" Daniela buttoned up her sweater.

"This . . . like the end of an epic love story: and they lived happily ever after." Emmaline held Daniela's hand, then blushed. "I'm sorry about everything—the lies, starting fights with your mom, antagonizing you about your religious beliefs, and the gun pointing. You never deserved any of that. I understand now that a good ending requires an even better beginning—a beginning that starts with intention and kindness."

"That's my Emmaline Darbyshire—a real classy dame, and . . ." Daniela paused, wiping a tear from her eye. "I love her, and that's the beginning and end of everything."

"Ditto, my Orphan Dreamer—my Great Gatsby." Emmaline rested her head on Daniela's shoulder. "It's at funerals when I think that maybe your God isn't so bad."

A smile peeled across Daniela's face. "That's a change."

Emmaline shrugged. "I never knew the Bible contained so many cool and complex stories. Nephilim. Prophecies. Crazy dreams. The list goes on."

Claire waltzed down the middle aisle, her arm held by a handsome young man as though she were a blushing bride marching to the altar to take wedding vows instead of giving a eulogy at her mother's funeral. "That's Claire Amilee."

"That's it?"

"In the flesh." Daniela couldn't expend the energy necessary to hate Claire. Besides, a girl who just lost her mother deserved compassion. With her beau at her side, Claire sat in the front row. "To making it count." Daniela squeezed her kindred spirit's hand.

The funeral dragged on with bad singing, a long-winded sermon, and a contrived eulogy.

During the last few minutes of the funeral, a scruffy man dressed in a black coat, a baseball cap, and dungarees plopped down on the end of their pew nearest a duct-taped stained-glass window.

A gust of body odor slammed into the side of Daniela's right cheek. She gasped for breath. Evil spilled from his pale eyes. Grinning, he leaned down and reached for the floorboard.

Daniela froze.

Where was the president's security?

His entourage was most likely scouring the grounds, looking for troublemakers. *Catch the butterflies and calm down.* Daniela took a deep breath. The man snapped to attention, then focused on the eulogy.

She'd been wrong to judge. She released her breath.

An hour later, the funeral service ended. "Shall we walk to the graveside and lay our dear sister to rest?" the pastor asked. The choir began to sing "Nearer My God to Thee."

Emmaline leaned closer to Daniela. "How near exactly are we to God?" She raised her brows, directing Daniela's attention to the stinky man. The scraggly man leaned down again, reached for the floor, and lifted the red carpet. Glaring at the Orphan Dreamer, he removed a long black object from a hidden compartment.

"Gun." Barely audible, Daniela's voice sank between ocean waves of fear.

She sat paralyzed. Was she dreaming? After blinking twice, she reached for the snowflake diamond beneath the neckline of her shirt. It was still there.

The man aimed the gun at the back of a young girl who sat in the pew in front of him. With blonde hair and a round face, she resembled a younger version of Claire.

Lips moving, he glared at Danicla. "You shouldn't have come." With yellowed eyes and a mouthful of tartar-stained teeth, he shouted, "You people wanna see my young'uns and wife so bad? Join 'em both in hell."

Time froze, as did the attendees.

Scraggly beard grabbed the helpless girl's ponytail and yanked her up over the bench into his lap. He then stood and backed up against the wall. "Consider me doin' the world a favor by cleanin' up God's house."

"Stop!" The minister charged the man.

"Daddy, let Polly go!" Claire screamed, then hit the

deck as the scraggly man mowed down the pastor with a spray of bullets. He dispatched to eternity any mourner who dared breathe or move.

Parishioners scattered, but few who moved escaped. Blood splattered the walls and stained-glass windows shattered.

Bullets pummeled the baptistery.

Water sloshed down the pulpit. Mute but no longer paralyzed, Daniela yanked Emmaline beneath their church pew. They crawled under church benches toward the door. Bullets splintered wooden pews in their wake.

"Daddy, you're hurting me," the little girl whined. "I'll be good—promise."

"Shut up. Yo mamma wudn't nuthin' and your brat sister wudn't nuthin' but a hussy, but Claire had a sweet little mouth."

Daniela froze. Images of the sad boy from her dreams flashed through her mind. "Limy . . . how does Claire's dad know how her mouth tastes?"

"You're a smart girl, Danny." Emmaline crawled beneath the pews, but Daniela grabbed her friend's foot, stopping her escape.

Bile shot up into Daniela's throat. Claire's father had raped her, and insecure people made the best bullies. "We have to help Claire and her sister."

"This isn't your fight." Emmaline grabbed Daniela's arm. "The president's security team won't waste time killing anyone who appears to be a threat to the Commander in Chief. We have to get out of here."

Flesh slapped flesh. "No—Daddy. Please don't do that to me." The little girl's cries ripped the steeple off the church. "I'll be a good girl."

"What's he doing?" Daniela's face flushed hot with rage.

"He's raping her, Danny-girl. Right in God's house, that monster. Do you think he's a Nephilim?"

"He's gotta be!" Daniela's world spun.

"Jerk-face. He's raping his own little girl . . . and do you smell that?"

Daniela sniffed. "Gasoline. Fire." She peeked above the last pew. The front pews were burning. Her blood ran cold. Standing, she glared Death in the face.

"Are you crazy?" Emmaline tugged at her friend's pant leg. "Get down."

"Go to the back of the church, get your gun out, then put your metal where your mouth is!" Beneath the pew, Daniela inched toward Claire's dad, her sights trained on his bowed legs.

She stopped and peeked above the back of a pew.

Belt unbuckled, the man had hoisted the whimpering girl under one arm and was sprinkling gasoline on the altar with the other. He knelt down in front of the communion table and retrieved a clump of dynamite that had been taped under it. "Coming to worship, Daniela?"

"Let her go." Daniela stood up as Claire ran to the back of the church, tripping and falling, all tangled up with her beau. Finally they reached the back of the church, and for some odd reason, Daniela just wanted to laugh.

"Make me, little nigger girl." He doused the altar with fuel, struck a match, lit the stick of dynamite, then dropped it into the pool of gasoline.

Hearing the N-word made Daniela want to laugh again.

"You're calling me that with your pants unzipped and semen running down your leg after raping your own elementary-school daughter in God's house. You are some kind of stupid." Daniela mocked.

Fire licked up fuel and inched up the wick. Somehow, when a man who raped his own daughter in God's house and then set fire to his wife's casket calls you the N-word, it's a compliment.

The intruder retreated, his back toward Daniela.

She took cover.

The altar exploded, sending shards of glass in all directions. Ash rained down on her body.

The girl screamed.

"King of the Fight, empower me to defeat this beast!" Daniela marched down what was left of the center aisle.

The demon-possessed man dropped the girl, grabbed Daniela's wrist, and flipped her onto her back. "Run!" Daniela screamed to the little girl.

But covered in ash, the girl just sat down on the floor, confused and shocked while calling for her sister. "Claire! Claire! Claire!" She never came.

Hot ash scorched Daniela's skin.

Outside, lightning flashed. Thunder clapped. The heavens rumbled, and a wall of rotating black sky screeched and careened toward the chapel. *A tornado.* A swish of hot air blew past Daniela's ash-laden frame.

Legna?

A firecracker exploded by Daniela's ear, throwing her off balance. The drunk stumbled backward, blood spilling from his right shoulder.

She looked up.

Emmaline stood above her, legs spread. Smoke rose from the tip of her Glock.

"Thank God," Daniela whispered. "It's loaded this time, Limy."

The little girl dressed in a thin white dress mimicked an angel as she ran from the bowels of hell into Daniela's embrace.

"What's your name?" Daniela asked.

"Polly."

"Go with my friend Emmaline." Sirens wailed outside, and voices echoed within the chaotic noise.

"Danny Rose, watch out!" Emmaline raised her gun.

Behind the Orphan Dreamer, the devil man sprayed bullets into the church fire, murdering his own demons before turning the gun toward his daughter's angel, Daniela.

"Take Polly—now!" Daniela's thoughts raced faster than her legs.

She smirked as she yanked the Glass Tattoo from around her neck, then buried the powerful diamond into her right palm.

Something powerful filled her body.

Her muscles hardened into steel cables. Bones solidified to iron. Her legs moved faster than a gazelle's. "It's my party now," she said in a calm voice, then ran straight toward the assailant, throwing a punch that cracked bone.

His neck twisted ninety degrees, and his head hung at an angle incompatible with life. Defying death, he reached inside his jacket and removed a brassy, round object—a grenade.

Storm!

Something slammed the pervert so hard into the concrete foundation that his body splintered the floor ten feet in each direction.

Then that same someone grabbed Daniela from behind and expelled her from the church. Legna's words flooded her soul. *You may not see me, but I'm here—fighting, protecting—just call me.*

Standing outside, drenched by a torrential rain, the warmth that had accompanied the angel's presence ebbed.

No good deed goes unpunished: camera flashes blinded her eyes. Microphones held by eager reporters pummeled her face. She raised her arms as police officers rushed to her side. Did they suspect her of murder—attempted murder of the President of the United States of America?

She didn't see the Beast, the president's limousine.

Boom!

A blast catapulted her across the lawn. The air buzzed, then a black curtain slid down, obliterating her world.

In that moment, one snowflake fell from heaven to quench hell's thirst. Ethan's Rosebud closed her eyes and sank beneath the surface of black and cold water. She took a deep breath and dived deep. "Take me to the stars, Yahweh."

"Dinna be afraid," a Scottish baritone voice said. "It's almost nightfall, and the river's a wee bit deep."

Who did this new voice belong to? "I can't swim," she seemed to reply.

"Take my hand, Rosebud. I'll not be lettin' ye drown. I'm a strong swimmer, lass. In time, ye'll see that I'm strong—not scraggly or weak."

"Oily boy?"

"I'm here wi' ye, now."

"But I'm scared . . . of you. You could be the antichrist—Six. Six. Six!"

"Dinna be afraid of me. I'll be the ruthless one, pushing back the darkness so ye can be kind. Earth will be balanced, rotating on its axis because of your compassion, Daniela, *a rún mo chroí*—secret of my heart. Trust me, *mo nighean donn*."

She grinned from ear to ear, pursed her lips, and blew the air from her lungs as she submerged herself beneath the water.

Daniela translated the Scottish Gaelic—*mo nighean donn*—to English: "My brown-haired lass." That was who she was.

"Take me to the stars, oily boy . . ." She dived into the Jordan River beside him, and the Glass Tattoo took them to a faraway place, to a desert place and then to a cold hospital room.

49—Nomed

The Present the End . . .
Nighttime, May 10
North Syria

EAGER TO STOKE YET ANOTHER intercultural offense, and still invisible to the Wraith and his Orphans, Nomed traipses across the desert, looking for a mutant human—a Nephilim—code name Abu Bakr al-Baghdadi.

Nomed's message for Baghdadi is simple: The assassin—an American patriot, the eagle—is coming.

Run.

Hide.

50—The Orphan

The Present the End . . .
Nighttime. May 10
North Syria

THREE MONTHS AGO, A TALIBAN fighter tried to spit a mouthful of blood into Wraith's face, though he missed by a long shot. Gasping for breath and gurgling blood, the dying Afghani soldier uttered his last words, "You Americans have all the watches, but we . . . we have the time."

Wraith had glanced at his military watch, then glared into the Afghan boy's eyes. "Sorry, lad, but yer time's up." He then slit the teenage boy's throat wide open, ghosting him, silencing another warrior—a son, a brother, and an heir to some Afghani family.

Once again, the assassin had stamped a period at the end of another fragile life.

Time is mercurial.

Death is reliable, even predictable.

But Yeshua had warned His disciples: "Those who live by the sword, will die by the sword." One night, Wraith would be required to pay the piper.

Has my time run out? Will the piper demand payment tonight?

Could a ghost be ghosted?

An apricot sulphur landed on the dead boy's nose.

51—THE ORPHAN

THE PRESENT. THE END . . .
NIGHTTIME. MAY 10
NORTH SYRIA

WRAITH FOLDS HIS PMC LETTER and stuffs it into a front pocket of his uniform, hiding it from the six other Orphans riding with him in the belly of the MH-47 chopper.

The special-ops warrior slides his fingers across the face of his watch.

Ancient proverbs: watches versus time.

Current realities: ghosts and aliens.

If Wraith's time on Earth has indeed run out, he could accept that. Yeshua's dimension would serve as a coveted tradeoff to Earth, the planet where dead men and women walk with their heads held high, fooling themselves about their self-importance and their self-determination.

Wraith understands that it's appointed for a man to die once and then face judgment.

But what would become of his *nighean donn*—his brown-haired lass—Danny Rose, his wife, the Orphan Dreamer? If he died, what would become of her and their daughter, Adelaide Rose? Life and death offered no perfect solutions.

All around him, night stalks the Syrian Sahara like a thousand-pound grizzly bear waiting to ambush a hunter who had just shot its only cub. Over six thousand miles away, his wife sleeps alone in the dark. Ever since Daniela was a little girl, she had despised nighttime—and deep waters even more. Fast-moving or meandering, the speed of the currents didn't matter, only the depth.

He had heard the news.

DELUGE FOLLOWED BY EARLY SPRING SNOWFALL AND WARMING TEMPERA- TURES THREATENS TO FLOOD NORTH CAROLINA'S MOUNTAIN RIVERS.

EVACUATE NOW!

A large lake sat behind their North Carolina chalet. If the lake's depth swelled to dangerous heights, would his wife be too sick to evacuate?

At the end of her spring semester at Exeter, Adelaide would arrive at her mother's side. Until then, Daniela would never attempt to leave the chalet without their daughter.

The MH-47 helicopter loses altitude, then regains it in less than five seconds, jarring Wraith's insides. He begs the One who holds the stars in one hand and the ocean tides in the other, "Dinna ask her to cross the river alone, Yeshua. She canna swim. She'll drown."

He inhales.

Lilac, her favorite scent, seems to fill his nostrils, washing away the acrid stench of jet fuel from his lungs.

If his time ran out, could he and his family swim the treacherous journey together, up the Jordan River—the mysterious path to ultimate freedom?

A ghost or spirit who swims the length of the ancient river will find a narrow passage into a peaceful world, where earthquakes, volcanos, and forest fires no longer devastate and where assassins no longer slit throats in the night.

Wraith studies his hands. He sees the blood of human life drenching his palms. He inhales again. This time the stench of human fear and the metallic scent of blood assault his nose. What had he become?

Do I deserve a second chance?

"Yeshua, forgive me," he whispers. But neither forgiven nor unforgiven murderers deserve access into a kingdom of peace with the Prince of Peace. "Surely, you know that I never wanted this life, Lord. It found me, not the other way around. My freedom in exchange for killing." He wants to weep, but he doesn't dare show a sliver of emotion in front of his brothers-in-arms.

"I see you. This day you will be with me in paradise." Yeshua speaks the words deep inside Wraith's soul, uttering the same reassurance given to a humbled thief who faced imminent death on a Roman cross beside the Messiah—the Christ, the Son of the Living God.

Something more costly than a swim up an ancient river is required to access this alien kingdom where the Prince of Peace reigns.

Redemption is the key that unlocks the portal.

Hope surges inside Wraith's heart, and he whispers a tender message to his wife: "Daniela, *mo chridhe*, if time has run out for me, dinna be afraid of the river. Jump in, lass. I'll not be leavin' yer side. Ye'll not drown." His mother isn't present with her paddle or switch, so he fully unleashes his Scottish burr. "Weel not be swimmin' for long." He tucks a smile into his Celtic-Anglo-lips—thin, pink, and soft. "Weel walk on water beside the Master, across the splintered back of an old rugged cross—redemption's key."

Wraith pours the water from his canteen onto his hands and washes the invisible blood off. Somewhere inside his tangled web of thoughts, he hears a mezzo soprano, Natalie Grant, singing the forgiving words of "Clean."

An angel couldn't have sung the lyrics any better. The compassionate song soothes his frayed nerves. Swallowing hard, he glares at the chopper's door.

In a few minutes, the door will open.

It'll be okay.

Because there's nothing too dirty that He can't make worthy.

52—The Orphan

TIME CAN BE THE BEST of friends and the worst of enemies. She tells no lies, but eventually she reveals all secrets.

Since Wraith's teenage years, he had dreamed that he would marry his best friend—a mesmerizing woman who he could talk to and reveal his scars to without fear of mockery or disdain. He would show his strengths, protecting her in one moment, then caressing her tired body in the next.

"Boys and books don't mix" and "Armageddon before puberty" had been his parents-in-law's approach to teenage romance for their only child, Daniela Rose Cavanaugh.

"Thank you, Almighty One," he whispers. The short-sighted mantras planted in the soil of parental fear had failed to poison her destiny.

His Orphan Dreamer had grown up and become his Orphan Tree—with deep taproots nourished by Eternal love, anchoring their family during life's storms.

She had defied Claire Underwood's incessant harassment, eclipsed puberty, then found her oily boy—him—an abandoned orphan who had been forced into the underworld of human trafficking and eventually the life of an assassin.

Armageddon before puberty.

Yet puberty had come and gone.

Tonight, beyond the helicopter's door, Armageddon looms on Earth's horizon in the form of seven black MH-47s and MH-60s tailing Wraith's lead chopper.

In total, the choppers carry seven Orphans and sixty-five special-ops soldiers of the 75th Ranger Regiment and Delta Forces counterterrorism units.

"Ramp door!" the jumpmaster of bird one barks his command to the Orphans over the roar and whine of the helicopter's engine and blades.

Sakura, an Orphan born in China, slides the aircraft's door open. Her waist-length black hair has been secured into a bun.

Cold night air careens into the cabin, propelling stray pieces of paper and fabric into the blackness while chilling the tips of Wraith's ears. The thump of the rotor hammers in sync with the pulse of his heartbeat.

A skullcap, black face paint, and night-vision goggles shift him from loving father and doting husband to menacing character.

Desert camouflage masks his ghostly Black Irish features.

Black Irish.

What an oxymoron—an Irishman with the palest Caucasian skin, raven-black hair, and sky-blue eyes. He's a genetic rarity, according to his scientist wife. Something about genotypes and phenotypes.

He grins from ear to ear. His Danny Rose is the very definition of a nerd.

A bookworm.

A scientist.

A medical doctor.

Intelligent, and not stuck on racial ignorance. She defied her da's prejudices and let Wraith pour his cream into her coffee. His Daniela Rose chose to judge him on the content of his character, not the color of his skin.

She's proud of me.

Loves me.

Fights for me.

Lingering thoughts about her make his heart beat wild with a cacophony of emotions. He adjusts a black glove that fits snug over his left hand and hides an unsightly scar—Bushcroft's sadistic gift.

"Stand up!" The jumpmaster commands. Seven Orphans rise like phoenixes from the Arabian desert.

Strapped with over a hundred and fifty pounds of gear, each man's face is illuminated by the glow of ChemLights.

Each soldier's focus hard and unflinching.

Standing beside the jumpmaster, Wraith gazes beyond the open door into the nighttime abyss, seeing nothing except a bank of clouds that blots out the village below and erases the horizon. He flips his night goggles over his eyes, shading the landscape in a palette of fluorescent green. Little green men skitter across the ground.

Fast in.

Fast out.

F-15E Strike Eagle jets pace the skies above, each providing backup for his team in the form of four Lockheed Martin Raytheon AIM-9LM infrared-guided Sidewinder air-to-air missiles or a BLU-118/B Thermobaric Bomb—a grisly weapon that burns oxygen from the lungs of its victims, effectively flushing out ISIL fighters hidden deep inside mountain-cave networks.

Like a bald eagle, the lead chopper—his bird—swoops toward the ground. The other choppers follow.

The loss of altitude feels like bricks slamming into Wraith's gut.

It's go time.

Harnessed to his master's front, Spook's ears stand at attention.

Closing in on their target—a compound located near Barisha, Idlib, a province four miles from the Turkish border—Wraith mutters his last desperate prayer: "I've returned to the killing fields. I am what I am. This isna their fault, Yeshua. Take care of my wife and my Adelaide Rose." Cold dread drips from his voice.

He embraces Spook as he whispers a love letter to his wife: "I've been the ruthless one, pushing back the darkness so ye could be kind. Earth will be balanced, rotating on its axis because of yer compassion, Daniela, *a rún mo chroí*—secret of my heart."

Will the African currents carry his message in a jet stream across the Atlantic Ocean to the slopes of North America's Blue Ridge Mountains?

He kisses a sliver of pink silk that he had cut from his

wife's favorite nightgown, then lets it go, releasing their fate to the One who said "Let there be" . . . and then there was.

The void of night swallows the silk.

Wraith faces his team—the Orphans—the warriors that arrive when the Navy SEALs, US Rangers, or Delta Force dial 911.

"Watch your six!" Chad Prevington, the second jumper and Wraith's spotter, shouts into the sniper's ear.

He glares into the lethal eyes of the man standing behind him and shouts, "You're my HOG. That's your job, cowboy." More lethal than a male hog, a HOG is a hunter of gunmen—a sniper who has killed an enemy sniper in combat.

"I've got it." Chad nods, but a glint of deception skitters behind his gaze.

Wraith studies his spotter's face—the flat lines, the lack of expression. "I'm trustin' you, pig man. My wife's trustin' you."

Chad grabs his friend by the shoulders and kisses him hard on the right cheek.

Wraith pulls away.

Reality washes the warmth of blood from his face, leaving the fever. Before Yeshua's crucifixion, Judas betrayed his Master with a kiss. In a friendship, there's room for secrets but never lies. One lie could erase a million truths. Wraith's stomach sinks into his boot-clad feet.

How does it feel to be crucified?

The vicious flogging and the spike through the hand he already knew about. He curls his left gloved hand into a fist. *No respectable woman would want you caressing her in the night with a hand like that.* Bushcroft had been wrong. Wraith grins.

"Hook up!" the jumpmaster barks. *Go time.*

Wraith and his Orphans clip their parachutes' red static lines to a steel cable running above their heads. He strokes Spook's head. *It's me and you, old boy.*

Fur bristles beneath his touch. The dog wags his tail.

Gently, Wraith holds a cloth drenched with the scent of the doomed terrorist to Spook's nose. "You're a good boy," he reassures his military working dog. "Find." His voice falls sharp and succinct.

The Belgian-Malinois's hackles rise. Harnessed to the front of Wraith's muscular frame, the canine gazes up at his master and pants. A cautious smile settles on his master's lips. "You're a good boy," he says again.

"Thirty seconds." The jumpmaster summons the Orphans' attention once more.

Ten seconds later, a light by the door darkens to red. The jumpmaster starts counting down, "Ten . . . four . . . three . . . two . . . one." The hiss of the chopper's engine plays a haunting soundtrack to the night's events.

Time is a blind wench. Eventually she'll run into a brick wall, knocking out all who rely upon her.

Red light turns green. *Ready or not, here we come!* Wraith and Spook jump in tandem.

If he had known his ending, how would he have lived his beginning?

No time to answer the philosophical questions of his Orphan Dreamer.

Because tonight, al Baghdadi will die, and Wraith will be the terrorist's executioner. The ghostly assassin smirks as he faces the wind. An oxygen mask fitted over his muzzle, Spook pulls close to his master's reassuring and fatherly embrace.

Ghosts never die—that is, if they're even real in the first place.

After the Messiah—Yeshua—was betrayed by his friend and crucified, He had refused to stay dead. Neither Time nor Death could hold him in the grave.

Plain.

Definitely simple.

Put that in your pipe and smoke it.

Yeshua had risen from Death's grave, gifting to those humans who hear His truth—receive and accept it—eternity in a world where war, hatred, and death do not exist.

Wraith lands on the desert floor with a soft thud, gathers up his parachute, releases Spook, and gives the command again: "Find."

53—Orphan Dreamer

To the Stars, the Very End . . . Maybe
Gainesville, Florida

AFTER EMMALINE, MY KINDRED SPIRIT, lied to me during our hiking trip in the Jemez Mountains of New Mexico, she did penance for months afterward, helping me rebuild my trust in her. Tonight is my turn to do penance—but my crime is murder.

An hour ago, I left Adelaide Rose, my daughter, curled up in a ball, sleeping on our hotel's king bed near the University of Florida.

Ever since she returned from boarding school, she'd been exhausted. Her dad had been missing for weeks. We expected to find him alive, not mourn him.

I snuck out of the hotel room because I couldn't bear to tell her where I was going.

In time, when she learns the truth, she'll mourn

him—wailing, screaming, and punching walls for hours and hours. But not now. Five hours ago, I gave her a dose of melatonin. It always does the trick.

I inhale restricted airflow as a Florida Gator mask covers my nose and mouth.

A virulent strain of the virus that typically causes the common cold roams Earth once again, engineered to wipe out the untouchables of the world—people with brown skin, the disabled, and the elderly.

After President Sheldon Covington lost his most prized asset, the Wraith—my husband and fallen hero—he tried to cover up the fact that American military operatives were spying in Russia.

In order to sidetrack Russia's president, Sheldon orchestrated an elaborate ruse, welcoming home a fallen soldier's body and claiming it was my husband's. The body belonged to John Hanson, who had been KIA during a conflict in Afghanistan.

I sent orchids to his family.

Yesterday, Wraith's brothers-in-arms, members of Delta Force and the Orphans, returned Wraith's body from Russia—bruised, battered, and tortured. He had survived Afghanistan, but then Sheldon Covington had sent him on a mission to Siberia, Russia.

So here's my newest reality: a brain-dead husband cursed with a beating heart.

I gaze down at the midnight-blue snowflake inked onto my palm. Am I dreaming? If so, here we go again.

I grip the foot of my husband's hospital bed, holding on for the ride.

After nightfall, my husband's heart will no longer beat for me; his warrior's heart will beat for another: a middle-aged man widowed over a year ago. A man who lives as a hermit in the Alpine Lakes Wilderness of Washington—an isolated region dotted with smoky-blue lakes and evergreen meadows.

This is a place where the hermit thrush sings a haunting yet breathtaking song to the Creator who dusted the bird's breast in powdered silver, then said, "Fly."

Three thousand miles north and west of my location—in a cold, quiet hospital room—the hermit thrush warbles as it dives deep and then soars through a forest carpeted with Douglas firs and western hemlocks.

The middle-aged hermit waits in the same region where the silver-chested bird flies.

I'm also waiting.

Still dressed in yesterday's outfit, I stand stock-still straight at the foot of my husband's hospital bed.

Grief yanks my back muscles tighter than a piano's soprano wires. I clench the front of my lavender sweater. Hospital chill soaks through the cashmere and drenches my flesh with frosted sweat.

Rubbing my arms, I fail to warm my skin.

I wrap a hospital blanket around my shoulders and tuck my grandmother's patchwork quilt around Spook. The dog lays at his master's feet, waiting for a go command that will never come.

I cradle Spook, burying his head into my embrace. When I see a dog, I see the heart of God. Taking comfort in my companion, I stare at my husband, who looks so alone. Did he look like that as a child? Long before I'd met my husband, he existed as an orphan.

Unwanted.

Discarded.

Homeless.

Rejected and desperate for a place to belong. Yahweh created my heart to love this orphan, my oily boy.

My hands were destined to heal his heart and stop the bleeding. One snowflake fell from heaven and quenched his hell's thirst. I rest my trembling hands on the middle of my chest. "You belong here—forever, my darling." I grip his hand, then dare to remember our beginnings.

Tears run down my cheeks.

Quiet has replaced the steady and reassuring masculine Scottish burr spiced with a bit of Irish brogue that had once answered me while he lived.

"You were brave. Took chances. I-I-I was afraid—so afraid to believe. If I hadn't been so afraid, maybe you would have come to me sooner, and we would have had more time together. Forgive me." I pause. "You're safe now. No more torment or shame. I've been left behind to fight Lucifer's army, then swim the Jordan River without you." I force a fleeting smile across my face. "I'm not sure if I'm strong enough."

It's true: unbelief—the devil's most powerful weapon outside of discouragement and human slander—poisons the mind, delaying the arrival of life's gifts. But grace, God's undeserved favor, remains the antidote for unbelief. Still, His grace is sufficient for me, so even when I am weak, He is strong.

Numb, I gaze beyond the hospital room's square window.

It's almost time for the sacrifice.

Ironically, it's almost time for my least favorite time of the day.

Nightfall.

One question nags me: Does the hermit deserve the

benefit of my husband's sacrifice for his family, his country, and his God—the sacrifice of a man who was once a little orphan boy, my oily boy?

I recall Yeshua's words as He hung battered and bruised from that old rugged cross, then whisper my own prayer of forgiveness: "Abba, Father, forgive them. For they didn't know what they were doing."

Can I forgive my husband's assassin? I can, but do I want to? I don't even know who killed him after he left Afghanistan.

It's true that in time, a dark cocoon releases an apricot sulphur, and its butter-yellow wings cast flickers of hope against the gray.

A roost of bright-yellow butterflies flies past the lone hospital window. My mother always told me that butterflies are the heaven-sent kisses of an angel, and if a butterfly lands on your hand, it means that the spirit of a dead loved one lives on.

Heaven. Kisses. Legna. Legna's master, Yahweh—my Father. In this moment, I yield my oily boy's spirit to my God, my Daddy.

Then, through gritted teeth, I make a demand of the middle-aged hermit who waits for my oily boy's sacrifice— the man who lives three thousand miles away from where I'm standing with a brain-dead husband: "Earn this."

Hour after hour. Minute after minute. Second after second. He lies so still, so helpless.

Some people connect with you in their free time, and others free up the time to connect. Freeing up the time to connect had been my oily boy's legacy.

Spook and I continue to stare at the plastic tube attached to a ventilator that juts out from between my oily boy's lips, silencing him forever.

His breathlessness drains me of breath.

One flesh.

One heart.

One soul—one breath.

My body convulses with tremors of grief. I inhale a misted puff of oxygen emitted from the nasal cannula. Gingerly, I rest my hand over the middle of my oily boy's chest and close my eyes. "Just one more time . . . say you love me while I listen to your heartbeat."

Silence whispers an answer—*no, mo chridhe. Not this time.*

"It's okay, my darling. Your heartbeat sings the melody of our lives together." My words vanish into the algid, thin hospital air. "For Adelaide." I force a smile through chattering teeth. "For Earth's survival." I grit my teeth. "I will fight again."

My phone continues to play music. Sam Cooke's song about being born by the river in a little tent—"A Change Is Gonna Come"—plays through the Bose speakers. It was Cillian's favorite song to dance to. I embrace myself and sway to the soulful melody.

When, Yahweh?

When will this change come—the *good* pandemic, the one when Yeshua calls me home? Unlike Sam Cooke, I'm not afraid to die.

My oily boy's Malinois whines. I massage his neck. "I won't abandon you. I'll fight as long as I can. Promise. Then one day, you'll come home with Mommy to where the lion lies down beside the lamb; the place where your father and Kian live."

It's true.

I was born with two ovaries more stubborn than a mule, and both have refused to release one single viable egg, choosing instead to leak ovarian cancer's venom into my young and childless body. Pressing my hand into my belly, I flinch as I exhale.

I am barren.

But I am a mother.

Grateful, I whisper my daughter's name, and a slip of a smile pushes dimples into pools of saffron-tinted chocolate. "Adelaide Rose, my sweet girl. Mommy loves you." A lonely chill snakes up my back, leaving a trail of sweat and reminding me of my version of reality.

My perception: I am alone.

My truth: I am never alone. Because Yeshua said, "I will never leave you or forsake you."

Still, I fail to quieten my shivering frame.

I dare to remember Kian, my brave boy, then gaze down at his father's lifeless face, and my smile vanishes faster than sunshine at sunset. "Daddy's coming. Take care of each other." I wipe a tear from my face. "Your sister and I will be fine . . . just fine."

Know this. If I continue to fight this war—a battle that must be fought and won in order to save Earth's current occupants from complete extermination—my fight will be for my daughter's sake.

Not mine.

Not yours—not anymore.

I am exhausted.

I am disappointed with humanity—or the lack thereof.

One day soon, the moment after my Adelaide Rose hears and responds to the Master's call—*Come to me all of you who are heavy and are heavy burdened, and I will give you rest*—I will lay down my weapons and no longer fight for Earth's survival. And then the day of the Lord will come as a thief in the night, and the heavens will pass away with a great noise, and the elements will melt with fervent heat.

Today is the day of salvation, because the Rapture—the *good* pandemic—could happen in ten seconds, ten minutes, or ten years, so make your decision now.

Beyond the ICU room's glass door, nurses and doctors busy themselves in the corridors, patient rooms, and at the nurses' station.

Doctor Rogers, one of the intensivist doctors, passes my husband's hospital room, stops, retraces her steps, then tiptoes into the room. "Daniela." She hugs me. "Oops, social distancing." Mask over her lips and mouth, she awkwardly backs away.

"It's okay, Renee."

"You okay?"

"I'm fine." I'm lying, and we both know that I am. But there is no purpose in unravelling emotionally in front of an overworked, yet concerned colleague. "Have you eaten lunch, Renee?" Shift the focus away from me, from my story. I loathe the idea of being front and center—the story's protagonist.

"No."

"Not even breakfast?"

"Toast." She smiles with her eyes—amber brown and glistening with hints of youth and optimism—though a chronic lack of sleep leaves black shadows beneath them.

"A full English breakfast," Daniela jokes, and Renee laughs.

"We docs are constantly wading through a perpetual swamp of paperwork, worrying about our patients infected with that darn virus, and facing decreased payments while being expected to pay our staff. There's no time to take care of ourselves." She keeps talking to me, refusing to leave me alone, and I love her for this simple act of kindness.

"Eat something, Renee." I reach into my overnight bag and offer her a turkey sandwich topped with lettuce, asiago cheese, and stone ground mustard. "Take it."

"But—"

"Please. I made the sandwich this morning, and I don't have much of an appetite."

"I could eat my fist." She gobbles down the sandwich while I snuggle beneath the hospital blanket's embrace.

"You really are famished."

"You'd think that I'd be losing weight, not gaining flab." She massages her bat wings.

"Stress, lack of sleep, too many twenty-four-hour shifts at the hospital, and no time to exercise. It's the job." I take her sandwich wrapper and toss it into the trash can.

"Not a job—a calling. Why else would we choose to wade through a swamp infested with gators, mosquitoes, and snakes?"

"By mosquitoes and snakes, you mean hospital administration and the federal government?"

"Add a few malpractice lawyers and unrealistic patients to the mix and you've got the gators." She winks, and I smile.

"Finish your rounds, Renee. I'm okay. I'll see you later tonight. Then, go to sleep. Promise me!"

"After the honor walk, I'll sleep . . . if I can." Renee chews the last bite of sandwich. "I wouldn't miss your husband's honor walk for the world." She fidgets with the stethoscope wrapped around her neck.

"It's not the Chicago fair." I force a chuckle, realizing my comment may have come off sarcastic. I'm feeling edgy and tired. "I'm sorry. I didn't mean to snap at you." I count the linoleum squares between us.

"You're exhausted." She touches my arm. "We're not God, Daniela."

"Tell that to some of my patients."

"We have feelings too. Weak moments when we need to be cared for. And, Daniela, what you're doing tonight"—tears well up in her eyes—"is more important and more memorable than any World's Fair or—"

"I'm only honoring my husband's wishes. I'm no hero." I inhale, then sigh deeply. "He gave enough in life, Renee." Emotion seeps into my voice. I pause and steady my resolve. "Why does he have to give even more in death?" Words clam up inside my throat.

"Because someone needs his strength—his heart—in order to live. In life, he made this choice. You must honor it."

"He's dead, and now, I'll be living with the nightmares." I shake my head. "I'm tired of dreaming, traveling to lost worlds."

"I once heard a preacher say that if your dreams don't scare you, they're not big enough."

"Quotable but not entirely true." Daniela slinks back and forth like a caged tigress in the ICU room. "I hope the man living as a recluse in the forests of Washington is worthy of my husband's gift and appreciates receiving the last living part of my heartsong." Silently, I whisper my mantra: *In life, he dies, but in death, he lives forever.*

But mantras don't stitch up shredded hearts, only love does that, unconditional love—Yeshua's agape love. *Love me, Yeshua . . . I need to feel Your love all the way down in my toes.*

"Your husband was an extraordinary man." She flashes a quick smile. "A much better catch than my deadbeat ex."

"Was," my voice breaks. "*Was* is the part killing me." I cover my mouth with my hand and turn my back to my colleague, so she can't see my silent scream. I take a deep breath, then paint a fake smile across my face. "How is Howard?"

"Dead."

"As in six feet under?" A crease runs down the middle of my forehead as I glance over my shoulder.

"Is there any other kind?" She shrugs. "A heart attack killed him on his fiftieth birthday. I wasn't at home, so I couldn't perform CPR."

"I'm so sorry, Renee." Instinctively, I rest my hand on the center of my chest and look down at my heartsong. I wasn't there either.

"One of us had to actually go to work and pay the bills. More oxygen for the rest of us." She steps closer to me. "Don't judge me, Daniela. I once loved him, but our marriage wasn't like yours." She releases an exasperated sigh. "Every day equaled torture—a job with absolutely no vacation or sick leave."

"I understand."

"No, Danny Rose. You don't understand, but you don't have to. You have experienced a love so rare and precious." The warmth of her hand on my shoulder melts my heart, followed by a plaintive squeeze before the *click-clack* of her heels sounds across the linoleum floor as she runs away from her demons.

I stand alone with Spook at my side, cradling a Southwestern-inspired mug filled to the brim with my favorite brew. My hands tremble and my grip loosens, threatening to drop my Christmas present onto the hospital's unforgiving floor. Instead, coffee sloshes over the rim onto the floor. I take a knee and clean up my mess.

It is a pitiful way to die.

Shattered across a cold hospital floor where bacteria and viruses infest cracks and divots.

After I finish my clean-up job and catch my breath, I sit beside my oily boy, sipping the rest of my coffee. Blends of cocoa infused with hints of molasses, butterscotch, and a splash of pear drench my taste buds with holiday memories—memories of him and our happy family.

I study his face.

"Maybe this isn't real." I place the empty mug on the bedside table, then push back his pale, paper-thin eyelids. Fixed and dilated, black pupils have filled his irises, leaving little room for his natural pale-blue ones. I bite my lip until the metallic taste of blood seeps between my teeth. This is real, no different from the night Ethan died.

My oily boy's heart beats, but his brain is deader than my dreams.

It's your fault, Daniela Rose, a sinister voice ricochets off the haunted hallways of my mind, and World War III commences across the bloody battlefield of my vulnerable psyche.

Mistake number one: I agree with the voice.

Mistake number two: I punish myself even further, adding more verbal poison, half-truths, and guilt to the accusing voice.

"I didn't protect him. I was supposed to, but I didn't." Sweat beads up across my back. "I should have been praying—fighting on his behalf. I'm a failure. Unreliable. Undeserving of his love. He protected me. Both of you did, Yeshua," I cry out. "Fly."

Spook raises his furry head, opens his maw, and releases

a whine that threatens to disembowel me. He remembers this version of his living father as well.

"Lemon curds and stale milk, Spook!" I embrace the trembling dog. "Shh. Don't cry. We'll be okay. Promise. Mommy will keep you safe." In a friendship, there is room for secrets but never lies.

The truth.

I don't possess the strength necessary to keep Spook safe like my heartsong had done. He once took the brunt of a high-caliber round that ISIL militants had intended for Spook's chest. What father wouldn't think twice before taking a bullet for his orphaned puppy—a puppy he had raised to become a war dog and a loyal friend?

My breath eases. I stroke Spook's head and relish the simple act of breathing. "Together, we'll remember him." Voice raspy, I breathe in another puff of oxygen. "It'll ease the pain."

Spook's gaze asks: *Does remembering really make the pain go away?*

"It's worth a try." I cradle his left paw between my hands and kiss it. "Besides, didn't anyone ever tell you? Legends—like your father—are impossible to forget. Legends were created so we could remember the good of humanity and make sense of the world when inhumanity closes in around us."

The four-year-old Belgian Malinois rests his head on my heartsong's chest. Spook's usual happy and engaged expression registers listlessness, so I dig inside my knapsack and offer him his favorite homemade treat—peanut butter and pumpkin cookies.

He turns away.

Rejection barbs pierce my heart.

But this isn't rejection.

It's unrequited grief, and I understand grief. Talk to him. Like his father had when he was only a puppy and afraid of thunderstorms.

"You're a good boy, Spook." The military working dog pants while gazing into my eyes. A flicker of joy registers behind his chestnut irises. I'll tell you a secret. A human's appearance doesn't tell the whole story of where they come from. It's why bigotry based upon skin color is the science of the uneducated. "He's beautiful, isn't he?"

Spook gazes into his father's face as though he sees the same beauty that I see. "You see it as well." A rugged face chiseled from granite, then forged in pain. Spook whines.

I lie down beside my oily boy. Spook pushes his sixty-five-pound body into mine.

Nestled between two warriors, I am safe.

Spook rolls over onto his back.

Seconds later, he logrolls onto his stomach and lunges at my face. Shooting out his tongue faster than a king cobra, he kisses me directly on the mouth. He waits, panting, his eyes shining brighter than the moon as endorphins pulse through his body.

He's happy.

I'm happier. "That's such an oily boy move!" I slide my cashmere sleeve across my mouth, removing the dog slobber but not the love.

He spreads his maw into a canine smile, then rests his paw on my shoulder, sliding it up and then down, comforting me and telling me, *Love you, Mom.*

"Love you too." Giggling, I embrace my dog.

I trace the outline of the Glass Tattoo inked into my right palm, then sweep a stray black hair from across my oily boy's forehead.

"After our first night together, I was no longer afraid of

your father's raw physical power or his quiet mental focus, so I gave him another name: heartsong, the man for whom love songs had been penned. Still, he was created to be an African giant swallowtail, not an apricot sulphur."

Spook locks eyes with me and listens. I stretch out my arms. "Swallowtails have a wingspan of over nine inches, and their wings are painted blood-orange and rimmed in black. They possess no natural enemies, and their sleek skin contains a toxin. The swallowtail is a beautiful assassin."

Spook knows the rest of the story.

He was there. Plus, Charlie had called me and spilled the details.

Two days ago, after nightfall, my heartsong and six of his Orphans, accompanied by Rangers and Delta Force warriors, executed their assassination mission in the bowels of an underground tunnel carved beneath the North Syrian desert.

After Cillian gave the command, his team of Orphans detonated precision munitions, blowing three man-sized holes into the eastern wall of a booby-trapped tunnel before he and his team entered.

Wraith gave the go command.

Spook, equipped with high-tech cameras and a bullet-proof vest, hunted the terrorist through narrow and dark passageways until he cornered al-Baghdadi at a dead-end alcove. Two other military working dogs sniffed out additional booby-traps and hostile personnel. Delta Force and the Orphans followed.

The Orphans, including Cillian, flanked right.

Delta Force flanked left.

Rangers charged down the middle.

Trapped but not alone, al-Baghdadi—the self-proclaimed

Muslim caliphate and leader of ISIL—refused to face his enemies. Instead, the coward terrorist activated his suicide vest laced with more dynamite than threads and seams, obliterating his portly frame and the futures of two of his children.

Why must children pay for the sins of their parents? The war dog rests his paw in my hand. I cup it and kiss it. His war wound has healed.

Children dying at the hands of adults.

Why?

Where is the hope?

Where is the Prince of Peace in this crazy world?

The preacher says that joy comes in the morning, but when does morning come?

Harness the butterflies—my runaway thoughts. Morning comes at its appointed time: when the sun rises again.

In the morning after the mission, the Syrian desert sun rose, splaying rose-gold streamers across Earth's horizon. Our ailing planet's heart ticked slow and steady, matching the purposeful and metered beat of my brain-dead husband's pulse as he traveled home by helicopter. The military still refuses to tell me when, where, and who injured Cillian. *That is classified*, was the response from top brass.

"Bring his body back to me—to my hometown hospital. We'll do what's been asked of me here, not at Walter Reed." That was my only request of Lieutenant Colonel Ryker.

Body bruised.

Lungs ventilated.

Brain dead.

Yet . . . my heartsong's heart still beats.

The hospital room emits a quiet buzz broken up by the chirp of my heartsong's cardiac monitor.

Slow and steady.

Nuclear bomb detonators beep with the same cadence. A wry expression twists my face into something most likely hideous. I massage Spook's back. His muscles contract, then relax beneath my maternal touch.

54—Orphan Dreamer

AN ACHROMATIC SCALE OF PALE gray shades the pre-dusk sky as though the Creator is gifting me a blank canvas.

Paint a Renoir or a Monet, Daniela Rose. Give them something to talk about.

"When they see my heartsong's scars, they'll have plenty to talk about. Gossip will roar through the corridors of the community hospital of my hometown like a one-legged tsunami riding a bullet train." I laugh, and a spark of happiness ignites within.

Suddenly my weight involuntarily shifts as though I'm standing on a bed of marbles.

I stumble forward. Rhythmic vibrations jar the room. What's this? An earthquake in Florida? I peer through the glass door facing the nursing station. Nurses sit at their computers, charting, talking, and laughing.

Nothing is amiss.

Yet I can feel rhythmic waves vibrating the room like a portly belly jiggles during a belly laugh. *He's laughing.* The Creator of the universe laughed at my pathetic joke. But why not? It's a fact: adoring fathers take pleasure in their daughters' joy.

Cradled inside his dog bed, Spook rolls onto his back. "He's laughing too." A jagged scar that zigzags down the middle of his belly expands and contracts as he laughs. The scar tells its own story.

I trace the lightning bolt scar with my forefinger.

Soldiers fight battles. Battles inflict scars. "Scarred and battered, you and your father understood each other." The Belgian Malinois snaps to attention, sits on top of his doggy bed, and pushes his deep chest forward. "You were born to fight." The military working dog whines. "But this battle isn't yours."

Spook wags his tail. *Mom, take me with you.*

"I wish you could fight beside me. You're dependable, a friend who sticks closer than human friends. But this war is a human war. We're fighting for our humanity, and we won't win this battle with conventional weapons."

Spook tilts his head.

"This war requires a powerful weapon, and most humans are too proud to wield it." I sigh, then wink at Spook. "Just be my friend. I'll need one."

The war dog glares at me. His gaze softens as he slowly wags his tail. In my deepest sea of motives, I believe that my husband's murderers don't deserve a merciful death. A violent shudder rattles my frame.

Exit the graveyard. There's nothing here except dead bones. Shift gears. Now! Before it's too late.

Thoughts precede actions, Danny Rose. Capture your thoughts.

"Yeshua, help!" My voice grates with raw emotion. "I don't want to murder anyone, not even in my thoughts. Send someone. Anyone. I need to talk to a person, not a dog. Don't let me cycle down into the abyss of depression—not now. Please. Not before the honor walk. Touch my heart. Stop the bleeding."

A miracle saunters around the corner, opens the glass door, and strolls into the room.

"Chad Prevington."

"That's my name, Daisy Rose." My husband's brother-in-arms, his spotter, and a member of the special-ops team—the Orphans—enters the room and stands beside me. "Good to see you."

"Thank God! You're here." I slip my arm into the crook of his.

"I'm here. You're not alone." He kisses my forehead. "Not anymore. How's my brother?" He looks down at his brain-dead brother-in-arms.

"He's swimming home, following the Master through the Jordan River."

"Then he'll be alright. Always was a strong swimmer. And if he tires of swimming, the Shepherd will help him walk on water like Peter. Jesus flexes like that." Chad flashes a wholesome country-boy grin.

I blossom, briefly opening my heart to every possibility. "Yea, though I walk through the valley of the shadow of death, I will fear no evil for thou art with me; thy rod and thy staff they comfort me . . ."

Chad recites the rest of Psalm 23 with me.

But then a thought goes through my mind. "While walking on water to Jesus, Peter began to sink beneath the waves."

"He called for help, and immediately Jesus snatched him from under the waves. Daisy Rose, Peter's faith was not in his feet, it was in Jesus's hand.

55—Orphan Dreamer: It's Nightfall

DUSK YIELDS TO NIGHTFALL, CASTING shadows across the dimly lit hospital room. Beyond the room's bank of windows, two hundred billion stars form a posse and chase the sun's warmth and light out of town.

But as always, the sun whispers over its shoulder, "Goodnight, Danny Rose" and swipes a kiss with painted lips of golden lavender across Earth's horizon, then skitters down the backside of the western sky—out of sight and out of mind, leaving a swath of shadows and darkness for those eager to get on with their diabolical plans. Namely, one man and his posse: Asher Bushcroft and his Sons of Venus.

Chad Prevington stands to my right.

Exhausted, I inhale a ragged breath, smelling the man before I see him. A veil of flowers—much too floral a scent for a man—trails behind him like Princess Diana's wedding veil, drowning my olfactory nerves.

I glance over my shoulder.

Alive and in the flesh, the wickedly handsome and small-statured Asher Valerian Bushcroft strolls into the room singing a strange tune: "If I could be a minnow, minnow, minnow. If I could be a minnow, I'd swim out to the deep blue sea." He then leans against the hospital room's doorframe behind Chad and me. A smirk creeps into the corners of his well-proportioned lips, and at the corners of gray-blue eyes, crow's feet scrape delicate lines into his tanned skin.

Tell me that I'm dreaming.

No, this is no dream!

"He struts into my husband's hospital room wearing a ten-thousand-dollar suit," I whisper to Chad, "but he can't afford to buy a sliver of shame." Bile rises in my throat, and I ball my hands into two pathetic, tiny fists.

"Are those for me, Miss Cavanaugh?" Bushcroft points at my fists.

"It's Doctor Cavanaugh or Mrs. Finn-Barry to you."

"So many aliases. One would think you were a spy."

Chad reaches for my hand, uncurls my fist, and clasps my frigid fingers inside the warmth of his bear paws. "I'll do the fightin', darlin'. Put down roots, Daisy Rose." He swaggers toward the intruder, dwarfing the five-foot-something man with his over six-foot frame.

Chad's facial muscles tense ever so slightly. His wheat-colored eyebrows slant downward, almost brushing the ridge of his freckled nose. He shifts his weight and smiles at Bushcroft. Bushcroft dodges past Chad and inches toward me.

"You're a daisy if you do."

Chad's warning stops Bushcroft dead in his tracks.

In tone, accent, and cadence, Chad's voice mimics Val Kilmer's portrayal of Doc Holiday in *Tombstone*. But he isn't acting. Roots planted deeper than hundred-year-old palms growing in Georgia's red clay, Chad Prevington is a Southerner, polite but meaner than a rattlesnake if disturbed.

Dressed in a taupe duster, plaid shirt, and denim Wranglers, he looks every bit the part. The only prop missing is an old Winchester double-barreled shotgun—a weapon the Second Amendment was written for—slung across his right shoulder with his forefinger resting on the trigger.

"Last time I checked, Mister Prevington . . ." Bushcroft grins, flashing a hedgerow of bright white teeth. "America is still a free country. Besides, where's your loyalty to the leader extraordinaire of the Orphans—the protectors of American freedom?"

Leader extraordinaire? Who calls themselves that? I roll my eyes. More like Satan's sadist.

"I give my loyalty to those who've never made me question theirs." Chad allows his accusation to sink in.

"You're making such a fuss over him." Bushcroft tips his head toward my brain-dead husband. "Yet there's nothing left of him except a bag of skin and bones."

"And muscle."

"But not enough to get up and be of use."

"He'll always be with us."

"No, Mister Prevington. The Wraith ghosted you, and that's that, but wraiths usually disappear, so what's new?

'There's no time to change your mind. The Son has come, and you've been left behind.' " He sings the theme song of *A Thief in the Night,* a 1970s movie about Earth after Christians are raptured, then resumes his verbal taunting. "He was abandoned, just like your mommy and daddy left you in a rickety station wagon while they shot up meth. I saved you, Chaddy-boy. How does that make you feel?" Bushcroft crosses his arms. Muscles flex beneath polished wool.

"Jealous . . . of my parents."

"I can make you disappear, Doc."

"Try it."

"Is that a challenge?"

"It's a request."

"You're an orphan, no different than him." Bushcroft points to my oily boy. "You're both disposable—replaceable."

"And you're a broken record. I've met some pricks in my life . . ." Smirking, Chad rotates a silver coin between his forefinger and middle finger. "But you, sir, are a cactus."

"Cacti evolved to survive the heat of hell. What about you, Prevington?" Shoulders back, Bushcroft struts from the room, leaving his scent of wildflowers behind.

A peacock could take lessons on catwalking from that man.

Every square inch of my one-hundred-and-five-pound frame throbs. I dare to blink. A drip of emotion moistens the corners of my eyes, belying my feigned bravery. Sour milk and mushrooms! I hate crying over rude people.

"Don't cry, Daisy Rose. Not here." Chad rests his arm around my shoulder. "Not in front of the cactus."

"Daisy Rose," I whisper to myself. Chad's got a thing with flowers too. Each year for my heartsong's birthday,

Chad would deliver a dozen red roses mixed with white and yellow daisies.

But he's right. Weeping in front of Asher Valerian Bushcroft would be a fatal mistake. Sharks smell blood, but the soulless fish really lusts for tears, because tears usually represent fear.

Sadists exist on fear.

Relishing the salty taste of his homeland—the ocean—Bushcroft plays with his victims before the kill.

I can handle death, but not a prelude of taunts.

"It's nightfall." I lean against Chad and tug my sweater together in the middle. His arm isn't as muscular as my oily boy's, but Chad was and still is just as deadly.

"Nightfall. She's all shadows and secrets, but nothing to be afraid of." He fingers his handlebar mustache. "She's quite lewd, actually."

"Or mysterious." I chuckle. "Nightfall used to be my least favorite time of day."

"What changed?"

"I met him." I point to my heartsong, noting the quiet serenity etched across his chiseled face.

"He quelled your fears in the dead of night like any good husband should?" Chad winks at me.

I ignore his insinuation. "He understood them. Didn't judge me because of them, then gave me the time to heal. He was my heartsong—my essence, my kindred spirit." I clear my throat, pouring wet concrete into my weakening voice. Forget about crying, there's no time. It's time to buck up and fight.

"You created a family—Kian and Adelaide. Something my ex and I never did."

"Do you regret that?"

"I do."

"I'm sorry. I wish life was fair." An earthquake of emotion rocks my body, pulverizing the concrete and steel foundation of my bravery into dust.

"We all make our choices."

"True." Kian looked like an eight-year-old version of his father, and Adelaide . . . well, she's breathtaking. "Our little bunch of kindred spirits." I wrap my arm around Chad's waist. "You've lost weight. Why?"

"Stress."

"Why don't you retire from the Orphans? You're one of us. Adelaide and I are your family, especially because Cil's gone. Don't allow stress to win."

"You're sweeter than pecan pie, always have been so kind to me, Daisy Rose." He pecks the top of my beanie—a rose pink crocheted number that hides my bald head. "Knowing you both has been the honor of a thousand lifetimes. Life's given me way more than I deserved."

Seconds vanish into the quiet eternity of minutes. Nurse Jocelyn, my heartsong's ICU nurse, enters the room. My heart skips a beat and then another before deciding to keep up the mundane task of delivering blood to my tissues.

"Good evening." I flash a meager smile.

"Good evening, Doctor Cavanaugh. We're going to start getting him ready. First, I'll check and flush all the lines, suction his endotracheal tube, then give him a chlorhexidine bath. Would you like to stay or leave?"

"We'll stay." I close my eyes. *Wake me up, Yeshua. Let this be nothing more than a nightmare.* I open my eyes. My heartsong is still lying in his hospital bed—brain-dead and vulnerable.

Reality sucks lemon-drop sours.

As though sensing my distress, Chad squeezes my shoulder, then says in a calm Southern twang, "That day,

Daisy Rose . . ." His baritone voice teeters on the edge of a fault line beyond which a cauldron of untouched and dark emotions rage. "I begged the good Lord to take me instead."

"Survivor's guilt mauls more savagely than a bear. It's okay that you're still here, Chad. I'm not angry with you."

"But I am, and the good Lord didn't listen to me, no different from my ex-wife."

"He's listening, but Yahweh still must have work for you to accomplish." Standing straighter than a ballerina, I hold my breath as Nurse Jocelyn prepares to suction my heartsong's endotracheal tube.

Will he cough due to the tracheal stimulation? If he does, he's not brain-dead. There's hope.

She suctions.

He doesn't flinch or gag. Brain-dead people don't gag. *Accept reality, Danny Rose.* Again, I rest my head on Chad's shoulder. "Whether you retire or not, finish his legacy—assassinate the antichrist, Chad. Promise me."

"How can a mere man fill the shoes of a giant?"

"He grows."

"Or he stuffs both feet into one shoe and then stumbles over himself." Chad chuckles and wipes his hand across his forehead.

I glance up at Chad, my human anchor. "He never sucked up the oxygen in the room." My voice cracks. "He never spoke when not necessary and always left before his welcome ended."

You've outstayed your welcome on Earth, Daniela. End it—now! A devilish voice shrieks across the battlefield of my mind.

I listen, then act. Intentional and with purpose, I hold my breath, but lungs riddled with idiopathic pulmonary hypertension defy my pitiful attempt at suffocation while standing. The effects of hypoxia reach my brain stem faster than lightning strikes the ground, triggering an involuntary gasp for breath.

I've tried before, but I can't die on my own terms. Then again, why should I be able to? I didn't create myself, so why should I be able to destroy myself?

To live is an act of courage. Yahweh will decide when and where to pull the plug.

Chad glances down at me. "Refusing to breathe . . . it's still deadly, Daisy Rose." A cowboy's smile spreads across his face. "Flowers clean the air, sucking up pollution and gifting the rest of life with oxygen when they breathe. Keep on breathin', Daisy Rose. We need your breath."

"Living without my sunshine, I'm not going to be a healthy photosynthesizer."

"You're such a nerd." He chuckles. "It's true. You may feel weak, but you're not, and sacrifice remains quite necessary for Earth to keep on spinnin'." Chad adjusts his ten-gallon cowboy hat.

"Understood." Gingerly, I find his gaze. "Tell me about the mission. Why did my sunshine have to die?" Yep, I'm using Emmaline's deceptive tactics. Deception for the purpose of finding the truth. Will his story corroborate Charlie's?

"Sacrifice."

"Cliché."

"But the act defines the truest American spirit, and it defined our last mission." Chad salutes his brother-in-arms. "Sacrifice is the steel in our bones, the heartbeat of this great land, and its blood courses through the veins of any real American. It's coded into our DNA. The act of sacrifice stamps the pages of our past and hopefully our future, but less so our present."

"You believe that Americans are more selfish now?"

"Many are, and if this country is to survive, she must be populated with those willing to sacrifice instead of just take."

"My ancestors sacrificed their dignity and even their lives while clearing the path for me to pursue life, liberty, and happiness."

"You've done the same, so don't give up now, Daisy Rose. United we stand, divided we fall." Quietness hangs between us. "Where do your people hail from, Daisy Rose?"

"Everywhere." I shrug. "I'm a mutt."

"The intelligent ones usually are. Inbreeding never did much for the brain or looks. Ever seen a Habsburg jaw?"

"Poor guy."

"At least he was a king, so people couldn't tell him what they really thought."

"Motives—the peasants were afraid the king would order the executioner to lop off their heads."

"Motives," Chad says. "Tricky buggers."

Nurse Jocelyn removes my heartsong's green hospital gown and covers him with a clean sheet. She rips open a plastic package containing chlorhexidine gluconate-soaked cloths, then begins to bathe my husband's bruised and battered body.

My God, what did they do to him? I want to look away, but I refuse to obey my internal fears. Lower lip trembling, I answer Chad's question. It's my turn to make nervous small talk. "M-m-my Irish grandmother escaped the Irish famine."

"Then the blood of the Irish courses through your veins the same as his."

"Yes . . . My Cherokee forefathers walked the Trail of Tears," I say, sniffling hard, "and my African ancestors crossed the Atlantic Ocean, packed like sardines inside a slaver's wooden tomb." The room quietens as though some unspoken burial of the past is taking place.

"Daisy Rose . . ."

"Yes?" My voice comes small and timid.

"I didn't put 'em in shackles, but I'm sorry my ancestors did."

"Why bring this up now? Slavery wasn't your personal sin."

"When my grandmother died, leaving me an orphan, people talked about the strangest things at her funeral." Chad nervously smiles.

"They were contemplating their mortality."

"You're right, and I'm thinking about taking the long walk down that dusty road leading into a sunset that will never turn into a sunrise again." He faces his friend. "Daisy Rose, I've benefited from America's history of discrimination, and sometimes I still do."

"You're so . . . honest, and I respect you for it. Thank you."

"Any pale-skinned American who says they don't benefit from systematic discrimination is either inbred or just plain tone-deaf. The system of slavery and peonage in this great country is one of its greatest sins. I acknowledge that. Every continent that my ancestors landed on, they brought death to the natives." His voice falls off into oblivion, so I fill in the silence.

"Guilt doesn't heal the victims. The emotion's quite useless, actually. Maybe even destructive."

"Then, what does a white man with a conscience do to ease the shame—the regret, the plain embarrassment?"

"Compassion, coupled with passion."

"Both of 'em?"

"One without the other is useless, like a car without an engine and an engine without a car. It's the desire to understand the other side, not feel sorry for them. We must acknowledge the challenges—not endlessly rehash them— then make a plan for reconciliation, together."

"I can do that."

"Is not repentance turning around and going a different way? Repentance, not guilt, is the salve that heals the atrocities of any savage part of history."

"Do unto others as you would have them do unto you. The Golden Rule."

"You choosing to be here with me defines the Golden Rule. You're in good practice."

"You're a rose." He wraps his arm around my shoulder.

"A rose bush or just a rose? Rose bushes bear thorns."

"Thorns meant to protect delicate velvet petals from probing strangers." Chad strokes Spook's head as Nurse Jocelyn finishes washing my heartsong's legs, then moves up to his torso.

"My ancestors were not all saints. A few of them bore more thorns than roses too."

"You don't say." A big ol' Georgia-peach smile spreads across his face.

"I am also descended from one of the world's most ruthless conquerors, Genghis Khan."

"One of the most successful conquerors in the history books. A lord of the Earth, according to Nietzsche."

"Should we really trust Nietzsche's philosophies?"

"Probably not."

"Onto a happier note . . . speaking of memories, during our night patrols, Wraith never stopped talking about Mongolia."

"What did he say?" Spook focuses his attention on Chad as well, then pulls back his lips, revealing his teeth. "It's okay," I say, patting Spook's head. The dog relaxes.

"A determined lad will hunt for a desert's secret oasis until he finds it, drinks, and quenches his thirst," Chad says in a faux Gaelic accent, repeating my heartsong's romantic sentiments.

"Was I his desert oasis in Mongolia?"

"You were his waterfall, running wild and free."

"I love that song by Chris Tomlin."

"You and your music. Cil said, 'If ye believe me about an oasis hidden in a barren land,'" Chad continues his really bad Scottish burr, "'then ye'll be trustin' me again, Chad. It's true that snowflakes fall in the desert, filling secret valleys with life givin' water.'" Chad smiles. "I challenged him to prove it."

"Did he prove his theory?"

"An hour before the bullet ripped into his pelvis, he said to me, 'One hellish summer, a delicate snowflake fell for me, my Daniela Rose—*rún mo chroí*, secret of my heart. She quenched my desert thirst.'"

A faint smile creases my lips. "I'll tell you a secret."

"Pray tell."

"Snowflakes melt faster in heat, Chad."

"I'm an orphan, and it's colder than Alaska in this room. Do I stand a flippin' chance?" Chad brushes against me, closing the gap as his piercing gaze lingers longer than it should.

I avert my eyes and study the white tips of my tennis shoes—again. He faces me, then gently cups my chin with his right hand. "We're not that different, Daisy Rose. Take away the Mongols. Add a few Scots. We're 'bout the same."

"None of us are that different at the DNA level, but that doesn't mean I can marry any and every man in the world."

"Didn't ask you to. I'm not everyone or anyone. I'm someone—a man who's admired you from a distance for years."

"Admiration is the gutsiest form of flattery, but flattery doesn't mend shattered hearts." I walk to my heartsong's side, then hold his hand. "I'm not ready to love like this again."

Chad's face flushes red. He readjusts his hat, hiding a bit more of his forehead.

"I'm part English, as well." I break the silence. "My English ancestors traveled on the Mayflower, escaping the yoke of the British crown while seeking religious freedom in the New World. Then on July 4, 1776, they signed the Declaration of Independence and cast their chains off forever."

"Let freedom ring. Daisy Rose . . ." He stands next to me.

Two additional nurses dressed in bright red scrubs enter the ICU hospital room. Each wears a backpack slung onto their slight shoulders. One holds an ice cooler marked with the telltale biological hazard symbols—the collection basket for my late husband's generous offering.

Offering time.

Pass the plates.

The clock is ticking. *Do something!* I demand of my brain-dead husband. *Show me that you're still alive.*

Chad sits in the pleather chair stationed at my heartsong's right side. The pink flush of blood drains from his face, leaving a sickly sallow green. Even an anchor can rust. He's losing his steely courage.

"You okay?"

"Give me a flash."

"Okay." I pour him a glass of water, deliver it, then lean against the wall.

After bravery returns to Chad's demeanor, he says, "Wraith stamped his legacy on the hearts of the next generation—his children."

"Did you know that a fifty-five-foot-deep foundation supports the Empire State Building, yet the steel and concrete never asks to be seen? Without fanfare, he poured their foundations, securing their future."

"You, the kids, Paul, and America gave him a second chance—a redemption of sorts, and he loved you all for it. No matter what Professor Jakob's letter accuses him of."

How did he know about the professor's letter?

Chad notes my curious face and explains, "Wraith showed me a copy of the letter, wanted to know what I thought. If you don't believe me, I have a copy with me."

"Let me see it," I demand, and Chad removes the letter from his wallet.

My Darling Rosebud,

I need your help.

The approaching four blood moons and Jewish holidays are related. The four lunar eclipses coincide with Passover and Sukkot in 5775—the Gentile dates of March 2014–March 2015.

The year 5775 will be big; it is the start of the final countdown.

Your interest in and perspective of my traditions and culture make sense to me now. You possess a mission given by YHVH. To ensure your success, find Ezekiel's blueprint of the final temple and the Ark of the

Covenant; they will be useful as you fulfill your mission. The rebuilding of the third and final Jewish Temple is a clock in its own right. Has its rebuilding not been prophesied at the end of all ends? Follow your Mongolian ancestors' footsteps to the lost tomb of Genghis Khan. There you will find your treasure—the blueprint, the Ark, and the treasure of the Copper Scroll.

Your heartsong possesses espionage ties and swims in a sea of liquid gold. Blood stains his hands and cries from the ground. The statue is the key that solves the mystery of who?

B'shalom,
Professor Jakob
Director of Israel Antiquities Authority

"Talk about not keeping secrets. Sheesh!" Suppressing a growing unease, I recall the details of Professor Jakob's letter. *Your heartsong possesses espionage ties and swims in a sea of liquid gold. Blood stains his hands and cries from the ground.*

"They say music heals a broken heart, and mine's about ripped to shreds watching these nurses hover over my best friend's bed like vultures sniffing for a cadaver."

My face flushes with embarrassment. "I apologize, Jocelyn."

"It's not necessary," Jocelyn says. "I've loved listening to your memories of Mister Barry. He is—I mean was—one fine man."

"He was a fighter, tenacious about protecting America's Constitution." Chad removes a folded American flag from its protective covering.

"My son joined the army. Some days, I wish he hadn't." Nurse Jocelyn looks up from her duties of giving Cillian a bed bath. "America's citizens are so entitled, and our government leaders are so full of themselves, believing they're the owners of human destiny, deciding every single detail of our lives."

"I wouldn't trust the US Congress on both sides of the aisle to run my drinking water, much less the details of my life," Chad quipped. "The rise of socialism in America, whether National Socialism or Communist Socialism, would equal the biggest betrayal of the citizens of this great union—and that's what Cillian believed, and that's why he fought."

"He never wanted his kids to be anyone's slaves, like he had been," I say. Jocelyn pauses, then continues the longest Chlorhexidine scrub ever.

"I didn't know that you knew," Chad whispers back.

"How couldn't I have known? I made love to him." I tilt my head. "I loathed the feel and look of his scars, but I adored him for surviving."

Nurse Jocelyn's hands tremble. "I'm done with his bath, Doctor Cavanaugh. Are you ready for us to wheel him down to the operating room?"

"Give me a bit of time." I walk to my heartsong's side. "Jocelyn . . ."

"Ma'am?"

"What's the recipient's name?"

"Normally we don't tell the donor's family." The older of the two nurses clutching backpacks adds, "The transplant surgeon has arrived. I just received the text."

"Okay. Just five minutes." With trembling hands, I trace the starfish-shaped scar that mars his left hand. Evidence of the rusty spike. As I perform my ritual, he lies deathly still. I hold his hand and hide his scar from any onlookers beyond the glass. I massage a patchwork of scars at the base of his neck.

Chad watches as I say goodbye to my heartsong—the man whom love songs had been written for. The man who loved me as I was—nosebleeds, big hair, and disorganized thoughts. His mouth comforted me. His touch calmed and awakened me. I gaze at his lips, willing him to speak to me one last time.

After the surgical team harvests his organs, will my colleagues notice his scars? Will they gawk? Will they recoil? Will they ask questions?

No.

We are professionals. We see, but we don't really see—at least not to remember.

Chad glares across the hall at Bushcroft. The small-statured man has taken up residence there, flanked between two male nurses. Other healthcare providers, military personnel, powerful politicians—including the First Lady—and plainclothes members of Delta Force and the Orphans gather for my oily boy's honor walk.

"Promise me, Daisy Rose." Chad grips my arm as he looks toward the gathered politicians. "Don't vote for Sheldon Covington, whatever you do."

"Why?"

"He's a mole."

"Really?" Nurse Jocelyn glances at me, trying to read my face and silently asking if I'm okay. I flash a smile, showing her that I'm fine.

"Promise me, Daisy Rose." Chad's face registers something dark and moody. "Do. Not. Vote for him."

"I thought you were riding the Sheldon train?"

"I am . . . being on the train doesn't mean I don't want to get off."

"If you were going to vote for him, why shouldn't I? Who's the alternative?"

Chad glances at the nurses who have become nothing more than Nosey Nellies. He leans in, and I can smell his breath—a mixture of cherry tobacco and eggs. "You."

"Me?" I burst out laughing.

"Yes—you."

"I've lived as the Orphan Dreamer for more than thirty years. I'm tired of all it: the pandering, the patronization, the politics. The lies. Celebrities weighing in on the common Joe's life and vice versa. I'm close to being done—forever."

Suddenly, a redhead whose cheeks are splashed with freckles appears inside Cillian's hospital room. "Adelaide Rose, my darling." I reach for her, but my hand goes through air. "Adelaide!" I frantically search high, low, behind me and in front. "Adelaide, where you are you? Please. Come to Mommy. "It's time to honor Daddy." I reach for a hand, but she never grabs mine.

Fingers dig into my arm. I look up into the pale-blue eyes of Chad Prevington. His expression says everything—I've lost it. "Daisy Rose. She's not here. Okay?"

I nod. "I thought I saw her."

"Go see your psychiatrist. Promise me."

"Still want me to run for president?" I smile weakly.

"Schizophrenia. Dementia. Narcissism. Pathological lying." Chad shrugs. "I'd take the schizo Orphan Dreamer any day." He hugs me, then releases.

"Thanks for the backhanded compliment." I cross my arms, protecting my heart. "Democrats. Republicans. The parties are nothing more than fake realities. You don't get it. Neither do they. The statue tells the background story of *who*."

"Who is he?"

"You don't need to know, but you'll find out when the rest of the world does—if I don't stop him."

"Go see your doctor, Daisy Rose."

"I'm fine. This is real, and you know it."

"Okay. Okay. Is *who* President Covington?"

"No. But tell me: what mission to Siberia did Sheldon send my husband on?" I lock eyes with Chad. He's hiding something. My gut twists into knots, confirming my suspicion. "Tell me the truth."

"Ask Covington's wife—Claire." A harshness ruffles his tone around the edges. "She's standing right there." He tips his head toward the glass door.

"She isn't the brightest tool in the shed, so asking her promises no sensical answer."

"A zebra's stripes never disappear. The animal ages, the stripes sag, then spread. That's all."

"A lovely visual."

"Claire Underwood Covington is still a bully."

"And a genius at manipulation and betrayal. I should know."

"Remember this. Liars are dangerous, and women can make their egotistical men feel invincible. She's dangerous, and so is her buddy."

"Who's this buddy of hers?"

"The cactus. Asher Bushcroft. The commander in chief of the Sons of Venus."

"What do Bushcroft's Sons of Venus really want?"

"That's easy. A leader for their cause—an antichrist . . . the Wraith."

"He's dead."

"Is he?"

"Stop it!" I massage my temples while sucking in ragged breaths.

"Daisy Rose, they need someone to execute their new world order, another Tower of Babel. Your Bible's one-world government."

"I'm tired, especially of your riddles." I shuffle close to the familiar and kiss my heartsong's cheek, then hold his hand. I see Adelaide standing at her father's side, and she's crying. "Do you want to say goodbye, Adelaide?"

"No." Her face contorts into an expression more hideous than a gargoyle's.

"Sit down. I'll walk with your dad alone."

"Thanks, Mummy."

"Daisy Rose, who are you talking to?" Chad inches closer.

Ignoring him, I whisper to Cillian, "Yeshua waits for you, Cillian Joseph Barry-Finn. Swim the Jordan—I'll be right behind you." I release my husband's hand, and Chad sniffles behind me. I turn and face him. "It's time. Time to let him go."

"I hate that it's come to this. But you need to rest, Daisy Rose."

"Tonight, we honor my heartsong. He fought for the right to exist as an individual, and we honor his courage." I swallow my fears. "I can handle the truth, so tell me. Who assassinated him, Chad?"

Chad Prevington ignores my question again. Instead he unfurls, then drapes an American flag across my husband's washed and gowned body, then looks at me. Regret flickers behind his hazel eyes.

I step backward.

His gaze darkens. "I'm your huckleberry, Daisy Rose." A hail of thorns pierce my heart.

"Jocelyn." I can't catch my breath. "Might you nurses please give us a few more moments?"

"Of course, Doctor Cavanagh. We'll be back for your husband in ten minutes." The ten-minute countdown begins. Monitors beep, high-pitched and regular, as though they're bombs set to explode in exactly ten minutes.

"You killed him?" If I were a dragon, I'd spew fire and burn Chad Prevington's beautiful face to a char. I clench my abdominal muscles, bracing for his answer.

"That's my game."

"He was your friend." Steel laces my voice.

"No, Daisy Rose. You're wrong—"

"Don't ever call me that again. The name's Daniela!"

"He was more than a friend."

"You think I've lost my marbles?"

"He was my brother." His voice falters. "He was all that I had left in this godforsaken world."

"Then why?" My entire body shakes the floor beneath my feet. "Lots of people have friends and even brothers, but they don't murder them unless they're jealous or just plain stupid."

"I'm no Cain. He's no Abel. You saw the scars, right?"

"You know the answer to that question. I was his wife!"

"We called him Wraith, but he's no ghost. He's made of flesh and blood, and he can feel pain."

"Your point?"

"I couldn't let that beast torture him again, so I gave him all that I had left."

"And what's that? A bullet to the gut?"

"Mercy."

"Do you expect me to thank you?" I shift my weight away from Chad Prevington. He's no longer my anchor, but a lead noose that threatens to suffocate me while I drown in grief's stormy seas. I clench my husband's cool feet with clammy hands. *Wake up!* I scream on the inside. *Before they take your warrior's heart. Fight with me. Avenge your blood.*

"I promised him that I had his six."

"More like six feet under."

"He would have done the same for me." Chad snorts down a nose full of snot, then walks to the foot of the bed and rests his hand on my back. Judas Iscariot's touch would have been less revolting.

I recoil. "What's wrong with you? Have you gone plum crazy? Don't touch me."

"Please, Daniela. Don't reject me. He knew about murder. It's what he did when he wasn't making money on Wall Street, giving you a posh life."

"I'm not naïve, or a hypocrite. I know what he did, but I made my own money and then spent my own money. I'm not a kept woman. Plain. Definitely simple." Tears cascade down my face.

"I'm sorry."

"And you think that I'm crazy."

For five minutes I can't swallow, much less speak, but time is running out. Two minutes left. "He never killed for fun. He only assassinated the bad guys, America's enemies."

"America's enemies are someone else's brother, sister, mother, or father."

"You're not consistent, Chad! Whose side are you on? America was his home—his family's home. What man refuses to defend his family and his homeland?"

"He who lives by the sword will die by the sword. I didn't write the holy book. Your God did."

"Then you know your destiny." I look Chad square in the eyes.

"Yes, I do."

"Leave!"

"I'm not leaving my brother to take his last walk alone. I've got his six."

"Your brother?" If I was outside, I would spit. "In a cold operating room down the hall, a surgeon sharpens his scalpel, preparing to remove my husband's organs, then divvy them up between strangers like the Roman soldiers divided Yeshua's garments at his crucifixion. Now I find out that my heartsong's best friend *is* Judas Iscariot."

"I never betrayed him, Daisy Rose."

"Don't call me that. To you, I'm a rosebush, full of thorns. You stand here wearing that silly cowboy hat, telling me that my husband is dead because his best friend— you—murdered him?" A cold dread ices my resolve. Chad removes his hat, revealing a mop of sandy-blond hair. "You betrayed him, Chad." Steel sharpens my voice. "Admit it."

"I did not betray my brother."

"I hate liars, people who gossip, and those who betray their friends." Raw anger boils over, spewing ash and fire in the form of a guttural cry. "Why?"

"I told you."

"People have lots of friends—and brothers—and they don't murder them."

"I don't." He locks eyes with mine.

"It's no wonder you're alone. Who are you? What are you?"

"You're still a rose." He hides his eyes beneath the brim of his cowboy hat. "Always have been and always will be. But it's time that you learned something. Your heartsong's brothers-in-arms nicknamed him Wraith for a reason. What do you think that reason is?" He tips his cowboy hat. "Good day, Daisy Rose. Don't stop bloomin'." Chad opens the glass door and prepares to leave the room. "I'm still going to read his favorite poem before they take him. That's final . . . and another thing: the next election relates to Cillian's death because once the president is gone, his wife—the real monster—can execute her plans."

"What?"

Chad removes a crumpled-up sheet of paper from his pocket and leaves the room.

I quickly process what I know.

The Orphans had called him Wraith—the pale ghost.

The Orphans themselves are an elite group of special-ops soldiers orphaned at a young age, trained to kill, and they answer only to the Sons of Venus, a powerful clandestine group chaired by none other than Asher Valerian Bushcroft.

The call sign had been meant to honor my heartsong's quiet and stealthy demeanor, as well as his striking looks.

Had the call sign been prophetic, just like Daniel's vision about the statue constructed of different metals, the Skeleton Key?

Ghosts promise one thing: to vanish, eventually.

I hear a voice—quiet and very Irish with a hint of a Scottish burr, say, "If I die without tellin' you, Danny Rose, that yer the pulse of my heart, then ye'll know that death beat me to the draw. Dinna worry yerself much. I'll even the score wi' her on the other side for being such a nasty wench."

"Who said Death is a she?" I had playfully challenged, refusing to believe that such a strong man could ever die.

"A man could never sneak up on an unsuspectin' victim without making a wee sound. Death's a lass. She's a huntress."

"You're wrong about one thing."

"Only one?"

"If Death takes you before she takes me, I'll be the one scratching her eyes out."

"A catfight?" He had laughed. "Goodness, Daniela Rose." Then he had reached down and stroked a few strands of stray hair from my brow before kissing my forehead. "I'll be doin' the fightin' for ye, *mo chridhe*." *My heart.*

Whether male or female, Death was and still is an entitled citizen of the underworld, taking without thinking, taking without asking, and taking without considering what others have given so that she could take something that never belonged to her—a life, but never a legacy.

Releasing his hand, I ball my hands into fists. I want to fight Death, but she's a coward. She hides, and I can't find her.

My eyes burn, but I refuse to cry.

Not here.

Not now.

Be strong. Be brave.

But I can't. Not anymore, so I cry on the inside while the world beyond the glass doors watches me.

I am with you always, even unto the end of the world. A calming voice pours salve into the crevasses of my shredded heart. "Yeshua, tell me that I'm dreaming," I whisper. "Tell me this nightmare is just another Glass Tattoo–inspired hallucination. Wake me up before it's too late. Before they make his heart bleed."

I reach up to fidget with the snowflake diamond that usually rests at the base of my neck. I forgot. It's gone.

One more precious thing taken without my consent. I open my palm. It wasn't taken. A midnight blue snowflake inks my pale skin.

Another surge of grief crashes over me, burying me beneath a tsunami of pain. Nervous twitches invade my face, seizing my tiny muscles and twisting my mahogany skin into an expression that I imagine looks hideous.

Head buried between his paws, Spook lies beside his master. Afraid to move. Afraid to feel.

"It'll be okay, Doctor Cavanaugh." Nurse Jocelyn re-enters the room and insulates my husband's head with a warm blanket while she assures me.

"It won't be okay." I dig my fingers into the front of my shirt, protecting my heart.

Outside the safety of his ICU room—a usual place of noise and chatter—all is deathly quiet.

No cell phones.

No chitchat.

Just the soft hum of the hospital's air conditioner and the beep of the monitors promising the transplant team that my husband's heart hasn't stopped beating. In life, he sacrificed and gifted freedom to millions. In death, he gives the rest of himself.

Nurse Jocelyn enters the room, again. "Are you ready?"

"What's his name?"

"Delbert Blythe." Nurse Jocelyn replies. "He's a widow, and he's getting your husband's heart."

"His wife died . . ."

"Excuse me?"

"I once rescued Delbert Blythe at an icy lake in New Mexico, and now Cillian rescues him, again." I smile. "Isn't life something else?"

56—Orphan Dreamer:
The Orphan Walks with Honor

SPOOK STANDS AT ATTENTION BESIDE me. Christian artist Phil Driscoll plays his trumpet and sings his version of "America the Beautiful" via my Bose speakers.

Chad reads the last stanza of Cillian Joseph Finn-Barry's favorite poem—"Let America Be America Again"—to the crowd.

"Let America Be America Again"

O, let America be America again—
The land that never has been yet—
And yet must be—the land where *every* man is free.

The land that's mine—the poor man's, Indian's,
Negro's, ME—
Who made America,
Whose sweat and blood, whose faith and pain,
Whose hand at the foundry, whose plow in the rain,
Must bring back our mighty dream again.

Tears stain every face, even Asher Bushcroft's and Claire Underwood's stoic mugs.

If I hadn't been Cillian's hero, could he have ever become America's hero? If my parents hadn't been my heroes, could I have ever become Cillian's hero? And if Yeshua had never been our hero, could we have survived the fight?

The answer to this riddle is no, no, and no. A trifecta.

Nurse Jocelyn finishes detaching my heartsong from the wall monitors: electrocardiogram, arterial line, pulse oximetry, capnography, and an intracranial pressure monitor. She unplugs the medication pump. Now running on batteries, the pump pushes a cardiac stimulant, Dobutamine, into his veins.

I step outside the safe haven of my heartsong's room. Now muzzled, Spook follows. Bushcroft skitters to the left, finding another perch between two politicians.

Go home. Please.

Dressed in crisp white coats, crumpled blue scrubs, skullcaps, and wool suits, my colleagues line the corridor walls of our community hospital. I scan their faces, afraid to look into their eyes, the windows of their souls.

I'm not ready to cry in public.

Not yet.

Maybe not ever. I'll most likely shed my first tear in public after I reach Yeshua's side in the great up yonder. I peer through the wall-to-wall telescopic glass doors. Nurse

Jocelyn wipes liquid from the corner of my husband's eyes. Does he know what's going to happen?

Are those tears? Can't be. He's brain-dead—right? Tenderly, she strokes strands of hair away from his brow as though he were alive and cared about his appearance.

An orderly and two nurses push my husband's oversized bed out of his intensive care room and into the bowels of the hospital's cold, bright, and stark passageways.

Silently I follow the processional with Spook at my side, studying the floor tiles more than the familiar faces of hospital staff, community members, and the incognito soldiers of Delta Force, the Rangers, and the Orphans.

My tongue clings to the floor of my mouth. How do I thank my colleagues without blubbering? I need to share a verbal expression of my grief, but most of my kindred friends—those who have loved me as I am and understood my motives—are gone.

What would the Reverend Billy Graham say, or what grand speech would Doctor Martin Luther King Jr. deliver to this mourning crowd?

What would Yeshua say? *Shalom. Be still, my friends. I'm going away to prepare a place for you. I'll come back again and welcome you into my presence, so that you may be where I am.*

How much longer before I can go home, hide in my empty bedroom, and cry?

The nurses, orderlies, and an anesthesiologist continue to push my oily boy's ICU bed down the hospital's corridors.

Chandler—a certified registered nurse anesthetist and a US Marine veteran—salutes as my late husband's American-flag-draped body passes by and Phil Driscoll's trumpet blows the notes of the patriotic song.

Doctor Riley, my fellow anesthesiologist and friend,

squeezes an Ambu bag, inflating and subsequently oxygenating my husband's exhausted lungs. He gave his last breath for me, for us. For every human being on Earth.

Remember this.

To me, he was and still is an American of Americans.

A soldier. A brother.

A father. A husband.

A friend. A businessman who employed thousands.

Last night, Yeshua called his name louder than I ever could, and my heartsong abandoned his mangled body. After the betrayal of a friend, he followed the Light of the World through the valley of the shadow of death and into the warm embrace of eternal bliss, where my Grandma Gertrude, my rafiki, Kian, my mother, and Ethan wait.

The hospital team approaches the operating room's double doors and stops. Nurse Jonathan taps a metal plate on the wall. The double doors unlock and clank open.

"Doctor Cavanaugh," the anesthesiologist whispers, "it's time."

"It's time to let go, then forget," I say.

"To let go, but never forget," the anesthesiologist replies.

I brush my lips across my heartsong's left ear. "Sorry for calling you oily boy. You never deserved that, not even when we were kids. But I was so scared of meeting you." My voice quivers. "To be honest, I was more frightened that you were only a figment of my imagination. Thank you for being real."

I press my cool, moist lips into my dead husband's warm, dry lips, awkwardly kissing him around his endotracheal tube for the final time.

The medical team wheels him past the double doors and into the operating room's corridors. The doors slam in my face, and an automatic lock engages. If I could bury myself alive, I would.

Depression sucks.

It's like breathing through an endotracheal tube your whole life.

Still, letting go of my kindred spirit—not to mention living to tell the tale—sucks even more.

He's gone.

And every square millimeter of my body aches for his touch. My lips twist, but my vocal cords refuse to form words.

You're a failure, Daniela. Can't even speak when there's so much to say.

I dare to look up and face the crowd. I want to tell them everything. I want to tell them how he fought for freedom against the beings trying to take our freedom—the Sons of Venus, Lucifer, the Nephilim, and the antichrist.

I want to tell them about the secret war he fought. I want to tell them that the monsters—the Nephilim—are real, not fairy tales, and that they're coming for us. Actually, they're already here, roaming Earth, killing, stealing, and destroying.

Their physical power has been diluted over the centuries, but not their motives. They're master manipulators, and they still exist.

And they're hiding behind the silent rise of the Fourth Reich. A globalist force constructed of religion—three Abrahamic religions mixed like iron and clay—married to politics, National Socialism, and Communist Socialism. They have one goal: oppress, then murder every single man, woman, and child.

But I say none of these things. I just stand here, mute and embarrassed by my inability to speak.

Then something rises within me. It's the God Factor. The same power that made brothers fight to annihilate the bonds of slavery.

As heaven's orchestra seems to accompany my mezzo-soprano voice, I sing the soulful Whitney Houston version of "Battle Hymn of the Republic," a Civil War–era piece written by Julia Ward Howe—an abolitionist, poet, and social activist—and sung by Northern soldiers during the bloodiest days of the Civil War.

"Battle Hymn of the Republic"

Mine eyes have seen the glory of the coming of the
Lord
He is trampling out the vintage where the grapes of
wrath are stored
He hath loosed the fateful lightning of his terrible
swift sword
His truth is marching on.
Glory! glory! Hallelujah!
Glory! glory! Hallelujah!
Glory! glory! Hallelujah!
His truth is marching on.
He has sounded forth the trumpet that shall never call
retreat
He is sifting out the hearts of men before his
judgment seat
Oh, be swift, my soul, to answer Him! Be jubilant, my
feet!
Our God is marching on.

Feet tap. Hands clap. Heads nod as sad eyes shed tears. Minutes later, the crowd dissipates and leaves the hospital.

Except for my dog, I stand alone near a bank of windows, staring at the helicopter pad. Waiting.

Several minutes pass, and the two nurses with coolers strapped onto their backs rush into a waiting medical transport helicopter. The helicopter blades start their rotational dance, and the bird lifts into the night sky.

It's my least favorite time of day.

"Nightfall," I whisper to Spook. He barks.

In a few hours, my husband's heart will beat for another—that hermit-man living in the Alpine Lakes Wilderness, Delbert Blythe. Only God knows what Delbert will do with the life gifted to him by the beating heart of a hero.

In life, Cillian dies. In death, he lives.

The helicopter disappears into the ink-black horizon, but a speck of yellow appears where the chopper vanishes. The yellow speck approaches the hospital window. I gasp. "It's an apricot sulphur!" I palm the window. Bravely, the butterfly flies toward my hand.

It's not stopping!

Don't let it die, Yeshua. Not in front of me—please.

Wings spread, it pierces the glass, leaving no cracks or signs of its entrance. The winged insect flits left and right, playing hide-and-seek. In the empty alcove of the hospital, I hold out my hand. Maybe the butterfly will choose to land. Spook jumps up, then dives right.

"Sit, Spook. Don't hurt the apricot sulphur." I open my right hand. A dark-blue snowflake tattoo stains my palm. The dainty insect plants its feet in the center of the snowflake tattoo. "It's not magic, little one. Not at all."

The butterfly's presence resembles one thing—redemption, a second chance—for me, for us, and for my oily boy.

I recall Chad Prevington's admonition: "We nicknamed him Wraith for a reason."

Ghosts are not real.

The truth collides with my perception of reality.

"Spook, my oily boy will live in my dreams, because he never died outside of my dreams. And even if he's not real, at least he's not dead." I smile—wild, free, and full of hope.

Believe early.

Believe often.

Just believe.

"One day . . ." The butterfly crawls up my arm and perches on top of my shoulder. Apricot sulphur butterflies truly are the mascots of dreamers. I smile. "If you're real, I'll meet you, oily boy, outside of my dreams."

Spook barks, agreeing with me . . . or so I thought.

"Bye, mom." My holographic vision of Adelaide waves, then disappears.

"I'll see you in my future, my darling one."

A man walks up behind me—coal-black skin and violet eyes. "Legna, you're here!" I reach out and pinch his arm.

"Ouch! What was that for, Rosebud?"

"Making sure you're real."

"Just ask next time, because unlike humans, I never lie."

"Sorry. If you're here, that means this isn't real. But you've never come to Earth in the present. Why are you here?"

"To drive the point home before you go back to your hospital room where they're waiting for you."

"What do you mean?"

"It doesn't have to end this way—your heartsong's end could look quite different."

"So it's true, Legna?" As my right hand trembles, I reach for Yahweh's powerful warrior. "The man they wheeled into the operating room is the boy trapped inside my dreams—my oily boy, a kid who one day becomes my heartsong, a warrior?"

"Yep. That's him." Behind a smile, Legna's gorgeous eyes register disappointment.

"What's wrong?"

"He's handsome. Isn't he?"

"Yeah . . . I guess." My face and neck heat up as I look down and away.

"You don't know?"

"I do, Legna." I rest my hand on the center of my chest as Spook nuzzles closer to my leg. "It's just that he's taken my breath away, and I-I-I am breathless and speechless."

"Sort of like how someone in this alcove makes me feel." Legna chortles, and Daniela's face feels hotter than a scorching summer day. "He—your Wraith—will not die of old age. That's for sure. What assassin does? Because those who kill by the sword will die by the sword. Remember?"

"I do."

"But he could die a less tortured death . . . if you so choose."

"If I choose? It's appointed that a man die once, and after that, face judgment. Hebrews chapter nine, verse twenty-seven. So I don't choose. He will die, and so will I."

"Since you're quoting the Bible, don't forget the passage your parents used to read to you about how the fervent prayer of a righteous person can accomplish anything."

"You've got my attention."

"It's true that humans can't avoid death—and trust me, I'm glad of that."

"Stop." I playfully slap Legna's arm.

"Excluding your demise, of course." He grins at me, and I grin back. "Maybe a person's final curtain call could be tweaked a bit."

"With prayer?"

"My Master likes listening to you humans. I still don't know why. Bad breath. Boring. Bat-dumb stupid. But Yeshua still says, 'Again I say to you that if two of you agree on earth about anything that they ask, it will be done for them by My Father in heaven.' "

"I'm game."

"You'll need to find another human to agree with you, maybe your mom, your dad, or Limy?

"I don't know who will agree with me, but my oily boy—I mean my heartsong—deserves a rewrite in his story line. He's constantly tormented in my dreams. He needs a break, even in death."

"Then pray, Danny Rose. Don't be so busy gaining the whole world while losing your own soul—your heartsong—a man born to love you as you are. Change Wraith's ending, right here and right now. It's your job, not mine."

Then pray for him. My rafiki's words also remind me of my responsibility. "Legna."

"What's up?"

"Do you like me like a guy likes a girl?"

"That will never happen." A smile cuts pleasure into the pain that shadows his chiseled face.

"I know, but it doesn't mean a person doesn't want what they can't have."

"Focus on what you can have, your heartsong."

"I hope you find happiness in every way, and I get the point. Prayer is the glue that links chronos time and kairos time, God's appointed time."

"Rosebud . . ."

"What?"

Legna leans down, pecks me on the lips, then vanishes.

Something so very amazing, something I've never experienced before, begins no different than a spark.

A match strikes the head of another match, igniting a flame that charges throughout my being—pulsing and contracting, methodically yet chaotically—until I'm catapulted onto the highest mountaintop and all valleys vanish.

"Legna!" I gasp.

"Rosebud, focus on what you can have—Wraith."

I recall Legna's words. "Could my heartsong, Wraith, make me feel this way?"

"Yahweh." I lift my eyes to heaven. "Show me his face once more." The face of the handsome soldier willing to give his heart to a stranger completely vanishes from my memory. The bruised face of a teenage boy replaces it.

Spook vanishes.

I am alone. Content. Happy. Hopeful. This isn't isolation, but insulation. And this I know: my oily boy and my heartsong are connected. I'll find them both in kairos time, Yahweh's perfect timing.

"Abba, my Father, please protect my oily boy wherever he may be. While we're apart, give him hope and wisdom. Make his second chance at life worth it—for him. Not for me, not for us, but for him. And if I could bring him happiness, let us meet one day . . . maybe I could make him feel the way Legna made me feel?"

I reach for Spook, forgetting that he's gone. Maybe my canine friend will exist in my future too. I hope so. "Time to go home. Beam me back down, Scotty."

I open my eyes.

The midnight-blue snowflake tattoo fades, and a snowflake-shaped diamond ejects from my right palm.

57—Orphan Dreamer

"PLEASE DON'T DIE, DANNY ROSE." A finger tapped her cheek. "Wake up, Lozen."

Shivering, Daniela opened her eyes, then surveyed her surroundings: white walls, fluorescent lights, and the scent of antiseptic. "Where am I?"

"In the hospital. The burn unit at Shands Hospital." Red hair and green eyes blurred in and out of focus. "It's me—Limy—and you're going to be just fine."

Emmaline's normally alto and calming voice landed sharp inside Daniela's ears.

"Are you okay, Limy?" Daniela reached for Emmaline's hand and found it.

"I am now."

"Where are my parents?"

"On their way." Emmaline cradled her friend's bandaged left arm. "You've been asleep for a little while."

Another man was in the room, and he seemed to be staring at Daniela. A five o'clock shadow added a ruggedness to an otherwise handsome face. "Who's that?" She pointed at the man.

"My dad. He flew from Boston right away. He wanted to be here for you and for me." Emmaline said, then faced Daniela and mouthed, *play dumb and nice.*

Daniela nodded. "Thank you, Mr. Darbyshire." She smiled weakly at the man.

"You're welcome," he said, then found his seat across the room.

"My parents will be worried." Daniela surveyed her body. Bandages hid Daniela's arms and the scent of charred flesh haunted her. "What happened?"

"An explosion. You were burned—second degree."

"Feels like my arms are on fire. And my face?" Daniela glanced left and then right, looking for a mirror.

"Your mug? It's still flawless and beautiful." Emmaline smiled.

"Can I trust you?"

"Secrets. Lies. Friendship. Remember?" She kissed Daniela's forehead. "You'll walk the fashionista's catwalk one day. Trust me." Daniela's face relaxed into a smile that eventually gave way to a laugh.

"What's so funny?" Emmaline asked.

"When I was a little girl, I scrubbed my arms raw, trying to remove my brown skin. Today I'd give anything to grow back my beautiful brown skin. Life's one big fat irony."

"What doesn't kill you . . . the scars will accent your beauty." A mischievous smile settled into Emmaline's full lips. "What about the orphan boy? In your mental fog, you talked about him incessantly."

"For real?"

"Yep. So do you love yourself enough to find him and then fall in love with him?"

"You won't give up, will you?"

"I'm your friend. Real friends never give up." Emmaline cupped Daniela's hands inside hers.

"I'm glad, because I'm not giving up either. Do me a favor, Limy." Daniela's voice dropped to a whisper. "Unwrap them."

Emmaline glanced down the hallway. "The nurses will scold me, possibly kick me out. Then what?"

"Please."

"I'll stand watch." Emmaline's MI6 dad leaves the room and guards the door.

"If you get me in trouble . . ." Emmaline carefully unwrapped the bandages. Bloodied white dermis glistened in contrast to a background of flawless mahogany skin.

Daniela ran her finger over Emmaline's arm. It was soft, covered by pale, freckled skin. "You tried to suntan again."

"Tried is the key word."

"How is the girl—Claire's sister, Polly?"

"Well."

"Then the scars are worth it."

"Oh, Danny Rose!" Emmaline burst into tears and embraced Daniela. "I love you."

"Our skin tells a story: Yours tells the stories of Vikings who braved the wintery tundra of Northern Europe. Mine tells the stories of an African man who ran with gazelles and lions, an Irish woman who escaped the Irish Famine, a Cherokee woman who lived in harmony with the land,

and an English woman who crossed the great Atlantic Ocean seeking religious freedom."

"Poetic."

"I'm feeling poetic." A plump tear formed in the corner of Daniela's eye. "I love your skin—because I love mine."

Emmaline rebandaged Daniela's arms with fresh gauze that had been left on a table stocked with tape and salve.

"Help me out of bed, Limy." With support from her Anne with an *e*, Daniela knelt down beside her hospital bed and breathed, "Protect oily boy, Yahweh. Thy will be done on earth as it is in heaven."

Emmaline pulled her friend back into bed. "We'll find him."

"Limy." Daniela pulled the sheet under her chin. "It's true. I travelled while I was sleeping."

"Your eyes were tracking back and forth so fast, I thought they'd jump out of their sockets. Where did you go?"

"Home—the place of my birth, Alachua General Hospital—where I learned that my oily boy's heart beats for another."

"What do you mean?"

"I don't know exactly, but I don't believe he's the antichrist. He's too compassionate to live as a tyrant who longs to kill everyone—but he did slice a boy's throat wide open. Still, it's time to take a chance and give him another name."

"Drumroll." Emmaline beat her hands on the edge of Daniela's mattress.

"I gift him the name heartsong."

"A boy who love songs were written for?"

"Indeed. But he'll stay as our secret—at least for twenty-four hours."

"Pinky swear." Emmaline interlocked her pinky with Daniela's.

"Also, there's a chance that I could change his ending—his method of death."

"How?"

"If someone will agree to pray with me and ask Yahweh to change the way my heartsong will die—not tortured, beaten, and then shot when some Russian spy mission goes wrong, it will be done."

Seconds later, Daniela's parents entered the hospital room with a bouquet of red roses. Emmaline's father followed.

Mama Cavanaugh arranged the flowers in a vase while her husband sat down on Daniela's bed.

The Orphan Dreamer's friend sat on the other side of the bed beside Daniela and said, "I'll do it, Danny-girl. I'll agree with you."

Emmaline's dad strolled up to Daniela's father. "These girls are heroes." The man extended his hand. "Charles Darbyshire. Sorry for the intrusion."

"Pleasure's all mine." Mr. Cavanaugh shook his hand while Daniela imagined horrid things about the mysterious man.

Was he the monster who would rule Earth with an iron fist?

Playfulness danced behind his eyes—not what she'd expected from a megalomaniac. "I apologize to you, Daniela, if I came off as a stalker when we spoke on the phone." Daniela glanced at her mom and dad. "It's my job to know important people."

"I'm not important."

"You are. I arranged the president's attendance at the funeral. The goal was for him to meet you—the Orphan

Dreamer charged with stopping Armageddon. We didn't think that a seventeen-year-old girl would want to fly to Washington, DC. And we never expected the senator to go postal. So here I am. When you recover, I hope you'll accompany Emmaline and me to the White House."

"I'll think about it." Daniela squeezed her father's hand, and her mother rested her hand on her daughter's shoulder.

"Who told you about our Daniela?" Mrs. Cavanaugh rotated her shoulders back and lifted her chin.

Mr. Darbyshire paused, then answered, "My daughter." He caught Emmaline's expression—a face painted in ruby red with matching splotches splattered across her chest. "It's harmless, just father-daughter talk." He looked at Mr. Cavanaugh. "You can understand."

"I do." Austin got up, walked around the bed, and stood between his daughter and Emmaline's father.

"Daniela won't be able to fly to Washington." Her mother stood tall, shoulders back. "From now on, she'll focus on her medical school—no politics, no saving the world, and no cuddling up with you or your friends. She's not a show-and-tell project, Charles."

"In a year, she'll turn eighteen," he said.

"And?" her mother asked.

"We'll wait for her, Mr. and Mrs. Cavanaugh." Mr. Darbyshire sat back in the hospital's recliner. Interlinking his fingers, he cleared his throat. "Emmaline tells me about a boy that you're keen to find, and I'd be delighted to help you in your quest."

"My Father will help me find him."

"Emmaline never told me your father was a member of intelligence." A puzzled look crossed Mr. Darbyshire's face as he glanced at Daniela's dad, no doubt seeing just a gray-haired black man leaning on a cane.

"He's a genius—my Father created the world." She winked at her rafiki, who understood that she wasn't speaking of him. "I imagine He can decipher my dreams."

"Interesting." Mr. Darbyshire smirked. "Emmaline tells me that you've struggled with depression *and* schizophrenia."

"It's time for you to leave—now!" Daniela's father ushered the MI6 agent to the door. Before Emmaline's dad left, he asked his daughter, "Are you coming, Emma?"

"In a bit. I drove the Jeep." Emmaline shifted her weight from left to right.

"I'll see you back in Boston tomorrow at eighteen-hundred sharp."

"Yes, Daddy." Emmaline gnawed the corner of her lip until her father left for good.

"Relax." Daniela's dad lifted Limy's chin. "Overbearing dads and presidents may rule—but the King of Kings reigns. Trust Him."

Until midnight, the foursome shared stories and laughed. Then the mood turned serious.

"Daddy, what about oily boy?" Even a seventeen-year-old girl could speak in riddles while mining her dad's honest opinion. "What if no matter how hard I pray, he's destined to be bad—like Mr. Darbyshire, the leader of the Sons of Venus?"

"In time, you'll learn that it'll be the size of his heart that matters most."

"Tell me more." Daniela grinned—wide and free.

"Ah then," Mr. Cavanaugh nodded, giving his approval. "Emancipated from a dam of selfishness, he'll love you like a waterfall, flowing wildly free. So, my brave daughter—tormented by nosebleeds, obsessed with the idyllic story of *Anne of Green Gables*, illuminated with the sensibility of science, and blessed with the magic of what-ifs—you'll one day be loved by this man. He'll adore you, our Orphan Dreamer."

"Poetic," Mrs. Cavanaugh said, as Daniela wrapped her grandmother's patchwork quilt around her shoulders.

Her father gently held his daughter's hands, his eyes fixed on her arms. His voice found a cadence and tone similar to Doctor Martin Luther King's. "Your scars will lend more compassion to your embrace, and he will be the lucky one."

Daniela sniffled.

"You'll understand his pain, Daniela." Letting go of his daughter, he buried his hands inside his beige polyester pant pockets. "By loving him, you'll heal his wounds and soften his heart—the Mr. Hyde we all possess."

"Six-six-six?"

"Yes." Mr. Cavanaugh cleared his throat of emotion. "Finish medical school. Then find him, grow—don't go fallin' into love with him, make oily boy your passion, your soul, Daniela Rose."

"My heartsong . . . that's what he'll be to me."

"Indeed," her dad said.

Daniela smiled, her future so full of hope. Her dad would become an ally in all things heartsong, no matter how much cream was in her heartsong's DNA.

Sporting a pair of spit-shined Stacy Adams, her dad paced back and forth like Perry Mason working a courtroom. "Pray for him, Daniela, protecting him from the wiles of our enemy, Nomed, and his human agents."

Daniela inhaled a deep breath. "Daddy, you know my heartsong's skin is white."

One second elapsed into ten, then a full minute.

"I know." Chaplain Austin Cavanaugh pointed to the glistening white dermis of her burns. "But so is yours." The five of them laughed, and Mrs. Cavanaugh wrapped her daughter's forearms, burying Daniela's pale skin beneath thin layers of cloth.

"You're my rafiki—my kindred spirit, my ally. Thank you, Daddy." She pecked his cheek.

* * *

The next morning, after breakfast, Emmaline and Mrs. Cavanaugh stood beside Daniela's hospital bed—her rafiki on the opposite side. He removed a crinkled envelope from his cabana shirt's front pocket.

"This letter came for you—from the professor."

"When, Dad?"

"Two days ago, but I didn't want to deliver the letter in front of Emmaline's dad." He faced Emmaline. "Sorry, Limy, but we don't know your father or what his intentions are."

"No, you don't." Emmaline looked down and away. *She's still hiding something.*

"But you do?" Austin asked.

"I'll understand a bit more about my father's and the Sons of Venus's involvement in this whole pandemic after I complete my reconnaissance."

Chaplain Cavanaugh crinkled his brow, and Daniela opened the letter while teasing her friend. "Limy's spying on her dad."

"Why?" Austin crossed his arms.

"To keep Daniela Rose, our Orphan Dreamer, safe," Limy said.

"Thank you." Jeanette Cavanaugh poured Emmaline a glass of water. "Visit us often, okay?"

"I'll stay in Danny's room . . . if it's okay with you, Mr. and Mrs. C." Emmaline sat on Daniela's hospital bed.

"It is," Daniela's parents said in unison before the Orphan Dreamer read the letter.

My Darling Rosebud,

Fact or legend?

Some Islamic and Catholic historical accounts suggest that when Mohammad was between the ages of nine and twelve, he accompanied a Meccan caravan to Syria where he met a Catholic monk, Bahira, who lived in a Jesuit monastery.

For the next several years of Mohammad's youth, the Islamic tradition loses track of his whereabouts, making it impossible to separate truth from historical legend.

Did Mohammad remain within the monastery with Bahira?

And what concepts did Bahira teach Mohammad before the young boy grew up, found his cave, had his vision, then penned the text of his new religion, Islam—a post-Judaic and post-Christian system of beliefs that formed the second largest religion in the world? This religion instructs almost two billion people on how they should live and how they should interact with the rest of humanity.

Six hundred years after Christianity was birthed by the fulfillment of the testaments of several ancient Jewish prophets, this brand-new religion, Islam, was born—founded only by one vision given in one cave to one illiterate man, with no corroborators to verify that his testament and his interpretation is truth.

Why?

Who knows? But before the Catholic monk Bahira left Mohammad's company, he reportedly said, "We rise together, or we fall together. Either way, Jerusalem will be ours."

B'shalom,
Professor Jakob
Director of Israel Antiquities Authority

"It matches what I read about Bahira as well, so that settles it then. Unless I can go to the Vatican and speak with those who can prove a different story and interpretation." Daniela's hands trembled violently. "But it's final—the founder of Islam was the Catholic Church."

"You're sure about this?" Emmaline asked.

"I am. The iron legs, feet, and toes in the Skeleton Key represent political Rome and religious Rome. The intermixed clay in the Skeleton Key's feet and toes represents Islam—the religion of the people of the desert and the political system that supports it."

"Why Islam instead of Hinduism or Buddhism?" Emmaline massaged Daniela's legs.

"The Bible was written by Judean Semitic men within

their cultural context and not with Western or Eastern cultural or religious influences like Hinduism or Buddhism."

"Why does this Islamic-Catholic union matter?"

"The political arm of the Fourth Reich will use this union to their advantage. Understanding the ancient offense between two half brothers—Ishmael and Isaac, Abraham's sons—the one-world government, i.e., the Fourth Reich, will pit Israel and the Arabic world against each other and start World War III, Earth's Armageddon as shown in the Book of Revelation. Then the occupants of Wormwood will invade and finish cleaning up the stragglers."

"If Bahira was responsible for the birth of Islam by feeding Mohammad Catholic-inspired knowledge and rituals, then is Bahira the one most responsible for fulfilling the iron-and-clay Bible prophecy? And if he's the instigator of the story, is he a Nephilim?" Emmaline asked.

"I don't know—not yet. But I will."

Emmaline sipped from her water bottle. "Three Abrahamic religions: Judaism, Christianity, and Islam. For some, Christianity identifies the Messiah of its parent religion, Judaism. What question of Judaism does Islam answer?" She pushed back into the reclining seat to the left of Daniela's hospital bed.

"Islam tells us the identity of the antichrist. Ishmael was the jealous stepbrother who wanted the destiny of the promised child, Isaac. Lucifer wanted to become God. Possessing the antichrist—six-six-six—will be his last chance to attempt to be like God," Daniela said.

"Limy, the Arabic people and the Jewish Hebrews have been at odds since the days of Ishmael and Isaac," Mrs. Cavanaugh added.

"After Mohammad left the company of the Jesuit monk

and experienced his visions inside that dark cave, Mohammad told his wife that he wasn't certain if his visions were from Satan or Allah," Daniela said.

"That sucks," Emmaline replied.

"After Yeshua was born, lived, died, and resurrected, the age-old prophecies written by the prophets Isaiah and Jeremiah answered the question of Judaism—who is the Messiah? Islam answered the question of who the antichrist is. After forming the newest warring branch of Roman Catholicism, Islam promised perpetual conflicts between Isaac's seed, Israel, and Ishmael's seed, the Arab people," Daniela explained.

"And?" Her mother held her breath.

"The antichrist and his—or her—Sons of Venus will use that situation to their advantage."

"The antichrist could be a girl?" Her mother gasped, then pulled her daughter close.

"It's okay, Mom. It's not me." The Orphan Dreamer smiled slightly.

"It couldn't be you or Dad, either . . ."

"Daniela . . . what are you saying?" Emmaline's face turned tomato red. "It's not me—right? I couldn't kill every man, woman, and child. I *am* studying biological weapons, but not to mass murder, just to protect our home, America, from everyone else."

"I'm not calling you the antichrist, Limy," Daniela reassured. "After you all left last night, I couldn't sleep, so I started playing with the Skeleton Key."

Daniela crawled from her bed, unzipped her small suitcase, then removed the Skeleton Key and gave her dad a wink. He'd brought it after visiting hours last night. She shook the statue. Inside, a liquid moved—heavy and lazy.

"What are you thinking, Danny-girl?"

"The liquid is mercury." The light goes off in Daniela's head. "The relic has a compartment filled with mercury, and somehow this heavy liquid will function as a key. Ezekiel's message written on the small stone tablet makes even more sense now." Daniela handed Emmaline the translation. "Read it again, Limy."

> "In kairos time, insert the Skeleton Key into a lock that secures a ruler's tomb beyond the Jordan River. Find King Solomon's temple treasure that was lost after my people were taken captive by the Babylonians. The Copper Scroll is nothing more than an inventory of temple treasure and a decoy. Travel safe, my alien friend—Mistress Daniela."

"Somehow this statue will function as a key and unlock the door or a tomb that leads to the Jordan River where lost treasure—and possibly the Ark of the Covenant—can be found," Daniela said.

"Are you sure, Danny-girl?" Emmaline took the object from her and shook it as well. "You're right."

"It's not only a key and a projector, but also something else . . ."

"You're kidding." Emmaline leaned closer.

"Watch." Daniela turned the golden head of the statue twenty clicks to the right, then she dialed the silver chest five clicks the other way.

Working it like a high school locker's combination lock, she rotated each portion of the statue, solving another mystery hidden inside the Skeleton Key.

"It's the simple number-to-letter code that was in Lozen's letter to my great-great-grandfather!"

"I thought you girls located that cipher in a cave?" her mother challenged.

"We did, but we didn't." In less than a minute, Daniela disclosed the short-story version to her parents, and Mr. and Mrs. Cavanaugh both crossed their arms in an attempt to not harm Emmaline. "It's okay, Mom and Dad. We survived."

"Lying is never okay," her dad stated plainly.

"I know." Emmaline did penance once more. "I repented, and Daniela forgave me."

The Orphan Dreamer's parents looked at their daughter the same way, their eyes asking only one question: why?

"Forgiveness," Daniela said, understanding their look. She shrugged. "It's sort of a Bible thing." She flashed a wicked grin.

Checkmate!

After uncrossing their arms, her parents' facial expressions softened into smiles, then beamed with pride. "Finish showing us what your statue can do."

"It twists and turns like a Rubik's Cube, but it hides mysteries more like a Russian doll." Daniela grabbed both ends of the Skeleton Key, then pulled, separating each component of the statue and revealing metal rollers imprinted with letters. "Limy, please give me my journal." Emmaline complied, and Daniela turned to the last pages of the tattered book and then showed them how it worked.

She rolled the individual cylinders across paper and a silvery substance formed Hebrew words and sentences. "Here's what it says."

"Who translated it for you?"

Daniela glanced at her rafiki. "My dad. Last night."

"You read Hebrew, Mr. C.?"

"Me growing up on a peanut farm and only having

access to a sixth-grade education doesn't mean I'm an idiot. A seminary man taught me. He thought reading Hebrew would be good for my chaplain calling."

"Cool." Emmaline looked at Mr. Cavanagh, then at the journal. "Your dad reads Hebrew, and the Skeleton Key isn't only an actual key, but it's also an ancient printer and a projector. Life couldn't be more strange or unbelievable!"

"Believe it." Mr. Cavanaugh chuckled.

"So read it, Danny-girl."

"Here it is. Translation number one . . . written by John, an apostle of Yeshua, while he languished on a desolate island, far away from the comforts of Rome."

> Little children, it is the last hour: and as you have heard that antichrist shall come, even now are there many antichrists; whereby we know that it is the last time (1 John 2:18).

> Who is the liar but the one who denies that Jesus is the Christ? This is the antichrist, the one who denies the Father and the Son (1 John 2:22).

> By this you know the Spirit of God: every spirit that confesses that Jesus Christ has come in the flesh is from God, and every spirit that does not confess Jesus is not from God. And this is the spirit of the antichrist, of which you have heard that it is coming; and now it is already in the world (1 John 4:2–3).

> Many deceivers have gone out into the world, those who do not confess that Jesus Christ has

come in the flesh; any such person is the deceiver and the antichrist! (2 John 1:7).

A bit unsteady on her feet, Emmaline sat on the foot of the bed before collapsing onto her back. "So then according to this little Russian doll, I'm the antichrist because I don't say that Jesus is the Christ—the messiah."

"Anyone who denies that Yeshua—Jesus—is from Yahweh possesses a spirit of antichrist, but that doesn't mean that they are *the* antichrist, the lawless one who was prophesied to trick humans into initiating their own mass genocide," Mr. Cavanaugh comforted his daughter's best friend.

"So by refusing to accept Yahweh's gift of eternal life through Yeshua, the Christ, humans effectively have chosen eternal death?" Emmaline asked.

"Refusing to accept Yeshua and then dying is like jumping into a raging river without a life raft," Mrs. Cavanaugh said. "Of course, the life raft is Yeshua."

"So the pandemic we need to stop is really eternal suicide?" Emmaline rolled onto her side, then curled into the fetal position.

"That's one way to interpret the Apostle John's sayings," Chaplain Cavanaugh added. "But it's also true that natural disasters and manmade disasters will reduce Earth's human population as well."

"Am I a Nephilim—genetically predetermined to reject the Jesus-thing and do nothing but evil deeds the rest of my life?" Emmaline asked.

"Most humans who don't choose Yeshua's path for salvation are just plain-Jane humans—nothing more. Who knows if those humans are more inclined to be influenced by evil?" Mrs. Cavanaugh said.

Daniela scooted from the head of the bed to the foot.

"But you, Limy, don't have to commit eternal suicide . . . no one does. Nor do you have to live separated or in rebellion against Yahweh by not listening to His voice."

Daniela's dad took on his preacher's stance. *Uh oh. Sermon time.*

"It's simple, Limy. The Bible shares the truth, but we don't have to embrace it. Can you deal with truth?"

"Try me."

"The penalty for evil deeds is death—eternal separation from God. But God laid a bridge in the form of an old rugged cross, laying it across the river so we could pass from death into life because of the sacrifice of Yeshua—Jesus, the Messiah. Walk across the bridge or drown."

Raised in the harshness of America's Jim Crow South, this was Austin's style whenever he shared the good news—plain, definitely simple, and to the point.

Take it or leave it.

"But why should I be punished like the Nephilim? I'm not the one running around deceiving the masses. According to Daniela, Lucifer's agents are the ones telling lies and tricking people into not taking a raft or crossing your invisible bridge to heaven."

"We're born into a state of punishment—on our way to our deathbed. Yeshua simply takes what is already dead—removing the penalty of sin which is death—and infuses life into us. Without Him, we're dead people walking, the walking dead."

"That's a visual."

"It's a precious gift. One day the antichrist and his false religious leader will pay the piper as well," Daniela's mom said. "The Book of Revelation promises those two monsters their dues." She opened the book and read ominous words.

And the devil who had deceived them was thrown into the lake of fire and sulfur where the beast and the false prophet were, and they will be tormented day and night forever and ever.

"That's Revelations 20:10."

"Trust me, being burned alive isn't fun." Daniela held up her arms as proof.

"We don't need to fear those who can kill our body," Mr. Cavanaugh expounded his wife's point. "Instead we must reserve reverence for Yahweh, the One who can kill the body and the soul, releasing us to eternity without His presence."

"Limy, Dad's right."

Emmaline lay still, then sighed heavily. "I believe but following Yeshua scares me. I'm not like Daniela. I need to live a little, have fun. Not shrivel up into a prude . . . sorry, Danny-girl. That's how I feel, though. I'll fight alongside you, but in my own way and on my own terms."

"Then we'll fight." Daniela didn't want to lose her best—her only—friend.

"But she'll not possess any weapons, Daniela Rose," her mother said.

"I have a gun."

"Yes, I know." Mrs. Cavanaugh rolled her eyes. "But a gun won't cut it."

"Daniela's a quick shot with her bow and arrow." Emmaline quickly stated, thankful that Daniela's mother didn't say anything more about the gun.

"Not going to kill the Orphan Dreamer's foe and his army." Mr. Cavanaugh buried his hands in his pockets.

"What kind of weapon are you talking about?"

"Daniela's most powerful weapon—prayer. The fervent praying of a person who has surrendered to Yahweh is the most powerful force on Earth. It can stop wars, break chains, and infuse hope into hopeless hearts."

"Humans have lost their focus on the real war, the battle meant to defeat the occupants of Wormwood." Daniela said, lying on her back beside her best friend.

"Where is this planet, Danny-girl?"

"It's out there, hidden inside a wormhole. In time, its occupants—hordes of demons—will come for us."

"But humans will call it an alien invasion?"

"Yep. Aliens—a human's favorite word for a being it doesn't understand."

Her parents abandoned the comfort of their chairs and stood beside the Orphan Dreamer. "We know what you're saying is true," her father said, "but we possess an ace."

"What's that?" Daniela asked.

"You, our Orphan Dreamer." A symphony of emotions moved his lips into an awkward smile. Pride. Fear. And thanksgiving because Yahweh hadn't forgotten His dear children or left them drowning in chaotic, raging seas.

"But, Dad, who will listen to me? And I got my butt blown out the front door of a rickety church after fighting just one Nephilim! Besides, the antichrist's false prophet will promote a universal religion, promising unity and peace."

"Clay mixed with iron—at best a temporary union." Chaplain Cavanaugh wagged his head. "A false promise designed to lead humans off the narrow path that leads to eternal life."

"Iron and clay could never fully join together," her mother added.

"But it's true, girls," Daniela's dad said, "that in the

middle of Earth's chaos—wars and promises of war, famine, ethnic conflicts, increasing in intensity and frequency—our neighbors will want—actually, need—clay and iron, two incompatible substances to fuse, driving desperate people to embrace fake unity and false peace."

"But when they say peace and safety, then sudden destruction will follow," Mrs. Cavanaugh quoted a Bible passage.

Both girls shivered, and a cold sweat chilled the Orphan Dreamer's skin.

She whispered, "I need to answer a personal question," then shared her heart with her parents and best friend. "Dreams and visions can trick and mislead a gullible and desperate mind, becoming nothing more than daydreams and little-girl fantasies."

"What's your plan, Danny-girl?" Emmaline slipped her arms around her friend, and her breathing slowed.

"In chronos time, in real life, I need to know once and for all if my oily boy will become my heartsong—or the dreaded antichrist."

"The truth always sets us free, Daniela." Her rafiki held out his hand to his little girl.

"I know, Daddy. But like Milton said, 'The mind is its own place, and in itself can make a heaven of hell, a hell of heaven.' Sometimes climbing out of bed and choosing to breathe are the bravest parts of my day." She reached up and held his hand.

The deepest things of God are the simplest, like "pray for your future husband—your oily boy whom you desire to become your heartsong. The only question for you to answer is: will you stay faithful and pray for your heartsong year after year without giving up?"

"I'll have to."

"Okay." He squeezed her hand. "How can we help you, Daniela?"

"Pray for me. Pray that I won't be blinded by lust and deceived by promises of a grand romance. Pray that I don't become an Eva Braun."

58—THE ORPHAN

JULY 11, 1998
MONGOLIA

IT WAS PAST MIDNIGHT AT Sumrall's restaurant. Paul tidied up the dining room while Cillian and Sam washed a never-ending tide of dishes in two stainless steel sinks.

The reason?

Mr. Sumrall had secured a large supply of seafood from his distributor and was offering his customers the rare treat of an all-you-can-eat seafood boil. All you can eat equaled a bottomless pit filled with pots, pan, plates, and cutlery.

Cillian's hands cramped. He had removed his left hand's protective glove as he scrubbed. Two hours had passed, and still a mountain of soiled dishes remained. Too exhausted to talk, the boys worked quietly, their only companions the stench of saltwater and rotting seafood, and the sound of a newscaster's voice coming from the TV that was anchored to the wall.

Sweat poured down Cillian's face. He blinked, but his briny perspiration only stung his eyes. Proteinaceous slime coated his previously white button-up shirt and the slippery floor. He stood on a perforated mat, fighting to stay upright each time he shifted his weight.

Behind him, emulsified fish and crustaceans oozed toward the floor's drain. With his feet in rubber boots, Sam wiped his brow while trying to remain upright at the sink next to Cillian. "Cil, how can you wash dishes day after day?"

Inwardly, Cillian chuckled. "Aye, it's a bit of a promotion."

"Is that possible?"

"Trust me."

"I never go anywhere besides school, home, and the campsite. Tell me a story about your adventures. What did you see, hear, taste, and smell?"

"It's not wise to venture into hell. Ye may never return again, Sam."

"What do you mean?" Sam stopped washing dishes, and Cillian wished that he would continue cleaning, or neither of them would sleep before the restaurant reopened in the morning.

"The dining room's spotless, Cil," Paul reported. His shoulders slumped as he gripped the handle of his mop. Cillian did a double take. In that moment, Paul looked just like John had before he died. "Sit and rest, Paul." Paul didn't hesitate. He leaned against a rusted metal stool.

"What about me?" Sam asked.

"Take ten minutes." Cillian scrubbed another soiled pan, uprooting the char of burnt scallops. He vowed to never eat another shellfish again. With his back to his brother—his only friend in the world—the orphan gagged.

Needing a distraction, he focused on the headline scrolling the television screen.

PREMED STUDENT SAVES CHILD FROM ENRAGED
US SENATOR
AS CHURCH FULL OF MOURNERS LOOKS ON

A photograph of a breathtaking girl—long dark brown hair accented with skin as cinnamon-brown as Mama Kelley's—lingered on the screen.

"Turn it up," Sam said. Paul dashed toward a coffee stand, grabbed the remote, and increased the volume. Cillian cut off the water. The reporter interviewed the girl. Both of her arms were wrapped with bandages.

As he ogled the girl, something strange and warm started growing inside him.

"That's her, Cil!" Paul exclaimed.

"She's your type of girl." Sam playfully punched Cillian's shoulder, intensifying the ache that had taken up residence in his bones.

"I dinna ken what my type of lass would be—or even if a lass could ever be likin' me, especially one smart enough to become a doctor." Cillian's face warmed as his heart filled with hope that maybe his life wouldn't always be like it was now.

The life of a vagabond. A dishwasher. A caretaker. A life without the affections of a compassionate, beautiful woman.

"I know what kind of girl suits you, Cil." Paul perched back onto his stool. "Smart. Brave. Kind. An introvert."

"The girl survived a bomb and saved a little girl while the president's Secret Service kept their hands clean." Sam slapped Cillian on the butt with his dishtowel. "She's a kick-butt hero. Could you handle her?" Sam watched Cillian's face.

"It's no secret . . . the lass is breathtaking."

Sam slapped his wet dishcloth over his shoulder. "I took a cute girl out to a movie once."

"What happened?" Paul stared at the television.

"She broke my heart."

"Maybe we should stay to ourselves, Cil." Paul filled a mop bucket with water. "Stay safe."

"Better to have yer heart broken, than to refuse to use it." Cillian dropped a deep boiler onto the dishwasher rack, splashing water over the edges of the sink.

"Careful. I've got to clean that up." Paul filled his bucket with hot water and bleach, picked up a mop, dipped the head into the commercial-sized bucket, and started scrubbing the slime off the floor.

Cillian kept glancing at the television as he washed dishes, hoping the girl's face would appear again. Where was she from? Would she like a guy like him? Maybe she'd already fallen in love with another boy—smarter, richer, and cleaner.

"Cil's in love." Paul threw a drying towel at his brother's face, then dipped his mop into the bleach water and continued cleaning the floor. "He can't keep his eyes off her."

"Mop the floor." Cillian scrubbed.

An hour later, the kitchen's floors and surfaces gleamed and smelled of bleach.

Paul sauntered into the room while holding a tattered paperback. "I dedicate these words to my brother, my best friend: 'She was beautiful,' he paused, 'but not like those girls in the magazines. She was beautiful, for the way she thought. She was beautiful, for the sparkle in her eyes when she talked about something she loved. She was beautiful, for her ability to make other people smile, even if she was sad. No, she wasn't beautiful for something as temporary as her looks. She was beautiful deep down to her soul. She is beautiful.' "

Paul closed the book and looked at his brother. "Still, she'd be the lucky one, Cil."

Cillian washed his hands in the sink. Water ran over his scarred hand, and he remembered Bushcroft's words. *No respectable woman would ever want your limp, mangled hand stroking her in the night.* "No, Paul. I'd be the lucky one, luckier than a leprechaun."

Tonight, the memory of the insult had an odd effect: every part of his being longed for the touch of the girl who had saved the child from the crazed and disgraced politician. Standing in the back kitchen of a Mongolian restaurant, the orphaned boy imagined the feel of her skin and the scent of her hair.

Sensual warmth flooded his body from his head to his toes.

He closed his eyes, relishing the sensation. *When the day comes, and I've made something of myself, I'll be findin' ye, lass.*

So until then, stay safe.

Wait for me.

I'm beggin' you to, mo nighean donn—*my brown-haired lass.*

59—Adelaide:
#Feels Like Home to Me

SNOW FALLS ALL AROUND ME, damping my skin, clothes, and hair. Top down on my periwinkle-blue 1969 Mustang GT Convertible, my ginger curls blowing in a cold night wind, I swerve into the driveway of the Cavanaugh-Finn mountain chalet, open a door to the five-car garage, park, and cut the engine.

I click off my recording device, giving myself a breather from retelling this portion of my parents' stories—an orphan tree and a vanishing skeleton key. I'll gift the recordings to Cordelia Gray when we set sail on the *Rose of the*

Ocean, so she can begin writing her breakout novel about my family's secrets.

I recall the last details of Mother's letter.

My Dearest Adelaide Rose,

My life is a Georges-Pierre Seurat painting—and I'm mortified . . .

Inside the wooden case, hidden beneath layers of shipping paper, you'll find the original study of Seurat's Sunday Afternoon on the Island of La Grande Jatte. Initially I was angry with your father for spending so much money for the masterpiece. I don't mind so much anymore, since now it's yours. If destiny is to take a mother and a father from you, then maybe this priceless masterpiece will soothe your heart, reminding you of us.

Your second gift is a quilt, made by my great-grandmother. There was a time when fabric squares hid mysteries, telling an escaped slave how to find a train that would escort them underground to freedom.

Escape before it's too late.

Keep your last gift inside its special case. It is the original score of "Blessed Assurance," my mother's favorite hymn. Harriet Tubman, a conductor on the train of bravery and freedom, understood that a song wasn't all notes, words, and tempo.

A riddle: Follow the lead in a rich, soulfully syncopated rhythm of C major. CeCe Winans sang the hymn best when your father and I attended the Cicely Tyson Kennedy Center Honors, where we said hello to the First Family for the last time.

Escape from where and escape from whom?

★ ★ ★

Adelaide Rose Cavanaugh-Finn has never been bone-of-my-bone or flesh-of-my-flesh—no, she's much more than skin, bones, or even breath. She exists as the fuel that sustains a forest fire of love raging inside my soul. She is my reason for living. For fighting.

She whispers to my heart, "Keep on beating. We need you." Adelaide touches me without even touching me, and what mother wouldn't save the universe, much less Earth, for her daughter's sake?

Strangers call me the Orphan Dreamer.

Adelaide calls me Mummy. I grin—wide, free, and proud.

My soon-to-graduate daughter—who will always be my little girl—has returned home. We sat up all night, talking, laughing, and drinking hot chocolate, instead of me researching while she worked on writing her essay: What question of Judaism does Islam answer?

I blow my nose, throw away the tissue, and wash my hands.

Darn COVID-20.

A few nights ago, he—not the virus, but my heart-song—disappeared.

Vanished.

I rest my hand on the center of my chest and shield my heart. My fingers quake as my heart pounds beneath my ribs. *Stay strong. You can do this, Danny Rose.*

I take a deep breath, then exhale. When Adelaide Rose gets up in the morning, I have to look her in the eyes and tell her everything. Her dad is gone, and I had a terrifying dream that he arrived back from the battlefield and gifted his beating heart to a stranger. But Emmaline and I had prayed for him. Cillian will keep his heart.

But what was the meaning of the dream?

Some questions refuse to give answers.

I'm dying, but that truth isn't the scary part of my revelation. Every human has an appointment with the grim reaper, and I know my ultimate destiny at the end of my journey.

The scary part of my secret is that on November 3, 2009, a two-headed beast that drinks the blood of the followers of the Way reawakened.

Hands jittery, I pace the hallway outside of Adelaide's bedroom. Should I wake her?

No. What mother wakes her daughter to talk about weird dreams about heart transplants, odd dates, skeleton keys, and missing dads? With the letter about Bahira, the Catholic monk, in hand, I walk toward a wall of floor-to-ceiling windows and face the world.

Beyond the glass, a Blue Ridge Mountain sunrise paints the sky. I haven't seen a morning quite so fine in a long time. Snow cascades down, cloaking evergreens that rise like spires, and silver-white flakes stick to the cabin's stained wood.

The world is on mute.

Silence echoes for miles.

This scene looks almost exactly like the town of Los Alamos that fateful morning, almost twenty years ago when I stood beside Emmaline Georgiana Winterlyn Darbyshire and looked out the picture window of our studio apartment.

That morning, we'd watched a springtime winter storm just like this one, then left the next day to camp in the remote Jemez Mountains where I was almost kidnapped and tortured.

Shivering, I press my face into the chilly windowpane.

It fogs.

I wipe the fog away.

If only the purposes behind life's challenges could be revealed as easily. What do I know for sure?

It's May.

Just like twenty years ago, it's much too late in the spring season for a snowstorm to blow into the mountains. I inhale a misted puff of air emitted from the nasal cannula.

Pulmonary hypertension doesn't play favorites. Neither does ovarian cancer. And for the last few months, the two diseases have danced a lethal jitterbug inside my skeletal body. I never told Adelaide about my condition. God didn't create children to worry about their parents' problems.

I inhale again. Cinnamon and spice waft from the Yankee Candle sitting on the coffee table.

Positioned in front of a stone fireplace, the table anchors the room. Scents of winter and Christmas happiness intermingle with oxygen and tunnel into my lungs before diving between the cotton fibers of my favorite taupe couch.

On this couch he held me in his arms while whispering words of love and affection.

Cupping my mug, I open a book.

A sound followed by silence. I glance over my shoulder. No one. *She's still asleep.* I smile, then gingerly drink a cup of English tea before my Highlander Scottish nurse wakes. She'll read me the Riot Act if she catches me in this act of treachery—daring to drink a tea named after her ancestors' oppressors.

But I relish the taste of English black tea.

Simple.

Straightforward.

No deception in its plain black flavor.

The fireplace pops and crackles as a gust of snow beyond the windows romps west, then east—only to blow north again while spewing snowflakes like a leaf blower onto the glass. "It's just snow," I whisper.

What had moments ago stimulated feelings of peace now stirred up anxiety. Wind stoned on ecstasy—that's what I call these ill-timed mountain storms.

Don't worry.

I don't take drugs, never smoked, and never even drank a drop of liquor, for that matter. Eating mixed nuts chased by marshmallow-topped hot chocolate while reading literary classics—such as *Jane Eyre* or *Anne of Green Gables*—this is my vice.

It wasn't liquor or cannabis that got Emmaline and me into trouble after that Los Alamos blizzard.

No, just a lack of common sense. A frequent disease that plagues a teenager's mind.

While looking up at the three-story ceiling, I pop a handful of warmed mixed nuts into my mouth, then turn another page of *A Voice in the Wind*, a novel by Francine Rivers. Hadassah, a Hebrew slave girl surviving Rome's oppression, has tied my stomach into more knots than a ship's deckhand ties in a year.

But no literary distraction will change this fact: tonight may be my last night with Adelaide. I dab my eyes with a tissue. No need to mourn.

I haven't shared all my story with you. But before I do, may I tell you a secret?

If I hadn't lived, humanity wouldn't have survived. Beyond the windows, a hermit thrush sings his morning song. Is he agreeing with that assessment of my legacy?

He sings again.

Something's moving! Beneath the couch. No, under my hips. My pulse shoots through the roof, and cold replaces the heat inside my living room.

I rub my hand beneath my backside. It's the pillow cushion, and it's vibrating. My hand runs across an object, and my heart skips a beat. The vibrating object is flat.

I roll my eyes.

It's your cell phone, Danny. Apocalypse aborted.

I pick up the phone, and the rattling of my withering butt cheeks ceases. A grin spreads across my face as I glance at the caller ID. "Limy, you called!"

"Of course I did!"

The familiar voice warms my soul, and my heart rate slows.

"How are you, Danny-girl?"

"I'm talking to my kindred spirit. The sun must be shining somewhere!" Goodness! I'm talking on stilts—a high-pitched tone echoing inside my head. I lower my voice. "My little rosebud came home from boarding school last night."

"Cooking all her favorite meals?"

"I'm not up to it, but Beatha is. We had girl talk, and I thought that I'd died and gone to heaven. This morning, we're going to eat Adelaide's favorite breakfast—avocado toast with fruit salad—while we research and she works on her final-exam paper." My tone turns reflective. "How are you, Limy?"

"Depends what I'm focusing on." She forces a splash of cheer into her tone. "SARS-Cov3—a.k.a COVID-20, sightings of a dark matter planet—probably your Wormwood—Claire's threats of eugenics, this new fad religion that preaches tolerance but refuses to tolerate anyone who doesn't want to join up, which is probably your clay and iron. FYI, the world's falling apart, Danny-girl."

"Seems like it does that periodically."

"Is this just another cycle or the end?"

"Time tells all secrets, but she doesn't always give you the opportunity to change your mind."

"So make my decision for eternity today, before there's no time to change my mind because the Son has come, and I've been left behind. That's what you're going to say, right?"

"What else would a true friend say—'hasta la vista, baby'?"

Silence, then, "I love you." Emmaline sighs. "But I'm not ready to make that kind of commitment. I'm too scared for my children's futures."

What an oxymoron.

Emmaline prattles on: "The same virus that causes the common cold—the coronavirus—has singlehandedly ravished the stock market—again. School's suspended, and the kids insist on driving me crazy." She laughs timidly.

"Send them outside to play. Sunshine's the best antidote for any mischievous soul."

"Have to peel their fingers from their iPads first." We both laugh.

"How's Paul?"

"Since Cillian disappeared, he's barely spoken to me or the children."

"They were closer than brothers joined by blood. Their bond was formed by choosing to love, sacrifice, then survive. Give him time, Limy."

"He's my husband—he's got all the time in the world. If this pesky virus doesn't wipe us clean off the map."

"This virus is only a prelude, not the big one," I say. "Marital counseling still isn't helping?"

"Can toothpicks prop up the Empire State Building?"

"Yes, if the toothpicks are surrounded by concrete and steel rebar."

"You're a great friend, Danny Rose—the steel and the concrete. Thank you for the years of propping me up."

"We're part of the same foundation. You're the concrete. I'm the steel."

"Concrete crumbles."

"Steel corrodes."

Emmaline laughs, then changes the subject. "Still choosing to stay on a keto diet when carbs equal Fox News or CNN?"

"I don't read the tabloids or social media gossip—nor do I watch their cousin, cable news." I type in an internet search on my Android phone, then read her the result:

```
"The FCC regulates broadcast
networks, since the airwaves
are free and public. But cable
channels, which rely on sub-
scribers, viewers, and adver-
tisers, are beyond government
control.

Since cable runs through pri-
vate providers, the FCC plays
no role in issuing or revoking
licenses, and it has no say on
what the channels can air.

The FCC does have regulations
regarding   the   distribution
```

of false information, but again, this only applies to over-the-air programs on networks such as ABC, CBS, NBC, or Fox Broadcasting, but **not** Fox News Channel or CNN."

"Ah, got it," Emmaline says.

"So . . . any questions?"

"Nada."

"I rest my case, Perry Mason," I tease. "It's crazy the amount of weight I've lost since cutting out the garbage," I say, while playing with my pajama's loose-fitting elastic band.

"Not funny, Danny-girl. You need to eat, gain some weight, and give the cancer a real honest-to-goodness fight," Emmaline protests.

"I'm dying, Limy." I shrug. "Plain. Definitely simple."

"You've always been too pragmatic."

"Someone has to be. Besides, I know where I'm going after I die. And just an FYI, we're both dying."

"Thanks for the info."

"What are you going to do about it?"

"Beg . . . I'll beg my best friend not to abandon me or leave her battle station." She adds an unsettling soprano-shrill to her tone. "Don't die on me, Danny Rose. I can't . . . I can't imagine you gone."

"I don't decide when I die. The appointment's already been set, and like everyone else, that's an appointment I won't be missing or arriving too late. But I can choose where I go after I die."

"I can't lose you." Emmaline ignores my theological subtext, but time is running out.

"Limy . . . one day, you will lose me, but if you choose

the Way—the narrow path that leads to life in Yeshua, we could live with each other again for an eternity where the Son always shines."

"Serving the main course?"

"Dessert doesn't keep a body strong."

"I already told you that I'm just not ready to embrace the reality of you dying. Danny, what about us—the ones you were destined to protect? When the next cycle starts, who's going to wield the Glass Tattoo? I'm . . . I'm scared, Danny Rose. Terrified, really."

"Limy, listen to me carefully. You're a biological weapons expert and an honors graduate from the Air Force Institute and MIT. Remember who you are and what you know. Has the same virus that causes the common cold got you stumped and scared out of your wits?"

"Puzzled, not stumped. And, yes, I'm scared like everyone else. It will kill the young and the old. Murdering like the Spanish flu in the spring, but the worst will be in the fall. I need something bigger than vaccines and antivirals for my family—and I don't have the weapon that you possess."

"Receiving or not receiving Him has always been your choice."

"Too much fairy tale, too few facts."

"Truth supersedes facts. The truth: If you had taken the sword, you would've known that God has not given us the spirit of fear, but of power, love, and a sound mind. You don't have to be afraid, Limy. Fear is a choice. Fear is simply faith in the wrong what-if. Remember?"

"But only you can wield the power of the Glass Tattoo, Danny."

"You don't need it to obtain peace. Yahweh will give you peace that passes all understanding if you ask Him to be with you, then follow him with a thankful heart. I'm begging you, Limy." My voice fractures. "Follow the Way before it's too late."

"You and Billy Graham would've been a power couple."

"He was fifty plus years older than me. And I didn't earn the secret weapon. It was a gift given to me from the Creator."

"Your Bible tales are all too weird. What about evolution? Science?" Emmaline sighs, then serves up her own main course—the real reason for her call. "Danny-girl, do you remember Li Xiu, the postdoctoral fellow working in our lab at LANL?"

"Family lived in China. Cooked killer ramen. Tall, gorgeous, blessed with a timid smile . . . always hogged the electron microscope, though."

"Identity confirmed."

"Why do you ask?"

"I've been ordered to engage in a scavenger hunt, following the trail of this newest strain of coronavirus."

"The diameter of the virus is only 120 nanometers. Gonna be hard to see." Bad joke, but I'm desperate to lighten the moment.

"Don't quit your day job, Danny-girl. But I'm not following the virus per se, more like following the handler of the virus."

"Okay, I'm listening."

"After Li Xiu left Los Alamos, she continued her postdoc work at the National Institute of Allergy and Infectious Diseases in Washington, DC—researching viruses in the disease-modeling-and-transmission section of the lab."

"Are you attempting to link her to the SARS-CoV-3 pandemic?"

"Not directly . . . at least, not now."

"It's a weighty accusation."

"I'm not judging, just asking you to brainstorm with me. You're a thinker. You ask questions. Make few statements. And you're rational—"

"Pragmatic."

"Not an emotional rollercoaster. A breath of fresh air. Now why would a PhD waste their time studying coronavirus in a lab that studies superbugs like the filoviruses—Ebola's parent virus, or bunyaviruses, arenaviruses, and flaviviruses?"

"Without going completely conspiracy theory, I don't have a clue. But you can answer your own question. Just keep some perspective. Keep your feet glued to the ground. Then, after you recall the facts, use your scientific brain and create a hypothesis. Okay?"

"Fine."

"What are you afraid of, exactly?" I ask.

"It's a fact. SARS-CoV-3, SARS, and MERS are all caused by strains of coronavirus, and maybe SARS-CoV-3 is a result of a mutation of the coronavirus that caused SARS, SARS-CoV-2, and MERS. If so, will it mutate again, becoming even more aggressive?"

"It's a virus. They mutate. It's why the flu vaccine isn't that effective from year to year. Limy, you're agitated. Why? So far, the rate of mortality is less than the mortality of MERS—with the exception of Italy, which has limited access to healthcare and an elderly obese population that smokes like chimneys."

"Remember that great minds discuss ideas, average minds discuss events, small minds discuss people."

"Right, à la Eleanor Roosevelt."

"Danny, over the last twenty years, you've preached that to me ad nauseum."

"Guilty." I sigh. "So we're not gossiping about Li Xiu, only an idea about our previous mentor?"

"Bingo."

"Okay, so your hypothesis and your idea rest on this question: Did Li Xiu Ying, after leaving the NIH and moving back to China, take classified research from the NIH and help create a superbug at the Institute of Virology in Wuhan?"

"It's a good start. Back to what I originally asked. Why would a PhD waste their career studying coronavirus—a virus that causes the common cold—in a US lab that studies super viruses like the virus that causes Ebola?"

"I'll play your game," I say. "I agree that it seems reasonable to conclude that if a PhD postdoc is studying coronaviruses in a lab that studies super viruses, they might be working on how to make the coronavirus mutate into a super virus." I inhale a lung full of oxygen. "Limy, are you insinuating that the virus causing the common cold is being developed as a biological weapon? That's your gig, right? Biological weapons created to decimate humans?"

"It is," she says quietly. Her voice is laced with shame. "Protesting is American. For goodness sakes, America was built on one big protest, The War of Independence. But looting mom-and-pop stores?"

"It's hideous. I agree with you, Limy."

"Someone has to keep the population from spiraling out of control. Too many dependents on those actually pulling the weight. That's the motive." My best friend finally comes clean. "What if I could help Li Xiu and the Sons of Venus finish developing a virus that could get rid of the world's dead weight? We'd create our own version of heaven right here on Earth."

"Limy, I'm disappointed—no, livid—with you. All this time, you lied to me."

A space of time elapses.

"Danny, I didn't lie."

"Tell me the truth."

"Only yesterday I started to fully embrace eugenics after I watched looters destroy Chicago's Magnificent Mile—the place where you and Cil were engaged! Look at the world, so full of stupid little people. Dad invited me to a meeting with the Sons of Venus. I went." She pauses. "And I spoke with Asher Bushcroft. He's an amazing man—smart, innovative, a forward thinker, and I learned so much from him."

"No longer spying on your dad—you've joined the ranks?"

"First and foremost, I promised to protect you." She pauses. "But that's not all."

"This isn't Double Jeopardy, Limy. Spit it out. My cabin is bomb-proof. Cillian made sure of that. Population control of who, exactly—poor people, brown people, pale people, young people, or the elderly?"

"You're a physician. You know that respiratory viruses are more likely to cause death in the elderly and chronically ill—the biggest drivers of healthcare costs. It's like the rise of the Third Reich all over again."

"The Fourth Reich," I challenge her. "In your world of shadows and daggers, remember that over twenty million Americans contracted influenza A this flu season. Eighty thousand Americans died."

"How effective was the flu vaccine—yet every hospital and government agency practically forced us to get stabbed in the deltoid?"

"It's true . . . the influenza vaccine isn't that effective. The virus mutates too fast." I agree.

"Bingo." Emmaline's tone weighs heavy with premonition. "Then add on socialized medicine. It takes two years in Canada to see a kidney specialist or a lung doctor. Italy can't keep up financially with their sick and dying, nor do they possess the personnel. And every single institutionalized system in America—healthcare, education, finance, law enforcement, politics—fails one major group in America: people who look like you, Danny-girl, especially the ones not as rich as you are."

"Methodical evil has motivated humanity, Limy. Infect them. Remove access to healthcare via socialized medicine, then thin the herd. Eugenics has been and always will be."

"Exactly. And thank you, Danny, for not thinking that I'm crazy."

"That's why I'm your kindred spirit." I close my eyes and visualize Emmaline's shoulders relaxing. "And what America doesn't realize is that when people who look like me stop fighting for America, this country is finished."

"Different soldiers for different wars." Emmaline sighs.

"Yes, and the soldiers marching in the Sons of Venus's army are slow-spreading viruses, infecting the world's citizens with a mutating virus."

"This isn't conspiracy, Danny-girl. It's just that Fox and CNN don't know what's really going on. You're right not to get your information from the talking heads—or from the diarrhea pile, social media."

"Ecclesiastes, chapter one, verse nine. 'What has been will be again, and what has been done will be done again; there is nothing new under the sun.' If the idea can be imagined, it has happened before. So I don't believe you're a conspiracy theorist. Point the masses in the wrong direction, then watch them walk off a cliff."

"Are you going to take the vaccine, Danny-girl? Some have said that blacks should take it first because they're more susceptible to the virus."

"Of course they did," I say. "Besides, I'm not black—"

"I'm brown," Emmaline finishes my mantra, then chides me, "*Now* who's the conspiracy theorist?"

"I'm almost dead, Limy. I don't need the vaccine. But conspiracy theory aside, the science behind two of the vaccines is rock solid and will save lots of lives, no differently than childhood vaccines. I will make sure Adelaide takes it. But Claire isn't almost dead, and remember her eugenics plan?"

"I'm not like Claire, Danny-girl."

"See it your way." I sigh. "Besides, it can cost a billion dollars and ten years to bring one new drug to market. A vaccine is being produced in less than a year—what's the price tag? And will an ever-increasing socialist culture in America value the intellectuals in our society, understanding that scientists and doctors need to be paid for their work? How will the country pay for distributing the vaccine for free? How will America attract bright minds to develop a future vaccine if her government refuses to value the scientists and doctors of the present and pay them for their work? Look at Italy, a socialist country bankrupt of scientific innovation."

"Big pharma can't be expected to give the vaccine away for free, Danny-girl."

"Unless Claire and her bunch possess an ulterior motive for issuing the vaccine."

"Like what?"

"You see, Limy, the various strains of socialism—national socialism and communistic socialism—can bleed a culture of the love of science, reason, and morality."

"I understand."

"The world's citizens have constantly been bombarded with chaos and a longing for law and order. So they've been primed to embrace your dad's Sons of Venus one-world government and religions. Then when they're ravaged by economic losses via frequent pandemics, they'll be primed once again . . . ready to take the mark of the beast. The mark of the Fourth Reich, an identity chip in the new power structure that will allow a person to buy or sell without having to work."

"It's always about the money."

"Always. Because when we love money, it's difficult to love God and avoid evil habits, especially when we divorce ourselves from the work required to earn money."

"Listen to the rich girls talk," Emmaline says.

"Having money doesn't equal loving money. A pauper can love money more than a billionaire. Ask Claire's family."

"She makes me sick!" Emmaline pauses, realizing the irony of her last sentence. We both break into laughter.

I hold my side, then laugh some more. Half-snort-laughing and half-talking, I ask, "Limy, you're not in your lane. Conspiracy theories aren't usually your thing."

"Because, my Lozen, you're my best friend—my kindred spirit. I trust you with my life. You're wise. Able to decipher the weird stuff."

"It's because I'm a soldier of an invisible world—an alien of sorts, a foreigner in this world."

"Different soldiers for different wars. You made contact, Orphan Dreamer."

"It's less sci-fi than that, Limy. Rather simple, really . . ."

"Tell me."

"Emmaline Georgiana, the masses are fighting the

visible war but losing the most important conflict: the invisible war. They've forgotten the end of the story. The end where the invisible world collides with the visible world and Earth vanishes."

"Then don't forget us. Fight on. Remind us to discover the invisible world, the place where the supernatural is the norm."

Emmaline pauses, so I say, "It's time for all of humanity to fight. Accept Yahweh's sacrificial gift—His one and only son, Yeshua—and follow Him. Praying that we can defeat Lucifer's army together. I can't win this war alone."

"Okay," the last bits of defiance vaporize from Emmaline's voice. "Remember our trip to the Jemez Mountains? Let's go again, just me and you. I'll hire a babysitter. We'll hike, swim, and eat marshmallows by the campfire."

"I'll never go hiking right after a snowstorm with you again." I laugh.

"Don't blame you. But you solved the functions of the Skeleton Key."

"With your help and Yahweh's wisdom." I clasp the Glass Tattoo hanging from my leather necklace. "But the Sons of Venus seem to have found their 'who.' And after they unleashed SARS-Cov-4, the SARS-Cov-3 pandemic will feel like a walk in the park."

"You're right, Danny-girl. My dad and his Sons of Venus are lurking behind the smoke and mirrors of this pandemic, never allowing chaos to go to waste. Meanwhile they're eager to announce their leader to the world." I can hear Emmaline swallow. "You know him." Emmaline's voice wavers. "You love him—adore him—and I know who he is. Will he agree and accept the position?"

"Unfortunately, he's a Nephilim," I whisper. Cold sweat bubbles up across my brown skin. "Why wouldn't he accept the position?"

"Are you going to tell Adelaide Rose everything, even about your illness?"

"Yes . . . tomorrow. After dinner, after we finish writing her research paper."

"What will she do?"

"Fall apart."

"I'm scared for you, Danny-girl."

"I'm scared too." I refuse to cry. I don't have any more tears anyway.

"Why do you think it had to be a pandemic to kick off the end of the world?"

"Economic failure. It's the prelude to the one-world government's common currency, the mark of the beast. And the antichrist is that beast." My mouth dries as I quote a passage from Revelation: " 'That no one may buy or sell except one who has the mark or the name of the beast, or the number of his name.' "

"What does it profit a man if he gains the whole world but loses his own soul . . ." Limy's voice trails off, then comes alive like spring. "Danny-girl, you're our warrior, so fight."

I exhale, exhausted but not completely spent. My heart still beats. "I never stopped." For Adelaide's sake. For the sake of the children, I continue to unsheathe my sword and fight.

"Good. Because 666 5th Ave New York, New York, just sold."

"Who the heck would purchase a property with that address?" I ask.

"I don't know, but Claire Amilee Covington-Underwood—America's First Lady—did say that if she ran for President of the United States of America, she 'could stand in the middle of Fifth Avenue and shoot somebody and not lose any voters.' "

"She did. And when we flip the political party coin, the other side declares that unborn people possess absolutely no rights . . . just a bunch of murdering narcissists on both sides hankering to run America six feet under."

"Pray for healing, then run for president, Danny Rose. I'm begging you."

"That won't work." Daniela chuckled. "People want to be led North, yet they stubbornly face South—when they should find a compass and then take the initiative to turn around, travel at least Northeast before asking a leader to take them North to the promised land."

Half-asleep, Adelaide stumbles into the living room. "Hi, Mummy." She kisses my cheek. "Love you."

"I'll talk to you later, Limy." I hang up the call and reach for my daughter. "I love you, darling." I bear-hug her with all my strength. "We need to talk." I clear my throat, release her, and pat the couch beside me.

"About?"

"Your daddy."

"Is he coming back?"

"No. We're going to him." My knowing tells me where my heartsong has disappeared to.

"Where?"

"New York City."

"Let's go shopping on Fifth Avenue."

"If we have time." I gift Professor Jakob's letter that reveals the historical link between a Catholic Jesuit monk, Bahira, and Mohammad—representatives of the Catholic

Church and Islam—to my daughter. "Take it, darling. Read it. This letter will help you write your research paper."

She reads the letter. "If religion is causing all the wars in the world, should we ban it?"

"I've never known a religion to start a war—only people, darling." I blow a kiss at my beautiful daughter, then smile. "What happened to your eye?"

Adelaide scoots away. "N-n-nothing."

"You only stutter when you're lying, Adelaide Rose. I'm your mother. Never lie to me."

"Oh, Mummy." Her face contorts into an expression of the purest pain—the kind when innocence has been stripped from the eyes of the innocent. She bursts into tears and throws herself on top of me. "It was Levi."

"As in Leviathan?" I seethe while holding my daughter.

"Yes, Mummy." She pushes back. "And I saw Sakura at the airport."

"Okay." Jaw set, I stand up, tuck my baby girl beneath a blanket, yank the Glass Tattoo from my neck, then ball my hands into tight fists. "Where is he?"

"Mummy, your eyes. They're scaring me."

"My eyes—they're not for you." I am the Orphan Dreamer—a mother with a steel fist tucked inside a velvet glove.

"Mummy, sit down and hold me for a while." Adelaide cuddles with me. "Let's listen to music, okay?"

"Your choice," I say.

She rests her head on my chest as she connects her cell phone to our Dolby Atmos Bluetooth sound system.

Natalie Grant's "My Weapon" plays. My Adelaide Rose has found the way of the Master, Yeshua.

I grin—wide, free, and so very thankful. As violinists' melodic notes soar throughout the expansive living room,

I remember these words: *But You are holy, enthroned in the praises of Israel.* Another Biblical promise fills my heart: *The heartfelt and persistent prayer of a righteous man (believer) can accomplish much [when put into action and made effective by God—it is dynamic and can have tremendous power].*

"We should pray for your dad, Limy."

"Okay, Mom." She grips my hand.

"You first, baby girl."

"Dear Yahweh, it's been a couple of days, but I haven't stopped thinking about You after I chose to follow you. I hope you prove to be just like my da—powerful yet loving Mummy and me. But it's my da who needs You, now. Protect him. Don't take him away from us—not yet." Her prayer ends.

There are no words left for me to add, so I pull my grandmother's quilt over us both and close my eyes.

Less than ten minutes later, my cell phone vibrates. *Unknown number*, but something tells me to answer it. "Hello?"

"Daniela, *a rún mo chroí.*"

I would recognize that deep baritone Scottish burr mixed with Irish brogue any day of the week. "Cil? Babe? Are you okay?" I bolt up, Adelaide almost tumbles onto the floor; still, my voice weighs nothing more than a breath. "Is it you? Is it my heartsong?"

"It is. Trust me, *mo nighean donn.*" The call ends as quickly as it came. The memory of his scent, my heartsong's essence, fills my nose—aquatic, woody, and aromatic all at the same time.

"Cil?" I jump up from the couch.

"Mummy." Adelaide faces me, her face registering desperation. "Is Daddy okay?"

"I don't know." I kiss her forehead. "But we'll be fine."

I remember what Wraith—no longer a ghost but my hero in the flesh and my husband—always told me: "I'll be the ruthless one, pushing back the darkness so ye can be kind. Earth will be balanced, rotating on its axis because of your compassion. Love me once more, *mo nighean donn*."

"Adelaide Rose."

"Yes, Mummy." My daughter rests her head on my shoulder.

"If you learn nothing else from me, learn this. In a world where you can be anything, be kind."

"Yes, mummy."

Wake up, world, the Watchers have arrived. Warriors, unsheathe your invisible swords before it's too late.

The world is not all bad. There are good people out there. And if you can't find one, then be one.

> And because lawlessness will abound, the love
> of many will grow cold. But he who endures
> to the end shall be saved. And this gospel of
> the kingdom will be preached in all the world
> as a witness to all the nations, and then the
> end will come.

> —Matthew 24:13-14

Motives

Who can I love without regret? I've learned that no human heart can be fully trusted—including my own. I chose to love Yeshua, for He is the essence of love, 'God is love. God is light and in Him there is not darkness at all.'

I can love and trust in the light—so I choose to trust the One whose name is Truth—I Am the Way, the Truth, and the Life, no one comes to my Father except through me.

Love His truth, like His truth, or hate His truth, but He only speaks the truth because He defines truth—the embodiment of the purest motives.

Take my hand, step out of the darkness and into the Light where unconditional love can be found!

—J. Nell Brown

The dream sequence showing Cillian's Honor Walk was written in memory of Jacquez Welch, a seventeen-year-old angel who played high school football in St. Petersburg, Florida. When the Creator whispered his name, Jacquez gave life to others via organ donation. His legacy will live forever.

Thank you to my kindred spirit—Steph—for gifting me the story of such an incredible young man. Keep on teaching America's kids to move and eat healthy. And to my best friend, S.T., waiting to go on the heart transplant list be brave because you are loved . . .

—J. Nell Brown

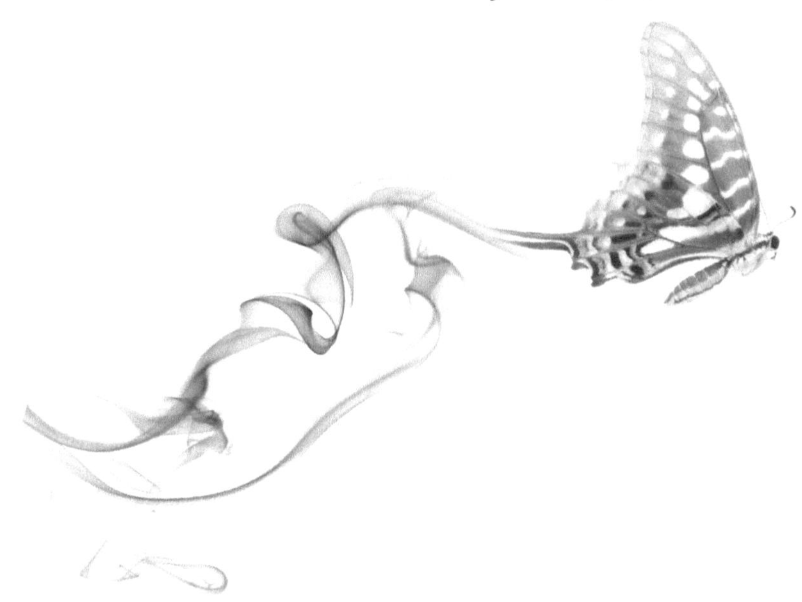

Acknowledgments

Yeshua, thank you for inspiring this book through my imagination at a time when I needed it most. You've always been faithful to me.

Special thanks to my late father, Chaplain Austin Brown; my mother, Mrs. Jeanette Brown; and my sisters and friends.

To my ancestors, thank you for your bravery.

To my editors, Ann Castro at AnnCastro Studio, Lisa Gilliam at LisaGilliam.com, and Courtney Rae Andersson at Elevation Editorial, and my proofreader, Emily Dings—thank you all for your eagle-eye talents.

To my readers, especially Amber Kolb, thank you for loving this story. These characters exist for you.

Dear Reader,

Thoughtful reviews about an author's work are like a pay raise or a tip to employees in traditional jobs. If you enjoyed this novel, *Orphan Dreamer and the Vanishing Skeleton Key*, please take a moment to tell all of your friends via social media and place a review wherever you purchased this novel, sharing with other readers what you've learned. Your feedback is invaluable.

The A21 Campaign, a nonprofit organization to abolish the human trafficking of children, is my charity of choice. When you purchase a novelette or novel in the Orphan Dreamer saga, ten percent of the profits will be donated to the A21 Campaign or to organizations with a similar mission.

I look forward to saying hello to you via my newsletter. Please sign up for my semiannual newsletter, and I will notify you about future releases, sales, and special events.

With gratitude,
J. Nell Brown

A Legacy Remembered

After September 11, 2011 and until September 13, 2011, the FAA issued a no-fly mandate. The entire airspace above the United States and Canada was eerily quiet as the vast skies remained closed to domestic and international flights alike except for military, police, and medical flights.

Karl Rove said that on September 14, 2011—the Friday after 9/11—with restricted airtravel and a no-fly mandate still in effect above Washington, DC, "One aircraft, [a] civilian aircraft, is in the skies above the United States, and it bears [The Reverend] Billy Graham."

A pastor to the world, Reverend Billy Graham's message of love and redemption etched his legacy in the annals of history. In the light of the reverend's legacy, I ask, what is my legacy?

Who so desperately needs the gift that I have nurtured and now can offer to a hurting world? What talent and gift have I allowed to grow, so that even the rigid demands of the FAA are suspended for me to offer what I possess to the world?

Do I speak words of truth, words of hope, and words of compasssion to a hurting nation and a chaotic world, or do I dabble in the destructive practice of killing everything around me with my careless words, instilling fear and hatred into the hearts of the masses?

I believe that Love wrapped in words of Truth are still the antidote to any nation's fear or hopelessness. "Jesus said, 'I am the way, the truth, and the life. No one comes to the Father except through me.' "

So in a world where those holding the proverbial

microphone—politicians, activists, and the media—have made hatred, fear, and distrust popular with their careless verbal banter, I dedicate this book to a leader who chose his words very carefully, gifting a message of love and truth to the world.

Thank you to the late Reverend Billy Graham—the preacher of the century. Like Doctor Martin Luther King Jr., you possessed a dream "to share the good news to the whole world."

A non-politicized, non-radicalized, non-monetized, and non-sensationalized human being whose divine message was simple—God loves you and He has a plan for your life. He remained faithful to his call until death arrived to the woods of Montreat, North Carolina, penciling in a comma behind February 21, 2018, when the Creator said, "Come home" and ushered the Reverend Graham into eternity where he lives beside my late father—Chaplain Austin Brown, a preacher and chaplain to the imprisoned around the world.

Yes, *I Can Only Imagine*!

What's your legacy?

—J. Nell Brown

Dear Reader,

All religions are basically the same—right?

Is there an equally simple answer to this seemingly simple question? No. Plain. Definitely simple, as Adelaide Rose or Daniela Rose would say.

I have studied and examined many of the religions of the world in order to answer my question, contrasting and comparing each religion's representative to Earth.

For instance, Yeshua (Jesus) versus Mohammad.

What Did Yeshua (Jesus) Claim?

Yeshua claimed to be the Son of God—God in the flesh, one part of a triune God.

He claimed to have existed from the beginning: "In the beginning was the Word, and the Word was with God, and the Word was God . . . And the Word was made flesh, and dwelt among us, (and we beheld his glory, the glory as of the only begotten of the Father), full of grace and truth" (John 1:1, 14).

He came to Earth from an extradimensional space in the form of a child with no genetic earthly father. After he grew up, he healed the sick, raised the dead, cast out demons, set people free, and fed the hungry, among many other miracles.

During His thirty-three years of earthly life, He fulfilled every single Messianic prophecy recorded in the Hebrew scriptures (the Old Testament), answering the question: who is the Messiah—humanity's redeemer?

Mathematically speaking, this accomplishment alone would be impossible for any human to fulfill. Thus, Jesus must be something more than a mere human or prophet.

What Did Muhammad Claim?

Muhammad claimed to be a prophet—nothing more, nothing less.

He was born in 570 CE—the year of the elephant—in the city of Mecca. Orphaned at six years old, Muhammad's uncle Abu Talib and his Aunt Fatimah raised him. As a young man, he faithfully worked as a merchant.

Yeshua's (Jesus's) Story Continued.

One night, Judas Iscariot, Yeshua's disciple, betrayed Him. Alone in the Garden of Gethsemane, Yeshua pleaded with His Father, "Let this cup pass from me."

In the end, He surrendered His will to His Father's, which required Him to carry an old Roman cross to Golgotha, where He was crucified. Before He died, He cried, "Father, forgive them for they do not know what they are doing."

At that moment, as the curtain separating the Holy of Holies in the Jewish temple was torn from top to bottom, removing the separation between God and man, Jesus cried, "It is finished!"

But the Messiah had not finished His final task.

After being buried in a borrowed tomb, on the third day, Jesus defeated death and the grave. Coming back to life, He appeared to His disciples, telling them, "My kingdom is not of this world."

Yes. Yeshua was an alien in some peoples' vernacular—or an extradimensional being in other peoples' perception.

He defied time and space, ascending to heaven where He now sits at the right hand of God the Father—Yahweh—where He prays for His children day and night and promises to return for them on one highly anticipated day known as the Rapture or the great escape.

Even on the copyright date of this novel, Yeshua lives.

Muhammad's Story Continued.

In Mecca, Mohammad married Aisha when she was six or seven years old. He consummated the marriage after his pilgrimage from Mecca to Medina, when Aisha had reached the age of nine or ten years old.

At times, he would seclude himself in a mountain cave named Hira for several nights of prayer.

At the age of forty, Muhammad reported that the angel Gabriel had visited him inside a dark cave and gave him his first revelation from Allah that became the basis for the Qur'an and the foundation of Islam.

After this experience, Muhammad became deeply disturbed, believing that he might be demon-possessed. Three years later, and after contemplating suicide, Muhammad started preaching his cave visions publicly, proclaiming that "God is one." Not that God is a triune being, as Christianity had taught.

He told his followers how to work their way to Paradise—the garden of pleasure, the presumptive home of Allah.

By 630 AD he had unified most of Arabia under a single religion—a new Abrahamic religion, a post-Judaic and post-Christian faith—before he died in 632 AD.

In 630 AD, after many wars and conflicts, Mohammad marched on Mecca with ten thousand Muslim converts and seized control of the city.

He gave amnesty to some of his enemies for past offences, except for some men and women found guilty of murder or disrupting the peace. Most Meccans converted to Islam, and Mohammad destroyed all the statues of Arabian gods in and around the Kaaba.

According to most reports collected by Ibn Ishaq and al-Azraqi, Mohammad spared frescoes of Mary and Yeshua, but others suggest that he erased all images of Yeshua.

A few months after his farewell pilgrimage to Mecca, Muhammad became ill with fever.

Resting on his wife's lap, Muhammad died Monday, June 8, 632, at the age of sixty-three. After asking his wife to dispose of his last worldly goods—seven coins—he spoke his final words, "O Allah, to Ar-Rafiq Al-A'la—exalted friend in heaven.

Are Yeshua and Muhammad the same in mission, persona, and deity?

Yeshua claimed to be the Messiah.

Muhammad claimed to be a prophet who was not sure if his visions were inspired by evil or good.

If Yeshua and Muhammad are not the same in mission, persona, and claims of deity, how could both Yeshua and Muhammad lead their followers to the same goal: the same God, the same state of eternity—heaven?

They could not.

Plain.

Definitely simple.

Are Allah and Yahweh the same God?

Yahweh

We have spoken about the differences between Yeshua and Muhammad. Let's explore the major difference between Allah and Yahweh.

Would you agree that America has one president? Of course you would. But what if I tell you the president's name is Bugs Bunny, but you believe the president's name is Donald Duck?

It is true: we both believe America has only one president.

And it is also true that we profoundly disagree on the identity—the character, the essence—of the President of the United States of America.

Yes, followers of the Ways (non-secular Christians) and Muslims agree about the existence of God, but there is a clear disagreement on the character of this God.

The characters of Yahweh and Allah lie at opposite ends of the spectrum. Yahweh is a personal God who wants a personal relationship with His creation—humans—and thus willingly made a huge sacrifice to secure this opportunity, the sacrifice of His only begotten son, Yeshua, as payment for the consequence of human imperfection.

This act solidifies Yahweh's claim, "God is love."

Allah

Allah is not a relational being. He is not personal. He does not claim that his essence defines true love, a.k.a. sacrifice. Thus, he has never made any overtures of sacrifice to bridge the gap between fallen humanity and his claimed state of perfection.

Muslims must earn their way to paradise which literally translates to *gardens of pleasure.*

Yes, some humans have gone to extreme lengths to earn their passage to place of pleasure where male martyrs are rewarded with seventy-two virgins.

And this process of earning of one's salvation is the major link between traditional Catholicism and Islam—the Bahira-link, as I call it.

Of course, for the Catholic believer, their soul will either go to heaven, hell or purgatory, depending on their behavior on Earth. But can a dead human make themselves live again by good works?

I doubt it.

As a medical doctor, I've never seen a dead patient perform CPR on themselves, someone else—an advocate—performs CPR on their behalf.

While I have only explored the three Abrahamic religions in *Orphan Tree and the Vanishing Skeleton Key*, all proposed pathways to God—the Creator of the universe—are not equal or the same.

This same exercise can be completed with any religion.

Compare and contrast. Search until you find the Truth, not tradition or culture. Your future depends upon this quest.

Be brave,
J. Nell Brown

Fact or Fiction

Fiction

Abu Bakr al-Baghdadi, ISIL's leader, was assassinated on October 26, 2019, not May 10 as depicted in this novel.

Daniel's Animal Farm Vision was actually given to King Belshazzar and not Daniel. The author modified that detail for the purpose of the story.

"Surrounded (Fight My Battles)" was written by Elyssa Smith and released April 10, 2020, not 1998.

The **Charlemagne Prize of the City of Aachen** has been won by modern-day European leaders such as Winston Churchill, Roman Herzog, Henry Kissinger, Pope Francis, and Emmanuel Macron.

Caves in the Jemez Mountains: Puebloan Indian tribes have lived in the Jemez Mountains, not necessary Apache Indians.

Phillips Exeter released students from school due to COVID-19 in March 2020, not May 2020, though *OT and the VSK* focuses on a variant of coronavirus, COVID-20.

Fact

Compassion versus love is pointedly demonstrated in Yahweh's (God's) sacrifice for human sin. He gave His most beloved gift, Yeshua (Jesus), His only Son. Yeshua was misunderstood, mocked, beaten, and then crucified. To this day, He remains the greatest love story ever told.

Prayer is the mechanism for human communication with Yahweh. A prayer of repentance is the first one a person must humbly utter after recognizing their sinful nature in contrast to that of the holy, all-powerful Creator of the universe.

A **blood moon** is a lunar eclipse. The moon appears red or orange when the Earth passes between the sun and the moon and casts a shadow on the moon.

Many 2014-to-2015 blood moon hypotheses exist. The lunar eclipse on September 28, 2015, was visible from Jerusalem. "And there shall be signs in the sun, and in the moon, and in the stars" (Luke 21:25).

Scholars anticipated a significant event in Israel or pertaining to Israel during this period. The only significant event I think may have occurred was that the antichrist—666—appeared on the scene, but their identity is not crystal clear—yet. Only Yahweh knows if this hypothesis is correct. The Bible says in Matthew 25:13, "Watch therefore, for ye know neither the day nor the hour wherein the Son of man cometh." The novel explores a plausible meaning of this text. Luke 21:36 reads, "Be always on the watch, and pray that you may be able to escape all that is about to happen, and that you may be able to stand before the Son of Man."

Live as though Yeshua will return tomorrow—and love as though He will return in a thousand years. If you are interested in astronomy, you may enjoy studying about the Jubilee year in the middle of the twenty-first century.

Spiritual warfare can be a spooky topic. It shouldn't be. We are made in the image of God. As a result, every human has three parts—soul, body, and spirit.

Spiritual warfare describes elements in the spirit realm. Lucifer rebelled against Yahweh with one-third of the sons of God. Since Lucifer was created by Yahweh, the battle outcome is determined. Yahweh has already won.

Yahweh created humans for fellowship. He never desired humans to be influenced by Lucifer and bend to evil tendencies. However, free will allows the recipients of love to decide if they will return love to the giver. Our parents, Adam and Eve, chose disobedience. Yahweh created a path of redemption for any human who desires a relationship with God.

Human trafficking has been slowly coming onto the radar of Americans. The recent spotlight cast upon a sex trafficking ring that serviced the powerful is a groundbreaking success story.

"Why do you have to be so graphic?" people have asked me. Trust me. The descriptions in the novel are minimal. The actual atrocities these children experience are ghastly. Read a few books about the topic. Talk to child services' case workers.

Meet a trafficked child, and then we may revisit the question. This novel actually paints a rosy story. Cillian would most definitely have contracted an STD and died a lonely death. Our "God Factor" prevented this outcome. Of course, I need the character for the other books in this saga.

If Harriet Beecher Stowe wrote *Uncle Tom's Cabin* with rose-tinted glasses, would the public have acted? I doubt it. Emotion has more benefit than enabling us to enjoy our favorite forms of entertainment. Emotion should also be used to propel us to action and to protect the voiceless in every society.

Molech (Set, Ba'al, Moloch, etc.) was a god created by human hands.

The worship ceremonies included child sacrifice and

orgies. Loud music drowned out the screams of infants and children. The top of the statue was a bronze bull head with arms outstretched. As parents placed their babies on Moloch's hands, the babies would roll down into the fire belly of the god.

Research Carthage and you will discover archeological findings of mass graves of infant skeletons.

The hard truth is that most cultures have participated in child sacrifice—infanticide—to a god. If an archeologist were to dig in "civilized" twenty-first-century graveyards, more than fifty-five million preterm-to-term skeletons would be unearthed.

The deity worshiped: convenience. Let's put that in our pipes and smoke it—meaning, let's change our ways.

If you are being human trafficked or know someone who is and would like help . . .

- **National Human Trafficking Hotline** offers 24/7 confidential support to all victims and survivors of sex and labor trafficking. https://humantraffickinghotline.org/
- **Office for Victims of Crime** provides access to a database that can be searched for various services offered to victims of all forms of human trafficking. https://ovc.ncjrs.gov/humantrafficking/index.html
- **U.S. Department of Justice**. https://www.justice.gov/humantrafficking

Characters and Pronunciations

Bushcroft: Bush-crawft
Cillian: Sih-lee-an
Daniela: Dan-yeh-la
Emmaline: Em-ma-line
Limy: Li-me
Jakob: Yah-kub
Legna: Lee-g-nah
Lucifer: Loo-suh-fer (Satan, Devil)
Nighean donn: Neein Down (Gaelic translation for Brown-haired lass)
Yahweh Adonai: Yah-weh Ah-doh-nie (Lord God)
Yeshua: Ye-SHOO-ah (Jesus)
Yeshua HaMashiach: Yeh-SHOO-ah Ha-Mah-SHEE-akh (Jesus the Messiah)

Definition of Proper Hebraic Names of God

Yahweh (YHVH)
Adonai (Master)
Emmanuel (God with us)
Elohim (The Supreme One) for God
Yeshua (Jesus)

Author Biography

J. Nell Brown, the daughter of a chaplain and a teacher, is a Florida native.

Her relationship with Yeshua (Jesus) is fused with experiences in life, travel, extensive Bible study, and people's stories, and she combines all of this to create characters, plots, and settings for her novels and short stories. An involuntary insomniac, Brown practices medicine and writes in her free time.

She is a self-proclaimed nerd and loves all things scientific. Her love of science is demonstrated by her research at Los Alamos National Laboratory, the site for the development of the atomic bomb. She graduated with honors from the University of Florida (U of F) College of Agriculture and received her medical doctorate from the same. After completing an anesthesia residency at The University of Chicago Hospitals, she began practicing in Florida.

Her heart overflows with compassion for people who are hurting, particularly children. A portion of the proceeds from this book will go to the A21 Campaign, a rescue charity for human-trafficked children, and Bethany Christian Academy in Gainesville, Florida, a school that J. Nell Brown attended as a child that promoted love, values, and a solid educational curriculum for children whose parents would not otherwise be able to afford an alternative school education.

Her first nonfiction book, *Shhh, My Father Is Speaking, and I Am Listening*, is about her prayer journey. The Bible is her favorite literary masterpiece. You may follow J. Nell Brown on her author website, JNellBrown.com.